Arthur Francis Leach

English Schools at the Reformation

Arthur Francis Leach

English Schools at the Reformation

ISBN/EAN: 9783741187018

Manufactured in Europe, USA, Canada, Australia, Japa

Cover: Foto ©Andreas Hilbeck / pixelio.de

Manufactured and distributed by brebook publishing software
(www.brebook.com)

Arthur Francis Leach

English Schools at the Reformation

ENGLISH SCHOOLS

AT THE REFORMA

ARTHUR F. LEAC

late Fellow of All Souls' Co

WESTMINSTER

ARCHIBALD CONSTABLE

& CO 1896

BUTLER & TANNER,
THE SELWOOD PRINTING WORKS,
FROME, AND LONDON.

CONTENTS

PART I

PART II

ENGLISH SCHOOLS AT THE REFORMATION.

1. Edward VI.: Spoiler of Schools.

NEVER was a great reputation more easily gained and less deserved than that of King Edward VI. as a founder of schools.

If the ordinary educated person were asked to whom our system of secondary education was mainly due, and who was the founder of most of the Grammar Schools on which it chiefly rests, he would answer, without hesitation, Edward VI. The magnificent foundations of Christ's Hospital and Birmingham Grammar School, and the numerous Edward VI. Grammar Schools which stud the country, would rise up before his mind, and he would give the credit of them to their reputed founder. Even to those people who credit William of Wykeham with the foundation of our public school system in founding Winchester, and credit Henry VIII. with the cathedral schools, such as the King's School, Canterbury, Edward VI. still stands out as *par excellence* the founder of schools and patron saint of industrious schoolboys.

So widespread is this reputation that even such an authority as Mr. J. R. Green, in his famous *Short History of the English People*, burns incense before the shrines of Edward VI. and of his father and sister, as the founders of English education. Summing up the state of learning in the reign of Edward VI., he says :—

"All teaching ceased at the Universities; the students, indeed, had fallen off in number, the libraries were in part scattered or burnt, the intellectual impulse of the New Learning had died away. One noble measure indeed, the foundation of 18 Grammar Schools, was destined to throw a lustre over

1

the name of Edward, but it had not time to bear fruit in his reign."

Again, *apropos* of Dean Colet's Foundation of St. Paul's School in the early part of the reign of Henry VIII., we read :—

" But the example of Colet was followed by a crowd of imitators. More Grammar Schools, it has been said, were founded in the latter years of Henry than in the three centuries before. The impulse grew, happily, stronger as the direct influence of the new learning passed away. The Grammar Schools of Edward VI. and of Elizabeth—in a word, the system of middle-class education, which by the close of the century had changed the very face of England—were the direct results of Colet's foundation of St. Paul's."

These statements are an amazing reversal of the real facts. The authority for Green's "it has been said " seems to be a passage in Knight's *Life of Colet* (p. 100, ed. 1724). " Within thirty years before it " (the Reformation) " there were more Grammar Schools erected and endowed in England than had been in 300 years before." But by " the Reformation " Knight meant the whole movement which began with the Dissolution of the Monasteries in 1535 ; that is the earlier, and not the latter years of Henry VIII. Knight's own statement is of questionable accuracy, but Knight's statement, as altered by Green, is unquestionably quite inaccurate. Even on Knight's statement it is difficult to see how Colet came to be looked on by Green as the originator of a Grammar School movement, since Colet's foundation was long after many of the 14 schools instanced by Knight, several of which indeed do not fall within his 30 years at all. Knight, it is clear (and in this he is perfectly right), did not consider that Colet originated the movement for founding schools, but, on the contrary, that he was himself following, if also improving on, the example of others, and partaking in a general movement already begun.

If Green was wrong as to Colet, he was also wrong as to Edward VI. What Green meant by 18 Grammar Schools founded by Edward VI. it is hard to say. The number may be derived from Strype's *Ecclesiastical Memorials* (II. part ii. p. 178), where a list is given of Schools founded by Edward VI. Green has, however, variegated his Strype. Strype's list gives 22 schools. But it includes Macclesfield, which Green had just read of in Knight as having been founded 45 years before Edward's accession; Tonbridge, which he no doubt knew was founded by Sir Andrew Judd; St. Alban's, which he imputed to the Abbey; and Shakespeare's School at Stratford-on-Avon, which is well known to have been kept by the Guild there long before, as its so-called foundation charter by Edward VI. shows. It is greatly to Green's credit, and shows with what care he used his authorities, that he did not swallow the 22 Edwardian Schools whole, as Canon Perry has done in his *History of the Church of England*, repeated in divers editions, even so late as 1891. Strype, however, did not profess to give an exhaustive list, and it is strange that Green should not have perceived this.

Green is, of course, not alone in his error. He is only selected for animadversion, because he is the most brilliant and best known of its propagators.

Canon Dixon, in his *History of the Church of England* (III., 458, ed. 1885), though in a note he points out three cases where schools existed before Edward which were continued or destroyed, repeats the common cry: "Not less than in Hospitals," (of which also a word could be said,) "in schools, the name of Edward VI. is famous for the great foundations that he planted in the nation: in the number of them he exceeded any of his predecessors." The learned Canon then proceeds to quote the inevitable Strype, and also, as he supposes, a former headmaster of Birmingham; but the latter quotation is really the passage already cited from Knight's *Life of Colet*.

In *Social England*, edited by Dr. H. D. Traill, we were promised the latest light on all English history, and "a combined history of research and education." Research on education has enabled Mr. J. Bass Mullinger (vol. iii., p. 229) to raise the number of Edwardian Schools. "Upwards of 30 Free Grammar Schools," he says, "founded at this time have permanently

associated the reign of Edward VI. with popular education."
He mentions 23 by name (including Christ's Hospital, which
whatever it was founded as, was certainly not founded as a Free
Grammar School) with "and others" at the end. He has added
to Strype's list no less than 11, thus bringing the total to
"upwards of 30," or, to be precise, to 33.

But this list includes Crediton, which appears on the face of
its charter to have existed before Henry VIII., and to have
been in course of re-foundation by him; Buckingham, of which
the earliest document printed states it to have been founded
before Edward VI.; and Pontefract, which in the printed official
source of information appears in an order of the Duchy Court
reciting an order *temp.* Edward VI. for its continuance.

Since this was written, a French writer, M. Jacques Par-
mentier, a Professor of Letters, has entered the field with a
Histoire de l'Éducation en Angleterre (Perrin & Cie., Paris,
1896). This author still believes that Alfred the Great founded
Oxford University, but, at the same time, that the English before
the Norman Conquest were merely a drunken lot of dissolute
barbarians, that York Minster was tenanted by monks, and so
forth. However, he at least goes, not one, but eleven better than
Mr. J. B. Mullinger, though attributing to Edward, or the
government, a more active share than some other writers have
done. "The *amour propre*," he says, "of the schismatic or
Anglican sovereigns mingled in it" (a movement for education).
"Catholic England, united to Rome, had had schools; it was
necessary that Protestant England, separated from Rome,
should have them too. If the reckoning is correct, there were
founded 49 under Henry VIII., 44 under Edward VI., and 150
under Elizabeth."

The "true truth" about the matter is that all these attempts
to assign a particular number of Schools to the creation of
Edward VI. are waste labour and beside the mark. With
Edward VI. personally, of course, we are not concerned. The
only foundation with which he is even reported to have had any
personal connection is Christ's Hospital, and that was not
founded as a Grammar School, but as a Foundling Hospital,

and, as I have shown elsewhere, he gave it little but his name. Even in that, he was but the mouthpiece of Ridley. The expression "Edward VI." is, it must be understood, only a short form for the predominant protector of the moment. The poor, rickety, over-educated boy, who was only 16 when he died, was not responsible for either the good or the evil that was done in his time. Edward VI. means first the Protector Somerset, then Dudley, Duke of Northumberland, and under them Paget, Sir Walter Mildmay, Lord Chancellors Audley and Rich, and others.

With this explanation, we may say that in point of fact Edward VI. either did not found a single Grammar School, or, if he did, he founded Grammar Schools, not by units or tens, but by scores. 51 is the number attributed to him in the report of the Schools Inquiry Commission, which in this respect is almost entirely a compilation from the Report of Lord Brougham's Commission of Inquiry into Charities, published between 1818 and 1837. But this list is by no means complete. 82 appear as continued or re-founded by him in the records now printed, most of which are not contained in the list referred to ; and there are quite as many more which do not appear here.

To thoroughly appreciate how very little Edward VI. or his father really did for education, we have first to realize the extraordinary antiquity of many of our existing schools. Grammar Schools, instead of being comparatively modern, post-Reformation inventions, are among our most ancient institutions, some of them far older than the Lord Mayor of London or the House of Commons.

The records appended to this book, show that close on 200 Grammar Schools (and the Schools of Winchester and Eton are included in the term Grammar Schools), existed in England before the reign of Edward VI., which were, for the most part, abolished or crippled under him. It will appear, however, that these records are defective. They are only the survivors of a much larger host which have been lost in the storms of the past, and drowned in the seas of destruction. They do not give, they could not from their nature give, a complete account of all the Grammar Schools then existing in England. Such an account is probably irrecoverable. The materials for it do not exist. Enough, however, can be gathered from other sources of information to permit the assertion to be confidently made that these 200 Schools do not represent anything like all the Grammar Schools which existed in, or shortly before, the reign of Edward VI. Three hundred is a moderate estimate of the number in the year 1535, when the floods of the great revolution, which is called the Reformation, were let loose. Most of them were swept away either under Henry or his son; or, if not swept away, plundered and damaged.

The Grammar Schools which existed were not mere monkish Schools, or Choristers' Schools, or Elementary Schools. Many of them were the same Schools which now live and thrive. All were Schools of exactly the same type, and performing precisely the same sort of functions, as the Public Schools and Grammar Schools of to-day. There were indeed also Choristers' Schools and Elementary Schools. There were scholarships at Schools, and exhibitions thence to the Universities, and the whole paraphernalia of secondary education. Nor was secondary education —not that the wretched, ambiguous term was then used—then understood in any different sense to that in which it was understood up to fifty years ago. It was conducted on the same lines and in the main by instruments of the same kind, if not identically the same, as those in use till the present generation.

I am not going to attempt, in the present book, to prove the whole of this thesis. This volume is limited to the provision for secondary education as it appears in the official records taken in the last two years of Henry VIII. and the first two years of Edward VI., though excursions have been found necessary into the earlier and later histories of some of the institutions concerned.

The official records themselves are here printed, because mere references to them are not, in a case of this kind, convincing. The sort of feeling one has to meet was exemplified in the airy remark of a critic on the announcement of this book. "'It will, (they say), revolutionize our views as to the condition of national education at the period named.' One is getting accustomed to that kind of thing. What a lot, to be sure, we have to un-learn!" He went on to compare it to a book which is said to be going to whitewash Herod the Great.

Whether the comparison is just or not depends on whether the whitewashing of Herod the Great—who, by the way, in mediæval plays always appeared with a black face, and therefore may be supposed to need whitewash—is to be accomplished with new materials, or merely a new stirring up of the old. It is one thing to move for a new trial, at the bar of history, on the ground that the verdict recorded is against the weight of evidence, and another to appeal on the ground that fresh evidence is forthcoming, which must needs alter the finding. This last is the present case. It is hoped to substitute for a theory based on hearsay evidence, mainly as to character, one founded on facts placed on record at the time the transaction took place.

In the records, specimens of all the kinds of Schools then existing in England appear, from the ancient Cathedral Schools to the not yet completed foundation of Berkhampstead ; from Winchester and Eton, with their well-paid masters and 70 scholarships apiece, to Cirencester, with two scholarships, and Launceston, where an old man is paid 13s. 4d. a year by the mayor, to teach young children the A, B, C.

There were 7 classes of Schools at that time, classifying them according to the institution with which they were connected. There were Schools connected with Cathedral Churches, with Monasteries, with Collegiate Churches or Colleges, with Hospitals, with Guilds, with Chantries, and lastly, independent Schools, existing ostensibly and actually for themselves as independent entities.

2. Cathedral Schools.

The Cathedral Grammar Schools of the Cathedral Churches "of the Old Foundation," some of which, as I have elsewhere shown, trace their descent from time immemorial, from the beginning of the Churches themselves, long before the Norman Conquest,

and others from the age immediately succeeding it, do not figure
largely here. Indeed, they ought not to appear at all. That of
Lincoln appears incidentally as the place at which divers scholarships, founded by divers Bishops of Lincoln, were held. Thus
Bishop Burghershe, *temp.* Edward II., founded a Chantry for
five chaplains at the altar of St. Katherine, and "for the maintenance of 6 poor boys professing the art of grammar, from the
age of 7 years till they have completed 16 years." They got
£10 among them for their commons and liveries. A further part
of the foundation was the distribution of £8 6s. 8d. a year in
pennies to the astounding number of 2,000 poor people present
at his Obits. Bishop Gynwell, called by an error in the record
Hymwell, about 1350, provided an unspecified number of scholarships for boys " at the Grammar School in the Cathedral Church
of Lincoln " ; and Bishop Buckingham, between 1362 and 1397,
founded still other scholarships for " 2 poor boys at the Grammar
School." These were all being maintained in 1548, except that
there was only one boy instead of two on Buckingham's foundation. A subsequent Bishop, Smith, had founded other exhibitions for choristers in the Song School. The Lincoln Cathedral
Grammar School has a long and interesting history from the
11th century. "But that is another story," and not to be told
here.

Wells and Chichester Cathedral Grammar Schools are included
in the returns here given, and the account of them is not remarkable for official accuracy, that of Wells being inaccurate in
a very essential particular.

As to Chichester the account given is: "Anthony Clarke,
Schoolmaster, Prebendary in the said church of the prebend
called Vyley "—a mistake for Highleigh—"impropriated for a
Grammar School for ever ; whereof the said Prebendary, of his
benevolence, alloweth towards the finding of an usher, yearly,
£4. Also the Dean and Chapter have granted and paid since
Michaelmas, 1547, to the finding of an usher, £2 12s. 4d., and
have granted to continue the same accordingly out of the livings
of the said Dean and Chapter for ever." A note adds, apparently as to the £4, "Not thought within the compass of the

Act," *i.e.*, the Act for the Dissolution of Colleges and Chantries. As the Cathedral Churches were exempt from the Act, the whole endowment being a prebend of the Cathedral must surely have been excluded also. This School is one quoted by Knight in his *Life of Colet* as founded by Story, Bishop of Chichester, who gave a bequest to it in his will in 1502. What Story did, in fact, was to procure the annexation to the School, which existed long before, of a canonry and prebend in the Cathedral, in February, 1498, and it is therefore still called the Prebendal School. An usher was contemplated by him in his statutes, and it does not quite appear where the benevolence of the master came in.

Wells has a longer ascertained history, with a sad conclusion, the sadness of which is largely due to the Chantry Commissioners having been led to report the thing that was not. They said, "The Dean and Chapter, of their free will, keep and maintain a Free Grammar School, and do pay to the master yearly for his stipend and wages £13 6s. 8d., and to the usher £6 13s. 4d."

That Wells, in common with other Cathedral Churches, was bound to maintain a Grammar School, appears from its earliest statutes in the 12th century. In 1229 there occurs a deed among the muniments of Wells Cathedral, for lending which I must express my thanks to Canon Church, whose excellent book on the early history of Wells Cathedral is well known. The deed is made by Roger of Chynton, Chaplain of Jocelyn, Bishop of Bath, Thomas Lock and Agnes his mother, and apparently represents what is now called an "equitable mortgage." The Chaplain having purchased the house from Lock as executor of his father, Adam Lock, mason, for 10 marks, and paid half the purchase money, it was provided that the title deeds should remain on deposit in the Treasury of Wells Cathedral, and be delivered to the purchaser, when he had paid the other 5 marks. This house was by another deed conveyed by Roger, now described as Canon of Wells and Rector of Chynton, "to God and the Church of St. Andrew, and the Chancellor of Wells, for the use of the School of Wells, so that the Chancellor may confer it, together with the mastership (*regimine*) of the

School (*scholarum*, plural as usual), on the Schoolmaster for the
time being."

This house was confirmed as part of the Chapter property,
"for the use of the School," by Archbishop Peckham, in 1281.
In 1410 it became the College of the Vicars-Choral, called
Mountery, which still exists; another house in Torrelane being
provided in exchange, for the use of the master of the Grammar
School (*eo nomine*). The "commons" of the Schoolmaster,
£1 10*s.* 4*d.*, appear in the Communar's or Bursar's accounts for
1327. In 1457 the Fabric Rolls show an expenditure of £3,
a considerable sum, in repairs at the school house.

There can be no doubt, therefore, that the Chapter maintained a School and that they held endowments for it. Nor
was this School a mere Choristers' School. There was a
Choristers' School, but it was a distinct institution. The
Choristers' Master was appointed not by the Chancellor, but
by the Precentor; and they had a separate School on the
opposite side of the Close, and a boarding house, the statutes
of which were confirmed by Bishop Beckington in 1457.
Very quaint are these statutes, showing that the boys slept
three in a bed, two smaller ones with their heads to the
head of the bed, and an older one with his head to the
foot of the bed, and his feet between the others' heads;
that their play-time was only half an hour, or at the most
an hour, before supper in winter, after it in summer. Minute
directions are given that the boys were to cut their bread at
dinner, not gnaw it with their teeth or tear it with their nails;
drink with their mouths empty, not full, and not pick their teeth
with their knives; and to take up their meat like gentlemen, not
ravenously. But this is an excursus. Suffice it to say that there
was no justification for the statement that the Grammar School
was kept by the "freewill" of the Dean and Chapter. It is possible indeed, nay, probable, that the amount to be paid to the
masters was a matter of discretion, and so far of free-will. But
there can be no doubt that a Grammar School, and an adequate
Grammar School, the Dean and Chapter were bound to maintain.

In the time of Elizabeth the same master seems to have been

employed to teach the Grammar School and the Choristers'
School, and then the two became fused; with the result that in
1852 there were thirty boys in it besides the eight choristers,
and in 1876 it ceased to exist: which sad ending is related
by the Chapter themselves in one of the Cathedral Commission
Reports.

3. Early College Schools.

The next class of Schools was that of the Grammar Schools
of the Collegiate Churches or Colleges, which figure largely in
the records under examination.   They would figure still more
largely than they do, had not many of them been suppressed at
the time of the suppression of the monasteries—"daily devoured
apace and nothing said."

Some of these Colleges were amongst the most ancient and
important of ecclesiastical institutions, when ecclesiastical institutions were the most important institutions in the country.
The Colleges, for instance, of S. John of Beverley; S. John
Baptist, Chester; of S. Cross or Holyrood, Crediton; of S.
Wilfrid, Ripon; of S. Mary, Shrewsbury, and S. Chad, Shrewsbury; of S. Mary of Southwell; S. Mary of Stafford; S. Edith
of Tamworth; S. Mary of Warwick; S. Mary of Wimborne—to
name some of those which appear in these records—all appear
in Domesday, and are so ancient as to be of unknown legendary,
prehistoric, or only semi-historic origin in Early English, i.e.
præ-Norman times.   They were, in fact, the same in constitution, and hardly distinguishable in purpose from Cathedral
Churches, and some of them were, perhaps, founded to be
Cathedral Churches.   Crediton was actually a Cathedral till the
see was removed to Exeter by Edward the Confessor.   But as
these colleges did not remain in direct connection with Bishops,
or become the principal seats of Bishops, they were not reckoned
as Cathedrals.   They were staffed, however, by the same class
of people as the Cathedrals, the secular canons; that is, ordinary
clergymen, who, like the canons of our Cathedrals now, married
and gave in marriage, and did not find domestic life inconsistent
with the worship of God or the service of man.   For their con-

B

stitution in detail, I am fain to refer to my *Visitations and
Memorials of Southwell Minster* (Camden Society, 1891), or to
my paper on *The Inmates of Beverley Minster* (Transactions
of the East Riding Antiquarian Society, 1894). Suffice it here
to say that a primary duty and an essential attribute of these
Colleges were the maintenance of a Grammar School.   In
ancient days their principal officer, after the Dean—and in many
places he existed before there was a Dean—was the Schoolmaster,
in later days called Chancellor, and, when so called, devolving
his duty of grammar teaching on a deputy commonly called
the Schoolmaster (*Magister Scholarum*), or, in full, "The
Master of the Grammar School of the Collegiate Church of
N.," or sometimes " of the town of N."

This College School was open to all lay folk, as well as church
folk. The College of Southwell, commonly called Southwell
Minster, one of the oldest and largest of these collegiate churches,
which survived as such even down to 1848, has been discussed at
length in the book above mentioned. Its record in the present
book (pp. 101–4) has therefore been cut down so as merely to show
that part of the possessions of the Church, out of which any
payment was made for the Grammar School, viz., the Common
Fund, divisible among the Residentiary Canons, in addition to
their separate prebends, and the prebend of Normanton annexed
to the Chancellorship. The common lands produced an income
of £33 net, applicable to certain wages of deacons, choristers,
incense-bearers, and "for the relieving of poor scholars thither
resorting for their erudition either in grammar or song." The
prebend of Normanton was worth £27 a year net, out of which
was paid the Prebendary's Vicar or deputy, "besides 40s. given
to the Schoolmaster of the Free School there." In a second
document the Song Schoolmaster appears separately as the
"Master of the Queristers," receiving 20s. wages, while the
Grammar Schoolmaster is called simply the Schoolmaster. The
parishioners " present that the said Parish Church of Southwell
standeth in the middle of the shire, accompted as a chief
church " (" Archbishop's see " Henry's commissioners called it),
" wherein is and hath been kept a Grammar School most apt

for the same time out of mind, and towards the maintenance thereof is given 40s. by year out of the Prebend of Normanton." So they beg " that our Parish Church may stand. Also that our Grammar School may also stand, with such stipend as appertaineth the like, wherein our poor youth may be instructed, and that also by the resort of their parents, we, His Grace's poor tenants and inhabitants there, may have some relief, whereby we shall be the better able to serve His Grace at time appointed." Whence it may be inferred that the School was a Boarding School, and the boarders (in those days when there was no Civil Service or Army and Navy Stores) profitable to the town and neighbourhood by the money spent on food and other necessaries. This is further evidenced from the delightful complaint made at a visitation in 1484, that " the Grammar School master does not attend to the teaching of his scholars in School at the proper hours, and gives his scholars indiscriminate remedies (holidays) on ordinary week-days, so that they learn nothing as it were in time, spending their parents' money for nothing. And they do not talk Latin in school, but English." The master at this time, John Barre, had been admitted master on the presentation of the Prebendary of Normanton in 1475. The earliest mention of the Grammar School master in the only two Southwell documents which survive is 1415, when he witnessed a chapter document. There is a statute of the Minster in 1248, providing that Schools of Grammar or Logic are not to be held within the prebends of the canons, except according to the custom of York. If there were Grammar Schools in the small dependent townships in Nottinghamshire, which formed the prebends of the canons, it may be safely affirmed that there was a Grammar School at the then important town and archiepiscopal seat of Southwell itself. Again, in 1238, the Chancellor of Southwell asserted his right to appoint the master of Newark Grammar School against the Priory of S. Catharine by Lincoln, to which Newark Church was appropriated. From this, again, we may reasonably infer that the home-town had its Grammar School. It is certain that the Chapter felt bound to keep up the Grammar School properly. For, by a document of 1504, when one of the best Chantries in the Minster (S. Cuthbert's), worth no less than £13 6s. 8d., fell vacant, which had been held by a deputy Grammar School master, the senior Vicar-Choral claimed it, but waived his claim at the Chapter's request, in order that it might be bestowed on another, who undertook to teach the Grammar School.

It is owing to this fashion of eking out what had, in the course of time, become the inadequate salary of the Grammar School master, that at Stafford, Tamworth, and Wimborne, we find the School treated not as a charge on the general resources of the Church, but on particular Chantries. Both at Stafford and Tamworth, it was the "Morrow-Mass Priest," who was Schoolmaster, as was the case also at Southwell in the transaction quoted in 1504. In our records we find very commonly that the Schoolmaster is also morrow-mass priest. The morrow-mass priest had to say mass at 4, 5, or 6 a.m., for the benefit of travellers and workmen before going to their business. His selection for Schoolmaster was probably due to the fact that he had to get up extra early, and therefore was on the spot to teach boys, those early-rising abominations, which plague even the modern household with their unseemly hours.

At Wimborne a Chantry called, in 1535, "the Schoolmasters' Chantry," is said (p. 56) to have been founded by Margaret Countess of Richmond and Derby, mother of Henry VII., well known still at Oxford and Cambridge as the Lady Margaret, whose name is commemorated in Boat Clubs, Ladies' Halls, and Divinity Professorships. Reginald Pole, by the way, afterwards Cardinal and persecutor, was Dean of this College in 1535. The incumbent of the Chantry was to "say mass for the souls of the founders, and to be a Schoolmaster, to teach freely all manner of children grammar within the same College." There was in 1548 "no School kept now . . . by the death of the late master; nevertheless it is very requisite and necessary to have said School maintained, for the town of Wimbourne is a great market-town and thoroughfare, and there is no Grammar School kept within 12 miles" of it. There is added a "memorandum for the appointment of the Schoolmaster,

Symond Smith, M.A., recommended by Mr. Cheke," this Mr.
Cheke being "Sir John Cheke, Who first taught Cambridge
and King Edward Greek," and became a Secretary of State.

At Ripon, however (p. 295), we still find the " Scolemaster of
Gramer " paid " yearly, forth of the common of the said church,"
that is out of the common fund; and his stipend is the same as
that at Southwell, viz., £2 a year.

At Crediton, in Devon, no less than 3 out of the 13 prebends
were used apparently as exhibitions at the Universities, one of
the three exhibitioners, however, being described as "scholar
of Exeter," which may mean at Exeter Grammar School.   The
Grammar School master is not mentioned.   He was probably
one of the Vicars-Choral.   The Song School master, " teacher of
children and queresters (choristers)," got £4 a year.

Before leaving the collegiate churches, it should be added that
at Warwick we find (pp. 231-2) a Guild selling lands at ten
years' purchase, to find the money to re-purchase the town's
parish church and Grammar School from the Crown, which
School was called "The King's New School of Warwick."   This
School was that of the Collegiate Church, in regard to which
occurs the actually oldest record of post-Conquest times, referring
to a school.   The church is mentioned in Domesday Book.   In
1123, Earl Roger purports to give " to the Church of St. Mary
of Warwick the School (scolas) of the same church, that the service of God may be improved by the attendance of scholars."
About the same date is a writ of Henry I., directing that " the
Church of All Saints at Warwick," a college of canons in the
castle, " should have all its customs as they (sic) did in the time
of Edward, and in like manner may have the school."   A few
years later the establishments of these two collegiate churches
were united by the same Earl Roger in St. Mary's; and to the
united churches is granted "the School of Warwick," a school
which is still in the front rank.

4. Schools in Connection with Monasteries.

In spite of the superior usefulness of the collegiate churches,
for some reason which no Gibbon has yet arisen to explain, the

Western world, and England especially, was in the 10th century seized with a craze, like that under which the Eastern world had long lain, for celibacy, fastings, floggings, and other forms of self-torture of the same kind as, and perhaps not very much less in degree than, the fanatical performances of Indian fakirs now. Such things are incompatible with matrimony and a married clergy. So in the era of Dunstan before the Conquest, and of Lanfranc after it, a movement sprang up in favour of monks and the so-called regular canons, in preference to the ordinary clergy and the secular canons. In England it went so far, that in many even of the cathedrals, as at Canterbury, Winchester, and Worcester, the clergy were displaced to make way for monks, and the Bishop's Chapter became one of monks instead of canons; a thing unknown abroad, where from St. Peter's at Rome to the furthest corners of Norway and Spain, the cathedrals always remained in the hands of the clergy. For nearly two centuries the creation of colleges in England almost entirely ceased, and in many cases the existing ones were suppressed and transferred to regulars. This happened at Bedford, at Christchurch, Hants, at Derby, at Leicester, at Oxford, at Waltham, and in many other places; and, wherever it happened, the neighbourhood as a rule lost, or was in danger of losing, the benefit of a school.

Mr. Mullinger indeed in *Social England* quotes (from Strype) the speaker of the House of Commons, telling Queen Elizabeth, in 1562, that "at least 100 Schools were wanting in England which before that time had been." "An allusion," adds Mr. Mullinger, "which, we may safely assume with Strype, had reference to the Schools of the monasteries." The assumption would, however, be extremely unsafe.

It is true that several Schools are mentioned in our records in connection with monasteries. Thus, at Evesham "it was presented that since the reign of Edward III. there hath been paid by the Abbots of the late monastery yearly the sum of £10, with meat and drink freely within the said late monastery, to one Schoolmaster, for keeping a Free Grammar School in the said town of Evesham, until the surrender of the said late monastery." This School has reached the historians, and they generally tell us that it ceased with the monastery. But what says this record? "Since which time the king's majesty's receiver of his highness' revenues there for the time being hath likewise paid yearly to the said Schoolmaster £10 for his teaching of the said Free School, until the Feast of Annunciation last past." At Whitsuntide the Schoolmaster departed "for lack of wages," owing perhaps to the Chantries Act. The inhabitants ask that the vicar should be appointed to be Schoolmaster as well as vicar, as his income has been diminished "by £4 a year," through the loss of the "privy tithes and offerings" of "some score and more" of the hangers-on of the dissolved monastery. Appointed he was accordingly, in spite of a neighbouring knight saying that he was "not so meet" as the departed master, and the stipend of £10 a year was continued to him and his successors (p. 280). £10 a year, one may as well say here as elsewhere, was very good pay for a Schoolmaster in those days, being that of the headmaster of Eton College himself.

Canon Dixon plunges, in a note to his history, (II., 460) into the matter of Evesham School, and makes the sweeping assertion: "A School was now erected at Evesham. . . . Evesham Abbey School was celebrated in its day, but it was swept away at the Dissolution, and the place was left without a school until the reign of James I. and the year 1605." This is quite unfounded. The School was, as we have seen, not swept away at the Dissolution, and when James I. gave a charter to the borough of Evesham, confirming the corporation which they already enjoyed, though its rights had, it seemed, been disputed, he also confirmed the corporation and governors of the Grammar School. While directing it to be called "The Free Grammar School of Prince Henry," he expressly confirms as part of its possessions, "for and towards the maintenance of the Master of the School aforesaid, for the time being, a certain annuity of £10 by the year, heretofore by us and divers of our predecessors and ancestors allowed and paid to the Master of the said School, as appears to us from several records, remaining in our Court of Exchequer."

Canon Dixon may of course call the School the Abbey School if he pleases. Its endowment, however, did not come out of the general funds of the Abbey, but was a special foundation, dating only, as the record shows, from the reign of Edward III. This was also the case at Bruton, in Somersetshire, where it appears (p. 193) the School was built on the north side of the monastery, but separated from it by a highway, and was endowed by Bishop Fitz-James, of London, in 1520. The lands were vested in the monastery in trust for the School. Nevertheless, in spite of the trust, the inhabitants had to get a grant of them from the Crown in 1549, and the School was called the Free Grammar School of Edward VI.

At Cirencester, "till the dissolution of the monastery of Winchcombe, there was granted and paid out of the same monastery, one yearly pension of £10 to and for a Free School, there to be maintained and kept," but, unlike Evesham, "since the Dissolution, the same hath been withdrawn and not paid, unto the great discommodity of the same town of Cirencester."

At Lewes, Agnes Morley had founded a Grammar School in 1512, and given the nomination of the master to the Prior. This too was in danger of perishing with the monastery, though the monastery was only a Trustee. It was seemingly saved by the Commissioners, who ordered the School to be continued. Again, the great Public School of Sherborne clearly existed before 1550, but it was not maintained by the monastery. Out of an endowment of some £1,200 a year, the Abbey of Our Lady of Sherborne spent, in 1535, just £5 2s. 8d. on education, in the " Exhibitions " of " three scholars in the Grammar School at Sherborne." At Bridgwater, where " the inhabitants make their most humble petition to have a Free Grammar School erected," had been a Priory. This Priory had maintained and educated 13 poor boys. Out of its general revenues? No ; but out of two rectories appropriated to it by Robert Burnell, Bishop of Bath and Wells, on that condition.

On the other hand, at Leominster and Launceston, where there had been priories, there was seemingly no School in connection with them. At "Leymster," which, we are told (p. 94), is

" the greatest market town within the county of Hereford, there is a Grammar School, kept by one Edward Allen, being a man of honest behaviour, and well learned, who hath no other living but that he hath of his scholars weekly." Yet " ever before this time there hath been School kept in the same town." The inhabitants ask (p. 102) " that they may have part of the stipendiaries and Chantry toward the maintenance of a Grammar School." But they asked in vain, until in Edward VI's. last year, and in his last month, 20th June, 1553, they paid £100 to buy £10 a year worth of lands of the monastery (which was worth in all £500 a year), and got an order for the grant. Edward died on 6th July, and the grant was not therefore completed till 1554, so that this School is credited to the Roman Mary instead of the Protestant Edward. How far any credit is to be given to either, more than to any other vendor of property, the reader may decide for himself.

Whether the monasteries themselves did anything for education and the learning of others, however learned some of their inmates may have been, is a question the answer to which again " belongs to another story." The instances of Schools in connection with monasteries before us certainly do not show that they did. That as ordinaries in their " peculiars," as rich landlords, and as trustees for other people, they may have controlled or even founded and maintained some Grammar Schools, is certain. The common belief and often repeated assertion, that all the education in the Middle Ages was done by the monks, is quite wrong. Whether the monks ever affected even to keep a Grammar School for any but their own novices, among whom outsiders were not admitted, is doubtful. Is there a single instance on record in the days of records of a monk teaching an ordinary Grammar School? There are divers cases recorded where a secular Schoolmaster was employed to teach the novices. Certain it is, that at the period with which we are concerned monks had little to do with general education, and less with learning.

5. Later College Schools.

By the middle of the 13th century the monastic *furore* had spent its force, and a new era of Colleges began. The first symptom of the awakening was the institution of the orders of friars, who were not, like monks, supposed to be confined to their cloisters, but to be in and of the world. They took the universities by storm, they gave an enormous impetus to learning, they stayed the tide of monkery, and at the same time woke up the secular clergy—who, by this time, were enforced celibates like the monks—to the need of combination in corporations, if they were to hold their own in the duties and emoluments of Church and State. Hence a new era of collegiate churches, and a marvellous new crop of Colleges arose. In modern parlance, the term College is confined to the collegiate church, or chapel rather, at the Universities; but the corporation of canons, fellows, secular priests, or clerks, which formed the staff of the collegiate church outside the Universities, was just as much a College as the similar body in the University, and was very commonly so called. The College of S. Thomas of Glasney, near Penrhyn, in Cornwall, is a fairly early specimen of the second crop, having been founded (or perhaps only augmented) in 1271, while Thornton College, Lincolnshire, only founded by Henry VIII. in 1542 out of the suppressed priory of Thornton, was one of the latest. In this suppression and conversion Henry, as is well known, was only following excellent papal precedents. His Holiness himself in 1415 gave his sanction to the creation of another College on our list, that of S. John the Baptist at Stoke-by-Clare, by a similar conversion of the priory there; to say nothing of the wholesale suppressions out of which Winchester and Eton Colleges, All Souls' and Magdalen Colleges at Oxford, were founded. How far the later Colleges were bound to keep Grammar Schools does not appear quite clear. From the instance of Pleshey it would almost appear that they were not; as there seems to be no provision for any but a Song School master. Perhaps the keeping of a Grammar School depended on the place where the College was. If it was populous, a Grammar

School was kept; if not, not. Certain it is that at Stoke-by-Clare there was kept not only the Song School master directed by the statutes (which are given by Dugdale), called in our records the Schoolmaster in the College, but also the master of the Free School, with a salary of five times as much, being indeed more than was paid to any vicar-choral, and more than was paid to at least one of the prebendaries. This College was granted to Sir John Cheke.

Of the Colleges mentioned in our records the majority, 24, excluding Oxford and Cambridge, or 31 including them, belong to the later crop. Oddly enough, the earliest of them is one founded wholly for educational purposes, the College, namely, of the "Scholars de Vawze" (p. 255), i.e., the Valley Scholars, at Salisbury. It does not seem to have borne any relation to one of the Regular Orders called "de Valle Scholarium," who had a convent at Paris about 1250, as it was presided over by a Canon of Salisbury, and consisted apparently of secular clerks, "studying divinity and the liberal arts." It was a very remarkable institution, no less than the first recorded University College in England. Its foundation by Egidius (Giles), of Bridport, Bishop of Salisbury, in 1261, preceded by three years that of Merton College, the oldest College at Oxford.

"Its early history was very much the same. Merton's House of Scholars was founded at Maldon, in Surrey, where certain bailiffs and priests were settled to manage the property and pray for the founder's soul, and apply the income for the support of scholars living at Oxford University. By 1274 Merton House was transferred to Oxford itself, and became Merton College. The College of the Scholars of the Valley at Salisbury was not thus divided at first; for the warden, who managed the property and the scholars in the schools alike, lived at Salisbury, and the Cathedral records show that in 1278 the Chancellor of the Cathedral (who still maintained his statutory Grammar School) asserted his authority over them as the Chancellor of Notre Dame at Paris asserted his over Paris University. In 1325 the majority of the scholars were sent to Oxford, where they lived in Salisbury Hall. The College at Salisbury seems to have become practically a nursery for a few scholars attending the Cathedral Grammar School at Salisbury, and so remained until the Reformation." (*Winchester College* 1393–1893, *Contemporary Review, July,* 1893.)

This College had already disappeared into the pockets of Henry VIII., as it is described as " late College " in the certificate of his Commissioners. It is only mentioned for a Chantry in Salisbury Cathedral maintained out of its former revenues.

The next College in point of date was also a University College, and was also at Salisbury—the College of St. Edmund. The certificate says, " Who is the founder of it does not appear, but many benefactors." We know better, thanks to the publication of *Sarum Documents* in the Rolls Series. It was founded by Walter de la Wyle, Bishop of Salisbury, in 1269, for 13 scholars in theology, but seems to have had at the time of dissolution only 4 Chaplains or Fellows, a Barber and a Laundress, a Steward of the Manors, and a Rent-Collector, with an income of £93 16s. 4d.

Glasney has been already mentioned. The next oldest to it was a collegiate church of the ordinary type, that of Trinity College, Stratford-on-Avon, founded, at his native place, in 1331, by John of Stratford, Archbishop of Canterbury. The head here was called not Dean, but Warden. The Schoolmaster was apparently a Song School master only, as he is described as " Schoolmaster and Organ-player," the School of the Guild of Stratford maintaining the Grammar School.

In 1334 Bishop Grandison, of Exeter, purchased from the Dean and Chapter of Rouen the Manor and Church of Ottery S. Mary, which had been appropriated to them at or before the Conquest, and founded a collegiate church therewith. A Grammar School master was a part of the foundation. This College was surrendered to Henry VIII. under a special commission in 1545, and among the pensions appointed to the warden, prebendaries and others, duly appears " to Sir John Chubbe, Priest, being Schoolmaster there, £10." The Song School master was probably the "chapel clerk," John Parke, who held by patent under the Chapter seal.

In 1384 William of Wykeham laid out a new line of development for these Colleges by constituting a Grammar School, the main, instead of a subsidiary, object of one. This precedent of College Schools (not without plenty of pabulum derived from suppression of monasteries) was followed by Henry VI. in Eton, on an even more gorgeous scale than Winchester, in 1440.

The record of Eton reminds us that, rich as it was—£1,066 a year against Winchester's £947, and both may be multiplied roughly by 20 times now—it had been largely plundered by Edward IV. He, in a spirit we now impute only to Celtic revolutionaries, could not endure the foundations of a deposed *régime*, and transferred all its possessions to "Windsor College." Much was recovered by William Waynflete's exertions, yet some never was. The story is told by Mr. H. C. Maxwell Lyte, C.B., now head of the Record Office, in his standard *History of Eton College* (Macmillan, 1875, pp. 60–78). Hence, in 1546, there were only 7 fellows at £5 a year instead of 10 at double that sum; 5 chaplains at £4, instead of 10 at £5; while the Schoolmaster only got £10 instead of £16. The "Conducts" had £2 a year instead of £4 a year. One of the Conducts was also organ-player, and his stipend should have been £6 a year; in fact, he only got £3 6s. 8d. The Usher was the only person who did not suffer, but, on the contrary, gained, unless, as seems probable, there is a mistake in the record, for he got £10 a year instead of £6 13s. 4d. *Apropos* of these Conducts, as their name still subsists at Eton, and has been mis-explained by Dr. Sharpe in a note in his *Hustings Wills* to mean a "conductor," it may be of interest to observe that they are mentioned several times in these records. They appear, for instance, in London (p. 145) and at Winchester College (p. 87), whence they were copied at Eton under the same name. The name is simply an Englished form of the Latin *conductitius*, as it appears in the statutes, meaning a hireling; and was applied to the chaplains, who were not, like the fellows, an integral part of the corporation, and had not, like them, freeholds in their posts during good behaviour, but were hired servants dismissible at pleasure.

A few years after Eton, in 1448, but on a much humbler scale, as befitted its founder, Spone, who was only an Archdeacon instead of a king, came Towcester College, "founded for two priests, one a preacher, the other a teacher of grammar"; the former having £8 19s. 10d.; and the latter, "well-learned, of the age of 45 years, and teacheth daily freely," £7 13s. 2d. This was re-purchased by Spone's trustees from Edward VI., and continued, and is the present Towcester Grammar School.

A more gorgeous foundation of the Winchester type was the Jesus College at Rotherham, founded by Archbishop Rotherham, an early Etonian, in 1484, with a Provost, £14 4s. 8d.; and three Fellows, who were a Schoolmaster of Grammar, £10 19s. 4d.; a Schoolmaster of Song, £7 12s. 2d.; and a Schoolmaster of Writing, £6 6s.; but instead of 70 scholars boarded, there were only six. There were a butler and a cook; and the College paid for barber and laundress. Not far off in Yorkshire, was the College of St. Andrew at Acaster, in the parish of Stillingfleet, founded by Bishop Stillington, of Bath, about 1480; also for a Provost and 3 Fellows, "whereof one doth keep a Free School of Grammar according to the foundation." This, however, was not a large foundation, though it too had its Free Schools of Song and of Writing, and the Scrivener's art. Total income, £37 15s. 6½d. The Grammar master here, poor man, had only £5 a year, and is described (p. 299) as "indifferently learned in grammar." He was, however (p. 304), "appointed to remain as Schoolmaster, and also to serve the cure there; And, because he must do both, allow him £8." He, at least, could have had little reason to be dissatisfied with dissolution. His clerical duties were not heavy, as "the necessity" of the College "is for the inhabitants of Acaster, being in number 200; the river Ouse, which is a great stream, running betwixt the said College and the parish church, and in that place without a bridge." Even far-distant Cumberland had its College of this kind, founded yb Lord Dacre, at Kirkoswald, with a Provost and five Brethren, two of whom were Schoolmasters, who received £2 apiece more than the other three, or £8 13s. 4d. each.

6. Schools in Connection with Hospitals.

Next to College Schools come Hospital Schools, both in regard to antiquity and importance.   But the subject of Hospital Schools is more difficult to work out, as there is less information available about Hospitals, and the connection of Schools with them is somewhat obscure.   A Hospital meant generally an < Almshouse, for the poor rather than for the sick.   Not very many of the ancient Hospitals appear in this book, as they were exempt from the Act of Edward VI., and their Schools would not, as a rule, be noted under Henry VIII.   The oldest Hospital mentioned is that of St. Cross, by Winchester.   Our record is, by the way, in this instance (as in many others), very ignorant on the subject of the Founders, for it imputed the foundation to "Henry Bowford, sometime Bishop of Winchester, and Cardinal, for a master, thirteen brethren, six priests, six clerks, and six querysters," and also for alms to 100 poor daily, and we find " the wages of the Schoolmaster, 46s. 8d."   But the true founder was not Henry Beaufort, uncle of Henry VI.; he was only a benefactor, whose beneficence was greater in intention than in fact.   The real founder was Henry of Blois, "sometime Bishop of Winchester, and Cardinal," and uncle of Henry II., and the date of foundation was 1132.   The Schoolmaster was probably only a Choristers' master in Henry VIII.'s time.   In Edward III.'s time it was given in evidence, before the foundation of Winchester College, that "13 poor scholars, named by the Master of the High School at Winchester," were reckoned among the hundred poor who were daily fed there.   Being so near Winchester, however, it is probable that there never was a real Grammar School at the Hospital.

This feeding of the poor scholars shows how natural it was to connect Schools with Hospitals.   It appears from Mr. Rashdall's *History of Universities*, that the oldest quasi-collegiate establishments in connection with Paris University consisted in this sort of provision for poor scholars.   At Pontefract, where the School was confirmed about 1090 to the College of Secular Canons of S. Clement in the Castle, it is recorded in 1266 that

S. Nicholas' Hospital was bound to find "40 loaves a week for scholars of the School of Pontefract," and this was still done in tho 15th century, subject to the proviso, "except in vacations." None, however, of the Hospital Schools mentioned in these records seem traceable to a very high antiquity. Some indeed have had a very high antiquity attributed to them, not always with good reason. A remarkable instance of this is S. Anthony's Hospital in Threadneedle Street, London, the School of which was very famous in the reign of Henry VIII., and is said to have produced Sir Thomas More, Dean Colet, and other worthies. It appears in the records, both in London, where it stood, and in Berkshire, because it was appropriated by Edward IV. to St. George's, Windsor, in that county. It is there said (p. 8) to have been "founded to find one master, two priests, one Schoolmaster, and 12 poor men," the Schoolmaster having for his stipend £16. Stow, followed by Strype, and other writers on the History of London since, have repeated this statement, as if it referred to the original foundation, about 1231, when, according to Stow, Henry III. granted a Jewish synagogue for its establishment. The history of this Hospital is extremely interesting; and thanks to the facility of access to the documents afforded me by Canon Dalton, of S. George's, Windsor, I have worked it out in detail, and hope some time to tell it. It was originally founded as a cell to the Hospital of S. Anthony at Vienne, in France (not Vienna, as Stow), served by Regular Canons, and was severed therefrom as an Alien Priory, in Henry VI.'s time, and handed over to the secular clergy. The School is, in fact, a very late incident in its history, not having been founded till 1441, after the transfer to the secular clergy, when John Carpenter, Provost of Oriel, and afterwards Bishop of Worcester, who was master of the Hospital, procured for it the appropriation of the church of St. Benet Fink, which stood next door to it, for the purpose of establishing a Free Grammar School. Copies of the deeds are extant at Windsor in Denton's Register.

Oddly enough, the end of this School has been as much misrepresented as its beginning. According to Strype, it was plundered by the Canons of Windsor, and extinguished by its own Schoolmaster, Edmund Johnson, in 1561. As the latter was a Wykehamist, I am glad to be able to say that this is a mere slander. The school flourished amazingly under Johnson, went on until the reign of James I., gradually declining, and, so far as can be gathered, lingered on as a poor sort of parochial Grammar School until the reign of Charles II. The building was destroyed in the Fire of London, and it was then it came to an end, the Windsor people probably not thinking it worth while to rebuild it. Yet over and over again it has been positively asserted that it began in 1231, and ceased in 1561, thus adding on 200 years to its career in front, and curtailing it by 100 years behind. Such is local history.

Among the few Schools recorded as attached to Hospitals will be found that of Banbury, where the Hospital of S. John Baptist was said to date from the reign of King John. The School was at one time so famous that it became a model for others, and from it issued a Grammar which became a standard work. The foundation deeds of Manchester Grammar School, in 1515 is expressed to be for a master " to teach and instruct children in grammar, according to the form of grammar then taught in the School in the town of Banbury." This is insisted on again in statutes in 1525. The High Master shall be " able to teach children Grammar after the School-use, manner and form of the School of Banbury, in Oxfordshire, now there taught, which is called Stanbridge Grammar." In fact, then, as before in the reign of Henry VI., when Eton was founded, and as afterwards when Dr. Arnold made Rugby the model School, the model Schoolmaster of the age proceeded from Winchester. John Stanbridge, Scholar of Winchester College, Fellow of New College, 1451, was the author of this Grammar. He was first Usher, then Head-master of Magdalen College School, and in 1501 was collated to the mastership of the Hospital of S. John Baptist at Banbury. He died in 1510. He was succeeded, so it is said, as Schoolmaster, though not as master of the Hospital, by his " brother, or near relative," Thomas Stanbridge, who was an M.A. of Magdalen College, Oxford, in 1518, and died 1522. He is spoken of by Wood in *Athenæ Oxonienses* as " an eminent Grammarian," and " a noted Schoolmaster of Banbury," and " was much frequented." Sir Thomas Pope, founder of Trinity College, Oxford, is said to have been educated there, and the statutes of the College, in 1556, gave Banbury School a second preference for Scholarships. The historian of Banbury (Alfred Beesley, London, 1841, p. 196), from whom these particulars are taken, then proceeds : " It is deeply to be regretted that no subsequent information can be traced respecting Banbury School. Its endowment and even its site are unknown, and all the advantages of this celebrated foundation have for ages been lost to the inhabitants. The school-house is imagined by some to have stood on the north side of the churchyard, where an old building was standing until 1838, but then taken down with the view of adding the site to the burial ground. This building had 64 feet frontage, and was 16 feet in breadth. In 1603 this is described as having sometimes been called the Church-house."

Our records throw some light on the disappearance of this comet among Schools, which shone so brightly for so short a time. Edward VI.'s commissioners make a " memorandum, that there is a Free School within the town of Banbury, called St. John's School, or Hospital ; the Schoolmaster, Nicholas Cartwright ; he having the profits for his wages, and for an usher to teach children there their grammar. The revenue of the lands belonging to the same is £15. Item, it is very meet that the said Incumbents may abide there to minister to the people, and aid the curate there ; for it is a great town replenished with people, and a great market town." Then, later on in the Certificate is a special entry, that " lands and tenements with all other commodities unto the said house or hospital belonging, lying within the said county, are now let by the said master by Indenture for the sum of £6 3s. 4d. Sir Nicholas Cartwright, clerk, master of the said Hospital, a man of honest behaviour." In another hand is written " Pension, 100s." Then follows another memorandum to the effect that this Hospital was not included in the former Certificate ; viz., of Henry's commissioners.

It is clear, therefore, that Cartwright held the Hospital as a Schoolmaster. It appears he was presented in 1541 to the mastership. His predecessor had been Dr. Thomas Brynknell, who held the Hospital at the time of the *Valor Ecclesiasticus* in 1535. Now Brynknell, like Stanbridge before him, had been Head-master of Magdalen College School, and was appointed master of Banbury after John Stanbridge's death, in 1511. It would therefore appear that 3 successive masters held the Hospital for a School endowment, and that their services were appreciated, as the commissioners reported in favour of their retention. However, Cartwright took his pension and retired. He died, according to Wood, in 1558, and was buried at Banbury. In 1554 he was assigned to dispute against Latimer, so he would appear to have been of the Roman persuasion. Yet he must have kept on the School, either in person or by a deputy or usher, in 1556, or Sir Thomas Pope would not then have coupled the School with Eton, and ranked it before Brackley or Reading Schools, as a place from which Trinity College was to be recruited. At his death it may have come to an end. Here, however, is a gap to be filled by the Oxfordshire Archæological Society, or some Banbury antiquarian. I have gone into it chiefly for the reason, that it was impossible to believe that a town of the importance of Banbury would have had no School in the early part of the 16th century, whatever gaps might be left by the carelessness of after times in the matter of education.

Another singular story of the disappearance of an ancient foundation is that of Heytesbury School attached to Heytesbury Hospital in Wiltshire. This was (pp. 256, 262) the "Hospital of S. John Baptist of the foundation of Margaret Lady Hungerford, which she was empowered to endow and incorporate by Letters Patent of Edward IV., in 1472, in pursuance of her husband Robert Lord Hungerford's will." "In which Hospital," say Henry VIII.'s commissioners, "yet remain 12 poor men and a woman, for whose maintenance the said Margaret Hungerford granted certain lands, the rents and profits of which, over and above the maintenance of the said poor, come to the hands of John

Benet, servant of William Sherington, Esquire." Worth by
year £43 3s. 7½d. "Abuse appears, because by the first foundation was founded a Grammar School, beyond the maintenance of
the said 12 poor, the governor of which School should annually
receive for his salary £10; and now there remain neither Schoolmaster nor scholars in the same." The report of the second
commissioners is to the same effect. "There hath been no
Schoolmaster by the space of these 5 or 6 years. Sir W.
Sheryngton [sic] perceiveth the issue of the same, but by what
authority we know not. The perfect survey of the premises
we have not taken, for the cause afore declared."

Somewhat similar was the report of the commissioners
nearly 400 years afterwards. "There has not been a Schoolmaster for many years. The present Trustees gave the present
Custos the option of acting as Schoolmaster or not. As the
option was given him, he declined, and no one has since been
appointed." This last remark is probably still true, as this
ancient School escaped notice in the report of the Schools
Inquiry Commission in 1867, and of the Royal Commission on
Secondary Education in 1896. Yet there is no doubt that the
School was an essential and integral part, if not the primary
part, of the trust. For there is some reason to believe that
the School existed before the Hospital. The Letters Patent of
the King, and the foundation deed of Lady Hungerford, 4th
April, 1472, have been printed in Sir Richard Colt Hoare's
magnificent County History of Wiltshire (I. "Heytesbury
Hundred," p. 128, ed. 1822). In these the foundation is expressed to be only for "an Almshouse of one chaplain, 12 poor
men and one poor woman, of whom the same chaplain shall be
warden (custos), to pray for the souls of the king, the founders,"
and a long string of other people, "and to do certain other things
according to the ordinance of Margaret" and two others. There
is here, as in so many foundations of Chantries and Hospitals,
no indication of any but the "chantry" purpose proper of
praying for souls; and that is why so many Schools perished,
because the foundation deed did not specify any but a "superstitious use." But we might be sure that Henry's commis-

sioners would not have reported the School as a part of the foundation if it was not. This inference has since proved to be in accordance with the facts. In Sir R. C. Hoare's monumental work the founders' statutes, which are extremely interesting, are not given ; they were apparently unknown to him, and indeed said not to exist. A copy of them, however, made in 1613, is preserved in the Bodleian Library (MS. Rawl. D. 812), for a reference to which I am indebted to Dr. Furnivall, of Early English Text Society (and many other Societies) fame. They appear to have been in English, and are full of curious details as to the poor and their mode of living. It plainly appears from these statutes that the School was as important a part of the foundation as the Almshouse. This is shown by the statute as to the appointment of the warden, or keeper, as he is called. I give it in modern English, as the Jacobean spelling is not that of the original.

"And also we will and ordain that the chancellor of the cathedral church of Saresbury, for the time being, or the Dean and Chapter, he not residencer, shall do (*sic*) present an able keeper and a sufficient teacher of grammar at every avoidance. Which shall, every feastful day in the year, give his good will to be at the parish church of Heytesbury in time of divine service-saying, and to help forth the choir to his power, if there be no reasonable cause to let him. And all other days, that he intend and do his diligent labour to teach and inform all such children and other persons that shall come to the place, which is ordained and depute[d] them, to teach in, within Heytesbury. And that the said keeper and master shall teach fro the beginning of learning until such season as they learn sufficient or competent [knowledge] of grammar ; no School hire take of no person or persons, or take [save of] such as their friends may spend £10 or above, or else that will give freely. And that he daily attend and keep his School, without any infirmity or other cause as is above said may be reasonably understood.

"And if it so be, that an able keeper and sufficient teacher of grammar cannot be provided within the space of eight weeks after the decease or avoidance of any of the forsaid keepers, that then we will that the chancellor for the time being, or in his absence the Dean and Chapter, and the dean be not resident, then the Chapter, put in a convenable and honest priest there to rest and to abide, and to do in all things as it is above rehearsed, unto such season that an able keeper and a sufficient teacher of grammar may be provided and had, according to the wills and ordinances of the founders of the same."

This is plain enough. Still more significant is statute 14. This provided that if the Keeper is incapacitated by sickness, he should provide an honest priest to say the masses he had to perform, "and over that, provide an usher to teach in the School, and to have the oversight to the poor men, and to execute the office of the said keeper in all things like as he should do himself, except only saying of mass." The School deputy was clearly more important than the clerical deputy. Again, the oath of the Keeper on admission was "to keep all the statutes and ordinances made for the conservation and good rule of the said School and Almshouse," putting the School first. The reason for the suggestion that the School was an earlier institution than the Hospital is a queer provision in statute 48. "Whereas the usher of the School, called Park Miles, now blind and may not see, is received into the Almshouse, and there hath meat and drink and other necessaries like as other poor men have, we will and ordain that never hereafter, whosoever be usher of the said School, be not received into the said house; for by the receiving of the usher into the said house, the Schoolmaster that now is, or shall be hereafter, would think that such as be usher should have meat and drink of the said Almshouse, the which we would in no wise they never have." If an usher had already got so old and decrepit as to have been a successful candidate for the Almshouse, the School must have been already going on some time. It is clear that the master was expected to supply an usher out of his own income. Well he might, for his pay was superb. The 13 poor received 6s. 8d. a week among them for "bread, beer, and victual," if the price of wheat per bushel was under 10d. a bushel, and 7s. 8d. if it was 15d. or above. The Keeper was to receive not only the

£10 a year reported by the Chantry Commissioners, but £1 for his servant, besides other yearly sums specially assigned to him, irrespective of the two manors which formed the Hospital endowment, amounting in all to £5 16s. a year. Besides this he had two cartloads of wood out of 20 provided for the Almshouse. He got therefore nearly as much as all the almsfolk put together. It was therefore an extremely good berth, adequate even for Sir W. Sheryngton, who, as master of the mint at Bristol, robbed the Crown to the extent of £4,000. The Hospital was within the Act of Henry VIII., but not within that of Edward VI. ; and Sir W. Sherington would seem not to have got a grant of the whole Hospital from Henry, but only of the keepership. At all events Cardinal Pole, who was much interested in Wiltshire, interfered in 1557 to effect its restoration, and then described Sheryngton as master *de facto sed non de jure.* He enjoined that the warden should teach a Grammar School there, and selected John Lybbe, B.C.L., as warden, for that object. During James I.'s reign, the usual attempts were made by informers,—who alleged "concealments" of the lands of Colleges, Hospitals, and Schools, which had survived the Edwardian plunder, and got grants from the Crown under pretext that they ought not to have survived,—to plunder or at least levy blackmail on the Hospital. The result was a re-foundation by James I., in which again the teaching of a Grammar School was made an essential part of the foundation, though the Keeper was now allowed to perform the duty by deputy, paying him £15 a year, less even than the amount of the salary in Edward IV.'s time. The School, however, seems to have flourished in 1765, when the Free School, together with the Hospital and its chapel, and 65 houses were burnt down. It did not exist when Sir R. C. Hoare wrote, as he expressed a hope that as the Hospital was now so rich the School might be restored. Instead of which, as has been seen, the Trustees gave it, or affected to give it, its *coup de grace.*

7. Guild Schools.

' After, if not before, Hospitals, Guilds were the most ancient source of Schools. It is unnecessary nowadays to explain what a Guild is. Its simplest, and perhaps most adequate definition, is that it was a corporation or association in the nature of a club. As with clubs, so with Guilds, their objects were endless, from governing the community to giving soup to the poor. In mediæval times the corporate unity was generally expressed in a religious form. At Beverley, for instance, one of the chief signs and tests of a Craft Guild was that it took part in the Corpus Christi procession on Corpus Christi Day, and performed, either by its members or at its members' expense, a scene or act in the Corpus Christi play.

Of the 33 Guilds mentioned in these records, excluding the Craft Guilds of London and Shrewsbury, and the Merchants' Guild at York, 28 kept Grammar Schools ; and to them may be added the Drapers of Shrewsbury, who kept a Grammar School ; while the Mercers of London were trustees for three Schools mentioned, and the Goldsmiths for two.

It is difficult to hunt down the real date of these Guild Schools. There would seem to have been no actual foundation of them as such. But a Guild being established, and maintaining, as it almost invariably did, one or more priests or chaplains to say grace and to pray for the souls of its members, which office, like that of burial of their bodies, was one of the chief objects of Guilds, the priest, either *proprio motu* or at the discretion of the Guild, kept a School. Afterwards the maintenance of a School, free for members' sons or the community at large, became part of the regular duties of the priest, or one of the priests, or special benefactions were given for that purpose.

Take, for instance, the case of Ashburton, in Devonshire, the Grammar School of which is given by the Schools Inquiry Commission as of the date 1593, but historically reputed to date from 1314. Here, we are told by Henry's Commission, is the Guild called S. Lawrence's Guild, "founded by [*blank in the original*] For the continual finding of a priest, as well to pray for the donors of the lands belonging to the said Guild and other benefactors of the same, as also to keep a School for the erudition of children freely for ever ; which hath for his wages or salary £6 13s. 4d., going out of the lands." The lands are valued in all at £10 15s. 8d. "The remainder and overplus of the lands," we are told, "is bestowed upon the reparation and maintenance of leads" (*ledes*, a translation apparently of *conductus*, or conduits) "for the conduction of wholesome water to the town of Ashburton," and upon the relief of people stricken in time of plague. Dr. Oliver, in his *Monasticon Diocœsis Exoniensis*, published in 1846, prints an abstract of this Chantry Certificate, with notes, and in the margin fills the blank of the founder's name, with the statement : "Bishop Stapledon was the founder. See his deed dated Monday after the Feast of S. Lawrence (August), 1314, copied into Bishop Brantyngham's Register, I., p. 12." This statement, so specific, and appearing to be based on the actual document, appeared absolutely trustworthy, and I ventured to assert this School to be one of the models which might have guided William of Wykeham in founding Winchester College.

Dr. Oliver having proved untrustworthy in other historical matters, it seemed desirable not to trust him, without verification, on the question of Ashburton. Information kindly given by Mr. H. R. Burch rendered Oliver's statement more than suspect. Now, with special kindness, the Rev. Canon Hingeston-Randolph, whose editions of the Registers of the Bishops of Exeter are marvels of research and editorial accuracy, has let me have a full copy of the document in question. And behold there is not a word about any School in it; nor, which is more unexpected, is there a word about the Guild of S. Lawrence. The document is headed "Confirmation of a Chantry in the Chapel of Our Lady " (*Beatœ Mariœ*) "in Aschpertone." Bishop Brantingham recites and confirms in 1371 a Patent of his predecessor, Bishop Walter Stapledon, and the Chapter of Exeter, dated Monday before S. Lawrence's Day (10th August), 1314. Stapledon says : "At the instance (*excitati*) of the Bailiff and Commonalty (*Prœpositum et Communitatem*) of the Burgesses of our town of Ashpertone, and after careful and adequate discussion with our Chapter of Exeter and their consent, we grant and assign all the oblations and obventions " (*i.e.* contributions such as Easter offerings and Whitsuntide pennies, and the like) " of the Chapel of S. Lawrence, situate within our manor (*curiæ*) of Ashpertone, to a Priest celebrating divine service for ever in the same Chapel (viz., of S. Lawrence) for our good weal, and for our soul when we are taken from this light, and for the souls of all our predecessors and successors, Bishops of Exeter ; on condition (*ita*) that the same Priest be under bond to the Bailiff and Commonalty to that service, and be presented every year to the official of the Peculiar of the same town, and be admitted (by him) if he be fit, having sworn obedience and that he will not diminish the rights of the Rector or Vicar ; but he is to obtain no title of his own in the said office," *i.e.*, it is to be a yearly appointment only, not a freehold ; " and on the condition that the said Bailiff and Commonalty of the Burgesses be bound to supply the maintenance, support, and yearly stipends of the said Priest, so far as the said obventions and oblations are not enough, and to repair, and keep in good repair, the chapel, books, and ornaments, and to give a sufficient bond for the same on presenting the said Priest every year. The Priest is to be present in the Parish Church every Sunday and feast of nine Lessons, or when the choir is ruled " (*i.e.*, on the greater feasts, and when there is an elaborate musical service), " at Matins, High Mass, and Vespers, singing and intoning (psalms, etc.) with others there ; nor on such days may he celebrate or begin Mass till after the Gospel has been read and the Offertory sung at High Mass in the Parish Church, unless for some special reason, with leave of the Vicar, he has to celebrate Mass sooner."

Now it is clear from this that both the Chapel of S. Lawrence —and if the Guild of S. Lawrence was a merchants' Guild, and the same thing with the Bailiff and Burgesses' Corporation, which is not only possible but probable—then the Guild of S. Lawrence, existed before Stapledon's time. The chapel appears in a visitation made at Ashburton by the Dean and Chapter (Ashburton being appropriated to them) in the time of Bishop

Bytton, his predecessor, on 1st July, 1301 (*Stapledon's Register*, ed. Hingeston-Randolph, p. 185), where it appears that in the parish church there was "a chalice too small, scarcely weighing half a mark, and another still smaller, belonging to the Chapel of St. Lawrence."

Why our document is headed "a confirmation of the Chantry in the Chapel of St. Mary" it is difficult to say. It looks like a mere error, as it seems quite clear from the terms of the document that the Chantry priest was to perform his service, in the Chapel of S. Lawrence, which was in the Bishop's manor, and is a considerable distance, for the size of the place, from the parish church.

Anyhow, there is nothing to show that Bishop Stapledon founded the Guild or the School, or when the School began. Ashburton being a Bishop's manor, it is quite possible that the priest in question was intended to and did keep a Grammar School, in, or before, Stapledon's time. On the other hand, it is also quite possibly a fifteenth or sixteenth century adaptation of the old endowment. All that can be concluded with certainty is that the people (probably the inhabitants) who made the Certificate said "that the priest was founded to keep a Free School," and that John Predyaux, deputy of the Particular Surveyor of the Court of Augmentations in Devonshire, continued the School; that the inhabitants bought back the lands from the Crown in 1593 and that it glows with all the latest lights of Technical and Agricultural education on the site, and under the shadow of the tower of the old chapel. A somewhat lame and impotent conclusion historically!

At Burford, in Oxfordshire, where there is an existing and flourishing Grammar School, credited to Simon Wisdom in 1571, we find the entry: "The Guild of our Lady in the parish church. Certain lands and tenements given by divers persons to the finding of a priest, and to give to poor people of the town yearly, and to the mending of highways, and of the common bridges of the same town; and the said priest to pray and sing for the founders and all Christian souls for ever. Thomas Plumtree (Plomtre), incumbent there, of the age of 40 years, a

man well learned, able to keep a cure, had for his salary yearly
£7, and hath none other living or promotion, but only this
stipend. The value of all the lands, £16 10s. 10d."

Then come some "Memoranda: That the said town of Burford
is a very great market town replenished with much people, and
needful to have a School there. Item that the Brethren of
the said Guild at their cost and charge did build a chapel of
our Lady annexed to the parish church there, of their devotion,
and did find a priest to minister there and to teach children
freely. *And after that* at certain times certain men of their
devotions did give by will and feoffment unto the said Guild
the lands and tenements aforesaid, amounting to the sum of
£16 10s. 10d., to find a priest and to help poor people [&c.], and
so it hath been always used." Now this Guild, according to
Gross (*The Guild Merchant*, i. 5), is one of the two merchant
Guilds (the Chapman's Guild, Canterbury, being the other) to
which the earliest known references are made. In the Guild
Certificate at the Record Office is a fragment of what purports
to be a copy of the Charter of Robert FitzHamon, who is said
(on the authority of *Dugdale's Baronage*) to have died between
1087 and 1107, and to have granted the burgesses of Burford
the Guild. As the grant gives Burford its privileges by reference to the Guild of Oxford, it of course establishes the
Oxford Guild as still earlier.

The Burford Guild only perished, by a combination of *felo-de-
se* and murder, under a private Act of Parliament in 1863.
The Lady Chapel, built by the Guild, still stands at the S.E.
corner of the church. It contains many traces in its archi-
tecture of Early English work, and is therefore as old as
the 13th century. It was, in all probability, not at first struc-
turally connected with the church, though standing in the
churchyard. But the church was much enlarged in the time
of Warwick the King-maker, who was lord of Burford; and in
Henry VIII.'s time the Lady Chapel was perpendicularized, and
joined bodily to the church, the symmetry of which it spoilt,
being a monstrous wart growing out of the nave, and concealing
a lovely Perpendicular south porch.

A vast mass of deeds belonging to the Guild, *rudis indigestaque moles*, are still in the possession of Dr. Cheatle, the son of the last alderman of the Guild, and he kindly allowed me to look at them. Time was limited, and I cannot be sure that there is nothing earlier; but the earliest deed in which the Guild priest is mentioned, so far as I could see, was a deed of 9th November, 23 Henry VII., *i.e.*, 1507, whereby lands were conveyed from one set of persons to another by a Latin deed, under which is written a declaration of trust in English to the effect that the proctors of Our Lady Chapel should take the profits and apply 11 marks to the support of an honest priest to do service in the chapel. This 11 marks, or £7 6s. 8d., corresponds so nearly with the £7 specified in the Certificate, that there can be little doubt that this priest is the Schoolmaster. Judging from the analogy of other deeds, this deed was only a conveyance on the appointments of new feoffees.

For with the deeds of another charity there is a deed of 7th February, 7 Henry VII. (1493), by which John Hyll conveys two messuages in S. John Street to four persons, described as "chamberlains of Burford," the rents to be applied " to the profit of the town, when taxes or fifteenths of the king are called for." At first sight it would appear that this was a foundation deed, and as such it is recorded in the report of Lord Brougham's Commission. But quite by chance I happened on another deed tied up in a bundle of leases belonging to different property, in which John Winrych and Thomas Spycer, "seniors of the Guild of Borford," with consent of their brethren, grant two cottages in S. John Street on the very same trusts; and this deed is dated in August, 16 Richard II., or 1392. So that more than 100 years before the deed, hitherto regarded as the foundation of this charity, the property was held by the Guild on the same trust; and its origin may well be another hundred years further back again. The curious thing is that the commissioners report that the charity had not been applied because no fifteenths were now levied; but as the trust was to meet any taxes, the reason seems hardly a good one. Considering, then, that the priest's deed of 1507 is a transfer from one body of persons to another body, we may safely infer that this too was not the original foundation, but only a conveyance on the appointment of new trustees; and the priest and his School may be as old as the Lady Chapel or the Guild itself. Certain it is that in the present Grammar School building on the Church Green there is a buttress of early Perpendicular date, perhaps of the latter part of the 14th century.

Moreover, if the origin of priest and School had been of later date, it is probable it would be still extant. There is still in evidence, for instance, the Letters Patent of Warwick the King-maker granting a licence to Henry Bishop to "erect, build and maintain an almshouse on Church Green," opposite the Grammar School, on condition that he and Anne his wife are called founders. The deed is dated in London, 26th of February, 34 Henry VI., *i.e.*, 1456, and is sealed with a magnificent armorial seal, and signed, apparently, in the King-maker's own hand. This signature is, according to Mr. Oman, his biographer, to whom I am indebted for a knowledge of this document, only the second specimen of his handwriting extant. The deed evidencing a grant of lands by the real founder, Henry Bishop, of Burford, is also extant. My Lord of Warwick had his desire, for he is duly writ down as founder of the Almshouse, known as the Great Almshouse, which still exists,— with windows and doorways of the 15th century, though largely rebuilt in 1828,—by the latest historian of Burford, Mr. W. J. Monk. True, Warwick did found it, precisely as much as Edward VI. founded Tonbridge Grammar School; but no more.

Simon Wisdom had possibly rather more actual share in re-founding Burford School in 1571, but he has certainly had far more credit than he was entitled to. The first deed of re-foundation is not Wisdom's at all. His deed is dated 20th October, 1571. On 24th May, nearly 6 months before, the two bailiffs of the borough, three of the burgesses, and William Sylvester, "alderman," and Thomas Appar, "taillour," co-feoffees of the parish lands, "have had consideration, and yet do consider, what great number of youth and young children have been, and yet are, and in time to come may be within the said town of Burford, whereof many of their parents have not been, nor at this present time are, of ability to find them at school, whereby the most part of their youth hath idly spent their time and have been traded and brought up in no order of learning or knowledge, whereby they might better apply their selves to know their duties as well towards God as their parents, and obtain increase of virtue in themselves. Which thing hath much moved the consciences of the said " persons "To have a Free School erected within the said town of Burford, and to have some order towards the stipend or salary of such persons as shall be Schoolmaster or usher there." They therefore conveyed to 10 other persons, 5 of whom are described as burgesses, certain houses and plots of land, including the significant item of " the Clerks' chamber," for the purpose of the "stipend or salary of a Schoolmaster to teach a School within the town of Burford." The yearly value of the lands conveyed was £3 12s. Rules are said to be annexed, but they have disappeared.

Simon Wisdom's deed begins with a recital in precisely the same terms as the earlier deed; and be it observed he was alderman, that is, of the Guild. He conveyed lands, including three houses by the bridge, (which still have a stone which says that he gave them to the Free School,) of the value of £5 a year in all; but the deed was to be void if a Free School and master's house was not erected within two years. The rules attached are said to be made " by the advice of the said Simon Wisdom, being one of the first founders, and by his learned counsel." He does not therefore even affect to claim to be founder, but only one among others, and it is quite possible that he conveyed in reality as alderman, and not in his private capacity. Certain it is that he was a tenant of the Guild in 1549. The two School-wardens, who were to govern the School, were to be one a burgess and the other a commoner, to be elected yearly by the alderman, steward, burgesses, and four of the best and most ancient commoners nominated by the alderman, steward, and two bailiffs. This surely shows that it was a joint town re-foundation and not the foundation of an individual.

Another Guild School which still flourishes is that of

Wisbech in Cambridgeshire, the only place in that county which appears in our records. This is an interesting case because it is the only specimen of its kind preserved. In all other cases we have the return of the Commissioners, prepared from papers presented to them by the various parishes. In this case we have the actual paper presented to the commissioners of Henry VIII. by the vicar and churchwardens of the parish. In Wisbech they say there was only one foundation within the Chantries Act, the Trinity Guild. This was founded in the second year of Richard II. by divers persons named, all of whom were clerks. There were four stipendiary priests attached to it headed by " Master Henry Ogle, being Schoolmaster." The Guild, they say, was founded for the maintenance of God's service in the parish church of S. Peter and S. Paul (which had been appropriated to the monks of Ely, and so deprived of due service), and also to pray for the souls of the " brutherne and susterne " of the Guild. Wherefore they kept "one priest, being learned, to preach," whereby the inhabitants "and others doth better know their duty towards God and their true and faithful obedience towards the king's majesty. And also keep a Grammar School freely to teach and instruct children continually in godly and virtuous learning, so many as doth or will repair to him for such purpose."

Now in this case the antiquity of the Guild was perhaps understated. In William Watson's *Historical Account of Wisbech* (Wisbech, 1827)—for reference to which I am indebted to the Head-master, Mr. A. W. Poyser—it appears that there is an account book of the Guild beginning in the year 1379, the existence of which no doubt led to the belief that the Guild began in that year. The first year's accounts suggest that the Guild was going on before. Among the receipts are 26s. 8d. from 64 brethren, and 46s. 8d. from 14 newly-admitted brethren. This does not look like a new foundation. Nor does the item of 26s. 8d. for "mending the image of the Trinity." A new Trinity Guild would have had a new image of the Trinity, not mended up an old one. The historian is not implicitly to be trusted, as he makes fearful havoc of the Latin. He even transforms what, according to his mangled version of the original, is clearly a payment of 8*d*. "for burying a man who was hanged," into the payment of that amount (which was more than a full day's wages for skilled workmen) to a man "for hanging up the burial things," whatever he may have thought that to mean. This historian says in one place, under date 1508, and, in another, under date 1506, that in that year occurs the first mention of the Schoolmaster in the entry. "The Schoolmaster shall have from Midsummer next 8 marks for his wages," an entry which, as he justly remarks, does not look like a new foundation. A Schoolmaster, he also says, is mentioned by name in 1446 in Cole's MSS. in the British Museum; and so it is. A survey was made when the Guild possessions were bought back by the town from Edward VI. at twenty years' purchase of the net rent; the town undertaking to maintain the Schoolmaster, the poor, and the sea banks, all of which are mentioned in our records. The Schoolmaster then received £10 a year. As he was the chief and best paid of the four priests of the Guild, it is also probable that he was the earliest; and so the School may well date at least from 1379.

Oddly enough the Guild out of which came the richest and largest of all existing Grammar Schools, that of Birmingham, is the only one given in detail in our records which is not stated to have kept a Grammar School. The Guild of the Holy Cross of Stratford did keep a School; but the Guild of Stratford, at least in that form, is not a very ancient one, purporting, as it does, to have been founded by Henry IV. In fact, it was much older, as the Guild returns, under Richard II. in 1389, show it then existing under the same name. Its accounts show a rent from John Schoolmaster, in 1402, for his chamber. The next step was to give him a chamber rent-free, and in 1427 a School—still part of the present School—was built for him in the yard behind the chapel and almshouses. It was not, however, until 1482 that a chaplain of the Guild endowed the School as a Free Grammar School. In 1552, the people of Stratford had to buy back from the Crown their Guild, with its

School and Almshouses, and so Edward VI. has the glory of having founded Shakespeare's School at Stratford-on-Avon.

The Guild of Birmingham, according to the Certificates, claims a high antiquity : the 16th year of Henry II., according to one Certificate; of Edward II., according to another. But in the documents published in Toulmin Smith's *English Guilds* (Early English Text Society, No. 40, 1870) it appears as founded in the same year of Richard II., and this is the real date, as there was a patent granted in that year for the foundation. If it did not keep a School, it kept most other objects of public utility; an almshouse, two great stone bridges, and divers foul and dangerous highways ; wine, wax, oil, and other necessaries for the church, including three chaplains and an organ-player, a keeper of the clock and chimes. The Guild was prepared to usher its members into the world through its "common midwife," to ring them out of it with its "common bellman," and bring them to an end with dirge and mass.

It seems probable that for a School the people of Birmingham relied on a Chantry or Guild at "Deritend in the parish of Aston and Lordship of Birmingham," which kept two priests, "whereof the one serving the cure, and the other teaching a Grammar School." Thereby hangs a tale. Mr. Toulmin Smith, like other writers on the dissolution of Chantries, has, through ignorance, wasted much good wrath on this matter. "So entirely unprincipled were the proceedings" of the Commission, "that the property of the old Guild of Deritend and that of the chapel endowment were mixed up together, and were both described as belonging to a Chantry," and so perished, whereas, he says, in the chapel foundation nothing is said about masses for the dead. Again, in a note, "It is interesting to catch unprincipled people tripping. In one document I find the words, 'Sive Gilda.' Thus the truth got blurted out . . in a moment of inadvertence, or conscience-smiting." Yet in Edward VI.'s Chantry Certificate, not printed here, the Chantry of Deritend is simply described as "a Chapel of ease for the same town of Deritend, being divided from their Parish Church with a great river." The attack, too, is beside the mark. Chapel of ease, Guild, Chantry, or stipendiary priest, all were included in the Chantries Act, and it made no sort of difference which it was called.

Mr. Toulmin Smith goes on in the same sort of way about the Guild of Worcester, which kept a Grammar School. This was in the "Trinity Hall," a Guildhall, "time out of mind a Free School." Edward VI.'s commissioners remarked, "The School may cease, for there is one other in the town of the King's foundation, and this is no School of any purpose, as it is credibly said." The other School was, of course, the Cathedral School, founded by Henry on the re-foundation of the Cathedral. The disparaging remark was perhaps true, though the Guild Certificate had said that Oliver had "above a hundred scholars." Mr. Toulmin Smith, however, flies off. "This was put in order to gloss over the intended seizure of the property of this Guild. The teaching of the youth of Worcester was, of course, a matter of too small importance to be allowed to interfere with the designs of those needy men who were bent on seizing the property of the Guild to their own uses. . . The plunder of the Guild seems to have been entire. So far as I can learn, not a trace or tradition of this great School of the Guild of S. Nicholas had remained."

Did Mr. Toulmin Smith really suppose that the commissioners, Sir John Pakington, Sir Robert Acton, and others, mostly country gentlemen, whose names he gives, were going to pocket the Guild lands themselves? Besides, what are the facts? The officers of the Court disregarded the remark of the commissioners; and under the Act continued the Schoolmaster and his salary. And what is more, the School continues to this day.

The Palmers' Guild of Ludlow is of great antiquity. It is stated to have been "founded by the most valiant and victorious king, of 'famous' memory, King Edward, grandfather to Richard II., and afterwards augmented ('aftemented') by Richard II., and also by now our most sovereign lord Henry VIII." Its formal foundation may only date from Letters Patent, 17 November, 3 Edward III., yet it does in reality date

from before 1284. This latter is the year of foundation given
in the Guild's return to Richard II., but in the same return it
is said, as Mr. Toulmin Smith pointed out, that it had lands
before the Statute of Mortmain, which was passed in 1279. But
non constat when the Schoolmaster appears. He may be in
those early times as unsubstantial as the ghosts that Mr. Toulmin Smith, by a most amusing blunder, has raised. The Guild,
it seems, kept "wakes" (*vigiliæ*) at the death of its members,
and these "wakes" were of the Irish order, for among the
ordinances is one prohibiting women from taking part in
them, though any male is allowed to do so "so long as he
neither calls up ghosts, nor makes sport of the corpse or its
good fame, or plays any other indecent games." *Apropos* of
these ghosts, the learned editor gives a long disquisition, and
refers to Icelandic sagas in illustration. But the original Latin
is *inducere monstra larvarum*, or "put on monstrous masks."
It was horse-play, not witches of Endor, the good Palmers
wished to put down. Perhaps they did not even believe in
ghosts ; the result of a sound Grammar School education.

Another Guild, dating, if not from Edward I., yet from
Edward II.'s time, was the Bablake Guild, sometimes called a
college, and now called the Bablake Hospital, at Coventry.
This Trinity Guild kept eight chaplains, two singing clerks,
two singing boys, and " a Schoolmaster of a certain School called
a Grammar School." It is to be noted that the Schoolmaster
got £6 13s. 4d. a year, while the chaplains only got £4 13s. 4d.
In March, 150¾, John Bond, of Coventry, draper, added to
this "a substantial almshouse, with a chapel " for ten poor men
and one woman, to dress their meat and drink, and also one
priest, " being a D.D. or else M.A., bound yearly to preach forty
sermons within the city, or ten miles compass of the same."
Sermons were then a rarity, and the excellent draper may be
strongly suspected of Wicliffite opinions for thus insisting on
sermons. The beautiful almshouse which still adorns Coventry
is no doubt that which he built. Here again there is nothing
to show when the Schoolmaster began to be, or whether he was
always there, an integral part of the Guild as one of the
chaplains.

It is strange that with all this wealth of Guild Schools the only Guilds mentioned in Chantry Certificates, in which I have definitely been able to establish a Grammar School before 1400, are Nottingham and Northallerton in Yorkshire; and singularly enough, the early mentions of these are not in connection with the Guilds. I have put together elsewhere the references to Nottingham School from the town archives and those of Southwell Minster. They do not begin earlier than 1382; and though they show both a Schoolmaster and usher, seem to point to a connection rather with S. John's Hospital than the Guild, though the two are not of course incompatible. As regards Northallerton, a series of entries in the Prior of Durham's Letter Books from 1321 contain appointments of the master of the Grammar School there by the Prior as "Ordinary of the spiritualities of S. Cuthbert in Yorkshire." There is no mention of pay, and the Guild may well have paid the master, so far as he did not live on fees. But the Guild is not mentioned.

8. Chantry Schools.

We now come to the latest and largest class of institutions in connection with Schools, the Chantries. A Chantry (*cantaria*) was an endowment for a priest to sing for the soul of some dead person. In a sense all the monasteries were nothing but large Chantries. It is almost invariably one of the expressed and primary objects of the founder of a monastery that the monks or canons regular should pray for him. Thus, as we learn in the Meaux Chronicle (Rolls Series, I. 90), William Crassus or Le Groos, otherwise the fat, Earl of Albemarle, "had founded St. Martin D'Auchy, or D'Aumale, in Normandy, of the Cluniac Order; and St. Mary of Thornton of regular canons of the Order of St. Augustine; and two monasteries of Vaudry and Meaux, of the Cistercian order." "When he crossed the sea, and met, as he often did, with sudden storms at night, threatening shipwreck to him and his," he had a sleepless time till midnight. "But then as his monks of St. Martin and canons of Thornton were accustomed to get up to matins, confiding in their prayers, he despised the storm and slept soundly. Then about cockcrow, the vigils of the monks and canons being over, if he woke up, confiding in the prayers of the monks *de Valle Dei* and of Meaux, who hastened to wake up at that very hour of the night, again despising the storm, whether sleeping or waking, he awaited the daylight without anxiety." From which security doubtless he was able to acquire his title to his cognomen.

In the same way a Deyncourt founded Thurgarton Priory in Nottinghamshire, by the advice of Thurstan, Archbishop of York, for the souls of himself and his mistress (*muliere*).

The term Chantry is, however, usually confined to an endowment, generally of one or two priests only, to pray for the soul of an individual, his family, and friends. If there were more than two priests on the same foundation, the foundation was often called a College. In common parlance, the word Chantry is used as if a building, a chapel, or at least a separate compartment of a chapel or church, were the essence of it. But it is by no means necessarily the case that a Chantry should be attached to or located in any specific or special building. The earliest Chantries seem to have been in those cathedral churches which were not monastic, and there might be several founded at the same altar. They were also founded in monastic churches, as the Nine Altars at Durham show, the Chantries being served sometimes by monks, but more often by secular priests. As a rule, however, in later times, each Chantry was founded at a particular altar, and in many cases, but not in the majority of cases, a separate chapel was built for the separate Chantry—either an actual annex to the main building, as in many parish churches, or, as in the case of William of Wykeham's, Edingdon's, and other bishops' tombs in Winchester Cathedral, merely a separate partition in the main building.

How early Chantries began it is not easy to say. Included in the present book is an entry of a Chantry said to have been founded before the Conquest. At Ashton Keynes, in Wiltshire, Adam de Purton, Kt., is said to have given, " by his deed made before the Conquest," all his lands in Crudwell to the Vicar of Ashton Keynes, " to the intent the said vicar for the time being should find a priest to sing for the soul of the said Adam, Cicely, and Sarah, his wives, within the said church for ever." The lands were said to be worth 35s. a year; but the vicar denied the Chantry, and said that he was charged with that sum as part of his vicarage.

There is, of course, no impossibility in this date; but in early days, before and after the Conquest, before the land was fully occupied, when it was still a drug in the market, and population was scanty, foundations were ordinarily made for communities like Colleges and monasteries rather than for individual Chantry priests. It seems hardly likely that lands given before the Conquest should only have been worth 35s. at our date; for the land which would have been only an adequate endowment for a single priest in the days of Edward the Confessor would, through the progress of population, have been enough for a rich College in the days of Edward VI.

However that may be, Chantries are known to have been founded in Chichester, Lincoln, St. Paul's, Wells, and York in the 12th century, by bishops and other great folk. At Southwell Minster 10 out of 18 Chantries were founded before 1372. The great bulk of the Chantries recorded here seem to have been founded in the 14th, 15th, and 16th centuries, and went on in increasing crowds, with the spread of wealth among the trading classes, right up to the Reformation. It is well known that Henry VIII. himself directed in his will the foundation of chantries for his own soul.

As one specimen of a Chantry foundation conveys more information about Chantries than much talk around them, I give, culled from the archives of All Souls' College, the foundation of Barton's Chantry at Thornton, Bucks (p. 14), in 1440, the merit of which is that it is in English and not Latin. Its origin is rather peculiar. Its full history appears in a Latin deed of two years later, 4th May, 1442. In the course of endowing All Souls' College, the founder, Henry Chicheley, Archbishop of Canterbury, bought some settled estates at Crendon, Morton, and Foxcote, from John Barton, the husband of Isabel Barton, to whom they belonged. They were duly conveyed to the king by the trustees of the Bartons' marriage settlement, and the king conveyed to the first warden, Richard Andrewes, this being the method by which All Souls' became entitled to be called a royal foundation. The estates were conveyed subject to the life interest of Isabel, who survived her husband. The price paid was 200 marks, and the provision for a Chantry is set out in the deed of 1440 in English, and of 1442 in Latin. The Chantry was further secured by a grant by the College of an annuity of £20 a year, to be paid only in the event of the Chantry not being duly maintained. The Chantry therefore formed the best part of the consideration, as, valuing the annuity at twenty years' purchase, the usual number in those days, it was worth £400 as against £132 18s. 4d. paid down in cash.

"This endenture, made at London, the 3ᵈᵉ day of Juyll, in the xviii. yeer of the regne of Kyng Henry the Sext, after the conquest of Ingland [1440], betwixt the right worshipfull fader in God, Henry, Archebishopp of Caunterbury, and Richard Andrewe, Wardeyn, and the College of Alle Soules in Oxenford, on that oon partie, And Isabell, late the wife of John Barton, of the counte of Buk[ingham], on that other partie.

"Witnesseth" (the deed then recites the circumstances already stated). "And the seyd Archebisshop, Wardeyn, and College, will and graunten be this endenture that they by the said feste of Sainte Andrewe next comyng shall fynde and make sufficient securte, by the avys of John Vampage and William Tresham, thereto named indifferently for both parties, to the said Isabell, for to fynde 3 prestes dailly and perpetually to synge for the soules of the said John Barton and Isabell, and for the soules of their fadres and modres, and for alle their frendes, and for all cristen soules.

"Of the whiche 3 prestes two shall synge in the said college of Alle Soules, and the thridde in the chapell of Our Lady, withyn the chirche of Thorneton, in the said countie of Buk[ingham], where the said John Barton liyth.

"Of the whiche two prestes that shall so synge in the said college, oon shall dailly seye for the soules aforesaid masse, that is to wite :—

" On the sonday, of the Trinite,
the monday, of Requiem,
the Tuysday, of the holy gost,
the Wednesday, of the angeles,
the thursday, of Corpus Christi,
the friday, of the holy crosse,
and the saterday, of oure lady, yf thay or oon of hem be disposed therto.

"And in their said masses they shall seye Placebo and
Dirige with commendation.

"And that the said Wardeyn and College shall yeerly kepe
and observe the obyte of the seid John Barton and Isabell in
the said College, the last day, sauf oon, of Janyver, with 2
tapres weyeng 6 lb., brennyng duryng Placebo and Dirige, and
the masse of Requiem atte same obyte, the whiche Placebo
and Dirige and masse of Requiem shall be said by note in the
seid College by a felowe of the College, the Wardeyn or his
depute, and the felowes of the same College.

"And the said preest that shall synge in the seid chapell of
our lady in the said chirche of Thorneton shall dailly kepe alle
the same observaunces aforewritten in the fourme aforesaid,
except the lymytacion of the said masses, and moreover he
shall every wike sey the sauter of seint David, except the
tyme of lenton yeerly.

"And in his masses he shall seye the 2 Collets aforeseid, and
every yeer keep the obyte of the seid John Barton and Isabell
withoute note, in the seid chapell at the seid day, and if he
have help he shall do hit by note, wyth 2 tapres weyeing 6 lb.,
and brennyng in the forme aboveseid.

"And that the seid Wardeyn and College and her successours
shall every yere in the day of the said obyte dispose, or do be
disposed, vi[s.] viij[d.] amonge pore folk at Thornton aboveseid to
pray for the soules aforeseid."

The deed concluded with a proviso that if the College lost the
lands, or the lands became of less value without their fault,
"that thanne so moche of the seid charges and suffrages after
the rate of the seid dymminycion be abbregged and dymminute,

by the discrecion of the archebisshop of Caunterbury that tyme beyng."

This is a very good instance of a Chantry foundation. It shows how entirely the thing was a matter of bargain and *quid pro quo*. The land was bought cheaper in consequence of the obit and the Chantry. The excellent Isabel laid herself up treasure in the other world, besides getting 200 marks and retaining her estate for life in this. The two provisoes at the end show how the amount of spiritual assistance out of purgatory was measured with "a nicely calculated less and more" by the amount of temporal benefit conferred; and how if the one was by any accident reduced, the other would be cut down proportionately. When it required so much money to get out of purgatory, one cannot but reflect on what a select place the mediæval heaven was thought to be. Nobody would be there under a lord of a manor, or a merchant who had "thriven to thane right," and could afford his Chantry like a lord. The poor would be left to "lie howling."

The Indenture, it is satisfactory to say, was duly observed by the College. In the College Accounts, in 1546, the chaplain at Thornton duly appears under the heading of annuities as receiving £6 a year; while 6s. 8d. is spent for alms at Thornton, and 3s. 4d. for wax there, for the candles. In 1547-8 the amount is paid to the chaplain at Thornton "and the collectors of the king, for the Chantry lately come to the king's hands. There appears in the same account "4d. for sweeping up and cleaning the choir after the last deportation of images." In 1550 the alms and wax at Thornton no longer appear in the accounts, so that the College gained at least 13s. 4d. a year by the cessation of the Chantry.

How early the Chantries began to be utilized as endowments for Grammar Schools, it is hard to say. The foundation deeds, and licences in mortmain—even when it is known from the statutes, where extant, that a School was intended—do not, as a rule, mention a School.

In 1414 Thomas Langley, Bishop of Durham, founded two Schools—one of Grammar, the other of Song, to be kept on the

Palace Green, in Durham, the open space between the Bishop's Castle and the Cathedral Abbey Church. The masters were to be Chantry priests singing at the altar of our Lady and S. Cuthbert in the exquisite late Norman Chapel, at the west end of the Cathedral, called the Galilee, which Langley had at great expense just restored, and in restoring given us one of the few mediæval specimens of deliberate imitation of older work. As Bishop he had to give two licences to himself, through two of his chaplains, in a double capacity : first, in his ecclesiastical capacity as Ordinary ; second, in his temporal capacity as Earl of a County Palatine, exercising the royal rights and powers. The episcopal licence merely empowers the founding of two Chantry priests to pray for his soul, the king's and others, and to make ordinances for them. The Palatine licence, by the hands of his temporal chancellor, is a licence in mortmain with the usual powers to grant lands to the Chantry and to make the Chantry priests a corporation. In neither licence is there a word about the Schools which the Chantry priests were to maintain, and for which they were created and endowed. But a lengthy deed, dated 14th June, 1414, the day after these two licences, sets out in elaborate detail the emoluments, position, and duties of the two priests ; and discloses that their main duty was to keep the two Schools, of Grammar and of Song, " teaching gratis the poor who ask it humbly for the love of God, but charging the rest moderate fees, such as are usually paid in other Grammar or Song Schools."

It is typical, by the way, of the little care with which, in local Histories, Schools have been treated that in the face of the deeds, which plainly show that the ostensible founders were only Langley's chaplains and agents, they have been by several local historians treated as the real founders to the exclusion of poor Langley himself.

Now if, as is usually the case with Chantry Grammar Schools in ordinary towns, the foundation deed has disappeared and no copy has been preserved, and we are thrown back on the licence in mortmain enrolled on the Patent Rolls or Close Rolls, we can never know whether the Chantry was really founded as a

School or not. As it was to the interest of the town that a
Chantry should not be held to have been founded for a Grammar
School, and the returns were very carefully scrutinized by the
Crown officials, we may feel pretty sure that wherever a Chantry
priest is reported as keeping a Grammar School "according to
the foundation" or "from time immemorial" the Chantry was
really founded for that purpose, and not merely applied to it in
later times.

With Chantries may be ranked such foundations as "the
Service of our Lady," or "So-and-so's stipendiary," which are
plentifully distributed through our pages as Grammar Schools
or Grammar School masters. The line between a Chantry, or a
service and a stipendiary is rather hard to draw. It would seem
that "a service" of a particular saint, commonly of Our Lady,
was an endowment not so much for the benefit of a particular
person's soul as for the maintenance of services subsidiary or
additional to the main services of the Church. Saturday was
specially devoted to Our Lady's service, and Our Lady was, from
the 12th century onwards, by far the most popular saint in
the "company of heaven," as is shown by the immense prepon-
derance of dedications to her of Colleges, Guilds, Chantries
and services ; while a Lady chapel became a necessary append-
age to every large church and almost every small one. The
great rise in Virgin-worship was coincident with the enforce-
ment of celibacy on the clergy at large. Perhaps they took to
the worship of the Virgin, as ideal woman, when the domestic
worship of a real woman was denied them. The stipendiary
was the same foundation as the service, looked at from the
point of view of the agent instead of the object. The priest
who performed the service was the stipendiary, and he might
either be called Our Lady's priest, from the name of the service,
or Smith's stipendiary (as at Saltash), from the name of the
founder. Perhaps, also, a technical difference may be found
in that a Chantry priest was a corporation created under a
licence in mortmain, and was, like a rector or vicar, his own
governing body ; while a stipendiary drew his stipend from
lands placed in the hands of trustees, who were the governors

of the goods and possessions of the foundation, and sometimes of the priest himself, over whom they were given a power of dismissal. We may illustrate the difference from " our Lady Chantry " at Wokingham, " founded by Adam Mullen, late dean of Sarum," 1441–5, " to maintain a priest for ever," compared with " A stipendiary priest, called our Lady priest, founded within the town " of Newbury, "perpetually to celebrate in an aisle there, called our Lady chapel, to the maintenance of which, and for reparation of the said aisle, certain lands and tenements were given unto a corporation there, called the corporation of our Lady chapel." A later stage of the stipendiary is seen at Kinnersley, in Herefordshire. "Certain lands and tenements given by Ann Delabore, widow, and enfeoffed to Thomas Mony-ington, Esquire, and other co-feoffees, to maintain a priest's service to sing at the altar of our Lady there." The founder of the stipendiary, who kept the Grammar School at Newbury, called Henry Wormestalls' priest, in 1466, actually anticipated modern ideas so much as to empower his feoffees " to alter and change the same foundation from time to time as to their discretion should seem good."

9. Independent Schools.

The foundations of stipendiary priests prepared the way and were the immediate precedents for foundations like Dean Colet's and Archbishop Holgate's, where the School was the expressed object ; and it was not thought necessary to conjoin it with a service or Chantry, or any other purely ecclesiastical function, or even to demand that the teacher should be a priest. Such foundations were, of course, comparatively modern. Perhaps the earliest specimen in these records is Chipping Campden Grammar School in Worcestershire, if it be correctly reported, and has not been incorrectly reported for the purpose of saving it from the Chantries Act. · This was " the Schoolmaster service, *alias* Ferby's service, founded by one John Ferby and Margery his wife, and the lands put in feoffment to the intent to find a priest to maintain a Free School in the said parish for ever." The words, "to find a priest," have been struck through, and then the whole entry cancelled with cross-lines. The foundation deed was lost, as so many others have been. It got into the hands of the lawyers in the course of a Chancery suit, and has not been seen since. Still the excision of the reference to a priest, the cancelling, in consequence, of the whole entry, and the retention by the School of its property till plundered in the beginning of the reign of Charles I., may be taken as very strong *primâ facie* evidence that this master was not required to be a priest, or perform any ecclesiastical functions, but to be a Schoolmaster only.

It is possible that Oswestry School, a School of Public-School rank in Shropshire, may be another and earlier instance, but there is no direct authority for it. It is said to have been founded in 1407 by David Holbeach, a Welshman and a lawyer, credited also by Leland with the foundation of Davies or Davy's Inn, one of the old Inns of Chancery in Holborn.

I have tried, but failed, to find the Letters Patent for the foundation. It is quite possible there was no patent; and if there were none, it would go some way to proving that there was no Chantry business about the foundation, and that it was merely and sincerely for a Schoolmaster, who was no priest. Unfortunately the earliest evidence extant is a very corrupt 17th century copy of an undated deed in Latin. This deed witnesses that Guinevere, as we may spell her in Tennysonese, or Gwenwhyvar, as she is spelt in the Welsh Latin, widow of David Holbadge, has granted the corn mill of Measbury and all property which she had in the manor of Two Parts (a part of Oswestry) to certain trustees, clerks and laymen mixed, and mostly Welsh. They covenant that therewith "the intent of David Holbeach shall be observed," viz., that the profits "shall be applied to the maintenance and sustenance of a Schoolmaster in the town of Oswestry yearly for ever." With scant reason, in face of the explicit declaration that Guinevere's grant was for the purpose of the husband's will, she has been erected into a co-founder. The deed is said, in the School book, which the Head-master, the Rev. J. Lloyd Williams, kindly lent me, to have been made about 9 Henry IV., *i.e.*, 1409. But it appears that David Holbeach's will was dated Wednesday after September 8, 1421, the last year of Henry V. This deed, therefore, cannot be earlier. In the same School book is a statement of " the names of the feoffees that were put in trust by David Holbadge for the School lands, 6 Henry IV." This, if correct, would make the School earlier, 1404–5. In our records there appear two priests of the service of our Lady, founded by Thomas, Earl of Arundel, in Oswestry parish church. The School is only mentioned in-the words, " To the augmentation of a Free School there, besides £6 by the foundation, 40s.," the forty shillings being apparently paid out of Our Lady's service. As usual, the details of the property in the Henrician and Edwardian Certificates differ. As the School is mentioned and not included in the Certificate, the presumption certainly arises that the Schoolmaster was not to be a priest, or he would have been a stipendiary within the Act.

It is, of course, not at all impossible that in those days, when Wickliffism was still strong, that a Welshman and a lawyer may have had views in favour of lay education. He is recorded, it is true, as founder of " the stipendiarie of David Holbache to celelebrate mass with other divine service at the altar of our Lady within the parish church of S. Mertin's," now called Saint Martin's. This is not, however, against his having founded a lay School. He may have changed his views when old and sick, or he may have objected to priests in education, but not in priestly functions.

The founder of Sevenoaks Grammar School, in 1432, said, point blank, that the Schoolmaster was not to be a priest *in sacris ordinibus minime constitutus*. It has been shown elsewhere how three successive Head-masters of York Cathedral Grammar School in the 15th century were laymen, and how the Head-master of Winchester College in 1535 was one also.

Colet, it is well known, in founding S. Paul's School, said that his Head-master was to be a layman, "a wedded man or a single man, or a priest that hath no benefice with cure "; and Lily, the Head-master he appointed, was a layman and married. At Manchester, in 1525, the Master was to be " a single man, priest or not priest, so that he be no religious man." So, too, Archbishop Holgate, for his three Schools in Yorkshire, only one of which—that of Malton—appears here, provided that the master might be married and a layman.

Fortunate, indeed, were those Schools in which their founders had so provided, for they escaped the meshes of the Chantries Act, and retained their endowments unassailed.

10. The Chantries Act of Henry VIII.

Such, then, was the provision for Schools when the Reformation swept like a deluge against all ecclesiastical foundations. At its beginning, and in its intention, the Reformation was certainly not hostile either to learning at large, or to Grammar Schools in particular. Still less was its particular manifestation in the dissolution of religious houses hostile to education. As we have cursorily noticed, the suppression of religious houses was largely connected with the founding of educational institutions; and Wolsey, as papal legate, gave Henry, with the full benediction of the Pope, his first lesson in the dissolution of monasteries. Nor is there any doubt that Henry did not intend to damage education. There is proof enough of this in his re-foundations of the cathedral churches of Canterbury and Durham, and of other cathedrals of the "new foundation," and his conversion into cathedral churches, with Grammar Schools attached, of Gloucester, Bristol, and Peterborough. He distinctly improved the position of the Cathedral Schools. At Durham, for instance, the Grammar School master was converted from the Chantry priest of S. Cuthbert in the Galilee, an outsider, into an integral part of the foundation, with the position and pay equal, or almost equal, to that of a residentiary canon.

So, too, in regard to the collegiate churches which Henry founded or refounded. There may, or may not, have been a School at Thornton Abbey, in Lincolnshire, before Henry converted it into a collegiate church. He certainly gave a very prominent position to learning in the collegiate church. So, too, at Westminster; for the present School was, it must not ba forgotten, originally his foundation. Further, in the year that witnessed the dissolution of the smaller monasteries, the Universities, and the Colleges of Eton and Winchester, which "ecclesiastical" foundations were included in the Valor Ecclesiasticus and the Act for payment of first-fruits and tenths, were exonerated from such payments—an exoneration which, no doubt, paved the way for the subsequent convenient and beneficial decision in James I.'s reign, in the teeth of all history, that they were not ecclesiastical foundations.

While the dissolution of the smaller monasteries damaged learning to a very small extent, if at all, the Act confirming the dissolution of the larger monasteries unfortunately included Colleges and Hospitals, and other "ecclesiastical" institutions, as well as "religious" institutions strictly so-called. In the dissolution of Colleges and Hospitals many Schools were therewith destroyed. Southwell Minster was dissolved and refounded with its School, but Chicheley's College, of Higham Ferrers, a smaller Winchester, fell, as did Cardinal College at Ipswich, and many more with them. However virtuous Henry's intentions may have been, the lack of money, which is the root of all evil, was too much for him and them. Besides, the example set by the Crown had private imitators. The mesne lords took to following the lord paramount, and suppressing Colleges and Chantries on their own account.

Hence came the Chantries Act of Henry VIII. In the absence of reports of debates in Parliament in those days, we are thrown back for an explanation of it on the statutes themselves. As this statute has been the subject of much writing without reading, and is only to be found in the Statutes of the Realm (III. 988), not in the Statutes at Large, a full account of it may not be amiss.

It is chapter 4 of 37 Henry VIII., *i.e.*, was passed fairly early in the Parliament which began in November, 1545. It is so curiously compounded in compartments that it would almost seem to have been the result of a compromise, or else to represent the consolidation of two distinct Acts into one. It is entitled on the Parliament Rolls, "An Acte for Colleges, Chan-

tries, etc.," and so it may have begun. It is entitled on the
Chancery Rolls, "An Acte for the Dissolution of Colleges,
Chantries, and Free Chapels, at the king's pleasure"; and, as
such, it certainly ended.

It began by reciting : "That where there have been diverse
Colleges, Freechapelles, Chantries, Hospitalles, Fraternities,
Brotherhedds, Guilds, and Stipendarie Priests having perpetuity
for ever within this your Realm.

"Sithens which time divers and many of the Donors, founders
or patrons, or such as pretend to be, of their own avaricious
and covetous minds, and of their own authority, without your
gracious licence, have of late entered into the same and have ex-
pulsed the Priests, Wardens, Masters, Ministers, Rulers, Governors, and Incumbents of the same, and do occupy the Masters'
houses, and do convert the rents to their own proper uses.

"And some of the said Incumbents by agreement between
them and the Patrons have also sold all or part of their lands,
belonging to their said Colleges [&c.]; and some by the assent
and consent of the Patrons [&c.], and some without, have now
of late made leases for lives or for terms of years, and have
not reserved the accustomable rent ; and some of them by
entries have made conveyances of all or part of their said
possessions; by reason whereof divers of the said Freechapels
[&c.] ben clearly extincted or determined, contrary to the
purposes of the Founders, and to the great contempt of your
Majesty and of your authority royal.

"And we, your Grace's subjects, right well knowing and
perceiving the great and inestimable charges which your
Majesty hath had and sustained, and daily doth sustain, as
well for the maintenance of these present wars against the
realms of France and Scotland, and for the preservation and
defence of us, your said subjects, against the invasions and
malice of your enemies, the French and Scots; as also for the
maintenance of your most royal estate, honour, dignity, and
estimation, which all your said loving subjects of natural duty
ben bound to conserve and increase by all such ways and
means as they can devise.

"Do therefore beseech your Majesty that it may be enacted in manner following."

Accordingly it was enacted: "That all the said Colleges [&c.], by what name soever they were founded or known, and all the mansion houses, &c., belonging to any of such Colleges [&c.] which between 4th February, 27th year of the King, and 25th December, 37th year, by reason of any such entry, expulsion, lease, or other conveyance thereof had or made ben dissolved, other than such as now be in the possession of the king, or that ben granted by his Highness to any other person, and have been lawfully obtained by any former title without fraud, or by license, shall from henceforth be in the possession and seizin of the King, and of his heirs and successors for ever; the said entries or other assurances notwithstanding."

I have given the exact words of the Act, merely omitting the legal verbiage and vain repetitions. It will be seen that the reasons for the Act are: firstly, that other people are devouring the Chantries without licence; and secondly, that the king's wars are devouring his substance, and therefore the plunder may as well go into the pockets of the king for the benefit of all, instead of the pockets of a few for the benefit of themselves. That other people were devouring the Chantries was not a mere idle pretext, as some historians have insinuated, is certain. There are four Certificates of unlicensed dissolutions in as many different counties still preserved. All such Chantries are, therefore, absolutely vested in the king without reserve. Sections 2 to 5 of the Act are merely amplifications of the saving words, and confirmatory of surrenders to and grants out again by the king, and need not be discussed.

The sixth clause begins the second part of the Act, and proceeds to deal, not with the Chantries which have been suppressed, but with those that survive. "And where also at this present time there are a great number of Chantries" [&c., in the same words as before], "having perpetuity for ever, and being charged or chargeable to the payment of First Fruits and Tenths according to the statute, and all Colleges as well chargeable or not chargeable to the payment, having divers manors [&c.] to the same annexed by the Patrons of them, to the intent that alms to the poor people and other virtuous and charitable deeds might be done.

"And for so much as it is well knowen that the said Governors, or the greatest number of them, hitherto have not, ne yet do use their said Chantries, ne yet bestow the rents of the same in alms and other deeds of charity, according to such virtuous and godly intents and purposes as the said Chantries were first founded, to the great displeasure of Almighty God and to the discontentation of the King.

"And for that the King's Highness, of his most godly and blessed disposition, entendeth to have the premises used to more godly and virtuous purposes, and to bring them into a more decent and convenient order for the commodity and wealth of this his realm, and for the surety of his subjects.

"Be it further enacted that the King's Majesty shall and may during his life make his Grace's Commission under his great seal upon a warrant signed with his Grace's hand, to such number of persons and into such counties, shires, and places as shall be thought expedient, giving unto the said commissioners, or two of them at the least, full power to enter into all chantries, [etc.], named in the said commission, and to seize and take the same chantries unto the King's hands To hold to the King's Highness his heirs and successors for ever.

"And that the said Commissioners or any two of them after such entry shall certify and return the said Commissions making mention in writing of their doings in the same, into the chancery, at such day, as shall be limited in the said commissions, there to remain of record for ever."

The rest of the Act is merely ministerial.

This second part of the Act, be it observed, does not give the Colleges and Chantries to the king out and out *instanter*, as the former part did. It only gives him power to issue commissions and take what he pleased. Presumably the form intended to be followed was that of the commission under which Crediton and Ottery S. Mary Colleges were dissolved before the Act (p. 47), 7th May. But Crediton was certainly, and Ottery

S. Mary most probably, intended to be re-founded, the School
and Church being granted to the inhabitants in the same way
as Warwick was. The actual money (£200) which the people
of Crediton had to pay for the re-foundation was paid to Henry,
though the Letters Patent were in fact only issued in Edward's
reign.

The most striking thing about this part of the Act is that
while, as regards Chantries, Hospitals, Brotherhoods and Guilds,
only those that were liable to first-fruits might be dissolved;
as regards Colleges, all might be destroyed, whether they paid
first-fruits or not. That is to say, almshouses or hospitals
—the terms were coterminous—which were under purely lay
control, such as, for instance, those under municipal corporations,
would be exempt, as would also all craft or municipal guilds,
as such. On the other hand, the Colleges in the Universities,
and Winchester and Eton, which only ten years before had been
expressly treated as non-ecclesiastical, were deliberately swept
into the net. It is to be hoped that the intention was only to
re-found the Colleges, sweeping away the "superstitious uses,"
e.g. Chantries, like Barton's Chantry at All Souls'. But in
view of the results of Henry's virtuous intentions with the
monasteries, the Colleges were none too safe.

When exactly the Act was passed is not known. The commissions under it seem to have all been issued on the same day,
14th February, 37 Henry VIII., i.e. 1546, according to our
reckoning. As a specimen of the commission itself, that for
Yorkshire is given. These commissions were as a rule for the
counties in couples, thus: Bedford and Buckinghamshire, Berkshire and Hampshire, Devon and Cornwall, Cumberland and
Westmorland, Durham and Northumberland, Oxford and Northamptonshire (with Rutland thrown in), Warwickshire and
Leicestershire; but Lancashire and Yorkshire, Essex and Kent,
enjoyed commissions to themselves separately.

The commissions did not authorize the commissioners to enter
on the Chantries, but only to survey them and report what there
were.

The Certificates thus made furnish the first part of the records

with which we are now concerned. Unfortunately only a few
are preserved; and most unfortunately those for Oxford and
Cambridge are not preserved. From the specimen of a parochial return given at Wisbech (p. 20), it appears that as late
as 17th May the returns were not sent in to the commissioners;
and it would no doubt take some time for the commissioners
to draw up their certificates from the parochial returns and
local inquiries, and to send them on to the Court of Augmentations of the revenues of the Crown.

Canon Dixon says (II. p. 381): "Before the end of the year,
Colleges, Hospitals, Chantries, and Free Chapels were falling
rapidly to the king." He gives a list; but the list does not
contain a single College, Hospital, Chantry, or Free Chapel
which fell under the Act. All but three, on his own showing,
fell before it. Of these three, two were Thornton College and
Fotheringhay College, which appear in our records, and were
still flourishing in 1547. Had the Canon taken the trouble to
read Rymer, whom he quotes as his authority, he would have
seen that those two Colleges merely granted to the king—
Thornton one, and Fotheringhay two—out-lying rectories. The
third institution, a Hospital at Arundel, did not fall under the
Chantries Act, but was surrendered under the second Act for
the dissolution of monasteries, which specifically included Colleges and Hospitals.

Rymer does (xv. 99) give one veritable instance of a foundation which was seized under the Chantries Act. This the
Canon has omitted. It was S. Edmund's College, Salisbury,
and the return in the case expressly refers to the Statute. Mr.
W. H. Page, in his Introduction to *Yorkshire Chantries*
(Surtees Society, 1895), doubts whether any Chantries fell under
the Act. The only instances known—and very likely there are
no more—of entry under the Act, besides the one mentioned, are
the Colleges of Tong, Shropshire; Pleshy; Hastings; the Hospital of S. Bartholomew the Great; and Chantries at Ald-
winckle and Lufwick, Northants; and Bakewell, Derbyshire.
These were not taken till the last three months of 1546.

They appear among the *Miscellaneous Rolls of Chancery*

(Bundle xiii., File 5); and for knowledge of them I am indebted to Mr. E. Salisbury of the Record Office.

But apparently Henry had a fit of reaction after the Chantries Act was passed. He is reported to have dissolved Parliament with a speech in which he said he was going to reform Chantries, not destroy them. Dr. Crome was nearly burnt for abusing Chantries in a sermon. If any were seized beyond the few mentioned, they were very few.

Henry died in January, 1547. With him died the power to seize the Chantries, the power to issue a commission to enter being, as we have seen, limited to his life and to a warranty under his hand. The Chantries were thus respited.

11. The Chantries Act of Edward VI.

One of the first Acts of Edward VI.'s first Parliaments (1 Edward VI. c. 14) was a new Chantries Act. This went on quite a different basis. At the very time Henry was dissolving the Chantries he was prosecuting people for not believing in Purgatory. The Parliament of the Protector Somerset placed their action on religious grounds. They dissolved the Chantries because they condemned the objects of Chantries. They considered " that a great part of superstition and errors in Christian religion has been brought into the minds and estimation of men, by reason of their ignorance of the very true and perfect salvation through Christ Jesus, and by devising and fancying vain opinions of purgatory and masses satisfactory to be done for them which be departed, the which doctrine and vain opinion by nothing more is maintained and upholden than by the abuse of trentals, Chantries, and other provisions made for the continuance of the said blindness and ignorance." They also considered " that the alteration, change and amendment of the same, and converting to good and godly uses, as in erecting of Grammar Schools to the education of youths in virtue and godliness, the further augmenting of the Universities, and better provision for the poor and needy, cannot in this present Parliament be done," and can only properly be done by the king, " with and by the advice of his most prudent council."

They also remembered and recited the two chief clauses of the Act of Henry. They, therefore, vested in the Crown as from Easter, 1548, " All Colleges, Free Chapels and Chantries," " All Lands given for the finding of a Stipendiary Priest for ever," " All rents and annuities for the maintenance of any Stipendiary Priest for ever," if within 5 years before the first day of Parliament they existed or were so applied. All these were included in the former Act. By other sections were now added lands given for anniversaries, obits, lights or lamps, kept within 5 years before. As regards fraternities and brotherhoods the Act is difficult to construe. It gave the Crown all payments made by " corporations, guilds, fraternities, companies or fellowships of mysteries or crafts," for priests, obits, etc. ; and also " all fraternities, brotherhoods and guilds—other than such corporations, etc., of mysteries or crafts above mentioned." The words are not very well put, but the intention would appear to have been to exempt from the Act all Craft Guilds and Town Corporations.

Hospitals are not mentioned in the Act. Hence such as had not fallen as monasteries through being served by canons regular, or had not been surrendered, escaped further molestation, though a good many of them appear in the Certificates. There were also specially exempted from the Act, Colleges, hostels, and halls of the Universities, and Chantries therein ; the Free Chapel of St. George the Martyr in the Castle of Windsor; S. Marie's College of Winchester by Winchester of the foundation of Bishop Wickham ; the College of Eaton ; the parish church called " Chapel in the Sea " in Newton, Isle of Ely. Then comes a very big exception of " any chapel of ease " or " such like," " whereunto no more lands or tenements than the churchyard or a little house or close door belong," and lastly, " any Cathedral Churches or Colleges where a Bishop's see is." The Chantries in Cathedrals are, however, confiscated, not " to be altered," as in the Universities. A commission was to be issued under the Great Seal to survey all lay corporations, etc., "as all other the said fraternities, brotherhoods, or Guilds," to know what money was paid for priests, obits, and also to inquire what lands were given to the king by the Act.

As regards Schools, section 2 of the Act said that the " Commissioners, or two of them at the least, shall have full power to assign, and shall appoint, in every place where a Guild or fraternity, or the priest or incumbent of any Chantry, by the foundation ordinance, or the first institution thereof, should or ought to have kept a Grammar School," and has done so since Michaelmas last, "lands, tenements, and other hereditaments of any such chantry, to remain and continue in succession to a Schoolmaster for ever, for and towards the keeping of a Grammar School, in such manner as they shall appoint." To meet this clause in the Act, the Commissioners of Edward VI. took special note of all Grammar Schools, and in some cases of other Schools as well.

Preachers were included with Schools; while other special clauses provided that a vicar should be endowed sufficiently in every parish church which was a College, Free Chapel or Chantry; and that in great towns lands should be assigned for one or more priests.

The commissioners were, further, " to make ordinances and rules concerning the service, uses and demeanour of every such priest and Schoolmaster, as also by what names he shall be called."

The same commissioners were also to assign pensions to the incumbents whose office was abolished; and, by a further clause, to continue any money or other benefits which the poor had out of the dissolved institutions. By another special clause, they were to assign to fraternities, brotherhoods, or Guilds, lands for the maintenance of piers and sea-walls. Their assignments and ordinances were to have the force of an Act of Parliament. Lastly, every commissioner was solemnly charged by the Act, " as he will answer before God, to execute the commission beneficially towards " the incumbents aforesaid—which term included Schoolmasters—the poor, and the maintenance of piers and sea-walls.

Now, if this Act had been carried out as was intended, and

the Schools treated "beneficially," it would have been difficult
for the most ardent upholder of the viciousness of the Re-
formers to attack it. It suited Froude to run down the statesmen of Edward's reign by way of foil to Henry VIII. But
this Act is a far more statesmanlike Act than that of Henry,
which trusted everything to the arbitrary will of that arbitrary
monarch. It bears traces of discussion and amendment while
passing through Parliament, as in the insertion of the clause
in favour of sea-walls, which was inserted to meet the opposi-
tion of the members for Lynn, and, we may suppose, of others,
whose Guilds carried out a great number of public works by
effort more or less voluntary, which are now done by municipal and other local governments. That it was a good thing,
per se, to abolish the bulk of the Chantries, there can, to every
reasonable man, Catholic or Protestant, be little question.
No form of charitable endowment could be less defensible in
theory, or less beneficial in practice, than that of the Chantry
pure and simple. To set one, two, or even three or more, priests,
educated men, or supposed to be educated, to spend his or their
days in singing psalms, or saying masses at a salary of £5 a
year, (say £60 to £100 a year of our money,) for the soul of
some one who had "emigrated from this light" perhaps two or
three centuries before, and was in most cases far better known
by his Chantry when dead than he had ever been by his
charity when alive, was perhaps as great a waste of men and
money as could well be conceived. Prayers for the dead may,
or may not, commend themselves as useful or meritorious; but
hired prayers for the dead are surely superstitious. Already in
Chaucer's time the poor priest who—

> " Ran unto London, unto St. Poules,
> To seken him a chanterie for soules,"

was an object of well-merited contempt. The records of Southwell Minster and of Wells Cathedral, and those hitherto un-
published at York, show the sort of life those people led, a life
not tending to edification. It was probably an unmixed good
to abolish the great majority of them, mere living prayer-

wheels to extract the well-to-do departed from the purgatory which they had no doubt amply earned.

Bishop Gardiner himself approved of the Chantries Act. In a sermon before the Court, he said : " If Chantries were abused by applying the Mass for the satisfaction of sin, or to bring men to heaven, or to take away sin, or to make men of wicked, just, I like the Act well. I that allow Mass so well, and I that allow praying for the dead (as, indeed, the Dead are of Christian charity to be prayed for), yet can agree with the realm in the matter of putting down Chantries." (Blunt, *The Reformation*, II. 141, quoting Foxe, VI. 87–93.)

But there was a large proportion of Chantry priests, who, as these records show, were not mere chanters of masses. Many of them were curates of the parish church, incumbents of chapels of ease, and Guild chaplains who no doubt did useful work. For these due provision was made by the Act.

The abolition of the Guilds was a measure of far more doubtful policy. The Craft Guilds and Town Corporations were exempt. But many Guilds were swept away, which, though nominally perhaps religious Guilds, performed in fact many of the functions of a modern municipality. Many more were at the least Burial Clubs and Social Clubs, in which the superstitious use was a mere adjunct, which could and would have been dropped without materially affecting the constitution or objects of the Guild. It was very hard on Stratford-on-Avon and Birmingham to have to buy back their bridge funds and clock funds and poor funds, and, in the case of Stratford, their School funds. The same exemption that was extended to funds for sea banks maintained by Guilds ought to have been extended to funds for bridges and all other objects of public utility.

As regards Schools too, though the Act provided for Grammar Schools, it made no provision whatever for Song Schools or Elementary Schools, whether they were called Song Schools or Writing Schools, or were merely old men to teach the A B C. This was a grievous omission. The Song School, no doubt, was capable of being represented as a seminary of superstition. Even the Reading School might be so looked upon. The pro-

fessed object of Primers was " to teach a child to help a
priest to sing." But it must have been perfectly well known
that some were for the most part mere Musical, and others mere
Elementary, Schools. The Grammar Schools throughout were,
as we have said, fairly provided for in the Act. The only blot,
and it is a grave one, was that the Act protected only Grammar
Schools which were so by "the first foundation or ordinance
thereof "; and it does not seem to protect a Grammar School
which was part of the foundation of a college. Section 11 only
speaks of places where "Guild, Fraternity, the priest or incumbent of any Chantry," should or ought to have kept a
Grammar School, whereas in other sections Colleges are expressly coupled with Chantries. Perhaps, however, this was
only a slip in the drafting or copying of the Act, because in
most Colleges the Grammar School is reported and is preserved,
as in Acaster (p. 304), Rotherham (p. 305), Southwell (p. 171),
Thornton (p. 138).

The other omission was more fatal, and accounts for the destruction of many Schools which were in fact maintained by
Chantries or Guilds, whether these were bound by foundation
to maintain them or not. Besides, the Act had it both ways.
If the School did not appear in the foundation, it was suppressed, even if one was in fact kept. On the other hand,
though one ought to have been kept according to the foundation, yet if in fact it was not kept, it was suppressed. Such
was the case of the wily Hugh Sherwood, master of the
School founded by Bishop Fitzjames at Bruton, who, "endea-
vouring himself rather to live licentiously at will than to
travail in good education of youth according to the godly
foundation of the said School," "surrendered the lands to
the king's majesty 6 or 7 years past," and "found means to
obtain by decree out of the Court of Augmentations for term of
his life one annuity or pension of £5, and the Schoolhouse with
a garden," and 4 acres of land, "discharged thereby of any
further free teaching or keeping of School there." The
inhabitants represented this to be " to the great decay of virtuous bringing up of youth of the said shire in all good learning,

as also of inhabitants of the King's said town of Bruton, of great relief that came thereby." Whence we may infer that the School was a boarding School, or, at least, that boys lodged in the town to attend it. Bruton was not continued by the Commissioners, and no doubt others were in like case. Bruton was in fact afterwards restored, but no thanks to Mr. Hugh Sherwoode.

Subject to these exceptions the Act bid fair not to harm Schools.

12. Execution of the Act.

Canon Dixon's account (II. 498 seq.) of the proceedings under this Act is highly confused and erroneous. "Instead of commissioners or visitors it would seem that injunctions were sent by the Council into every parish to four honest persons at the least. These persons were enjoined to inquire," and so on. "In this artful and quiet manner there was wrought a ruination, which was only inferior in extent to that of the monasteries themselves." Then he proceeds to give an instance : "The old College and sanctuary of St. Martin le Grand was now given to the Chapter of Westminster. They in turn sold the bells, etc." Surely Canon Dixon might have taken the trouble to ascertain the facts as to his specimen cases. The College of St. Martin le Grand was not " given to the Chapter of Westminster," but had been handed over to Westminster when Westminster was still an Abbey, by Henry VII. The general statement is founded on even a less sure foundation than the particular example. The Canon refers in a note to a single document in Burnet's *Collectanea* (II. xxvii.) as his authority. It will be hardly believed that this very document, printed at full length, is dated 4th February, 27 Henry VIII., and yet the Canon builds on it an account of what happened in the reign of Edward VI.! It is true that the year is wrong; it should be 37 Henry VIII., as is clear by the fact that the first signature to it is by Robert Holgate, Archbishop of York, who was not appointed till 1545. The document, signed by Archbishop Holgate, and by 9 others, is, in fact, a specimen of

the inquiries addressed by the Chantry Commissioners under
Henry VIII.'s Act to the parson and others in each parish in
Yorkshire, to furnish the information on which their Certificate
was to be based.

It shows, therefore, so far as Henry VIII.'s Act is concerned,
the direct opposite to what Canon Dixon asserts. Instead of
working in the dark and quietly, the county Commissioners
sent a document to every parish to get on the spot an exact
account of the foundation with which they were concerned.
They sent to the people who ought to know best, being also, it
must be remembered, those who would be most interested in
preserving the foundations, especially if they were useful to the
parish, or commended themselves to the parishioners. Among
our records there is a single specimen of one of these parochial
returns—that for Wisbech. It is the only return under either
of the Acts for Cambridgeshire, and makes us wish we had
many more of them. To make confusion worse, the Canon has
referred us for specimens of commissions for Chantries, to commissions for inquiries as to church goods, not issued till February
1549. So that different reigns, dates, and subjects are treated as
all one, if only a fling at the Reformation party can be got out
of the confusion.

The "artful and quiet manner" in which the Chantries were
dissolved is quite imaginary. Of the high-handed and hasty
way in which the Act was carried out, complaint might be
possible; but artful and quiet are about the last epithets
which are applicable. The commissions under the later Act
were made in precisely the same way as those under the former
Act. Separate commissions were issued for the counties either
singly or in couples, apparently on the precedent of Henry's
commission. They were dated 14th February, 1548, just two
years after the former commission. Some of the commissioners
were the same persons. They were selected from the knights
and other country gentlemen of the counties concerned, with
one or two officials thrown in. Partly to show the class
of persons, partly as a concession to the genealogists, I have
given the names of the commissioners, whenever they are

attached to the Certificate made by them. The only marked difference appears to be that bishops were as conspicuous by their absence among Edward VI.'s commissioners, as they were by their presence among Henry's. Here are the lists of the two sets of commissioners for the grouped counties of Bucks and Beds as a specimen; those marked with a star being officials:—

HENRY VIII.	EDWARD VI.
John, Bishop of Lincoln.	Sir John St. John, Kt.
Sir John St. John, Kt.	Sir Laurence Lee, Kt.
*Henry Bradshawe, Esq.	*Sir Robert Drury, Kt.
*Robert Drury, Esq.	Sir Thomas Rotheram, Kt.
George Wright, Esq.	*Henry Bradshawe, Esq.
*Hugh Fuller.	George Gifford, Gent.
	*William Smyth, Gent.

There is nothing hole and corner about the composition of either commission; and the latter is the stronger of the two. To show the terms of the commission, that for Kent, which is still annexed to the return of the commissioners, is printed in Part II. as a specimen.

If the returns under these commissions had been as full as was contemplated, they would have given us a very accurate notion of the nature and date of these foundations. The returns are, in fact, little more than summaries, and are especially defective on the heading of foundation.

They are, for the purpose of Schools, however, more illuminating than the Certificates under the first Act, by reason of section 2 quoted above.

13. Commission for Continuance of Schools.

Apparently the Act intended that the same commissioners should both inquire into and continue the Schools, and should give them the lands of the institution which had before maintained them, or other lands to form an adequate endowment. Unfortunately it was not so interpreted. The continuance was not left to the commissioners for the different counties,

who being for the most part natives of the counties, would
have taken, and in many cases show by their recommenda-
tions that they did take, a liberal view of the requirements
of the localities. It was reserved for a different commission,
given to two officials of the Crown. As this commission, of
great importance in the history of these transactions, is quite
unknown to or unnoticed by the historians, it has been
printed at full length, so far as it is legible, though it is of
portentous bulk. The Certificates of the county commissioners
were to be all in by 31st May. This commission is dated 20th
June. It appoints Sir Walter Mildmay, the general surveyor
of the new Court of Augmentations; and Robert Kelway,
"surveyor of our liveries in our Court of Wards," commissioners. Sir Walter Mildmay is of course a well-known person.
He was a Cambridge man, became afterwards Chancellor of the
Court of Augmentations, and in Elizabeth's reign Chancellor
of the Exchequer. He turned to good use the acquisitions,
which, in common with other statesmen, by no means ex-
cepting the Romanizers, he got from the confiscated lands by
founding Emmanuel College, Cambridge—a college suspect of
Elizabeth as puritanical, and which turned out very advanced
indeed. He even himself wrote, according to Mr. Mullinger, Latin
poems. His sympathies therefore were likely to be with the
encouragement of learning and the maintenance of Grammar
Schools. Still, an official charged with getting in money at
a time when the State was avoiding bankruptcy by depre-
ciating the currency, was only too likely to take an "official
view." Still more so was his coadjutor, Robert Kelway.
Kelway was an Oxford man, took no degree, went to the Inner
Temple, wrote Kelway's Reports *temp.* Henry VII. and Henry
VIII., and became in 1552 a sergeant-at-law. He was one of the
county commissioners for Beds, Berks, Devon, Dorset, Lancashire, Somerset and South Wales, so that he probably played a
more important part in the matter than Mildmay. He seems
to have been a mere lawyer and official, not likely to care much
to save Grammar Schools.

To these two was practically committed the settlement of the

whole question of Secondary Education at this crisis. The
scope of their commission included not only the continuance of
Schools and preachers, but also the assignment of vicars and
curates, where needed, in places where there were Colleges or
Chantries, money for the poor and for sea-banks, and also the
assignment of pensions to those who were disestablished. The
Schools are made quite a subordinate part of the business they
had to do. First and foremost is put the question of pensions.
Only when that is disposed of are the commissioners to " cause
any of the particular surveyors of our lands, or any of the
auditors of the Court of Augmentations, to make collection of the
number of Grammar Schools and preachings in every county
that have been kept of the said lands, and of the yearly value
of the lands which have been yearly bestowed towards the
maintenance thereof, and deliver them to you ; and you to make
declaration thereof to us, or to our most dear uncle, to the
intent thereupon to take order for the continuance or alteration of the same Schools and preachings, or for the same or
other to be newly erected in such places in every county as
shall be thought meet."

Then " We, or our said uncle, may signify unto you our pleasure, by word of writing, how many Grammar Schools shall be
erected and have continuance in every county, and how much
lands and other yearly pensions, annuities, or other profits,
shall be appointed for the maintenance of every one of the
same." The commissioners are empowered to assign lands
and tenements, or else rents and yearly pensions "toward the
keeping of so many Grammar Schools " and Hospitals, as the
"dear uncle" shall appoint. "Books," i.e. deeds, are to be
made of the same, under the advice of the Attorney and
Solicitor-General, and the Attorney-Generals of the Augmentations, and Wards and Liveries, and Court of First Fruits, and
others. The "books" are then to be presented " to us and
to our Council," to be signed. This was all very well, especially
as it was prefaced by a declaration that " We, minding to
erect divers and sundry Grammar Schools in every county in
England and Wales, for the education and bringing up youth

F

in virtue and learning and godliness, by the advice of our dearest Uncle Somerset the Protector, will and command you " to do all this.

But the whole thing was vitiated by the fatal addition : " And forasmuch as present order and direction cannot be had and taken, for and concerning the said Grammar Schools and preachers, and for the continuance or alteration of the same " and all the rest of it : " Our pleasure is that so much money as heretofore hath been yearly employed towards the maintenance of any such Schools, preachings, Schoolmasters," etc., " shall be paid from Easter last, to the sustentation of the same, in such manner as the same has been used to be paid ; until such time as other order and direction shall be taken therein, in manner afore rehearsed." And so they were directed to issue their warrants accordingly, on the strength of the certificate of any of the said auditors or particular surveyors, or any of their deputies. It therefore came down to this, that the question of Schools was really settled by the clerk of a person who occupied the same sort of position as a local agent of the Woods and Forests now. He took out of the Certificates what Schools were kept and were to be kept, and Mildmay and Kelway signed the warrants, which the deputy of a deputy of a deputy drew up. No wonder that the whole business was polished off in a month, and the continuance warrants all duly signed and done with on the 20th July.

In such a fiasco ended the great promises of Henry to his Parliament, and the expressed will of the Parliament of Edward VI. for the reform of Chantries and the advancement of learning. For most of the Schools the " other order " never came.

It is to the proviso of this commission that we owe the two sets of documents which complete our records. First, the Brief Certificate, or abstract of the County Commissioners' Certificate, drawn up by the local surveyor :—a good specimen is that for Cornwall (p. 9). Second, the Warrants for continuing Schools (which included also vicars, preachers, sea-banks, and the poor) signed by Mildmay and Kelway. These are all in the same form as that given in full for Bedfordshire (p. 5).

It should be added that the Duchy of Lancaster was treated separately in accordance with the Act, and the Certificate for Schools in the Duchy was not signed until the 11th of August (pp. 123, etc.).

An interesting point about these commissions is that it lays down a fixed scale on which pensions are to be awarded to the dispossessed, showing that it was not left, as seems to have been generally supposed, to the arbitrary discretion of the commissioners in each case. The scale is a liberal one on the whole. A person with an income of £5 and under got a pension to the whole amount:

Above £5 and under £6 13s. 4d., £5.

£6 13s. 4d. and under £10, £6.

„   £10 and under £20, £6 13s. 4d.

This last sum seems rather small, but as £5 was an adequate livelihood, perhaps it was thought that £6 13s. 4d. was luxury, and you could want no more. These pensions were to be paid without fine or fee—a necessary provision in those days of fee-paid officials, the officials being paid out of the " suppressed lands." The pensions seem to have been very fairly paid on the whole.

The erroneous account given by Canon Dixon of the Commissions of Inquiry under the Chantries Act has been criticised. That account was accuracy itself compared to the extraordinary version given by a writer in *Social England* (iii. 265) of the Schools Continuance Commission. " The suppression of the monasteries was seriously felt in the matter of the education of youth. The monks had always taken care of that; and the sudden failure in this respect was so felt that in 2 Edward VI., Letters Patent, dated 20th June, 1549, were issued, appointing certain commissioners to take diverse orders for the maintenance and continuance of 'scollers, priests, and curates,' and other matters relating to the poor—which necessarily embraced the question of education. We hear all over the country of Edward VI. Grammar Schools—and many were provided by his Letters Patent, but they mostly received very little, if any, endowment from the forfeited estates, and were like Christ's Hospital and the other London hospitals, cheap advertisements of their royal patron and his advisers."

The writer thus imputes a commission, arising from the confiscation of Chantries and Colleges, to the confiscation of monasteries nine years before; he treats the commission as if it were an isolated measure of reform, and not a mere ministerial resultant of the Chantries Act; he or his authority had misread "scolemⁿ" into "scollers"; while, instead of the Schools re-founded by Letters Patent, receiving little, if any, endowment from the forfeited estates, they received it all from these estates, and very good endowments too.

The only pity was that so few were re-founded by Letters Patent. There can be little doubt that the Protector Somerset intended to make the "further order" contemplated by the Continuance Commissioners' Warrants. Wars abroad, risings at home, a constant struggle for power and for life, and the resulting empty exchequer, prevented the "further order" being made.

14. Re-foundation of Schools.

Among people interested in education there was great dissatisfaction at the way the Act was carried out. Latimer frequently refers to the matter in general terms, while the sermons of Lever, Master of St. John's, Cambridge, before Edward VI. in 1550 (p. 81, Arber's Reprint) go into particulars. "Pleaseth it your Majesty with your honourable council for the reverence of God, the pity of the poor, and the godly zeal that ye have to good learning, hear what hath been done in your time." He then quotes the Act as to Schools, and continues: "But now many Grammar Schools be taken, sold, and made away to the great slander of you and your laws, to the grievous offence of the people, to the most miserable drowning of youth in ignorance, and sore decay of the Universities. There was in the North country, amongst the rude people in knowledge, a Grammar School founded, having in the University of Cambridge of the same foundation 8 scholarships, ever replenished with the scholars of that School, which School is now sold, decayed, and lost. Mo[re] there be of like sort handled. But I recite this only, because I know that the sale of it was once stayed by charity, and yet afterwards brought to pass by bribery, as I heard say. . . . For God's sake, you that be in authority, look upon it. For if ye wink at such matters God will scowl upon you." In another sermon, in December the same year, he refers to the same subject. "Look whether there was not a great number of both learned and poor that might have been kept . . . in the Universities! Yea, and in the country many Grammar Schools, founded of a godly intent to bring up poor men's sons in learning and virtue, now be taken away by reason of the greedy covetousness of you that were put in trust by God and the king to erect and make Grammar Schools in many places; and had neither commandment nor permission to take away the Schoolmasters' living in any place. I know what ye do say and brag in some places, that ye have done as ye were commanded, with as much charity and liberality towards both poverty and learning, as your commission would bear and suffer.

"Take heed whom ye slander. For God's word and the king's laws be open unto every man's eyes; and by every commission directed according unto them, ye both might and should have given away much, whereas ye have taken much away.

"Take heed unto the king's statutes. There ye shall find that the Nobles and Commons do give, and the king doth take into his hands Abbeys, Colleges, and Chantries, for erecting of Grammar Schools, the godly bringing up of youth, the further augmenting of the Universities, and better provision for the poor. This shall ye find in the Acts of Parliament and in the king's statutes. But what shall be found in your practice and in your deeds?

"Surely the putting down of Grammar Schools, the devilish drowning of youth in ignorance, the utter decay of the Universities."

It was no doubt owing to such appeals as these, public and private, that the restoration of some Grammar Schools began. Sedbergh was the School referred to in Lever's sermon, having been founded by Dr. Lupton of that College (p. 303) 9th March,

152⅞; and Sedbergh was ordered to be re-founded on 20th February, 1551. " Make a grant of the premises for a Free Grammar School to be erected in Scadburgh (*sic*) in consideration of a School there before, the lands whereof are sold by the King's Majesty." The re-foundation was a fair instance of robbing Peter to pay Paul. The new endowment was made up of the following fragments :—

			£	s.	d.
The whole possessions of a Chantry in All Saints', York			6	8	4
„	„	„ Coley Chantry in Halifax parish	1	13	4
„	„	„ Rood Guild in Sedburgh . .	1	6	8
Part of the possessions of Hunter's Chantry in Halifax Parish Church			0	19	9½
The whole possessions belonging to maintenance of a lamp in Fishlake			0	3	10½
Part of the possessions of Our Lady Chantry in Thurne Parish Church			0	8	0
„	„	our Lady Chantry in Barnby-upon-Don . . .	2	18	10
„	„	the College of Jesus at Rotherham	2	3	0
„	„	S. Nicholas Chantry, Ilkley .	4	7	0
			£20	13	10

It is these warrants which form the last class of documents given in this book. They are not strictly within its title : but they have been collected at the Record Office in the same bundle with the Continuance Warrants, and shed so much light on the methods of precedure, adopted in the re-establishment of those schools which were re-established, that they have been included. There are only 14 in all, and nearly all in the fifth year of Edward's reign, *i.e.* 1551-2, but the first in 1550.

It is the fashion to abuse Dudley, Duke of Northumberland, because he tried to prevent Mary from coming to the throne, and from creating a reaction, or, perhaps, undoing altogether the Protestant Revolution. Yet Mary's reign should give pause to those who blame him, and raise a doubt whether he did not possess true insight, when he tried to prevent her from reigning. At all events he, if any one, is entitled to what credit there is in Edward VI.'s School foundations. Except for a few Colleges like Crediton, St. Mary Ottery, and Maidstone, where the arrangements for re-foundation had been made under Henry VIII., there was scarcely a School re-founded till the Duke of Northumberland came into power. The Protector Somerset was sent to the Tower in January, 1550. Among the first Schools to be re-founded was Sherborne, the charter for which became a model for the rest. "The King's Majesty, by the advice of his Privy Council, is pleased and contented that a Free Grammar School shall be erected and established in Sherborne," on 29th March, Edward VI., 1550. The actual Charter was dated 13th May, 1550. The lands, as in the case of Sedbergh, were not the lands which had previously supported the School. They were the lands of the Chantries of Martock, Somerset ; S. Katherine's Chantry, Gillingham ; Gybbon's Chantry in Lychett Matravers ; the free chapel of Thornton in Marnehull parish ; and thirty acres of land belonging to S. Katherine's Chantry at Ilminster. The clear yearly value was £20, with 13s. 4d. reserved as rent to the Crown. "A Bill" was "to be devised" to vest these in a corporation of governors "of the inhabitants of the town and parish." The School itself had existed long before the dissolution of S. Mary's Priory.

When people talk of such endowments as "small," they talk ignorantly. £20 a year was a very good endowment—the pay of a well-paid canon. The endowments of Sherborne School, even in these days of agricultural depression, are worth £1,270 a year, or sixty times the original value ; though, according to Carlisle, they were "formerly much neglected, if not abused." If all the Schools which had £20 a year in 1547, or even those which had £10 a year, or £5 a year, had been left in possession of their lands, they would have been amply endowed. The Guild of Birmingham bought back its £21 a year clear. In this case, as a specimen, I have set out all the "parcels." They were tenements in Dalend, Chapel Street, English Market, New Street, High Street, Mulle (? Mill) Street, Edgbaston Street,

Mercers' Street, the Bullring, Well Street, Park Street, and the Foreign (*forennseca*, the part outside the old borough), by the Lake meadow, Rotten Field, the Butts, producing their 1*s.*, 3*s.*, 5*s.* a tenement, or 8*s.* to 36*s.* 8*d.* for a piece of meadow or pasture. These same lands, growing with the growth of Birmingham, now produce more than £30,000 a year, keeping the High School and half a dozen other flourishing Grammar Schools for both sexes. Call you that a small endowment? Yet it is with little exception, if any, nothing but the old endowment, developed with the development of the place.

Take again Macclesfield Grammar School. Its original lands were given back to it, together with part of the endowment of the great College of St. John Baptist, Chester, the original Chester Cathedral, a magnificent building standing on Dee side, the tower of which the negligence of modern times has allowed to go to ruin in the present century. The total value of the School endowment was £21 4*s.* It has not received any notable or known increment, but its income is now £1,600 a year, according to the Secondary Education Commission, and its Grammar School is in a highly flourishing condition.

Stourbridge had only £17 10*s.* 8*d.*, clear, given it, but it now has close on £900 a year. In some cases, as in Crediton, Ottery S. Mary's, Wimborne, where in the re-endowment School and Church were mixed, the School has been sacrificed to the Church, but even the endowment of Crediton School is £830 a year, and of Wimborne £482. It is really sickening to think what endowments have been lost to education by the fatal *quousque* order. If the State had benefited, it would not have mattered so much. But the "unearned increment" has not come to the State, but to the private purchasers; and the loss is incalculable. All honour then to John Dudley, Duke of Northumberland, who at least saved from the wreck all that was saved. Whatever his other demerits may have been, even to the pardonable weakness of recanting his views on the other world for the sake of remaining a little longer in this, he should be regarded as the true patron saint of the Grammar Schools of Grantham, and Louth, and Morpeth, of Birmingham

and Macclesfield, and of the "Public Schools" of Sedbergh,
Sherborne, and Shrewsbury. By their wealth and by their good
works we can measure the loss sustained by their contem-
poraries and compeers, which was restricted to a fixed sum,
adequate enough, in some cases, at the time, but long since
shrunk into a miserable pittance.

15. Documents of Dissolution.

Under the general heading of Certificates of Colleges and
Chantries, there have been collected and catalogued in the
Record Office three distinct sets of documents. The calendar or
catalogue gives no indication of the set to which any particular
document belongs. They are :

1. The Certificates under the Chantries Act of Henry VIII.

2. The Certificates under the Chantries Act of Edward VI.

3. Abstracts of the Certificates under the Act of Edward VI.,
compiled for the purpose of the assignment of pensions ; or, in the
case of those persons, such as Schoolmasters, Vicars, and Curates,
who were continued, an order to that effect, and the amount of
salaries assigned to them.

In these documents the whole of North Wales is treated as a
single county, and the whole of South Wales, with Monmouthshire, as another. There are several cases of linked battalions,
Berkshire and Hampshire being joined in a single commission,
as are also Bucks and Beds; Oxford with Northampton and
Rutland ; while Lancashire is treated apart in the records of
the Duchy of Lancaster. But, on the other hand, York and the
East Riding of Yorkshire are regarded as a separate county, and
the West Riding is so vast as to occupy several rolls, separately
numbered as Certificates, while there is a distinct document for
the Island of Jersey. Allowing for these divergencies, there
should be, on an average, a Certificate of each class for each
county, treating North and South Wales as one county, about
120 in all.

There are, in fact, about 110 documents classed as Chantry
Certificates. Unfortunately, they do not include anything like
one Certificate of each class for each county.

In the first place, there are a large number of documents included which have nothing to do with the Colleges and Chantries under the Acts, including reports of commissions for inquiry as to certain monasteries in Hampshire and Wiltshire, in Norfolk and in Surrey; and as to Friars' Houses in Hampshire, Wiltshire, and Gloucestershire. One so-called Chantry Certificate is a Rental of some former Chantry land so late as 1610. Three are account rolls of the College of Fotheringhay; another is a commission and return as to the surrender of the College of Ottery S. Mary, dissolved at least 6 months before the Chantries Act. These last have, however, yielded evidence of Schools, and have been used. Perhaps the most interesting of these extraneous documents is a statement of the " Possessions of late erected Colleges and Cathedral Churches to be surrendered and assigned to the king's two Colleges in Oxford and Cambridge." Then there are divers duplicates, in whole or in part, of various Certificates; and special Certificates, such as one for Warwickshire taken in Henry VIII.'s reign, of Chantries dissolved without licence. There are only 8 counties which are fully represented in the three classes, viz., Cornwall, Essex, Gloucestershire, Northumberland, Staffordshire, Warwickshire, Wilts, and the North Riding of Yorkshire. In the other extreme, Norfolk has no Certificate, though 2 documents, so-called, are included: one an account of religious houses, the other a valuation of stone, timber, etc., of a College near Norwich. Surrey is represented by a fragment of a return as to religious houses. Cambridge has no county Certificate, and only a single return from Wisbech; while Huntingdon is represented by nothing at all. Of the Certificates under Henry VIII.'s Act) only 23 remain; of the Certificates under Edward VI.'s Act, 31 exist; but of the Pension Certificates, only 20.

It is extraordinary that these Chantry Certificates have not long ago been printed and published in full. They are mines of information about the fabric and history of the churches, and would be invaluable to the topographer, the genealogist, and the historian generally. For one thing they very frequently give the number of howseling people or communicants in various places, from which a very fair estimate can be formed of population. In London especially the number is given parish by parish, and with an absence of round figures which inspires confidence for the formation of a complete census of the London of that day. One would have thought that any county archæological society would have chosen these Certificates to be amongst its earliest publications. Yet the only societies that have printed any are the Chetham Society for Lancashire, the Somerset Archæological Society, and the Surtees Society for Yorkshire. That Lincolnshire and Warwickshire should have neglected theirs, full as they are of the most curious and interesting details, is inexplicable. To Mr. W. H. Page, the Editor of the *Yorkshire Chantries*, I am indebted for being able to "lift" bodily the extracts bearing on Schools, relying on their accuracy; to the Somerset Society also. The Chetham Society's volume, though distinguished by a mass of genealogical annotation, is edited in such a confused fashion, not distinguishing between Henry's and Edward's Certificates, and not giving the latter, except by reference, that I had to go to the originals.

In the other counties, where the Certificates have not been published, I have perforce gone to the originals and extracted all that I could find relating to Schools and exhibition foundations. It is hoped that no Grammar Schools are omitted, though it is hardly to be expected that none have been overlooked. Several Song Schools, or choristers' exhibitions, have been passed over, as I had not realized the desirability of including them all till my search was far advanced.

For the transcripts of the extracts I am indebted to Miss Edith Salisbury. Her transcripts have only one fault—that they spoil the printer through the excellence of her caligraphy. They are most trustworthy. Wherever I have challenged her rendering, because *aliunde* I knew a wrong statement was made, or because from internal evidence it appeared to be wrong or doubtful, a reference to the original has invariably proved that if there was an error, it was not hers.

The extracts have, as a rule, been confined religiously to the pertinent part of the Certificates, though a few lapses from the rule have taken place for special reasons. The extracts also, as a rule, abstain from giving the details of the property of the Schools. In most cases the details are not given in the original Certificates, but in schedules which were either attached to or sent with them. Where they are given, they swell the bulk of the entry too much for its special purpose, however useful they might be to the local topographer or the local genealogist. An indication is given where these details are omitted by placing the words "rents" or "farms" (*redditibus,* or *firmis*) in brackets. In the case of the grant of Birmingham Grammar School, the whole details of the lands are given as a specimen; and in the case of the Trinity Guild at Coventry, the names of the streets in which the property lay. I have also yielded to temptation in Shrewsbury, and given the Certificates as to the pre-Conquest collegiate churches of S. Mary and of S. Chad, and the Craft Guilds connected with them, as somewhere amongst them ought to be, but is not, found the Grammar School, which must have preceded Edward VI.'s foundation of the present School, with the spoils of those churches. I have yielded also to a similar temptation in giving all the Chantries at Walsall, in Stafford-shire. A curious thing happened in this case. The original Certificate, which misled me, had already misled Edward VI.'s commissioners. Against Walsall apparently was written in the margin *Continuatur Schola quousque,* "the School is continued till further orders." Accordingly a continuance warrant was made out continuing Walsall School, and assign-ing to the master the salary of £3 2*s.* 2*d.* When, however, it came to transcribing, it appeared that the words did not apply to Walsall at all, but to the next entry below it, and that Walsall, which really had no School, was thus enriched at the expense of Eccleshall. To make the matter still more complicated, the officer of the court said, *apropos* of the Chantry School at Shenston, "This School is thought meet to be re-moved to Walsall, a great town about three miles thence." Owing however (apparently) to the muddle about Eccleshall this was not done, and Shenston School was continued at Shen-ston. Walsall afterwards procured a grant of its own Chan-

tries early in Mary's first year, which looks suspiciously as if
it had been arranged by Dudley, Duke of Northumberland, in
Edward's reign; but whether poor Eccleshall ever recovered
its property and its School, thus taken from it in error, I am
not aware. Walsall School now divides its income between two
flourishing Schools, one for each sex.

The extracts show that the merit of the various Certificates
from the School point of view is most unequal. It is quite clear
that the commissioners varied very much in their desire to preserve such of the threatened institutions as were really useful
for educational purposes. In the Certificates under Henry
VIII.'s Act, which paid no particular attention to Schools and
did not profess to regard them, Schools are but seldom mentioned, except in such cases as Winchester and Eton, Rotherham and Stillingfleet, where the whole purpose of the foundation
was educational, and the stipends of the educational officers had
to be stated. Even in these cases—at least at Winchester—it
is noticeable how the School portion is thrust into the back-
ground as far as possible. At Winchester, for instance, the
Choristers', or Song School master is put before the Head-master,
or, as he is called, the Grammar School master; and both are
relegated to a quite inconspicuous and subordinate position.
Was the object to treat the College as being merely one of the
usual type of collegiate churches—a place for the multiplication
of services and devotions, in which a School was quite a subordinate institution,—so that it might perish as a mere abode of
superstition, instead of being saved as a home of learning? In
the whole of Hampshire not a single other School is mentioned,
not even the Grammar School kept by the ancient Brotherhood
of the Holy Ghost (holly goost, they call it) at Basingstoke,
existing at least from the 13th century, which had been specially re-incorporated and re-constituted under Henry himself,
through the patronage of Bishop Fox of Winchester. He, by
the way, has been therefore absurdly credited with having
founded it. If the Chantries and Colleges had actually disappeared under the hands of Henry VIII., we should perhaps
never have known how large a provision for secondary education was made through them.

There are great differences, even among the Certificates taken under Edward VI.'s Act, in the way in which Schools are treated. It is obvious that the Edwardian commissioners in Essex were interested in education. While the Henrician commissioners, headed by Bonner, who, as a Bishop, might have been supposed to be interested in education, mentioned only one School—that at Walden (now Saffron Walden)—the later commissioners, of whom only one had served on the former commission, presented no less than 17 places as having Schools ; two of them, Chelmsford and Great Badow, having apparently either two Schools—one Grammar, one Elementary—or perhaps only two Schoolmasters, one of whom was the Head-master, and the other an usher or assistant. It would appear doubtful, as to some of these Schools, whether they were not in the nature of private adventure Schools ; the Chantry priest, or stipendiary priest, teaching School merely to fill up his time, and eke out his living. Unfortunately there is no Schools Continuance Warrant for Essex, except for "Much " or Saffron Walden, which happened to be part of the possessions of the Duchy of Lancaster, so we do not learn how many of these Schools were recognised by the officials of the Court of Augmentation as established Grammar Schools. Equally full is the return for Hereford, in which 15 Schools are found. In this case the officials only recognised and continued ten, while an eleventh, Leominster, was re-endowed and re-founded. Why Weobley, Much Cowern, Kington, and Staunton were left out in the cold to perish does not appear. Compare with these Certificates the meagre record in Kent, where only the School of Wye College and a small School recently started by S. John's College, Cambridge, in the little chapelry of Ospringe in Faversham, appear, though there was one attached to Maidstone College, and there were Grammar Schools at most, if not all of the Cinque Ports. We know of one in Sandwich apparently as early as 1392; and at many other places in the county—Faversham and Sevenoaks, to mention no more.

In Derbyshire not a single School is recorded, though a Certificate under the Act of Henry VIII. is extant. Yet Chesterfield, with its Guild, must certainly have had a School;

and so in all probability had Ashbourne, Bakewell, and other places. Derby School, endowments for which appear in the 12th century, having been transferred to the guardianship of Darley Abbey, would probably not appear, though commissioners, zealous for education, would have ensured its mention, as was done in a similar case at Tewkesbury in the Gloucestershire Certificate, or Launceston in that of Cornwall. So, too, it is hardly credible that in Bedfordshire there should only be one, and in Hertfordshire only two Schools. Bedford must have had its Grammar School. Indeed, in the account of the possessions of the Corpus Christi Chantry, in the parish of S. Paul's, the mother church of the town, a collegiate church of canons before the Conquest, there is an incidental mention of "the farm" (*i.e.* rent) "of three cottages in Scole Lane in the tenure of three poor folks, 12s." Is this School Lane other than the lane by which the School of the Harper foundation afterwards stood? It appears in a British Museum MS. that particulars of sale of the Chantry property had in 1549 already been handed to "one Mr. Harper." This foundation, it must be remembered, owes its present magnitude and consequent celebrity to the bulk of its property having been in Holborn, London, and not in Bedford itself; and to the fact that New College, Oxford, had the appointment of the master, which secured it a succession of Winchester scholars, including the present Head-master, under whose reign it has so abundantly multiplied. But S. Paul's, Bedford, was one of the instances of the canons of a pre-Conquest collegiate church (it appears in Domesday) having been dispossessed, and their church (as at Derby) handed over to regular canons. The School may therefore have temporarily disappeared with Newenham Abbey. Since this was written, I have found conclusive evidence of the existence of the School before the transfer to the regular canons—that is between 1160 and 1170.

Buckinghamshire is almost as scurvily treated. The first Certificate gives only two Schools—Eton and Thornton. The second gives also only two—Thornton and Great Marlow; Eton, like Winchester, having been expressly exempted from the second Chantries Act. This is absurd. Buckingham had a School, the Chantry of Thomas "the Martyr." Aylesbury School was still, in 1818, held in a Chantry attached to the parish church. High Wycombe Grammar School was a Hospital School, and so outside the Act.

It must not therefore be assumed that the lists of Schools are exhaustive, even in the 8 counties which are represented in each class of Certificate. In Staffordshire, for instance, there is no mention of the Grammar School at Rolleston, founded with a great flourish of trumpets by Robert Sherborne, Bishop of Chichester, in 1520–3. He was a Wykehamist, and founded the School in his native place in thankfulness for his success, to be as far as possible on the model of Winchester. Even the *preces* (prayers) which were to be used at the opening and closing of the School every day were to be those used at Winchester, and a copy is carefully appended to the statutes. This School was omitted, either because the Warden of New College appointed the master, or because there was no requirement that he should do any actual Chantry business, though he had to pray for the founder's soul in School. Unfortunately for the School, Sherborne says that he could not get any land to buy for the endowment, and he therefore arranged with the Dean and Chapter of Chichester to pay a fixed sum of £10 a year. His School, with all its elaborate statutes insisting on the highest education, has dwindled therefore into a mere Elementary School. In Kent Sevenoaks School escaped altogether, probably because the founder, a London citizen, in 1432, had said, as we have seen, that the master was "by no means" (*minime*) "to be in holy orders," consequently he could not be a Chantry priest. For the same reason the newly-founded Malton School, in Yorkshire, may have been thought not to be "within the compass of the Act," because Archbishop Holgate had provided that he might be a layman, like the High-master of S. Paul's. For similar reasons, no doubt, S. Paul's, London, Wolverhampton, Northampton, and Sutton Coldfield Grammar Schools are not recorded, while Oswestry and Nottingham are only incidentally mentioned. Numerous other Schools that are known to have existed at this time do not appear, either because they were kept at the discretion and cost of the inhabitants or Guilds of the towns without any fixed endowment, as at Richmond, Yorkshire, or because the commissioners did not think they were Chantries, or because they were "concealed" from the commissioners.

The Warrants for Continuance of Schools have not survived the shocks of time any better than the Chantry Certificates. Of the forty-four that there should be, treating Wales as two counties, and each Riding of Yorkshire as one, there are only 23 extant among the bundle at the Record Office, called "Edward VI. Grants for Schools."

In the same bundle, out of an unreckoned number of actual grants for Schools, re-founded by or under Edward VI., the orders for the preparation of the "Book," as the Letters Patent were called, are to be found in only 14 cases. It may well be that others lurk in the voluminous papers of the Court of the Augmentation of the Revenues of the Crown, but they have not come out of their hiding-places.

16. Statistics from the Documents.

The broad results of these extracts amply prove the thesis laid down at the beginning. In all 259 Schools appear in these records of 1546 and 1548. Of the ~ Schools mentioned, 193 were Grammar Schools. 140 of them are so-called. Of 21 which are only called Free Schools, 15, including Berkhampstead, are either positively known or reasonably believed to have been Grammar Schools; of 16 which are simply called Schools, 11 are thought to be Grammar Schools; of 4, in which only a Schoolmaster is mentioned (which include Eton), all are reckoned as Grammar Schools; of 25, in which the teaching of children or simply teaching is recorded, 20 were, in all probability, Grammar Schools.

There are 23 Song Schools, besides 5 which, being also called Grammar Schools, have been reckoned among Grammar Schools.

There remain 22 Schools which may, perhaps, be regarded as Elementary Schools. Of these, 6 are called Free Schools,

G

5 are called simply Schools. In 5 only the fact of teaching
being given is recorded. 6 others are mentioned—teaching
A B C (3), Reading (2), Writing (1). There are really more
Schools in which Reading and Writing are mentioned, but 3
of them are also Grammar Schools, and have been counted as
Grammar Schools. In three of the Reading Schools, Writing
is also mentioned. There is only one Writing School under
that name (*simpliciter*), which is the Writing School of
Rotherham College. The Song Schools were in part also Elementary Schools of a rather higher type than the ordinary
Reading and Writing School—Higher Elementary Schools, in
fact. Including them, the Elementary Schools mentioned reach
the very respectable total of 45.

As has been said before, by no means all Endowed Schools
are here included. Besides these, there were no doubt many
Schoolmasters who were not endowed, like that one who came
to Rotherham about 1415 "by some divine chance," and
taught Thomas Scot, who went thence to Eton and King's,
and became in his turn the founder of that striking foundation, Rotherham College.

These 259 Schools enjoyed a total income of £1,677 5s. 0½d.,
excluding the incomes of Winchester and Eton. These two
Colleges between them had £1,951 11s. 3½d., a year, or more
than all the rest put together. But this is a somewhat
misleading piece of statistics; for if we reckoned the whole
income of Winchester and Eton as School income, so ought we
to reckon the whole income of Rotherham and Acaster, of
Brecon and Thornton. But whereas in those Colleges the
Schoolmasters' incomes are separately given, at Winchester and
Eton the general staff are mixed up together with the scholars
and masters. The incomes of the Schools attached to Colleges
and Hospitals ought properly to be augmented by the allowance
for commons, liveries, lodgings, and so on. It is not possible,
without excessive labour, if at all, to arrive at what this
allowance should be; so the mere bare stipend paid to the
master and, in the case of Brecon, to the 20 scholars, has been
reckoned in the total. It was on this meagre basis that

Edward's commissioners went, in assigning stipends to the
masters who were continued, except that in the case of Southwell they seem to have allowed the value of a vicar-choralship
in addition to the statutory £2 a year.

Taking, then, the bare stipends, the average pay of a Schoolmaster works out at £6 9s. 6d. a year. On the one hand, some, like
the master at Thornton College, got £20 a year, besides board,
lodging and gowns; and the master of S. Anthony's School, London, got £16 a year, with the like allowances. On the other
hand, several teachers of the A B C appear, who only received
a mark (13s. 4d.) a year; and the ordinary Song School master
did not receive more than £5 a year, though one at Thornton
College got £10. A good many small Grammar School
masters did not receive more than £5, while some who received
that, or less, looked to fees to make up their livings to the
ordinary standard. The Schoolmaster was decidedly better paid
than the ordinary Chantry priest, whose salary commonly ran to
£5 or under. In the Edward VI. re-foundations, £20 a year seems
to have been the standard aimed at, which, with outgoings for
repairs, allowance for an usher, and the like, would give about
£12 a year to the Head-master. That is about the sum the
larger Schools, though not the largest, paid before the Reformation.

For educational payments other than Schools there should be
added £25 18s. 9d. for various Exhibitions at Schools, excluding
Winchester, Eton and Brecon; and £179 18s. 1½d. for exhibitions at the Universities, making a total sum of £1,883 1s. 11d.
This represents, in round figures, £37,660 a year of our money;
and if the allowances mentioned were included, the sum would
not be less than £45,000 a year.

17. Exhibition Foundations.

The School and University exhibitions absolutely disappeared. Most of the latter were perversions, excellent perversions, of the original foundation. For instance, the Chantry
at Fisherton Anger, founded, it is said, in 1324, was held by "a
very honest man"; it was "given unto him for, and to his

exhibition to School, albeit he is no priest." The reader may
perhaps say, Why is this called a University exhibition, not a
School exhibition ? For the excellent reason that though the
words "to School" may mean University or Grammar School,
this exhibitioner being 36 years old, it may fairly be assumed
that he was not a schoolboy. Two prebends in the quasi-collegiate church of Chumleigh were applied as School exhibitions,
one being "employed to the maintenance of Storye, being a
little child who goeth to School, and hath no other profits towards his finding and sustentation." Three prebends at Crediton
were treated apparently in the same way. The free chapel of S.
John in Dorchester, by virtue of Letters Patent 32 Henry VIII.,
i.e. 15 years before the return, was held by Edward Weldon
towards his exhibition at the University in Oxford ; so he held
his exhibition for some time. The free chapel of Denton, in
Gloucestershire, is returned as "now in the hands of one William
Tracy " ; and this is said to have been actually "founded to find
to School one of the younger brothers of that name, of their issue
successive, for the time he shall be bachelor." So, too, a pension
of £2 a year from Nenweneck's or Menwenyck's Chantry, in
South Petherwin, was founded "towards the finding of á scholar
at Oxford." The free chapel of S. Nicholas, in Holbeach, is said
to have been given "from time immemorial" to a University
student, and was then held by a *"scolaris studiosus"* (which
should probably be translated not studious but University scholar)
at Queen's College, Cambridge. The free chapels of Calne and
North Wraxall, Wilts, were treated in the same way. Another
free chapel was held by the Warden of All Souls' College,
Oxford. At the Collegiate Church of Norton all the eight
prebends were treated as University Exhibitions; and this is
said in an MS. [Harl. 605] in the British Museum to have been
an ancient custom. It would seem, then, that when Mr. Massing-
ham suggested, two or three years ago in the *Contemporary
Review*, that the canonries of cathedrals should be given as
rewards for research in all branches (including persons like
Professor Huxley) and not confined to the clergy, that, after
all, he was not making a new suggestion, but only proposing to

revert to the practice of our unreformed ancestors of pre-Reformation times. This sort of application is presumably what was meant when Henry promised Parliament to utilize the Colleges for the advancement of learning. What a chance was missed!

18. Song Schools and Elementary Schools.

The Song Schools were not mere singing Schools. Often, indeed, in small places, the Song School, the Reading School, and the Grammar School, were combined in one person. Such was the case at Northallerton in Yorkshire (pp. 286–7, 289), where, from 1377 onwards, appointments of the master to teach boys " as well in grammar as in song," made by the Prior of Durham as "Ordinary of the Spiritualities of St. Cuthbert in Yorkshire," are preserved in the Durham Registers. Similar appointments at Hemingborough, a College in Howdenshire, Yorkshire, from the same date, show the same mixture. We see the combination in these records, at Barnard Castle, in Durham (p. 61); Blackburn, in Lancashire (p. 107); Bosbury, in Herefordshire (p. 93); Giggleswick, in Yorkshire (p. 297); Kingsley, Staffordshire (p. 200). The master was intended to combine both duties at Montgomery, in Wales (p. 312), but actually only taught young " beginners to write and sing, and to read so far as the accidence rules, and no grammar." It is possible that song may be included in the " other sciences," that the Free Schoolmaster at Walden (Saffron), in Essex, was (p. 62) to teach besides grammar, though it would more properly mean " dialectic" and " rhetoric."

As a rule, however, the Song School master was a different and inferior person to the Grammar School master. In the colleges, of course, he was always present, chiefly to teach the choristers. He appears, and still exists, at Winchester College. He is mentioned at Brecon, Crediton, Fotheringhay, Lincoln, S. David's, Pleshey, Southwell, Stoke-by-Clare, Stratford-on-Avon, Thornton. At Alnwick and at Durham and in many other places, we may suspect, twin Schools were established—one of Grammar, the other of Song.

It was a strange measure to make no provision whatever

for saving or continuing these Schools and their like. The mischief caused by this was immeasurable. Before the reign of Edward VI., England was *par excellence* the land of song. Erasmus describes the English as the musical, the Germans as the drunken people. If nowadays in common repute the epithets are reversed, is it not largely owing to the abolition of the Training Schools of song and music? For the Song School was not confined to singing. Often "teaching to play on the organs" is included in the description of the Song School master. Such was the case at Bosbury, in Herefordshire, where the Grammar School is now only an Elementary School. The Schoolmaster there was "to bring up youth in learning and to play at organs," and in the Colleges the singing and playing was, of course, a very important part of the whole business. It is remarkable, by the way, that even then two of the Song School masters in London whose names are mentioned are Welshmen. Was Wales even then a nation of songsters?

Of all the wealth of Song Schools which then existed outside the Cathedrals, the Oxford and Cambridge Colleges, and Winchester and Eton, all have perished, except the Song School at Newark, which, being a new foundation, or re-foundation, together with the Grammar School of Dr. Magnus, escaped being reckoned as a Chantry, and has survived, though in a mutilated form, to this day. How many Purcells have we lost, how many Wesleys, not to guess at Beethovens and Mozarts, for lack of the proper endowment of organists and of Song Schools!

An evil blow, too, was struck at the education of the masses by the destruction of the Elementary Schools,—of Schools like the Writing School at Rotherham. Many of them were very small affairs. Still, 13s. 4d. given to an old man to teach children their A B C was a great deal better than nothing. It is probable that a great many more of the Chantries than here appear were used as endowments for Elementary School masters. It was mere robbery of the poor to abolish such foundations. Why, instead of annihilating those that were definitely kept as such, did the reforming council not convert other Chantries to the purpose of Elementary education?   It was all very well for Henry VIII. to sack the Chantries.   He did not regard it as the business of the multitude to read the Scriptures and discuss them; though it is noticeable, how many of the "baser sort," as tinkers and tailors and the like, were able to read the bibles set up in the churches.   But the party of Cranmer and Cheke, of Somerset and Latimer, could have had no such views.   What a chance they lost in not revising the policy of Henry and saving some of the Chantries for Elementary, and the Colleges for Secondary, Education!   We might have been a singing people and an educated people three centuries ago instead of just beginning to be so in the nineteenth century.

19. Numbers attending Grammar Schools.

If the lower classes lost a chance of being levelled up educationally, the middle classes were distinctly levelled down. People have talked and written as if the Grammar Schools of the middle ages and of the new learning were little better than Elementary Schools, scattered in small numbers about the land, and attended by a very small number of scholars, who just learned to stumble through *hic, hæc, hoc*, like Master Page in the *Merry Wives of Windsor*, or to have a dim idea of the meaning of the mass.

The proportion of the population which had opportunity of access to Grammar Schools, and, as we can see, used their opportunities, was very much larger then than now.   Certainly it was larger than the proportion at the time of the only authoritative statistics on the subject; viz., in 1865-6, as given in the Schools Inquiry Commission's Report.   The Report gives some 830 Secondary Schools of all grades.   This included a large number, little, if at all, above the merest Elementary Schools (and Elementary Schools were then for the most part very elementary), and many of those decrepit, and on the verge of extinction.   That number was no more than one Secondary School for every 23,750 people, among the then population of 19 millions. "In at least two-thirds of the places in England named as towns in the census, there is no public School at all above the Primary School; and in the remaining third, the School is often insufficient in size and quality."

It is difficult to arrive at a precise estimate of the proportion of Schools to population at the Reformation, because, while it is difficult or impossible to ascertain the exact number of Schools, it is equally difficult, and perhaps impossible, to ascertain the population of England at any given date in the Middle Ages. Professor Thorold Rogers sets the population of England and Wales at not more than a million and a half before the Black Death, of 1349, and says that "it is certain that the rate of production precludes the possibility of its being more than two and a half millions." In 1377, up to which time, owing to successive plagues, it is pretty certain that no increase of population had taken place, a poll-tax was levied on all persons 14 years old and upwards. The return for it gives an indirect census of the population of England. The laity and clergy are assessed separately; all classes are included except manifest paupers among the laity, and the professed paupers—the friars— among the ecclesiastics; but Durham and Cheshire are excluded, having, as counties palatine, separate collectors. 1,376,442 lay people and 29,161 ecclesiastics paid the tax. It is assumed, in estimating the population, that one-fifth of those who ought to have paid did not (a very large proportion indeed); and that one-third of the whole population was under 14, and therefore exempt. This would give just over $2\frac{1}{4}$ millions, which it is pretty certain would be an over- rather than an under-estimate.

It is commonly said that the population did not increase between the Black Death and the reign of Elizabeth. It is a doubtful, and an almost incredible statement, when the great development of manufactures and of wealth is considered, and the cessation of perpetual internal war, for the wars with France and the Wars of the Roses were very poor Malthusian substitutes, as population-thinners, for the private wars which preceded them. Still, for the present purpose, we may accept the

statement, and compare the Schools of 1546 with the population of 1377. Take, say, 300 Grammar Schools among 2½
million people. This gives one for every 8,300 people instead
of one for every 23,000, as in 1865. In the Poll-Tax returns of
1377, forty-two towns are given, which ranking, in modern
parlance, as county boroughs, were assessed separately from
the counties they were in. They had a total population of
166,000. Of the 8 most populous towns, 6 were cathedral
cities, each with its Cathedral or Episcopal Grammar School.
London, with 44,000 people, had at least four Schools: S.
Anthony's, S. Paul's, S. Martin's-le-Grand, S. Mary-le-Bow.
York, with a population of 13,500, had its Cathedral Grammar
School, with its Abbey Boarding House for 50 boys; and small
Schools, perhaps only Song Schools, in St. Leonard's, and the
Trinity or Fossgate Hospitals. Bristol, with 12,000, had a somewhat misty School, said to have been kept by the Kalendars'
Guild; its undoubted Free Town Grammar School founded by
purchase of S. Bartholomew's Hospital, and after 1540 the
Cathedral Grammar School; while there was another in
the famous chapel at Redcliffe; to say nothing of minor
Schools, probably more or less elementary in character, such
as that in connection with S. Nicholas Church. All the other
towns of the 42 had a population under 10,000, and 26 of them
had a population under 4,000. Yet, with the possible exception
of Dartmouth, with its 949 people, every one of these towns had
its Grammar School.

To take a single county. The population of Herefordshire, as
shown in the Poll-Tax return, was some 25,000; in addition to
Hereford city, 3,568, and Ludlow, then reckoned in Herefordshire, 2,198; or some 30,000 in round figures in all. Hereford
had its primæval Cathedral Grammar School, besides a lesser
one, perhaps more or less elementary, in St. Owen's Church;
Ludlow its Guild School, Ledbury its Chantry Grammar School
in connection with its collegiate church, the flourishing state
of which has already been commented on, sunk now to
Elementary education. Besides these there were Leominster,
unendowed, and the thirteen others mentioned in our records,

of which nine alone were continued. That is, there were 17 Grammar Schools for a population of 30,000. Assume even that the population was not the same, in 1546, but doubled; cut off a fourth of the Schools as really Elementary; yet where should we find a population of 60,000 in 1860, or in 1896 for that matter, with 13 Grammar Schools at its command? It is possible that in Herefordshire the Schools were exceptionally thick upon the ground. But in Essex there were 17 Schools, Colchester not being mentioned, its School being maintained with Chantries granted by Henry VIII., in 1539, for that purpose. The population of all these places but one is given in houseling people, meaning communicants,—generally by scores of houseling people. Taking 14 as the age at which people were eligible for becoming communicants, the age under which they were exempt from Poll Tax, you must, according to the calculations, add one-third for all those under that age. The number of houseling people given in the different places varies from 240 in Gosfield, to 800 in Bocking and Chelmsford, and 1,000 in Coggeshall. The total number is 8,300 houseling people, to which a third added brings the population to 11,000 in round figures, a sufficiently small number for 16 Grammar Schools.

It is certain, then, that a very large proportion of the population had the opportunity of attending Grammar Schools. How far did they avail themselves of their opportunities?

As regards the numbers attending these Schools, wherever numbers are mentioned they are surprising for their magnitude. Winchester and Eton, we know, had 70 scholars apiece, besides their commoners and oppidans, who, at Winchester, within 10 years of Wykeham's death, numbered 100. These numbers were by no means extraordinarily large. At Worcester the Guild School in the Town Hall had "above the number of 100 scholars." At Taunton there was a "fair, large and goodly house now builded, erected and made for a schoolhouse about 25 years now past," or 1522, the date which was still—at the time of Lord Brougham's commission, on the School, and may be there now. In that year also the Pipe Roll of the Bishops of Winchester records that a schoolhouse at Taunton was built

at the cost of the very large sum of £226 5s. 10d., or of
£4,000 of our money. In this School there were "a Schoolmaster and usher found, the space of 12 or 14 years, for the
virtuous education and teaching of youth as well of the said
town of Taunton as of the whole country, to the number of 7
or 8 score (140 to 160) scholars, by the devotion of one Roger
Hill, of the same town, merchant, now deceased." Since his
death, however, there being no regular endowment apparently,
in spite of Taunton being the chief town of that part, and an
important seat of the learned Bishops of Winchester, it was in
abeyance "to the great prejudice, hurt and discommodity of
the commonwealth of the said shire." Crewkerne meanwhile
had thriven, perhaps on the misfortunes of Taunton; for John
Byrde, with an endowment of £8 1s. 3d. only, "well learned
and of good judgment, has at this present 6 or 7 score (120 to 140)
scholars." We pass across the country to Skipton, in Yorkshire,
and there we find Stephen Ellis, a pluralist, holding the Chantry
of S. Nicholas in the parish church of Skipton-in-Craven, worth
£4 13s. a year, and also the service of our Lady in the parish
church of Kildwick-in-Craven. He was "42 years of age, a
good grammarian, having scholars to the number of 120, and
hath kept school there these five years past." Or, if we go
back to Worcestershire, there at King's Norton, "be three
stipendiaries or services, whereof one has always taught a Free
Grammar School." First was "Harry Saunders, M.A., 40, of
honest conversation and well learned, Schoolmaster," and second,
"John Peart, being no priest but usher of the said School," also
"well learned." He had only "been found within 2 years
past to aid the same Schoolmaster, now being charged with
the teaching and instructing of 120 scholars." The third
stipendiary acted as curate-in-charge of a chapel of ease at
Moseley. They were continued; Saunders with £10 a year;
Port, as he is called, with £5 a year—adequate sums then. In
Carlisle's time the School had sunk to an Elementary School of
15 boys. It has now further subsided to an exhibition fund in
connection with the Elementary School. Carlisle, by the way,
credits Edward with the foundation, instead of spoliation, of this

once great School. He gives a legend that the inhabitants of King's Norton had the choice of an endowment either in land or money, and preferred money; Birmingham had a similar offer, and preferred land, and we see the difference. But we know how much to believe of that tale. The King's Nortonians of Edward's day never had the chance of keeping their lands. No one in his senses could have chosen a fixed charge instead of the lands, when the lands were let on fixed rents on beneficial leases, and every few years great fines came in, reckoned not on the fixed rent, but on the improved value.

In Gloucestershire, at Chipping Campden, founded 1487, there " hath been time out of mind kept within the said parish a Grammar School freely taught, commonly furnished with the number of 3 or 4 score scholars." At the neighbouring Newland we are told that the School is "very well haunted," but unhappily we are not told by how many scholars. Equally vague is the account of Godshill, a charming spot in the Isle of Wight. The master, an M.A., teaches "grammar to many young children." At Kinnersley, the stipendiary at our Lady's altar " is now employed to the keeping of a School, there now being there 60 scholars." Income, £6 2s.

Essex tells us more of the numbers than any other county, but unfortunately not in its largest towns. Chesterford, with 500 "howseling people," has " 20 scholars and more." The "Guild priest of the Trinity Guild," in Finchingfield, Sir William Atkinson, clerk, of the age of 60 years and above, literate, and teacheth a Grammar School there, and hath the number of 30 scholars." In Gosfield, with 12 score of howselyng people, " Sir John Hornesey, clerk, of the age of 36 years, hath to the number of 40 scholars, and hath taught the said School by the space of 7 years." So at Blisworth, in Northamptonshire, where the endowment was considerable —£12 a year—" houseling people 200," " the Schoolmaster well learned, hath 30 scholars." At Brackley, Magdalen College, Oxford, had erected a Free School, " in which many children are taught, to the great commodity of the county."

That there were considerable numbers at School would also

appear from such entries as this at Ledbury. The stipendiary of the service of the Trinity there, was "daily occupied in teaching of children grammar, which hath for his salary the clear yearly revenue (£4 1s. 4½d.), and none other living but the little reward of the friends of the scholars." This then was a Grammar School, but not a Free Grammar School. Is is said, nevertheless, that "the inhabitants have not only had profit and advantage by the keeping of a Grammar School there, as in boarding and lodging his scholars, but also the country thereabouts in uttering of their victuals by means of the said scholars." They therefore, "humbly beseech that it may please the king's majesty, with the assent of his honourable Council to his bountiful goodness "—they knew well enough that the king was only a name—"to grant that the said School may there still be kept, a charitable deed, if so it may please his highness." It did please his highness to suffer the School to remain, but it also pleased him to put the endowment of the School in his pocket, so that this still important town in Herefordshire has now no Grammar School, and an Elementary School takes the Crown stipend. Similar petitions were presented all over the kingdom, mostly with a similar result.

20. Learning in Grammar Schools.

As regards what the boys learnt in these Schools, very little direct information is to be found in the records before us.

It is a thousand pities that the Inventories of the goods which belonged to the Schools included in the Chantry Certificates are not extant. They might show what books belonged to them. The inventories seem to have disappeared. Only one specimen is here given from what is called a "survey and rental roll," and that for the distant and wild county of Westmorland. At Appleby there seems to have been only one mass-book. But at Burgh-under-Stainmore, now Brough, a mountain town among wild moors, there were "6 books of the Bible, called *glosa ordinaria*," i.e., a commentary used in the stated University lectures on the Bible, "price 13s. 4d. The whole Bible in Latin, 20d. 9 other books," and there the exasperating inventory-maker, instead of giving the names, only adds, "an ortus vocabulorum et catholicon, 20d.," the two mentioned being dictionaries. It is possible that the master provided the books in most places, in which case they would not appear.

The only other kind of evidence afforded as to the standard of Schools is in the way of complaints as to inefficiency on the part of some masters. One of them alone is quite sufficient to knock on the head the notion that the Grammar Schools were merely elementary. At Montgomery it appears " by the depositions of the Proctors, Wardens and Presenters there, that these same did find and hire one priest or learned man "—not necessarily a priest, be it remarked—" continually by the space of 30 years by past, to keep a Free School in the said town." But "Sir William Ilkes, being chiefly hired for that purpose, taught but young beginners only to write [and sing, and to read so far as the accidence rules, and no grammar, since Michaelmas." We have quoted in another connection remarks on the demerits of the Vicar of Evesham as compared with the late Schoolmaster there. Again, at Witney, Oxfordshire, a great manor of the Bishops of Winchester, and therefore no doubt an ancient site of a Grammar School, "The inhabitants desireth to have a Schoolmaster to teach youth there, but the said William Dalton doth little service there now." At Much Cowern, too, the stipendiary priest is described as "indifferently learned," which is perhaps why Much Cowern School was not continued; and at St. Owens, Hereford, the incumbent was 80 years old and "indifferently learned," which School also ceased. At Wotton, the schoolmaster there, is said to be "of 60 years, being unwieldy, and for that purpose neither meet in discipline nor behaviour." But this School was fortunately not thought to be within the Act; so that the delinquencies of the master did not cause the loss of the School or its endowments, though it was severely attacked and much plundered in the reign of James I., as having been a Chantry concealed from the Crown.

Now surely the inhabitants of these places would not have taken the trouble to find Schools and Schoolmasters, and make

great efforts for their continuance, if they were merely Schools
to teach half a dozen choristers to read and sing and construe.
Yet, according to Mr. Bass Mullinger, in Schools "the average
acquirements were limited to reading and writing, to which,
in the Cathedral Schools, there were added chanting, and an
elementary knowledge of Latin." This sentence shows that
the writer has not yet acquired an elementary knowledge of
Cathedral Schools. He is still in the hopeless condition of not
knowing that the Grammar School and the Song School are
wholly distinct, under different masters, different management,
with different endowments, and, for the most part, different
scholars. It was precisely the Cathedral Schools and the other
great Schools, the Schools of the quasi-cathedral collegiate
churches, where the strongest distinction was drawn between
the Song School, in which chanting, reading, and writing were
taught, and the Grammar School,—to which boys were not
admitted until they had learnt their accidence,—where Latin,
dialectic, and rhetoric were taught, which enabled a youth
of 16 to 18 to go straight to the University, or to a
learned profession. The learned professions required a competent knowledge of Latin far more directly then than now
A need for Latin was not confined to the church and the
priest. The diplomatist, the lawyer, the civil servant, the
physician, the naturalist, the philosopher, wrote, read, and to
a large extent spoke and perhaps thought in Latin. Nor was
Latin only the language of the higher professions. A merchant, or the bailiff of a manor, wanted it for his accounts;
every town clerk or guild clerk wanted it for his minute book.
Columbus had to study for his voyages in Latin; the general
had to study tactics in it. The architect, the musician, every
one who was neither a mere soldier nor a mere handicraftsman,
wanted, not a smattering of grammar, but a living acquaint-
ance with the tongue, as a spoken as well as a written language.

For all practical knowledge of the language, for readiness
in reading, in writing, and still more in speaking Latin, the
young Beckets, or Mertons, or Wolseys might be safely pitted
against their modern successors.

We are always hearing about the barbarous jargon of the Schoolmen, and "monkish Latin" is used as a byword, as if it were ungrammatical and unintelligible stuff. So far as grammatical errors are concerned there are few or none. The impression that mediæval Latin was either ungrammatical or corrupt is due mainly to the sad hash made by ignorant modern transcribers, who could not read the writing or understand the abbreviations used by mediæval scribes. Take for a specimen the beginning of the licence in mortmain & the foundation of Pocklington School, in 1526:

Md qd xxiii die Maij Anno rr subscr. istud bre libat fuit Dño canc. Angl apud Westm̄ Oxeguend. Henricus dei gra Rex Anglie et Francae et Dns Hibnīe Rewendissimo in xp̄o p̄ri Willmo Cantuar Archriepo . saltm̄ . . Et quod fraternitas . . cum sic erecta . fuit sit unum corpus integrum in re nomine ħeat qz successionem ppetuam ͺet nomie . . ac per nomen fraternitatis . . ñois Jħu . in . . Poklyngton fundat appellat nomietr.

Who would suppose that this garbled rubbish, which appeared in the *Yorkshire Archæological Journal*, 1896, represented the following intelligible and grammatical legal Latin, as it stands in the original?

Memorandum quod xxiiij [the date even was misread] die Maii, anno regni Regis subscripto, istud breve liberatum fuit Domino Cancellario Angliæ apud Westmonasterium, exequendum.

Henricus, Dei gratia, Rex Angliæ et Franciæ et Dominus Hiberniæ, Reverendissimo in Christo patri Willelmo Cantuariensi Archiepiscopo . salutem. . Et quod fraternitas . cum sic erecta . fuerit, sit unum corpus integrum in re et nomine, habeatque successionem perpetuam et nomen . ac per nomen fraternitatis . nominis Jesu . in Poklyngton fundatæ, appelletur, nominetur [*etc.*].

The stuff above, and worse than that, has been passed off on us as mediæval Latin, and our poor ancestors have been treated as the boy in the lower form of a preparatory school treats his Cæsar and Ovid. They are not expected to have written sense, and so it does not matter how much nonsense is made of what they did write.

That Chapter-Act Books and Charters should be Ciceronian
in style is neither to be expected nor desired. The English
language of the Law Courts, and of marriage settlements, is not
(and we may be thankful that it is not) that of *The Ring and
the Book*, or *Sartor Resartus*. But it is astonishing how well
the legal Latin of Justinian and Gaius is preserved in its
purity far down in the centuries. As for the "jargon of the
schoolmen," one can hardly expect a treatise on the Trinity to
be written in the style of Burke's speech on the Impeachment
of Warren Hastings. There are not wanting those who would,
and do, describe the diction of Herbert Spencer or Hegel as
jargon. The mediæval schoolmen sinned no more against pure
Latinity than the modern scientific writer sins against English
undefiled, if such there be.

We need only turn to Wolsey's statutes for Ipswich school,
to see what they learnt in good Schools. This School had
existed as a Free Grammar School from 1483, when Richard
Feldw endowed what had hitherto been a fee-paying School,
and was in 1528 made part of "Cardinal's College" at Ipswich. There were to be eight classes in the school, for which,
besides their Lily's Grammar—which was still the recognised
school grammar in the schooldays of men yet alive—divers
authors were prescribed. In the 3rd form from the bottom they
were to read Æsop, "quis facetior?" Terence, "quis utilior?"
In the 4th they got to Vergil, "prince of poets"; in the 5th
they read Cicero's *Select Letters*"; in the 6th, Sallust, or Cæsar's
Commentaries; in the 7th, Horace's Epistles and *Ovidii Meta-
morphoses* or *Fasti*, and had to write verse-tasks; in the 8th
form they abandoned Lily for Donatus, and read Valla, and
other ancient Latin authors. They also returned to Terence,
and were to discuss his life, style, and so forth, with a view,
perhaps, to performances like the Westminster Play. They
were also to learn précis-writing and to write essays. This,
by the way, is a much more liberal intellectual *menu* than
that provided by Colet, ten years or so before, for S. Paul's
School. Colet, like Gregory the Great, seems to have had a
holy horror of "the classics," as represented by Vergil, Ovid,

and Terence; and though he wanted "the very Roman tongue" of their time, puts Saint Jerome and Saint Austin on the same level with them, and prescribes Sedulius, Juvencus, and such like who wrote "Easter Hymns," and Gospels in verse, like Clement Marot in Browning,

> "Whose faculties move in no small mist
> When he versifies David the Psalmist,"

and even (save the mark!) Baptista Mantuanus, a Carmelite Friar, who died in 1516, and composed Eclogues.

It may be said Ipswich was a School of the new learning. True, but no one who has ever read the clever rhyming Latin verses of earlier times, or the quotations from all the authors mentioned above, which abound in the mediæval writers of the most solemn order in all times, can doubt that the classical authors were studied as a matter of course in the ordinary Schools, and studied to profit. Moreover, who took up the new learning with most zest? Wolsey, who had been Head-master of Magdalen College School; Fox, who had been Head-master of Stratford-on-Avon Grammar School; and earliest and most famous of Greek scholars in England, Grocyn, scholar of Winchester, Fellow of New College; with them Colet and Sir Thomas More, who are alleged to have been at S. Anthony's Hospital School in London. It was the three Wykehamical Colleges, New College, All Souls', Magdalen; Grocyn, Linacre, Latimer, Colet, Wolsey, Lily, recruited and inspired from Winchester and other old Grammar Schools, that introduced the new learning. How could they have done so if they had merely learnt at school to stumble through the church service?

21. The Class attending Grammar Schools.

We may approach this matter from another point of view, and ask whether it is likely that, in days when the labouring classes were still serfs, and Parliament actually petitioned the Crown against their being allowed to go to the Universities or Schools, that bishops and lords and country gentlemen would, at great expense and labour, found elaborate educational insti-

tutions for the benefit of half a dozen poor choristers? The
poor who are spoken of in these old foundations are not
the poor in our sense, the destitute poor, the unsuccessful
among the labouring classes, but the relatively poor, the poor
relations of the upper classes. That occasionally bright
boys were snatched up out of the ranks of the real poor
and turned into clerics, to become lawyers, civil servants,
bishops, is not to be doubted. But it was the middle classes,
whether country or town, the younger sons of the nobility and
farmers, the lesser landholders, the prosperous tradesmen, who
created a demand for education, and furnished the occupants of
Grammar Schools. When Archbishop Rotherham, of Eton and
King's, founded (1487) Rotherham College, it was in thankfulness for the Schoolmaster, who by some divine chance had found
his way to Rotherham and taught him. But he was a son of
a substantial landowner. When John Percivall, knight, "and
late maire of the city of London," founded his Grammar School,
in 1502, in Macclesfield, "fast by the which I was born,"
where "God, of his abundant grace, hath sent and daily
sendeth to the inhabitants there copious plenty of children,"
but "few Teachers and Schoolmasters in that country," he
founded it as " a Free Grammar School, teaching there gentlemen's sons and other good men's children of the town and
country thereabouts." The good men, the *probi homines* of
earlier times, were not the poor labouring folk, but the substantial yeomen and burgesses. At Liverpool, John Crosse
founded a School, of which Humphrey Crosse, a relation no
doubt, was master, the trust being for Chantry priests at the
altar of S. Katharine, " to teach and keep one Grammar School,
to take their advantage of scholars, saving those that beareth
the name of Crosse, and poor children." This prosperous merchant would not lump his "founder's kin " with the children of
the gutter, any more than William of Wykeham did at Winchester, or the "nobles" of Hampshire, who sent their sons to
live with the scholars or commoners there. So at Eardisley
(p. 99) the Grammar School was "founded by Sir James
Baskervyle, knight, to instruct and bring up his children and

other men's in learning of Grammar." The Schoolmaster took
fees, as he had "for his wages or stipend the clear yearly
revenue of the lands" (£4 13s. 2d.), and "the advantage of his
scholars."

22. What was a Free Grammar School?

This brings us to another point: What was the meaning of
Free School, or Free Grammar School at this time? Dr.
Johnson defined it to mean, and that is the obvious meaning
of it, a School that is free,—where no payment is made for
tuition fees.

It has been alleged that Free School did not mean free or
gratuitous, but (1) a Grammar School, (2) free from ecclesiastical jurisdiction, (3) giving a liberal education, (4) immediately dependent on the Crown, (5) free from the statute of
mortmain. There may be other fanciful explanations devised to
escape the obvious meaning. None of them can survive when
confronted with the facts. The first explanation is annihilated
by a single entry in our records, p. 279: "The College of Jesus
in Rotherham was founded for a preacher to preach 12 sermons
every year, three Schoolmasters of Free Schools, viz., Grammar,
Song, and Writing, 6 poor children, a butler and a cook." On
p. 193 we learn: "The same Schoolmasters be bound to continual residence, and to teach all children, freely, resorting to
the said College." The six poor children were boarded and
lodged as well. Here, then, a Song School and a Writing
School are called Free, as well as a Grammar School. So at
Durham. A Chantry was founded by Bishop Langley (1414) "to
keep two Free Schools, one of Grammar, one of Song." Therefore Free School was not merely a synonym of Grammar School.
Indeed, as the common phrase is Free Grammar School, it is
absurd to suppose it was. Of course Free School may be, and
is, used for short in referring to a Grammar School already
mentioned, or in a context in which Grammar is assumed to
be implied. Naturally, when the great bulk of Schools were
Grammar Schools. But there were Grammar Schools which were
not free, and Free Schools which, so far as is known, were not

Grammar Schools. Moreover, the common alternative phrase for "keeping a Free Grammar School" is "teaching Grammar freely."

It is part of the case of those who say that Free School does not mean free of fees, that it could not mean it, because, before the Reformation, all Schools were free of fees. The two cases already quoted of Liverpool and Eardisley disprove this. But to prove it again, take the following instances. At Ledbury, the stipendiary kept a School, continued as a Grammar School (p. 106), while (p. 93) it is said that the Master hath the stipend "and none other living but the little reward of the friends of the Scholars." It is not called a Free School. At Leominster, a Grammar School is kept by one who "hath no other living but that he hath of his Scholars weekly." At Kingsland the stipendiary, founded "to teach children," "keepeth a School, having for his salary the clear revenue, and the profit of scholars."

On the other hand, at Wisbech the Schoolmaster is "to keep a Grammar School, freely to teach and instruct children in godly and virtuous learning." At Week S. Mary the Chantry priest is "to teach children freely in a School founded by Lady Percivall," and the Continuance Warrant says that "a Grammar School hath been continually kept in S. Mary Week."

At Wimborne, where, according to the foundation, the School-master was to teach "after the manner of Winchester and Eton," he was, "to be a Schoolmaster to teach freely all manner of children Grammar within the said College." A memorandum says "it is very requisite that the said School may remain still for the bringing up of young children in learning *freely, without any thing paying, as it was in times past.*" This foundation was 1497, statutes 1510. The Continuance Warrant says, "A Free Grammar School hath been kept in Wimborne," and continues it.

At Darlington was "a Free School of Grammar for all manner of children thither resorting." "Wootton Free School" (1384) was for finding a master "freely to teach Grammar," and the original foundation adds, "without any benefit or gain for his pains" beyond his stipend. At Chipping Campden "the Schoolmaster's service" was founded "to maintain a Free School," and in a memorandum it says, "a Grammar School freely taught."

Bishop Langley, besides his Durham Schools, founded another School at Middleton in Lancashire, though his name has been forgotten in that of one of his scholars, Dean Nowell, who further endowed it in Elizabeth's reign. The incumbent there was to teach "a Grammar School, free for poor children."

At Stamford we get the phrase in Latin, and it is part of the adverse case that the phrase originated in Latin in Edward VI.'s charters, and was translated into English. The Stamford Certificate says that in 1532, 15 years before Edward VI., the School was founded for a secular chaplain, sufficiently learned "to pray [etc.] and freely to teach (libere docturum) and instruct the art of Grammar." At Towcester, described (p. 153) as "a Free Grammar School," the master is said on p. 146 "to keep a Grammar School," and on p. 151 "teacheth daily freely, and hath no other living." We have already seen how the Schoolmaster at Bruton School, founded in 1520 for a "Free Grammar School," was by surrender to the Crown "discharged of any free teaching or keeping of School there."

At Cannock the priest of our Lady's Service "for 30 years hath kept a Grammar School, and taught children of the said parish, for the most part freely," while at the neighbouring Bromley, a stipendiary priest "hath always kept a School, but not freely."

To conclude with two crucial instances. In Newland, Gloucestershire, by licence of King Henry VI. (1446) Robert Gryndour, Esq., founded a Chantry "to the intent to maintain a discreet priest, being sufficiently learned in the art of grammar, to keep a School half-free ; that is to say, taking of scholars learning grammar 8d. the quarter, and of others learning to read 4d. a quarter." This is the Edwardian finding. It was more shortly put in the Henrician Certificate : "to find a priest, and a Grammar School half free for ever." In Harl. MS., 605, it is added that its discontinuance would be "a great loss to all

the country thereabouts, for there is not any other Grammar
School free, neither otherwise, not by a great distance."

At Stourbridge the stipendiary "stood charged to teach the
poor men's children of the same parish freely," and "hath
always used, and yet doth use, to keep a School." This School
was one of the earlier of Edward VI.'s reputed creations. The
lands had been all sold, but were supplied from other Chantries,
and, 1st June, 1551, were ordered "to be granted to certain
persons and to their heirs to have continuance for ever, for
the free teaching of children within the town of Stourbridge,"
and in the Letters Patent, 19th June, 1552, it is called *Libera
Scola Grammaticalis*, a Free Grammar School for the instruction of boys and youth in grammar. Instead of saying labori-
ously, as the old founders did, that the master was to teach
"freely without taking anything for his pains," it was all
expressed in the neat formula, "There shall be a Free Grammar
School."

After these samples of what Free School meant to the very
people who were supposed to be creators of the phrase, it is not
necessary to dispose in detail of the adverse theories. It cannot
mean free from ecclesiastical jurisdiction, for not one of the Free
Grammar Schools was free from the jurisdiction of the Ordinary,
whose licence was a necessity until within the last century. It
cannot mean that the master or the School, was free from every
one but the Crown, for even in Edward VI.'s foundations, notably
Shrewsbury, the statutes had to be approved by the Bishop, and
the master was almost invariably appointed by the Governors,
or a College, or some other person or body, not the Crown; and
the phrase was used by private founders, whose heirs were born
Visitors. It does not mean a School which gives a liberal education, for in the three Free Schools in Yorkshire, founded by
Archbishop Holgate, the word for liberal knowledge is used,
and it is not *libera*, but *liberalis*. It cannot mean free from
the statute of mortmain, because when a licence in mortmain
was embodied in the Letters Patent or Charters, it was a
licence to a limited amount only, and the School was not
freed from the statute generally. It is impossible, if the

phrase is regarded in its historical development (which cannot be gone into now), that it could have meant anything but
what it was popularly supposed to mean—free from payment of
tuition fees. Entrance fees, and all sorts of extras and luxuries,
such as fires, light, candles, stationery, cleaning, whipping,
might have to be paid for ; but a free School meant undoubtedly
a School in which, because of the endowment, all, or some of the
scholars, the poor or the inhabitants of the place, or a certain
number, were freed from fees for teaching.

23. Specimens of Edwardian Spoliation.

The Grammar Schools were not destroyed by the Chantries
Acts. It is perhaps the case even that the statesmen of the
day did not realize the full effects of their action in taking
away the lands of the Schools and substituting fixed stipends
from the Crown, especially if they really intended to re-endow
at that future golden moment which never came. Yet they did
in fact sign the death-warrant of scores of Schools.

How unfortunately the "quousque" warrant, never followed
up by any further order, worked for destruction a few particular
cases may show.

One of the first Schools on our list is Newbury, Berkshire.
The Schools Inquiry Commission Report dates it only "before
1677." That particular year was chosen, because in that year
a Crown payment of £12 being "the stipend of the Master of
Newbury Grammar School," was, with other such payments,
ordered to be reserved on the sale of Crown lands. Lord
Brougham's commission had, however, mentioned the Chantry
Certificate continuing the School, though they say that they
had enquired for it at the Augmentation Office in vain.

That Certificate is now printed. It shows that a stipendiary
priest, "called Henry Wormestall's priest," was "founded by
Henry Wormestall, which, by his last will, dated 2nd March,
1466, willed that certain men should stand seized of and in
divers lands and tenements in Newbury and Greenham upon
condition that they and the heirs of them should keep repara-
tions, etc., and hire an honest priest to pray for his and all

Christian souls for ever, and keep a yearly obit of 10*s.*; with this addition, that it should be always lawful to the said cofeoffees " (pronounced, we may say for the benefit of lay-readers, not fĕŏffees, but feffees) " to alter and change the same foundation from time to time as to their discretion should seem good. Which lands and tenements be of the yearly value of £13 9*s.* 8*d.* Whereof in Redditi resoluti (*i.e.*, fixed rents payable) "by year 15*s.* 3*d.* The tenth " (*i.e.*, the tithe of the annual value payable to the Crown by virtue of a statute of Henry VIII. on all ecclesiastical benefices), "12*s.* 0½*d.*; 27*s.* 3½*d.* Remaineth unto one Thomas Evans, Schoolmaster, teaching a Grammar School there, whereof that town hath great need, £12 2*s.* 4½*d.*" The Commission further reported that there was another paper showing a payment of £4 to a priest from S. Bartholomew's Hospital, an ancient foundation, which was, as far back as King John's reign, granted the right to a Fair. The corporation, it seems, claimed that this £4, which was usually paid to the master of the Grammar School, was part of the £12. A reference to our records would have shown at once that this was not so, for the Crown having, in right of the Chantries Act, taken the lands, the School was continued (though in this case the original warrant is not forthcoming), and the Master was paid the full amount of his salary, deducting only 2*s.* 4½*d.* for fees. On the other hand, the Hospital being exempt from the Act of Edward, retained its lands. The result was, that while S. Bartholomew's Hospital, Newbury, the lands of which were worth £21 a year, as stated in the Chantry Certificate of Henry VIII., had 60 years ago seen its income augmented to some £500 a year, the School, with only the fixed sum of £12, had fallen into abeyance. The schoolhouse was let, the Crown payment itself taken by the Corporation, and, on the principle of "To him that hath, to him shall be given," applied in aid of the rich Hospital. A scheme afterwards reversed the process, and set the School on its own legs again. But for something like a hundred years Newbury was deprived of the chance of higher education, for which one if not two endowments had been given, because the Schoolmaster was left with a fixed stipend instead of his endowment.

Another instance, while illustrating the historical importance of these documents, shows how deeply rooted in the minds of country communities is the memory of ancient charities. Lord Brougham's Commission reported of Week S. Mary, or S. Mary Weke, as it used to be called, in Cornwall, that "much excitement has existed respecting certain lands called the Commons, which are reported to have been given for charitable purposes by one Thomasin Bonaventure, *alias* Percival. No will has been found, though repeatedly searched for; and we could discover no evidence of any charitable trust in connection with them." Is not this a vague reminiscence of the Grammar School at Week, founded by Thomasina Lady Percival, wife of Sir John Percival, Knight, Merchant Tailor and Lord Mayor of London, who himself founded what is still the very flourishing Grammar School at Macclesfield (pp. 23, 24)? Her London will, made by her 12th February, 1508, as a freewoman and citizen of London, enrolled in the Hastings Court in 1512, showing, probably, that she was then dead, is abstracted in Dr. Sharpe's *Calendar of Hastings Wills*, ii. 618. She founded "a Chantry at the altar of S. John Baptist, in the north aisle of the church," "called Dame Percival's Chantry," "to find a priest for ever, not only to pray for her soul within the parish church, but also that he, the said priest, do teach children freely, in a School founded by the said Dame Percival, not far distant from the parish church"; and "to find a maniple also, to instruct and teach children under the said Schoolmaster." The Schoolmaster got £12 6s., and the maniple £1 6s. 8d. a year. A memorandum says, "The said Chantry is a great comfort to all the country there, for that they that list may set their children to board there, and have them taught freely, for the which purpose there is an house and officers appointed by the foundation accordingly." The maniple, of course, whose title is still preserved in Oxford Colleges, was one of these boarding-house officers, as well as Elementary School teacher.

The "comfort to the country" was no doubt the view of the

parishioners of Week S. Mary. Edward's commissioners give
a very different account. While they praise the master,
William Chalwell, or Cholwell, as " a man well learned, and a
great setter forth of God's word," they say " the said School is
in decay by reason it standeth in a desolate place, and far from
the market, for provision of scholars." The number of " houseling people," or communicants, is given at 150 only, repre-
senting a population of, say, 200. The endowment income was
£15 11s. 4d., besides some lands which one of the founder's
feoffees kept in his own hands, paying to the manciple in respect
of it £4 yearly, and 13s. 4d. to the laundress of the schoolhouse,
so that the whole came to the very respectable sum of £20 a
year, or £400 a year of our money. But in the borough of
Launceston, "the shire town" with a population of 550,
there was a stipendiary priest to teach children grammar,
who received £6 for his salary, while 13s. 4d. was given to " an
aged man, chosen by the mayor, to teach young children the
A B C." Of this the Commissioners say : "The commons of
the same town of Launceston be greatly charged for binding
of prisoners in the king's common gaol there. Adjoining to
the town be 12 parish churches, whereof the king's majesty
is patron, by reason of the late dissolved monastery of Launceston, and no vicar endowed, for they were wont to be served
with the religious persons of the said late monastery. Item,
there is a very meet place to establish a learned man to preach
and set forth the word of God to the people, and also to teach
children their grammar, and other necessary knowledge. And
where the said School of S. Mary Week is now in decay for
lack of convenient relief for the scholars, this is a very meet
place to have the foundation of the School removed unto, for
both the said towns of Launceston and Week standeth within
7 miles distant." In the Schools Continuance Warrant we find
that the Grammar School maintained out of the Chantry of S.
John Baptist of Week is ordered to be continued, "and that
there shall be paid yearly to the sustentation or maintenance
of the said School, £17 13s. 3½d."

The School was continued not at Week, but at Launceston,

as appears from the Pension certificate. The manciple usher was pensioned off with 66s. 8d. a year, and his wife, the laundress, with 13s. 4d., while it is said "At Launceston, *continuatur quousque* (*i.e.*, till further or other order be made) with the accustomed wages"; and a note adds: "appointed by my Lord Protector's Grace's letters to be moved hence to Launceston, and there to have continuance, if it shall appear to be more necessary there than at Week. And upon letters directed to certain of the worshipful of the shire it is certified that the same is more meet; whereupon it is ordered *quousque.*" Meanwhile the Launceston stipendiary was abolished, "the pension of the priest to be borne by the inhabitants of the town, because the Schoolmaster of S. Mary Week, by their own suit, is removed hither." Presumably there were difficulties afterwards as to this transaction, for Lord Brougham's Commission report, under heading of Launceston, that "A Grammar School in this Borough was endowed by Queen Elizabeth, with an annual payment of £16 13s. 4d., payable out of the revenues of the Duchy of Cornwall to the master, who has always been appointed by the Corporation." Thus was Queen Elizabeth credited with the good deeds of Edward VI., who took the School endowment, but gave a fixed stipend instead.

This case is a remarkable instance of the Protector Somerset's advanced views, in thus authorizing the removal of a School from a small village, where it was doing no good and was not wanted, to a larger neighbouring town, where it was wanted, and did so after consulting the local authorities. It is creditable, too, to the local authorities, who thus supported the doctrine that the best way of carrying out the founder's wishes was to apply her endowments in the way most calculated to advance education.

It was not a condemnation of the Protector's policy in removing the School that in 1837 it was in abeyance, and the Crown stipend not paid for 16 years, for lack of a master. But it was his fault that the endowment, which, if the actual lands had been continued or restored, would have been found amply sufficient for a flourishing First Grade School, was found to be so insufficient that it had to be converted into an exhibition endowment. Thus has poor Thomasina's memory faded from the memory of man.

Very sad has been the history of nearly all these ancient Schools in Cornwall, where new founders have not come forward, as in other parts of the country, to make up for the Edwardian spoliation.

Our records show us the College of S. Thomas of Glasney, founded, or augmented rather, by Walter the Good, otherwise Bronescombe, Bishop of Exeter, about the year 1271, in or near the town of Penryn (Peryn, it is called), with its staff of a Provost, 12 canons and prebendaries, and 7 vicars choral, a chapel clerk, a bell-ringer, 4 "querysters"—a term still understanded by Wykehamists—and 3 Chantry priests, standing "upon a fair haven named Falmouth," where sometimes "repair for harbour 100 great ships, which, being there, have always used to resort to the said College to see the ministration there; and the walls of the said College on the south side well fortified with towers, and ordnance in the same for the defence of the said town," in the same way as the walls of New College, Oxford, were also the town walls. The College, of course, kept its Grammar School, one of the vicars choral being master; but he was "late deceased" in 1548, "for the which the people maketh great lamentation; and it is meet to have another learned man, for there is much youth in the said town." A somewhat mystic note (p. 30), "Nota pro Raufe Coche Mr. Hobbis Stole," appears to mean that Coche, the "chapel clerk, of the age of 50 years," who "hath for his salary in the said College £6 12d., besides his meat and drink, and hath no other promotions," should succeed to the place or stool (or perhaps it is scole for school) of the late Schoolmaster, named Hobbs.

Nor was the elementary education of the place unprovided for. "John Pounde, bell-ringer there, of the age of 30 years, hath for his salary there 40s., as well for teaching of poor men's children their A B C as for ringing the bells." The yearly

value of the College was £228 4s. 7d., or somewhere about
£4,500 a year. The whole was swept away, including the poor
children's A B C teacher, and the stipend of the Grammar
Schoolmaster, £6 18s., alone continued.

It is true that £9 out of £228 devoted to education was not
a very large proportion. A School building was, however, provided, and no doubt a very much better Schoolmaster than
would otherwise have been the case. Moreover, while the
endowments of the College remained, they were ready at any
time to be applied to more useful purposes than the maintenance of canons, mostly non-resident, and vicars choral, whose
singing and praying allowed them, as we know from other
like places, a great deal too much time and inclination for
dicing, drinking, and damsels. The commissioners say that " it
is a meet place to establish a learned man to teach a Grammar
School, for people thereabouts be very ignorant." But Glasney
shared the common lot. It was recited that " a Grammar
School has heretofore kept at Penryn, in the parish of Glavias,
with part of the revenues of the late College there, which
School is meet and necessary to continue," and " assigned that
the School in Penryn aforesaid shall continue, and that the
Schoolmaster there shall have and enjoy the £6 18s. for his
wages yearly." That was all that was saved from the wreck,
and in this way did the commissioners exercise their full power
and authority to appoint " lands, tenements, and other hereditaments " for the keeping of a Grammar School for ever. Short
is the record of this School in Lord Brougham's Commission
Report. " Queen Elizabeth gave the annual sum of £6 13s. 4d.
to a Grammar School at Penryn,"—again the sister is credited
with the good deed, such as it was, of the brother,—" which is
stated to have been secured under the Pension Act of 22 Car. II
c. 6, sec. 14, by deed bearing date 5th June, 1677, and payable
at the Land Revenue Record Office. As there is no Grammar
School in Penryn, and consequently no master to whom payment
can be made, it has been withheld several years." The Royal
Commission on Secondary Education records a melancholy blank
under the heading of Penryn Grammar School.

Similar is the record for the Grammar School at Bodmin, "called Nayler's or S. John Baptist's Chantry, to find a priest for ever to celebrate in the said (parish) church and teach young children grammar." Lands, £7 19s. 8d., of which Priest's salary £5 6s. 8d. "This town of Bodmin," say Edward's commissioners, "standeth in the midst of the shire of Cornwall, the king's majesty lord and patron thereof, . . being the greatest market town that is in all the shire; great resort thither, as well for the said market as for sessions two times in the year, there kept. A very meet place for a learned man . . for the Lord knoweth the said 2,000 people are very 'ingnorant.'" The School was continued with the salary of £5 6s. 8d. But the Crown payment, credited as usual to Queen Elizabeth, who seems to have been the "common vouchee" of Lord Brougham's commission, "is now" (1837) "discontinued." The commission of 1867 says, the School was "formerly held in S. Thomas' Chapel," and is in abeyance. A simple reference to this report is the record in 1895.

At Saltash, lands held by the mayor and burgesses, given by John Smith and others "to pray for them, their fathers and mothers, and to teach children there, born within the borough," were swallowed up. The Schoolmaster's salary, £7 a year, reduced by taking fees (which the Chantries Act expressly said were not to be taken) to £6 17s. in 1837, and to £6 4s. 9d. later, continued to be paid till shortly before 1867, and has not been paid since for lack of one to receive it.

The case of Truro is better. There the old Grammar School master was "a stipendiary in the parish church, of the benevolence of the mayor and burgesses, to find a priest for ever to minister in the parish church and to keep a school there." He received £6 13s. 4d. Being "of the benevolence," it would appear doubtful whether the School fell within the Act, and in the pension list, though a pension of £6 is entered, it is added, "The said pension is paid of the benevolence of the mayor and brethren yearly." The corporation stuck to the lands, and in 1837 paid the master £35 a year, which, though not too magnificent a salary, was yet more than five times as much as he would have been paid, if he had fallen under the tender mercies of Edward VI.

Such is the doleful record of the havoc wrought in the educational provision of a single county.

The reader would be wearied if many more examples were piled up of Edward VI.'s method of founding Schools. He can turn over the documents and see for himself how the 226 Schools recorded fared, many of them destroyed at once, many more fading away under the tender attentions of that careful educational planter. To aid the reader, a table is appended of the Grammar Schools mentioned, showing their date of foundation or earliest mention, and whether still subsisting as Grammar Schools, sunk into Elementary Schools, converted into Exhibition Funds, or perished altogether. The record is not complete, and much local and special knowledge is required to complete it. Imperfect as it is, it is enough to establish that the received notions of the provision for education in England are extremely erroneous, and that the history of many of our Schools is much longer than is commonly supposed.

As for poor Edward VI., meaning thereby the ruling councillors of his day, he cannot any longer be called the founder of our national system of Secondary education. But he, or they, can at least claim the distinction of having had a unique opportunity of reorganizing the whole educational system of a nation from top to bottom, without cost to the nation, and of having thrown it away.

PART II. DOCUMENTS.

BEING COMMISSIONS, EXTRACTS FROM CERTIFICATES AND WARRANTS UNDER THE CHANTRIES ACTS 37 HENRY VIII. c. 14 AND 1 EDWARD VI. c. 4

COMMISSION OF ENQUIRY

UNDER CHANTRIES ACT, 37 HENRY VIII.

Yorkshire. Certificate 66.

KING Henry the Eight by the grace of God King of Englond, Fraunce, and Irelond, Defender of the Faythe and of the Churche of Englond and also of Irelond, in erthe, the supreme hedd to the most reverend father in God, Robert, archbishopp of Yorke, and to his trustie and wellbelovyd Syr Mychaell Stannop, knyght, Syr Leonard Bekwith, knyght, Wyllyam Babthorp, esquyer, Robert Chaloner, esquyer, Robert Hennage, esquyer, Richard Whalley, esquyer, Thomas Gargrave, gentylman, Richard Norton, gentylman, and Humfrey Bowland, gentilman, and to every of theym, Greating.

Where by one acte in our Parliament, holden at Westminster in the 37th yere of our reigne, for certeyne causes and consyderacyons, conteyned and specyfyed in the same acte, there is gyven and graunted to us full power and auctoritie to assume and take into our hands and possession, at our will and pleasure during our naturall lyfe, all chauntries, hospitalls, colleges, free chappells, fraternyties, brotherhedds, guylds, and sallaries of stipendarie priests, within this realme of Englond and Wales, and the Marches of the same, having perpetuytie for ever, and beyng charged or chargeable to the payment of the fyrst frutes and tenthes, and all colleges chargeable and not chargeable to the payment of the first frutes and tenthes, and all the mannours, londs, tenements, heredytaments, and possessyons, unyted, annexed, or belongyng to theym, or to any of theym, as in the seid acte more at large may appere.

We, ernestlye sekyng and wysshing that the due and true execution of th' aucthorytie and powre to us gyven and graunted, as is aforeseyd, shulde hoolye tende to the glorye of Almyghtie God, whose honor we chieflye seke in this thing, and to the comon welthe of this our Realme, accordyng unto the truste and confydence that our wellbeloved and obedyent subjects have conceyved in us and commytted unto us in that behalfe, have thought good, before we shulde procede to th' execucyon of anything therin conteyned, to have a trew and certeyn declaracyon and certificat made unto us, as well of the number and names of the seid chantreis, colleges, fraternyties, brotherhedds, hospitalls, and other the seid promocyons, as also of th' orders, qualities, degrees, uses, abuses, condycyons, estates, and necessities, concernyng theym or any of theym; wherof being certeynlye, fullye, and crediblye enformed and instructyd, we shall be the more able with expedycyon to do and accomplysshe those things whiche the necessitie and ymportance of this matter requireth.

Know ye, therefore, that we, trusting in your fydelyties and approvyd wysdome, have appoynted and assigned you to be our commyssioners, gevyng to you nyne, eight, seven, syx, fyve, fowre or thre of you full power and auctoritie to assemble yourselfes in suche place or places within the countye of York, the cytye of Yorke, and the towne of Kyngeston uppon Hull, and at such daies and tymes as you, nyne, eight, seven, syx, fyve, fowre, or thre of you shall thinke mete and convenyent, and examyne, serche, and enquyre, by all wayes and meanes that ye can, what and how manye chauntries, hospitalls, colleges, free chappells, fraternyties, brotherheadds, guylds, and stypendarye prestes havyng perpetuytie for ever, by whatsoever names, surnames, corporations, or tytles, they be commonly called or knowne, accordyng to ther severall natures, kindes, qualities, and degrees, be within the seid countye of Yorke, the cytye of Yorke, and the towne of Kingston uppon Hull; and also to examyne, serche, and enquyre, by all waies and meanes that ye can, by your discrecyons or by the discrecyons of nyne, eight, seven, syx, fyve, fowre, or thre of you, to what intentes, purposes, and dedes of charytie the same chauntries, hospitalls, colleges, and other the seid promocyons, or any of theym, were founded, ordeyned, or made; and howe and in what manner the revenewes and profitts of the possessions of the same be used, expended or imployed; and whiche and howe manye of them be paroche churches; and howe farre dystant every of the seid chappells or chauntries bene from the paroche churche, within whiche paroche any of theym stondyth and be sett, to th' intente we may knowe whiche shalbe mete to stond and remayne, as they nowe be, or to be dissolvyd, altered or reformyd, making to us a perfyte certyficatt of every particuler poynte therof accordinglie.

And, further, we gyve full powre and auctorytie to you, our said commyssyoners, and to nyne, eight, seven, syx, fyve, fowre, or thre of you, to repayre to the pryncypall howses of all the seid chauntreis, hospitalls, colleges, free chappells, fraternyties, brotherheddes, guylds, and sypendarye prestes in the seid countye of York, the cytie of Yorke, and the towne of Kingston uppon Hull, and to make a survey of all the landes and tenements, possessyons and revenewes unyted, annexed, or apperteyning to theym and to every of theym, or whiche at any tyme syth the 4th day of Februarye in the 27th yere of our reigne, dyd aperteyne or belong to the seid promocyons or to any of them, making mencyon of the resolutes and deduccyons going owte of the same.

And we give unto you, nyne, eight, seven, syx, five, fowre, or thre of you full power and auctorytie to enquyre, serche, and examyne howe manye chauntries, hospitalls, colleges, free chappells, guyldes, fraternyties, brotherheddes and other promocyons aforesaid, sith the fowrth daie of Februarie in the seid 27th yere of owre reigne, have bene dissolvyd, purchased, or by any other meane obteyned by any of our subjectes of their owne auctoritye, withoute our speciall lycence, and to survey truly the same, and the yerely value therof, with the goodes and ornamentes of the same, with all the deductyons and resolutes thereof, and to make certificate accordinglie.

And to th' intentes that the plate, jewells, ornamentes, goodes, and catalles of the seyd chauntries, hospitalls, and other the seid promocyons, by the maisters, governers, mynysters, and incombents of the same, shulde not be wastyd, spoyled, or otherwise embeseyled, but that the same shulde remayne to such godlye ententes and purposes as we shall hereafter appoynte for the same, our wyll and pleasure is, that you, our seid commyssyoners, nyne, eight, seven, syx, fyve, fowre, or thre of you, shall make severall inventories indentyd between you, nyne, eight, seven, syx, fyve, fowre, or thre of you and the maisters, rulers, governors, or incombents of the seid chauntries, hospitalls, and other the said promocyons, of all the plate, jewells, ornaments, goods, and cattalls merelye perteyning or belonging to any of the seyd chaunteries, hospitalls, and other the seid promocyons, and thereuppon to gyve charge and commaundment, in our name, to the seid maisters, rulers, governers, mynysters, and incombents of the seid chauntries, hospytalls, and other the seid promocyons, safelye to kepe and preserve the same untyll our further pleasure be knowne in that behalfe.

And, further, oure pleasure and comaundment is that you, our seid comyssyoners, nyne, eight, seven, syx, fyve, fowre, or thre of you, shall not onelye certefye unto our Chauncellour and Counsell of oure Courte of th' augmentacyons of the revenewes of our Crowne, in writing, in parchment, under your seales, the nombre and names of all the seid chauntries, hospitalls, colleges, and other the seid promocyons, but also shall lykewyse certefye the survey of the landes, tenementes, revenewes, and possessyons, goods, catalls, ornaments, and jewels of the same, to be made in forme aforesaid; and also one part of the inventorye indentyd to be made of the seid plate, jewells, ornaments, goods, and catalls of the same chauntries, hospitalls, colleges, and other the seid promocyons, as is aforesaid, and all other things commytted and comaunded to you to be done and executyd, by vertue of this comyssyon, togyther with the same comyssyon, so that the same may remayne of record in our seid Courte of the Augmentacyons, and to th' entente that trewe declaracyon therof shalbe made to us by the Chauncellor of the same Courte.

And we commaunde to all mayers, sheryffs, baylyffs, constables, and all other our offycers, mynysters, and subjects, that they, and every of them, shalbe aydyng, obedyent, and assistaunte to you, and everye of you, in all things touching th' execucyon of this our comyssyon, as it behoveth, and as necessytie from tyme to tyme shall requyre in that behalf.

In wytnes wherof we have caused these our lettres to be made patent. Wytnes our self at Westminster, the 14th daie of Februarye in the 37th yere of our reign [154⅔].

Southwell.

COMMISSION OF ENQUIRY
Under Chantries Act, 1 Edward VI.
Kente. Certificate 28.

Edwarde the sixte, by the grace of god Kynge of England, Fraunce, and Ireland, Defendeur of the Feythe, and of the Churche of England, and also of Ireland, in earthe the supreme heade, To our trustie and Wellbeloved Rafe Vane, Anthony Aucher, Walter Hendle, and James Hales, knyghtes ; Henry crispe, Thomas Spilman, Paule Sidnour, and Thomas Wotton, Esquiers ; Cristofer Nevison, William Hyde, and John Lendall, Gentilmen ; greatynge.

Whereas by an acte, made in our Parliament begonne and holden at Westminster, the fourth daye of Nouember, in the firste yere of our reigne, Colleges, Chauntreis, Frechappelles, Fraternities, Brotherheddes, and guyldes, Manours, landes, tenementes, hereditamentes, and certeyne other thynges mencyoned in the said acte, Were, and are geven vnto vs in suche sorte as in the saide acte more playnely dothe appeare ; And by the same acte, power and auctoritie is geven vnto vs to make and directe fourthe our commissions for the survey, and further doinges, of and concernynge the aforesaid Colleges, Frechappelles, chauntries, and other thynges geven vnto vs by the said acte.

Wee, myndynge trulie, playnely, and certeynly to be enformed of all the thinges geven vnto vs by the said acte, To the entent that aswell we for our parte maye be truly and iustely aun-swered of suche and so moche of the same as by the said acte to vs apperteyneth, As also vpon enformacyon by the survey of the same, procede the better and more vprightly to an order for the satisfaccion and accomplishement of suche rightes, duties, and allowaunces as by the same acte to any our subiectes apperteyneth, Haue thought convenyent for the confidence We haue in your honesties, Wisdomes, and true dealynges, to appoynte, ordeyne, and make you our Commissioners.

And by these presentes do auctorise you, tenne, nyne, eight, seven, sixe, fyve, foure, three, or two of you, to enquire, survey, and examyn, aswell by the othes of suche persones as you shall thynke convenyent, as otherwise, by your Wisdomes and dis-crecyons, What Colleges, Chauntreis, Frechappelles, Brother-heddes, Fraternities, and Guyldes, Manours, landes, tenementes, hereditamentes, and other thynges Within our countie of Kent, and the Cities of Canterbury and Rochester, ought to come to vs by vertue of the said acte; And also the foundacions, vsages, contynuaunces, vses, qualities, values, condicions, and state in euery degree of the same, and euery of theym.

And of your doinges and procedinges therin We Woll and commaunde you, tenne, nyne, eight, seven, sixe, fyve, foure, three, or two of you, to certifie vs before the laste daye of Maye nexte comynge, into our Courte of Augmentacions and reuenues of our crowne, at Westminster, of somoche thereof as is oute of our Duchie of Lancaster, And of suche and somoche of the premisses as is Within our said Duchie, We Woll ye shall certifie vs into our courts of our Duchie of Lancaster, into our Duchie Chamber at Westminster, before the same daie. And that ye faile not hereof as ye tender our pleasure and Will aunswere to the contrary.

And We Woll and Commaund all Mayres, Sheriffes, Bailifes, Constables, and all other our officers, Mynysters, and subiectes, that they and euery of theym shalbe obedyent, aidynge, fauorynge and assistinge to you and euery of you frome tyme to tyme in all thynges touchynge, or in any Wise concernynge, the execucion of this our Commission, as the case shall requyre,

and as they shalbe on our behalf by you commannded, upon the
perill therof to fall.

In Witnes Wherof We haue caused these our letters to be
made patentes. Witnesse our selfe at Westminster, the foure-
teneth daye of February, the seconde yere of our reigne. [154⅞]

SOUTHWELL.

B.

COMMISSION FOR CONTINUANCE OF SCHOOLS
Preachers, etc., and Pensions,
UNDER CHANTRIES ACT, 1 EDWARD VI.

Patent Roll. 2 Edward VI. Part iv., m. 22 (d.)

Edward the Syxt, etc. To oure trustie and welbelouyd Walter Mildmay, knyght, one of the General Surveyours of oure
Courte of the Augmentacions and revenues of oure Crowne, and
Robert Keylwey, Esquyer, Surveyoure of oure lyueries in oure
court of Wardes, greatyng.

Where in the acte of parliament made in the first yere of oure
Reign, by the wich diuerse Colleges, Frechappelles, Chauntries,
Guyldes, Fraternytes, and Stipendes of priestes, ar dissolued,
and the landes and tenementes and possessions of the same, together with diverse other landes, tenementes, and possessions
mencyoned in the same acte, ar come to our handes and possession, it is expressed and declared that at oure Will and
pleasure we myght direct oure Comission or Comissions, under
our greate seale of England, to suche persons as it shulde please
vs, for the assignement and appoyntment of landes and tenementes for and towarde the sufficyent fynding and manetenaunce
of Scolemasters and preachers in such places where the same
were founded or ordened to be kepte ; and for and towarde the
sufficyent fyndyng and maynetenaunce of priestes within such
Townes or parisshes, where there is necessite to haue mo priestes
then one for the mynistracion of Sacramentes, and for the makyng vicars to haue perpetuyte for ever in parishe Churches,
wiche first day of the said parliament were Collegies, free chappelles, or Chauntryes, or wiche were appropried, annexed, or
vnited to any Colledge, Free Chappell or Chauntrye that shuld

come to our handes by vertue of the said Acte; And for the suffioyent indownent of suche vicars hauing respect to other Cures and Chardges.

And for the assignement of yerelie pencions, annuites, or other recompenses to the Deanes, maisters, Wardens, provostes, and other Incumbentes and mynisters of the said Colledges, Frechappelles, or Chauntries dissolued or determyned by the said Acte, and to stipendarie priestes and other priestes whose Salaries we shuld be intitled unto by the said acte, and to all fellowes and pore persons hauyng relyef out of any the said Colleges, Frechappells, or Chauntries, duryng theyre severall lyves.

And for the assignement and appoyntment of landes, tenementes, and other hereditamentes to and for suche money, profettes and commodite, as any pore personne or persons within fyue yeres next before the begynnyng of the said parliament had or inioyed 'out of any Colledge, Frechappell or Chauntrie, or other thing, lymytted or appoynted to us by the said Acte by vertu of any conveyaunce, assuraunce, composicion, will, deuyse, or otherwyse heretofore had made or intended or mente to haue contynuance for euer. And for the appoyntment of landes, tenementes, and hereditaments to and for the mayntenaunce of peers, guttes, Walles or bankes, agayne the Rages of the See, hauens and brekes, as by the said Acte of parliament, amongestes other thynges therin more playnelie appereth.

And were we haue lately directed oure severall Comissions vnder oure greate Seale of England to diuerse and soundrye persons into all places of this, oure Realme of England and Wales, to examyne, serche and enquyre; and also to certifie, what maners, landes, tenementes, possessions, profettes and hereditaments shuld come to vs by reason of the said Acte, And also to enquyre and certyfie diuerse other matters, causes, and thinges mencioned in the said Comyssions, as by the same comissions more playnelie appereth.

We myndyng to erecte diuerse and sundrye Grammer Scoles in euery Countie in England and Wales, for the Educacone and bryngyng uppe of youth in vertu and learnyng and godlynes, and also to make prouision for the releif of the pore, in such wyse as shall be thought mete and convenyent: And myndyng also al thynges mencyoned in the said Acte of Parliament, touchyng any chearytable or godlie Acte, purpose or intente to be done, executed and performed, towardes al persons accordyng to the true meanyng and ententes thereof:

Knowe ye that for diuerse causes and consyderacons, vs and oure Counsaill at this presente speciall moving, We trustyng in youre fydelyties and approvyd wysdomes, have assigned and appoynted you to be oure Comissioners, and by these presentes, by the aduice of oure moiste derest and entirely belouyd vncle and Counsaillour, Edward Duke of Somersett, Governour of oure person, and protectour of oure Realmes, Domynyons and subiectes, and of other oure Counsaillours, do gyve vnto you full power and auctorite by youre discrecions to assigne and appoynte as well to euery Dean, Maister, Warden, Prouoste, and other Incumbent and mynystre of euery of the said Collegis, Free chappells and Chauntries, wich be dyssolued and determyned by the said acte of parliament made in the said first yere of oure Regne, Wiche Deanes, maisters, Wardens, provostes, Incumbentes or ministers, had seuerallie for theyre seuerall lyuynges vnder the yerelie value of twenty poundes, as to euery Stipendarie prist and other priest Whose salarie beyng under twenti poundes yereley We be entitled unto by the same Acte, and to euery fellow and pore persone wich had yerelie any relief vnder the yerelie value of twentie poundes out of any the said Colleges, Frechappelles, or Chauntries, such seuerall yerelie annuytes pencions or other recompenses, to be graunted to theym by vs by letters patentes in due forme, to be made vnder the greate Seale of oure Courte of the Augmentacions and Revenues of oure Crowne, duryng theyre seuerall lyves: The same to be paied by the handes of any of the Receyvours of the revenues of the said Courte of the Augmentacions and Revenues of oure Crowne for the tyme beyng, of oure Revenues frome tyme to tyme remaying [sic] in theire handes, as by you shall be thought mete and convenyent, with a promiss to be conteyned in the same letters patentes that, yf any such persone to whome any suche pencion annuyte or recompense shall be graunted, be hereafter promotyd by vs to any promotion, dignite, or other thyng of the clere yerelie value of such pencion annuyte or recompense, so to be graunted in forme aforesaid, or better, that then the same letters patentes or graunt From thensforth to be voide and of non effect. And where the promocion or lyvyng of any person which shall haue any such pencion or recompense was but for terme of yeres, so that, after the expiracion of the same yeres, We shall not enioie the same promocion, or lyvyng, or the landes, tenementes, or other thinges appoynted to the same; that in suche case the pencion or recompense to be graunted or assured to such person, shall be but duryng the same yeres, yf such persone so long do lyve.

And oure pleasure is and by these presentes we do auctorise you that in the assignament and appoyntmentes of the said pencions and recompenses, you shall and maye assigne and appoynt to euery person wich had for his lyving £5 yerelie or under, a pencion, annuyte, or recompense to the yerelie value of the hole therof;

And to euery personn which had for his lyuyng yerelie aboue £5 and vnder £6 13s. 4d. yerelie, a pencion, annuyte, or recompense of £5 yerelie;

And to euery persone wich had for his lyvyng yerelie £6 13s. 4d. or aboue, and vnder £10 yerelie, a pencion, annuyte, or recompense of £6 yerelie;

And to euery personne whych had for his lyvyng £10 yerelie or aboue, and under £20 yerelie, a pencion, annuyte, or recompense of £6 13s. 4d.

And oure Will and pleasure is that [you] shal (*sic*) and procede in the assignament and appoyntment of the said pencions, annuytes, and recompenses vppon the certificattes of eny of oure particuler Surveyours of landes of oure Courte of Augmentacions and Revenues of oure Crowne or any of theyre deputies, or any two of oure said Comissioners appoynted for the examinacion or survey of the landes, tenementes, and other thinges wich came to vs by the said Act, Within the lymittes of theire comissions, to be made of the yerelie lyvinges of such persons as ought to haue the same recompenses, annuytes, or pencions, and the same

certyficattes to be to you sufficyent Warraunt and Discharge in
that behalf.

And further, we woll, and by the aduise of oure said Counsaill, do graunt by these presentes that a bill or billes, warraunt
or warrauntes, to be assigned or subscribed with youre handes,
mencionyng suche pencions, annuyties, or recompenses, to be
concluded and appoynted by youe in forme aforesaide shall be
good and sufficyent warraunt and warrauntes to the Chauncellour of the said Courte of the Augmentacions and revenues of
oure Crowne, and to all other oure offycers and mynystres of the
same Courte for the tyme beyng, for the makyng furthe, sealyng,
and delyueryng of our seuerall letters patentes thereof in due
forme, to be made to the persons to whome the same shall be so
made and graunted, without any further or other Warraunte to
be had or obteyned in that behalf : And that the same letters
patentes so to be made and sealed shall be as good and effectuall
in the law to all intentes and purposes as yf the billes or
Warrauntes theire of were or had byn assigned by oure owne
hand, and that without any fyne or fynes, fee or fees, to be
payed to vs or to oure vse, or to any oure officers or mynysters
what soeuer they be, or to their use ; any law, statute, or Acte
heretofore had or made, or any other matter or cause to the contrarie in any wyse notwithstandyng.

And also we woll and commaund you vpon the certyficattes to
be made of the said Comissions made for the inquerie and certificatt of the said manours, landes, tenementes, possessions,
hereditamentes, and other thinges wich are comme or ought to
comme to vs by the said Acte ye do cause any of the particuler
Surveyours of oure landes, or any of the auditours of oure said
Courte of the Augmentacions and revenues of oure Crowne, or
any theyre deputies, within theire seuerall Officyes, to make
colleccion of the numbre of Grammer Scoles and prechinges in
euery Countie of England and Wales that haue byn kepte of any
of the said landes, tenementes, or other proffettes or Reuenues,
wiche came or ought to come to vs by reason of the said Acte,
and of the yerelie value of the landes, tenementes, or other
Revenues or proffettes wich haue byn chargeable or yerelie

bestowed towardes the mayntenaunce therof, and to delyuer the same to you; And you to make declaracion therof to vs or to our said moist dere vncle; to the intente there uppon, by aduise of oure said vncle and any other of oure said Counsaill, we may consider and take order for the contynuaunce or alteracion of the same Scoles and prechynges, or for the same, or other, to be newelie erectyd in suche places in euery countie as shall be thought mete and convenyent.

And also that lykewyse ye do cause the said particuler Surveyours or Auditours to make colleccion of all suche money, or other yerelie proffettes or commodite, as hath byn ymployed yerelie toward the fyndyng of any poore persone or persons, to have contynuaunce for ever, within fyue yeres next before the begynnyng of the said parliament, out of any College, Frechappell, Chauntrye, or other thing graunted or appoynted to vs by the said Acte, and to delyuer the same to you, and you to make relacion therof to vs or to oure vncle.

So that thereuppon we, or oure said vncle, maie signifie unto you oure pleasure by worde or wrytyng how many Grammer Scoles shall be erected, and haue contynuaunce in euery Countie, and how moche landes and other yerelie pencions, Annuyties, or other proffettes shall be appoynted for the mayntenaunce of euery one of the same, and also what nombre of prechers of Goddes Worde shall be appoynted to be in euery countie within England and Wales to haue contynuance for euer, together with the stipendes or yerelie proffettes appoynted to theym for the same, and how many hospitalls or places for the sustentacion and releif of the powre shall be erected, founded, or made to have contynuaunce for euer in euery countie, and what and how moche landes or other proffettes shall be appoynted to the mayntenaunce of euery of the hospitalles or places for relief of the poore.

And we gyve to you full power and auctorite that, after oure said pleasure to you declared in the premisses, by vs or oure said vncle in forme afore saide, you, for vs and in oure name, shall and may appoynt and assigne by youre discreccions as moche landes, tenementes, Rentes, or other possessions or hereditaments of such as came to vs by reason of the said Act, or elles rentes,

annuytes, or yerelie pencions, to go and remayne in Successione
for euer towarde the keping of so manye Grammer Scoles and
preachynges, and so many hospitalls and houses for the relief of
the poore as by vs or oure said vncle shall be named and
appoynted in forme aforesaid.

And we gyve to you full powre and auctorite to assigne and
appoynt in oure name Tythes, pencions, and annuyties or other
yerelie proffettes to and for the sustentacion and endowment of
vicars perpetuall, to haue contynuaunce in succession for euer, in
parishe churches, wich the first daye of the saide parliament
were Colleges, Frechappells, or Chauntries, appropried, vnited, or
annexed to any Colledge Frechappell or Chauntrie, wich is come
to oure handes by vertu of the said Act; And to endowe euery
suche vicar sufficyentlie hauing respect to his cure and chardge.

And also assigne and appoynt landes, tenementes, tithes, and
other possessions or hereditamentes, wich came to us by the said
Act, or elles yerelie pencions or annuytes or other yerelie proffettes
for and to the Stipende and fyndyng of any prist or priestes for
the mynistracion of the Sacramentes in any Towne or parishe,
wiche hath necessite to have mo priestes then one for that purpose ; The same to haue contynuance in succession for ever, for
and towarde the finding and mayntenyng of the same priestes.

And also to assigne and appoynt landes tenementes and hereditamentes to go towardes the maynetenaunce of peers, Jutties,
Walls, or bankes ageynst the Rage of the See, hauens, or breekes,
in suche places where necessite requyreth, as shall appere to
you, vppon the certyficattes therof to be made by any of the
said particuler Surveyours or Auditours or theire deputies
within theyre seuerall offices ; the same landes, tenementes, and
hereditamentes to be assured and graunted in fee simple, and to
contynew in successyon for ever, to suche vses and in such maner
and as you shall thyngke mete reasonable and convenyent.

And that youe cause bokes and Warrauntes to be made and
devysed of the premisses, in suche maner and forme as you shall
thyngke mete and convenyent, and accordyng to the true
meanyng of the godlie ententes and such purposes of the said
Act of Parliament.

And also we wolle and commaunde that oure Attorney generall,
our Attorney of oure Courte of the Augmentacions and revenwes
of oure Crowne, and oure Solicitour generall, oure Attorney of
oure Duchie of Lancastrie, oure Attorney of oure Courte of
Wardes and lyueries, oure Attorney of oure Courte of first
frutes and tenthes, oure Solicitour of oure said Courte of the
Augmentacions and revenues of oure Crowne, and oure clerke of
the same Courte of the Augmentacions and Revenues of oure
Crowne, for the tyme beyng, shall be attendaunte vpon you for
the Drawing, Survey, and examinacion of the bokes, wrytinges,
and Warrauntes to be deuised and made of the premisses,
accordyng to the rates and conclusions therof by youe to be
agred and concluded :

And the billes, Writtynges, bokes, and Warrauntes therof to
be ingrossed and subscribed with the handes of the same
persons, or two of theym at the lest, shall be to you sufficyent
Warraunt and Discharge to assigne and subscribe likewyse with
youre handes the same Warrauntes, billes, and bokes, and
thervpon to exhibite them to vs and oure Counsaill, to be signed
by vs and oure Counsaill at oure will and pleasure.

And for as moch as present order and direccion cannot be had
and taken for and concerning the said Grammer Scoles and
preachinges, and Scolemasters and preachers, and for the contynuaunce or alteracion of the same, And for suche yerelie
profett and commodite as ought to be payed or imployed toward
the fyndyng of poore persons to haue contynuaunce for euer, And
for such yerelie pencions or Annuyties or sommes of money as
heretofore haue byn paied to the fyndyng and mayntenaunce of
Curates in places where the parsonages be appropried to vs, and
no vicar indowed in the same to serue and bere the charge of
the Cure, and the fyndyng and mayntenaunce of priestes in
townes or parishes were necessite is to haue moe priestes then
one for the mynystracion of Sacrementes, and for such money,
profette or commodite as heretofore hath byn bestowed to the
mayntenaunce of peers, Jutties, or banks ageynst the see, hauens,
or creeks, Oure pleasure and comaundement is that such and
and so moch money profett and commodite as heretofore hath

byn yerelie ymployed or bestowed towarde the mayntenaunce
and sustentacion of any such scoles, preachinges, Scolemaistiers,
preachers, Curates, priestes or poore personnes, or to maynetenaunce of any Jutties, peers, or bankes ageynst the rages of the
see, havens or Creekes shall be imployed and payed from the
feast of Ester last past furtwarde To the sustentacion of the same
Scoles, preachinges, scholemaisters, preachers, priests, and pore
parsons, and of Jutties, peers, or Bankes agaynst the Rages of
the See, haven, or Creekes, in suche maner and Forme as the
same heretofore hath byn vsed to be payed and ymployed; vntill
suche tyme as other order and direction shall be taken therein,
in maner and forme before rehersed.

And therefore we gyve vnto you full power and auctorite that
vpon the certificatt of any of the said Auditours or particuler
Surveyours of the saide Courte of the Augmentacions and Revenues of oure Crowne or any of theire deputies Within their
seuerall offices, declaryng how moche hathe byn yerelie or otherwyse bestowed or imployed to any of the vses, ententes and
purposes aboue mencioned, you shal and may by vertu herof
make and directe your Warraunt or Warrauntes to oure Auditours, Receyuers, particuler Surveyours of landes or any other
oure officers or ministres of the said Court of the Augmentacions
and Revenues of oure Crowne, or to any of their [deputies] for
the payment and allowaunce of the same as shall appear to you
by any of the

*Seventeen lines illegible. Some words at end of lines
legible, but not sufficient to make sense.*

to give there attendaunce vpon you, oure said Comissioners, as
well for the makyng of certificattes to youe of suche oure
manors, landes, tenementes and other thynges [as] are appoynted
to be bargayned and sold, or of any other thyng appoynted to
be executed or doune by you for vs, by vertu of oure Comission
to you directed, beryng [date] the 27th day of Aprill last past;
as also for makyng of certyficattes to you of, for, or concernyng
such matters, causes and thinges as are appoynted to be executed and doune by you by vertu of this our Comission.

We therefore are pleased and contented that the certificattes
of any of the deputies of eny of oure Auditours or particuler Surveyours or the Surveyours of oure Woodes, heretofore made, or
hereafter to be made to yow, as well of the yerelie values of any
oure manours, landes, tenementes or other thinges, appoynted
to be bargayned and sold by vertue of oure said former Comission to youe directed in forme aforesaid, or of any thyng appoynted to be executed or doune by you by vertu of the same
Comission, as also of any matter or cause expressed or mencioned in this oure Comission, shall be as good and sucffiyent
Warraunte and Discharge for and to you to procede to the
execution or doyng of eny thing or thynges mencioned in the
said former Comission, or in this oure comyssion, as hit shulde
haue byn yf the same certyficattes had byn made by the said
Auditours or particuler Surveyours or Surveyours of oure
Woodes or eny of them, any thyng in the said former comyssyon, or in this oure Comission, to the contrarie therof, in eny
wyse not withstandyng.

And were, in consyderacion of the pouertie of the said
Chauntrye priestes and other parsons appoynted to haue pencions and recompenses of vs for theire lyvynges in forme aforesaid, Oure pleasure is that they shud haue the same made
and assured to them frelie, withoute any fyne, or fee, or other
thing therfore to be paied to vs or any oure Officers or mynysters ; yet neverthelesse, in consideracion of the Wryttyng of
the same, We ar pleased and contented that oure Thresaurer of
oure Courte of the Augmentacions and Revenues of oure Crowne
for the tyme beyng, of such oure money or treasure as frome
tyme to tyme shall be or remayne in his handes of the sale of
oure landes, shall apon Warraunt or Warrauntes from you,
subscribed with your handes, content and pay to oure Clerke of
the same Courte of the Augmentacions and revenues of oure
Crowne foure shillinges of lawful money of England, for the
Wryttyng and Inrolment of euery letters patens of annuyte,
pencion, or recompense, to be made and graunted vnder the said
greate [scale] of the Courte of the Augmentacion and revenues of
oure Crowne, to any Deane, maister, warden, prouost, or other

Incumbent or mynyster of any of the said Colleges, Frechappelles or Chauntries, or to any stipendarye prieste or other priest, or to any persone wich shall haue pencions, annuities or recompences graunted to theym in forme of this oure Comission; or a duplicate therof shall be to the same Treasaurer a sufficyent Warraunt and Discharge in that behalfe.

And we gyve vnto you full power and aucthoryte by youre discreccions to make and gyve allowaunce of money as well to messyngers as to all other such personnes, wiche by youre commaundement shall travell, or take any payne in and aboute the busynes and execution of this oure Comission, or of oure Comission to you latelie directed, touching the sale of our landes; the same money and allowaunce to be paied by the handes of oure Treasaurer of oure saide Courte of the Augmentacions and revennes of oure Crowne for the tyme beyng, of suche our Treasure and money as frome tyme to tyme shall be and remayne in his handes of the sales of oure said landes; And that you shal and may make and direct your Warraunte or Warrauntes to the same Treasaurer for the payment therof; Wich Warraunt and Warrauntes shall be to the same Treasaurer sufficient discharge in that behalf.

And oure Will and pleasure is that this oure Comission shall endure and continew vntil such tyme as we shall declare oure pleasure in Writyng to the contrarie.

In Witteness, &c., Teste Rege at Westminster, 20 die Junii [1548].

EXTRACTS FROM CHANTRY CERTIFICATES AND WARRANTS

Comitatus Bedfordie. Chantry Certificate 4.
(Henry VIII.)

For date and names of commissioners, see under Bucks, p. 13.

THE PARYSHE OF HOUGHTON REGIS.

The Chauntrye of Houghton Regis: fownded by William Dyue, of London, Mercer, wiche haithe no perpetuytie, but

K

att Wille, to the entente to fynde a Preiste to synge within the seid churche of Houghton, And teche 6 poore childeren.

Also to be given to another preiste to singe for the seid William Dyue, and other in the manour of one Lues Dyue Esquier, within the chapell of Sawell.

And also certeyne other monye to be bestowed to diuerse poore people at the obittes kepte for the seid William Dyue, and Also certeine other monye to the helpe of diuerse poore people whan the Kinges majestie shalle chaunce to have anye 15 graunted, Whiche are not able of theme selves to paie Redilye, Whiche is nowe imploied and bestowed (as the feofers affirme) by theire othes ; Accordinge to the laste Wille of the seid William.

This Chauntrie haithe no foundacione, but there is one preiste singethe for the soule of the seid William Dyue, in the seid churche of Houghton Regis, Accordinge to the Wille of the seid William.   Also An other Preiste haithe 40s. to singe Masse for the seid William in the chapell of Sawell within the manour of the seid Lues Dyue, Whiche Hamelecte of Sawell is within the parishe aforeseid : And the seid Preiste Hathe this Stipende to singe masse in Wynter only for the ease of the seid Hamelecte, Whiche is A myle and more frome the seid parishe churche ; And ther be within the seid parishe of Houghton 280 house-lynge people.

The seid Chauntrie is of the yearelye value of £20 16s. 5d. Wherof

Paied to our seid Lorde the Kinge as in the Righte of his Priory of Dunstaple, by yere, 28s. 9d.

Paid to our seid Lorde the Kinge for the seid 15 when thei chaunce, ~~24s. 8d.~~ [sic].

Paied to our seid Lord the Kinge for tenthes, 41s. 7¼d.

Paied to diuerse other persones for Rentes Resolute, 53s. 9d.

£6 4s. 1¾d.

And so Remayneth, With £11 6s. 8d. for the seid preistes Wages, and money Distributed to the poore folkes, £14 12s. 3¼d.

There is neither Goodes, Catalles, Ornamentes, Juelles, ap-perteninge to the seid chauntrie; for the chalice and other necessaries are fownde by the parishioners of the seid churche.

The feofors of this Chauntrie hadde neuer more landes in
Value then is before said to the performaunce of the Wille of
the seid William Dyue; And also there is neither Chauntrie,
Colledge, Hospitalle, fraternytie, Guylde, or Stipendarye Preiste
havinge perpetuytie Within the churche or parishe aforeseid
(Savinge they saie ther is certeyne londe lyenge Within the seid
parishe called Chauntrye lande, Whiche the Ladye Braye dothe
occupie).

The countye of Bedforde. Certificate 1.
(Edward VI.)

p. 1. The certyfycat of Syr John Saynt John, Knyght, Syr
Thomas Rotheram, Knyght, and Wylliam Smyth, Gent., Commyssyoners wythin the countye of Bedford, Amonges other
authorised by the Kynges mayesties letters patentes of commyssyon, beryng date the 14th day of February, in the second
yere of the raign of our souerayn lord Edward the syxt, by
the grace of God Kyng of Ingland, Fraunce, and Ireland, Defendour of the Fayth, and in Erth of the churche of Ingland
and Ireland the supreme Hed [154$\frac{7}{8}$].

To Sir John Saynt John, Sir Laurence Lee, Sir Robert Drury,
Sir Thomas Rotheram, Knyghtes, Henry Bradshawe, Esquyer,
George Gyfford and Wylliam Smyth, Gent., directed : For the
survey of all colledges, Free chapells, Chauntries, Fraternyties,
Brothereddes, Guyldes, Stypendaries, Obytes, Anniuersaries,
lightes, and other like within the countyes of Bedford and
Buckes, havyng or beyng at any tyme within 5 yeres next
before the fourth day of November last past.

Viz., Touchyng as well the yerely value of all the Manours,
landes, possessyons and heredytamentes, stockes of money,
stockes of cattell, Juells, plate, ornamentes, and other goodes to
theym or any of theym Wythin the said countye of Bedford,
or els where belongyng or apperteignyng ; With the yerely
reprises and deduccions goyng out of the same. And also the
aunswering to suche articles of Instruccions as they, the said
Commyssioners, receyvid from the Kynges most royall maiestye
for the better procedynge in that behalf as here after folowyth.

The Chantry of Kynges Houghton (p. 33).

The landes and tenementes to the sayd chauntry of Houghton, belonging [*value in all*] £20 12s. 2d.; thereof,

Reprises,

In rente resolute, to our souereign lorde the Kynge at [*sic*] to the Maner of Dunstable, by yere, 26s. 9d.

To the lorde Bray, by yere, 10s. 8d.

To the Deane and Chapiter of Poules, by yere, 4s. 8d.

To the prebende of the Churche of Saynt [*blank*], by yere, 8d.

To Lewes Dyve, by yere, 2s. 1d.

To George Alworth, by yere, 3d.

To the Maner of Cardington, by yere, 4½d.   45s. 5½d.

And so remayneth clere by the yere, £18 6s. 8½d.

Money payd to dyuers pore folkes of the Town of Hoghton aforesaid in ayde of the 15, by yere, 20s.

Money payd to John Couper for teaching of 6 pore Folkes children there, by yere, 26s. 8d.

Memorandum that all the landes aforesayd were put in Feffement by Wylliam Dyue, Citezen and Mercer of London, in the yere of our lord God, 1515, to the intent that the said Feoffees shold perceyve and take the profettes of the landes and tenementes aforesaid, and there with to Fynde 2 prestes: the one to syng in Houghton, and the other to syng in a chapell at Sewell in the said paryshe of Houghton, and to kepe yerely 2 obites for the sayd William, and also to pay yerely to a prest to teche 6 of the poore men's children of Houghton aforesaid, and the sayd prest to haue for his syngyng in the said Churche of Houghton, £6 a yere ouer and besydes 26s. 8d. for the teachyng of the sayd 6 poore children, vnto the end and terme of 99 yeres. And if the said feoffees could obtayn the Kynges letters patentes of lycence to mortmayn the sayd landes and tenementes, that then to contynue for euer; if not, that then within six or seuen yere of the end of the sayd 99 yeres the sayd feoffees to make sale of the said landes and tenementes, and the money therof comyng, to be bestowed as herafter is declared; that is to say, the third parte therof to be bestowed

by the churchwardens of Houghton aforsayd and by the said
Feoffes, vppon Ornamentes most necessary for the sayd churche
of Houghton and reparacyons of the same. One other parte to
be bestowed by the said Wardens and Feoffees vpon mendyng
of a certen high way called Pynder's Hill, and of poore folke
and poore Maydens' mariages wythin the sayd parishe of
Houghton, And the other parte to be delyuered to the Abbesse
and Generall confessors of Syon, as in the sayd last wyll
remaynyng at large doth apere.

Also John Couper is incumbent there, of the age of 40 yeres,
but meanely lerned, and teacheth six poore children, and hath
for his stipend 26s. 8d. as is aforesayd.

The Countye of bedforde. Certificate 2.
(Edward VI.)
HOUGHTON REGIS (p. 3).

The Chantry of Kynges Houghton is worth aboue all the
reprises, by yere, £18 11s. 8½d.

John Couper is Incumbent there, of the age of 50 yeres,
lerned, and hath no other lyuing, but for teaching of 6 poore
children in the said parishe of Houghton 26s. 8d., and his
stipend of the sayd Chauntry, which is, by yere, £6.

Gramer Scole of 6 poore children is founded in the said
chantry, and the chauntry prieste doth euer teache theym, and
hath for his stipend, by yere, 26s. 8d.

Continuatur schola with the wages of £6 quousque.

Preacher mayntened, none.

Poore people of the said parishe haue out of the said
Chauntry in ayde of the 15 and other, by yere, 20s. And to
poore peple, at 2 obbittes yerely, 8s. 8d.

William Smyth.

Bedfordshire. Schools Continuance Warrants,
Edward VI. Warrant 16.

Wee, Sir Walter Myldemay, Knight, and Robert Keylwey,
Esquyer, Commyssioners, appoynted by the Kinges maiesties

Commyssion, vnder the greate seale of England, bearyng date
the 20th day of June last past, touchyng order to be taken for
the mayntenaunce and contynuaunce of Scoles and preachers,
and of preestes and curates of necessitie for seruynge of cures
and mynistracion of sacramentes, and for money and other
thinges to be contynewed and paide to the poore, and for
dyuerse other thinges appoynted to be done and executed by
vertue of the same commyssion. To the Audytour and Receyvour of the Revenues of the court of The augmentacions and
Revenues of the Kynges maiesties crowne in the Countie of
Beddford, and to either of them greatyng.

Forasmoche as it appearith by the certificate of the particuler
surveyour of landes of the saide court, in the saide countie, that
the churche of the late colledge of our lady, in the parisshe
of Norell, in the countie of Beddford aforesaide, is a parishe
churche, and that there is no parsone or vycare endowed therin
for the discharge of the cure of the same. Wherfore it is
necessarie to haue a vycare to be endowed there,

And that a grammer Scole hath been contynnuallie kept in
Howghton, in the saide countie, with the Revenues of landes
and tenementes, gyven and appoynted to the fyndyng of a
Chauntrie preest there, And that the scolemaster there hathe
had for his wages yerelie sixe poundes.

We therfore the saide commyssioners by vertue and aucthoritie of the saide commyssion have assigned and appoynted that
the churche of the saide late colledge of our lady in Norell,
afore rehersed, shall contynewe to be a parisshe churche, And
that John Carter, one of the Fellowes of the saide late colledge,
shall be in the Rowme and place of vycare there, and shall haue
for his stipende and lyvyng yerelie tenne poundes.

And that the saide grammer scole in Houghton aforesaide,
shall contynue; and that John Cowper, scolemaster there, shall
haue and enjoye the Rome of scolemaster there, and shall haue
for his wages yerelie sixe poundes.

And we, the saide commyssioners in the Kynges maiesties
behalf, by vertue of the saide commyssion, do requyre you,
the saide Receyvour, that of suche the Kynges money and

Revenues as from tyme to tyme shall be and remayne in
your handes, you do content and pay yerelie, from Easter last
forthwarde, the saide seuerall sommes of money and wages
before mencioned to the persones before rehersed, and to suche
other persone and persones as shall haue and enjoye the saide
Romes and places of the same persones, to be paide wekelie, or
quarterlie, or otherwise, as necessitie shall requyre, vnto suche
tyme as further or other order shall be taken for the same.

And this warraunte shall be to you, the saide Receyvour
and Audytour, sufficient discharge for the payment and' allowaunce of the same accordynglie.

Youen the 20th day of July, in the seconde yere of the
reigne of our soueraigne lorde Edwarde the sixt, by the grace
of god Kyng of Englande, Fraunce, and Irelande, defendour of
the faithe, and of the Churche of Englande, and also of Irelande,
in earth the supreame Heade [1548].

Wa : Mildmay.

Robt. Keylwey.

Examinatur per R. Duke.

Berks. Certificate 51.

(Henry VIII.)

For names of commissioners, see under Hampshire, p. 86.

40. THE PARISHE OF LAMBORNE.

One Chauntre of the Trinitie: founded by John Isbury, by
the Kynges Majesties lycence that nowe ys (as yt ys Reported),
to the entente to haue a prest, to saye masse 4 tymes wekely
in the parishe churche of Lambourne, and to helpe to synge
the devyne seruice there, and Also to teche the scolers of the
Frescole in Lambourne aforsaid ; Whyche ys done and obserued
Accordynge to the Foundacion.

The said Chauntre ys scituate within the parishe churche of
Lambourne.

The Value of the londes and tenementes belongynge vnto the
said Chauntre, £10 0s. 20d.; wherof

For the Kynges majesties tenth, 20s. 2d.

And so Remayneth £9 0s. 18d., Whych Walter Burnell,

Chauntre prest and scole master there, Doth receyve for ys
stypend or salarye.

Ornamentes, plate, Juelles, goodes and catalles, merly Apperteynynge to the said Chauntre, as Apperyth by an Inventorie
therof made, not praysede.

41. THE PARISHE OF CHYLDREY.

One Chauntre, with an Almes house therunto Annexed,
founded by William Fetepas, by the Kynges lycence (as the
Commyssioners ben enforemed), to the entent to haue one prest
and 3 pore men, which prest ought (by hys foundacion) to
kepe and teche the gramer scole there; And the poure lykwyse
ought to be dayly at masse, and there to saye certen suffrages
mencyoned in the same Foundacion (as yt ys Reported). And
Also the said prest to haue for his stipend or salary £8 by
yere, And euery of the said pore men to haue Wekly, 9d., ouer
and besydes, to euery of them 6s. yerely, for and in the name
of there lyuery.

The said Chauntre ys scytuate within the parisshe churche
of Childrey in the said Towne.

The Value of the said Chauntre with the Almes House, in
mony nombred, payd by the Warden of the quens colledge in
Oxford, £14 15s.; Wherof

For the Tenthe, 16s.

For the Preste, £7 4s.

For the 3 pore men, £6 15s.   £14 15s.

Ornamentes, plate, Juelles, goodes, And catalles, merly ap-
perteynge to the said Almes House, as apperyth by an Inventorie therof made; not presede.

48. THE PARISHE OF SEYNT BENNETTES FYNCKE, LONDON.

One Hospytall of Seynt Anthonye; founded
To Fynde one Master, 2 prestes, one scolemaster, and 12 pore
men there, perpetually to serue and saye the devyne seruice,
and to praye for the soules of there founders, and to haue for
theyr stipendes as herafter Foloweth: Whyche Hospitall ys
Annexede vnytede And Appropriatede vnto the collygyatt
churche or Freechaple of Seynt George in Wyndsore, As yt ys

Reportede by Sir Anthonye Baker, clerke, master of the said Hospytall.

The said Hospytall ys scytuat wythein the citie of London, in the parishe of seynt benetes fynck, nyghe vnto the parisshe churche.

The Value of all the landes, tenementes, and other possessions to the said Hospitalle apperteynynge or belongynge, £55 6s. 8d. ; Wherof

For the Kynges Majesties Tenthe, 32s.

For Rentes Resolutes, 47s. 5d.

For procuracions and sinodalles, 2s.

For Brede, Wyne, Wax, and Oyle, £4 0s. 2d.

For stipende of 2 prestes, £16.

For the stipend of the steward, 100s.

For the scolemasters stipend, £16.

For the stipend and commons of 12 pore men, £31 17s.

For the stipend of the Clerke that kepyth oure ladye masse, £9.

For the pencion of the Curate of seynt benet Fynkes, £8.

To the sexten, 40s.   £95 18s. 7d.

And so lackythe For the proporcion of the same House, £40 11s. 11d., Whych ys borne by the Deane and Cannons of Wyndsore, wherunto this Hospytalle ys Annexede Vnytyde as ys abouesaid.

Ornamentes, plate, Juelles, goodes, and catalles, merly apperteynyng to the said Hospytall, ys, as apperyth by A Invetory made and delyuered to the Comyssionours.

Comitatus Berks. Certificate 3.

(Edward VI.)

The Certificate of Sir John Mason, knyght, Thomas Denton, Esquire, and Roger Amyer, gentilman, Comissioners appointed, emonges others, for the Survey of Colleges, Chaunteries, Free chappelles, Guildes, Fraterniteis, and suche like, in the Counties of Bark and Southamton, as well of all ande singuler suche Colleges, Chaunteries, Fre chappelles, brotherheddes, Fraternites, Guildes, and other thinges within the saide Conntie of Bark, which oughte and be commen unto

the kinges maiesties handes, by vertue of the acte of parliamente begon and holden at Westminster the 4th daye of
Nouember, in the Firste yere of his maiesties reigne [1547]; As
also the yerly values, condicions, state, and degree of the same
and euery of them according to the tenour, purporte, and effecte
of his highnes Commission and instrucions vnto vs and others
in that behalf Directed, bering Date at Westminster the 14th
daye of February, in the seconde yere of the Reigne of our
saide souerain Lorde Edwarde the 6th, by the Grace of God
king of Englande, Fraunce, and Irelande, defendour of the
Feithe, and in Erthe supreme hed of the churche of Englande
and Irelande. [154$\frac{7}{8}$].

OKYNGHAM (p. 5).

Oure Lady Chauntry; Erectid and Founded within the
parishe churche there by Adam Mullen, late Deane of Sarum
and other, to mainteigne a priest for ever.

Is woorthe by yere, as apperith by the Suruey, £16 0s. 6½d.

Whereof in Rentes resolute by yere, 58s. 0½d.; Tenthe
reseruyde, 20s. 7d.   78s.

And so Remayneth To Robert Avys, Clerk, Master of Arts,
Incumbent there and teaching a Grammer scole within the
said Chauntrie, being of the age of 36 yeres, able to kepe Cuer,
not hauing anny other lyuing, £12 2s. 6½d.

Goodes Geuen and solde sythe the 23th daye of nouember
anno Regni Henrici VIII 27mo none, sauing certeine woodes
solde by the saide Incumbent to the value of £7 towardes the
payment of his first fruictes; Remayning the 8 daye of
December last paste in the custody of the saide Incumbent
none, besides A chalice poiz 10 ounces. *Examinetur.*

CHYLREY (p. 14).

A Chauntry of the blessid Trinite and Saincte Katheryn,
within the paroche churche ther, And one Aulmes house for
3 poore men vnto the same anexed, claymed to be parcell of
the Quenes College in Oxenford.

Founded by William Fetiplace, who enfeoffed certeine persons
in the moitie of all his manor lande and tenementes Callid

Ledcombe, to the intent that his saide Feoffees, or the prouoste
and Scollers of the Quenes College in Oxford, shulde not only
paye £8 yerly to a preste of goode conuersacion to praye perpetually for his, and his Frendes within the paroche churche
of Chilrey, But also shulde finde habitacion for 3 honest poore
men, And paye unto euery of the saide poore men wekely 9d.;
and yerly to euery of them for his lyuery with lynyng and
making of the same, 9s. 4d. And also for woode and Cooles to
euery of them in the hole yere, 2s. 8d. As by his Laste will
dated the 20th of July, anno 1526.

Amounting in all by the whole yere, As apperith by the
Suruey, £23 13s. 7d. Wherof in

Rewarde to a precher, 6s. 8d.

To Ambros Lancaster, clerke, incombent, teaching a gramer
scole ther, and praying for the founder, of the age of 36 yeres,
able to serue cure, not hauing besides this any other lyving,
£8 13s. 4d. cum 13s. 4d., de dono Thome Fetiplace defuncti.

Almes to 3 poore men, euery of them after the rate of 9d. by
the weke, 9s. 4d. for his lyuery and 2s. 8d. for woode and cole,
with 13s. 4d. emonges them of the geifte of Thomas Fetyplace;
in all per annum £8 6s. 4d. Almes emonges the poore of the
paroche at the obite daye, 7s. 6d. Reparacions of the almeshouse, 13s. 4d.

Reparacion, 6s. 8d.; Renewing of bedding, 6s. 8d.; Releif of
poore men in an almes house at Wantage, 6s. 8d.; per annum, 20s.

Releif of poore Scollers of the Quenes college in Oxford,
40s. Fees of the Suruewor and Stewarde per annum, 13s. 4d.
£22 0s. 11d. And So

Remaineth to the vicar ther for an yerly obite, 4s. 4d. To
the churche wardens of Wantage for an obite, 10s. To the
mayntenaunce and Reparacions of Belles within the paroche
of Chilrey, 6s. 8d.

To the mayntenaunce of lyghtes within the same churche, 5s.
To the parisshe Clerke ther for his Fee, ringing the courfewe
bell euery night, by the yere, 6s. 8d. 32s. 8d.

Goodes Solde, geuen, or spoiled sithe the 23th of nouember
anno 37mo Regni Regis Henrici 8ui [1545], none.

Remaining the 8th of December laste paste nowe committed
to the custody of John Bouncy and Roberte Newbury, 62s. 4d.,
ouer and besides a chalice poiz 11 ounces. *Examinetur.*

*Memorandum vppon sighte of the evidence of the saide
College shewyd by the prouoste of the same vnto sir Walter
Mildemay, Knighte, and Roberte Kelwey, Esquier, and vppon
conference by them had with the Jugges concerning the same :
It semyth that this chauntery is not within the compas of the
statute ; And therefore it is ordered by the saide Sir Walter
Mildemay and Roberte Kelwaye that the proueste and Fellowes
of the same College shall Receiue the Reuenewes of the same
Chauntry, vntill better matter may be shewed for the Kings
maiestie.*

NEWBURY (p. 14).

A Stipendary preste callid our Lady preste. Founded within
the Towne ther perpetually to Selebrate in an Isle ther, callid
our Lady chappell, to the maintenaunce of whiche and for reparacion of the saide Isle certeine Landes and tenementes be
geuen vnto A corporacion ther, callid the corporacion of our
Lady chappell, to the yerly value of £13 0s. 20d.　Wherof

Rent Resolute, 3s. 6d.

The Tenth, 19s. 1d.

Reparacions of tenementes, 9s. 1d.

Almes to 12 poore men Releved in an aulmes house ther,
66s. 8d.　　　　　　　　　　　　　　　　　　　£4 18s. 4d.

And so Remayneth to Thomas Forscote, incumbent, of the
age of 60 yeres, teacher of the Gramer Scole ther, with 3s. 4d.
for wine and waxe, having nothing elles towardes his lyving,
nor is able to teache cure, £8 3s. 4d.

Goodes to the same belonging, none.

One Stipendary preste, callid Henry Wormestalles preste.

Founded by Henry Wormestall, which, by his laste will dated
2⁰ marcij anno 1466, willed that certeine men shulde stande
seased of and in diuerse Landes and tenementes in Newbury
and Greneham, vppon condicion that they and the heires of
them shulde kepe reparacions, &c., and hire an honest preist

to praye for his and all cristen soules for euer, and kepe an yerly obite of 10s.; with this Addicion, that it shulde be alwayes lawfull to the saide cofeoffees to alter and change the same foundacion from tyme to tyme as to their discrecion shulde seme goode, whiche Landes and tenementes be of the yerely value of £13 9s. 8d. Wherof in

Redditus Resoluti by yere, 15s. 3d.

The Tenth, 12s. 0½d.   27s. 3½d.

Remayneth vnto one Thomas Evans, Scole master, techyng a Gramer scole ther, wherof that towne hath grete nede £12 2s. 4½d.

Goodes to the same apperteining, none.

LAMBORNE (p. 23).

The Trinite Chauntry.

Founded within the paroche churche ther by John Isbury, to the entent to haue masse 4 tymes euery weke saide within the same, and also to teache a Free Scole.

Is worth by yere, as apperith by the Suruey, £10 0s. 20d. Wherof

The 10th, 20s. 2d. And So

Remaineth to Arthur Elmes, incumbent, of the age of 50. yeres, able and apte to serue cure, and not having any thing elles towardes his Lyving, £9 0s. 18d.

Goodes Remaynyng ther the 23th daye of nouember laste paste committed to the custody of [blank], 20s. 1d., ouer and besides one chalice, poiz 10 ounces. Examinetur.

Comitatus Buck (et Bed). Certificate 4.
(Henry VIII.)

A brief certificate of the Survey of alle the londes and tenementes belonginge to all and singular Chaunteries, Hospitalls, Colleges, Fre Chappells, Fraternities. . . Guyldes sett and being within the counties of Buckyngham and Bedforde aforeseid surveyed by the Reuerend father in God, John, Bysshopp of Lincolne, Sr John St. John Knyght, Henry Bradshawe,

Esquier . . . the Kynge, Robert Drury, George Wright, Esquyers And Hugh Fuller, one of the Kinges maiesties Auditours, in the [monthes of march and aprill of the 37th and 38th yeres] of the raigne of our Soueraigne Lord Henry the eight, by the grace of God [Kyng of] Englond, Fraunce, and Ireland Defendour, of the faith, And in erthe of the churche of Englonde and also of Irelonde the supreme head, by vertue of our said soueraign Lord the Kinges Maiesties Commission, dated the 14th day of February in the 37th yere aforesaid, [154$\frac{5}{6}$] to theym directid and here vnto affyled and annexid ; as folowith.

Buck.

10. The Parishe of Thorneton.

Bartons Chauntrye, fownded by one Roberte Ingleton, to the intente to fynde a prieste for euer. And that the said prieste shalle gyve yearly to 6 poore folkes contynually 6d. the weke for euery of theyme. And to gyve for the lyuerey of 6 poore children euerye yeare to euerye of theyme, 4s. And also the said prieste to teache the children of the said Towne.

The said Chauntrye is fownded within the parishe churche of thornton aforesaid, and is obserued accordynge to the fowndacyone before declared, And so is verye necessarye.

The said Chauntrie is of the yerly value of £21 11s. 6d. wherof

Paide to the Kynges maiestie for Rentes Resolute, 13s. 4d., and for tenthes, 43s. 1$\frac{3}{4}$d.

In the hole, 56s. 5$\frac{3}{4}$d.

Paied to [   ], yerely, 3s.   59s. 5$\frac{3}{4}$d.

And so Remayneth for the accustomable paymentes as is before mencyoned, viz., for the priestes salary, £9 12s. 0$\frac{1}{4}$d. ; in Almesse to 6 poore folkes, £7 16s. ; and to 6 poore childeren, 24s. ; in all, £18 12s. 0$\frac{1}{4}$d.

The ornamentes of the seid chapell, or Chauntrye, be estemed to be worthe as itt appereth by the inventory, 33s. 4d. The Juelles of the said chapell or Chauntrye, that is to saye, A chalyce of siluer and guilte, weinge 18 ounces, Remayninge in the handes of William Abbotte, Incumbent there.

There is a mansyone howse belonginge to the said chauntrye Prieste, whiche is nowe in the handes and occupacyone of one Humfray Tirrell, And the said chauntrie prieste nor his predecessors had itt this 14 or 15 yeares Which is worthe yearly [*blank*].

And there hathe bene none other dissolucyone purchace or obteignynge of anye parte of Possessiones or goodes of the said chauntrye sithe the fourthe daye of Februarye, in the 27th yeare of our souereigne lorde the Kinges maiestes Reigne [153⅘].

16. ETON COLLEGE.

Founded by Kynge Henry the sixte.

Robert Aldridge, Bisshop of Carlill, is provest there.

The seid college is a parishe churche.

The seid college is of the yerely value of £1066 16s. 9¾d. wherof

Paide for collectours fees and rentes resolutes, and suche other as doth appere in the Ministers accomptes, £62 13s. 1¼d., paide to the provest for his stipend, £30; to 7 felowes at Cs. the pece, £35 ; to 5 chaplaynes, at £4 the pece, one of theyme havynge 13s. 4d. more by yere, £20 13s. 4d.

To the Scoole Master, £10; the vssher, £10 ; and to 10 clerkes callid conductes, wherof one is an organe player, £21 6s. 8d; in all, £121.

Paide to the vice provest, £4; to the chaunter, 26s. 8d. ; to the sexten, 26s. 8d. ; to the under sexten, 13s. 4d.; to the 2 bursarres, £4; and to the clerke of the londes, 53s. 4d. ; in alle, £14.

Paide for the kepyng of 5 obbites for the founder, and for Kinge Henry the First [*sic*] and Quene Kateryne, his wife, quene Margaret, the founder's wife, and for william waynflete, late bisshop of Wynchester, £14 0s. 4d.   £211 13s. 5¼d.

And so Remaynyth, £855 3s. 4½d.

For the whiche some, there is yerely borne the diettes of the provest, vice provest, felowes, chaplaynes, 70 scollers, 13 poore children and 10 choristours, and 5 of the provest his seruauntes, and other seruauntes of the house, And also for liueries, and

Wages, and Reparacions and other charges, as well ordynarie as extraordynarie.

The ornamentes or goodes apperteynynge to the seid college be worth, as by the Inventorie therof more playnly it may appere, £373.

Plate gilte and enamylid, poice, 314¼ ounces.

plate gilte not enamyled, 1,000 ounces.

place parcell gilte, 847½ ounces.

And White plate, 152¼ ounces.

Remaynynge in the handes of the Reuerend father in God, Roberte Aldridge, Bisshop of Carlill, and provest of the college there.

The provest and Felowes, with other stipendaries of the seid college, had by the old foundacions, for their stipendes as folowith, that is to saye, the provest, £75; 10 felowes, euery of theym £10, £100; 10 chaplaynes, euery of theym 100s., £50; the scoole master, £16; the ussher, £6 13s. 4d.; 10 conductes, wherof one is an organe player, and his stipend by yeare, £6, to 3 other at £4 the pece, £12; to the clerke of the revestre, 66s. 8d.; the parishe clerke, 66s. 8d.; And 4 other clerkes at 40s. the pece, £8; in alle, £280 6s. 8d.

Of the which some, the seid college doth paye for like stipendes at this present, as apperith before, in the title of the Volour of the College, but £121; for rewards to the vice provest and other, £14; And for keping of 5 obbites, £14 0s. 4d.: in all, £149 0s. 4d.; bicause that moche of their londes was takyn from theym and given to Wyndesour College by Kynge Edwarde the 4th.

Comitatus Bukingham.   Certificate 5.

(Edward VI.)

14. THORNETON.

A Chauntrie of oure Ladie in Thornton called Barton's Chauntrie.

Certeine landes, tenementes, Rentes, and Fermes belonginge to the said Chauntrie within the said Towne worth by yere £21 11s. 2d.

A Chauntrie in Thorneton called also Bartons Chauntrie.

One Annuitie or yerely stipend, goinge oute of certeine Landes and tenementes, of the colledge called Alsoulne Colledge in Oxforde, paide to a chauntrie priest in Thorneton, geven by one John Burton, by yere, £6.

Obett Rente.

An yerelie Rent paide by Alsoulne Colledge in Oxforde aforesaid, for an yerelie obett to be kepte within the said parishe, worth by yere 6s. 8d.

Item the Incumbent of the said Chauntrie of oure Ladie is called Sir William Abbott, and is of the age of 60 yeres, hauing none other promocion but onelie that, whoo hath doune heretofore, and yett doth, teach a Free schole of grammer according to the Foundacion of the same.

Item there are within the said parishe of Thorneton 60 housling people And one Sir Roberte Bartlett is nowe stipendarie priest there, and is at the eleccion and putting oute of the saide Alsouline Colledge in Oxforde, and is of the age of 80 yeres, &c.

77. GREATE MARLOW.

Obett lande.

Certene landes and Rentes there given for kepinge of Diuers obettes within the saide Towne, worth by yere, 37s.

Lampe lande.

Certeine landes and Rentes there, geven for the kepinge of a lampe light within the said parishe, worth by yere, 9s.

Landes geven for diuers vses.

Certaine landes, tenementes, Rentes and Fermes belonging to the saide vses within the saide towne; worth by yere, £10 6s. 10d.=£12 12s. 10d., wherof in Reprises oute of the saide landes there £7 17s. 6d. and so Remayneth £4 15s. 4d.

Memorandum : that the priest called Sir James Graie, Founde of the said Landes, hauing £6 13s. 4d. yerelie for his sallarie, hath ben and is admitted to teach children, and to helpe to minister in the quier; for that the saide parishe is 4 myles of lengeth and 17 or 18 miles compas, and there be aboue 500 housling people within the saide parishe, &c.

Comitatus Buckinghamie.   Certificate 77.

(Edward VI.)

HUNDREDUM DE BUCKINGHAMIA.

1. THORNETON.

The Chauntrie of oure Ladie in Thorneton aforesaide called Bartons Chauntrie worth by yere, ouer and bysides certeine Reprieses, £19 8s. 0½d.

Sir William Abbott ys Incumbente of the saide Chauntrie.

The saide Incumbent of the age of 60 yeres hath yerelie cominge of the saide Chauntrie, over and besides all Reprises, by yere clere £10 8s. 0½d.

The saide Incumbent dothe teach a grammer Schole according to the fundacion, and hath no other lyving but this saide Chauntrie.

Continuatur the Schole quousque.

Memorandum: there is paide oute of the saide Chauntrie by yere vnto six poor foulkes wekelie, to everie of theyme 6d., which doth amounte vnto the yerelie Somme of £7 16s.

Item paide also to six Childerne yerelie for everie of their lyveries 4s., which doth amounte to the yerelie somme of 24s.

Continuatur to the pore quousque.

The Chauntrie in Thorneton called bartons Chauntrie mainteined by Alsoulne Colledge, in Oxforde, ouer and besides Certeine Reprises worth by yere 108s.

Sir Roberte bartlett, clerke, ys Incumbent of the saide Chaunterie.

The saide Incumbent, of the age of 80 yeres, hath one annuitie or yerelie pencion cominge of the said Chauntrie paide by the said Alsoulne Colledge by yere clere 108s.

The said Incumbent hath no other living but this saide Chauntrie that is presented.

Pencion 108s.

HUNDREDUM DE CHILTERNE.

GREATE MARLOWE (p. 5).

A Chauntrie of our Ladie of great marlowe aforesaide is worthe, bysides Certeine Reprises, by yere £8 17s. 11d.

Sir James Graie, Clerke, is Incumbent of the saide Chauntrie.

The said Incumbent, of the age of [blank] yeres, hathe yerelie for his Salarie or Stipende cominge of the said Chauntrie, by yere clere £6 13s. 4d.

And the said Incumbent is well Learned and teacheth childern there, having no other lyvinge but this.

Pencion £6.

Memorandum : there is to be Allowed for 2 poor foulkes Rentes whiche hath sytt Rent Free this 7 yeres, because thei be verie olde ympotent poor, and not able to paie their Rentes, which is by yere 13s.

HUNDREDUM DE COTISLOWE.

IVINGHOO (p. 10).

The Chappell or Chauntrie of seint James in the hamlett of Aston within the said paryshe of Ivinghoo, worth by yere clere, above all Reprises, 66s. 3d.

The said sir Thomas Barker incumbent there.

The saide Incumbent hathe yerelie coming of the said Chauntrie, over and besides all Reprises, by yere clere 66s. 3d.

And the said Incumbent dothe teach Childerne there *etcetera*, *and haue no other living then is before declared.*

Pencion 60s.

Buckinghamshire. Schools Continuance Warrant. 8.

Forasmoche as it appearith [&c.] that a grammer schole hath been contynuallie kept in Thorneton [&c.], with the Revenues of the late Chauntery of our ladye there, called Bartons Chauntrye And that the scholemaster there hath had [&c.], £10 8s. 0½d. [&c.]

We therefore [&c.], haue assigned [&c.], that the saide grammer schole shall contynewe and that William Abbot, scholemaster there, shall haue [&c.] £10 8s. 0½d.

Cambridgeshire.   Q.R. Anc. Misc. Aug. $\frac{77}{29}$

(Henry VIII.)

WYSBECHE.

The certyfycate of sir Thomas prest, curate of the towne of Wysbeche, John Awsten and Henry Johnson, churche wardens of the churche of wisbeche, to certen articles sent from the right reverende father in god, Thomas, by his permyssyon byshoppe of Ely, and other the Kinges magestyes commissioners, for the survey of all chauntreys, Hospitalles, colleges, fre chappelles, fraternites, brotherheddes and gyldes, and other spyrituall promosyons within the sayd Ile, in the cownte of cambridg, made the 17th day of maye, the 38 yeare of the Reygn of owr Souerreygne lord Henry the eyght, by the grace of god, Kinge of England, Fraunce, and Ierland, Deffendour of the faythe, and of the churche of England and Ierland supreme hedd [1546].

(1) In primis the sayd sir Thomas and the other, to the furste article, saythe that ther is nether chauntre, Hospitall, college, fre chappell, fraternite, brotherhedde, Gylde, or other spyrituall promosyons within the towne of wisbeche, but one Guylde or brotherhedde in the paryshe churche of wisbeche aforsaid, named the Trinite Guylde, and to the same ther is 4 stipendarye prystes, whose names are called Master Henry Ogle, beyng scholmaster, sir Thomas Chameron, sir Roberte Lyne, and sir William Smythe.

(2) Item, to the seconde article, they saye that the sayd guylde was Fownded and begonne in the secounde yeare of the Reygne of Kynge Richard the Secounde, by William sporell, of wisbeche, in the cownte of cambridge, clarke, philippe stanton, of the same towne, clarke, with other clarkes, John clarke, of the sayd towne of wisbeche, and Richard sutton, of the same town, with other mo, the whiche fowndacion was Renued and confirmed by Kinge Henry the sixthe, Kinge Edwarde the fowrthe, and also by Kyng Henry the Seuenthe, and also by our souereygne lord King Henry the Eyght, nowe Reyninge in the 20th yeare of his most gracyous Reygne, as

more planly by ther seuerall charters here redy to shewe, shal
appere.

The Ententes and purposes of the sayd fowndacion is this—

Furste, for the mayntenaunce of godes Service, to be kepte
and celebrate in the parishe churche of saynte peter and pawle,
in wisbeche aforsayd, with certen chapplens or pristes, with
other mynisters electe, and chosen by the Alderman and
brythern. Also to pray for the preseruacion of the Kinges
most Roiall magesty, for the Quenes grace, the prynces grace,
with al his most noble progenye. And for the good estate of
the Alderman, Bretherne, and Sisterne of the said gilde.

Item, to pray for the sowles of the Kinges most noble progenitors nowe beyng departed, And for the sowles also of the
brutherne and susterne of the sayd Gylde, and al christen
sowles.

In consideracion wherof that the sayd Ententes and purposes of the sayd fowndacion myght be better mayntayned,
fulfilled, and kepte to godes honor, their Edifyenge, and Discharge of ther conscyens, they the sayd Alderman and brothern
have hyered, kept, and dothe kepe one priste, being lernid, for
to declare, preche, and teche the worde of god, wherby not only
the Inhabitauntes of the sayd towne of wisbeche, but also
diuerse other thether Resortinge, doth better knowe ther duty
towarde god, and ther trewe and faythfull obedience towardes
the Kinges magestye And also kepe a gramer scole, frely to
teache and instruct childern contynually in godly and vertuos
lerninge, so many as dothe or wil Repare to him for suche purposes.

Also they say that the guylde was fownded for the releffe
of certen pore and Impotent peple, as conserning the same
purpose ther be certen mansyons and howses called the Almes
howses, ordeyned and prepared at the costes and charges
of the sayde guylde, with other distribucions to the pore and
Impotente persons within the sayd towne, as more largly shal
appere by the byll of charges here Redy to sheue. Moreouer,
yf it fortune that any of the sayd bruthern and sustren of the
Guylde falle in to decaye and come to pouertye, the sayd person

or persons so Impouerysshedd hathe 8d. euery weake of the sayd guylde towardes ther Fynding.   Furthermore, as conserning the sayd Ententes and purposes before mensyoned, they say that if the churche steple, or any thing therto apperteyning, stand in nede of making, Reparyng, Renueyng, or other necessary charges as conserning the premisses, that then the sayd guylde hathe alwaye ben so benyfycyall in suche nedes, that by the helpe therof bothe the pouertie hathe ben well spared from beyng contributors vnto the sayd charges, And also the sayd steple and churche, with other necessaries, by the helpe therof, wel and sufficyently buylded, Renued, and provided for.

Finally, wher the sayd towne of wisbeche is bothe muche Replenisshedd with people, and also in great daunger of the waters bothe freshe and salt, They say that the Guylde hathe, and is alway, a great helpe, not only for the administracion of seruice and sacramenttes to the sayd parishoners by the prist and Mynysters therof, but also standithe charged for the reparacions and Mayntenaunces of the bankes, to kepe the sayd waters, for the sauftie bothe of the sayd towne and 14 other townes adyoyning thervnto, the whiche, if any breche schowld chaunce, as god forbydd, showld be vtterly ondone for euer.

.   .   .

(6) Item to the sixte article, thei say that ther is in the sayd Guylde at this present day one Master Henry Ogle, Scolmaster and precher, sir thomas cameron, sir William smithe, and sir Roberte Lyne, and that ther is no mansyon or habitacion other then is here sertyfyed by the sayd Rentall here all Redy shewid.

Cambridgeshire. Schools Continuance Warrant. 21.

Forasmuche as it apperith [&c.] that a grammer schole in Wisbiche [&c.] hath been maynteyned [&c.] of the reuenues of the Guylde there, and that the scholemaster there hath had [&c.] £10 6s. 8d. [&c.].

We therfore [&c.] haue assigned [&c.] that the said schole in Wisbiche aforesaid shall contynue, and that Henry Ogle, scholemaster there, shall haue [&c.] £10 6s. 8d.

Cest?. Certificate 8.

(Edward VI.)

Hughe Cholmeley, William Brereton, Knyghtes; John Arscote, James Starkey, George Browne, Thomas Carns, Esquyers ; John Cheching, Thomas Fletewoode, and William Laton, Gentlemen ; commyssyoners.

11. NAUNTWYCHE.

The Chauntery within the sayd churche.

John Brasenett, of the age of 60 yeres, Incumbent there.

The yerely valewe, £7 6s. 8d.

In Almes to poore Folkes, 26s. 8d.

The clere Remayneder, £6.

Plate and Jewells, 10 ounces.

Goodes and Ornamentes, none.

Leade and Belles, none.

Memorandum : the said town of Nantewiche is a gret towne and hath 1,800 hoslyng people within the same, and is very necessary to haue a grammer scolle within yt, and also A Vicar and Assistaunt to serue the cure accordingly.

21. MACCLESFELDE.

The servyce of 3 Prestes, called the Rode servyce, Jesus seruyce, and the Trenyte servyce.

Charles Alexander, of the age of 56 yeres, and Randall Pykerynge, of the age of 40 yeres, Incumbentes there.

The yerely value, £8 13s. 4½d.

Reprises yerely, 26s. 6¼d.

The clere remayne, £7 6s. 10d.

Plate and Jewelles, none.

Goodes and Ornamentes, none.

Leade and Belles, none.

Being a chapell of ease, is distaunt from the parishe churche two myles, and hath oon Assistaunt appointed to serue the cure there, And hath oon gramer scole alredy within the same.

31. MALPAS.

The Stipendary in the said churche. Richerd Maddokkes, of the age of 51 yeres, Incumbent.

The yerely value, 106s. 8d.

Plate and Jewelles, 7½ ounces.

Goodes and Ornamentes, none.

Leade and belles, none.

Memorandum : within 10 yeres last past there was A Gramer Scole erected in this seyd Towne of Malpas, and the Scolemayster therof haveyng landes and tenementes Assygned for hys Stipende to the yerely value of £12. The same landes nowc beyng resumed and taken awey by one Sir Roger Brereton, Knyght, So that at thys present there ys no scole there kept, Albeyt yt were verey necessary to have a Scole there.

CHESHIRE. Stockport, see post p. 144.

Comitatus Cestrie. Particulars for Schools, Edward VI. Roll 14.

MACCLESFIELD GRAMMAR SCHOOL.

Scola Grammaticalis de Macclesfelde, in Comitatu Chestre, cum terris et Tenementis datis tam pro oracionibus animarum quam pro sustentacione scole predicte.

Terre et possessiones dicte Scole pertinentes valent In [Redditibus]. £11 2s. 8d.

Exeuntes de terris prædictis annuatim, videlicet,

Ad baliuum de Macclesfelde predicta, 10s. 1½d.

Ad Reve Rente, 2s. '

per me Jacobum Starky, Supervisorem ibidem

Summa totalis per annum, £10 17s. 8d.

Parcelle Terrarum et possessionum nuper Collegii Sancti Johannis Baptistæ in Ciuitate cestriæ, videlicet;

Parcellæ Terrarum vocatarum [th]e Prebendes landes in Comitatu Cestriæ valent in [Firmis], 107s. 4d.

Nuper Cantaria [vo]cata le Pettye Chanon [in] Ciuitate Cestriæ valet in [Firma], 100s.

Summa Totalis Valoris, £10 7s. 4d.

examinatur per me Willelmum Rygges,

auditorem.

Sum total of all the premysses, £21 4s.

(In margin) $\left\{ \begin{array}{l} \textit{[faded]} \text{ die Februarii Anno } \textit{[faded]} \text{ Edwardi vj}^{ti} \\ \text{pro libera scola grammaticali } \textit{[faded]} \text{ d in Maccles-} \\ \text{felde in } \textit{[faded]} \text{ Che[stre].} \end{array} \right.$

Make a graunte of the premyssis to certeyne persones to be incorporated for a Fre grammer Scole to haue contynuaunce for ever in Macclesfelde aforesaide, in suche fourme and sorte as other Free Scoles haue ben erected by the kinges maiestie ; Reservyng to the kyng 25s. yerely vpon the same graunte. And the proffittes of the landes to be graunted from mychaelmas last.

(*Signed*)

Ry. Sakevyle.

(On the back is a copy of the original foundation by Sir John Percivall.)

The Countye of Cornwall.   Certificate 15.

(Henry VIII.)

(For date and names of Commissioners, see under Devon, p. 145.)

73. SAYNT MARYE WEKE.

The Chauntrye called Dame percyualles Chauntrye.

Founded by Dame Percyuall to Fynde a pryste for euer, not onlye to praye for herr sowle within the paroche churche of saynt Marye Weke aforesayde, But also that he the sayde pryste do teache children ·freelye in A scole foundede by the sayde Dame Percyuall, not farr distant from the sayde parishe churche.   And he to perceyve for his yerelye stipende or salarye, £12 6s., to be levyed of the landes gyven, amonge other vses, to that entent and purpose.   To Fynde A mancyple also to instructe and teache children vnder the sayde Scole mayster, And he to have for the mayntenaunce of his lyving yerelye, 26s. 8d.   To gyve to a laundresse to wasshe the clothes of the aforesayde Scolemaystre and Mancyple for herr rewarde yerelye, 13s. 4d.

And the remayne of the sayde landes the above-namyde Foundresse wyllede (all charges of reparacions, aswell of the tenementes and houses As also of the chalys and ornamentes belonging to the sayde Chauntrye being firste susteyned and allowed) shulde be expendyde in the keping of an obytt yerelye for herr within the paryshe churche aforsayde.

The yerelye value of all the landes and Possessyons belonging or appertaynyng to the Chauntrye aforesayde, £15 14s. 8d., wherof

Defalked :

For rente resolute yerelye going owt of the sayde landes to dyuerse and sondrye parsons, 21s. 7d.

For the yerelye stipende of Wylliam Chalwell, now Incumbent and Scolemayster there, £12 6s.

For the yerelye salarye of [blank], now Mancyple there, 26s. 8d.

For the rewarde of the laundresse by the yere, 13s. 4d.

£15 7s. 7d.

And so Remayneth clere, the 10th in this Value not reprysed, 7s. 1d., whyche The sayd Foundres wylled to be expendyde yerelye in the celebratyng of an obytt, As is before declarede.

The value of all the ornamentes, Jewelles, plate goodes or catalles belonging or appertaynyng to the sayd Chauntrye Founded by the abovenamyde Dame Percyvall, As by a particular Inventorye therof made at large, and redye to be shewede more playnlye maye appere, 37s.

Memorandum: that the sayde chauntrye is a great comfort to all the countre there, for that they that lyst may sett their children to borde there and have them tawght freely, for the which purpose there is an House and Officers appointed by the Foundacion accordynglye.

77. SOUTHEPEDERWYN.

The Stipendarye, callede Nenweneckes Stipendarye.

Founded by [blank] Nenwenecke, clerke, who enfeoffed dyuerse

Parsons in certayne landes and tenementes to the entent that they shulde Fynde a pryste to have contynuance for euer to celebrate masse, dirige, and other dyvyne servyce for His sowle, and all christian sowles within the parysshe churche of Southepederwyn aforesayde, and he to have for his yerelye stipende or salarye, 106s. 8d., to be taken of the revenuez of the sayde landes enfeoffede amongst other vses to that entent and purpose. To gyve also to the mayntenaunce of a scholar at Oxforde for his exhibycion yerelye, 40s. To gyve to the fyndyng of a poore man yerelye for his releyf and sustentacion, 30s. 4d.

And, fynallye, the abovenamyde Foundar wyllede his sayde Feoffees, being put yn trust on this behalf, to lay vpp and safelye kepe 20s. yerelye of the profyttes of the sayde landes, for the reparacion of the chalys and other necessarye ornamentes for the celebracion of masse belonging to the sayde chauntry.

The yerelye value of all the landes and Possessyons belonging or appertaynyng to the sayde Stipendarye, £9 10s. 8d.

Against the which defalked:

For rente resolute yerelye going owt of the sayde landes, 28s. 7½d.

For the yerelye stipende of [blank], now Incumbent there, 106s. 8d.

For the exhibicion of a Scholar at Oxforde, 40s.

For the fynding of a pore man yerelye, 30s. 4d.

For the reparacion of the chalys and other ornamentes, 20s.

$$£11\ 5s.\ 7\tfrac{1}{2}d.$$

And so Remayneth nothyng, bycawse the charges wherewith the sayde landes arr burdened surmounte the revenuez of the same by 34s. 11¼d. Whyche commythe so to passe by cawse the premysses came in sute, and a greate parte of the issues of the sayde landes have byn expendyde in the sute of the same. Nil.

The value of all the ornamentes, Jewelles, plate, gooddes and catalles belonging, or in eny wyse appertaynyng, to the sayde stipendarye Foundede by the abovenamyde Nenwenecke in the sayde paroche churche of Southepederwyn, As by a particular Inventorye therof made at large and redye to be shewede more playnlye maye appere, 27s.

83. Salteasshe Boroughe.

The stipendarye callede Smythes stipendarye.

Founded by John Smythe For the perpetuall Fyndyng of A pryste Aswell to teache children freelye in A schole buyldede within the towne of Salteasshe aforsayde As also to praye for his sowle and all Christian sowles in a chappell scituate within the sayde towne Distant from the parysshe churche three quarters of a myle or more, and to be assistant yn the mynysterye of Dyvyne servyce ; for that in the sayde paroche (which is large and ample) is but one pryste more besydes the sayde schole mayster, who hathe for the mayntenaunce of his lyvyng £7 yerelye, payable by the mayre and Burgesys of the sayde towne, to whom certayne landes were given by the above-namyde Foundar to that vse and purpose. The remaynder of the sayde landes to be vsede after the goode discretyon of the sayde mayre and other the burgeses for the tyme beyng (all reparacions vpholden and maynteynede) As may be thought beste for the wealthe of the sowle of the sayde Foundar.

The yerelye value of all the landes and Possessyons belonging or appertayning to the sayde stipendarye As by particular bookes therof made and redye to be shewede more playnlye maye appere, £10 11s. 6d., wherof

Defalked :

For rente resolute yerely going owt of the sayde landes to dyuerse parsons, 6s. 6d.

For the yerely stipende of [blank], now Incumbent there, £7.

£7 6s. 6d.

And so Remayneth clere, the 10th not reprysed, 65s., whiche The sayde Foundar willed (all yerelye charges of reparacions beyng susteynede and allowede) to be expendede As the sayde mayre and burgeses shulde best devyse for his sowles wealthe.

The value of all the ornamentes, Jewelles, plate goodes or catalles belonging or appertaynyng to the stipendarye afore-sayde As by a particular Inventorye therof, made at large and redye at all tymes to be shewede, more playnlye maye appere, 26s. 8d.

The County off Cornewall.   Certificate 9.

(Edward VI.)

William Godolfyn, Knyght ; John Graynfeld and Henry Chyverton, Esquyers, Commissioners.

1. THE TOWN OF PERYN,

wherin are Howselyng people, 400.

The Colledge of seynt Thomas of Glasney, standyng in the said Towne, being the parishe churche.

Off the Foundacion of Walter Goode, sometyme Bysshoppe of Exceter, to fynde a Provost and 12 prebendaryes (wherof the said provost and 7 of the said prebendaryes be nowe Residente, And 5 not residente), 7 vicars, a Chapell Clerke, a Bell rynger, 4 querysters, and 3 Chauntre prestes to celebrate in the said colledge.

Memorandum : that this colledge standeth vpon a fayer Havyn, named Falmouth, Where, aswell all kynde of straungers, as other, vpon any Arryvall in to that parties Haue there accesse ; so that sometymes in the yere there Repayreth to the said Haven for Herborowe 100 greate shypes, whiche, beinge there, have allwayes vsed to resort to the said colledge to se the Mynystracion there. And the Walles of the said Colledge on the Southe syde, well fortyfied with Towere and Ordinaunce in the same for the Defence of the said towne, and the ryver commynge to the same, Whyche Ordinaunce perteyn to the men of the said Towne.

This colledge standeth Dystaunte Frome the parishe churche Half a myle and more, Whyche parish churche ys very litle for the nombre of the People in the said Towne.

This ys a meate place to establyshe a learned man to teache scollers and to be a precher.

John Sybbe, a man well learned, Provost there, of the age of 60 yeres, hathe for his sallarye in the said colledge £40, bysides his promocions in other places, £10.   £40.

Rauff Trelobbes, of the age of 70 yeres, hathe for his sallary

in the said Colledge £11, bysides his promocions in other places,
£20.   £11.

Thomas Vyvian, of the age of 70 yeres, hathe for his salary
in the said Colledge £12, bysydes his promocions in other places,
£6.   £12

Mathewe Newcombe, of the age of 60 yeres, hath for his
salary there £11, besides his promocions in other Places, 40s.
                                                           £11.

Mathewe Broke, of the age of 45 yeres, Hathe For his salarye
there £11, besydes his promocions in other places, £20.   £11.

Gerens John, of the age of 46 yeres, hathe for his Salarye
there £11.   And hathe other Promocions, 100s.   £11.

John Harrys, of the age of 80 yeres, Hathe for his Salarye
there £11.   And Hath other promocions, £8.   £11.

Nycholas Nicolls, of the age of 45 yeres, Hathe for his Sallary
£11, besydes his promocions in other places, £20. Whiche
Nicholas was admytted in the said colledge but one daye
before our commynge to take the survey there.   £11.

Prebendaries not Resident.

Henry Kyllyfree, Thomas Molsworthe, Rauf Cocke, euery
of them not resident, hath yerely for their salaryes, 26s.   78s.

Nota for Raufe Coche m^r· Hobbys stole.

The twoo other places be nowe voyde.

The Names of the Vicars.

William Kneben, of the age of 55 yeres ;

John Kylsye, of the age of 35 yeres ;

Robert Morsse, of the age of 40 yeres ;

William Hawton, of the age of 50 yeres ; and

Robert James, of the age of 30 yeres ; euery of them hathe
for their salarye in the said colledge £7 10s. The 2 other
places of the said 7 vicars be nowe voyde, and other promocions
none.   £37 10s.

The Names of 3 Chauntre prestes.

John Chymowe, of the age of 40 yeres, Hathe for his Salarye
in the said colledge, £7 10s.

Thomas Michell, of the age of 35 yeres, Hathe for his salary in the said colledge, 100s.

Rauff Rychard, of the age of 30 yeres, Hathe for his salarye 100s.

And other lyvynges have they none. £17 10s.

The Chapell Clerk.

Rauff Coche, chapell clarke, of the age of 50 yeres, hath for his salary in the said colledge £6 12d., bysydes his meate and drinke, and hathe no other promocions. £6 0s. 12d.

The Names of the querysters.

Henry Mychell, of the age of 10 yeres.

Thomas Wykes, of the age of 12 yeres.

Henry Couche, of the age of 14 yeres.

Henry Goodalle, of the age of 12 yeres.

Euery of them hathe for his sallary 20s., and other lyuynge haue they none. £4.

The Bell Rynger.

John Pownde, bell rynger there, of the age of 30 yeres, hathe for his salarye ther 40s.; aswell for teachynge of pore mens children there A. B. C., as for ryngynge the Belles, 40s.

The yerely value of the landes, and yerely profettes perteynynge and belongynge to the said Colledge, together with 5½ acres of Woode, £228 3s. 7d. Whereof

Paied oute in Reprises to diuers persons, £6 5s. 3d.

The Clere Remayn yerely, with the sallaryes of the Incombentes and other mynysters in the said colledge, and Fees and Annuities, £221 18s. 4d.

Plate and Jewelles, weying, ounces, 493;

in Gylte, ounces, 210;

parcell gilte and syluer, ounces, 283.

Ornamentes valued, by estymacion, £26.

Leade conteyning, by estimacion, 40 Foder; Wherof 8 foder ys taken by vertue of a commission for the fortificacion of the Iles of Sylye.

Belles weying, by estimacion, 4,000 weight.

Other goodes, valued by estimacion, left in the said colledge, as vestmentes, Aulter clothes, orgaynes, and other lyke neccessary for the mynystracion there, £4.

Stockes, none.

Memorandum, that this churche aboute a twelmoneth past, by reason of the open standynge of the same vpon the see, by tempest of Whether fell in to suche decaye that the provost there was Dreven to Borowe £40 to repayer the same churche. And as the said provost and other deposed before vs the comyssionours, the said provost nowe standith bownden for the payment of the saide somme.

Item, this ys a mete place to establishe A learned man to teache a gramer scole or to Preache godes Worde, for the people theraboutes be very Ignoraunte.

5.   THE PARISHE OF SOUTH PEDERWEN,
where are Howselynge People, 300.

A Chauntre within the saide parishe Churche.

Off the Foundacion of William Menwenyke, Clerke, for a prest to celebrate ther in the said Churche for euer, And for to distrybute towardes the fyndynge of a scoler at Oxford 40s. yerely, and to the pore, 30s. 4d.

Sir John Lucas, preste Incombente, of the age of 49 yeres, And hathe none other promocion, a man hable to kepe a Cure, and hath for his salarye, £6 13s. 4d.   £6 13s. 4d.

The landes and Tenementes, given to the said chauntre, are of the yerly value of £11 14s.   Wherof

In Reprises, 28s. 7½d.; vltra, 26s. 8d.; solutos heredibus [blank] pro redditu exeunte de terris vocatis le ford parcella Cantarie.

And so yerly Remanethe with the said 40s. apponted to the scoler & 30s. 4d. to the pore.   £10 5s. 4½d.

The ornaments belongynge to the said Chauntre valued at 3s. 4d.

The Nombre of the plate and Juelles belonging to the saide Chauntre, 7½ ounces.

Memorandum : that a certeyne parcell of landes and tenementes namyeḍ Forde, parcell of the possessions of this Chauntre, nowe in the tenure of Nicholas Glyn and John Helyour, Farmers of the same by Indenture, is charged at 63s. 4d. by yere, in the said somme of £11 14s., And for no more Rente vnto the tyme that the said farmers haue Receyued one Hundred markes whyche shalbe fully by them Receyued at the feast of Seynt Michell the archaungell, nowe next commynge, And Frome thens the same landes and tenementes to be charged yerly at £6 3s. 4d.

Memorandum : that Gentyll Graynfeld hathe the said Pencion of 40s. aboue specified, towardes his exibuscion at Oxford.

6. The Parishe off Weke Beate Marie,

in the saide Countie, where are howselynge people. 150.

A Chauntre at the Awlter of seynt John Baptyst in the northe yelde within the same church.

Off the Foundacion of Dame Tomysen Percivall, wyff of syr John Percyvall, knyght and Alderman of London, to celebrate there for euer, And the Incombent therof to teache chylderne frely in a scole not far Frome the Churche. The said Scole in Decay, by reason yt standith in a desolate place And far frome the markett for provision of the said Scolers.

William Cholvell, Incombent there, of the age of 55 yeres, hathe of the Reuenues of the same for His Salarye and lyvynge, with 26s. 8d. for the vaiges of an vssher, And none other Promocions, beynge a man Well learnede, and a greate setter forthe of Godes Worde, £14 3s. 1d.

The landes and tenementes belonginge to the said Chauntre be of the yerely value, £15 11s. 4d. Wherof

Reprises, 21s. 7d.; To the pore, 13s. 4d.

And so Remaneth clere by yere, £13 16s. 5d. *nota : the Duke of Sulffolke Claymyth 13s. oute of this Sume.*

The ornamentes belongynge to the same Chauntre be valued at 5s.

The value of the goodes or Housolde stuff belonginge to the same, 55s. 6d.

M

The nomber of ounces of plate and Jewelles to the same belongynge, 8½ ounces.

Memorandum : that sympson, parcell of the premysses, liethe
within the libertie of the Duchie of Lancaster.

Memorandum : that one John Deneham, of Lyston, in the countie
of Devonshere, one of the Feoffes of the Founderis of the said
Scole kepyth in his Possession one parcell of lande namyd Ashe,
lying in the parishe of Brodworthe, and other quylyttes thereto
Adioynnyng, parcell of the Possessions gyven for the mayntenaunce of the said Scole of Wyke. And the said John Denham with the profyttes therof payeth £4 yerely to the mancyple
ther, And 18s. 4d. to the launder of the said scole howse.

7. THE BOROWGHT OF LAUNCESTON,

Wherof in [sic] are of Howseling people, 400.

A Stipendarye in the Churche of Mary Magdalen there in the
said Borowght.

Certeyn landes named Bodman, alias Bodyman, geven by
Johne Corrdy, Rychard Coberthourne, and other to the mayre
of the same Borowgh for the tyme beynge and to his successours
Mayres there for euer to fynde a prest to celebrate within the
saide churche, And to teache chylderne gramer ; And also to
the Reparacion of the churche of mary Magdalyn, and further
to do suche dedes of charitie as by the discression of the said
Mayre shall seme most convenient.

Stephyn Gourge, Incombent and Scolemaster there, of the age
of 40 yeres, a man Well learned, mete for the Educacion of youthe
in the laten tonge, Hathe for his salarye and lyvynge of the
mayre and burgeses yerely £6, ouer and besydes a pencion out
of the Possessions of the late Monastery of Launceston, which
ys yerly £10 ; And 13s. 4d. yerly distributed to an aged man
chosen by the mayre to teache yonge chylderne the A B C.
John Bannek, nowe teacher there, of the age of 60 yeres.

                                                £6 13s. 4d.

The landes et Tenementes before rehersed be of the yerely
value of £9 6s. 8d., some tyme letten by yere for 76s. 8d.=
£9 6s. 8d. Wherof

In Reprises, viz., pauperibus, 20*s.* In Reparacions of the Churche, 10*s.* 30*s.*

And so Remayneth Clerely by yere, with £6 13*s.* 4*d.*, the salarye of the Incombent and techer, £7 16*s.* 8*d.*

Ornamentes belongynge to the same, None.

Plate and Jewelles ther nombred, 7 ounces.

Memorandum : that the comens of the same Towne or Borowgh of Launceston be greatly charged for byndynge of Prysoners in the Kynges common Jale there; And Also for Mendynge of Brydges and Relevynge of Pore people in diuers Almese houses there. Item that the said Borowghe of Launceston ys the shere Towne Wherunto all the said countie Haue contynuall Accesse. And Wekely a gret nombre do Repayre to the markettes holden there. And adionaunte to the saide Towne be 12 parishe churches, Wherof the Kynges maiestie ys patron, and hathe the parsonage by Reason of the late Dissolued Monastery of Launceston. And no Viker euer endued of eny of the said parishes, for they ware wonte to be serued with the Religious persons of the said late Monastery.

Item ther ys a verye meate place to establyshe a lerned man to preche, And sett fourth the Worde of god to the people ; And Also to teache Chylderne in theyr gramer and other necessarye knowledge. And where the said scole of Seynt Mary Wyke ys nowe yn decaye for lake of convenyent Reliff for the scolers, this ys a very meate place to Haue the foundacion of the said scole removed vnto, for bothe the said townes of Launceston and Weke standethe within 7 Myles Distaunte.

13. THE BOROWE AND PARISHE OF LYSKARD,
where are Howselyng people, 1,000.

A Stipendarye within the said churche of Liskard set within the same Borowgh.

Off the Foundacion of John Kempe the Elder to fynde a prest to Celebrate in the said Churche and to Helpe the quyer there.

Robert Chamlett, Incombent there, of the age of 55 yeres, And hathe none other promosion ; A man Hable to kepe a Cure, and Hathe towardes His salarye, 47*s.* 5*d.*

The landes and tenementes belongyng to the said stipendarye be of the value of 54s. 5d.   Wherof

In Reprises, 7s.

And so Remayneth Clere by yere, 47s. 5d.

Ornamentes, plate, And Jewelles to the same, None.

The chauntre, Called Clemens, in the parishe of Lyskerd, in the said Borowghe.

Off the Foundacion of one Thomas Clemens, to fynde a prest to celebrate in the sayd Churche, and to Helpe in the quier there.

Peter Waryson, Incombent there, of the age of 65 yeres, and Hathe none other promocion or lyuynge, beynge a very Honest preste, and Hathe all the profyttes to the said chauntre for his lyvynge, He paying almaner of charges, £8 2s. 3d.

The landes and Tenementes belonging to the said chauntre are of the eyrely value of £8 2s. 3d.   Wherof

In Reprises, 23s. 6d., *with* 10s. 6d. *for diuers pauperibus.*

And so Remayneth Clere by yere, £6 18s. 9d.

Ornamentes belongynge to the said Chauntre, 3s.

The Nomber of the ounces of plate and Jewelles, 6 ounces.

A Chapell of our Ladye, called Parke, in the said Towne of Lyskerd.

Certein londes gyven to the said Chappell: A garden with an orchard and one half acre of gronde.   And in the said Chapell was greate oblacions some tyme.

None Incombent ther.

The Value of the said landes belonging to the said Chapell 10s.

Ornamentes, None.

The Nomber of ounces of plate and Jewelles, 9½ ounces.

A bell weying by estimacion, 100 weight.

A Masse of Jesu to be said in the parish Churche of Lyskarde in the forsaid Borowgh.

Off the gyft Foundacion or Feoffement of the said John Kempe, mad to the parishens and theyr successours, to the entent to fynde a prest to saye the masse of Jesu euery Frydaye in the yere, within the said parishe churche of Lyskerd.

Thomas Mownse, Incombent there, of the age of 60 yeres, and Hathe none other promosion nor lyvynge, a man mete to serue A cure, 40s.

The landes and Tenements gyvyn for the said masse to be said there are of the yerely value of 51s. 10d., with 40s. for the stipend of the Incombent, and to the pore, 11s. 10d.

And so Remayneth, 40s.

Ornamentes, plate, and Juelles belongynge to the said masse, None.

Memorandum : that this ys An Aunciant Borowe Towne, Whereof the Kynges maiestie ys lorde and patron, The great nombre of the People, And the contynuall Accesse of the greater nombre Repayrynge to the same Towne considered, We thinke convenient to syngnyfie vnto your mastershyps that it ys a meate place to establyshe A learned man to preche Godes worde, or to Teache A Gramer scole ther, so yt myght stand with the Kynges maiesties Pleasure.

19. THE BOROWE OF SALTAYSHE,

Within the parish of Seynt Stephens,
Where are Howselying People, 600.

Certyn landes within the said Borowghe of Saltayshe,

Beyng of the gyfte and feoffemente of John Smyth and others to the Mayer and Burgises of Saltayshe, to the entent that a prest should be maynteyned to praye for them and their Fathers and mothers, and to Teache childerne there borene within the said Borowgh.

Sir Andrewe Furlong, Incombent there, of the age of 40 yeres, which hathe for his salarye of the said mayre and burges yerely goinge oute of the said landes, and Hathe none other promosion or lyvynge, £7.

The landes and Tenementes ys of the yerely value of £9 13s. 2d., Wherof

In Reprises, 6s. 6d.

And so Remayneth clere by yere, £9 6s. 8d.

Ornamentes belongynge to the said mayntenaunce be of the value 2s. 8d.

The Nomber of plate and Jewelles of the same, 18 ounces.

Memorandum : that the said Brughe or Towne ys dystaunte Frome the parishe churche a myle or more, And standith vpon the Seesyde and daungerouse in Warrè tyme yf the people of the same Towne shuld contynualy Repayer to the said parishe churche, for in tyme past the said Towne haith ben Brente with the Frenchemen when the people haue byn at churche, And for the defence of the said Towne beinge the Kynges maiesties Heneritaunce, ther ys an olde Key that defended the salte water, whyche ys nowe Ruened and sore in decaye, And for the mayntenaunce therof they haue but only the premysses.

23. THE PARISHE OF BODMYN,

where are Howselyng people, 2,000 persons.

A chauntre called Naylers Chauntre, other wyse the chauntre of Seint John Baptyst, founded in the parishe churche there within the Towne of Bodmyn.

Of the Foundacion of one Nayler to fynde a prest for euer to celebrate in the said churche, and to be distributed yerely to the pore 13s. 4d., at the discression of the Wardens of the same church, And also by the foundacion the said prest is bounde to teache yong chylderne grammer.

sir Nicholas Taprell, prest, the Incombent there, of the age of 57 yeres, and hath of the Reuenues of the said Chauntre for His salarye 106s. 8d., And Hathe none other promosion. 106s. 8d.

The landes and tenementes belongyng to the said Chauntre be of the yerely value of £7 19s. 8d., Wherof

In Reprises, 29s. 9d. (13s. 4d. to the pore.)

And so Remayneth clere by yere, £6 9s. 11d., with 106s. 8d. the stipend of the prest there.

Ornamentes belongynge to the said chauntre valued at 3s. 4d.

The nomber of ounces of plate and Juelles, None.

Memorandum : that thys Towne of Bodmyn standythe in the mydes of the shere of Cornewall, the Kynges maiestie lorde and

patron therof, and Hathe . . . the [parsonage] and the
more parte of the [Vicarage] therof. Beynge the greateste
Markett Towne that ys in All the said shyre, Greate Re[sorte]
thether Aswell for the said Markett As for Sessions twoo tymes
in the yere there kepte.

A very meate place for a learned man to be . . . goodes
worde, for the lorde knoweth the said twoo thousand people are
Very Ingnoraunt.

26. The Towne of Trerowe,

where are in Howselynge people, 600.

A Stipendary in the parishe church of Trerewe.

Of the Benyvolence of the Mayer and burges of the said Towne
to fynde a preste for euer to mynyster in the parish churche,
and to kepe a scole there.

sir Richard Fosse, prest, Incombent, and scolemaster there, of
the age of 50 years, hath for His Salarye £6 13s. 4d., and other
promocions none, £6 13s. 4d.

The landes belongynge to the corporacion to the value of £9,
wythe £6 13s. 4d. for the stipend of the forsaide Incombent and
scole master.

Ornamentes, plate, and Jewelles to the same, None.

The Countie of Cornewalle. Certificate 10.

(Edward VI.)

John Graynfylde, surveyor.

1. Peryn.

The Colledge of Saint Thomas Glasneye, standinge in the
Toowne of Peryn and in the parishe of Glavias, where are houseling people, 1,200.

A Scholemaster to contynew ther and to haue the wages of
£6 18s. quousque.

[*Here follow names of Provost, Prebendaries, Vicars, &c.*]

Memorandum : a Scoole there, one of the said vicars scolemaster
late deceased ; for the whiche the people maketh great lamenta-
cione, and it is mete to have another lerned man, for there is

muche youthe in the same Toowne. Also Beadmen and other poore people having any Relefe out of the premisses, none.

7. SOUTHE PEDERWYN.

The Chauntry within the parishe churche of Southe Pederwyn. John Lucas, incombent, for his salarye yerelye, £6 13s. 4d.

Pencion, £6.

Gentile Graynfelde, Scolar at Oxforde, hathe for his exhibicione yerelye out of the same Chauntrye, accordinge to the foundacione therof, 40s.

Pencion, 40s.

Scoles and preachers, none. To the poore people yerelye, 30s. 4d.

9. WYKE.

The Chaunterie of Saint John Baptist in the parishe churche of our Lady of Wyke.

William Cholwell, incombent and skolemaster, for his Salarye clere, £11 13s. 3½d.

[*blank*] vssher, for his wages, 26s. 8d.

George Sprye, manciple there, hathe for his Salarye or wages yerelye out of certayne landes in the handes of John Denham one of the Feoffies of the Foounderis, over and Besides the landes above specified, £4.

Pencion, 66s. 8d. (£16 19s. 11½d.)

The wife of the said George Sprye, laundres there, for hir wages out of the said landes in the handes of the said [*blank*] 13s. 4d.

Pencion, 13s. 4d.   £17 13s. 3½d.

At Launceston. Continuatur quousque with the accustumed wages.

A Scole there. To the poore people yerelye, 13s. 4d.

Appointed by my Lord protectours graces Letters to be removed hense to Launceston in Cornewall, and ther to haue continuaunce, if it shall apier more necessarie ther then at Sainte marye wike ; and vppon Letters Directed to certain of the worshipfull of the Shere it is certefied that the same is more mete &c., whervppon it is so ordred quousque.

10. LAUNCESTON.

The Stipendarye in the parrishe Churche of Mary Magdalene, in the Boroughe of Launcestone, houselyng people, 400.

Stephan Gourge, incombent and Scolemaster, for his wages and salarye, clere £6.

John Balmok, Scolemaster there, A teacher of poore mennes children there A!B C, yerely, 13s. 4d.

The pencion of the priest to be borne by the Inhabitauntes of the Towne, because the Scholemaster of Saint Marye wike by ther owne suete is removed hether.

A Scole there. To the poore people yerely, 34s. 2d., And to the Reparacione of the said Churche, 10s.

Sum of the Schole, £24 6s. 7½d.

20. SALTAYSHE.

A Chauntrie in the parishe churche of saint Stephan, in the Boroughe of Saltayshe. houseling people, 600.

Andrewe Furlonge, incumbent there, for his Salary yerelye £7.

Pencion [blank].

Continuatur Schola quousque with the wages of £7.

A Scole there, and the said Andrewe his Scolemaster, preachers none; poore people having any Relief out of the same, none.

26. BODMYN.

The Chauntry called Nailers in the parrish of Bodmyn. houselyng people, 2,000.

Nicholas Taprell, Incumbent, for his Salarye yerelye, 106s. 8d.

Pencion, [blank].

Appointed to be assistaunt to the cure quousque.

A Scole there, the Scolemaster being the said Nicolas; poore people out of the premisses yerelye, 13s. 4d.

Continuatur Scola quousque.

30. TREROWE.

The Stipendarye in the parish church of Trerowe and Toowne. houseling people, 600.

Richarde Fosse, incumbent there, for his wages or salary
yerelye, £6 13s. 4d.

Pencion, £6.

*The said pencion is paid of the benevolence of the maior and
brethern yerly.*

A Scole there, the said Richard being Scolemaster; preachers,
none; poore people having relief out of the premisses, none.

Cornwall.   Schools Continuance Warrant, 12.

Forasmoche as it apperith [&c.] That a grammer scole hath
been heretofore kept at Peryn, in the parishe of Glavias, with
parte of the revenues of the late colledge there [&c.].

And that a grammer scole hath been contynuallie kepte at
saynt Mary Wike [&c.], with the reuenues of the late Chaunterie of Saynt John Baptist there [&c.].

And that a grammer Scole hath been contynuallie kepte in
the Borough of saltayshe [&c].

And that a grammer scole hath been contynually kept in
Bodmyn [&c.].

And that a grammer scole hath been contynually kept at
Peryn [&c.], And that John Arscot, scolemaster there, had [&c.]
£10 [graunted] to hym by the late Abbesse of syon by wryting
vnder the Covent Seale of the late Monastery of Syon [&c.].

Wee therefore [&c.] haue assigned [&c.] that the said scole at
Peryn aforesaid shall contynue, And that the scolemaister there
shall haue and enjoy the £6 18s. for his wages yerelie.

And that the said scole at saynt Mary Wike shall contynue,
and that there shall be paid yerelie to the sustentacion and
mayntenaunce of the same scole £17 13s. 3½d.

And that the said grammer scole at saltaishe shall contynue,
And that Androwe Furlong, scolemaster there [&c.], shall haue
[&c.] £7.

And that the said scole in Bodmyn shall contynue, And that
Nicholas Taprell, scolemaster there [&c.] shall assist the cure
in Bodmyn aforesaid, And shall haue [&c] £5 6s. 8d. [&c.].

And that the said John Arscot shall teche scole as heretofore
he hath vsed, and shall haue [&c.] £10.

The Countie of Cumbrelonde.
(Henry VIII.)

Q.R. Anc. Misc. Aug. $\frac{76}{5}$. Rentals and Surveys. Roll, 846.

Roberte, bushop of Carlioll, Thomas lorde Wherton, sir John Lowther, knyghte, and Edwarde Edgore, esquyer, commyssioners.

KIRKOSWALD.

Glebe londe and spiritualities pertening to the colledge of *Kirkoswalde*.

Roland Threlkelde, clerke, proveste of the same.

Glebe [*of Kirkoswalde*], 46s.

Tithe Corne, £10 20d.

Tithe Heye, 25s. 11d.

All manner of tithes, 66s. 8d.

Ferme of Cherygarthe, 12d.

Tithe of Wooll, 109s.

Offeringes, £6 18s. 8d.

[*Glebe of Dakcr*], 46s. 10d.

Tythe Corne, £35 14s. 10d.

All manner of Tithe Hey, £4 2s. 8d.

Wool, 117s.

Offeringes, £9 4s.

Sum Totall of the Issues of the parishe churches of Kirkoswalde and Daker by yere, Communibus annis, £86 15s. 3d. videlicet:

Kirkoswalde, £29 9s. 11d.

Dacre, £57 5s. 4d. Whereof

Reprises

Paid for bred, Wyne, Wax, and other necessarie expenses in geythering Tithes of bothe parishinges as apperethe particulerlie by the accomptes therof, 105s.

Item paid for cenage, Pencyon to my lorde of Carlell, subsedie and Procter expences, 38s.

Item paid to sir Roland Thrilkelde, proveste of the colledge of Kirkoswalde, for his yerlie pencion, £20.

Item paid to sir John Skales, vicar of Kirkoswalde, and sir Roland Dawson, vicare of Daker, for ther yerlie pencion, £16.

And paid to sur Roberte thomson, Sir John blenkarne, sir Roberte Redshawe, sir William Sowdean, and sur William Harre, Fyve bretherne for ther yerlie stipende, ar pencioned after £6 13s. 4d. to euerye of them; £33 6s. 8d.

Item paid to sur John Blenkerne, and to sur Roberte Redshawe, two scolemaisters, ouer and besides ther pencions aforsaid, 40s.

And paid to John emerson, 40s., barber; Roberte Milner, butler, 40s.; John Baxster, Coke, 40s.,; and Jane Ewerdley, launderer, 40s.; for ther Wages yerlie, £8.

Sum of all the said deduccions yerlie, £86 4s. 8d.

Et Remanet, 10s. 7d.

And as for anye Jewels, plaite, Anowermentes, or Implementes, gooddes, or cattalles pertening to the said colledge of Kirkoswalde, ther is none, for ther was neuer maister ther that had any soche or euer kepte any House ther, by cause the House was vnfynished.

The Counties of Cumberlande (and Westmorelande). Certificate 11.

(Edward VI.)

Sir Thomas Wharton, knight; Alane Bellingham, Ambrose Middleton, [blank] Lamplay, Cuthbert Horseley, Anthony Barras, and Christopher Martyn, gent., commyssioners.

No. 12. COKERMOUTHE.

A stipendarye in the parishe there.

Vsed to kepe and teache a grammer schole there, And to pray for the soulle of the Foundour for ever.

Rowlande Noble, Incumbent and Master of the said schole, of the age of 36, hathe the clere yerely revenue of the same for his salarie, And his lyvinge besides is nil., 116s.

The landes and tenementes belonginge to the same be of the yerely value of 116s.; whereof

In Reprises, nil.

The Counties of Devon (Cornwall) and the Citie of Exetor. Certificate 15.

(Henry VIII.)

The Certificate of John, Busshopp of Exetor, syr Rychard Edgecome, Knyght, syr Hugh Trevanion, knight, syr Gawyn Carow, knyght, John Grenefeld, Esquyre, John Arscott, Esquyre, Nicholas Adams, gent., Philipp Lentall, gent., and John Ayleworthe, gent.

Commissionars assigned by our most drade soueraigne Lorde Henrye the eight, by the grace of god Kyng of Englande, Fraunce, and Irelande, Defendor of the Faithe, and of the Churches of Englande, and also of Irelande, the supreme Hedd, by force of his graces Highnes Letters patentes, beryng date at Westminster the 14th Daye of Februarye, in the 37th yere of his said graces raigne [154$\frac{4}{5}$] Aswell for the examynacion, serche and enquire of the nomber and names of all Chauntryes, Hospitalles, Colleges, Freechapelles, Fraternities, Brotherheddes, Guyldes, and stipendarye prystes, by what names, surnames, corporacions, or titles they be commenlye callyd or knowen by, accordyng to there seuerall Natures, kyndes, qualytees, and degrees, As to what ententes, purposes, and Dedes of charyte, the same and euerye of them were founded;

The yerely Value of all the landes and possessions to the same belonging, with the ornamentes, Jewelles, plate, goodes, and catalles, with a speciall remembraunce what Chauntryes, Hospitalles, Colleges, and other the sayd promocions sythe the 4th Daye of Februarye, in the 27th yere of the Kynges maiesties Raigne, Have byn dissolued or obteyned by any parson without the Kynges licence, with the clere yerely value of the possessions thereof, And the value of the goodes and catalles of the same. All whiche premisses were given vnto our sayd soueraigne lorde the Kynges maiestie by force of Acte of Parliament, holden at westminster, the sayd 37th yere of his most gracyouse Raigne, As in the same amongst others more plainlye apperythe.

The Countye of Devon.
[See also Addenda, p. 319.]
35. AYSSHEBURTON.

The Guylde called saynt Lawrences Guylde.

Founded by [*blank*], For the contynuall fynding of a pryste, Aswell to praye for the Donars of the landes belonging to the sayd guylde and other benefactors of the same, As also to kepe a scole for the erudycion of children frelye for euer ; who hathe for his wages or salarye £6 13s. 4d. yerelye, going owt of the landes appertayning to the guylde aforsayde.

The remaynder and ouerplus of the which landes is bestowede vppon the reparacion and mayntenaunce of ledes, for the conduction of holsome water to the towne of Ayssheburton, aforsayde, And vppon the releif and sustentacion of suche peple as arr infected, when the plage happenythe to be wythein the same towne, that they, being exemptede from all companye, maye not by theire Infectyon corrupte the hole.

The sayde towne of Ayssheburton is a boroughe towne, and is peplede by estimacion with [*blank*] houselyng peple.

The yerely value of all the landes and possessyons belonging or appertayning to the sayde Guylde, callede saynt Lawrences guylde, £10 15s. 8d. ; whereof

Defalked :

For rente resolute yerelye going owt of the sayde landes to dyuerse and sondrye persons, As by particular bookes therof made maye appere, 32s. 4d.

For the yerely stipende of John Fall, now Incumbent there, £6 13s. 4d.   £8 5s. 8d.

And so Remayneth clere ouer and above all repryses, the 10th to the Kynges maiestie in this value not deductyde, 50s. ; whiche Remaynder is imployede to the vses before declared.

The value of the ornamentes, Jewelles, plate, goodes, and catalles belonging or appertayning to the sayde guylde, with £33 8s. 9d. in redy moneye founde in the store of the same guylde, As by a particular Inventorye therof made at large more playnlye maye appere, £38 9s. 3d., ouer and besydes dyuerse syluer rynges, with other certayne Jewelles and ornamentes of smale pryce, which arr not here valuede.

71. CHUMLEGHE.

The prebende there callede Penelles, Founded by [*blank*]. For the contynuall fynding of A pryste or other lernede parson to be ayding or helpyng in the mynysterye of goddes holye servyce, to be celebratede wythe in the sayde paroche churche of chumleghe. And he to have for the mayntenaunce of his lyving the profytt of certayne landes Aswell spirituall As temporall appoynted owt by the Foundar to that purpose.

The yerelye value of all the landes and possessyons Aswell spirituall As Temporall belonging or appertayning to the sayde prebende callede Penelles, 100s., whiche Possessyons and yerely value byne ymployede to the mayntenaunce of [*blank*] storye, beynge a lyttle childe who goythe to scole, and hathe no other profyttes towardes his fynding and sustentacion, 100s.

There is no ornamentes [&c.].

The prebende there callede Denys. Founded by [*blank*] in lyke maner, for the entent and purpose that the Incumbent of the same for the tyme being shulde be assistant from tyme to tyme in the quyer of the sayde paroche churche of chumleghe, for the mynystracion of Dyvyne servyce there, havyng the profytt of the hole landes belonging to the sayde prebende for his sustentacion and lyving.

The yerelye value of all the landes and Possessyons belonging or appertayning to the sayde Prebende, callede the prebende of Denys, £4 6s. 8d., whiche Possessyons and yerelye value arr ymployede to the Fyndyng of Wylliam Harveye, being a childe at scole, who hathe no other rentes or profyttes for his exhibycion or lyving, £4 6s. 8d.

There is no ornamentes [&c.].

Comitatus Devonie. Certificate 80.

(Edward VI.)

BARNESTAPLE. *m.* 2 (*dors*).

A Stipendarie in the Chappell of Seint Nicholas there. Freholde £7 18s. 8d.

Copiholde nihil, *ouer and besides the Chappell their, valewed at the yerely rent of 2s.*

Memorandum : the same was founded to kepe a grammer scole.

Continuatur the Schole quousyue.

MARLEDON, *m.* 3. *Examinetur.*

A Chauntery in the parishe Churche there.

[*Incumbent*] Thomas Harrys, 100s.

Pencion 100s.

Freholde £12 5s. 10d.

Copiholde, *nihil.*

Memorandum : these premisses were given as well for the mayntenaunce of the seid Chaunterie as for the mayntenaunce of too poore men, every of them wekely to have 8d., And also for the mayntenaunce of a Grammer Scole.

Scole for the Children inhabityng At Marelden Aforeseid.

AYSSHEBURTON *examinetur.*

A Free Chappell of Seint Laurence in the said parishe.

[*Incumbent*] John Favell, £6.

Freholde, £13 11s. 6d.

Copiholde, nihil, *and a lesse of a merkett for yeres yet induryng.*

Memorandum : the Incumbent hereof vseth to teache a Grammer Scole.

Continuatur Schola quousque etcetera.

Per me Johannem predyaux, deputatum Anthonii Harvy, armigeri, particularis supervisoris ibidem.

Devon. Certificate 81.

(Henry VIII.)

CREDITON COLLEGIATE CHURCH. *m.* 1.

Henricus octauus, dei gracia, Anglie, Francie et Hibernie Rex, fidei defensor, et in terra ecclesie Anglicane et Hibernice supremum caput, Dilectis et fidelibus suis, Thome Leigh Militi, Mathie Colthirste, Anthonio Harvy, Humfrido Colles, et Roberto Keylwey, Armigeris salutem. Sciatis quod nos de fidelitate et proinde circumspeccione vestris plene confidentes assignauimus vos, ac tenore presencium damus vobis et duobus vestrum, plenam potestatem et auctoritatem faciendi, peragendi et exequendi ea omnia et singula, que in articulis et instruccionibus presentibus annexis exprimuntur et specificantur, iuxta formam, tenorem et effectum eorundem articulorum et instruccionum. Et quicquid in premissis feceritis nos inde, et de toto facto vestro in ea parte, in curiam nostram Augmentacionum reuencionum corone nostre inscriptum in pergameno sub sigillis vestris vel duorum vestrum indilate reddatis cerciores, remittentes nobis hoc breve vnacum instruccionibus predictis. In cuius rei testimonium has litteras nostras fieri fecimus patentes. Teste Edwardo Northe Milite, apud Westmonasterium, decimo septimo die Maij, Anno regni nostri tricesimo septimo [1545].

Duke.

Artycles and Instruccions for the Kinges Commissioners named in the Commyssion hereunto annexed. m. 2.

The saide Commyssioners shall repayre to the College of Credyton, in the countie of Devon, and also to the College of saynte Marye Otere, in the said countie. And there to cause and procure the Chaunters, Wardens, Treasourers, Deanes, Prebendaries, Bretherne, and fellowes of the said seuerall colleges or of anye of theym, by what name or names theye or any of theym be incorporate, named, or called, or the more parte of the persons of the said seuerall colleges, and all and euerye other person or persons hauynge or claymynge any right, tytle, or interest in or to anye of the said colleges, or in or to anye of the possessions of either of theym, to make seuerall surrenders and gyftes of the said Colleges, and of all the Manors, Lordeships, Landes, tenementes, tythes, heredytamentes, liberties, profyttes, Reuenues and possessions, whatsoever they be, whiche nowe be, or at any tyme hertofore haue been takyn or reputed for, or as parte, parcell or member of the possessions of the said colleges, or of eyther of them, to the Kinges Maiestie, to the use of his Highnes accordinge to the tenour of one Dede of Feoffament and gifte Dyvised and to be deliuered vnto Thomas

Lee, Knight, Robert Keylewey and Humfrey Colles, or to one of them havynge Auctorytie to take the surrendres and giftes of the premysses.

Item after the said surrendres and gyftes taken as is aforesaid, The said Commyssioners shall assigne and appoynte to the Chaunters, Wardens, Treasourers, Deanes, Prebendaryes, and to all and euerye other persone and persons of the said seuerall colleges, or being mynysters of any of the said colleges, havynge perpituyties or perpetuall stipendes, or lyvinges, such yerely pencions and annuytyes to be graunted to theym for their Lyvinges as by the discrecion of the said commyssioners shalbe thought mete or reasonable.

* * * * *

Item, the said commyssioners shall haue power and auctorytie to cause aswell the foresaid persons as all and euery other person and persons to brynge in to theym as well all and euerye of the charters, evydences and Wrytinges concernynge any of the premisses as all and euery other Charters, Wrytings, and evidences towchynge and concernynge any Duetye, pencion, charge, or somme of monye to be paide to anye of the said colleges, or towchinge or concerynge any Dyvyne seruyce, or anye other thinges to be hadde, doone, or suffred within anye of the said colleges.

Item, the custodie of the said colleges, with all the foresaid charters, evidences and wrytinges, and the leade and belles shall be also commytted to the said Mathewe Coltehyrst, Antonye Harvye, and Humfrey Colles, or to twoo of theym, safelie to be kepte to the Kinges vse, vntill suche tyme as the Kinges graces further pleasure be knowen in this behalf.

CREDITON. *m.* 3.

Compotus Walteri Mugge, clerici, Thesaurarij nuper Collegij Sancte Crucis, Crediton, Receptoris siue Senescalli omnium et singulorum prouentuum spectancium ad Sustentacionem vicariorum choralium ibidem de Recepta officij predicti a Festo sancti Michaelis, Archangeli, Anno regni Henrici octaui, dei gracia Anglie, Francie et Hibernie Regis, Fidei Defensoris, et in terra

Ecclesie Anglicane et Hibernice Supremi Capitis Tricesimo sexto usque ad 25^tum Maij, anno regni eiusdem domini Regis Tricesimo Septimo.

m. 3 (*dors.*). Summa totalis Recepte cum Stauro et arreragijs, £71 12s. 0¼d.

Stipendia Vicariorum et ceterorum ministrorum. Et in solucione facta Willelmo Renawdon, Capellano, Vicario Chorali, ibidem tam pro mensa sua quam pro stipendio suo per tempus huius compoti, £4 5s. 10d. . . . Et in solucione facta Philippo Alcocke, clerico Capelle ibidem, pro stipendio suo per tempus predictum, 66s. 8d. . . .

Summa omnium solucionum predictarum, £35 7s. 5½d.

Et sic debentur, £36 4s. 6¾d.

m. 4. Que sequuntur ad canonicos residentes in Ecclesia crediton nomine Distribucionum spectancia.

De ecclesia parochiali de Lanant in Cornubia, que dicte ecclesie collegiate appropriata est, per annum, £76.

Wolsegrove.

Prebenda Johannis Blaxston, precentoris Ecclesie collegiate sancte crucis, crediton, que vulgo Wollesgroue appellatur, valet per annum, £26 0s. 10½d.

Woodland.

Willielmus Hermon, scolaris Exonie, prebendarius de Woodland, cuius valor annuus est, £11 10s.

Aller.

Georgius Denys, scolaris, prebendarius de Aller, cuius valor annuus est, £18.

Stowford.

Edwardus Yerde, scolaris, prebendarius de stowford, cuius valor annuus est, £13 6s. 8d.

m. 4 (*dors.*).   *Vicarij Chorales.*

[*Four in number; stipend of each*], £7 6s. 8d.

Clerici secundarij.

Philippus Alcocke, clericus capelle, cuius Stipendium, £6 13s. 4d.

Egidius Rawe, clericus Secundarius, cuius Stipendium, £6.

Pueri Coriste.

[*Six in number ; stipend of each*], 26s. 8d.

CREDYTON *alias* KYRTON.

Hereafter ensuythe the pencyons appoynted and assegned by the Kynges Commyssioners in that behalfe to the master, prebendares, and other Mynysters to the college there as folowyth, that is to saye :

Fyrste to John Blaxton, precentor of Woolsegrove, £26 13s. 4d.

Item to Water Mugge, Thresarer of Tarswell, £16.

Item to George Mason, prebendary of Henstyll, £13 6s. 8d.

Item to George Carewe, Archedeacon of Totton, prebendary of West Samford, £5.

Item to Adam Traves, Doctor of Lawe, Archedeacon of Exeter, prebendary of Pole, £10.

Item to Thomas Sowtherne, Thresorer of Exeter, prebendary of Rudge, £6 13s. 4d.

Item to William Luson, chauncelor of Exeter, prebendary of Pruscomb, £5.

Item to John Holwyll, canon of Exceter, prebendary of Credy, £5.

Item to John Mason, prebendary of Crosse, £11.

Item to William Hermon, scoler of Excetor, prebendary of Wodland, £6 13s. 4d.

Item to George Denys, scoler, prebendary of Aller, £12.

Item to Edwarde Yarde, scoler, prebendary of Stowforde, £6 13s. 4d.

Item to John Donne, prebendary of Bursales, 40s.

Item to Richard Kenrycke, 40s. ; Richard Bramstone, 40s. ; Henry Hyll, 40s. ; William Horne, 40s. ; and Edward Sheppard, 40s. 5 other prebendaries Bursalles, £10.

Item to Philip Alcocke, clerke and teacher of cheldren and queresters, £4.

Summa totalis annualium pencionum predictarum, £140 6s 8d.

m. 7. The certificat of the Dissolucion of the late college of the Holy cros of Credyton dissoluid by Thomas Legh, knight,

mathew Colthurste, Anthony Hervy, and Humfre Coles, esquiers, the Kinges maiesties commissioners, auctorised for the
same and directed to the Righte worshipfull sir Edwarde northe,
Knight, chauncelour of the Kinges courte of the Augmentacions,
moste hartely Desiring hym to referre the contenttes therof (in
moste humbleste manner) to the Kinges Maiestie in our names,
and further to do as shall be thoughte good to His approuid
wisdome and discreccion in full accomplishement of our duties
in this behalf.

per me thomam Legh,
per Mathiam Coltehirste,
per Anthonium Harvy.
Humfridum Colles.

Collegium de Otery beate Marie in comitatu Devonie.

Q.R. Anc. Misc. Aug. $\dfrac{70b}{65}$

(25 May, 37 Hen. VIII., 1545.)

[*The commission, etc., are the same as for Crediton.*]

Summa Oneris tam Omnium temporalium quam spiritualium
collegij de Otery beate Marie predicta, £389 14s. 8¼d.

Inde in reprisis, £65 5s.

Et remanet clare, £324 9s. 8¼d.

Hereafter folowyth the pencions appoynted and assigned by the
Kynges Comyssioners in that behalff to the Master and
prebendaryes, and other Ministers of the college of seynt
Mary Otery.

Prebendaries.

Fyrst to John Fyssher, Wardyn there, £33 6s. 8d.

Item to Sir John Hount, clerke, Mynyster there, £12.

Item to Sir Roberte Peryns, clerke, Chauntour ther, £12.

Item to Sir Roger Stockeman, clerke, sexton there, £12.

Item to Sir John Tybbes, clerke, prebendary there, £10.

Item to Sir Harry Spycer, clerke, prebendary ther, £10.

Item to Sir Thomas Rowsewell, clerke, prebendary ther, £8.

Item to Sir John Lylle, clerke, prebendary ther, £8.

Stypendaryes.

Item to Sir Olyuer Southorn, parysshe priste ther, £8.

Item to one other parysshe preste, callyd Sir Richard Falbys, £6 13s. 4d.

Item to John Parke, chapell clerke, to hym grauntid by letteres patent vnder the common seale, £6 13s. 4d.

Item to Sir John Chubbe, preste, beyng scolemaster ther, £10.

Item towardes the Wagez of 2 parysshe clerkes, videlicet, William Martyn and Michaell Stonyng, 13s. 4d.

Summa Totalis, £137 6s. 8d.

The Countye of Dorsett. Certificate 16.

(Edward VI.)

Thomas Speke, Hughe Powlett, John Seintlowe, John Rogers, & Thomas Dyer, knights; Robert Kaylewey, William Morice, George de la lynde, and Robert Metcalf, esquiers; William Hartegill and John Hannam, gentillmen, Commyssyoners.

DECANATUS DE BRYTPORTE. NETHERBURY.

57. Cantaria de Netherburye in ecclesia de Netherburye, Johannes Neweton, incumbens, ibidem, £7 13s. 4d.; wherof

Deducted for money Payde for the obbyte of the funder And Distributed emongest the powre people, 20s.

And for the 10th, 10s. 9¾d.

And so Remaneth Clere, £6 2s. 6¼d.

All whiche he receyued yerely of Henry Powlet & Mary, his wife, but oute of what landes he knowethe not.

Ther is a Gramer Scole kepte by Sir Martyn Smythe, preste, and receuyth for his wagis 106s. 8d. yerelye, by the handes of John Herne and Henry Sawe.

Ther is no power people releved, nor yet precher founde of the premyssez.

Continuatur quousque.

DECANATUS DE WHITCHURCHE. LYME REGIS.

73. Seruicium beate Marie in Lyme Regis fundatum per diuersas personas, 38s. 11d.

All the said landes apperteynyng to the said seruice was geven to the mayntenance of our lady seruice in Lyme Regis abouesaid to the fynding of A clerke and children, as in ther certificate it will appere.

Respectuatur pencio.

MIDDLETON TREGONNELL.

81. Memorandum : that ther ys A fre Scole Foundyd by Sir John Leder, prist, with other in the paryshe of Middelton Tregonnell, the landes and Tenementes wherof are in the tenure of Robert Best, of Lytle Mayne, Amountynge to the summe of £8 by the yere ; whych sayd some of £8 ys yerelye payd to the scolemaster for his stypend, the whych landes stand in feoffes handes to the use of the sayd scole, and that many gentylmen of the sayd shire of Dorset be infeoffyd in the same landes to the use abouesayd, as in ther certyficate exhibityd to the Kynges comyssioners yt wyll appere.

Respectuatur quousque.

DECANATUS DE DORCHESTER.

84. Libera capella sancti Johannis in Dorchester. Edwardus Weldon, incumbens, ibidem, £10 4s. 6d. ; wherof

Deductyd for Rente resolute, 42s. 8d.

Decima, 6s. 5d.

And so Remayneth clere, £7 15s. 5d.

Whiche the sayd Edwarde Weldon Recauyth towardes his exhibiccion at the vniuersite in Oxford, by vertue of the Kynges letters patents, dated 3^{die} Augusti, Anno 32do nuper Regis Henrici 8^{ui}.

Pencion, £6.

JURISDICCIO DE SHIRBORNE.

91. Hospitale siue Domus leprosorum sancti Johannis Evangeliste in Shirborne, £35 8s. 6d. Wherof

Deductyd for Rente Resolute, £4 3s. 6d.

And so Remayneth clere, £31 5s.

Of the Whych the prest there hath yerely for his stipend, 106s. 8d.

And the resydewe beynge £20 19*s.* ys ymployed to the fyndynge of 12 powre impotent men and 4 powre women, accordyng to the foundacion therof, &c.

Memorandum for a Scole to be in Shirborne; continuatur quousque.

WYMBORNE.

106. Cantaria Margarete Comitisse Rychemond et Derbie, matris Domini Regis Henrici Septimi, nullus incumbens ad presens, £11 17*s.* 4*d.*

Deductyd for Rente Resolute, 15*s.* 3½*d.*

Decima, 19*s.* 1½*d.*

And so Remayneth clere, £10 2*s.* 11*d.*

Memorandum that this was foundyd to the intent that the incumbent therof shuld say masse for the solles of the founders, and to be a Scolemaster, to teche frely almanner of childern Gramer within the same College as in ther certyficate yt maye appere. In which sayd premisses ther ys no Scole kept now, by reason that yt ys in the Kynges handes, by the deth of the late [master] ther; neverthelesse, yt ys very requisite and necessary to have sayd Scole maynteyned, for the towne of Wymborne ys a greate market towne and a through fare, and hath many children therin, and ther ys no Gramer Scole kept within 12 myles of Wymborne aforsayd, at which place the poore men dwellynge in Wymborne and nere therabout are not able to kepe ther children; therfore yt ys very requisite that the sayd Scole may remayn stille for the bryngynge vp of yonge Children in larnynge frelye, without any thynge payinge, as yt was in tymes past.

Continuatur quousque.

Memorandum for a Scole to be hadd in Wymborne.

Memorandum for the appointment of the Scholemaster, Symond Smith, Master of Art, recommended by Mr. Cheke, appointed to be scholemaster there quousque.

[Note at foot of roll.] *The officers think most convenient to appoint a Schole and an Hospitall at Sherborne, and the like at Wimborne, being the places most met for the purpose.*

BLANDFORD.

115. Libera capella de Westhemesworth, Doctor Benett, incumbens, 53s. 4d.

Decima, 5s. 4d.

Remanet, 48s.

Whyche sayd some of 53s. 4d. the incumbent yerely receavyd to his owne vse.

Memorandum that the sayd Chappell was ordeynyd for a Scolemaster, to be maynteyned in Blanford aforsayd, as by an exemplyficacion vnder the seale of the Court of Augmentacions and Reuenues of the Kynges Crowne yt wyll appere.

Pencion, ~~58s. 4d.~~ [*sic*], 48s.

No cause of continewance there, but it may well be added the Schole at Wimborne.

Dorset. Schools Continuance Warrant, 23.

Forasmoche as it apperith [&c.] that a grammer schole hath been contynuallie kept in Netherbury [&c.] with the revenues of the late chauntrie of Netherbury, And that the scholemaster there hath had [&c.] 106s. 8d. [&c.],

And that a Fre grammer schole hath been kept in Wymborne [&c.], and that the Scholemaster there hath had [&c.] £10 2s. 11d. [&c.],

We therefore [&c.] have assigned [&c.] that the said grammer schole in Netherbury aforesaid shall contynue, And that Martyne Smythe, scholemaster there, shall haue [&c.] 106s. 8d. [&c.],

And that the said gramer schole in Wymborne aforesaid shall contynue, And that the Scholemaster there shall haue [&c.] £10 2s. 11d. And that John Dooe, late vicar of the firste pre-bende in the said colledge of Wymborne; John Clerke, late vicar of the seconde prebende in the same colledge; Walter Mathewe, late vicar of the thirde prebende in the same colledge; and John Goddyng, late vicar of the fourth prebende in the same colledge, shall be curates of the parishe churche of Wymborne aforesaid, and of the three chappelles annexed and belonging to the same, and that euery of the same curates shall haue wages yerelie, £6 13s. 4d.

Comitatus Dorsete.   Particulars for Schools.

Edward VI.   Roll 13.

SHERBORNE GRAMMAR SCHOOL.

22 die Marcii, Anno 6 Regni Regis Edward VI[u]. [155½].

Landes appoynted by the kinges maiestie for a Free grammer Scole in the Towne of Shirbourne in the Countie of Dorset.

Cantaria de Martocke in Comitatu Somersete.

Valet In [Redditibus], £14 5s. 4d.   Inde

Reprise In [Redditibus Resolutis], £6 18s. 4d.

Et valet clare, vltra Reprisas predictas, per Annum, £7 7s.

Memorandum : that all the landes belonging to the Chauntrie of Martocke abouesaid lyeth in the Countie of Dorset, except the Chauntrye house of the yerely value of 4d., as is aboue mencioned, and that ther is no other landes belonging to the said Chauntry then is above mencioned.

Cantaria Sancte Katherine infra ecclesiam parochialem de Gillingham in Comitatu Dorsete.

Valet In [Redditibus], £6 13s. 4d.

Cantaria in Lychett Matrauers, vocata Gybbons Chauntrie, in Comitatu Dorsete predicto, Valet In Redditu, 40s.

Libera Capella de Thornton, infra parochiam de Marnehull, in dicto Comitatu Dorsete.   Valet In [Redditibus], 54s.

Memorandum : that ther is no other landes belonging to the Chauntries in Gillingham and Lichett Matravers or the fre chappell of Thorneton, in the parishe of Marnehull, then is above Declared.

Triginta acre Terre in parochia de Symondesborowe, in Comitatu Dorsete, parcella Cantarie Sancte Katherine, ex fundacione Johannis Wadham, in ecclesia parochiali de Ilmynster, in Comitatu Somersete.   Valent In Redditu, 40s.   Inde

Reprise In Redditu Resoluto, 12d.

Et valent clare vltra Reprisas predictas per annum, 39*.

Summa Totalis Annui Valoris terrarum pertinencium Cantariis et liberis Capellis predictis, £27 12s. 8d. Inde
In Redditibus Resolutis ut particulariter superius patet, £6 19s. 4d.
Et Remanent clare per Annum, £20 13s. 4d. Inde in
Annuali redditu reseruando domino Regi, 13*. 4d.
Et sic remanent clare, £20.
Examinatur per me Henricum Leke, deputatum Auditorem.

29 die Marcii, Anno Regni Regis Edwardi VI". quarto [1550].

The kinges maiestie, by thadvise of his prevy Counsaill, is pleased and contented that [a] free grammer Schole shalbe erected and establisshed in Shirbourne in the Countie of Do[rset, an]d Landes to the yerely value of £20 to be geven and assured by his highnes to the maynetenaunce thereof.

And that there shalbe a Corporacion of 20 of the Inhabytauntes of the Towne and parishe of Shirbourne aforesaid to be enhabled to haue properties [in] succession as gouernours of the possessions, reuenues, and goodes of the same Scole, And to haue powre to Receyve the landes to be appoynted for the said Scoole, And to haue thorder and gouernaunce therof.

Wherefore there must be a bill therof devysed accordingly, and a graunte to be made of the landes aboue rehersed with the Issues and proffittes therof from the annuncyacion of our lady last, to the Gouernours of the possessions, reuenues, and goodes of the said Scole, and to their Successours with a Lycence also that they may take and Receyve by waye of purchase or gifte other landes and heredytamentes hereafter to the yerely value of £20.

(*Signed*)
Ry. Sakevyle.

Durham, Bishoprick of. Certificate 18.

(Henry VIII.)

(*For commissioners see under Northumberland, p.* 155.)

63. THE CHAUNTRIE OF OUR LADY AND SEYNT CUTBERT
(In the cathedrall churche of Durham).

The said chauntrie was founded by one Thomas Langeley, somtyme bisshopp of Durham, John Thoralbey and John Newton, chapleyns to the said bisshopp, to fynde 2 priestes to pray for their Sowles, and all christen sowles ; and also to kepe 2 Free Scooles, the one of Grammer, and the other of Songe, in the Citie of Durham, for all maner of children that should Repayre to the said scooles, and also to distribute in Almes yerely to poore people, 13*s.* 4*d.*, whiche ordynance hath ben so vsed hitherto.

The yerely valewe, according to the booke of fyrste fruytes, £19 15*s.* 5*d.*   The yerely valewe, according to this Survey, £20 13*s.* 4*d.*, as appereth by A Rentall; whereof is paid owt in Almes yerely, 13*s.* 4*d.*, and for the Kinge's maiesties tenths, 39*s.* 7½*d.*, as appereth by the said Rentall, 52*s.* 11½*d.*

And Remayneth clerely, £18 0*s.* 4½*d.*, whiche Robert Hertborne and William Cockey, priestes, Incumbentes of the same, kepyng 2 Scooles in maner and fourme aforsaid, haue yerely for their Stipendes.

The said chauntrie is founded in the cathedrall churche of Durham aforsaid.

The valewe of the Ornamentes, &c., £4 19*s.*, as appereth by A particuler Inventory of the same.

Ther were no other landes nor yerely prouffittes apperteynyng or belongyng to the said chauntrey, syth the 4th day of February, in the 27th yere of the Kinge's maiesties Reigne, more then is before mencyoned.

85. THE GUYLDE OF THE TRINITIE IN BARNARD CASTELL
(AFORESAID).

The said Guylde was founded and endowed with certen landes, by Gifte of the brethern and other benefactors of the

same, of auncyent tyme, to fynde A preste to be namyd the
Guylde preste, to say masse dayly at the 6th houre of the
clocke in the mornyng, and to be resident at Mattens, Masse,
and Evensonge, and to kepe A free Grammer scoole and A Songe
scoole for all the children of the towne ; and to kepe one Obitt
yerely for all the Founders and benefactors of the said Guylde
by Reporte.

The yerely valewe, according to the booke of the fyrste
fruytes, &c., *nihil*, for it doth not appere in the Abstracte
taken owt of the courte of the first Fruytes and tenthes to be
charged ther.

The yerely valewe, according to this Survey, £4 9s. 4d., as
appereth by the Rentall, whereof is paid owt for a Rent
resolute, 10d., and for one yerely Obitt, 7s. 6d., as appereth by
the Rentall, 8s. 4d.

And Remayneth clerely, £4 0s. 12d., whiche are employed
to the sustentacion and Relief of Peter Coward, priest, Incumbent of the same.

The said Guylde is founded in the chapell or churche within
the towne of Barnard castell aforesaid, Beying within the
parishe of Gaynford, 6 myles distant from the parishe churche.

The valewe of the Ornamentes, &c., *nihil*, for ther ben neyther
Goodes, catalles, nor ornamentes apperteynyng to the same.

Ther wer no other landes nor yerely proffittes apperteynyng
or belonging to the said chauntrie syth the 4th day of
February, in the 27th yere of the Kinges maiesties Reigne
more then is before mencyoned.

102.   The Chauntrie of all Sayntes, in the parisshe of
Darlyngton
(In the countie of Durham aforsaid).

The said chauntrie was founded by one Robert Marshall,
clarke, to Fynde a priest for euer to pray for his Sowl and all
christen sowles, and to kepe one yerely Obitt and A Free Scoole
of Grammer for all maner of children thider resortyng, and he
to haue the Reuenuez of the same for his seruyce. [The yerely
valewe, according to the booke of the fyrste fruytes, &c.], 114s.

The yerely valewe, according to this survey, £4 11s. 8d., as appeareth by a Rentall, whereof is paid owt for one yerely Obitt, 12s., and for the Kinges maiesties tenths, 11s. 5d., as appeareth by the said Rentall, 23s. 5d. And Remayneth clerely, 68s. 3d., whiche ben employed to the fyndyng of a Scoole master according to the order of the Foundacyon.

The said chauntrie is founded in the parishe churche of Darlington aforsaid.

The yerely valewe of the Ornamentes, &c., *nihil*, for ther be nether Goodes, Catalles, nor ornamentes apperteynyng to the same.

Ther wer no other landes nor yerely proffittes apperteynyng or belongyng to the said chauntrie syth the 4th day of February, in the 27th yere of the Kinge's maiesties Reigne more then is before mencyoned.

[See also Addeuda, p. 319.]

Durham. Schools Continuance Warrant, 9.

Forasmoche as it appearith [&c.] that there hath been a Grammer Scole contynually kepte in Darlyngton [&c.], with the reuenues of the late chauntrie of all sayntes founded within the parishe churche of Darlyngton aforesaid, And that the scolemaster there hath had [&c.] £4 8d. [&c.].

We therefore [&c.], haue assigned [&c.] that the said Grammer Scole in the paryshe of Darlyngton aforesaid shall contynue, And that Thomas Richardson, Scholemaster there, shall haue [&c.] £4 8d.

Essex. Certificate 20.

(Henry VIII.)

Commission annexed, directed to Edmund, Bishop of London, Richard Legh, Knt., Sir John Smythe, Knt., John Cocke, Esq., Nicholas Bristowe, Esq., and John Goldyng, Esq., dated 14th Feb. 37 Hen. VIII., 154⅚.

31. WALDEN.

A Free Scole ther, foundid,

To Find A priest for euer to teche and lerne young Childryn

both Gramer and other syences, per licenciam Domini Regis nunc Henrici 8ui.

The said Scole howse is Foundid by sides the Church yarde in Walden Aforesaid, And ther is taught in it Abought the Nomber of 60 childryn and Aboue.

And is Worth by yere £10 6s. 8d. Wherof

For rentes resolute, 6d.; For the 10th, 20s.   20s. 6d.

And so remaineth clere, £9 6s. 2d.

43. PLACYE.

Collegium ibidem, Foundid

To Find A Master and 8 priestes, 2 Clerkes, and 2 queresters, for euer, by licens of Kyng Rychard the Seconde, Whereof ther is at this Daye but A Master and 5 priestes, 2 Clerkes, and 2 queresters.

The said College is the Parishe Church of the Towne of Placye, and they haue none other Church ther but only the same.

And is Worth by yere £145 16s. 3d., wherof

For the Wages of the Curate of Whitstaple, £8.

For Rentes resolute, 24s. 7d.

For the 10th, £13 18s. 0¾d.

For procurator and Sinodalles, 2s. 6d.

For a pencyon to the vycar of moche Waltham, 10s.

For certen obites yerely, 23s. 5d.

For Fees grauntid by letteres patentes, £8.   £32 18s. 6¾d.

And so remaineth clere, £113 17s. 8½d.

Comitatus Essexie. Certificate 19.

(Edward VI.)

John Reinsforthe, Henrie Parker, and John Wentwoorthe, Knightes; John Cocke, William Bradburye, Fraunces Sowthewell, Thomas Goldinge, and Mathewe Coltehurste, Essquires; Reignolde Hollingworthe and Roger Challoner, gentlemen; commyssioners.

1. PRITWELL.

Laundes and tenementes in pritwel in the seid countie.

Putte in feoffament by 2 Wardens, one Master and one priest, and certeine bretherne and sisterne there, to diuerse persons, to Finde a priest callid Jesus priest their, for ever, by license of Kinge Edwarde the Fowerthe.

And one sir William Rowbothum, clerke, of the age of 52 yeres, of honest conversation, And teachithe a scole their, having none other lyvinge, is nowe Incumbent theroff.

The seide towne is a populous towne, havinge in yt 300 howselinge people.

The seid priest singithe within the seid churche of pritwell.

The yerelie valewe of the same amountith to the some of £7 17s.; whereof in

Rent resolute to diuerse lordes by the yere, 23s. 1d.

And so remaynithe cleare to the Kinges Majesties vse, £6 14s. 3d.

The valewe of the plate, Juelles, and other implementes, viz., One chalice poysaunt 10 ounces, the ounce at [blank] 10 ounces.

Four scochins of silver, poysaunt 2 ounces, the ounce at [blank], 2 ounces.

Item 28 spoons of silver, poysaunt 20½ ounces, the ounce at [blank], 20½ ounces.

One Seall of silver, poysaunt 2 ounces, the ounce at [blank], 2 ounces.

Item 2 Masers of silver poysaunt, without the wood, 12 ounces, the ounce at [blank], 12 ounces.

Diuerse other implementes, prysed togither at £4 5s. 2d., 153½ ounces.   £4 5s. 2d.

2. ORSETT.

Laundes and tenementes in orset in the seid county.

Put in feoffament by Thomas Hotofte, deceased, to finde a priest for ever to singe masse in the parishe churche of Orset aforeseid, and also to teache a scole, and to serve the cure.

And one sir Edmunde Talbote, clerke, of the age of 78 yeres or their abowtes, havinge none other livinge, and of Good conversacion, and teachithe chylderne their, is nowe Incumbent thereof. The seid Towne of Orset ys a populus towne, Havinge in yt by estimacion Fower Hundrythe of Howselinge people.

The seide Incumbente celebratythe in the seide churche of Orset.

The yerelie valewe of the same, with the Ferme of one tenement, gardine, and orcharde, Copieholde of the byshop of London as of his manour of Orsett aforeseide, doith amownte to the summe of £7 16s. 8d.; whereof, in

Rent resolute to diuerse lordes by the yere, 20s. 11d.

And so Remaynithe cleare to the Kinges majesties vse £6 15s. 9d.

Goodes, catelles, &c., *nulla.*

4. WRITTLE.

Londes and tenementes in Wryttle predicta.

Put in feoffament to diuerse persons to Find a priest callid Sewall bromefeldes, alias our ladies, chauntrie, the seid priest to say dyvine seruice in a chapple in the parishe churche yerde of wrytle aforeseide.

Ande one sir Robert Cowple, clarke, of the age of 47 yeres, havinge none other lyvinge, And teachith childerne in the seide Towne of Wyrttle, and of goode Conversacion, is nowe Incumbent their.

The seide Incumbente celebratithe in the seid churche of wryttle.

The yerlie valewe of the same chantrie doithe amount to the summe of £15 10s. 6d.; wherof in

Rent resolute to diuerse Lordes their By the yere, with 40s. to one clerke their, £4 3s. 3d.

And so Remainith cleare to the Kynges majesties vse, £11 7s. 3d.

The valew of the implementes their, viz. :

In yerne, glasse, stone and timber, 66s. 8d.

2 Bells poisaunte 3 cwt., metall, at 16s. the hundrithe, 48s.

One blewe vestment, with other diuerse implementes, praised at 6s. 10d.

In leade 6 foders and a quarter, at £4 the foder, £25.

£31 0s. 18d.

o

5. COGGESHALL.

Landes and tenementes in Coggeshalle in the seid county of Essex.

Put in feoffament by diuerse and sundry persons to the main-tenaunce of a preste forever, the seid priest to singe masse in Coggeshall aforeseid, and Also to helpe serue the cure.

Ande one Sir Thomas Frauncis, clerke, of the age of 56 yeres, hauinge none other promocion, and teachithe a Scole their, and of good vsage and conversacion, is nowe Incumbent therof.

The Seide Incumbent celebratythe in the seide churche of coggeshall.

The yerely valewe of the same doth Amownte to the summe of £7.

Rente resolute, *nullus.*

Goodes, catelles, &c., *nulla.*

Memorandum : it is to be considered that the same towne of coggeshall is a populus towne, and hauinge in yt to the nomber of a Thowssand of Howsellinge people, and haue no more but the vicar and the seid chauntrie priest to minister their, which is not able to doe the same without helpe.

8. BOCKYNGE.

Landes and tenementes in bockinge in the seide countye.

Put in Feoffament by william dorewarde to finde a priest their callid dorewarde's priest, to singe Masse and to helpe serue the cure in bockinge aforeseide.

And one Sir John Kinge, chauntrye priest their, of the age of 34 yeres, hauinge none other promocion, literate, And Teachithe childerne to wrytte and Reade their, And of good conversacion, is nowe Incumbent thereof.

The seide Incumbente celebratithe in the seid church of Bockynge.

The yerelie valewe of the same doithe Amownte to the summe of £8. Wherof in

Rente resolute to diuerse lordes their, by the yere, 2s.

To the poore, 6s. 8d.   8s. 8d.

And so Remaynithe cleare to the Kinges Maiesties vse, £7 11s. 4d.

The valewe of the plate and other implementes, &c., viz. :

2 vestmentes withe two olde albes, praysede at 3s. 4d.

Diuerse other impleamentes, praysede togither at 20d.   5s.

Memorandum : their is in the same towne of Bockinge to the number of 800 of howselinge people, which seid towne is a Thorowght-Fare and market towne.

10. BRAUNTRE.

Londes and tenementes in Braynctre, in the cowntye of Essex.

Put in feoffament to diuerse persons to Finde a priest callid Seinct John Baptistes priest, to singe Masse in the parishe churche of Braynctre aforeseide.

Ande one Sir John Homexstedow [?], of the age of 30, Ande teachithe a grammer scole their, and haithe one Annuytie or pencion of 100s. of the Kinges majestie owt of the londes of Waltham Holy Crosse, is nowe Incumbent thereof.

The Seide Incumbent celebratythe in the seide churche of Braintre.

The yerelye valewe of the same, with the rent of 2 Stalles, 2s., copyhold of the bysshop of london, doith Amownt to the summe of £8 2s. 3d.   Whereof in

Rent resolute to diuerse Lordes by the yere, 12s. 8d.

And so Remaynithe cleare to the Kinges majesties vse, £7 9s. 7d.

The valewe of the Belles, other implements, &c., viz. :

Two belles, price 8s.

One vestment of saye 4d.   8s. 4d.

Memorandum: it is to be considered that the same towne of Braintre is a great popullus and a market towne, Havinge in yt to the nomber of 24 score of Howselinge people and more, and the seid priest is aydinge the Curat their, who, without helpe, is not able to serue the seid Cure, for that their is none other helpe nor ayde.

13. FINCHINGFELD.

Londes and tenementes in Finchingfelde, in the county afore-seide.

Put in feoffament by Henry Onyon, William Sergeant, Richerde Walkefor, Richerd Mortimer, and [blank] Kempe, Gentlemen, to Finde a guylde priest their, callid the trinytie guilde; the Foundacion thereof cannot be shewid. The seide priest to singe masse, Ande also to teache a grammer Scole within the seide Towne of Finchingfeld.

And one sir William Atkinson, clerke, of the age of 60 yeres and above, litterate, and teachith a Gramer Scoole their, and haithe the nomber of 30 Scolers, And of goode conversacion and vsage, is nowe Incumbent thereof.

The seide town of Finchingeffelde is a populus town, and of a greate Circuite, conteynynge 20 Miles in Compasse, havinge in yt to the Nomber of 500 howselinge people.

The seide Incumbente celebratythe in the seid church of Finchingfeld.

The yerlie valewe of the same doithe Amownte to the summe of £6 14s. Whereof in

Rent resolute to diuerse persons by the yere, 32s. 3½d.

And so remayneth cleare to the Kinges majesties vse, 101s. 8½d.

The valewe of the implementes and monyes, &c., viz. :
In readie Monie, £4.
Diuerse other implementes praysed togyther at 22s. 1½d.

102s. 1½d.

17. THAXSTED.

Londes and tenementes in Thaxsted, in the county of Essex.,

Put in feoffament to diuerse persons to Finde a priest to singe Masse in the parishe churche of Thaxsted aforeseid.

And one Sir John Holder, clerke, of the age of [blank] yeres, And teachith chylderne their, Havinge none other promocions, is nowe Incumbent theroff.

The seid Town of Thaxsted is a greate and populus Towne,

And A market and thorowghe fare town havinge in yt by estimacion abowt the Nombre of 800 howselinge people.

The seid Incumbento celebratythe in the seid church of Thax-
etead.

The yerelye valewe of the same doythe Amownt to the summe
of £11 19s. 10d.

Rent resolute to diuerse lordes by the yere, 48s. 8½d.

And So Remaynyth cleare to the Kinges majesties vse,
£9 11s. 1½d.

The valewe of the Goodes and other impleamentes, &c., viz. :
One cheste to put the vestmentes in, price 12d.

Fyve vestmentes with the appurtenances and diuerse other
implementes praysed togyther at 37s. 8d.   38s. 8d.

One chalice of silver, poisaunt 12½ ounces, the ounce at [blank],
12½ ounces.

19. HORNCHURCHE.

Londes and tenementes in Hornechurch, in the county of
Essex.

Put in Feoffament by William Baldewin to the intent that
the Wardens of the Guilde their, comonly callid the Trynitie
Guilde, shulde Finde a priest to celebrate within the churche
of Hornechurche, within the liberty of Haveringe at bower, Ande
to keape serteine Obittes yerelie.

And one Sir Robert yerelonde, clerke, of the age of 44 yeres,
havinge none other promocion, Ande teachith the pore mens childerne their, And of good vsage, is nowe Incumbent thereof. The
seid towne of Hornechurche is a populus towne havinge in yt
abowt the Nombre of Six hundrethe of Howselinge people and
more.

The seide Incumbente celebratythe in the seid church of
Hornechurch.

The yerlye valewe Thereof doith Amownte to the summe of
115s. 8d.; wherof in

Rent resolute to diuerse lordes by the yere, 10s. 9d.

And So Remaynythe cleare to the Kinges Maiesties vse,
104s. 11d.

The valew of the plate, Juelles, &c., viz. :

One chalice of silver parcell gylte, poysaunt 5 ounces the ounce, at 4s. 5 ounces.

One vestment with redd and whit Flowers with the appurtenances, price 3s. 4d.

22. HARLOWE.

Londes and tenementes in Harlowe in the seid countye.

Put in feoffament by John Staunton, Clarke, some time parson their, to find a prieste to saie dyvine seruice, and to singe masse in the seide churche of Harlowe.

Ande one Sir William Butler, clerke, of the age of 60 yeres, and good lerninge, havinge none other promocion, and teachith a scole in the seid Towne of Harlowe, And of good conversacion, is nowe Incumbent thereof.

The seid Towne of Harlowe is a verye greate and populus Towne, havinge in yt abowt the Nombre of 400 howselynge people.

The Seid Incumbente celebratythe in the seid Towne of Harlowe.

The yerly valewe of the same doith Amownte to the summe of £9 0s. 10d. Wherof in

Rent resolute to diuerse lordes by the yere, 10s. 11½d., et vnum rasyne of Ginger.

And So Remaynyth cleare to the Kinges maiesties vsc, £8 8s. 10½d., and a rasin of ginger.

The valewe of the plate, Juelles, &c., viz. :

One chalice of silver parcell Gilte, poysaunte 10 ounces, the ounce at [blank], 10 ounces.

Diuerse other Implementes their praysed to Gyther at 14s. 3d.

26. BADOWE MAGNA.

Londes and tenementes in Badowe magna in the seid countey.

Put in feoffament by diuerse and sundry persons to Finde a priest, the seid priest to be aydinge and assystinge the cure of muche Badowe aforeseid, and also to singe Masse their before the alter their callid Trinytie Alter.

And one Sir Raeff More, clerke, of the age of fyftye yeres; and more, havinge none other promocion, and of good vsage and conversacion, and preachythe, And teachythe A gramer scole their, is nowe Incumbent thereof.

The Seid Incumbent celebratyth in the seid church of Badowe magna.

The yerely valewe of the same doth Amownte to the summe of £14 13s. 4d. Wherof in

Rent resolute to diuerse lordes by the yere, 40s. 8d.

For skoringe of the owt markes yerelye, 13s. 4d.   54s.

And So Remaynith cleare to the Kinges maiesties vse, £6 19s. 4d. [sic].

The valewe of the plate, Juelles, &c., viz. :

One chalice of silver white, poysaunte 12 ounces the ounce at [blank], 12 ounces.

3 vestmentes, with the appurtenances, praysed togyther at 9s. 8d.

2 corporas clothes and 2 Alter clothes, price 14d.   10s. 10d.

Londes and tenementes in muche Badow in the seide countye.

Put in feoffament by diuerse and sundrie persons to the fyndinge of a priest their, callid coggeshall prieste, the seid priest to singe masse in the seid churche of muche Badow, And also to be aydinge and assystinge the vicar their.

And one Sir William Knightbridge, clerke, of the age of 38 yeres, Havinge none other promocion, and of good vsage and conversacion, lernide, and Exersisethe him self in teachinge of yowthe their.

The seid Towne of Muche Badowe is a greate and populus Towne (and the most parte of theim dwell vplonde, and farr from the seid churche of much Badowe), having in yt abowt the Nombre of Fower hundryth of howselynge people and more.

The seide Incumbent doith celebrate in the seide church of much Badowe.

The yerely valewe of the same doyth Amownt to the summe of £20 16s. 8d.

Rent resolute, £10 14s.

And So Remaynyth cleare to the Kinges maiesties vse, £10 2s. 8d.

The yerlye valewe of the plate, &c., viz. :

3 vestmentes, with the appurtenances, praysed at 17s.

2 corporas clothes and 2 Alter clothes, price 14d.　　18s. 2d.

31. MALDON.

Londes and tenementes in the parishe of seinct peters, in maldon, in the seid county.

Put in feoffament by License of Kynge Henry the fyfte to Finde a priest to singe masse in the seid churche of Seinct peters, in Maldon, and to praye for the seid Kinge Henry, and also to keape a scole their.

Ande one sir Reignolde Legge, clerke, of the age of 35 yeres, Havinge non other promocion, and well lernid, and instructyth yowthe their, and of good vsage, is nowe Incumbent therof.

The seid parishe of seinct peters is a very greate parishe, havinge in yt the nomber of 12 score of howslyng people.

The seide Incumbent celebratyth in the seide church of seinct peters.

The yerly valewe of the same doith Amownte to the summe of £9 5s. 9½d. ; whereof in

Rent resolute to diuerse Lordes by the yere, 25s. 2¼d.

And so remaynyth cleare to the Kinge's maiesties vse, £8 0s. 7¼d.

The valewe of the plate, Juelles, &c., viz. :

One Chalice of Whyt silver, poysant 10 ounces the ounce at [blank], 10 ounces.

4 vestmentes, with albes and the appurtenances, price 13s. 4d.

36A. CHELMYSFORD.

[Londes and tenementes in the parishe of Chelmysford in the seid county.]

Put in feoffament by diuerse and sundry persons to the intent that the Wardens of the Guilde their, commonly callid our Morowe masse Guilde, other wise callide Corpus Christi

Guilde, iu Chelmysforde aforeseid, shulde Finde a priest to singe Masse ther at the alter callid corpus christi Alter, and to helpe serue the Cure their.

Ande one Sir Thomas Eve, clerke, of the age of 40 yeres and more, litterate, and of good vsage and conversacion, and is benefysed to the yerly valewe of Fyve powndes owt of the late dissolved Collige of plasshye, And teachith a Scole in chelmysford aforeseid, is nowe Incumbent thereof.

The seide Incumbente celebratyth in the seid church of Chelymesford.

The yerely valewe of the same doith Amownte to the summe of £8 15s. 6d.; whereof in

Rent resolute, 16s. 8d.

And so Remaynyth cleare to the Kinges maiesties vse, £7 18s. 10d.

[Londes and tenementes iu Chelmysford aforesaid.]

Put in feoffament by Sir John Mowntyney, knight, to the intent that the Wardens of the Chauntry their, callide Mowntneys chuntrye, alias our ladye chauntry, in Chelmysforde churche yerde aforeseid, shulde Finde a priest to singe masse in the Chapple of our ladie in chelmysforde churche yerde aforeseid.

And one sir peter Wyleigh, clerke, master of arts, of the age of 56 yeres, and hayth none other promocion, and of Good conversacion, and teachyth A Grammer Scole their, and hath done this Sixtene yeres and more, is nowe Incumbent thereof.

The seid Incumbente celebratythe in the seid chapple of chelmysford.

The yerly valewe of the same doythe Amownte to the summe of £11 10s.

Rent resolute, 20s.

And So Remaynythe cleare to the Kinges maiesties vse, £10 10s.

Goodes, catelles, &c., *nulla*.

Memorandum: the seid towne of Chelmysford is a verie Greate populus and a markett Towne, havinge in yt to the nomber of 800 of howsselinge people and more.

36B.   RAYLEIGHE.

Londes and tenementes in Rayleighe, in the county of Essex.

Put in feoffament, by diuerse and sundry persons, to Finde a priest to singe masse, and to helpe serue the cure their, and to Teache a fre Scole their, to Instruct yowth; Whiche seid Town of Rayligh is a very greate and populus Town, Havinge in yt about the nombre of 16 score howselynge people, and Fur from the churche.

The seid Chauntrie is now vacant without any Incumbent.

The yerelye valewe of the same doythe Amownt to the summe of £10 12s. 2½d.

Rent resolute, 8s. 2½d.

Goodes, catelles, &c., nulla.

40.   CHESTRESFORD MAGNA.

Londes and tenementes in chestreford, in the seid county of Essex.

Put in feoffament by William Holden to Finde a priest foreuer, the seid priest to singe masse in the churche of Chestreforde aforeseid, And Helpe serue the cure.

Ande one Sir John Craste, clerke, of the age of 58 yeres, and of good vsage and conversacion, and teachith a Grammer Scole, and haythe to the nombre of 20 Scolers and more, is nowe Incumbent thereof.

The seid town of Chestreforde magna is a greate ande populus town, havinge in yt to the Nombre of fyve hondrethe of Howselinge people and more.

The seid Incumbente celebratithe in the seid churche of chestreforde.

The yerely valewe of the same, with the Ferme and Rente of certein londes and tenementes in chestreforde, holden by copy of court Roll of diuers lordes ther, doyth amount to the summe of £9 9s. 7d.

Rente resolute, 14s. 11½d.

And So Remaynyth cleare to the Kinges maiesties vse, £8 10s. [sic] 7½d.

Goodes, catelles, &c., nulla.

41. GOSFELDE.

Londes and tenementes in Gosfelde in the seid county.

Put in feoffament by Thomas Rolff, Essquire, to Finde a priest For ever, the seide priest to saye dyvine service in the churche of Gosfelde aforeseid, and to helpe serue the cure their.

And one Sir John Hornesey, clerke, of the age of 36 yeres, and of good conversacion, and teachyth a Grammer Scole their, and haythe to the Nombre of 40 scolers, and hath Tawght the seid scole by the space of 7 yeres.

The seid Town of Gosfelde is a greate town having in ytt the nomber of 12 score of howselynge people.

The seid Incumbent celebratyth in the seid church of Gosfeld.

The yerly valewe of the same doyth Amownt to the summe of £6 13s. 4d.

Rent resolute, *nullus*.,

The valew of the plate, Juelles, &c., viz. :

One chalice of silver, parcell Gilte, poysant 5 ounces the ounce at [*blank*] 5 ounces.

One vestment with an albe, price 2s.

48. WALTHAM STOWE.

Londes and tenementes in Waltham Stowe, in the seid countye.

Put in feoffament by George Monox, gentleman, to the Maintenance of a priest, the seid prieste to singe masse in the Churche of Waltham Stowe, aforeseid, and Also to teache a free scole their duringe the term of 20 yeres.

And one Sir John Hogeson, clerke, of the age of 40 yeres, Ande of goode vsage ande conversacion, litterate, and teachithe a scole their, is nowe Incumbent thereof.

The seid Town of Waltham Stowe ys a greate town, and havinge in yt to the nomber of 18 score howselynge people, and more.

The seid Incumbente celebratyth in the seid church of waltham stow.

The yerly valewe of the same doyth Amownte to the summe
of £6 13s. 4d. Whereof in
Rent resolute, *nullus.*
Goodes, catelles, &c., *nulla.*

Comitatus Essexie. Certificate 83.

Ower ladies Chauntrie, alias Mountrieys, in Chelmesford,
£9 12s.

Sir pater wileight, clerke, master of arte, incumbent their,
and *hath taught a Schole bi the space of 16 yeres past hetherto,*
and yet continewes.

Pencion, £6. *Continuatur Schola.*

Essex.

Duchy of Lancaster.   Schools Continuance Warrant.
Div. XXV., Q. No. 8.

Forasmuch as it apperith [&c.] that a Free Scole hath been
heretofore continually kept in the parish of Muchwalden in
the county of Essex, with the revenues of a chauntry founded
there, And that the Scolemaster [&c.] £10, which scole [&c.].

We therefore [&c.] have assigned [&c.], And that the said scole
in Michwalden aforesaid shall continue, And that Christopher
Bland, Scolemaster their, shall be and continue in the same
towne, And shall have for his yearly wages, £10.

Comitatus Essexie.   Particulars for Schools.
Edward VI. Roll 7.

CHELMSFORD GRAMMAR SCHOOL.

Cantaria vocata Hilles Chuntry in Badowe magna.   Valet in
Firma, £14.   Inde in reprisis ; in
Redditu Resoluto, 40s. 8d.   Allocacione, 13s. 4d.   54s.
Et valet clare per annum, £11 6s.

Guilda siue fraternitas in Vltynge ; valet in
[Redditibus], 32s. 5d.

Parcelle Reuencionum nuper Cantarie, Vocate the Stonehouse,
in Estilbury ; valent in
Firma, £8. Inde in Reprisis, Redditu Resoluto, 7d.
Et valet clare per annum, £7 19s. 5d.

∴ ~~Chelmysford, in comitatu Essexiæ, valet in [redditibus], 21s.~~
[sic].

Summa Totalis Clari Annui Valoris, Omnium Reddituum et
Firmarum predictarum per Annum, £20 17s. 10d.

Examinatur per thomam mildemay, Auditorem, 10 die Februarii, anno 5 Regis Edwardi sexti. [155?].

Make a graunte of the premisses for a free grammer scole, to
be erected in the paroche of Chelmisforde, in the countye of
Essex, with a corporacion of 4 persones, to be Gouernours of the
possessions, revenues, and goodes of the said Scole, And that the
same corporacion be first made to Sir William Peter, Sir Walter
Mildemaye, Sir Henry Tirrell, Knightes, and Thomas Mildemay,
esquier. And as any of them shall fortune to dye, the survivour
to electe the nexte heire male of him so dieng, and for defaulte
of suche heire male to electe one other person, being of the order
and degree of a knight, and dwelling and hauing for the moost
part his familye in the Countye of Essex. And if all the
Gouernours happen to dye, then the Bisshop of the dioces within
which the Town of Chelmisforde shalbe, to electe 4 persons,
being knightes, and inhabiteng for the moost parte in the
countye of Essex, to be governours of the said Possessions,
Revenues, and goodes of the said Scole, with suche oother
clauses to be conteyned in the said ereccion, as in other scoles,
lately erected by the kinges majestie, And the Governours to
have the Issues of the premisses from michelmas laste.

And with a clause to be conteyned in the said ereccion, that
40s. 8d. shall be giuen and bestowed yerely to the poore people
in moche Badowe, as hertofore hath ben accustomed, of thissues
of the said Chauntrye, called Hilles chauntrie, and to reserve
yerelie to the kinges majestie, 17s. 10d.

(Signed) Ry. Sakevyle.

**The Cytie of Gloucestre, with the Countie of the
same and the Cytie of Bristoll. Certificate 21.**

(Henry VIII.)

John Carrell, esquyer, Richard Pate, and Edwarde Gostwyke
gentilmen commyssioners.

24. THE PARISHE OF NEWLAND,
within the Deanry of the Forest.

Gryndoures Chauntrye.

Foundyd To Fynde a preste and a gramer scole half free
for ever, And to kepe a scoller sufficientt to teche vnder hym
contynually, And he to have for his salary by yere £10 4s. 2d.

Gryndoures chauntery ys within the said churche.

[*Yearly value*], £11 16s. 8d.   Wherof

For the preste Stipende, £10 4s. 2d.

For Renttes Resoluttes, 2s. 10d.

For the Kynges Tenthes, 23s. 8d.

For 2 Obbyttes yerely, 4s.

For 2 Tapers yerely, 2s.   £11 16s. 8d.

And so Remanyth, *nil.*

[*Value of ornaments, &c.*], £15 3s. 9d.

31. THE PARISHE OF CAMPDEN,
within the Deanry aforesaid (Deanre of Campden).

Ferby servis, otherwyse callyd the scolemaister servys.

Foundyd and the landes put in feoffament To Fynde a preste
for ever to kepe a Fre Scole and to have for hys salary by
yere, £8.   To kepe an Obyt and to geve in almes yerely
40s.

[*Yearly value*], £13 6s. 8d.   Wherof

For the prest Stipende, £8.

For the poore Folke, 40s.   £10.

And so Remanyth clere, 66s. 8d.

49. THE PARISHE OF WOTTON VNDERHEDGE,
within the said Deanry (Deanry of Dursley).

Katheryn Vele Fre Scole.

Foundyd To fynd a Scole Maister and 2 pore scolers for ever, and the to have the value of the landes, which is worth by yere, £17 15s. 2d.

Vele Scole ys nere the said Churche.

[*Yearly value*], £17 15s. 2d.   Wherof

For the Maister, £10 0s. 19¼d. ; for one scoler, £4.

For Rentes Resolutes, 22s. 3½d. ; for Fees, 28s.

For the Kynges Tenthes, 23s. 3¼d.   £17 15s. 2d.

And so Remanyth *nil.*

57. THE PARISHE OF DEYNTON,
within the foresaid Deanry (Deanry of Hawkesbury).

The Frechappell of Denton, now in the handes of one William Trace.

Foundyd To Fynd to scole one of the yonger Brothers of that name, of ther Issue successiue, for the tyme he shalbe bacheler; by yere, 48s.

[*Yearly value*], 53s. 4d.   Wherof

for the said scoler, 48s.

for the Kynges Tenthes, 5s. 4d.   53s. 4d.

And so Remanyth *nil.*

The Countie of Gloucetur, with the Cities of Bristowe and Gloucetur. Certificate 22.
(Edward VI.)

Anthony Hungerforde, Walter Bucler, William Sharyngton, and Milez Partridge, Knightes; Arthure Porter, Richarde Tracye, Thomas Throckemerton, Esquyers; Thomas Sterneholde and Richarde Pates, Gentilmen; Commyssioners.

37. THE PARISHE OF WOTTON SUBTUS EDGE,
within the Deanery aforeseid (Deanerie of Durseley), where are of houseling people, 800.

Memorandum : that there is within the seid parishe a Free

Scole of the Foundacion of oone Ladie Katheryn Veele, Whoe gave certeyn landes and Tenementes to the yerelie value of £16 14s. 8d., for the Findinge of a mayster there to teache gramer Freelye, and for 2 pore Scolers there, also to be maynteigned and founde with the issuez and proffittes therof.

[*The following entry is cancelled*] :—

WOTTON FRE SCOOLE.

Founded by one Lady Katheryne Vele for the finding of a mayster there Frely to teache gramer, and for two poore scolers also there to be founde, with the profittes commyng of the same landes.

Sir Robert Coldwell, scolemaister there, of the age of 60 yerez, being vnweldy, and for that purpose neither mete in disciplyne nor behaviour, and hath no other lyving then the seid scolemaistershipp, which ys yerely [*blank*].

The landes and tenementes belonging to the same are of the yerely value of £16 14s. 8d. Whereof

In Reprisez yerelye, [*blank*].

And so remayneth clere by yere, [*blank*].

Ornamentes, plate and Juelles to the same, noone.

IN THE DEANERY OF CAMPDEN.
57. THE PARISHE OF CAMPDEN,
where are of houseling people, 600.

[*The following entry is cancelled.*]
The Scolemaister Servyce *alias* dictum Ferbye seruyce.

Founded by one John Ferbye, and margery, his Wiff, and the landes putt in Feoffment, to the entent ~~to fynde a priste~~ [*sic*] to maynteigne a Fre scole in the seid parishe of Campden for ever.

Sir Robert Glaseman, Incumbent there, of the age of 53 yeres, having no other lyving then in the seid seruice, which ys yerely   .

The landes and tenementes thereunto belonging are of the yerely value of £13 6s. 8d. Whereof

In reprisez [*blank*].

And so remaneth clere by yere [*blank*].

Ornamentes, plate and Juelles to the same, Noone.

This seruyce ys left oute in the other certificat.

Memorandum : that there hathe byne tyme oute of mynde kepte within the seid paroche a gramer Schole Freelie taughte, commenlie Furnysshed with the nombre of 3 or 4 score scolers. For mayntenaunce and kepinge wherof oone John Ferbye, and margery, his Wiffe, gave and put in feoffement the moytie of a certeyne manour, with the appurtenaunces, amountynge to the yerelie value of £13 6s. 8d., with which yerelic Rent comynge of the premisses the seid schole hathe byne alweys and yet is kepte and maynteigned accordingelie, The teacher having for his salarye sometymes £10, sometymes £12 by yere, as his learnynge, qualities, and behavyour byne. The residue therof hathe byne distributed and converted to the Relevynge of poore people, and in payeinge a Stuardes Fee of 20s. by yere.

In the Deanery of Cirencestre.

64. The parishe of Cirencestre,

where are of houseling people the nombre of 1,400.

Robert Ricardes seruice, *alias* St. Anthonies seruice or chauntry.

Founded by one Robert Richardes, and Elizabeth, his wyff, and the landes and tenementes thereunto belonging putt in feoffment, to the entent to manteigne a priste, being a singing man, to celebrate at the alter of St. Anthonye in the seid churche, and also to teache frely 2 children from tyme to tyme to singe, to helpe the dyvyne seruice there, and to praye for the Founders sowles and all christien sowles for ever.

Sir William Wylson, Incumbent there, of the age of 46 yeres, having no other lyving then in the seid seruice, which ys yerely, £6 0s. 14¾d.

The landes and tenementes belonging to the same are of the yerely value of £7 13s. 5½d. Whereof

In reprises yerely, 19s. 4d.

And so remayneth clere by yere, £6 14s. 1½d.

P

IN THE DEANERY OF THE FOREST.

70. THE PARISSHE OF NEWLANDE,

within the seid Deanery, where are of houseling people, 800.

The chauntry of Blakbroke, alias dicta Greyndours chauntry
or schole.

Founded by one Robert Gryndour, esquier, by licence ob-
teigned of Kinge Henry the sixt, and landes and tenementes
gyven to the same, to the entent to manteigne a discrete priest,
beyng sufficiently lerned in the arte of Gramer, to Kepe a
Gramer scoole half Free; that ys to seye, taking of scolers lerning gramer, 8d. the quarter, and of others lerning to rede, 4d.
the quarter; and to celebrate at the alter of St. John and St.
Nicholas, prayeng for the Founders sowle and all christien
sowles.

Sir Roger Forde, Incumbent and Scolemaister there, of the
age of 55 yeres, having no other lyving then in the seid
chauntry, which ys yerely, £11.

The landes and tenementes belonging to the same are of the
yerely value of £11 14s. 6d.   Whereof

In reprises yerely, 2s. 10d.

To the pore yerelie, 5s. 8d.

And so remayneth clere by yere, £11 6s.

Ornamentes thereto belonging, valued at £4 3s. 11d.

Plate and Jewelles to the same valued at 10 ounces, 40s.

Memorandum the Scole, &c.

Obytlandes and Rent in the seid parishe.

Certyn landes and Rent geven for the manteynaunce and
keping of an yerely obytte for Dame Isobell Hyott in the seid
parishe churche *for ever, and to distribute thereatt certeyn
money to the pore Scolars and other pore people of the same
parishe as here folowinge is mencyoned.*

The seid lande *is rented by yere at* 16s. 8d., *and the Rent so
gyven ys yerely,* 20d., *Which in the whole dothe amounte by
yere to* the value of 18s. 4d.   Whereof

Distributed to the poore people *dicte parochie and scolers*
yerely at the same obytte, *accordinge to the seid foundacion*

therof. And so ~~was bestowed yerelie on priestes and clerkes and lighte thereatt~~ [*sic*] *remaine clere by yere, 8s. 8d.*

The Countie of Glouceter, with the cities of Bristowe and Glouceter. Certificate 23.

(Edward VI.)

The aunswer and cetificat of Thomas Sterneholde, Partycular surveyour vnto the Kynges Maiestie, appoynted for the saide Countie and Cyties vnto certeyne Artycles here vnder wrytten, as doth hereafter ensewe.

32. ·IN THE PARYSHE OF NEWENT,
where are of howselinge people, 500.

Memorandum : that Newent is a Markett Towne, wherunto is muche resorte of people, And all the youthe of a great dystaunce therhence rewdlye brought up, and in no maner of knowledge and Learninge, Where were a Place mete to establyshe a Teacher and erect a Scole for the better and more godlye bryngynge vp of the same youthe.

34. IN THE PARYSHE OF NEWLAND,
where are of howselinge People, 800.

Grynedowres chauntrye.

The clere yerely value, £11 11s. 8d.

Roger Foord, Incumbent and Scolmaster there, hath for his yerely Stypende, £11.

To the pore yerely, 5s. 8d.

Continuatur the Schole quousque.

Memorandum : that the abouesaide chauntrey called Gryndours chauntrye was founded by one Robert Gryndowre, Esquyre, to the entente that there shulde be an Honeste, discrete pryste, beinge suffyciently learned in the Arte of Gramer, whiche shulde be bounde by the graunt of him the saide founder to fynde one Scoller to teache vnder him there, Gevinge him meate dryncke, clothe, and all other necessaries, And so the said chauntrye Preiste to Kepe a Scole, and teache there for euer in the howse

called the Chauntrye Howsse, or Scolehowsse, a gramer scole
half Free ; that is to saye, to take of Scolers Leringe gramer 8*d*.
the quarter, And of other quarterlye, 4*d*. And allso the saide
chaunterye pryste to Celebrate at saynt Nicholas Aulter in the
saide Parishe Churche of Newlande, and praye for the saide
founder for euer.

Off whiche saide chauntrey the aboue named Roger Foorde
is now Incumbent and Scolemaister, A man of Honest conversacion and good Learninge, and wholye geven and applyinge
himself in the vertuouse bryngynge vp of the same scollers,
wherof are at this present good store, and the Scole very
well Haunted, to the grete commodytie of the countrey theraboutes.

The Deanrye of Cirencester.

No. 40. In the parysshe of Cirencester,

where are of howselinge People the nombre of 1,400.

The chauntry or servyce of our Ladye.
The clere yerely value, £11 8*s*. 4*d*.
Thomas Taylour, Incumbent, hath for his yerely Stypend, £7.
A Schole taught by him at this presente.
Continuatur the schole with the accustumed wages quousque.
Memorandum : that this said towne of Cyrencester is an
Auncyent Boroughe Towne, The greate numbre of People and the
contynuall Accesse of the greater nombre Repayringe to the
same Towne consydered.

The Inhabytantes there are moste humble sutours, that it
maye please the Kynges Maiestie and His mooste Honorable
Counsell to lett theim haue therin stablysshed some learned
man to teache a Grammer Scole for the vertuouse bryngynge
vp of the youth there aboutes, where are many chyldren which
heretofore haue been very rudely, ignorantly, and, for lacke of
suche a teacher, symplye brought vp, and withoute knowlege,
tyll within these three yeres Paste, sythens which tyme the
aforesaide Parishoners, with their whole assentes, dryven therunto of grete necessytie, did appoynte one of the abouesaide

servyces in their saide Churche, called our Ladye servyce, to be
conuerted to the Kepinge of a Scole, And the Incumbent therof,
named (as is aforesaide) Syr Thomas Taylour, hath very dili-
gently applyed him self in teachinge of childrene, and hath hadd
for his Salarye yerely £7 and his Mansion howse.

In whiche saide Towne, till the Dissolucion of the Monasterye
of Wynchecome, there was Graunted and payed oute of the
same Monasterye one yerely Pencion of £10 to and for a Free
Scole, there to be maynteyned and Kept; sythens the Dissolucion of whiche Monasterye the same yerely pencion of £10
hath been withdrawen, and not payed, vnto the grete discom-
modytie of the same Towne of Cirencester.

THE DEANERY OF WYNCHECOMBE.

52. IN THE PARYSSHE OF TEWKESBURYE,
where are of howselinge people, 1,600.

Memorandum: that the saide Towne of Tewkesburye is a
verye grete markett Towne, where is kept Markett twyse euerye
Weeke, Wherunto is contynuall accesse of a grete numbre of
People, besydes those (which are no small nombre) that been
inhabyted within the same Towne, Havinge many children
likely and apt throughe good instruccion to atteigne to Learninge, Whiche the Premysses tenderly consydered, the Inhabytauntes of the same Towne are moste Humble Suters that it
maye please the Kynges Maiestie and his moste honorable
counsell to geve and appoynt some convenyent Stypend for the
mayntenaunce of a Free Scole there for euer, to be kept and
establysshed for the better educacion and bringynge vp of
the saide youthe in knowlege of vertue and good Learninge.

53. IN THE PARYSSHE OF CHELTENHAM,
where are of howselinge people, 600.

Saynt Kateryne Servyce.

The clere yerely value, 118s. 11d.

Edward Grove, Incumbent, hath for his yerelye stypend,
100s.

Memorandum: that the saide Syr Edward Grove, one of the Incumbentes, was charged by speciall Couenaunt betwene the Parysshoners of the ¡saide Towne of Cheltenham and him, alweyes to teache their children; which Towne is a markett Towne, and muche youthe within the same, nere wherunto is no scolle kept. Wherefore it is thought convenyent to signyfye vnto your Mastershipps the same to be a meate place to establyshe some Teacher and erect a Gramer Scole, So it might stande with the Kynges Maiesties pleasure.

Continuatur schola quousque.

Places for Grammerscoles to be newlye erected.

The townes of Newent, Cirencestour, Tewkesburye, Cheltenham, in the aforesaide countie of Glouceter.

Examinatur per me Humffridum Vlton, deputatum particularem supervisoris comitatus predicti.

Comitatus Southamptoñ (et Berß). Certificate 51.

(Henry VIII.)

Sir John Wellesborne, Kt., Walter Hendley, Richard Worseley, George Powlet, Richard Powlet, Esquyers, and John Hammond, gentylman, Commyssyoners.

3. THE SUBURBSE OF THE TOWNE OF WYNTON.

One Colledge of our lady there, founded by

William Wykeham, somtyme Bysshope of Wynton, by the licence of Kynge Rycharde the Secounde; For one Master or Warden, 70 Scolers, 10 felowes, beyng prestes, 3 Conductes, prestes, 3 clerkes, 16 queresters, one Scole master, and one vssher of the gramer scole, And Also one master of the songe scole for the queresters aforsaid.

All whiche nomber ar there Resydent, euery of them at this present to do His Offyce.

The said Colledge ys scytuate nyghe Wynton, almoste vnder the Walles of the saide Towne of Wynchester.

The value of All the londes apperteynynge or belongynge to the said Colledge, £947 7s. 7d.   Wherof

For Annuall Fees and for Rentes Resolutes, pencions, procuracions, and Sinodals, by yere, £96 6s. 11¼d.

For the Warden's Stipende, with His Commons, £101 18s. 8d.

For 70 scolers and 16 querysters for theyr porcion and Comons, £308 4s. 8d.

For 10 Fellowes For theyr porcion and comons, £154 2s. 4d.

For the porcion of 3 Conductes, 3 Clarkes, the Master of the songe scole, the Master of the gramer scole, the vssher, and other officers belongynge to the same Colledge, and for theyr Comons, £122 7s. 10½d.

For Wages and lyuers for certeyn seruauntes in the said Colledge, £32 17s. 4d.

For the stipend of one Chauntre prest, founded in the Cathedrall Churche of Sarum, £7 6s. 8d.

For Almes, £8 0s. 20d.

For diuers expenses for the said Colledge, as for the progresse, seruauntes lyuerye for progresse, Visitacions of the Bysshoppe, For Wex, wyne, oyle and candelles, £41 14s. 2½d.

The Tenth Reserued of all the Hole possessions of the said Colledge, £33 2s. 4½d.   £905 [sic] 2s. 8¾d.

And so Remayneth £42 5s. 10¼d., Whych ys ymployed towardes the Repayrynge of the tenementes and londes.

Ornamentes, plate, Juelles, goodes and catalles merely Apperteynynge vnto the forsayd Colledge, as Apperyth by the Invetory thereof made to the sayde comyssyoners, nott Praysed.

One Chauntre within the colledge of our Lady Aforsaide. Founded by

John Froreman [sic], and Mawde, hys Wyff, to the entente to haue a prest to synge in the chappell within the Cloyster of the saide Colledge three tymes in the Weke, And so to serue And singe in the quyer of the same Colledge one the Holydayes.

The said Chauntre ys scituate in the said Chapell, within the Cloyster of the said Colledge.

The value of the said Chauntre ys, in Mony nombred, £6 13s. 4d.

Whych the prest hath and dothe Receyve For His Annuall
stipend.

Ornamentes, plate, Juelles, goodes and catalles merly Apperteynynge to the said chauntre there are none, but yt ys
seruyd with the ornamentes of the said Colledge.

The Hospytale of Seynt Crosse nygh Wynton. Founded by
Henry Bowford, somtyme Bysshope of Wynton and Cardinall,
to the entent to haue one master, 13 Bretherne, 6 prestes,
6 clerkes, and 6 quyresters, to syng and say daly in the churche
There the devyn service, And Also they are bond by there
fondacion to gyve Almesse to 100 pore people daylye, Whyche
they do observe Accordyngly.

The said Hospytall ys scituate in the parishe churche of
seynt Fayth, one Myle Dystaunte From the Citie of Wynton.

The value of the londes and other possessions apperteynynge
vnto the said Hospitall, £293 0s. 6d. Whereof

For Rentes Resolutes, £23 12s. 3¼d.

For the Tenthe, £8 1s. 5d.

For the stipendes of 6 prestes with there lyuerys, £26.

For the wages of the 6 clerkes, £16.

For the wages of the Scole Master, 46s. 8d.

For the wages of the sexten, belrynger, and other manualle
seruauntes, wythe theyre lyuerys, £16 3s. 4d.

For the Commons of the said 6 prestes, 6 clerkes, A Sexton,
and other the seruauntes Aforeaide, £95 14s.

For the wages, lyuerys, and Comons of 13 men called
Bretherne, £43 6s. 8d.

For almes gyven to 100 pore people yerely, £18 19s. 4d.

£250 10s. 8¼d.

And so Remayneth £42 9s. 9¾d., Whych ys ymployed
towardes the Repayringe of the tenementes and londes.

Ornamentes, Plate, Juelles, goodes, And catalles merly Apperteynynge vnto the sayd Hospytall, as apperythe by the
Invetory therof made, nott Praysede.

Hampshire. Certificate 54.

(Edward VI.)

Sir John Mason, Kt., George Poulet, John Kingesmill, Nicholas Tichebourn, Esquiers, Edmund Clarke, Nicholas Vaux, and Richard Gifford, gentilmen, commissioners.

DECANATUS DE BASINGSTOKE.

2. BASINGSTOKE.

The Brotherhodd of the chapell of the Holly goost.

Founded of the deuocion of the inhabitantes at the begynnyng, there to fynd a prest for euer, and sythens employed to the intent to fynd a scole Master to teache children grammer, whiche hathe been so continually kept thes 10 yeres last past unto this daye ; whereunto belongen, viz. :

Landes and tenementes in basingstoke to the yerely value of £6 13s. Wherof

Resolute, 15s. 4d.   Et Remanet, £5 17s. 8d., Whyche is yearly paid to the said scole Master.

Ornamentes and plate belonging to the same brotherhod, Delyuered by Inventory Indented by the commissioners to the wardens of the said brotherhod, valued at 28s.

Memorandum : the said chapell of the Holly goost, and the yard environyng the same, is the common buryeing place for all the said parishe, And the Vicar there findithe a curate, And the same Vicarage is of the yerely value of £26 2s. 9d. benefice.

Houseling people there, 304 people.

3. ODIAM.

A stipendary prest in odiam.

Note ministracion and a scole.

Founded of the deuocion of the inhabitantes to haue continuance for ever there, to be assisting and aiding to suche ministracion as is required to be emonges the people, by the woord of godd, and to the intent to teache children gramer, whereunto belong, viz. :

Landes and tenementes in odiam to the yerely value of £7. Whereof

Resolute, 6s. 4d.

Et Remanet, £6 13s. 8d., Whiche is yerely paid to Hueghe Laner, Whose age is 40 yeres, for his salary, who hath none other lyving.

Memorandum : there is one George Flowre, vicar there, whose benefice is to the yerely value of £21 benefice.

And hathe in howseling people above 1,000 people.

Memorandum : there is a chapell of ease in Northwarnborough, being distant from the churche of Odiam, which is emploid in the tyme of the plage for ministracion to the whole, and for a place to teache children in.

Ornamentes and plate belonging to the furniture of the said stipendary priest, delyuered by Inventory, indented by the commissioners to the wardens of the said landes, valued at £3 7s. 4d.

DECANATUS DE ALTON.

12. ALTON.

A Stipendary Priest.

Founded by one John Chawnflower, to have continuance for ever, to the yntent to assist ministracion in the Churche of Alton, and to teache children grammer. Whereunto belong, viz. :

Landes and tenementes to the yerely value of £11 0s. 15d. Whereof

Resolute, 20d.

To the steward for his yerely fee, 6s. 8d. (Obits 11s. 8d.).

Et Remanet, £10 0s. 15d.

Memorandum: that Richard Ryder, Clerc, is Vicar there, and hathe in houseling people, 900 people.

Note ministracion and a scole.

Which Vicar cannot well satisfie the due ministracion without the assistance of an other minister, the Value of which Vicarage is £35 16s. benefice.

Memorandum : the stipendary prest hathe of the said landes for his salary yerely payd by the wardens of the same town, £6 13s. 4d., and hathe none other lyving, whose name is Gregory Bacon.

Ornamentes belonging to the said stipendary valued at 3s. 4d.

DECANATUS DE WINCHESTER.

36. THE NEW COLLEAGE AT WINCHESTER.

A stipendary priest.

Appointed to haue continuance for euer to serue in a chapell in the Manour of Barton, in the Isle of Wight, who hathe for his salary, paid yerely by the warden of the said colleage, £6.

Memorandum: the said Warden, &c., presented dyuers other Diriges and obites there in the said colleage to be kept yerely for certayn their founders, the proffit wherof only is employed vpon the scollers of the same house, and vpon poore people.

DECANATUS DE INSULA VECTE.

45. GODDSHILL PARISHE.

A chantry there.

Note, a pencion of the Kinges charge, And teaching of children.

Founded by Sir John Ligh, Knight, to haue continuance for ever, wherunto belong landes and tenementes of the yerely rent of £11 9s. 4d. Whereof

Resolute, 4d. To the poore yerely, 6s. 8d.

Et Remanet, £11 2s. 4d.

Ornamentes and plate thereunto belonging appere by Inventory Indented, deliuered by the commissioners to the churchwardens there, valued at 43s. 4d.

Memorandum: the incumbent therof is one Johne Griffithe, master of Arte, of the age of 40 yeres, and hathe besides, £6 pencion out of Hales monasterie during lief, who teachithe there grammer to many yong children.

Also George Cotes, Doctour in Diuinitie, is vicar there, the value whereof is £33 0s. 21d. benefice.

Who is charged with one curate vnder hym there, And with an other curate at Whitewell chapell, 2 miles from the parishe churche, Having of houseling people in the holl parishe, 600 people.

The Countie of Hereford. Certificate 24.

(Edward VI.)

William Crouche, William Grene, John Skudamore, and John Borne, Esquyers, Comyssionours.

3. HEREFORD (CITY).

The parishe of Seynte Owyns within the saide citie, Wher be of Howselyng people, 181.

A Chauntre called our ladye chuntre within the parishe churche of Seynt Owyns aforsaid.

Certeyn landes and tenementes gyven to the churchewardens and parishoners, to fynde a prest to celebrate in the chapell of our lady, and to pray for the founders and all crysten sowles.

Sir Phylipe Hye, of the age of 4 score yeres, Incombent, beinge a ryght honest man indyfferently lerned, and taketh paynes in kepying of a scole and bryngyng vp of chylderne, Havyng no other lyvyng but the clere yerely revenue of the same.

The landes and tenementes belongynge to the same be of the yerely value of £4 13s. 6d. Wherof in

Reprises yerely, 18s. 11½d.

And so Remayneth clere, 74s. 6½d.

Ornamentes belongynge to the same, valued at 20s.

THE HUNDRED OF RADLOWE.

9. THE PARISHE OF LEDBURY.

Howselynge People, 640.

A Stipendarye in the parishe churche there called the seruice of the Trynytie.

Certeyn landes and tenementes gyven by diuers founders to fynde a prest to celebrate there and to Pray for the founders.

Sir Rychard Wheler, Stypendary there, of the age of 54 yeres, a man of god conuersacion, and dayly occupied in teachyng of chylderne gramer, Whych hath for his salary,

the clere Reuenue of the same, And non other lyvyng, but
the lytle rewarde of the Frendes of the Scolers.

The landes and tenementes belongyng to the same be of
the yerely value of £4 9s. 2d. Wherof in
Reprises yerely, 7s. 10½d.
And so Remayneth clere, £4 0s. 16½d.
Ornamentes to the same belongyng valued att 3s. 4d.
Store in catell to the same valued at £9 16s. 8d.   £10.

Memorandum : that the Towne of Ledbury ys a very pore
towne ; And by the forsaid Sir Richard Wheler, Stipendary,
the Inhabitaunces of the same Haue nott only Hade profytt
and aduauntage by the kepyng of a gramer scole there, as
in bordynge and loggyng His scolers, but also the countre
therabowtes, in vttryng ther vytalles ther by mean of the said
scollers. In concideracione therof the pore Inhabytaunce of
the same Towne humbly beseche that yt may please the Kynges
maiestie, with the assente of his honorable counseill to his
bountefull goodnes, to graunte that the saide scole maye ther
styll be kepte, and the said Stipendary to Remayn for the
maynteynyng therof to the erudicion of yough, a charytable
dede yf so yt may please His Hyghnes.

10. THE PARISHE OF BOSBURY.

Howselyng people, 320.

A Scolemaster, to Brynge vp yought in lernynge in the said
parishe, and to play at the Organs.

Certeyn landes and tenementes gyven in Feoment by one
Rychard Poyke to Rychard Hope and other Cofeoffes, to them
and to their Heyres for euer, Declarynge no vse, Whiche
landes and tenementes, with the encrease of A stoke of money
and catall remaynynge in diuers mens handes, Hathe byn
alwayes imployed to the vse and Fyndynge of a scole master
to bryng vp yought in lernynge, and to play at Organs, and
to do other seruice in the said church.

Sir Thomas Keyling ys nowe Scole master, and hathe byn
4 or 5 yeres last past ; A man of good conuersacion and lernyng,

of the age of 75 yeres, a man nott able to ryde or to go
for deceases; Havynge the clere Reuenue of the premysses for
his salary, and no other promocion.

The landes and tenementes belongynge to the same be of
the yerely value of 58s. 4½d.   Wherof in

Reprises yerely, 8s. 7d.

And so Remayneth clere, 49s. 9½d.

Stoke of money, 51s. 8d.   Store in catall, 19s.   70s. 8d.

And it is presented vnto vs the Kynges maiesties comyssioners that Sir Rowland Norton, Knyght, hath gevyn vnto the
parishe of Bosbury a tenemente and 4 acres of arrable land, to
the entent that the parisheoners shuld Distribute the Reuenue
therof yerely to pore people, Reparacion of Hyghwayes, and
other cherytable dedes; And that hathe nott byn ymployed
any other wyse.

THE HUNDRED OF WOLFEY.

15.   THE PARISHE OF LEOMYNSTER.

Howselynge people, 1700.

And also we be certified that the said Towne of Leymster
ys the Kynges maiesties borowe towne, and the greatist
Markett towne within the Countie of Hereford, and the parishe
therof very wyde and brode.   In whyche towne ys a gramer-
scole kepte by one Edward Alen, beinge a man of Honest
behaver and well lernyd, who hathe no other lyvyng but that
he hath of his scolers wekly; And that euer before thys tyme
ther hath byn scole kepte in the same towne.

THE HUNDRED OF STRATFORD.

81.   THE PARISHE OF PEMBRIDGE.

Howselyng people, 500.

A stipendarye, called the seruyce of our ladye, at our ladye
Aulter within the same parishe churche.

Certeyn landes and tenementes gyven to the fyndynge of A
prest, to celebrate one masse wekely at the said alter, and to be

a scole master to teache chylderne borne within the said parishe Frely.

Sir John Roode, stypendary prest, a man of good conuersacion, A bacheler of Arte, well lernyd, whiche lernethe the Gramer-scole there, and the said seruice, Havynge for his salary the clere yerely Reuenue of the same and no other lyvynge, a man of the age of [blank] yeres.

The landes and tenementes belongynge to the same be of the yerely value of 104s. 3d. Wherof in

Reprises yerely, 31s. 3d.

And so Remayneth clere, 73s.

32. THE PARISHE OF WEBLEY.

Houseling people, 280.

A chauntrey in the chapell of seynte Nycholas within the same parishe church.

Founded by John Chapman and Alice Baker, whyche gave the manour of Blakehall, with the appurtenaunces, in the countie of Hereford, and other lands and tenements, for the fyndynge of a prest to celebrate there, and to pray for all the founders.

Sir James Morgan, Incombent, a man of Honest conuersacion, well learned, Hable to kepe a cure, of the age of 30 yeres, which doth kepe a scole, and doth teache chyldern, and brynge them vpe in vertue, Havyng only the clere Reuenue of the same, and the proffytt of the scole, and no other lyvinge.

The landes and tenementes belongynge to the same be of the yerely value of £6 17s. 7d. Wherof in

Reprises yerely, 4s. 6d.

And so Remayneth clere, £6 13s. 1d.

Ornamentes to the same, valued at 14d.

33. THE PARISHE OF KYNGESLANDE.

Howselinge people, 300.

Twoo stipendarys of the Aulter of oure Lady, in the said parishe church. The one of them dyscharged.

Certyn landes and tenementes, gyven by diuers persons to

the Fyndynge of A prest to celebrate there, and to Teache Chylderne.

Sir John Harteley, Incombent, stipendary preste, a man of goode conuersacion, of the age of 42 yeres, Whych doth celebrate, Helpe the Curate, and Kepythe a scole, and Dothe brynge vpe yough vertuesly, Havyn for His salary the clere Reuenue of the same and the profytte of His scolers, And no other lyvynge.

The landes and tenementes belongyng to the same be of the yerely value of £9 16s.   Wherof in

Reprises yerely, 31s. 9d.

And so Remayneth clere, £8 4s. 3d.

34. THE PARISHE OF DELWYN.

Howselynge people, 300.

A chauntre of Seynte Nicholas in the said parishe churche.

Certeyn landes and tenementes, gyven by certeyn Inhabit-aunces of the said parishe towardes the Maynteynynge of a prest to celebrate there morowe masse Dayly, And to Kepe a Obitt yerely.

Sir Thomas Nicholl, a man of Honest behaver, and competenly lerned, of the age of 60 yeres, Which bryngith vpe manye chylderne in vertue and learnynge, Havynge the clere Reuenue of the same, and no other lyvyng.

The landes and tenementes belongynge to the same be of the yerely value of £4 15s. 3d.   Wherof in

Reprises yerely, 15s. 3d.

And so Remayneth clere, £4.

Stores in catall, 55s. 8d.

37. THE PARISHE OF KYNNERSLEY.

Howselyng people, 140.

A stypendarye preste in the said parishe churche.

Certen landes and tenementes gevyn by Anne Delabore, wydowe, and enfeoffed Thomas Monyngton, Esquyer, and other cofeoffeis, to mayntayn a pryste seruice, for to syng at the Aulter of our lady there.

Incombent, None. The forsaid Stipendary ys nowe imployed to the Kepynge of a scole, there nowe beinge there 60 scollers. And that one Sir William Pyk, Clerke, ys scole master there, a man of Honest behavour and well learned, Hable to teach gramer, of the age of 30 yeres, Havyng no stipend but only the clere Reuenue of the same, and no other lyvyng.

The landes and tenementes belongynge to the same be of the yerly value of £7 18s. 2d. Wherof in

Reprises yerely, 36s. 2d.

And so Remayneth clere, £6 2s.

Plate, valued by estimacion, 5 ounces.

Ornamentes to the same, valued at 4s. 2d.

THE HUNDRED OF BROXASHE.

39. THE PARISHE OF MYCHE COWERN.
Howselynge people, 182.

A stypendary prest, called the seruice of our lady, within the said churche, and to the Maynteyning of a lampe.

Certen landes and tenementes, gyven by Diuers persons to Maynteine the said seruice and the prest, to celebrate and Helpe the Curate ther, And to Teache chylderne born within the said parishe frely.

Sir Thomas More, stipendary, of the age of 60 yeres, a man of Honest behavour, indyfferently lernyd, whyche takyth Payne in teachynge chylderne Dayly, having no other lyvyng but the clere Reuenue of the same.

The landes and tenementes belongynge to the same be of the yerely value of 47s. 11d., with 11d. for the Kepyng of a lampe light. Whereof in

Reprises yerely, 5s. 11d.

And so Remayneth clere, 42s.

Stores in Catall, 22s. 1d.

44. THE PARISHE OF BROMYARDE.
Howselyng people, 800.

A stypendary in the said parishe churche.

Q

Landes and tenementes gevyn to fynde a prest to celebrate there, and to Maynteyn and brynge vpe the chylderne borne in the parishe in Reading, Wrytynge, and gramer.

Sir John Bastenall, Incombente and scole master ther, of the age of [*blank*] yeres, a man of good conversacion and well lerned, which teachith chylderne, and doth brynge vpe vertuously in redyng, wryttynge, and in gramer, Havynge the clere Revenue of the same and no other promoscion.

The landes and tenementes belongyng to the same be of the yerely value of £4 3s. 2d.   Wherof in

Reprises yerely, 13s. 3d.

And so Remayneth clere, 69s. 11d.

Memorandum : that the Towne of Bromyard ys a markett towne, and greately Repleynyshed with People, and the parishe therof longe and large, that ys to wytt, 7 myles ouer some waye, and 15 myles compasse abowte, And that Diuers men, before the remembraunce of the Inhabitaunces the nowe, gave the said landes and tenementes, for the maynteynyng godes seruice, and bryngynge vp the chylderne borne ther in readyng, wrytynge, and gramer, Hyered and enterteyned 2 prestes for the Mayntenaunce of the same, and paied theyre salary with the Reuenues of the said landes and tenementes. In consideracion wherof the Kynges maiesties Humble subiectes, the Inhabitaunces of the same parishe, besechith that yt may please His Highnes with the assente of His most Honorable Counseill, the Mayntenaunce of brynge vp of yough in Readyng, Wrytyng, and in gramer, And the scole masters to Helpe the Devyn seruice in the said parishe churche ; the forsaid landes and tenementes, and other the premyssez gyven to that entente, as ys aforsaid, to Haue to them and theyr successours for euer to the same vse, And that in the reverence of god and in waye of charytie.

THE HUNDRED OF HUNTINGDON.

47. THE PARISHE OF YARDESLEY.

Howselinge people, 343.

A stipendary within the parish churche, And A gramerscole within the said parishe.

Founded by Sir James Baskervyle, Knyght, Which gave certeyn landes and tenementes to the fyndynge of a gramer scole
there, and a scole master to teache gramer, to instructe and
bryng vpe His Chylderne and other mens in learnyng of gramer,
And the said gramer scole hath byn euer sith continued and
kepe. And the said scole master to celebrat in the parishe
ther.

Sir William Storr, Incombent and scole master there, a man
of good behavour and well learned, Whyche hath for his waiges
or stypent the clere yerely Reuenue of the same, the advauntage
of His Scolers, and no other lyvynge.

The landes and tenementes gyven belongynge to the same be
of the yerly value of £4 13s. 2d., Whyche the said Incombent
Dothe yerly Receyue the same.

49. The parishe of Kyngton.

Howselinge people, 560.

A stypendary at the Aulter of our lady within the parishe
churche there, And 2 lampes in the same parishe churche.

Certen landes and tenementes gyven to the fyndynge of a
prest to celebrate there, to Helpe the curat, and to praye for the
Founders, and to teache chylderne, And to fynde 2 lampes
there.

Sir John Grene, stipendary prest there, of the age of 36 yeres,
a man of Honest conuersacion and a good clerke, and Hathe the
clere Reuenue of the same, and no other lyuynge.

The landes and tenementes to the same belongyng be of the
yerely value of £4 16s. 9d., with 7d. For the fyndyng of the
same 2 lampes in the said parishe church.

Store in catell valued at £8 13s. 4d.

The Hundred of Wygmore.

53. The parishe of Bucknell.

Howselinge people, 160.

A stipendary to celebrate in the said parishe churche and A
scole master.

Certen money gyven by Diuers and sundry persons, by
Whome yt ys vnknown, Remaynge in a stoke of £32 lying and
beinge in diuers of the parishoners Handes, And with the Increse therof to maynteyn the said stipendary to ayde the curate
there, and to teache chylderne theyr gramer.

Sir Lawrence Johnson, Incombent and scolemaster there, of
the age of 60 yeres, a man of Honest behavour and competenly
lernyd, which dothe celebrate in the parishe churche, and doth
helpe the curate there, Havyng for his Salary by the handes of
the parishoners, 106s. 8d.

The waiges of the said Stipendary, 106s. 8d.

Stoke of Mony, £32.

The Hundred of Webtre.

59. The parishe of Staunton.

Howselyng people, 152.

A seruyce of our lady within the saide parishe churche.

Founded by the parishenours there apon theyr Devocion, to
Have a prest to synge for all crysten sowles, to Helpe the curate
in His necessite, to visite the syke.

Sir Richard Cowley, the stipendary, an agid man of Honest
behavour, and conueniently learned, which dothe teache many
pore mens chylderne, Havying for His salary the clere Reuenue
of the same, and no other lyvynge.

The landes and tenementes belongyng to tho same be of the
yerely value of 17s. 2d.   Wherof in

Reprises yerely, 13d.

And so Remayneth clere, 16s. 1d.

Stokes in Money, £17 13s. 4d.

The Countie of Hereforde.   Certificate 86.

(Edward VI.)

A Breff declaracion of all and Synguler the late Colledges,
    Chauntryes, Freechapelles, Fraternyties, Guyldes, Stypen-
    daries, and Brotherheddes, with other licke in the saide
    Countie ; with the names of the Incumbentes, Masters,
    Governors, and other lyke, with their wages yerlye the

Tenth deducted, Scoles, prechers, Bedemen havinge Relieff goinge out of the premysses, which by the late Acte of parlyament Intitled to the Kinges maiestie As hereafter ensuethe.

THE HUNDRED OF RADLOWE.

LEDBURYE. *m.* 1.

Memorandum: that the saide parishe of Ledburye beinge a pore Towne . . . Richarde Wheler, Stypendarye and Scolemaster there, The Inhabitauntes of the same haue not only had proffytt and advantage by kepinge of A grammer Scole there as in bordinge and logginge his Scolers, but also the Countre thereaboutes, in vttringe there vytalles there by meane of the saide Scolers. In consideracion thereof the pore inhabitauntes there humblye besechethe that yt maye please the Kinges maiestie to graunte that the saide Scole maye there styll be kepte and the sayde Stipende to remayne.

BOSBURY.

The Scole in the parishe of Bosburye called the Frescole.

Thomas Keylinge, Scolemaster, for his wages or Salary yerly, 49s. 9½d.

Howselinge people, 320.

The parishenors there desierethe that the saide Scole maye styll remayne.

LEDBURY.

The late Stipendarie, or seruice, called the Trynytie service, in the parish churche of Ledburye. That is to saye:

landes and tenementes to the same, £6 14s. 10d. Whereof

In reprises yerly, 7s. 10½d.

And so Remaneth, £6 6s. 6½d.

Richarde Wheler, Stipendarie there, dyd receyve the saide clere remayne for his lyvinge, And hathe no other lyvinge, but only the same.

Memorandum: that where the same stipendarye was not in the First Certyficate vnto your mastershipe Certefyed as above is expressed, was by cause there was certen Arable landes beinge in diuerse mennes handes there, which should pay yerely after the rate of the thirde sheff unto the saide Chauntrie or stipendarie, was not heretofore rated or rented. But nowe the Foresaide Stipendarie hathe rated and rented euery mannes parte in moneye what they should paye, whiche Amountethe to the Sume of 45s. 3d.   Also the saide Stipendarie Saithe that he dyd neuer paye eny tenth vnto the Kinges maiestie, for the foresaide Stipendarie or Chauntrie was Removeable.

The Hundred of Wolfey.

Leomyster.   m. 2.

Memoranda : that the saide parishe of Leomyster beinge a greate Borough Towne belonginge to the Kinges Maiestie, yt is the gretest merket Towne within the Countie of Hereford, and the parishe thereof standethe verye wyde and brode, meate to haue a learned man to preche goddes worde, for the people is very ignorante.

Item the Inhabitauntes of the saide Towne and parishe humbly desiereth your mastershippes, yf it may stande with the kinges maiesties pleasure, That theie maye haue parte of the saide Stipendaries and Chauntre towardes the mayntenaunces of a Grammer Scole to be kepte within the saide Towne ; And that euer before this tyme there hathe been kepte A Grammer Scole in the saide Towne.   It would be a greate helpe to the same.   The Nomber of Howselinge people, 1,800.

Richard's Castle.

The Stipendary of the service of our lady and Saint John Baptist, in the parishe churche of Rychardes Castell.

Howslinge people, 300.

John parkynges, prest, incombent, for his salary Clere, £4 16s. 7d.

A Scole there, the Scolemaster the said John parkynges.

The parishenors desierethe that the said Scole maye styll remayne.

THE HUNDRED OF STRATFORD.

PEMBRIDGE.

The Stipendarie called our ladie service, in the parishe churche of pembredge.

John Roode, preste Stipendarye, for his Salarye yerelie, .73s.

Howseling people, 500.

A Scole there, the Scolemaster the saide John Roode.

Memorandum: that this parishe of pembredge beinge A Towne, there is kepte in the saide towne a merkett, and the saide parishe standethe wyde and large seven or eight myles aboute, mete to haue a lerned manne to preche goodes worde; the people there very ignoraunte. And also the saide Scole there to be maynteyned for the erudicion of the yough there.

WEBLEY.

The Chauntre in the Chapell of Saint Nicholas, in the parishe churche of Webley.

James Morgan, incombent, for his Salarie Clere, 119s. 8¼d.

Howselynge people, 380.

Memorandum: that the inhabitauntes of the saide parishe of webley desierethe to haue A Scolemaster to teche younge Childrenne there, and mete to haue a lerned man to preche goodes worde.

KINGSLAND.

The 2 Stipendaries at the Aulter of our ladie, in the parishe Churche of Kyngeslande.

John Harteley, Stipendarie, for his Salarie yerely, £8 4s. 3d.

A Scole there, the Scolemaster the saide John Harteley.

Howselinge people, 300.

Memorandum: the inhabitauntes in the saide parishe desierethe to haue the saide Scole to be styll maynteyned for the éducacion of the yough there. The other Stipendarie is nowe voyde, for the saide John Harteley, Scolemaster and Stipendarie, hathe the whole for his Salarie and teaching the Childrene there.

DILWYN.

The Chauntre of Seynt Nicholas, in the parishe churche of Delwyn.

Thomas Nicholles, incombent there, for his Salarie Clere, 71*s.* 6¾*d.*

A Scole there, The Scolemaster of the saide Scole.

Howselinge people, 300.

KINNERSLEY.

The Stipendarie or Scole, in the parishe of Kynnersley.

William Pyke, Clerke, Stipendarie, and Scolemaster, for his stipende and wages yerlie, £6 2*s.*

Howselinge people, 140.

Memorandum : the saide Stipendarie is now imployed to the Keping of A Scole, nowe being there 60 Scolers. And that the saide William Pyke, Clerke, is Scolemaster, a man well learned, And the Stipendarie was converted to be A Scole foure or fyve yeres past.

THE HUNDRED OF BROXFASHE.

BROMYARD. *m.* 3.

The Stipendarie in the parishe churche of Bromyarde.

John Bastenall, prest, Stipendarie, for his Salarie yerely, 69*s.* 11*d.*

A scole there, the Scolemaster the said John Bastenall.

Howselinge people, 800.

Memorandum : that this Towne of Bromyarde is a market Towne, and Greatlie replenished with people, and the parishe of the same longe and large, that is to wytt, 7 myles over some waye, And 15 myles cumpase aboutes ; And the landes, which was geven by dyvers persons as well to the maynteyninge of Goddes seruice as also to bringe vp Childrene borne there in readinge, wrytinge, and grammer. The inhabitauntes of the saide Towne and parishe humble besechethe that it maye please the Kinges maiesties highenes, with the assent of his most honerable Counsaile, to Graunte the saide landes to the mayntenaunce of the bringing vp of the yough there according to the

Foundacion thereof, And it is a mete place to establishe a learned man to preche Godes worde.

THE HUNDRED OF HUNTYNGTON.

YARDSLEY.

The Stipendarie and Gramerscole in the Towne and parishe of Yardesley.

William Storr, prest, Stipendarie, and Scolemaster, for his Stipend, £4 13s. 10d.

A Scole there.

Howselinge people, 343.

The Inhabitauntes of the saide Towne and parishe desiereth that Scole there according to the Foundacion maye styl be maynteyned; and mete to haue a learned man to preche Goddes worde, for the people there is very ignoraunte.

THE HUNDRED OF WYGMORE.

BUCKNILL.

The Stipendarie in the towne and parishe churche of Bucknell.

Laurence Johnson, Stipendarie and Scolemaster, for his wages, 106s. 8d.

A Scole there.

Howselinge people, 160.

Memorandum: that the saide Stipendarie and Scolemaster is payd his wages of dyuerse Menne of the said parishe of Bucknell of a certen Stocke of money of £32 remayning in there handes, the increse thereof geven to the mayntenaunce of the saide Stipendarie and Scolemaster, as well to mynyster and helpe the Curate there, as also to teche pore mennes Childrene within the saide parishe or Towne aforesaide there Grammer.

Herefordshire. Schools Continuance Warrant, 5.

Forasmoche as it apperith [&c.] that a grammer scole hath bene contynually kepte in Ledbury [&c.], with the revenues of the late chauntry called the Trynitie seruice there, And that the Scholemaster there hath hadd [&c.] 71s. 8d. [&c.].

And that a grammer schole hath bene contynually kept in Bosbury [*&c.*], with the revenues of the parishe there, and that the Scholemaster there hath hadd [*&c.*], yerely, 49*s.* 9½*d.* [*&c.*].

And that a grammer Schole hath ben contynually kepte in the parishe of Ricardes Castell [*&c.*], with the revenues of the Chauntery or seruice of our lady and saynt John Baptist there, And that the Scholemaster there hath had [*&c.*] £4 16*s.* 7*d.* [*&c.*].

And that a grammer Schole hath bene contynually kepte in the parisshe of Pembredge [*&c.*], with the revenues of landes and tenementes appointed to the seruice of our lady there, And that the Scholemaster there hath had [*&c.*] 73*s.* [*&c.*].

And that a grammer schole hath bene contynually kepte in Kynges lande [*&c.*], with the revenues of landes [*&c.*] appointed to the fyndyng of two Stipendaries at the aulter of our lady there, And that the Scolemaster there hath had [*&c.*] £8 4*s.* 3*d.* [*&c.*]

And that a grammer schole hath bene contynually kepte in Delwyn [*&c.*], with the revenues of the Chauntery of seynt Nicholas ther, And that the Scholemaster there hath had [*&c.*] 71*s.* 6¾*d.* [*&c.*].

And that a grammer Schole hath bene contynually kepte in Kynnersley [*&c.*], with the revenues of landes [*&c.*] appointed to the fyndyng of a prest there, and that the Scholemaster there hath had [*&c.*] £6 2*s.* [*&c.*].

And that a grammer Schole hath bene contynually kepte in Bromeyarde [*&c.*], with the revenues of landes [*&c.*] appointed to the fyndyng of a preest there, and that the Scholemaster there hath had [*&c.*] 69*s.* 11*d.* [*&c.*].

And that a grammer Schole hath bene contynually kepte in yardesley [*&c.*], with the revenues of landes [*&c.*] appointed to the fyndyng of a prest ther, and that the Scholemaster there hath had [*&c.*] £4 13*s.* 10*d.* [*&c*].

And that a grammer Schole hath bene contynually kepte in Buckenell [*&c.*], with the revenues of landes [*&c.*], appointed to the fyndyng of a prest there, And that the Scholemaster there hath had [*&c.*], 106*s.* 8*d.* [*&c.*].

Wee therfor [*&c.*] haue assigned [*&c.*] that the seid grammer

Schole in Ledbury aforeseid shall contynue, and that Richard Wheler, Scholemaster ther, shall haue and enjoye the rowme of Scholemaster there, and shall haue for his wages, yerely, 71s. 3d.,

And that the seide grammer Schole in Bosbury aforeseid shall contynue, and that Thomas Keylyng, Scholemaster there, shall haue [&c.], 49s. 9½d.,

And that the seide grammer Schole in Ricardes Castell aforeseid shall contynue, and that John Parkyns, Scholemaster there, shall haue [&c.] £4 16s. 7d.,

And that the seid Grammer Schole in Pembridge aforeseid shall contynue, and that John Roode, Scholemaster there, shall haue [&c.] 73s.,

And that the seid grammer Schole in Kynges lande aforeseide shall contynue, and that John Harteley, Scholemaster there, shall haue [&c.] £8 4s. 3d.,

And that the seid Grammer Schole in Delwyne aforeseid shall contynue, and that Thomas Nicholl, Scholemaster there, shall haue [&c.] 71s. 6¾d.,

And that the seid grammer Schole in Kynnersley aforeseid shall contynue, and that William Pyke, Scholemaster there, shall haue [&c.] £6 2s.,

And that the grammer Schole in Bromeyarde aforeseide shall contynew, and that John [Batteshall], scolemaster there, shall haue [&c.] 69s. 11d.,

And that the seid grammer Scole in yardesley aforeseid shall contynue, and that William Storr, Scholemaster there, shall haue [&c.] £4 13s. 10d.,

And that the seide grammer Schole in Buckenill aforeseid shall contynue, and that Laurence Johnson, Scholemaster there, shall be and contynue styll [&c.], and shall haue [&c.] 106s. 8d.

Comitatus Herefordie. Particulars for Schools.

Edward VI. Roll 4.

LEOMINSTER GRAMMAR SCHOOL.

Parcelle Possessionum nuper Prioratus de Leompstre, in Comitatu Herefordie, Celle nuper Monasterii de Redinge, in Comitatu Berkesire.

Cotage rente [in] Leompter, [in] comitatu Herefordie, valet in
Redditu, £22 15*s*. 4*d*.   Incremento Redditus, 28*s*. 10*d*.

£24 4*s*. 2*d*.

Inde Reprise, videlicet, in
Vadiis Collectoris Reddituum ibidem, 10*s*.
Et clare valent per annum, £23 14*s*. 2*d*.

Memorandum : the Lordishipp of Leompstre, lyinge within the
parishe of Leompstre, parcell, of the sayde late Pryorye, wherof
the premisses ys parcell, is of the yerely value of fyve hundreth
poundes, and above, in Rentes and Fearmes, besydes Casualties
per annum, etc.

Examinatur 12 Marcii, Anno 7 Regis Edwardi VI[u]., per me
Johannem Hanbie, Auditorem.   [155¾.]

2 Junii, Anno 7 Edwardi VI[u].   [1553.]

The kynges magestez plesser ys that the Baylly and the 24
Burgessez of the Towne of Leompster shall haue a new
Corporacyon, by the name of baylly and burgessez of the sayd
Towne, and that they shall and may chose yerly such one of the
sayd burgessez as they shall thynke mete to be baylly ther for
one yer, and they to haue such lybertese and Customese and
franchese as they haue heretofore lawfully had and vsede within
the sayd Towne, and also shall haue to the fayr day ther,
wyche they have alreddy ther had, wyche ys and hathe byne
kept yerly at the fest of saynt Peter the appostell, one other
fayr ther to be kept yerly at the fest of Symon and Jude, and
the same to Contynew That daye.

And also the kynges magestez plesser ys to geue and grant
vnto the sayd baylly and burgesses to the ereccion of a scole,
now and euer mor within the sayd towne and borow, of the
housez, cotages, and gardens aforesayd, as myche of them as
shall amonte to the clere yerly valew of £10, and shall haue
of the sayd howsez, cotages, and gardens as myche more of
them as shall amounte vnto other £10 by yer, after the rate of
tenne yers purchase, towarde the mayntenance of the sayd scole
in the sayd borow ; and of the resydew of the sayd howsez,
cotages, and gardens as myche as besydes the som £20 by
yer shall amonte vnto £16 17*s*. 3½*d*. the kynges magestez

plesser ys that the sayd baylly and burgessez shall haue to them and to ther successors payynge the yerly rent of £16 17s. 3½d. to thekynges magesty, his heyers and successers for euer.

And also the kynges magestez plesser ys that the sayd baylly and burgesses sh[all] haue lycence of hys hyghenesse, for the better mayntenance of the sayd scole and borow aforesayd, other lands and tenementes to the clere yerely valew of £10 by yer.

Therfore mak a grant to the sayd baylly and burgessez and to ther successors of the thynges before remembered accordyngly.   (*Signed*) Ry. Sakevyle.

The landes and tenementes, within mencyoned, to the yerely value of tenne poundes after the rate of tenne yeres purchace, purchaced by the bailiff and burgeses of Leompster, amounteth to the somme of one hundreth poundes, which was paided by the said bailiff and burgesses to Sir John Williamz, Treasaurer of the Courte of thaugmentacions, as appereth by an acquyetaunce shewed, dated the 20 day of June, Anno Regni Regis Edwardi vj^u. 7.

Nuper Seruicium Sancte Trinitatis in [Leom]pstre infra Wolsey, [in] Comitatu Herefordie ; valet in

[Redditibus], £6 7s. 4d.   Inde Reprise, videlicet, in [Redditibus resolutis], 2s. 10½d.

Et valet clare per annum, £6 4s. 5½d.

Nuper Seruicium [beate] Marie in Leompstre predicta ; valet in [Redditibus], 101s. 4d.

Nuper Seruicium [beate] Marie in Leompster vocatum Philipp ap organs landes, cum obitu ibidem ; valet in [Redditibus], 44s.

Summa claris valoris trium Canteriarum [*sic*] predictarum, per Annum, £13 9s. 1½d.

Inde in vadiis Collectoris Reddituum predictorum, per annum, 6s. 8d.

Et valent clare per annum, £13 3s. 1½d.

For the baylly and burgessez of Leompster.

Examinatur 12 Marcii Anno 7 Regis Edwardi vj^u., per me Johannem Hanbie, Auditorem.

The Countie off Hertforde. Certificate 27.
(Edward VI.)

Sir Henry Parker, Knyght, John Cokkes, Fraunces Southwell
and Robert Chaloner, Esquiers, Commissioners.

13. ASSHWELL.

A Gilde or fraternite founded within the churche of Asshwell
for the findinge of a preste for ever.

Valued in

Rentes of assise paid to the said Brotherhedd, viz.: John
Sewster, of Mordon, 2s. 10½d.; John Bill, gent., 5s. 1d.; James
Orwell, gent., 2s. 8d.; of Mr. Randall, 2s.; of Mr. Warde, gent.,
15d.; John Sewster, of Glitton, gent., 9d.; John Nicolles, 2s.;
William Lecheworthe, 12d.; John Shersmythe, 18d.; Thomas
West, 10d.; John Barlie the elder, 17½d.; of [blank] Colles, 3d.;
Thomas Sterlinge, 2½d.; of Mr. Eston, 10d.; of Mr. Avenon,
6¼d.; John Bigrave, of Glitton, 6d.; William Chapman, 5d.;
of St. Jones Colledge, in Cambridge, for Londes in the said
Towne of Asshwell, 2½d.; of Mr. Lambarte, for Londes in
Henxworthe, 12¼d.; Warren Payne, 4d., for Londes in Henx-
worthe. Also of Roberte Morgan, for Londes in Mordon, 3d.;
Thomas Bridgges, 6½d.; and of gunwell Hall, in Cambridge, for
Londes in Mordon, 2½d. In all by the yere, 26s. 8¾d.

The Ferme of a Messuage or tenemente called the Westburie,
with Londes, Meddowes, pastures, and Tenementes therto
belonginge, now in the Tenure of Thomas Goode, And payethe
yerelie, £9.

The Ferme of a Tenemente with the appurtenaunces in the
Tenure of Thomas Chapman by the yere, 20s.

The Ferme of a close containing 2 Acres lyinge in Swynewell,
in the tenure of John Waller by the yere, geven to the Brotherhedde to kepe an obite, 9s.

The Ferme of a Tenemente lyinge in the Hight strete at
Asshwell, in the tenure of Jone Bigrave Widowe, 2s. 4d.

The Ferme of 5 acres of Londe lyinge in Henxworthe filde, in
the tenure of William Chapman by the yere, 3s. 4d.

The [blank] of a Tenemente called the Brotherhedd howse
and one other tenemente wherin the prest of the said Gilde

dothe inhabite, and one close now in the tenure of John Letcheworthe, worthe, to be letten yerelie, 13*s.* 4*d.*

As yet not letten.

Inde sold to Reve and Johnson and Hendeson the prestes howse, 6*s.* 8*d.*

Copieholde londes.

The Rente of a Tenemente, with a garden lyinge in the weste ende, geven to the said Brotherhedde for the kepinge of an obite, now in the tenure of Thomas webbe, And payethe by the yere, 14*s.*   £13 8*s.* 8¾*d.*

Memorandum : that it was thought by diuerse of the honest men of Asshwell, which were before the Commissioners, &c., that certen parcelles of the Londes belongynge to this gilde to be copie-holdes ; but for as muche as at that tyme they were not hable to make certen declaracion therof, I haue here chardged all aswell Free as copie quousque, &c.   Whereof

Reprised in

Rente resolute to the Kinges maiestie yerelie, 4*d.*

Rente resolute to the Quenes grace at Lylington Courte by the yere, 1*d.*

Rente resolute payd to the Lorde bisshoppe of westminster, 27*s.* 6*d.*

Rente resolute to [*blank*] Hawtred, gent., to his Mannour of Westburie, by the yere, 31*s.* 4*d.*

Rente resolute to the Heres of [*blank*] Randoll, gent. 2*s.* 11*d.*

Rente resolute to Mr. [*blank*] Burgoyne by the yere, 6*d*
                                                          62*s.* 8*d.*

And so remayneth clere, £10 6*s.* 0¾*d.*

Inde pro Salario vnius Capellani, £6 13*s.* 4*d.*

And the rest to pore people, 72*s.* 8¾*d.*

Plate belonginge to the said Gilde wayethe 16½ ounces— viz. : *gilt* 2½ *ounces, parcell gilte* 10½ *ounces, white* 3½ *ounces.*

Goodes and Implementes of howseholde, as apperethe by an Indenture, ben valued at 69*s* 6*d.*

Memorandum : the parsonage of Asshwell is impropered to the Bisshopprike of Westminster. Doctour Taylour is vicare

there, who fyndethe but one preste to mynistre to the holle
cure or parisshe, wherein ben aboue 26 score of people, and of
them ther is aboue 200 pore people.

Item Thomas Daye, of the age of 54 yeres, is Brotherhedd preste, a Man of good behauour and well lerned,
excersysynge hym selfe in techinge of childerne franklie,
havinge non other lyuinge but the said salarie.

*Nota, that here is a necessite for a preste to assiste the curate
and to teche childerne.*

Comitatus Hertfordie. Certificate 87.

(Edward VI.)

2. ASSHWELL.

The Fraternyte there (whereunto are belonginge bothe Fre
londes and copiholde) is worthe clere, £10 6s. 0¾d., owt of
which

Thomas Daye, a man well lerned, beyng the brotherhed prest,
hade for his stipend, £6 13s. 4d.

*Thomas Daye appointed to be assistant to the cure, with
the accustomed wages quousque, etc., and to kepe the schole
there.*

The reste of the Revenneus was yerelie Distributed emounge
the pore people of the parisshe, which amountethe to 72s. 8¾d.

The Brotherhedd prest was bound to serue in the churche,
and to teche childerne of the parisshe frelye.

Item the parsonage is impropered to Westminster, And
Doctour Taylour, Deane of Lyncoln, is vicar there, who hathe
but one curate there at his chardge, unhable to serue the cure
without assistaunte.

3. BARKEHAMSTED.

A Free Scole ther founded by Doctour Incent, and endowed
with Landes and Possessions for the findinge of a Scole Master
and Vssher, and a chapleyn, to the clere yerlie valew aboue all
Rentes resolute, £31 3s. 8d.

Hertfordshire. Schools Continuance Warrant, 14.

Forasmuch as it apperith [&c.] that a Free Schole hath bene
contynually kepte in Aysshewell [&c.], with the revenues of the
Guylde or Fraternitie there, and that the Scholemaster there
hath hadd [&c.] £6 13s. 4d. [&c.].

We therefore [&c.] have assigned [&c.] that the seide Fre
schole in Aysshewell aforeseide shall contynue, And that
Thomas Daye, scholemaster there, shall haue [&c.], and shall be
assistaunt to the cure there, and shall haue [&c.] £6 13s. 4d.

Kente. Certificate 28.
(Edward VI.)

Commission annexed directed to Raffe Vane, Antony Aucher,
Walter Hendley, and James Hales, Knyghtes; Henry Crispe,
Thomas Spilman, Paule Sidnour, and Thomas Watton, Esquiers;
Cristofer Nevison, William Hide,.and John Lendall, gentilmen.

29. THE PARISHE OF WYE.

Churche land gyven by William [German gent.] to the
Churche of Wye for the helthe of his soule for euer.

The yerelye value of the same land is 8s., wherof in

Rente resolute, 18d.

And so remaneth clere, 6s. 6d.

Memorandum : there is a gramer scole ther kepte, latelie
maynteined by the late College there, which was surrendered
into the handes of our late soueraign lord Kinge Henry the
eight, anno regni sui 36to. And nowe the scolemaster there
recevith his stipend, which is £18 6s. 8d., at the handes of Sir
Moryce Dennys, Knighte, who doth enioye the possessions of the
said College, as assigned vnto Sir Walter Buckler, Knighte,
vnto whom the Kinges maiestie did graunte the same.

124. THE PARISHE OF FEVERSHAM (OSPRINGE)

A salarye or stipend of one preiste within the said parishe of
Feuersham, graunted by the late Master, the fellowes and

scolers of saynt James [sic] College, in Cambridge, to the entent and purpose that the said preiste shulde celebrate and synge in a certen chapell there, in Ospryngestrete, and to teache children there frely duringe his lyff.

The same salarye or stipend is by the yeare, £6 13s. 4d.

William Thompkynson, clerke, is Incumbent or Salary preyste there, of the age of [blank] yeres, and of honeste qualities and learninge ; and hath not any other thinge to lyve vpon, but only his service there, whiche he hath duringe his lif, as by the letters patentes of the said Master Fellowes and Scolers doth appere.

There is not any vicar endowed there, other then the vicar of the parishe there, whose name is Clement Norton, for that the said salarye is no parishe churche, nor yet any parishe churche thervnto appropriat. And that there are 900 houslinge people within the same parishe.

There hath not bene any gramer Scole kepte, preacher mayntened, or pore people relevid by the said salarie other then before is declared.

Goodes or plate belonginge to the same salarie, or Fre scole there is none, but one chalys gylded, weyenge [blank] ounces taken from the said salarie, by one doctour Bill, master of the College of St. Johns in Cambridge, sythens the feast of Ester laste paste ; but by what right, it is not knowen.

Kent. Schools Continuance Warrant, 3.

Forasmoche as it apperith [&c.[that a Free Schole hath been contynually kepte in Higham with the revenues of the late Chauntrie there, And that the scholemaster there hath hadd for his Stipend and Wages yerelie, £6 13s. 4d. [&c.].

And that a free Schole hath been contynually kepte in Osprynge in the said Countie, with the revenues of the late Chauntery there, And that the Scholemaster there hath hadd for his stipend and wages yerelie, £6 13s. 4d. [&c.].

We therefore [&c.] haue assigned and appoynted that the said free Schole in Higham aforesaid shall contynue, And that

John Cowper, Scholemaster there, shall haue and enjoye the Rowme of Scholemaster there, and shall have for his wages yerelie, £6 13s. 4d.

And that the said Free Schole in Osprynge aforesaid shall contynewe, and that William Thomson, Scholemaster there, shall haue and enjoie the Rowme of Scholemaster there, and shall haue for his wages yerelie, £6 13s. 4d.

Kent. Duchy of Lancaster. Schools Continuance Warrant. Div. XXV. Q. No. 8.

Forasmuch as it appeareth [&c.], And that a Grammer Scole hath beene heretofore continually kept in the parish of Tenterden, in the county of Kent, with the revenues of the Chauntry of Peter Marshall, founded in the parish church there, And that the scholemaster there had for his wages yearly £10, which scole [&c.].

Wee therefore [&c.] have assigned [&c.] that the Grammer Scole in Tenterden aforesaid shall continue, And that John Forset, scholemaster there, shall continue in the said rowme, And shall have for his wages yearly, £10.

Lancashire. Duchy of Lancaster.

Class XXV., Bundle V., 3rd portion, m. 45.

(Henry VIII.)

John, Bishop of Chester, Syr Thomas Holcroft, Knight, John Holcroft, Robert Tatton, John Kechyn, and James Rokeby, esquiers, commissioners.

23. LIVERPOOL.

The Chauntrie at the alter of Saynt Katherine, within the said chapell [of Lyverpole].

Humfrey Crosse, preist, Incumbent ther, of the Foundacion of John Crosse, to celebrate ther for the sowles of his said founder and his heires, and to do one yerlie obbet, and to distribute at the same 3s. 4d. to poore people ; and also the Incumbents herof by ther Foundacion are bounden to teache and kepe one gramer skoile, to take ther advantage of skolers, savinge those that beryth the names of Crosse, and poore children.

The same is at the altar of Saynt Katherine within the chapell of Lyverpole, in the paroche of Walton beforsaid, being distante from the paroche church 4 myles, and at this day the said Incumbent doth celebrate, distribute, and teache accordinge to his said Foundacion.

First, one chalez, poiz by estimacion 2 onces.

Item, 2 olde vestments.

Item, 1 masse boke.

Item, 1 superaltar.

Sum totall of the rentall, £4 15s. 10d.

36. MYDELTON.

The Chauntrie in the paroch churche of Mydleton.

Thomas Mawdesley, preiste, incumbent ther, of the foundacion of Thomas Langley, somtyme Bishopp of Durham, ther to celebrate for the sowles of the kinges of Englande, the said Bishop, and his ancestors; and the Incumbentes herof to teache one gramer skole, fre for poore children.

The same is at the alter of Saynt Cuthbert, within the paroch church of Mydelton, and the same prist, nowe Incumbent, doth celebrate and teache gramer accordinge to thentent of the saide foundacion.

First, one chalez of silver, poiz by estimacion 10 oz.

Item, thre vestiments.

Item, one masse boke.

Item, 2 alter clothes.

Sum totall of the rentall, £6 13s. 4d.

Sum of the annual reprises, 13s. 4d.

And so remanyth £6.

46. BLACKBURN.

The Chauntrie at the alter of Our Lady within the said paroch church (Blakborne).

Thomas Burges, preist, incumbent ther, of the Foundacion of the ancestors of th'erle of Derbie, to celebrate ther for ther sowles, and to maneteyne the one side of the quere to the uttermost of his power every holie day; and also the Incumbent herof, to be sufficientlie lerned in gramer and plane songe, to kepe a Fre Skole contynuallie in Blakborne biforesaide.

The same is at the alter of our lady within the said paroch church, and the said Incumbent doth celebrate and manetene the quere every holie day accordinglie, and also doth teache gramer and plane songe in the said Free Skole, accordinge to the statutes of his Foundacion.

Sum totall of the rentall, £5 10s. 8d. Whereof

Paid for a rent, 2s.

And so remanyth, £5 8s. 8d.

59. LEYLAND.

The Chauntrie within the paroch church of Leylonde. Thurstane Taylor, preiste, incumbent ther, of the foundacion of Heury Faryngton, Knight, to celebrate ther for the sowles of hym and hys antecessors, by which foundacion the Incumbents herof are bounde to kepe one fre Gramer Skoyle in the church biforsayde, as by the said foundacion it may appere.

The same ys at the alter of saynt Nycholas within the paroch church biforsayde, and the sayd Incumbent this day doth celebrate ther and kepe A Fre Skoyle accordinglye.

Plate [&c.], None.

Sum totall of the rentall, £4 5s. 1d., whereof payde to Sir Henry Farrington, knight, for cheif rente goinge forth of the same landes by yere, 4d.

And so remanyth, £4 5s. 9d.

64. PRESTON.

The Chauntrie at the altar of Our Lady within the said church.

Nycholas Banaster, preist, Incumbent ther, of the foundacion of Helene Houghton, ther to celebrate contynuallie for his sowle and all christen sowles; and the Incumbent thereof, to be sufficiently lerned in gramer to th' entent to have a fre gramer skole kept ther also, as by the sayd foundacion it doth appere.

The same is within the paroche of Preston, and the Incumbent biforsayde doth celebrate there, and kepe gramer skole at this day accordynglye. And by reporte of the Inhabitants of the saide towne the ordinaunce of the sayde foundacion hitherunto hayth be well kepte and usyd.

Plate, none.

Sum totall of the rentall, £3 2s. 4d.

Reprises, none.

68. St. Michael-upon-Wyre.

The Chauntrie in the paroch church of St. Myghell upon Wyre.

Willyam Harryson, preist, Incumbent ther, of the foundacion of John Butler, to celebrate there in the saide church for his sowle and all chrysten sowles, and the Incumbent therof to teache gramer Skole.

The same is at the alter of saynt Katheryne within the paroche churche of saynte Myghell upon Wyre, and the same preyst doth celebrate ther, and kepe gramer skole accordinglie.

Sum totall of the rentall, £5 15s. 8d.

Reprises, 5s.

And so remanyth over, £5 10s. 8d.

Hornby.

The supposedde Hospital or Bedhouse in Hornebey, in the paroch of Mellinge.

The same was willed and ordened by the lorde Edwarde Mounteigle, deceased, to have beene one hospitall, and to have hadde in yt two preistes, one clerke, 5 beydemen, and one Scole master perpetuallie, to have songe, prayde, and taughte one Fre gramer skole there.

For the trewe performaunce wherof he did infeoff Edwarde Stanley, son and heire of Thomas, late Erle of Derby, and other in certen his manors, landes, and tenementes in Hornebye, litle Harwoode, Preston in Amoundernes, Keverden, Walton in le dale, Penwertham, Tatham, Lancastre, Catone, Bolton in Londesdale, Oxclyff, Ovangle, Gressingham, Eskerige, in the countie of Lancastre, and Underley, in the countie of Westmorelande, as in the will of the sayde late lord Mounteigle apperyth, and for the establishinge of a foundacion of the sayde hospitall, (which nether in his lyf tyme nor none other tyme sithens was fynyshed), as by the sayde will apperyth.

Item, there ys none Incumbente there at this tyme, nether preyste, clerke, nor bedemen, nor at no tyme hertotore hayth beene; albeyt the lord Mounteigle that nowe is, doth of his owne benevolent good will and plesure kepe one skole master to teache gramer skole there, beinge one of his household servandes.

Item, For so moche as the sayde hospitall was not fullie fynyshed in the lyffe of the sayde lorde Edwarde he dide will his executors should performe and fynyshe the same, which they have not done, so that at this daye there is no such hospitall erected nor founded there, accordinge to the will of the said Lorde Edwarde Monteigle, decessed.

There is no perfyte rentall knowen, but onlie landes put in feoffement for the establishinge of the sayde hospitall as before is declared, which sayde hospitall was never fullie erected and fynyshed as by the said will apperyth.

Plate, &c., none.

Lancashire. Duchy of Lancaster.
Div. XVIII., vol. 26 B.
(Edward VI.)

The Certificat of all Colledges, Chauntryes, and other corporacions within the Countie of Lancaster, surveyed anno Edward VI. 2° by vertue of his Grace's Comyssion directed in that beyhalfe [1548].

THE TOWNE AND PARYSHE OF WARRINGTON. f. 5, p. 8, where there are houselinge people, 2,000.

The Chauntrie in the parishe churche of Warrington, called Butler Chauntrie.

Off the Foundacion of Sir Thomas Butler, knight, to celebrate there for his sowlle and the soulles of his auncestors for ever, which is observed accordinglie.

Robert Halle, incumbent, of the age of 70 yeres, a man decrepit and lame of his lymmes, hathe the clere yerelie revenue of the same for his salarie, £4 10s. 5d. And his lyuinge besides is *nil.*

The landes and tenements belongynge to the same are of the yerely value of £4 10s. 5d., whereof in reprises, *nil.*

THE TOWNE AND PARYSHE OF WALTON.   f. 9, p. 16.

Houselynge people, 1,000.

The Chauntrie at the alter of Saynt Katherine within the said chappell of Lyverpole.

Off the Foundacion of John Crosse, to celebrate there for his soulle, And to do one yerely obit, and to distribute at the same 3s. 4d. to pore people ; And also to kepe a Schole of Grammer free for all children bearynge the name of Crosse, and pore children, which is not observed accordinglie. And the graunte is for ever.

Humfrye Crosse, Incumbent, of the age of 50 yeres, hath for his Salarie the clere yerelie proffitts of the same, £6 2s. 10d. And his lyvinge besides is *nil.*

The lands [*&c. as in last entry*], £6 2s. 10d.

In reprises, *nil.*

The ornaments belongynge to the same are valued at 3s.

The number of ounces of plate belonginge to the same are, by estimacion, 12 oz.

THE TOWNE AND PARISH OF MIDDELTON.   f. 13, p. 24.

Howselinge people, 800.

The Chauntre in the parishe church of Middleton, off the Foundacion of Thomas Langley, sometyme Bishop of Durham, to celebrate there for the soulls of the Kings of Englande, the said Bishoppe and of his auncestors.

And also to kepe a Grammer Schole for pore children, which is observed accordinglie.

And the graunt is for ever.

Thomas Mawdesley, Incumbent, of thage of 50, hath the clere yerely revenue of the same for his salarie, £6. And his lyvynge besides is *nil.*

The lands [*&c.*], £6 13*s.* 4*d.*

Whereof in Reprises, 13*s.* 4*d.*

And so remayneth clere by yere, £6.

The stockes, goodes, Ornaments, &c., belongynge to the same be valued at 3*s.*

The number of ounces [*&c.*], 10 oz.

THE TOWNE AND PARISH OF BLACKEBORNE. f. 16.

Houselynge people, 2,000.

The Chauntrie at the alter of Our Ladie, within the said parishe churche.

Off the foundacion of the ancestors of therle of Derbie, to celebrate there for their soulls, to mayntayne th' one side of the Quyre, And to kepe a Fre Schole in Blakborne aforesaid, which is observed accordinglie.

Thomas Burges, of thage of 58 yeres, hath the clere yerely revenue of the same for his salarie, £5 14*s.*

And his lyvynge [*&c.*],

The lands [*&c.*], £5 16*s.*

Whereof in Reprises, 2*s.*

And so remayneth clere by yere, £5 14*s.*

Ornaments belongynge to the same be valued at 1*s.* 8*d.*

The number of ounces of the plate, *&c.*, 9 oz.

THE TOWNE OF LEYLONDE. f. 23, p. 44.

Houselinge people, 800.

The Chauntrie within the parish church of Leylonde, off the Foundacion of Henrye Farryngton, Knighte, to celebrate there for the soulls of hym and his ancestors. And also to kepe one Fre Grammer Schole in the said Churche, which is observed accordinglie.

Thurstane Taylor, Incumbent, of the age of 52 yeres, hath the clere yerely revenue of the same for his Salarie, £4 5*s.* 9*d.*

And his lyuing [*&c.*],

The landes [*&c.*], £4 6*s.* 1*d.*

Whereof in Reprises, 4*d.*

And so remayneth clere by yere, £4 5*s.* 9*d.*

THE TOWNE AND PARYSHE OF PRESTON. f. 25, p. 48.

Houselinge people [Number not stated].

Chauntrie at the altar of our ladie within the said parish [Preston].

Of the foundacion of Helene Houghton ther, to celebrate contynuallie for hir sowle and all cristen sowles.

And also to teach one Fre Grammer Schole, which is observed accordinglie.

Nicholas Banester, of thage of 42 yeres, hath the clere yerely revenue of the same for his salarie, £3 2s. 4d.

The lands [&c.], £3 2s. 4d., whereof Reprises nil.

THE TOWNE AND PARISHE OF ST. MIGHELL UPON WYRE.

f. 26, p. 50.

Houselinge People, 800.

The Chauntrie at thalter of St. Katheryne, within the parish church there.

Off the Foundation of John Butler to celebrate there for his Soulle and all Christen Soulles; And also to teach a Grammer Schole, which is observed accordynglie.

William Harryson, Incumbent, of the age of 54 yeres, hath the clere yerely revenue of the same for his Salarie,

And his lyvynge [&c.], £5 10s.

The landes [&c.], £5 15s.

In Reprises, 5s.

And so remayneth clere by yere, £5 10s.

THE TOWNE OF MANCHESTER. f. 32, p. 60.

A Chauntrie of two pryests within the parish church there.

Off the Foundacion of Alexander Bessike, merchant, to celebrate there for his soulle, And thone of the two Pryests to teach a fre schole, which is observed accordinglie.

Robert Prestwich, clerke, and Edward Pendilton, Schoolmaster, Incumbents there, have the clere yerely revenue of the same for their salarie, £8 12s. 3d.

And their lyvinge besides is nil.

The Landes [&c.], £8 12s. 3d.

A Stipendarye in the Chappell of Rufforth.

Off the Foundacion of Barthilmewe Heskethe, esquyre, to celebrate masse there, and to teache the scholers of the towne of Rufforthe. And that 6 marks or lesse of his morgage, landes, and bargaynes, and for terme of yeres, except Thornton landes, be taken yerely by his executors for the fynding of a pryest, and his stipende to endure as the landes in morgage and bargaynyes, and the yeres therof, and other landes for terme of yeres except Thornton landes, will endure.

Richarde Deane, incumbent, of thage of 40 yeres, hath the clere yerely revenue of the same for his salarie, £4.

And his lyvynge besides is *nil.*

Landes [*&c.*], £10 0s. 9d.

LANCASTER. f. 38, p. 73.

A Stipendarie in the parishe church there [Lancaster].

Ordeyned and founded by the Mayer and burgesses of Lancaster, with parte of the profitts rysinge and growinge of one Mill graunted to them by Indenture for terme of yeres, And the residue of the profitts are ymployed to the mayntenaunce of one Grammer Schole, for which purpose they say the Mill was graunted to them.

John Lunde, pryest, Incumbent, of thage of 54 yeres, hath yerely for his salary, goynge out of the said Mill, the some of £4.

And his lyvinge besides is *nil.*

The yerely value of the Stipende paid to the priest is £4.

Lancashire. Schools Continuance Warrant. Duchy of Lancaster, Div. XXV., Q. No. 8.

Wee, Sir Walter Mildemay, Kt., and Robert Kelway, Esquier. Commissioners appointed by the King's Majesty's Commission to us directed touching [*&c., as in p. 5 above*], To the Right Honourable Sir William Pagett, Knight of the Order, Chancellour of the Duchy of Lancaster, and to the chancellor of the same for, the time being greeting.

Forasmuch as it appeareth by the certificates of certaine of the particular surveyors of the kings majesties lands that the church of the late colledge of Manchester, in Manchester, in the countye of Lancaster, is a parish church, and that there is greate necessity to have a Vicar to be endowed there. . . .

And that a Grammer scole hath beene heretofore continually kept in the said parish of Walton, with the revenues of the chauntry of St. Katherine, founded in the said chaple of Liverpoole, and that the Scole Master there had for his wages £5 13s. 3¾d. yearly of the revenues of the same chauntry, which Scole is very meete and necessary to continue.

And that a Grammer Scole hathe likewise beene continually kept in the parish of Midleton, in the said countye, with the revenues of the chauntry, founded in the parish church there, And that the Scolemaster there had for his wages yearly £5 10s. 8d., which scole [&c.].

And that a Grammer Scole hath been heretofore continually kept in the parish of Blackborne, in the said countie, with the revenues of the chauntrey founded at the alter of Our Lady in the church there, And that the Scolemaster there had for his wages yearly £4 7s. 4d., which scole [&c.].

And that a Grammer Scole hath been heretofore continually kept in the parish of Leylaunde, in the said countie, with the revenues of the chauntry founded in the church there, And that the Scolemaster [&c.], £3 17s. 10d., which Scole [&c.].

And that a Grammer Scole [&c.], in the parish of Preston, in the said countie, with the revenues of the chauntrey of Our Lady founded in the church there, and that the Scolemaster [&c.], £2 16s. 2¼d., which Scole [&c.].

And that a Grammer Scole [&c.], S. Michaell upon Wyer, in [&c.], with the revenues of the Chauntry of St. Katherine, founded in the parish church there, And that the Scolemaster [&c.], £5 10s., which Scole [&c.].

And that a free scole hath beene heretofore continually kept in the parish of Manchester, in [&c.], with the revenues of the chauntry founded in the church there, And the Scolemaster [&c.], £4 1s. 9d., which scole [&c.]. . . .

Wee, therefore, the said Commissioners, doe signyfye to you, the said chancellor of the said Duchy of Lancaster, that by virtue of the said commicion to us directed in fourme aforesaid [we have assigned and] appointed . . .

And that the said Grammer Scole, in the said parish of Walton, shall continue as heretofore hathe beene used, And that Humfrey Crosse, Scolemaster there, shall bee and remayne in the same rome, and shall have for his stipend and wages yerely, £5 13s. 3d.

And that the said Grammer Scole in Midleton aforesaid shall continue still, And that Thomas Mawdesley, scolemaster there, shall bee and remayne in the same rowme there, and shall have for his wages yerely, £5 10s. 8d.

And that the said Grammer Scole in Blackborne aforesaid shall continue, And that Thomas Burges, scolemaster there [&c.], £4 7s. 4d.

And that the said Grammar Scole in Leyland aforesaid shall continue, And that Tristram Taylor, Scolemaster there, shall bee and remayne still in the same roome [&c.] £3 17s. 10d.

. . . [MS. torn] Preston aforesaid shall continue, And that Nicholas Banister, Scolemaster there, shall bee and remayne in the same rowme, And that he shall have for his stipend and wages fifty-six shillings and two pence yearly.

And that the Grammer Scole in the said parish of St. Michaell upon Wyre shall continue, And that William Harrison Scolemaster there, shall continue in the same rowme, and shall have for his wages yearly, £5 10s.

And that the said free scole in Manchester aforesaid shall continue. And that [blank] Pendilton, Scolemaster there, shall continue in the same roome of Scolemaster [&c.], £4 1s. 9d.

And that the severall wages, stipends, and sumes of money appointed to bee continued in forme aforesaid, and every of them shall be paid from Easter last past forthward of the rents and revenues of the said [Duch]y of Lancaster, by the hand of such of the receyvours thereof for the tyme being as shall bee thought most meete and conveynient for the payment of the same, to the personnes above rehersed, and to such other persons as shall be in their rowmes and places for the tyme being, untill fur[ther or] other order or direction shall bee had or taken [in the] premisses.

Wherefore wee the said commissioners doe require you the said chancellor of the said Duchie of Lancaster to make out severall warrants accordingly for the payment of the said severall wages, stipends, and sums of money appointed to bee continued and paid in fourme aforesaid, and every part [and parc]ell thereof, to such the receyvours, and other officers of the revenues of the same Duchy, as you shall thinke most meete and conveynient for the ease, quietness, and commoditye of the same persons.

And this warrant shall bee as well to you the said chancellor of the said Duchy of Lancaster, as to all auditors, receyvours, and other officers and [ministers] of the same Duchy for the [time] being, sufficient discharge for the payment and allowance of the said severall stipends, wages, and somes of money to be continued and paid in fourme aforesaid.

Writtne the eleaventh day of August, in the second yeare of the reigne of Our Soveragne Lord Edward the 6th, by the grace of God King of England, France, and Ireland, Defender of the fayth, and in earth of Church of England and alsoe of Ireland supreme head [1548].

W. Mildmay.
[R. Kelway.]

Leicestria. Certificate 31.

(Henry VIII.)

(*For Commissioners see under Warwickshire, p.* 225.)

65. Cantaria de Castell Donyngton,

in Comitatu predicto.

Valet In

Firma Manerij de Byllysdon, cum quatuor Mesuagijs et terris, simul cum omnibus alijs terris, tenementis, pratis, pascuis, pasturis, et suis pertinencijs vniuersis, dimissa Johanni Turvile

Armigero per indenturam, pro termino Annorum, Reddendo inde per Annum, £7 18s.

Firma Mancionis eiusdem cantarie, cum omnibus Domibus et edificijs eidem pertinencijs, scituate in Castell Donyngton, in Comitatu predicto, valuata per Annum, 6s. 8d.   £8 4s. 8d.

Reprise, Videlicet In

Stipendio Cantariste ibidem per Annum, £6 13s. 4d.

Decimis Domino Regi Annuatim, inde solutis per Annum, 14s. 5d.

Obbitibus pro Fundatore ibidem per Annum, 8s. 11d.

Denarijs Annuatim solutis pro pane, vino, et cera per Annum, 2s.

Elimozinis datis pauperibus Annuatim, 8s. 11d.   £8 7s. 7d.

Et sic videtur esse in superplusagio, 2s. 11d.

Founded by Harrold Staunton, to the entent to Fynde one preste, aswell to syng dyvyne seruyce in a chapell of our Lady Within the paroche churche there, And to pray For the Founders soule, as for to teche a gramer scole there For the erudycyon of pore scolers, within a scolehouse Founded by the seyde Harolde, Within the seyde Towne of Donyngton.

Leicestershire.   Schools Continuance Warrant.

Duchy of Lancaster.   Div. XXV.   Q.   No. 8.

Wee [&c.] Forasmuch as it appearethe [&c.], And that there is a Grammer Scole kept in the [*MS. torn*] Donnyngton, in the said countie of Leicester, with the reveneus of Harrold Stauntons chauntrey in the same parish, And that the Scolemaster there [&c.], £6 13s. 4d. yearly, which scole [&c.].

Wee, therefore [&c.].

And that the said Grammer Scole in the said parish of Castle Donyngton aforesaid shall continue, And John Taylor, scolemaster there, to continue in the sa[me] rowme, and have for his wages yerely, £6 13s. 4d.

Comitatus Lincolnie. Certificate 33.

(Edward VI.)

(Commissioners not named.)

ECCLESIA CATHEDRALIS LINCOLNE.

7A. CANTARIA VOCATA BURGEHERSHE CHAUNTRIE,
in Ecclesia predicta.

Fundata fuit per Bartholomeum, Henricum, et Robertum
Burgehersche, ea intencione vt quinque capellani perpetuo
Diuina celebrarent ad altare Sancte Katerine, in dicta ecclesia,
pro animabus dictorum fundatorum et aliorum, et vt sex
pauperes pueri artem grammaticam profitentes continue sus-
tentarentur ad Scolam ab etate 7 annorum vsque ad completos
Annos sexdecim annorum ;

Necnon vt quatuor solempnes obitus siue anniuersaria Annuatim obseruarentur, in ecclesia predicta, pro animabus
dictorum fundatorum et pro anima Regis Edwardi tercij,
quorum primus obseruaretur annuatim 2do die Januarij,
secundus 26to die eiusdem mensis, tercius tercio die Decembris,
et quartus 27mo die Julij.

Incumbentes dicte Cantarie modo existunt Thomas Cham-
berlayne, etatis 56 annorum, ad curam seruiendam minime
idoneus ; Henricus Norton, etatis 66 annorum, ad seruiendam
curam minime idoneus ; Nicholaus Cusworth, etatis 52 annorum, ad seruiendam curam minime idoneus ; Johannes
Bankes, etatis 40 annorum, ad seruiendam curam minime
idoneus ; Et Ricardus Bedforth, etatis 46 annorum, ad Curam
seruiendam satis idoneus, quorum quilibet habet pro salario
suo de exitibus terrarum subsequencium, £8 per Annum, nullas
alias habentes promociones.

Terre et possessiones eiusdem Cantarie valent per annum,
£67 11s. 4d.

Reprise inde, videlicet: dictis 6 pauperibus pueris pro commensalibus et liberaturis suis, £10 ; et in denariis distributis
in eliemosina duobus millibus pauperum ad obitus predictos
annuatim, £8 6s. 8d. ; in toto, £18 6s. 8d.

Clarus valor terrarum et possessiones dicte cantarie, reprisis
deductis, per Annum, £49 4s. 8d.

Bona, Catalla, et alia ornamenta dicte Cantarie, vltra duos

calices parcella deaurata, ponderantes 30 vncias, et vltra sex coclearia argentea, ponderantia 5 vncias; 51s. 9d.

Memorandum: that £6 14s. 4d. is hollie due vnto the Kinges maiestie for the 4th obit holden the 27th of Julie for this presente yere, wherof £4 3s. 4d. hath ben yearly distribute to a thousand pore people within the said citie; that is to saie, to euery one of them, 1d.

7B. CANTARIA VOCATA BUCKINGHAMS CHAUNTRIE,
cum obitu suo.

Fundata fuit per Johannem Buckingham, quondam Lincolnie Episcopum, ea intencione vt duo capellani perpetuo divina celebrarent ad altare Sancti Hugonis et Sancte Katarine, in ecclesia predicta, pro anima dicti episcopi et aliorum, ac vt 1 obitus annuatim observaretur imperpetuum pro anima dicti Episcopi, 25 die Junij;

Necnon vt duo pauperes pueri custodirentur ad Scolam grammaticalem ab etate 7 annorum vsque ad completos annos 16 annorum.

Ad quas quidem intenciones terre et possessiones inferius specificate concesse fuerunt, Decano et Capitulo Lincolnie et successoribus suis, videlicet: Rectoria ecclesie parochialis de Lilforde, in comitatu Northamtonie, adtunc existens clari annui valoris £16, Ac modo dimissa pro £8:

Et pro eo quod exitus et proficua dicte Rectorie ita minuuntur clausura terre infra parochiam predictam, circiter 40 annos elapsos inclusæ, vnus capellanus et vnus puer de numero predicto modo extinguuntur.

Modernus incumbens dicte Cantarie est Thomas palfreman, etatis 65 annorum, ad seruiendam curam minime idoneus, percipiens annuatim pro salario suo £6 6s. 8d., nullam aliam habens promocionem.

Terre et possessiones eiusdem Cantarie valent per Annum, £14 13s. 4d.

Reprise inde, videlicet: dicto pauperi puero, pro commensalibus et liberatura sua, per annum, 33s. 4d., et pauperibus in eliemosina ad diem obitus predicti, 24s. In toto, 57s. 4d.

s

Clarus valor terrarum et possessionum dicte Cantarie, reprisis deductis, per Annum, £11 16s.

Bona, Catalla, et alia ornamenta dicte cantarie, vltra 1 calicem parcella deaurata, ponderantem 15 vncias, 3s.

38. CANTARIA SANCTI JACOBI IN MAGNA GRIMMESBY.

Fundata fuit per quendam Rayner, ea intencione vt vnus capellanus perpetuo divina celebraret in ecclesia sancti Jacobi ibidem pro animabus fundatoris et aliorum;

Cuius Incumbens nuper fuit quidam Thomas Tomlynson, qui, pro certa pecuniarum summa sibi per Maiorem et burgenses dicte ville soluta, et pro alijs causis eum in hac parte moventibus, licencia Domini Regis, nunc Edwardi sexti, in hac parte prius habita et obtenta, dedit, concessit, et pro se et successoribus suis confirmauit, dictis Maiori et Burgensibus et successoribus suis, tam omnia Maneria, Dominia, terras, tenementa et hereditamenta quecumque, cum suis pertinenciis dicte cantarie spectantibus siue vllo modo pertinentibus, quam omnia bona catalla, Jocalia et alia ornamenta dicte cantarie pertinencia.

Habenda et tenenda, eisdem Maiori et Burgensibus et successoribus suis imperpetuum ad vsum et intencionem in literis patentibus dicti domini Regis specificata et declarata, videlicet :

Vt Iuventus dicte ville et patrie adiacentis in teneris annis, tam bonis moribus et sincera erga Deum fide, quam policioribus literis imbuantur et instruantur, et vt vna libera Scola Grammaticalis ibidem de vno magistro, preceptore siue pedagogo, et vno subpedagogo, pro pueris et adolescentibus in sciencia grammaticali instruendo instituatur, et pro perpetuo stabilietur et continuetur ; vt per literas patentes dicti Domini Regis, gerentes Datum 12 die Julij, Anno regni sui primo, et per Scriptum dicti Thome Tomlinson, capellani, gerens Datum 20ᵐᵒ die Septembris, Anno predicto, dictis Maiori et Burgensibus confectas plenius liquet.

44. GILDA SANCTE TRINITATIS IN LOUTHE.

Fundata fuit per Johannem Whittingham et alios, ea intencione vt vnus capellanus perpetuo diuina celebraret in

ecclesia ibidem, pro animabus fundatorum et aliorum, qui
temporibus congruis suam meliorem preberet diligenciam in
cotidiana manutencione diuini cultus in ecclesia predicta ;

Cuius incumbens est Robertus Beyverley, etatis quadraginta
annorum, ad seruiendam curam idoneus, percipiens et habens pro
salario suo per manus Aldermani dicte gilde 1 annuitatem,
£5 13s. 4d. sibi concessam ad terminum vite per scriptum Aldermanni Fratrum et sororum dicte gilde, sub eorum communi sigillo,
cum clausa districcionis, nullam aliam habens promocionem.

Et postea alia terre et possessiones concesse fuerunt dictis
Aldermanno fratribus et sororibus et successoribus suis imperpetuum per diuersas alias personas, tam vt vnus capellanus,
in arte grammaticali sufficienter eruditus, pueros dicte ville
et patrie adiacentis, tam bonis moribus quam policioribus litteris
instrueret imperpetuum ; Quam vt 6 pauperes viri aut mulieres
eiusdem ville annuale releuamen de exitibus terrarum predictarum per manus dicti aldermani imperpetuum haberent
et perciperent, videlicet : quilibet eorum 6s. 8d. per annum,
pro focalibus et commensalibus suis, et vnam domum vocatam
Trinity beid House, pro eorum cohabitacione ;

Que quidam Scola grammaticalis a tempore concessionis
terrarum predictarum vsque in hodiernum continuata fuit,
cuius instructor est Rogerus Ascue, alias bawnus, etatis 35
annorum, nullam aliam habens promocionem, Habens consimile
stipendium ei similiter, vt supradictum est, pro termino vite
concessum.

Terre et possessiones dicte Gilde valent per annum, £19 17s. 5d.

Feoda, vadia, redditus resoluti, et alie reprise exeuntia, extra
terras predictas, per annum, £16 7s. 3d.

Clarus valor terrarum et possessionum predictarum, reprisis
deductis, per Annum, £3 10s. 2d.

Bona catalla et alia ornamenta predicte Gilde, vltra 1 calicem
parcella deaurata, ponderantem 13 vncias, 29s. 4d.

85. LIBERA CAPELLA SANCTI NICHOLAI IN HOLBECHE.

Dicta Capella, distans ab ecclesia parochiali 1 miliare, fundata
fuit per quendam Laurencium Holbech, militem, ea intencione

vt 1 capellanus perpetuo celebraret in eadem pro animabus fundatorum et aliorum;

Tamen nullus capellanus ibidem celebrauit iuxta tenorem dicte fundacionis a tempore cuius contraria memoria hominum non existit; Sed capella predicta vna cum terris et tenementis eidem pertinentibus de tempore in tempus collata fuit per patronos eiusdem, vni Scolari studenti apud cantabrigiam vel Oxoniam;

Cuius incumbens modo est Ricardus Thorpe, ætatis 17 annorum, Scolaris studiosus in collegio Regine cantabrigie, qui habet et percipit exitus et proficua terrarum et possessionum subsequencium uersus exhibicionem, nullam aliam habens promocionem.

Terre et possessiones dicte capelle valent per annum, 40s.

Reprise inde, Nulle.

Clarus valor, Patet.

96. Cantaria vocata Curteys Chauntrie in Grantham.

Fundata fuit per Ricardum, Wintoniensem Episcopum, et Thomam quadring, Executores Testamenti Ricardi Curteis, ea intencione vt duo capellani perpetuo diuina celebrarent in Ecclesia parochiali ibidem, et orarent pro animabus Henrici et Ricardi Curteis et aliorum imperpetuum, quorum vnus instrueret pueros, tam in bonis moribus quam in arte Grammaticali, in quadam celebri domo ibidem adhoc constructa et edificata, et prope ecclesiam ibidem adiacente;

Que quidam Scola a tempore fundacionis predicte usque in hodiernum diem continuata fuit iuxta intencionem fundacionis predicte,

Cuius instructor est [blank] etatis quadraginta annorum, habens pro salario suo, vltra domum mansionalem suam, £5 6s. 8d., nullam aliam habens promocionem; Et alter incumbens est georgius Gibson, etatis Triginta novem annorum, consimile percipiens stipendium, ac nullam aliam habens promocionem, fungens officio subpedagogi scole predicte; qui percipiunt exitus et proficua terrarum et posses sionum subsequencium pro salariis suis.

Terre et possessiones dicte Cantarie valent per Annum, £13 9*s.* 4*d.*

Redditus resoluti et alie reprise, exeuntes extra terras et possessiones predictas, per annum, 56*s.*

Clarus valor terrarum et possessionum predictarum, reprisis deductis, per annum, £10 13*s.* 4*d.*

Bona, Catalla, et alia ornamenta dicte Cantarie pertinencia, 4*s.* 2*d.*

Memorandum : that the resolutes abouesaid of this Chauntrie be in the charge of the Fermour during the yeres that he hath in his leases, which is about 30 yeres.

119. Stipendium vnius Capellani celebrantis in parochia beate Marie in Staunforde.

Quidam Willielmus Ratclif, per ultimam voluntatem suam factam primo die Junij, Anno Domini Millesimo 1532, inter alia voluit et declarauit quod Rogerus Ratclif, Henricus Lacye, et alij feoffatores sui et eorum heredes, seisiti existentes de et in omnibus messuagijs, terris, pratis, pasturis, Redditibus et seruiciis, cum suis pertinentiis in Staunforthe, in comitatu Lincolnie extunc starent et essent seisiti, de et in premissis, sibi heredibus et assignatis suis imperpetuum, sub condicione tamen quod ipsi, eorum heredes aut assignati invenirent et sustentarent vnum idoneum capellanum secularem sufficienter eruditum, celebraturum et oraturum pro animabus dicti Willielmi et aliorum, ac libere docturum et instructurum artem grammaticam in Staunford predicta, quamdiu lex illud permitteret.

Et si liceret executoribus suis amortizare premissa Aldermanno gilde corporis Christi ibidem, quod tunc omnia premissa supradicta remanerent Aldermanno gilde predicte imperpetuum ad vsum predictum ; Et si non liceret executoribus suis obtinere premissa in manum mortuam ponenda, quod tunc omnia predicta Messuagia, et cetera premissa, venderentur per dictos executores suos, pro tanto quanto vendi possint, cum concensu et assensu Aldermani gilde predicte pro tempore existentis, et denarij proinde recepti disponantur pro salute anime sue et aliorum fidelium ad vsum superius specificatum, prout per dictum vltimam voluntatem plenius liquet ;

Quequidem terre et tenementa nunquam amortizata fuerunt iuxta intencionem vltime voluntatis predicte ;

Sed incumbens ibidem est Libeus Byard, etatis 36 annorum, qui non solum celebrat et orat pro animabus predictis, verumeciam instruit pueros dicte ville in arte grammaticali iuxta intencionem predictam, Habens et percipiens pro salario suo exitus et proficua terrarum subsequencium, nullam aliam habens promocionem.

Terre et tenementa, ad usum predictum concessa, valent per Annum, £10 3s. 1d.

Redditus resoluti et alie reprise exeuntes, extra terras predictas, per Annum, 17s. 8d.

Clarus valor terrarum et tenementorum predictorum, reprisis deductis, per Annum, £9 5s. 5d.

124. COLLEGIUM DE THORNTON, IN COMITATU LINCOLNIE.

Fundatum fuit per Invictissimum principem sacrosanctæ memoriæ, dominum Henricum octauum, nuper Regem Angliæ, ea intencione ut sacra Dei eloquia Sacramentaque nostre redempcionis pure ministrarentur, boni mores et discipline, sincere obseruarentur, senes et qui in publicis regni negocijs viribus destituuntur ibidem foveantur, et vt Iuventus in litteris liberaliter instruantur.

Exitus et proficua terrarum et possessionum dicti Collegij percipiuntur et disponuntur per Decanum et capitulum ibidem, iuxta statuta et ordinaciones dicti domini Regis, vt inferius patet.

Terre et possessiones dicti Collegij, tam in comitatu Lincolonie quam in comitatu Eboraci, valent per Annum, £616 10s.

Feoda vadia et aliæ reprisæ exeuntia, extra terras et possessiones dicti collegij, per Annum, £61 12s.

Clarus valor terrarum et possessionum dicti collegij, Feodis, vadiis, et aliis reprisis deductis, per Annum, £554 18s.

Bona, Catalla, et alia ornamenta dicto Collegio pertinencia, vltra Jocalia argentea ibidem inferius declarata, £34 7s.

Proporciones Decani, prebendariorum, ac aliorum Ministrorum quorumcumque eiusdem collegij, iuxta fundacionem et ordinacionem Dicti Domini Regis Henrici VIII., vltra alias promociones in manibus dictorum Decani, prebendariorum, et aliorum ministrorum ibidem existencium prout, inferius patet.

Decanus dicti Collegij, Roger Dalison, clericus, ætatis 50 annorum, habens 3 beneficia annui valoris, £30, habet annuatim per portione sua in dicto collegio, £101 5s.

Prebendarij Collegij predicti [4], £64 13s. 4d.

Canonici minores dicti Collegij [5], £60.

Magister scole grammaticalis ibidem, Johannes Gooddall, etatis quadraginta quatuor annorum, percipit annuatim pro porcione sua in dicto collegio, nullam aliam habens promocionem, £20.

Magister choristarum ibidem, Radulphus Wadeson, etatis quadraginta annorum, percipit annuatim pro porcione sua in dicto collegio, nullam Aliam habens promocionem, £10.

Lector Euangelij ibidem, £6 13s. 4d.

Lector Epistole ibidem, £6 13s. 4d.

Clerici cantantes ibidem, vocati singgingmen [4], £26 13s. 4d.

Subsacrista, £5.

Pincerna minorum canonicorum ibidem, £5.

Cocus minorum canonicorum, £5.

Pauperes ibidem, vocati the Kinges beidmen [4], £20.

Janitor ibidem, £5.

Choristæ ibidem, vocati Querysters [6], £16.   £351 18s. 4d.

Jocalia deaurata et argentea dicto Collegio pertinencia :

Imprimis, quatuor calices deaurati, ponderantes 92 vncias.

Item, tres calices parcella deaurata, ponderantes 33 vncias.

Item, duo lez Basins argenti, ponderantes 16 vncias.

Item, duo paria de lez cruettes, vnum par de le censer, vna crux lignea argentea cooperta, ponderancia 98 vncias.

Item, unus liber, vocatus a gospell boke, partim argenteus coopertus, ponderans 1½ vncias.   240½ vncias.

Ultra quatuordecim coclearia, ponderancia 21 vncias.

181. BOSTOUNE, IN COMITATU PREDICTO.

Guilda beate marie ibidem.

Terre et Tenementa nuper pertinencia, siue spectancia nuper·
guilde Beate Marie ibidem, jacentia in diuersis villatis,
videlicet; in Bostoune, Kirkton, Doningtoune, Quadring, Hol-
beche, Quaplode et alibi, vt patet per rentale penes superuisorem
remanens, £328 15s. 4d.

Redditu resoluto [&c.], £129 5s. 3d.

Et in denarijs solutis novem capellanis pro eorum salarijs,
videlicet: Willielmo Harrisoon, ludimagistro, £10 2s. ; Radulpho
Cokeler, £5 13s. 4d. ; Robarto Ellingtoune, £5 13s. 4d.; Johanni
Welles, £5 6s. 8d.; Richardo Robinsoon, £5 6s. 8d. ; Richardo
Spensley, 106s. 8d. ; Robarto Richardsoone, £6 ; Andree Headley,
£6 2s. ; et Christophero [blank], celebranti apud Hospitalem
sancti Johannis Jherusalem, 33s. 4d.   £51 4s.

Et in denarijs solutis Johanni gillmyn, Capellano, pro canta-
tione in choro beate Marie, 33s. 4d. ; et Willielmo Warde, Capellano, pro organizatione in dicto choro Beate Marie, 43s. 4d.
                                                      76s. 8d.

Et in denarijs solutis diuersis clericis, cantantibus quotidie in
dicta ecclesia, pro eorum stipendio, videlicet: Ricardo gillmyn,
£8 13s. 4d. ; Richardo gouche, £8 13s. 4d. ; Nicholas Blewet,
£6 ; Johanni Broke, 36s. ; Willielmo Neudik, £7 10s.; Stephano
Mighell, £6 ; et Johanni Newman, 13s. 4d.   £39 6s.

Et in consimilibus denarijs solutis Agneti Willerton, pro
annuitate sua, 20s.; et Johanne, Vetule, in domo pauperum,
6s. 8d.; Lotrici, 10s. 10d. ; Magistro mendicantium, 5s. 4d.;
Mancipulo capellanorum, 26s. 8d.; pro Commensalibus Choristarum, £10 16s. ; et Barbitonsori pauperum, 13s.   £9 18s. 6d.

Et in expensis forinsecis cum regardatis, £5 18s. 10d. ;
expensis in festo Corporis christi, £5 21½d.; et in solucione
pauperum, £22 4s.   £33 4s. 7½d.

Et in Feodo consiliariis villae, £13 13s. 4d ; Willielmo Kyd,
pro superplusagio anni precedentis, £26′ 14s. 6½d. ; eodem
Willielmo Kyd, exercenti officium Aldermanni per duos annos,
£6 13s. 4d. ; in denarijs accommodatis eodem pro negocijs ville,
£20 ; exhibicione Choristarum, £6 17s. 10d.   £73 19s. 0½d.

Et in custagiis cantarie beate Marie, £5 12s. 5d.   Expensis
necessarijs, cum emptione carbonum, pro pauperibus et capellanis
et pro subsidio domini Regis, cum alijs, £32 14s. 5d.

£38 6s. 10d.

Et in solutione pro obitu siue anniversariis hoc anno, ultra
obitum Johannis Robinsoon prædicti, £12 22d.   £391 2s. 9d.

Et sic in superplusagio hoc Anno, £67 7s. 5d.

136. GUILDA BEATE MARIE IBIDEM.

Incorporatur per concessionem Richardi Regis secundi geren-
tem Datam vicesimo tercio die Septembris, anno regni sui sexto-
decimo, per nomen aldermanni fraternitatis in honore dei et
beate Marie virginis, ad instantiam philippi Tilney, militis, et
aliorum, pro sustentacione duorum capellanorum celebrantium in
Ecclesia sancti Botulphi pro animabus eiusdem Regis Richardi
et Annæ reginæ.

Incorporatur similiter per concessionem Henrici Sexti geren-
tem datam anno regni sui vicesimo tercio, per nomen Aldermanni
fraternitatis Beate Marie in Bostonia.

Lincolnshire. Duchy of Lancaster. Class XVIII. 25, Book A.

LINNCOLN CANTARIE.

Cantaria Willelmi Smith, nuper Lincolniensis Episcopi.
Fundata fuit per executores Willelmi Smith, quondam Lincolniensis Episcopi, ea intentione ut unus Capellanus divina
celebraret ad altare S. Sebastiani ibidem orans pro animabus
fundatorum et aliorum omnium fidelium imperpetuum, Et ut
unus solempnis obitus sive anniversarium ibidem annuatim, 17°
die Januarii, perpetuo observaretur, una cum annuali exhibitione
12s., choristis dictæ ecclesiæ, ac duobus vicariis choralibus, 13s.
4d., cantantibus missam de nomine Jesu, singulis diebus Veneris,
qualibet septimana ibidem imperpetuum ; Ac Magistro Choristarum pro organizatione ad eandem missam, 26s.

Cujus incumbens nunc est Willelmus Patchet, etatis 44
annorum, nullam aliam habens promotionem, ac ad serviendum
curam minime habilem ; Qui habet et percipit exitus et proficua
omnium terrarum et possessionum subsequentium pro salario suo.

Terre et possessiones dicte Cantarie pertinentes, valent, per annum, £13 6s. 8d.

Reprise nulle. Clarus valor patet.

Bona, catalla, et alia ornamenta eidem cantarie pertinentia, 6s. 8d.

Lincolnshire. Schools Continuance Warrant, 18.

Forasmoche as it appearith [&c.] That a grammer Scole hathe been contynuallie kept in Thorneton [&c.], with parte of the Revenues of the late [Colledge there], And that the Scolemaster there hathe had [&c.] twentie poundes [&c.].

And that tenne poundes yerelie hathe been contynually paide to the fyndyng of six children at the grammer Scole out of the Revenues of the late Chauntrye called Burghersche chauntrye, [founded in the] Cathedrall churche of Lyncoln, and that Christopher Hunt, John Watson, David Newland, Robert Asgerby, Thomas Barker, and Thomas Aslaby, beyng Scolers, do nowe enjoye the same; and that 33s. 4d. hathe been yerely geven to the fyndyng of a poore childe to the grammer Scole out of the Revenues of the late Chauntery called Buckyngham chauntery, founded in the Cathedrall Churche of Lyncoln, and that Christofer Large, beyng a Scolar, nowe doth enjoye the same [&c.].

And that a grammer Scole hath been contynuallie kept in Louth [&c.], with the revenues of the Guylde or fraternytie of the holie Trynytie in louth aforesaide, And that the Scolemaster there had [&c.] 113s. 4d. [&c.] assigned to hym by dede dated the 17th daye of December, in the 36th yere of the reigne of Henry the eighth [&c.].

And that a grammer Scole hathe been contynuallie kept in Grantham [&c.], with the Revenues of the late Chauntery called Curteis Chauntery, in Grantham aforesaide, And that the Scolemaster and the ussher of the same scole have had [&c.] £9 12s. [&c.].

And that a grammer Scole hath been contynually kept in Staunforth [&c.], with the Revenues of landes geven to the fyndynge of a preest in the Churche of our lady in Staunforth

aforesaid, and to teche a grammer Scole in Staunforth aforesaide,
and that the Scolemaster of the same Scole had [&c.] £9 5s. 5d.

We, therefore [&c.], have assigned [&c.] that the said scole in
Thorneton aforesaide shall contynewe, And that John Goodall,
Scolemaster there, shall have [&c.] twentie poundes [&c.].

And that the payment of tenne poundes yerelie to the fyndyng
of the saide sixe children [&c.] shall be contynewed, And that
the payment of 33s. 4d. yerelie to the fyndynge of the saide
childe [&c.] shall be contynewed [&c.].

And that the Scole in Louth aforesaide shall contynewe, and
that Roger Bonno, otherwise Askue, scolemaster there, shall
have [&c.] £5 13s. 4d. [&c.].

And that the saide Scole in Grauntham aforesaide shall
contynewe, and that the Scolemaster which herefore hathe
contynewed and yet remaynith there shall enjoye the Rome of
Scolemaster there, And George Gybson, ussher of the same
Scole, shall haue and enjoye the Rome of ussher there, And that
the same Scolemaster and ussher shall have [&c.] £9 12s.

And that the saide Scole in Staunforth aforesaide shall contynewe, and that Lybeus Byarde, Scolemaster there, shall have
[&c.] £9 5s. 5d.

Lincolnshire. Duchy of Lancaster. Schools Continu-
ance Warrant. Div. XXV., Q. No. 8,

Forasmuch as it appeareth that [&c.].

And that certaine poore scollers att the Grammer Scole in the
Cathedrall Church of Lincolne there have had heretofore yearly
out of diverse obitts found there 40s., and 10d. yearly towards
the maintenance of theire living, and that the same poore scollers have heretofore had out of the obytt of John Hymvell, late
Bishopp of Lincolne, £4 3s. 4d., And that the choristers of the
said church have had heretofore yearly out of the said obytts
36s. 8d., And that 1,180 pore folke have heretofore had yearly
£4 15s. 8d. in almes out of the said obyts,

And that the said choristers have had heretofore yearly
towards theire living 12s. out of the possessions of late Bishopp

Smiths chauntry, And that also the Scolemaster of the said choristers hath heretofore had 26s. 8d. yearly out of the possessions of the said Bishop Smiths of the same choristers ;

Wee, therefore [&c.] have assigned [&c.].

And that the poore scollers at the Grammer Scole in Lincolne shall have yearly 40s. 10d. as they have beene accustomed to bee paid yerely to the hands of the Deane and Chapiter of Lincolne aforesaid, And that alsoe the said poore schollers shall have yearly £4 3s. 4d., as hath been accustomed to bee paid to the handes of the said Deane and Chapter, And that the said choristers shall have yearly 36s. 8d. [&c.], and that the said 1,180 poore fellows shall have yearly, as hath beene accustomed, £4 15s. 8d., to bee paid [&c.], And that the said choristers [&c.] 12s. [&c.], And that the Scolemaster of the said choristers shall have yearly for teaching the said choristers, as hath beene accustomed, 26s. 8d., to bee likewise paid to the hands [&c.].

Comitatus Lincolnie. Particulars for Schools.
Edward VI. Roll 7.

GRANTHAM GRAMMAR SCHOOL.

Nuper Cantaria Sancte Trinitatis in Grauntham, in Comitatu predicto ; valet In Firma, £6 16s. 8d.

Nuper Cantaria Beate Marie in Grauntham, in dicto Comitatu Lincolnie; valet In Firma, £7 6s. 5d.

Parcelle Terrarum Obituum in partibus de Kesteven, in dicto Comitatu Lincolnie.

Manthorpe, Grauntham, Hougheton et Spyttlegate, cum Pawnton magna in dicto Comitatu Lincolnie; valent In [Annualibus Redditibus], 15s.

Reprise videlicet in Redditibus resolutis, 18d. Reparacionibus, 13s. 4d.

Et Remanent clare, vltra reprisas predictas per annum, £14 3s. 1d. [faded].

Examinatur per me Willelmum Rygges, auditorem.

10 Marche, anno regni Regis Edwardi vj^u., 5 [155?].

The Kinges Maiesties pleasour is that the Aldermen and Burgeses of the towne of Grauntham, in the countye of Lincoln, shall have the premysses assuryd to theym and to their Successors for ever to thentente a Free Grammer Scole shalbe with thissues and proffettes of the same premysses fowndyd there of his maiesties ereccion [*faded*] for ever, And also a licence of Mortmain [*faded*] and tenementes given by bisshopp Fox to the college of Corp [*faded*] to the relief of the Scolemaster there, as by a p [*torn*] tripartite thereof made more playnlie appereth.

Reservying to his highnes, his heires and Successers, one yerely Rentt of xi. [*torn*].

Drawe a graunt thereof accordinglye.

(*Signed*) Ry. Sake[vyle].

Comitatus Lincolnie. Particulars for Schools.
Edward VI. Roll 1.

LOUTH GRAMMAR SCHOOL.

Parcelle terrarum et possessionum nuper cantarie sancte Trinitatis in Louth, vocate John Louthes Chauntrie, modo auctoritate parliamenti dissolute.

Terre et tenementa in Louthe et Somercotes, in Comitatu predicto ; valent In

[Firmis], £6 0s. 17d. ; Inde in Reprisis, videlicet in Redditu Resoluto, 2s. 11d.

Et valet clare, per annum, £5 18s. [6d.].

Parcelle terrarum et possessionum nuper guilde sancte trinitatis in Louthe, modo aucthoritate parliamenti dissolute.

Terre et tenementa in Louth, Thedilthorp, anderbie, et Skidbroke, in Comitatu predicto ; valent in

[Firmis], £5 16s. 3d.

Reprise, videlicet in Redditu resoluto, 15d.

Et sic valet clare, per annum, £5 15s.

Parcelle terrarum et possessionum nuper guilde beate Marie de Louth, modo aucthoritate parliamenti dissolute.

Terre et tenementa in Louth Thorphall infra parochias de Louth Thedilthorp et Garnethorp in Comitatu predicto; Valent In

[Firmis], £16 7s. 11d.

Reprise, videlicet in Redditu Resoluto, 7s. 7d.

Et valet clare, per Annum, £16 0s. 3d.

Parcelle terrarum et possessionum nuper guilde beate Marie de Garnthorp, modo aucthoritate parliamenti dissolute.

Terre et tenementa in Garnthorp et south Somercottes, in Comitatu predicto; valent in Firma, £4 13s. 9d.

Reprise, nulle.

Parcelle terrarum et temporalium possessionum nuper pertinencium episcopatui Lincolnie, [in] manibus domini Regis modo existencium.

Parcelle manerii de Louth predicta, in Comitatu predicto; valent in

Firma, £10.

Exitu, 3s. 4d.

Memorandum : that all the woodes growinge in hedgerowes about the premisses will not suffice for the necessarie repaire and fensinge of the said lands.

Item the most parte of the said lands be verie chargeable withe the yerelie   [faded]   Sea banks lying nygh adioyning to the same, and dothe amount yerelie [one] withe an other to the some of three poundes and above.

Examinatur per me L. Cresbie, deputatum supervisorem.

10 September, anno Regni Regis Edwardi vj[u]. 5 [1551].

The clere yerelie valew of the premisses, £42 11s. 10½d. Whereof diducted and allowed for yerelie chardges going owt of the premisses, towardes the mauntenance of freshe water drennes and sea banckes, as by the certificat of the surveyour doth appere, 51*s.* 10½*d.*

And so remayneth clere, £40,

which the kinges highnes is pleased to geve towardes the mauntenance of a free scole in Lowthe, and towardes the sustentacion of 12 poore folkes to continew for ever.

His highnes pleasur is also that there be a corporacion made to take and purchase ouer and lese [the] premisses, landes, and tenementes to the valew of £40. His further pleasur is that there shalbe there a scolemaster and an vssher for

[*faded*] frelie, and the scolemaster to haue for his stipend £20, the vssher £10,

To holde the premisses in Socage.

To have thissues and proffettes from the feaste of thanunciacion of our lady [la]st [pa]st.

(*Signed*)   Ry. Sakevyle.

London and Middlesex.   Certificate 34.
(Edward VI.)

55.   The paroche of St. Bennetts Finke.

There is of houselying people within the said parische the nomber of 300 and above.

Memorandum : the Deane and chapiter of the Colleage of Windesor is parson of the same parische churche, and the value of the same parsonage is £16 ; and that there is but one priest ther by them founde to serve the cure, which priest is very unhable to serve the same.

And that within the seid parische is a Gramer Scole, by the name of a Free Scole, called Saynt Anthonies, the Scole master whereof is nowe Master Edmond Johnson, and his wages paid by the Stewarde of Seynt Authonyes, and how muche is not knowen.

The Corporacions and Companyes within the Citie of London.

MERCERS.

John Abbot gave unto the Master and Wardens to finde a prest singing at Fingeringhoo [Farthinghoe], in the countie of Northampton, and also for keping of a Free Scole to teache younge children in the same Towne, lands amounting to £9 16s. 8d. Whereof

To James Collis, prest, by yere, for his stipende, £6 13s. 4d.

And then remayneth clere, £3 13s. 4d.

GOLDSMYTHES.

Thomas Fereby gave unto the same master and Wardens to thintent that £17 in monie shulde be imployed to finding of one prest in Longdondale, in Cheshire, for the ese of the people being fare distaunt from the paroche churche, and also in the finding of one well learned prest to teache a Grammer Scole in Topford [*Stockport*], and to kepe an obit there for euer, all his landes and tenements, amounting to £51 2s. 8d. Whereof

To the Kinge for quitrent, 13s. 4d.

To the Scolemaster of Topford, £10.

To the Chaplen singing at Langedon Dale, by yere, £4 6s. 8d.

Spent upon th'obbite, £2 1s. 4d.

To the pore yerely, 12s.   £17 13s. 4d.

And then remaynethe clere, £33 9s. 4d.

Bartilmewe Rede gave unto the same Master and Wardens to finde a prest, and kepe an obite for his sole for ever, within the Churche of Cremer [Cromer], lands and tenements amountinge to £50 10s. 8d.

Whereof to the same prest by yere, £12 3s. 4d.

Spent upon thobbite, £2 6s. 8d.   £4 10s.

And then remayneth clere, £36 0s. 8d.

The Citie of London. Certificate 88.

(Edward VI.)

THE PARISH OF SAINTE MARYE HILL IN BILLINGSGATE WARD. *m.* 1.

John Cawston Chaunterye, £20 17s. 8d.

Sir Edmunde Alston, Chaunterie priest, £8.

[*Other promocions*], none.

Pencion, 100s.

Respectuatur quousque Examinetur in Curia.

Ther is a priest, A master, and children, and certain Conductes founde of the churche Landes of the yearly value of
£24 3s., but the Kinges Title for lacke of Evidence cannot apier
vnto us.

John Bidham, chaunterie, £8 6s. 8d.

Of the landes.

Rice williams, Scolemaster of the Children, £8 10s.

Pencion, 100s.

Roberte Tanner, conduct, £8 10s.

Pencion, 100s.

Landes, the donors whereof vnknown, £24.

Founde by the parochianers.

Thomas Merten, parysshe Clerke, £6 13s. 4d.

Thomas Mundy, Sexton, £4.

william hamounde, £8.

Pencion, 100s.

SAINT DONSTON IN THE EAST. *m.* 2.

James Runyger, Master of the singing children and Organ
plaier, £17 10s.

Pencion, £6 13s. 4d.

SAINT MARYE WOLNOTHE.

Hughe Jones, Conducte ther, hathe for his seruice and teaching of singing childeren, by the Graunt of Hughe Brice and
other, £6 15s.

Pencion, 100s.

Comitatus Northamptonie (Oxonie, Rutlandie)
Certificate 36.
(Henry VIII.)

Robert, Bisshopp of Oxford, and John, Bisshopp of Peter-
borowe, Sir John wylliams, knight, Edward Griffith, Esquyer,
solicitor Generall, John Ooly, John Marsh, and Frauncis Sowthwell, Commyssyoners.

T

5. TOWCESTER.

The Colledg or Spones Chauntree.

Founded to maynteyne 2 Prestes, beyng men of good knoweledg, The one to preache the Worde of God, And the other to kepe a Grammer scole.

The valewe of the Londes and possessions apperteyning to the same colledg, with £16 paid by the Kinges Majestie out of the Courte of the augmentacion by the handes of Georg Gifford, one of the particular Receivers of the same Courte, £18 20d.; wherof

For the Masters or prouostes Salarye, £8 13s. 4d.

The Kinges tenthes, 38s. 8d.

The scole Masters or secundaries Salarye,   £7 6s. 8d.
                                          £17 18s. 8d.

And so Remaineth, 3s.

9. ALDEWYNCLE.

Memorandum : the same Towne is inhabityde with a Greate multitude of people.

Chambers Chauntre.

Founded to finde one preste, And the same preste to teache 6 pore Childerne of the Towne of Aldewyncle, And to distribute in almes yerely vnto 2 poure Bedemen of the Almes house in Aldwyncle aforeseid twentye syx shillings eight pence.

The valewe of the londes gyuen to the mayntenaunce of the same Chauntre, £10 15s. 6d.; whereof

Rentes Resolutes, 5s. 5d.

The kinges tenthes, 12s. 8d.

To poor people, 26s. 8d.

The prestes stypend, £8 10s. 8d.   Et equalis £10 15s. 6d.

The valewe of ye Juells, ornamentes, belongyng to the said Chauntre, 36s.

15. FARNYNGHOO.

One Chauntre there.

Founded to fynde one preste to teache and Instructe frelye The Childerne of The inhabytauntes of Fernynghoo.

The valewe of the Londes gyuen to the mauntenaunce of the seide Chauntre Apperithe not, for the preste Receyueth At the handes of the Master Wardons of mercers of London one yerelie Annuitie of £6 16s. 8d. ; wherof, cum 3s. 4d. de firma mansionis Capellani ibidem.   For the Kinges tenthes, 13s. 4d.

For ye prestes Salarye, £6 3s. 4d.   Et equalis £6 16s. 8d.

The Juells and oramentes belonging to the same Chauntre ar not valewed As apperith by the inventary.

16. BLISWORTH.

Roger wakes Chauntre and fre scole.

Founded to mayneteyne one preste, being A graduat of Oxforthe, As well to praye for the soles of the moste noble King Henry the 7th, And the founders of the same, as Also to kepe a fre Grammer scole for all that shall repayre Thither.

The valewe of the Londes and possessions apperteyning to the mayntenaunce of the same Chauntre and fre scole, £12 4s. whereof

For the Kinges Tenthes, 24s.

For the prestes Salarye, £11.   Et equalis £12 4s.

Comitatus Northampton.   Certificate 35.

(Edwarde VI.)

Syr John Williams, Knight, Edwarde Gryffyth and Richarde Cycyll, Esquyres, and John Mershe, Gentylman, Commissioners.

HUNDREDUM DE SPELLOWE.

1. THE PARISH CHURCHE OF ALL SEINTES IN NORTHAMPTON.

The Fraternyte of the Trynytie and our Lady there.

Founded by Thomas Pyrrye and John Atwell too mainteine 4 preestes too singe and praye for euer for the soles of the seyd Thomas and John and ther Aunceters, and for all the Bretherne and Systers of the same Fraternitie for ever.   Is worth by yere in Landes and Tenementes Lying and being in the Towne and

Countie of Northampton, as by the Survey therof made particulerly apperythe £72 0s. 12d.

Rente Resolute, £5 6s. 8d.

Too the pore yerely, 16s. 2d.

Too Anne prentice, wydow, verye pore, Sumtyme A syster
of the same Brotherhed, wekely 8d.; and so the hole yere
amountyth to 34s. 8d.   £7 17s. 6d.

Remaynythe to 3 preestes, daylly seruing and singing in the
foresayd parishe Church, videlicet: to William Suitar, of the
age of 51 yeres, £5 6s. 8d., by patent for terme of his lyffe
vnder the Comen seale of the seyd Fraternitie; Richard Wattes,
of the age of 54 yeres, £5 6s. 8d.; John Harvye, of the age of
57 yeres, £4. They are vnmete to serue cure, and haue no other
lyving.   £14 13s. 4d.

William Wood, of the age of 40 yeres, 40s. a yere, and one
howse of the valew of 10s. a yere, by patent for terme of lyffe.
William Cockin, Organ player, of the age of 54 yeres, hathe A
like Annuytie of 40s., and one howse of 10s., by a like patent,
And 26s. 8d. more for teachin Childerne to sing.   £6 6s. 8d.

Alsoo to 3 singingmen, videlicet: John Brightwen, of the
age of 62 yeres; Edmunde Kinwelmershe, of the age of 44
yeres; Thomas Chatton, of the age of 48 yeres; eche of them
having for his stipend for terme of Lyffe, by patent, 40s.   £6.

Simon Charelton, Sexton, of the age of 64 yeres, hathe for his
stipend 16s., and one howse of 16s. a yere, by patent for tearme
of Lyffe. 32s.

And so Remayneth clere yerely, £35 11s. 6d.

Goodes Remayning the 8th of December Last past, as apperythe perticulerly by an Inuentorye thereof, 18s. 4d.

Plate parcell gylte, weying 20¼ ounces.

Memorandum: preacher or Schole Master none; pore people
relevyed, none; other then douthe appere.

HUNDREDUM DE ROTHEWELL ET HOKESLOO.

12. ROTHEWELL.

The Chauntery of seint Nicholas ther.

Founded by Edwarde Saunders, to finde a preist to sing for

euer in seinte Nicholas Chappell, within the parishe Churche
there. Is worth in Landes and tenementes, £8 10s. 8d.;
whereof in

Rente Resolute, 22s. 6¾d.; And to

Roberte Worde, incumbent, of the age of 54 yeres, vnmete
to kepe A Cure, and hathe no other Lyving, £7 8s. 1¼d.

Goodes Remayning the 8th of December last past, as apperith
particulerly by an Inuentory thereof, 10s.

Memorandum: precher, Scole Master, or pore people relevyd
or maynteyned there, none; howzeling people there, 500.

A free Scole there.

Landes and Tenementes gyven by dyuers persons vnknowen
to the mayntenaunce of A Free Schole for euer, £4 2s. 9d.;
whereof in

Rente Resolute, 13s. 8d.

To the pore, 4s. 2d.   17s. 10d.

And so to Giles pikering, Scole Master, of the age of 38
yeres, well learnyd, And hathe no other Lyving, £3 4s. 11d.

16. WENDELINGBRUGH.

The Fraternitie or Guilde of our Lady there.

Founded in the parishe Churche there by William Topping,
Robert Fitz [Dier], William Spencer, and John Walgraue, to
the intent to do suche dedes of Charytie as shulde seme to the
masters of the same bretherhed most mete, whoo haue bestowed the same yerely apone the bridges abowt the same Towne,
whiche are yerely very chargeable. So that the same Towne ys
like to be muche impoueryshed onles yt maye pleas the Kinges
Maiestie to suffer the seyd Towneshipe to enioye the same,
£5 6s. 10½d.

Goodes Remayning the 8th of December last past, as apperith by the inuentory therof, 56s.

Plate gylte, weying 21 ounces.

Memorandum: yt is to be consyderyd that the Towneshipe
of wenlingbrughe ys A very preti merket Towne, and the
Kinges Towne; and to the intent yt might please the Kinges
maiestie to erect there a free Scole, apoynting the same Landes

towardes the same, The vicar there ys contentyd to charge
his benefyce for euer with 40s. a yere towarde the same, and
the Towneshipe offerith to purchas as muche more lande as shal
be conuenyent for the ereccion thereof.

HUNDREDUM DE SUTTON.

19. BRACKELEY.

Seint James Stipendarye preest.

Graunted by Lawrence Stubbes, president of the College of
seinte Marye Magdeleyne in Oxforde, And the Fellowes of the
same College, to haue a prest to sing within the parishe
Churche there for tearme of 40 yeres, as may appere by the
graunt thereof bering Date 8° Decembris, Anno Regni Regis
Henrici Octaui 19°, The tenor wherof folowythe in hec verba:

Omnibus Christi fidelibus ad quos presente litere nostre per-
uenerint salutem, in Auctore salutis. Sciatis nos Lawrentium
Stubbes, presidentem Collegij sancte Marie Magdelene in
vniuersitate Oxonie, et eiusdem socios seu scolares, vnanimi
consensu et voluntate nostris dedisse, concessisse, et hac presente
Carta nostra, confirmasse Roberto Barnard, arcium magistro, ac
olim predicti Collegij socio, quandam Capellaniam seu Canteriam aut sacerdotale seruicium in Ecclesia sanctorum Johannis
et Jacobi, in villa de Brackeley, in Comitatu Northamptonie,
ad celebrandum missas et alia Divina pro animabus Domini
Francisci de Lovell, pro animabus progenitorum eiusdem, ac pro
animabus omnium benefactorum dicti Collegii, et omnium fidelium defunctorum.

Et insuper nos predicti presidens et socij seu scolares con-
cedimus prefato magistro Roberto, nomine stipendij sui, octo
libras bone et legalis monete Anglie, Annuatim percipiendas
de exitibus seu Redditibus nostris in Brackeley predicto,
per manus balliui seu receptoris ibidem pro tempore existentis,
ad 4ᵒʳ. Anni terminos, videlicet: ad festum Annunciacionis
beate virginis Natiuitatis, sancti Johannis baptiste, Michaelis
Archangeli, et Natalis Christi, per equales porciones, ac
vnam Cameram Ecclesie . . . predicte ex parte Australi

contiguam, vna cum gardino eidem annexo, Habenda, tenenda et occupanda eandem Capellaniam Canteriam seu sacerdotale seruicium, vna cum Annuali stipendio octo librarum, vt permittitur, et Cameram predictam cum gardino eidem Annexo Ad terminum quadraginta Annorum, &c., £8 6s. 8d.

Memorandum : that sythe the Commyssion to vs directyd Roberte Barnarde, Clerke, who, by vertu of the graunt aboue said to hym made for tearme of yeres dyd then serue, ys deceassyd, sins whiche tyme the presydent and fellowes of the College aforesayd haue erected a Free Schole there, in whiche many Chylderne ar taught to the great commodytie of the Cuntrye.

Also howzeling people there to the number of 260.

HUNDREDUM DE GYLLESBOROUGHE.

26. TOWCETOR.

The Colledge there Callyd Spones Chunterye.

Founded for 2 prestes, the one A preacher, the other A Teacher of Gramer. The londes belonging to the seid College or Chunterye Is worth by yere, 51s. 8d. And also the haue a pencionem payed owt of the Kinges Coffers, videlicet : to the precher or Master, 13 marke ; to the secundary or teacher, 11 markes, by the Receyvor. £18 11s. 8d.

Rente Resolute, videlicet : Domino Regi pro Decima, 38s. 8d. And to

William Reignoldes, Master of the seyd College, and A preacher, of the age of 53 yeres, and hathe no other Lyving, £8 19s. 10d.

William Symondes, Schole Master, well learnyd, of the age of 45 yeres, and teachith Dayly freely, and hathe no other lyving, £7 13. 2d.

HUNDREDUM DE WYMERSLEY.

31. BLISWORTHE.

The Chunterye ther.

Founded by Roger Wake, Esquyre, and Lady Elizabeth his wyffe, to the intentes to finde a prest to sing there for euer,

and the seyd preest to be A schole master to teache a free schole
there. Is worth in Landes and Tenementes, as well in North-
amptonshere as Bukkinghamshere, £12 4s.

To John Curtes, Scole Master, of the age of 42 yeres, well
lernyd, and hathe at this present 30 Schollers, and is very mete
to serue Cure, and hathe no other lyving, £12 4s.

Memorandum : preacher or pore people relevyd, none. Howzeling people to the number of 200.

HUNDREDUM DE NASSABRUGHE.

35. STAUNFORDE.

Seinte John baptist Free Chappell apon staunforde Bridge.

Founded by whom it is vnknowen, to the intent to Finde
a stypendarye preest; is worth in Landes and Tenementes,
£11 4s. 11d.

Rente Resolute, 28s. 6d. And so
Remaynethe Clere, £9 16s. 5d.

Memorandum : that sythe the Survey Taken by vertu of the
Commyssyon, one John Stodderd hathe brought before the
Kinges Maiesties Comyssyoners, Dyvers Evydences proving
the same to be an hospitall, And requyrethe that the Certificate
made before the Commyssyoners may be Frustrated and
avoyded; but forasmuche as yt hathe not byn vsyd as an
hospitall in releving the pore, but the Revenues and proffyttes
therof hathe byn conuertyd only to the use of Thomas Stodderd,
sone of the seyd John, being an infant of the age of 13 or 14
yeres, Towardes his exhibicion at Schole as yt is sayd, The
Commyssyoners hathe Commyttyd the Determynacion therof to
this honorable Courte.

Northamptonshire. Schools Continuance
Warrant, 13.

Forasmuche as it apperith [&c.] that a Grammer Schole hathe
been contynuallye kepte in Rothewell [&c.], and that the Scolemaster there hathe had [&c.] £3 4s. 11d. [&c.];

And that a Free Schole hathe been contynuallie kepte in

Blysworth [&c.], with the revenues of the late chaunterie there, And that the Scholemaster there hathe had [&c.] £11 [&c.] ;

And that a Free grammer schole hathe been contynually kepte at Towcetour [&c.] with the revenues of the late chaunterye called spones chauntrie, and that the Scholemaster there hathe had [&c.] £7 13s. 2d. [&c.] ;

And that a grammer Schole hathe been contynuallye kepte in Oundell [&c.], with the revenues of the late Guylde of our ladie of Oundell aforesaide, And that the Scholemaster there hathe had [&c.] £5 6s. 8d. [&c.].

Wee, therfore [&c.], haue assigned [&c.] that the saide schole in Rothewell shall contynewe, and that Gyles Pykerynge, scholemaster there, shall haue [&c.] £3 4s. 11d. ;

And that the saide free Schole in Blisworth aforesaide shall contynue, and that John Curtes, Scholemaster there, shall haue [&c.] £11 [&c.] ;

And that the saide Schole in Oundell aforesaide shall contynewe, and that Wyllyam Irelande, Scholemaster there, shall haue [&c.] £5 6s. 8d.

Northamptonshire. Certificate 99.
(Henry VIII.)
FODRYNGHAY COLLEGE.

Compotus Magistri Johannis Russell, Clerici, Magistri Collegij ibidem, A Festo sancti Michaelis Archangeli, Anno regni Henrici octaui, dei gracia anglie, Frauncie et Hibernie Regis, fidei defensoris, et in Terra Ecclesie Anglicane et Hibernice supremi capitis, 36to usque idem Festum Sancti Michaelis extunc proximo sequentem, Anno regni eiusdem domini Regis 37mo, scilicet per vnum Annum integrum [1544–5].

Summa totalis Reddituum cum Arreragijs, £557 9s. 9½d. De quibus

Sellaria Magistri et Sociorum Collegij.

     *   *   * . . *   *

Et in feodo Thome Topeliff, per annum, cum 10s. pro tuicione choristarum, £4 10s.

     *   *   *   *   *

Stipendia Clericorum.

*   *   *   *   *

Et soluto Ricardo Bealle, pro stipendio, cum 20*s.* pro informacione choristarum, £4.

Summa Omnium Allocacionum [&c.], £71 3*s.* 10¼*d.*

Et sic habet superplusagium, £123 14*s.* 0½*d.*

Northamptonshire.   Certificate 93.

(Henry VIII.—Edward VI.)

FODRYNGHAY (COLLEGE).

Compotus Ricardi Ward, Clerici, presentoris Ecclesie Collegiate ibidem, Laurencij Sa . . . Roberti Shorys, Roberti Ryfham, Thome Topleff, Johannis Gilbert, Thome Thorp, Johannis Flynt, Thome Styrop, Johannis Stanyan et Roberti Webster, Administratorum omnium et singulorum bonorum, catallorum Jure Creditorum Magistri Johannis Russell defuncti, nuper Magistri ibidem, A Festo Sancti Michaelis Archangeli, Anno regni nuper Regis Henrici octaui 38^{uo} usque idem Festum Sancti Michaelis extunc proximo sequentem, anno regni Edwardi sexti, Dei gracia Anglie, Frauncie et Hibernie Regis, fidei Defensoris, et in terra ecclesie Anglicane et Hibernice supremi capitis, primo, scilicet per vnum Annum integrum [1546-7].

Summa totalis Reddituum, cum Arreragijs, £591 15*s.* 1¼*d.*
De quibus—

Sellaria Magistri et Sociorum Collegij.

*   *   *   *   *

Et in Feodo Thome Topcliff, per Annum, cum 10*s.* pro tuicione choristarum, £4 10*s.*

*   *   *   *   *

Stipendia Clericorum.

*   *   *   *   *

Et soluta Ricardo Bealle, pro stipendio suo, cum 20*s.* pro informacione Choristarum, £4 5*s.*

*   *   *   *   *

Summa Omnium Allocacionum [&c.], £70 12*s.* 9*d.*
Et sic debet, £21 2*s.* 4¼*d.*

The Countye of Northumberlande (and the Bishopricke of Durham). Certificate 18.

(Henry VIII.)

Robert Mennell and Henry Whitereason, Esquyers, and Humfrey Waren, gentilman, commyssioners.

41. THE CHAUNTRIE OF ALL SAYNTES IN MORPETHE (AFORSAID).

The said chauntrie was founded, by Reporte, to fynde a priest to say masse, and pray for all Christian sowles, and also to kepe A Grammer scoole for the erudicion and bringyng up of children, and hath ben so vsed.

[The yerely valewe according to the booke of fyrste fruytes &c.], *nihil,* for it was neuer charged to the payment of the fyrst Fruytes and tenthes.

[The yerely valewe according to this survey], £6 8s. 2d., as appereth by a Rentall, which hathe ben of long tyme vsed and employed to the fyndyng of A priest aswell to say masse and other divyne servyce ther as to kepe A scoole for the instructyng and bryngyng vp of children in learnyng, as is aforesaid.

The said chauntrie is founded in A chapell of all Sayntes, within the parishe of Morpeth aforesaid.

[The valewe of the Ornamentes, &c.], *nihil,* for ther ben nether Goodes, catalles, nor Ornamentes apperteynyng to the same.

Ther were no other landes nor yerely proffittes apperteynyng or belongyng to the said chauntrie syth the 4th Day of februarie, in the 27th yere of the Kinges maiesties Reigne [153½], more then is above mencyoned.

Within the Countye of Northumberland. Certificate 62.

(Edward VI.)

Sir Thomas Hylton, Sir Roberte Brandelinge, Knyghtes, Roberte Mennell and Henry Whyterayson, Esquyers, Comyssyoners.

30. ALNEWYKE.

Landes and possessyôns belonging to the vse and stypende of twoo preestes, the one Master of a gramer scoole, and the other master of a songe scoole, within Alnewyke, afforseyd.

Wylliam Hudson and Thomas Thompson, bothe of 54 yeres of age, well learned, of honest conuersacion and qualytes; The seyd Wylliam Hudson having one pencion of 100s. by yere, besydes his sayd stypend; The other having no other lyving, but onely the same stypend, And they kepe twoo Sckooles, the one for gramer, and the other for songe, to bring up children in learning according to ther fundacion.

And there ys no landes sold syth the 23 of November, anno 38 [*Hen. VIII.*]. Ther ys of Howslyng people 1,500 within the same parishe.

The yerely valewe of the seyd Stypendarys, as shall appere by the partyculer of the same, £12 3s. 4d.   Wherof

In Decaye yerely of the same, £4.

And so Remanethe clere, £8 3s. 4d.

37. MORPETHE.

Landes and possessyons perteyning to the vse and stypend of one prest, Master of the Free gramer scoole in Morpethe.

Thomas Husbande, Incumbent, of the age of 40 yeres, wel learned, of honest conversacion and qualytes, having no other lyving then the same stypend, and he kepyth the sayd Free Scoole there for erudicion of chyldren.

And ther ys no landes nor Tenementes solde sythe the 23 of November, dicto anno 38 [*Hen. VIII.*]

The clere yerely valewe of the same Chauntery, as appereth by the partyculer of the same, £6 12s. 10d.

And there be of Howselinge people within the same parishe, 1150.

The Countye of Northumberland. Certificate 94.

(Edward VI.)

Thomas Hylton and Robert Brandlinge, knyghtes, withe others Commissioners.

ALNEWICKE. m. 2.

Landes and possessions graunted towarde the Findinge of two prestes in the Towne of Alnewicke, whereof William Hudson and Thomas Thompson are Incumbentes, £12 3s. 4d.

In decaye yerelye, £4.

The cleare remayne, £8 3s. 4d.

Whiche The saiede Incumbentes receyved yearlie to theire owne vses for kepinge of two skoles in the saiede Towne of Alnewicke ; The one teachinge gramer, and the other Songe.

Pencion, William hudson, £4.

Memorandum of howslinge people there, 1500.

Continuatur Schola and the wages of thomas Thompson, Schole master there, as hathe bene vsed, videlicet, £4 20d.

MORPETHE.

Landes and possessiones Graunted For the Fyndinge A prest in the saide Towne of morpethe, wherof Thomas Howsebande ys Incumbent, £6 12s. 10d.

Whiche The saied Incunbent receyved yearlie For his owne vse for Teachinge of A Grammer Skole within the saied Towne.

Memorandum of howslinge people there, 1150.

Continuatur Schola, with the accustomed wages, quousque, etcetera.

Summa totalis to the poore, 46s. 8d.

Summa totalis to the scholes, £10 14s. 6d.

[*In dorso.*]

Townes mete for Scholes and Hospitalles :

Newcastle, Alnewike, Morpethe, Hexham.

Northumberland. Schools Continuance Warrant, 20.

Forasmoche as it apperith [&c.] that a grammer schole hath bene contynually kepte in Alnewicke [&c.], with the revenues of landes [&c.] appointed to the fyndyng of two preestes there, and that the Scholemaster there hath hadd [&c.] £4 20d. [&c.] ;

And that a grammer Schole hath bene contynually kepte in

Morpeth [&c.], with the revenues of landes [&c.] appointed to the fyndyng of a preest there, and that the Scholemaster there hath had [&c.] £6 12s. 10d. [&c.].

We, therfor [&c.], haue assigned [&c.] that the seid grammer Schole in Alnewicke aforeseide shall contynue, and that Thomas Thompson, Scholemaster there, shall haue [&c.] £4 20d. ;

And that the seide grammer Schole in Morpeth aforeseid shall likewise contynue, and that Thomas Housbande, Scholemaster there, shall haue [&c.] £6 12s. 10d.

In Comitatu Northumberlandie. Particulars for Schools. Roll 3.

(Edward VI.)

MORPETH GRAMMAR SCHOOL.

Nuper Cantaria de Morpethe, fundata in Capella omnium Sanctorum, infra parochiam beate Marie ibidem.

Terre et Tenementa pertinencia dicte nuper Cantarie; valet in

[Liberis Redditibus], [£2 18s. 8d.].
Firma, 26s. 8d.   [Redditibus], [8s.]   £4 13s. 8d.

Memorandum: the late Incumbente of the sayde Chauntrye hathe an yerlye Pencione of £4 2s. 6d., payde yerelye, by thandes of the kinges magestyes Receyvor of his Courte of Augmentacones, within the Countye of Northumberlonde.

Altera nuper Cantaria infra villam de Morpeth predictam.
Terre et tenementa pertinencia dicte nuper Cantarie in Morpeth; valet in
[Liberis Redditibus], [£4 1s. 8d.].   [Firmis], [12s.]
                                                        £4 13s. 8d.

Memorandum : the late Incumbente of the sayde Chauntrye hathe yerelye the hole Somme of £4 13s. 8d., in the name of an Annuall pencion payde by thandes of the kinges Magestyes Receyvor of his Courte of Augmentacions, in the Countye of Northumberlond.

Terre et possessiones pertinentes nuper ad vsum et stipendium presbiteri Magistri libere Scole grammatice in Morpethe predicta . . . valet in [Liberis redditibus], £6 12s. 10d.

Memorandum : the late Scolemaster of the sayde Scole in Morpethe ys appointed by Master Mildmey to teache and kepe the sayd Scole there, hauing yerelye the hole Somme of £6 12s. 10d. aforesayde.

Nuper Cantaria Sancti Egidii, Fundata in Capella de Witton, in parochia de Harteborne.

Terre et Tenementa pertinencia dicte nuper Cantarie Sancti Egidii; valet in [Firmis], 64s.

Memorandum : the late Incumbent of the premyses hathe an yerely pencion of 60s. 10d., payd by thandes of the kinges magestyes Receyvor, in the Countye of Northumberlond.

Terre et Tenementa nuper Spectancia ad vsum vnius presbiteri, vocati le ladye masse prest, in pont Ilonde . . . valet in [Firmis], 26s. 6d.

Memorandum : the late incumbent there hathe yerely, in the name of an Annuall pencione, the hole Somme of 26s. 6d., payd by thandes of the kinges magestyes Receyvor abovesayde.

Also the Premises afore Specifyed do agree with the Survey Taken by William Farewell, Surveyor, within the Countye of Northumberlonde aforesayde. And as tochinge anye Former Perticular, I have made none, but onlye thes, At the Sewte of the lorde Dacres, by vertu of master Chauncelers warraunte, but for what Intente he hathe them I know not.

Examinatur per Ricardum Hochonson, Auditorem.

1 Marcii, Anno 5 [155⁰⁄₁].

Make a grant of the Chantrez abovesayd, of the cler yerly valew of £20 10s. 8d., vnto the Bayleyffes and burgessez of Morpethe, in the County of northehumberland, and to ther successors, to the vse of a scole in suche forme as other scolez hathe passede, reservynge to the kynges magesty, hys heyrs and successors, 10s. 8d. yerly.

(Signed)   Ry. Sakevyle.

Comitatus Nottingamie (et Derbie).   Certificate 13.
(Henry VIII.)

Sir John Markeham, Knighte, William Cowper, Nicholas Powtrell, Esquyers, and John Wyseman, Gentilman Commyssioners.

26. THE PARISSHE OF EASTE RETFORD.

The Chauntries called the trynite Chauntrie and our ladye Chauntrie, in Este retforde, founded by the predecessors of the bailiffes, burgesses, and Commynalte of the said towne, in Consideracion that the said towne of Esterettford, being a markett towne, and greatlye inhabited withe people, and muche resortte therunto, to the intente that Godes seruice moughte be the better and the more honorabley mayntayned, and also for other Godlie purposes, as mor playnelye apperithe by the foundacyon to the Commyssioners shewed. [The yerlye valewes accordynge to the boke of the tenthes], 73s. 4d.

[The yerlye valewes as nowe surveyed, &c.], 73s., Goying owte of 9 decayed howses and 5 toftes in the said Burgage, whiche were for the moste parte consumed and brente, like as almoste the holle Burghe was; and sythens the tyme of the same fire there the moste parte of the said rent hath ben imployed towardes the Reedificacion of the same decayed howses, and the residewe ben imploied towardes the lyvinge and fyndynge of oon Discrette prieste, beinge a Scolle master there, for the Brynginge vpp of youthe in Godley lernynge, and to mynistre within the said Churche accordynge to the said foundacyon.

The said Chauntrie is no pariche Churche, but within the parisshe churche of Estretford aforesaid, and that there be 5 hundred howselinge people by estymacion, havinge no more priestes, but the vicar and this prieste there.

The mancion howses of the said two Chauntrie priestes were consumed and brente by casualtye of Fyer, and as yett not Reedyfyed.

There hathe ben no more Londes nor yerly profittes belonginge to the same syns the tyme abovesaid [the iiij^{th} daye of Februarye, in the xxvij^{th} yere of the Kinge reign] more then is byfore mencyoned.

[Jewells, plate, ornamentes, &c.], 44s. 8d., as apperithe by an Inventorie to this certificate annexed.

There hathe ben no chauntries, nor other like promocions there dissolued, purchased, or by anye other meane opteyned withoute the kinges licence sythens the tyme abouesaid.

29. THE PARISSHE OF MATTERSAYE.

The Chauntrie of Mattersey, so named in the Booke of 10ths.

Nevertheles, Robert Buttie, Stipendarie prieste there, Deposithe vppon his othe that the same is no Chauntrie, butt Certeyn landes gyven by diuerse men, as apperithe by Dedes of Feoffemente, to Fynde A prieste for helpinge of the vicare there and to teache Children, beinge no foundacyon therof, nor Donatyve perpetuall, butt a prieste to singe att the will of the parissheners.

[The yerlye valewes, accordynge to the booke of the tenthes], £4 6s. 8d.

[The yerlye valewes as now surveyed, &c.], £4 10s. 3d. clere, besides 2s. 2d. in Rente resolute to diuerse persons, Which is imployed to the lyvinge of Roberte Buttie, stipendarye pryste there.

The same is nott voide nor hathe anye mancion.

There hath ben no more londes [&c.].

There is neither chalis, plate, goodes, nor ornamentes to the same belonginge, butt a vestment of Grene satten of Briggis with an olde albe of smalle valewe, by the othe of the said incumbente.

There hathe ben no chauntries [&c.].

40. THE COLLEGIATT CHURCHE OF SOWTHWELL WITHE IN THE PARISSHE OF SOWTHEWELL.

The Collegiatte Churche of Sowthewell beynge Reputed and taken for the Hed mother Churche of the Towne and Countie of Nottingham, wherin is sedes archiepiscopalis, and so Allowed by the Kinges maiesties Grace 3 yers paste by an Acte of parliamente, and the Chapter of the same Churche have particuliere

U

Jurisdiccion, and is Exempted ab omni archiepiscopali pre-
terquam in causis appellacionum et negligencie.

Whiche Collegiate Churche of Aunciente tyme was founded
by the Righte famous of memorye Edgare, the kinges maiesties
moste noble progenitor, and by the Confirmacions as well of his
said noble progenitors as nowe of late by his moste excellente
maiestie, founded, Erected, and Establisshed in like manour
and fourme as itt was before; that is to saye, by the name of
the Collegiate churche of our blessid ladye the virgyn of
Sowthewelle, as by the said acte of parliamente therof made
maye appere.

Which said Collegiatte churche was at the Firste Chieffelye
founded for the mayntenaunce of Goodes worde and mynystringe
of the most blessid sacramentes, and for to have all Dyvine
seruice there Daylye songe and sayde, in the which Churche
there be Dailye att this Daye Resyaunte and Abydynge 47
parsons, wherof 3 Chanons residensaries, the parisshe vicar,
16 vicars choriall, 13 Chauntrie prystes, 4 Decons and sub-
deacons, 6 Choristers, 2 thuribulers, and 2 clerkes, dailye there
to mayntayn Godes seruice as is Abouesaid, withe other Godlye
causes and consideraccyons as by the Certificate of Edwarde
Bassett, John Fytzharbert, and John Adams, clerkes, prebendaries there, more att large maye appere; Withoute any foundacion in Writinge shewed to the Commyssyons.

[Yearly value in Book of Tenths], £39 5s. 6d., whiche is for
the landes in Comen to the prebendaries there.

[The yerlye valewes as now surveyed, &c.]   £33 Clere,
besides £7 4s. 2d. for diuersse Resolucions perpetualle, which
clere Reveneux ben imployed as well vppon the wages of the
Deacons, 66s.; Choristirs, 26s. 8d.; clerkes, 20s.; Thuribulers,
13s. 4d.; who hathe no more wages to fynde them meate and
Drinke then before is sett vppon their heddes, and also for the
Relyvinge of poore scollers thyther Resortinge for ther
erudycyon either in Grammer or songe, as for ther expenses
in hospitalitee, emongiste suche the said prebendaries as there
be resident, and partelye for the socoure of pore people thither
Resortinge, as by the said certificate dothe appere, wherunto
the said prebendes are sworne.

The said Collegiate Churche of Sowthewell is the parissho churche of Southewell, and to all the kinges maiesties soke of Sowthwell, in which soke be 13 Townes, villages, and Thorppis buylded, and ther be in the said parisshe of sowthwell, withe the thorppis aforesaid, 2 thousand howsling people by estimacion ; and further, the kinges maiestie hath a Goodlie manor ioynynge to the said Collegiatte Churche, which late was the busshopps of yorke.

All the promocions of the same Churche be fulle and nott voide, except the prebend of Rampton and oon of the vikers choriall, whiche be in the kinges maiesties handes to dispose att his pleasure.

There hath ben no more londes nor yerly profittes belonginge to the comens, syns the tyme abovesaid, more then is before Reherced, except diuerse tithes and offeringes there greatly decresid and mynysshed.

[Jewells, Plate, ornamentes, &c.], £19 0s. 8d. ; besides 633 ounces plate nott itt praysed, also over and besides A chalis of golde with a patente, a Crosse of Golde with a fote of Golde sette with diuerse stones, a tabernacle of our ladye of siluer and Gilte withe 2 tables of siluer and Gilte enclosinge the same, latelye delyuered by John adams, Clerke, to the kinges maiesties vse vnto sir Edward Northe, knight; and also ouer and besides 2 basens of syluer, weyinge 47 ounces, taken by the said John adams for his costes in the Cariage of the said plate, as apperithe by the inventorie of the premysses to this Certificate annexed, and also ouer and besides certeyn plate late belonginge to the same churche, which was solde and expended aboughte the sewtes and necessares of the newe Ereccion of the said college, as by the said Certifycate apperithe.

There hath ben no Collegis nor otherlike promocions [&c.].

The prebende of Normanton, withe in the said Collegiatte Churche of Sowthwell belongynge to Thomas White, prebendarie of the same.

The yerlye valewes, accordynge to the boke of the tenthes, *nihil*, forasmuche as the same is not charged in the copye of the kinges recordes of his 10th delyuered to the commyssioners.

The yerlye valewes, accordynge to this Survey, £20 6s. 8d. clere, withe 6s. 8d. for the prebendaries mancion howse, and besides £4 for the wages of John Trapps, oon of the vicars Choriall;

Also, besides 40s. given to the scole master of the Free Scole there, and 20s. for the vicars pencion of the parisshe Churche of Sowthewell.

Comitatus Nottinghamie. Certificate 37.

(Edward VI.)

Sir Giervayce Clifton, Sir John Hersey, Sir Antonye Nevile, Knightes, and William Bolles, Esquyer, Commissioners.

1. NOTTINGHAM TOWNE.

The Guylde of the Trynytie in the parishe of saint Mary.

Founded By Thomas Thurlande to Mayntayne 2 preistes to sing Masses for euer. Ys worthe by yere in landes and possessions, lying and being in Diuerse places of the saide Towne of Nottingham, as by the Survey therof made Remayning with the Surveyour of the said sheire particlerly appereth, £18 9s. 6d. Wherof in

Wages yerely paid to William Raynes, stipendary there, £6.

Rentes Resolute, 7s. 5½d.

Rentes Decaied and vacant, 9s.

Rentes given and paid yerely towards mayntaynaunce of a fre Scole, 8s.

The poore, 15s. 2d.   23s. 2d.   £7 19s. 7½d.

And so Remayneth to The Chambers of the said Guylde Due yerely, Over besydes all maner of Charges, £10 9s. 10½d.

Memorandum: Goodes Remayning to the Kinges Maiestes vse there, None.

HUNDRED OF NEWARKE, THE TOWNE EXCEPTED.

CASTRETFORD.

66. Twoo Chaunteries of the holie Trynytye and our Blyssed Ladye within the parishe of Este Rethforthe.

Founded by the Bailyff and burgieses there to finde 2 prestes,

and nowe converted to kepe a Scole for a certain tyme. Ys
worthe by yere in landes, Tenementes, and other possessions,
lying and being in Diuerse and sondrye places within the
parishe of Est Rethforth, As by the Survey therof made particulerly, yt dothe appere, 73s. 8d.   Wherof in

Rentes Resolute yerely, 9s. 8d., And so

Remayneth clere yerely vnto Charles Weste, Scholemaster
there, for and his finding in keping of a Scole there by yere,
64s. 5d.

Memoranda : Goodes Remayning or coming to the Kinges
maiesties vse by reason of this chauntery, over and besydes one
Challice of syluer waying 7½ ounces not deliuered vnto the
Master of the Kinges Jewell house as yet, 3s. 4d.

The Churchewardeines there haue vpon their othes presented,
That there ys one Annuall rent of 73s. 8d. apperteyning to theis
saide 2 Chaunteries comming and Growing of Ten decaied mes-
suagies and 5 Toftes in Estrethforthe aforesaide, Nowe in the
severall tenures of the Inhabitauntes of the Burgage there for
terme of certaine yeres, as appereth by a Rentall therof made,
Whiche houses about 20 yeres paste were burnte with the hole
towne, By reason wherof Richarde Beyoke and Robert mowbery,
Then Chauntery preistes there, were removed by the mutuall
consentes of themselves and the saide Bailyfes and Burgiesses
for a tyme vntill the saide Toftes and messuages were buylt and
Recdyfyed again, at whiche tyme it was, agreed, as before, that
they shoulde be restored vnto their hole lyvinges againe, whiche,
before the said burning chaunsed, was moche more then the said
somme of 73s. 4d.   And forasmoche as the said Baylyfes and
Burgiesses were not able to buylde the said houses and other
the premysses vnto the valiewe of suche a some as of long tyme
before was payeable to the said Chauntery preistes, They haue
employde and converted the said somme of 73s. 4d. by them
recouered (before this Survey) vnto the finding of one syr
Charles Weste, preste and scolemaster there, towards the Bringing vp of youth, And for bycause, in the meane season, the said
landes are commen vnto the Kinges maiesties handes by reason
of an acte of parlyament therof made, the saide 2 incumbentes

are vnprovydede of theyr said lyvinges vnto them promysde by
the sayd Baylyves and Burgiesses; And that Sir Robert mowe-
bury hath £16 yerely, That is to saie, being pencyoner of one of
the vicars chorals in southwell, and £10 being vicar of
Knesall.

106. SOUTHWELL COLLEDGE,

in the said Countye of Nottingham.

Landes and possessions being in common among all the
Cannons Residenciaries ther.

Founded by King Edgar to mayntayn Devyne Seruyce there
for ever. Ys worthe in Landes, Tenementes, Rentes, Tythes,
and Oblacions commyng and growing of diuers Manours And
Lordshippes within the saide Countie of Nottingham, As by the
Survey therof made, Remayning with Surveyour of the said
Shere, particulerly yt dothe appere, £48 14s .5d.   Wherof in

Fees and Annuyties, videlicet : To the Stewarde of Courtes of
the saide landes, 13s. 4d.

To the Registre of the Chapitre, 13s. 4d.   26s. 8d.

Rentes withholden and decayed, 20s.

Wages, That is to saie, to the mynystres serving in the
Churche at the Altares, 52s.

The master of the Queristers, 20s.

The Thuribularies servuing at the altare, 13s. 4d.

The 2 Churche Wardeins there, 26s. 8d.

The vierge berers, 3s. 4d.   115s. 4d.

Money paied to the vicar of vpton towarde the augmentacion
of his vicarage yerely, 26s. 8d.

Dilacion of Oyle and creme from Yorke, 12d.

Keping of certain Obites of the Revenues herof yerly, 14d.

Money paied to the prebendary of normanton for the one half
of certaine Offeringes of the hole shere of Nottingham alwaies at
pentecoste, by the yere, 100s.   £14 10s. 10d.

And so Remayneth Clere vnto the sayde Resydensiaries of
the saide Colledge in common, to be expendyd Amonges them
all yerely, £34 3s. [7d.].

THE PREBENDE OF NORMANTON.

Founded by the foresaide King Edgar, as parcell of the said Colledge to mayntayne Devyne Servyce there for euer. Ys worthe in landes, Rentes, and Tythes lying and being in diuers and sondry places within the saide Countie of Nottingham, As by the survey therof made particulerly doth appere, £27. Wherof in

Wagis yerely paide vnto the Vicar Chorall of this prebende, £4.

Wages yerely paid vnto the Scholemastre there, 40s.

Money yerely payed to the Vicar of Southwell towarde the augmentacion of his Vicarage, 20s.   £7.

And so Remayneth Clere yerely vnto Thomas White, Prebendary there, of the age of [blank] yeres, £20.

111. THE PARISHE CHURCHE OF SOUTHWELL,
being within the Collegiate Churche there.

Ys worthe in the Rent of a certaine house lying and being in Southwell aforesaide, graunted towardes the fynding of an obite there, 7s. ; wherof in

Money yerely payde vnto the queristers, Deacones, and other Clarkes in the colege of southwell aforesaid, 2s. 6d.

Remayneth Clere vnto the said parishe Churche yerely, 4s. 6d.

Memoranda : It ys presented by John Pallmer, John Wylloughby, Thomas Weldon, Edwarde Batheley, Henry Roberteson, and Richarde Banes, Churchewardens of the sayde parishe churche of southwell, within the saide Collegiate churche, That there ys a great parishe churche belonging to the Towne or Sooke of Southwell aforesaide, which heretofore, By reason of the nombre of prebendaries, with other preistes and mynysters, hathe ben vsed to be called a Collegiate churche, In whiche parishe churche are 16 prebendaries, 16 vicars Chorals, 13 Chauntery priestes, 2 Deacons, 2 sub-deacons, 6 Queristers, and 2 Thuribularies.

The same do presente that within the saide Towne of South-

well, and within 3 villagies therunto adioyning, called Esthropp,
West thropp, and Normanton, are Twoo thousande Crystened
soules or there aboutes, whiche haue none other parishe churche
or Chapell of ease, but onely the sayd paryshe churche of southwell, called the Collegiate churche of southwell.

And that within the saide parishe and Sooke of Southwell be
Ten villagies and hambletes Ouer and besydes the 3 villagies
aforesaid, whiche be called Hallam, Kyrtlington, Edingley,
Farneffelde, Hallaughton, alias Halton, Bleesby, Goverton,
Gybsmeere, vpton, and morton, which haue Chapelles of ease,
and be within the said parishe of southwell, And within the
said Villages or hambletes ben 2,000 christened soules and
more, So that the hole nombre of people within all the parishe
of Southwell doth amounte vnto about 4,000 persones.

And that 3 of the saide villagies, That is to saie, Hallaughton,
Halam, and Morton, haue ben vsed to be serued, and yet be, by
3 mynysters of the said Churche of Southwell ; And thei present
That there ys in Southwell aforesaide a vicar endowed, and no
mo, but he onely to serve the cure of Southwell and the three
villagies aforesaide, called Estthropp, Westthrop, and Normanton, wherin are 2,000 people, as before ys said, who is
lyving, consisteth in a mancion house, with a garden, and 20s.
yerely paide by the prebendary of Normanton, and 4 offering
daies; more he hath not, but of love offeringes and prevey
tythes at Ester.

And saie that the Tythes and other proffites perteyning to a
parishe churche ys not onely payde to the parishe churche of
southewell, as to their parson, by the inhabitantes of the said
towne, But also by the sayd villagies before rehersed, And that
the said 10 villagies, or the moste parte of them, do bury the
deade within the Churche yerde of the said Collegiate churche
of southwell, whiche ys the paryshe churche.

And that the seigniorie of the said towne, or manor of the saide
Towne of Southwell, and all the tennauntes therin apperteyning,
are the Kinges maiesties, wherunto belongeth 13 villagies
named Southwell Sooke, with many other Royalties here not
expressed.

Ann thei present that the said parishe churche of Southwell standeth in the mydle of the Shere, accompted as a chief Churche, wherin ys and hath ben kept a Gramer scole most apte for the same (tyme out of mynd), And towardes the mayntaynaunce therof ys given 40s. by yere out of the Prebendary of Normanton.

And that, in Respect of the Great nombre of people perteyning to the saide Sooke and Royaltie, there hathe ben 16 prebendes, and no preacher charged for the same.

In consideracion of the premysses and other moste vrgent not here alledged, We, the poore Inhabitauntes and parishioners, the Kinges maiesties tennauntes there, Do not onely make our requeste that our parishe churche maye stande, and to haue therin suche preachers apte and mete to enstructe vs our Dueties towardes God and our king, as his maiestie shall appointe, But also that our Grammer scole maie also stande with suche stipende as apperteyneth the like, Wherin our poore youth maie be enstructed, and that also by the resorte of their parentes we, his Graces poore Tennauntes and inhabitauntes there, maie haue some relief wherby we shalbe the better able to serue his Grace at tyme appoynted.

The Countie of Notyngham. Certificate 95.

1. SOUTHWELL.

A College Lately establisshed by the Kynges maiestie, beynge Also a parishe Churche, havinge Aswell the Cure of the hole Towne, as of 13 villages to the nombre of Two thowsande howselinge people.

Founded to have Divyne seruyce there Dayly songe and sayde, in the which Churche ther be at this presente resyante three Canons, Thyrtene Prebendaries now resydent, the Parishe vycar, 16 Choriall vicars, the said vicars kepynge hospitalitie togithers, and Distributing certeyn money to the Poore, Accordinge to theyer Foundacion, 4 Deacons and sub-Deacons, 6 Coresters, 2 Thuribilers, 2 Clerkes, And Children repayringe thither, taught theyer Grammer and Songe, And Also in the same Churche be 13 Chauntryes founded by seuerall Persones to have masses said for theyer Founders, £543 2s. 5d.

8. MATERSEY.

A Chauntrie within the parishe Churche there.

Founded to Fynde a priest to helpe the vicar And to teache Children, £4 10s. 4d.

[Plate and gooddes], None, but a vestyment of small value.

EAST RETFORDE.

The Trinytie Chauntrye and our Lady Chauntrye within the parishe Churche ther, wher Arr by estymacion Fyve hundreth houselinge people and no mo priestes but the vycarr and this.

Founded to maynteyne the seruyce in the Churche ther to bringe vp Children, and other Godly purposes not expressed, 73s.

[Plate and Gooddes], 44s. 8d.

The Countie off Notyngham. Certificate 96.

68. SOUTHEWELL.

A College latelye establyshed by the Kinges Maiestie, beynge also a parishe Churche havynge as well the Cure of the hole Towne as of Thirtene villages to the number of Twoo Thowsande howselynge people.

Founded to haue divyne service there daylie songe and said in the which Churche there be at this presente resydant three Canons, Thirtene Prebendaries now resident, the parishe vicar, 16 Choriall vicars, the said vicars kepynge hospitalite togyther, and distributyng certen monie to the pore accordynge to their foundacion, 4 Deacons and Subdeacons, 6 Coresters, 2 Thuribilers, 2 Clarkes and children repayrynge thither taughte their Grammer and Songe, And also in the same Churche be 13 Chauntries founded by seueral persons to have Masses said for their founders, £543 2s. 5d.

50. MATERSAY.

A Chauntrie within the parishe church.

Founded to fynde a priest to helpe the vicar and to teache Children, £4 10s. 3d.

[Plate and goodes], None but a vestyment of a small value.

Nottinghamshire. Schools Continuance Warrant, 2.

Forasmuch as it apperith by the Certificat. . . . That the Scolemaster of the Scole of Nottyngham hath yerlie hadd in augmentacion of his lyvyng the house called the Frescole in Notyngham, with a gardeyne, parcell of the late Guylde of Holy Trynytie in Our Ladie Churche, in Notyngham aforesaid, without paieng any rente therefore.

And that two Almeshouses, parcell of the late Chauntrie of Seynt John Baptiste, in Mattersey in the said countie, have been yerlie letten to twoo poore folkes to inhabite in without paiyng any rente therefore.

And that a Grammer Scole hath been contynuallie kept in Southwell aforesaid, with the revenues of the said late College of Southwell, whiche Scole is very mete and necessarie to contynue. . . .

We therefore . . . have assigned and appointed that the Scolemaster of Nottyngham for the tyme beyng shall enjoye yerelie the said house called the Scolehouse, with the said gardeyne in Nottyngham aforesaid, without any thing paying for the same.

And that the twoo poore Almesfolks inhabityng in the said twoo Almeshouses in Mattersey shall have and inhabite the same houses without any rente to be paid therefore.

And that the said Schole in Southwell aforesaid shall contynue, and that the Scholemaster there for the tyme beyng shall yerelie have for his wages £10.

The Countie of Oxford. Certificate 38.

(Edward VI.)

Sir John Williams, Knyght, John Doyly and Edward Chamberleyn, Esquyers, Commissioners.

11. THE PARISHE AND TOWNE OF BURFORD.

Howselyng people, 544.

The Guilde of our Lady in the said parishe Churche.

Certeyn landes and tenementes gyven by Diuers persons to the Fyndyng of a Prest, and to Gyve to pore People of the Towne yerely, And to the mendynge of highways And Comyn brydges of the same Towne, And the said prest to pray and synge for the Founders and all Crysten soules for euer.

Thomas Plomtre, Incombent there, of the age of 40 yeres, a man well learned, able to kepe A Cure, had for his salary yerely, £7, And hathe non other lyvynge nor promocion, but only this Stipend.

The value of all the landes and tenementes to the same belongyng ys, yerely, £16 10s. 10d.; whereof in

Repryses yerely, 32s. 9d.

And so Remayneth Clere [blank].

Plate and Jewelles, weynge by estimacion, 10 Ounces.

Ornamentes valued at 20s.   20s. and 10 ounces.

Obites there

Founded by Diuers persons whiche gave Certeyn Annuall rentes goinge oute of theyer landes to haue certeyn Obittes theyr for euer.

Incombent, None.

The said Annuall Rentes going oute of the said landes be of the yerely value of 30s.

Memoranda : that the said Towne of Burford ys a very greate merkett Towne Replenysshed with muche People, And nedfull to haue a Scole there, And the said landes was gyven to the mayntenaunce of hyghewayes and brydges, and to pore people.

Item that the Bretherne of the said Guylde At theyr Costes and Charge dyd bulde A Chapell of our lady annexed to the parishe Church there of theyre devosion, And dyd fynde a prest to mynyster ther, And to Teache Chylderne Frely, And after that, at diuers tymes, certeyn men of theyr devosions dyd gyve by will and feofment vnto the said Guilde the landes and tenementes aforsaid, amountyng to the somme of £16 10s. 10d., to fynde a prest, and to helpe pore people, And to mend hyghwayes

and the Comyn Brydges of the Towne, And so yt hath ben allwayes vsed so.

12. THE PARISHE AND TOWNE OF CHEPYNGNORTON.

How[s]lynge people, 540.

The Trynytie Guild there.

Certeyn landes and tenementes gyven by Dyuers and soundre
persons vnknowen, to the said Guilde, to Fynde a morowe masse
prest, A Scole master, and for Almes deades to be gyven yerely
of the Reuenues of the same in the said Towne.

Sir William Bryan, morowe masse Prest, of the age of 60
yeres, a man of honest behavyour, had for his salary, yerely, £6,
And had no other lyvynge nor promosion.

Sir Hamlet Malban, prest, Scolemaster there, of the age of 40
yeres, a man well learned in gramer, And doth kepe and teacheth
a Scole of Childerne of the said Towne, And hathe for his Stipend
£6 yerely, And hath no other lyvyng, but only the same.

The value of all the landes and tenementes to the same belongyng ys, yerely, £16 15s. 10d.; whereof in

Reprises yerely, 25s. 2d.

To the pore, 22s. 9½d.

Plate and Jewelles to the same, weying by estimacion 46
ounces, Remayning in the handes of John oppwood, of the said
Towne.

Ornamentes to the same, valued at 13s. 4d.

13s. 4d. and 46 ounces.

Memorandum: that the said Towne of Chepyngnorton is a
greate market Towne replenysshe with mnche People, And in
the said Towne is vpon the foundacion of the said Guild kepte
a Scole there by one of the said Guilde preasts, whyche ys nowe
the forsaid Amlet malban, chauntre preste there.

The Countie of Oxford. Certificate 97.

(Edward VI.)

BANBURY.

Memorandum: that there ys A Free scole within the Towne
of Banbury Called Seynt Johnes scole or hospitall; The

Scolemaster Nycholas Cartewryght, he havynge the profyttes for his waiges, and for an vusher to teache chylderne there their Gramer.

The Revenue of the londes belongyng for the same ys £15.

Item yt is very meate that the said Incombentes may abyde there to mynyster to the people and ayde the Curatt there, for yt is a greate Towne replynyshed with people, and a greate merkett Towne.

5. CHIPPING NORTON.

The late Guilde called the Trynytie Guild in Chepyngnorton Aforsaid.

William Bryan, Stipendary, had for his waiges and Salary Clere, £6.

Pencion, 100s.

Hamlet Malban, Scolemaster, for his waiges and stypend Clere, £6.

Stipendaries, £15 4d., ouer and aboue all Reprises.

A Scole there, and the said Malban Scolemaster.

Continuatur the Schole quousque.

Memorandum : the Inhabytaunces of the said Towne of Chepyngnorton desyereth that the said Scole maye be still kepte for teachyng yong chylderne. There ys muche yought in the said Towne.

6. BURFORD.

Memorandum : that the Towne of Burford ys a greate markett Towne Replenysshed with muche people, And it is verye necessary to haue a scole there, for ther is muche yought.

10. WITNEY.

The late Stipendary in the parishe church of Wytney.

Howselyng people, 1,100.

William Dalton, Incumbent, hathe for his salary, the Tenth Deducted, 116s. 4d. The said Incumbent dyd Receyue the same for his salary.

Pencion, 100s.

Memorandum : that the Towne of Wytney is a greate merket Towne, and Replenyshed with muche people, mete to have ayde for the Curatt there. The inhabytaunces desyereth to haue a scole master to teache yough there, but the said William Dalton doth lytle seruice nowe.

11. DEDDINGTON.

Ducatus Lancastrie.

The late Guild of the Trynytie in the parishe church of Dadyngton.

Howseling people, 300.

William Burton, Incumbent there, hath for his salary, the tenth deducted, £6.

[*The clere yerely valewe*], £7 18s. 10d. ouer and boue all charges.

A Scole there, the said william burton, Scolemaster.

The Towne of Dadyngton is parcell of the Duchie of Lancastre. The said William Burton ys A good Scole master, and Bryngyth vp yough very well in learnyng.

12. HENLEY.

The late Stypendary or Chauntre, Called seint Katheryns Chauntre, in the towne and parishe of Hendley.

Howselyng people, 500.

Roberte Bynkys, Incumbent, hathe for his salary, the tenth Deducted, £6.

Pencion, 100s.

£10 8s. 10d. ouer and aboue the Repryses.

To pore people oute of the premysses, and to the mendyng of Brydges, £4 14d.

19. BANBURY.

The Certificat of John Maynard, Surveyer there, for the house or hospitall of Seynt John's next Banbury, in the said Countie, as hereafter ensuyth, videlicet :

The landes and tenementes, with all other Commodities vnto the said house or hospytall lying within the said Countie, ar nowe letten by the said master by Indentur for the somme of £6 3s. 4d.

Sir Nicholas Cartwryght, Clerke, master of the said house or hospitall, a man of honest behavior, and had for his stipend the clere yerely value of the same.

Pencion, 100*s.*

Memorandum : that the said house or hospitall was not presented by fore the Kynges maiesties Comyssioners appoynted for the Chauntres, etcetera, in the said Countie.

The Countie off Oxford.

Q.R. Anc. Misc. Aug. $\frac{82}{17}$

CHEPYNGNORTON. *m.* 1 (*dors*).

The late Guylde called Trynitie Guylde, in chepyngnorton aforsaid.

William Bryan, prest, incombent, for his salary clere, £6.

Pencion, 100*s.*

Hamlett Malban, scolmaster, for his waiges and stipend clere, £6.

Stipendaries.

[*The Clerc Remaynder*], £15 0*s.* 4*d.* ouer and aboue all Reprises.

A Scole ther, the scolemaster the said Hamlett Malban.

Continuatur the Schole quousque.

Memorandum : the Inhabitaunces of the said Towne of chepyngnorton desyereth that the said scole may be still kepte for teachyng yong chylderne, for ther ys muche vght in the said Towne.

OXFORD. *m.* 3.

The servyce in The Chapell of our ladye, in the parishe Churche of Mary Magdalens, in Oxfford aforeseid.

Thomas Blauncharde, prest Incombent there, of the age of 40 yeres, a man of good conuersacion and well learnyd, and bryngethe vppe yowthe well, whoe hadde yerelye for his Salarye for Synging morowe masse daylye in the seyd Chappell, £4.

Pencion, £4.

The landes and tenementes gyven by dyvers persons vnknowen vnto the seid chappell for the finding of a preste in the seid chappell be off the clere yerelye value above all reprises goynge out off the same, £10 5s.

Memorandum: the cause that his name was lefte out of the certifycatt, that I delyveryd vnto your Mastershippe, was for that he was not at Oxforde when the Comyssyoners Satt there, but hadde bene absent From thens by the space of halfe a yere, And one Thomas Brewerne, his deputye, namyd him selfe Incombent, and because of the doubte who was trewe Incombent he was omyttyd and left owt of the Certyficatt that I made vnto yowe.

Per Johannem Maynarde, supervisorem.

WITNEY. *m.* 6.

The late stipendary in the parishe churche of Wytney. Howselyng people, 1,100.

William Dalton, Incombent, for his salary clere, 116s. 4d.

Pencion, 100s.

[*The Clerc Remaynder*], *nihil,* for that the incombent Receyueth it for his stipend.

Memorandum: that the Towne of Witney is a very great markett Towne and Replenyshed with muche people, mete to haue ayde for the Curat there. The inhabitaunces desyeryth to haue a scole master to teache yought there, but the said William Dalton doth lytle seruice there nowe.

DEDDINGTON.

The late Guylde of the Trynitie, in the parish of Dadyngton. Howselyng people, 300.

William Burton, Incombent, for his salary clere, £6.

[*The Clere Remaynder*], £7 18s. 10d., ouer and aboue all charges.

A Scole ther, the said William Burton, Scolmaster.

Ducatus Lancastrie.

The Towne of Dadyngton ys parcell of the Duchy of Lancastre. The said William Burton ys a very good Scole master, And bryngyng vp yough very well in learnynge.

m. 8. Summa totalis:

The Scholes, £12.

The Pore, £23. x

Oxfordshire. Schools Continuance Warrant, 15.

Forasmoche as it appereth [&c.] that a grammer schole hathe
been contynuallye kepte in chepingnorton [&c.], with the
revenues of the late Guylde there, called the Trynytie Guylde
and that the scholemaster there hath had [&c.] £6 [&c.].

Wee, therefore [&c.], haue assigned [&c.] that the saide,
grammer Schole shall contynue, and that Hamlett Malban,
scholemaster there, shall haue [&c.] £6.

Comitatus Rutlandie. Certificate 39.

(Edward VI.)

Richard Cicyll, Esquyre, and Thomas Hayes, commyssioners.

3. WHIGHTWELL.

One Chauntry within our lady chapell in paroche church ther.

Fownded by Richard Wyghtwell, prest, one of the Canons of
the Cathedral Churche of Lyncoln, for the Mayntenaunce of one
preest to singe ther for ever.   And hathe of landes and tenementes therunto belongyng lyenge in dyuers places within the
Counties of Rutland and Lincoln as maye appere by the Survey
therof to the yerly Value of 107s. 1d.; wherof in

Rente resolute to dyuers parsons, as apperyth by the Survye,
3s. 4d.

And so Remaynethe clere, for the porcion of the Chauntry
preest ther, namyd Sir Robert Sucklynge, of the age of 46 yers,
hauynge no other levynge but his sayd Chauntrye, who ys of
honeste conversacion and good report emonge his neighbors, and
hathe alwayes heretofore ben exercysed in the educacion of
youthe in lernynge, And yet vnable to serue a cure because he
is poorblynd ; by the yere, 103s. 9d.

Inde pro decima Domino Regi reservata, per Annum, 9s. 11d.

Et Remanet, £4 13s. 10d.

Memorandum :

Plate belongynge to the Furnyture of the sayd Chauntrye, as
apperythe by the Inventory : one Chales, poisant 20 ounces,
delivered to the Jwelhowse.   Ornamentes belongynge to the

sayd Chauntry, as apperyth by the sayd Inuentory, praysed at 13*s*. 11*d*.

The nombre of huslynge People ther, vnder the cure of the parson ther, Are 60.

The Tenauntes of Hambledon ther, nere adioynynge, do clayme owte of the landes ther, in Hambledon, in the tenure of William Fowler, to the payment of theire 15th, when yt chaunseth, 3*s*. 4*d*.

Comitatus Rutlandie. Certificate 99.

(Edward VI.)

WHIGHTWELL CHAUNTRYE.

Founded within our ladye chapell, in the paroche churche ther, for the Mayntenaunce of one preeste, ys of the clere yerly value of 103*s*. 9*d*. Inde

Pro decima domino Regi reseruata, per annum, 9*s*. 11*d*.

Remanet, £4 13*s*. 10*d*.

Memoranda. Sir Roberte Sucklinge, of the age of 46 yeres, is chauntry preeste ther, who ys of honeste conversacion and goodd report emonge his neighbors, albeyt vnable to serue a cure because he is pore blynde, and hathe of other leuynge besides this sayd chauntrye, none.

Scole, preacher, or povertye ther releuyd and mayntenyd, other then by the chauntrye preeste, Who hathe alwayes educatyd younge children in Lernynge, none.

The Counties of Salop (and Stafford), with the Towne of Salop. Certificate 40.

(Henry VIII.)

Richard, Bysshop of Coventrey and Lychfeld, Sir Phylyp Draycot, Knight, Edward Lyttleton, Esquyer, Anthony Bocher, gentilman, & Wylliam Sheldon, gentilman, Commissioners.

1. THE TOWNE OF SALOP.

The collegiat or parish church of Sainct Marie.

Founded by Kinge Edgar for the mayntenance of a Deane, 7 prebendaries, and a parishe preest, to celebrat and singe Diuine seruice daylie within the said parishe Church of saint Marie, and to dischardge the cure of the same..

The Reuenuez ben yerely imployed for

The porcions of the foresayd Deane and 7 prebendaries, according to there seuerall assignementes, with the dyvydent among them, £22 7s. 4d.

The stipende of a paryshe preest, £6 6s. 8d.

Wyne and waxe, 40s.

The Fee of a Collector of the Possessyons, 4s.

The 10th to the Kinge, by yere, 26s. 2d.   £32 4s. 2d.

The same is a paryshe Church, and the Deane and Chapter ben parsons there, and hath cure by estimacion of 1,500 houseling people.

The Possessiones theirof, being not chardged wyth any Rentes resolutes or deduccions going out of the same, ben clerely valued, by yere, at £32 4s. 2d.

And the dwellinge house of the Deane wyth the appurtenaunces, now vnletten, is valeved by yere at 8s., before not valued.

2. THE FRATERNITIE OF THE COMPANYE OF DRAPERS, WITHIN THE PARYSH CHURCH OF SAYNT MARIE AFORESAID.

Founded by The Company of the Drapers, and after confirmed by King Edward the 4th, to and for the mayntenyng of a preest to sing at the Altere of the Trinitye, within the paryshe Church or Colledge of saint Marie, and for the relef of 15 pore almes people.

The Reuenuez ben yerely imployed for

The stipend of the sayd prest, £4.

The Relyef of the said 15 pore people, videlicet : for the Master or Governor of them, at 2d. the weeke, and 2 Lodes of wood by yere, and euery of the other 14 a penny the weke, and one Loode of woood by yere. In mony, 53s. 4d. ; in wood, at 8d. the Loode, 10s. 8d.   64s.

Rentes resolutes, 10s. 2d.

Whatsoeuer remayneth to be spent in Reparacions and other charges or expences at the pleasure of the said Company, £8 0s. 12d. £15 15s. 2d.

The prest aforesayd is apointed to serve in the parysh Church *L* of saint Marie at the alter of the Holy Trinitie.

The Possessiones to the sayd Fraternitye belonging ben valewed by yere at £15 15s. 2d. Wherof

In Rentes Resolutes, by yere, 10s. 2d.

And so Remayneth, by yere, £15 5s.

And the 15 smal romes for the foresayd 15 pore almes people, now in their tenure, not Letten, ben valeued at 2s. 6d. by yere.

3. THE COLLEDGE OR PARYSH CHURCH OF SAYNT CHADE.

Founded by One Roger, Bisshop of Chester, for the mayntenaunce of a Deane, 10 prebendaries, and twoo parysh prests, to saye and sing daylye Dyuyne seruice within the sayd parysh or Collegiat Church of saynt Chad, and to dischardge the cure of the same.

The Reuenuez ben imployd yerely for

The 10th to the Kinge, 29s. 5¼d.

The porcions of the foresayd Deane, and 10 prebendaries, according to their seuerall assignementes. In all, £21 15s. 2¾d.

The Stipendes of the sayd twoo preestes, videlicet : to the one £6 13s. 4d.; and to the other, £4 6s. 8d. In all £11.

Wyne, 57s; wax, 6s. 8d.; the clerkes, 3s. 4d.; the Deacon, 2s.; the Maundy, 2s.; a reward to a Welshe preest at lent tyme, 6s. 8d. In all, 77s. 8d.

The Fee of a collectour of the Revenuez, 4s. £38 6s. 4d.

The same colledge is a paryshe Church of saynt Chad, and the Deane and prebendaries ben parson of the same, and haue the cure of, by estimacion, 1,600 howseling people.

The Possessions therof, wythout any yerely ordinary Rentes going out of the sam, ben valeved clerely by yere, £38 6s. 4d.

And The howse wherein diuers mynisters of the sayd

Colledge do now inhabyt, with the appurtenances, vnletten valued by yere at 10s.

Plate, whyte, 6 ounces.

Goodes and other implementes and small vtensylles belonging to the same appere in a Inventorye herwith redy to be shewed, not valued.

4. THE FRATERNITIE OF THE COMPANIE OF MERCERS WITHIN THE SAYD PARYSHE CHURCH OF SAYNT CHADE.

Founded by One John Begett to and for the fyndyng of a preste to synge at the altare of saynt Michaell, within the sayd paryshe or Collegiat Churche of saynt Chade, and for the Relyef of 13 pore Almes people.

The Revenuez ben yerely imployd for

The Stipend of the said prest, £4.

The Relyef of the sayd 13 pore people, videlicet: euery one of the 13 at 1d. the Weeke; by yere, in all, 56s. 4d.

An Obbett, 2s. 2d.

Rentes Resolutes, 7s. 10d.

Whatsoeuer remayneth to be bestowed in Reparacions and other chardges at the discrescression [sic] of the sayd Compenye of Mercers, 11s. 2d. £7 17s. 6d.

The sayd prest is appoynted to serve within the sayd paryshe churche of saynt Chad at the Alter of saynt Michaell.

The Possessions belonging to the sayd Fraternitie ben yerly valewed at £7 17s. 6d. Wherof in

Rentes Resolutes, 7s. 10d.

And so Remaineth by yere, £7 9s. 8d.

And the 13 smale romes now in the tenure of the sayd 13 pore people not letten ben yerely valewed at 13d.

5. THE FRATERNITIE OF THE COMPANIE OF TAYLOURS WITHIN THE SAYD PARYSHE CHURCHE OF SAYNT CHAD.

Founded by one Roger Wyke and William Walford to and for the mayntenaunce of a prest to sing within the sayd paryshe or Collegiat Churche of Saynt Chad, and to celebrat at the Alter of saynt John Baptist.

The Revenuez ben yerely imployd for

The Stipend of the sayd prest, £4.

An Obbett, 2s.

Rentes Resolutes, 3s. 4d.

Whatsoeuer remaineth to be bestowed in Reparacions and other chardges at the discressyon of the sayd Company of Taylours, 3s. 6d. £4 8s. 10d.

The prest aforesayd ys appoynted to serue within the sayd paryshe churche of saynt Chad.

The Possessiones belonging to the sayd Fraternitie ben yerely valewed at £4 8s. 10d. Wherof in

Rentes Resolutes, 3s. 4d.

And so Remaineth by yere, £4 5s. 6d.

7. THE FRATERNITIE OF THE COMPANYE OF WEVERS
WITHIN THE FORNAMYD CHURCH OF SAINT CHAD.

Founded by one John Begatt to and for the findeyng of a preest to synge within the sayd paryshe or Collegiat Churche of saynt Chad.

The revenuez ben yerely imploid for

The Stipend of the sayd prest, 47s. 1d.

Rentes Resolutes, 4s. 11d. 52s.

The prest aforsayd is appoynted to serve in the sayd paryshe churche of saynt Chad.

The possessiones belonging to the sayd Fraternitie ben yerely valeued at 52s. Wherof in

Rentes Resolutes, 4s. 11d.

And so Remaineth by yere, 47s. 1d.

8. THE FRATERNITIE OF THE COMPANYE OF SHOMAKERS
WITHIN THE SAYD PARYSHE OR COLLEGIAT CHURCH OF
SAINT CHAD.

Founded by Robert Endeslow to and for the fynding of a

preest to sing within the sayd paryshe churche of saynt Chad at the Altare of saynt Katharine.

The Reuuenez ben yerely imployd for

The Stipend of the sayd prest, 26s. 8d.

Rentes Resolutes, 19s.   45s. 8d.

The preest aforsaid is appoynted to serve in the sayd Church of saynt Chad.

The Possessiones of the sayd Fraternitie ben valued by yere at 45s. 8d. Whereof in

Rentes Resolutes by yere, 19s.

And so Remaineth by yere, 26s. 8d.

10. THE FRATERNITIE OF THE COMPANI OF SHERMEN IN THE PARYSH CHURCH OF SAYNT JULIAN.

Founded by

Whome they know not to and for the fynding of a prest to sing within the paryshe Church of saynt Julyan at the altare of our Ladye.

The reuenuez ben expended for

The Stipend of the sayd prest, 75s. 8d.

An Obbett, 2s.

The Fee of a Collectour of the Landes, 3s. 4d.

Rentes Resolutes, 4s. 4d.   £4 5s. 4d.

The foresayd prest is appoynted to serve within the sayd parysh Church of saynt Julyan.

The Possessiones of the sayd Fraternitie ben valued by yere at £4 5s. 4d. Whereof in

Rentes Resolutes, 4s. 4d.

And so Remaineth by yere, £4 0s. 12d.

8. [23]. THE PARYSHE OF OSWESTRIE.

The Service of our Ladie.

Founded by Thomas, Erle of Arundell, and afterwardes augmentid by diuers and sundrie persones, to and for the findeng of twoo preestes to Celebrate Masse, with other diuine service, within the Churche of Osewestre aforesayd.

The Revenuez ben yerly imployd for

The Salary of the sayd twoo preestes, £10 10s. 11d.

Rentes Resolutes, 25s. 2d. £11 16s. 1d.

The service is founded within the parysh church of Osewestre aforsaid, Wherunto belongeth the chardge of 2,000 housling people or theraboutes.

The possessiones belonging to the sayd service is valued by yere at £11 16s. 1d. Wherof in

Rentes Resolutes by yere, 25s. 2d.

And so Remaineth by yere, £10 10s. 11d.

Plate Gylt, 8 ounces.

13. [30]. THE TOWNE OF LUDLOW.

The palmers Guyld within the paryshe church of saynt Laurence.

Founded by the most valiant and victorius Kinge of Famus Memorie, Kinge Edward, graundfather to Richard the second, and afterward aftemented [sic] by Richard the second, and also by now our most souaraynt lorde King Henry the 8th, to and for the findynge of a warden, 7 preestes, 4 singyng men, twoo Deacons, syx Queristers, to sing diuine service within the paryshe church of saynt Laurence; And also for the Meyntenaunce of a Scolemaster of Gramer, and 32 pore Almes people.

The Revenuez ben yerly imployd for

The Salaries, Stipendes, or Fees of the predicted persons, with other Officers, accordyng to ther seuerall assingmentes; videlicet: to the sayd 7 preestes, £38 13s. 4d.; twoo singingmen, parcell of 4 after the Fundacion, £6 13s. 4d.; twoo Deacons, 40s. 8d.; 6 queresters, 34s.; the scolemaster of gramer, £10; The pore Almes people, 27s.; to one which Ringith the Almes bell, 2s.; the porter of the sayd Guild, 44s. 4d. In all by yere, £62 14s. 8d.

Diuerse Obbettes, £14 5s. 6d.; haloyd bred, 12s. 3d.; diuers lightes, 28s.; money geven to pore people, 8s. 2d.; The Reward to the warden, ouerseer of the workes and Reparacions, 46s. 8d.

The Collectour of the possessiones, 100s.   In all by yere, £24 0s. 7d.

Rentes Resolutes, £9 11s. 5½d.

Decayes and Defautes of Rentes, £19 19s. 3½d.

What soeuer remayneth to be bestowed in Reparacions and other expences, and charges at the discresion of the warden for the tyme being, £6 23½d.

But the reparacions (The Revenuez of the premisses lieing for the gretest part in howses) do yerly mych exced this sume as they afferm.   £122 7s. 1½d.

The sayd Guyld is wythin the parysh Church of saynt Laurence, within which paryshe ben 1,800 housling peple or theraboutes, but the Ministers of the Guyld be not chardgeable towardes the cure.

The possessiones of the Guyld, wyth the Decayes, ben yerly valued at £122 7s. 11½d.; wherof in .

The Fee of a Collectour, 100s.; Rentes Resolutes by yere, £9 11s. 5½d; Decayes and defautes of Rentes, £19 19s. 3½d.

£34 10s. 9d.

And so Remayneth by yere, £87 17s. 2½d.

And the Manscion howse wherin the said Ministers do dwell, with the Almeshouse whioh the foresayd pore people doo Inhabit, with the appurtenaunces, is worth by yere, to be letten, 20s., before not valued.

Plate Gylt, 93¾ ounces; Parcel gylt, 56¼ ounces; Whyte, 32½ ounces.   182¾ ounces.

Certen other plate being set and fastened to tre, glas, and stone, And other goodes or Ornamentes, with diuerse vtensylles, appere In an Inventory, redy to be shewed not valued.

The Countie of Salopp.   Certificate 41.

(Edward VI.)

Sir George Blount, Knyght; Reynold Corbett, Rychard Forssett, and Richard Cupper, gentlemen; Comyssyoners.

10. THE PARISHE OFF WELLYNGTON.

The Seruyce of our Ladye.

Founded off one preste to celebrate at the alter off our Ladye Wythin the parishe Churche off Wellyngton Afforeseyd, entended to haue Contynuance For euer.

The value, 114s. 6d.

The Reprises, 14s.

The Remainder, 100s. 6d.

Thomas Taylor, stipendary, aged 60, and other livinge, £10.

£4 17s. 6d.

The sayd preste kepte Alweys a grammer Schole ther freelie. Goodes, 3s. 4d.

15. THE PARYSHE OFF OSWESTRY.

The Service of our Ladye.

Founded off certen landes and tenementes heretofore geuen, to the Fyndynge off 2 prestes to celebrate at the Aulter off our Lady Wythyn the parishe churche off Qswestry, entended to contynue For euer.

The value, £13 11s. 10d.

The Reprises, 25s. 2d.

The Remainder, £12 6s. 8d.

John Mathew, stipendary, aged 32, and no other lyuynge, 106s. 8d.

Moryce Ap Edward, stipendary, aged 30, and no other lyuynge, £4.

To the augmentacion of a Free schole ther, besydes £6 by the Foundacion, 40s.

Goodes, 19s. 2d.

25. THE PARYSHE OFF SAYNT LEONERDES IN BRYDGENORTH.

The Chauntries Within the seyd Parishe.

Founded by the Ballyes and Burgeses off the towne off Brydgenorth, by dyuerse Kynges lycences, off 2 prestes to celebrate Within the parishe Churche there, entended to contynue for euer.

The value, £35 19s. 11d.

The Reprises, 38s. 3½d.

The Remainder, £34 19½d.

William Swanwyke, one of the Incumbentes, aged 68, and no other lyuynge, 100s.

Richard Knowles, the other Incumbent, aged 46, and hathe no other lyuynge, 100s.

To Roland Lymell, precher, 100s.

To a Scholemaster kepynge a grammer schole there, £8.

31. THE PARYSHE OF MADELEY.

The Seruyce of our Ladye within the seyd Parishe.

Founded of certen landes & tenementes heretofore by diuerse persons geuen and enffeoffed, to the use of a preste to celebrate at the Aulter of our Ladye there, entended to haue contynuance for euer.

The value, with 7s. 6d. of copie hold, 52s.

The Reprises, *nihil*.

The Remainder, 52s.

John Lye, stipendary, aged 40, and hath other lyuynge, (106s. 8d.), 52s.

The sayd Incumbent hath alweys kepte a gramer schole there.

34. THE PARYSHE OFF NEWPORTE,

whereyn be 800 hoselynge people hauynge, therfore, necessytie of the Indowment of a Vicar.

The Colledge off our Ladye there, beynge a parishe Churche.

Founded by one Thomas Draper, by the lycence off Kynge Henrye the VI., off one Warden and 3 Fellowes, to Celebrate daylie Within the seyd churche, to haue Successyon for euer.

The value, £33 0s. 2d.

The Reprises, 15s. 8d.

The Remainder, £32 4s. 6d.

John Moreton, clarke, Warden there, aged [*blank*], and other lyuynge, £8 5s. 5d.

Rychard Robyns, Fellowe there, aged 60, and other lyuynge, 100s.

Rychard Holynshedd, Fellowe, aged 60, and other lyuynge, 100s.

John Hall, aged 80, and other lyuynge, 40s.

John Barbor, organplayer, 26s. 8d.

The sayd Rychard Robyns hathe alweys preched the Worde off God, and kepte a gramer Schole there.

To the pore, 3s. 4d.

Plate, 14 ounces.

Ornamentes, goodes, and household stuffe, 26s. 8d.

Somerset. Certificate 42.
(Edward VI.)

Thomas Speke, Hugh Poulett, John Rogers, John Seyntlow, and Thomas Dyer, Knights; William Moryce, George Lyne, Robert Keylway, and Robert Metcalff, Esquires; John Hannan and William Hartegyll, gentlemen; Commissioners.

3. CRUKERNE.

The Free Scole ther, sometyme callyd the Chauntrie of the Trynitie ther, is yerely worthe in

Landes, tenementes, and other hereditaments, nowe in the holding and occupying of sondery persones, as may appere more at large by the Rentall of the same, £9.   Whereof in

Rents resolute paid yerely to sondery persones, 18s. 9d.

And so Remayneth clere, £8 1s. 3d.

Sir Hughe Paulet, Knighte, and Henry Cricke, holden of the Kinges Majestie certayne curstomary landes, parcell of his graces Manor of Crukerne, aforesaide, videlt.: too partes of the landes callyd Crafte, graunted unto them by copy of Court Rolle for terme of their lives, after the custome of the saide Manor, to the use of the trynitie and mayntenaunce of the saide scole, by the Surveiors of the late attaynted Lorde Marques of Exciter, then Lorde of the saide manor, whiche landes be worthe yerely, over and above £2, paide to the Manor of Crukerne aforesaide for the rent and farm of the same landes, £2.

John Byrde, Scole Master ther, a man of honest conversacion, well learned, and of goodly judgement, dothe moche good in the countrie in vertuouse bringing uppe and teaching of Children, having at this present 6 or 7 score scollers, receyved the hole proffects for his wages.

And thenhabitaunts ther be most humble Suters to have the saide Free Scole contynued, with augmentacion of the saide Scole Master his lyving.

5. CURRYVELL.

The Chauntrie or Free Scole, foundyd by Margaret, late Countisse of Richmond and derby, within the late College of Wymborne, in the Countie of Dorset, is yerely worth in

Landes . . . , £11 14s.

20. THE TOWNE OF TAUNTON.

Thenhabitauntes of the towne of Taunton aforesaide, the 6th daye of Aprill, anno regno regis Edwardi VI[u]., 2nd, [1548], made humble request unto the Commyssionors in manner and forme followinge: Wher ther is within the saide town of Taunton, beinge the greatest and best market towne in all that shire, in a verray holsome, good, and plentyfull soyle, a faire, large and goodly howse newe buylded, erected, and made for a Scolehouse about 25 yeres nowe past, wherin was a Scole Master and an Ussher founde the space of 12 or 14 yeres, for the vertuouse educacion and teaching of youthe, as well of the saide towne of Taunton as of the hole contrye, to the nombre of 7 or 8 score Scolers, by the Devocion of one Roger Hill, of the same towne, merchaunte, nowe deceased. A great Relief also to the same towne of Taunton. And nowe sythe the deathe of the same Roger Hill the saide Scolehouse standyth voyde, without either Master ussher, or Scolers, to the great preiudice, hurte, and discommoditie of the commen welthe of the saide Shire.

Whereuppon the saide enhabitaunts make most humble sute unto the Kinges majestie that yt may please his highnes to graunte and assigne suche landes and tenementes in perpetuytie as shalbe thought mete unto his grace and his most honorable counsaile, to the mayntenaunce and finding of a Maister and ussher to teache in the same Scholehowse, which no doubte is most bewtyfull and most necessarie place of all that shire.

66. The Towne of Bridgewater.

Thenhabitauntes ther make their most humble peticion to have a free grammer scole erected ther.

172. Brewton.

Memorandum : Thenhabitaunts of the towne of Brewton afore-saide, the 21st day of Aprill, anno regno regis Edwardi VI^u., 2do, made humble request unto the commyssionors in maner and forme following. Wher ther was within the foresaide towne a faire Scolehouse for a free grammer Scole, newly buylded, erected, and made in the 11th yere of the reigne of oure late soveraigne lorde of famouse memory, King Henry VIII. [1519-20] by Richarde, busshop of London, John FitzJames, and John Edmondes, Doctor of Dyvinitie, who did gyve and assigne to the maynten-aunce of the same Scole, landes and tenementes to the yerely value of £12, for the vertuouse educacion and teaching of the yewthe, as well of the saide towne of Brewton as of the hole contrie, nowe decayed by reason that Heughe Sherwoode, late Scolemaster ther, surrendred the saide landes into the Kinges Majesties handes 6 or 7 yeres nowe past, who, indevoring hym self rather to lyve licentiously at will then to travaile in good educacion of yewthe, according to the godly fundacion of the saide Scole, founde the meanes by his saide surrender to obtayne by Decre out of the Courte of augmentacions of the Revenues of the Kinges Majesties Crowne for terme of his lyffe one Annuytie or pencion of £5, and the foresaide Scolehowse, with a gardeyn and a close of lande therunto adjoynyng, contaynyng by esti-macion 4 acres, lying in Brewton aforesaide, discharged also thereby of any further Free teaching or keping of Scole ther, to the great Decaye as well of vertuouse bringing uppe of yewthe of the saide shire in all good lernying, as also of thenhabitaunts of the Kinges saide town of Brewton, of great relief that came thereby.

Wherfore the saide inhabitaunts made mooste humble sute unto the Kinges Majestie that yt may please his highnes, of his bounteouse liberalitie, to restore the saide Scolehowse, landes and tenementes, to the use, godly purpose and intent of the fundacion of the foresaide Byssop, John FitzJames, and John Edmondes.

175. YEUYLL.

Memorandum : . . . Ther is a chapell scituate within
the churche yarde of Yevill kevered with leade, contayning by
estimacion nighe one fooder praysed worthe to be solde, £4,
which thenhabitaunts ther desire to have for a scolehouse.
The towne is a great market Towne, and a thoroughe faire.

199. THE CATHEDRAL CHURCHE OF SAINCTE ANDREWE IN WELLES.

Memorandum : . . . The same Deane and Chapiture, of
their Free will, kepe and maynteyne a free grammer Scole ther,
and do paye to the Master of the same Scole yerely for his
Stipend or wages, £13 6s. 8d., and to the ussher of the same
scole yerely, £6 13s. 4d.

Somersetshire. Schools Continuance Warrant, 4.

Forasmoche as it apperithe [&c.] that a grammer scole hathe
ben continuallie kepte in Crukerne with the reuenues of the late
chauntrie of the Trynytie in Crukerne aforesaid, And that the
Scolemaster there hathe had for his stipende and wages yerlie
£8 6s. 8d. [&c.],

We therfore [&c.] haue assigned [&c.] that the said scole in
Crukerne aforesaid shall contynue, And that John Birde, Scolemaster there, shall haue and enjoy the Rome of Scolemaster
there, and shall haue for his wages yerelie £8 6s. 8d.

Comitatus Somersetie. Particulars for Schools.
Edward VI. Roll 2.

BATH GRAMMAR SCHOOL.

Parcelle terrarum et Possessionum nuper Prioratus de Bathe,
in Comitatu Somersetie.

Omnia terre, tenementa, Cotagia, gardina, et molendina infra
civitatem Bathonie et Suburbiis eiusdem, in Comitatu predicto,
valent in

[Redditibus], £54 5s. 4d.

Reprise in

Feodo, 40s.   Et in redditu resoluto, 3s. 6d.
Et in decasu siue defectu reddituum, £9 8s.   £11 11s. 6d.
Et Remanent vltra per annum, £47 13s. 10d.
Examinatur per me Henricum Leke, Auditorem.

28 die June, Anno Regni Regis Edward VI^u., Sexto [1552].
The kinges maiesties pleasour is that the Maior and citizens
of bathe shall haue the landes and tenementes above mencyoned,
of his highnes gifte to theym and their Successors for ever, to
thentent the said maior [and] citizens shall fynd one able Skolemaster with thissues and proffettes therof, to teache a free
grammer scole there, to haue continewance for euer, and also in
further consideracion that they shall with thissues and proffettes
of the saide premisses relieve 10 poore folke within the said
towne of bathe for ever.

The said maior and citizens to yeld to his highnes one yerely
Rentt of £10.

The tenure is free burgage.

To haue thissues from the feast of thanunciacion of our
Lady laste paste ; therefore make a booke therof accordingly.

(*Signed*), Ry. Sakevyle.

Comitatus Somersete.   Particulars for Schools.
Edward VI.   Roll 10.

BRUTON GRAMMAR SCHOOL.

Parcelle Possessionum [nuper] Monasterii de Brewton, in Comitatu [Somersete].

(*faded*)   Brewton   e   de blinfeld   Dors ac
      [War]myster   comitatu Wiltesire ; valent in

Firma Vnius Mancionis, scituate in Brewton, in boriali parte
nuper Monasterii siue Abbathie de Brewton, que quidem
Mancio ibidem edificata fuit pro quadam Schola gramaticali in
eadem imperpetuum tenenda, cum Curtilagio, gardino, et Duabus
parcellis terre adiacentibus inter quandam Communem viam,
inter dictam nuper Abbatheam et dictam Mancionem, videlicet :

Y

ante fenestram australis partis predicte Mancionis, quarum vna palis, et altera aliis Clausuris vocatis Barringes, ac eciam vnius acre terre mensura completa, boriali parte, inter Rivulum vocatum Brewe et dictam Mancionem, ac eidem Mancioni adiuncte, cum suis pertinenciis; per Annum, nihil, quia omnino reseruata ad vsum Schole ibidem; prout in quadam carta sub Sigillo Conuentali nuper Monasterii de brewton, cuius data est 20 die aprillis, Anno regni nuper Regis Henrici VIII[ul]. 19 [1528], inter alia plenius continetur.

[Firmis], £11 5s.

Memorandum: that the premisses in brewton, blinfild and Warmyster before mencioned were gyven to the　　　　(faded) of brewton to thentente that the profittes of the same shoulde be employed to the maintenaunce of a Schole in brewton for euer more, as by seuerall Dedes and Indentures quadrapartite (faded)　　　dothe appere.

Examinatur per me Henricum Leke, deputatum Auditoris.

The kinges maiesties plesser ys by the advyse of hys most honorable Consell, that　　(torn and faded)　　corporacion of a conuenyent nombre of the Inhabitantes of (torn and faded)　e perpetuall succession, And to haue the premysses assured to them　　　to purchas £12 by yere more. Wherfor make a boke therof　　　the maytenaunce of a free gramer scole to be called the free　　　of Kyng Edward the Sixt in Bruton, to be contynued for euer　　　　　　e a graunt of the issues of the premysses from Michaellmas, anno 3 [1549].

Ry Sakevyle, Wm. Hildman.

The Countie of Stafford. Certificate 40.

(Henry VIII.)

16. THE TOWNE OF STAFFORD.

The Collegiat and paryshe Church of our Lady.

Founded by The Most Excellent Prynce of Famouse memorye, King John, to fynd a Dean, Twelve prebendaries, fower preestes, vicars, and fower clerkes, vicars, to synge diuine service within the Collegiat and paryshe Churche of our Ladye, within the Towne of Stafford.

The Reuenuez ar yerely imployed for

The Tenthes, £6 13s. 9¾d.

The Salaries of the Deane and 12 prebendaries, accordyng to ther seuerall Rates, £43 12s. 10¼d.

The Salaries of 3 preestes, accordyng to ther seuerall Assingmentes found by the Deane, £14 6s. 8d.

The Salarie of a preest payd out of the prebend of Cotton, £6 ; the Salaries of 2 prestes payd out of prebend of Marston, accordyng to ther seuerall Assingnementes, £9 13s. 4d. ; The Salaries of twoo preestes payd out of the prebend of Salt, £9 13s. 4d.   In al, £39 13s. 4d.

The Stipendes of fower Clerkes, vicars, videlicet to euery of them, 8s.   In all, 32s.

The Deane of Staffordes pencion, 46s. 8d.

The procuracions of the sayd Dean, 2s. 2½d.

Wyne and wax payd out of the prebend of coton, 40s.

£96 0s. 11d.

The sayd Colledge ys a paryshe Church, and hath the cure of 3,000 howslyng people, being parson of the sayd paryshe.

The Possessiones therof, beyng not chardged wyth any ordinary resolucions or deduccions goyng out of the same, ben clerly valued by yere at £96 0s. 11d. ; wherof in

A pencion and proxes to the Dean of Stafford by yere, 48s. 10½d.

And so Remayneth by yere, £93 12s. 0½d.

And the howse, wherin diuerse Ministers dyd lye, is letten to on John ap Harry for terme of 60 yeres at 8s. by yere.

The Chauntrey wythin the Collegiat Church of Stafford.

Founded by Thomas Counter, Chappelleyn, to fynd a scolemaster to teach Chyldren, Whyche scolemaster, by cause he was presented before the Kinges Maiesties Commyssions as a Chauntrey preest, he was Chardged with the payment of the 10thes, and hetherto hath ben called by the name of a Chauntrey, wheras yt is none in deade.

The Reuenuez ben yerely imployd for
The Salarye of the sayd preest, £4 5s. 0¾d.

The 10th, 8s. 3¼d.   £4 13s. 4d.

The Possessiones therof, beyng not chardged wyth any
ordinery Resolucions or deduccions goyng out of the same, ben
clerely valued, by yere, at £4 13s. 4d.

17. THE TOWNE OF TOMWORTH.

The Colledge of Tomworth.

Founded by Kynge Edgare, to fynd syx prebendaryes to
syng diuine service within the Collegiat and paryshe Church of
Tomworth.

The Reuenuez are yerely imployed for

The Salaries of the sayd prebendaries accordyng to ther
several Rates, £55 17s. 9¾d.

The Tenthes, 114s. 8d.

The Wages of 6 preestes, videlicet to euery one of them, £6,
payd equally out of euery prebend.   In al, £36.

The Bysshopes visitacion, 22s. 2¼d.

Proxes and Synages to the archdeacon, 18s. 4d.

A custom callyd a cheff ale, 33s. 4d.

The Deacons wages, 60s.

A pencion payd to the prebend of Cotton out of the prebend
of Wyggyngton, 43s. 4d.   £106 9s. 8d.

The same ys a paryshe Church, and hath the cure of 2,400
howslyng people, beyng parsone of the sayd paryshe.

The Possessions therof, being not chardged with any ordinery
Resolucions or deduccions going out of the same, ben yerely
valued at £106 9s. 8d.

Plate, Whyte, 88 ounces.

Other Goodes and Ornamentes not valued ar reported in an
Inventory redy to be shewed.

27. THE CITIE OF LYCHFELD.

41. THE HOSPITALL OF SAYNT JOHN BAPTYST.

Founded by Wylliam, somtyme Bysshop of Lychfeld and

Coventry, to fynd a Schoolmaster and an vssher to teach chyldren, and a preest to say masse and other diuine seruice within the sayd Hospitall, and 13 pore men.

The Reuenuez ben yerly imployed for

The Salaryes or Stypendes of the sayd persons, videlicet the scolemaster, £10; the vssher, 100s.; the preest, 106s. 8d.; and 13 pore men after the rate of a 1d. the day, £19 14s. 4d. In all, £40 12d.

The Fee of a Baylyff, 60s.

The 10th, 17s. 6d.

Rentes Resolutes, £4 12s. 1d.

And so Remaineth to be dysposed at the pleasure of the Master of the Hospitall, 113s. 4d.   £5 13s. 10d.

The sayd Hospitall is no paryshe Churche, but only to the 13 pore men and the Inhabitans within the precinct of the sayd hospitall.

The possessions therof ben clerely valued at £54 3s. 10d.; wherof in

The Fee of a baylyf by yere, 60s.

Rentes Resolutes by yere, £4 12s. 1d.   £7 12s. 1d.

And so Remaineth by yere, £46 11s. 9d.

Plate parcell, gylt, 7½ ounces.

Other goodes or Ornamentes to the same belongyng, not valued, ar reported in an Inventory redy to be shewed.

Staffordshire. Certificate 54.

(Edward VI.)

John Talbott and George Blount, Knyghtes, Reynold Corbett, Richard Forssett and Richard Cupper, Gentilmen, Commys-syoners.

2. THE TOWNE OF STAFFORD.

The Chauntery or scole in the Collegiate churche of Stafford.

Founded by Thomas Counter, priest, of one priest perpetually to celebrate dayly masse within the Collegiate churche of Stafford, And also to kepe a free scole there.

The yerely value, £4 13s. 4d.

3. THE PARISHE OF TAMWORTH.

The Morowe Masse priest and scole master in Tamworth.

Londes and tenementes first gyven by dyuerse persones to-wardes the perpetuall fyndyng of a priest to syng morowe masse dayly in the chappell of Seynt George, within the Collegiate churche of Tamworth, And also to teche a free scole in the same parishe. And afterward other londes and tenementes purchased and assigned by Nicholas Agard and John Shepperd, executours of the testament of John Bayly, for the further amplification of the lyvyng of the same priest for euer.

The yerely value, £12 18s. 3½d.

Reprise, 35s. 3¼d.

Remayneth, £11 3s. 0¼d.

Plate parcell guylt, 6 ounces.

Ornamentes, 2s. 10d.

Vessell vsed to be letten out for reparacions of the tenementes belonging to the possessyons therof, 32s. 2d.

The free chappell of Seynt James, called the spittell chappell.

Founded by Henry Wylloughby, Knyght (but how and by what conveyaunce it is vnknowne), as a perpetuall free chappell of one priest, to syng and celebrate in the same chappell for euer.

The yerely value, 66s. 8d.

The seruyce or stipendary within the chappell of wilmecot.

Londes and tenementes, gyven and assigned to the perpetuall fyndyng of a priest, to celebrate in the seyd chappell, for the ease of the Inhabitauntes of the township of wylmecot, being two myles distaunt from their paryshe churche, And fowle ways betwene.

The yerely value, 36s.

Our ladyes chappell within the churche Collegiate, And an other chappell in the churche yard there.

Londes and tenementes gyven seuerally by seuerall parcelles, by Thomas Barwell and John Grene, to be perpetually prayed for, And for the mayntenaunce of the same two chappelles.

The yerely value, 5s.

The priests seruyce in Wyggynton chappell.

Londes assigned for hiring of a priest to syng in the seid chappell at suche tyme as for fowlenes of the wether the en-habitauntes there cannot convenyently go to their parishe churche of Tamworth, entended so to contynue for euer, whiche chappell is one myle from the parishe churche. There is none other seruyce maynteyned in the seyd chappell.

The yerely value, 2s. 8d.

The priestes seruyce and obite, founded by Rychard Bretten.

Londes and tenementes, gyven by Rychard Bretten, to haue a masse sayd in Tamworth churche euery fryday perpetually, and ones in euery yere one obite for euer.

The yerely value, 2s. 10d.

Memorandum : the hole londes gyven in fourme aforeseyd ben of the clere yerely value of 29s. 4d. Howbeit, bicause that the resydew, besydes the seid 2s. 10d., hath ben yerely imployed vpon the Morowe masse, priest or scolemaster aforeseid, and is there charged as parcell of his porcion, the value is here cer-tyfyed no more, but only 2s. 10d.

7. THE CITIE OF LYCHEFELD,

with the cathedrall churche there.

The Guyld of our lady.

Memorandum: that londes, to the clere yerely value of £6 19s. 5d. in Norton, grete wirley, litell wirley, and wall, were putt in feoffment in 36 Hen. VIII. [1544–5], by the maister and brethern of the seid guyld for perpetuall mayntenaunce of the conduytes in lychefeld, whiche somme is not conteyned within the somme of the yerely value of the seid guyld. Also dyuerse Annuyties ben graunted to dyuers persones for terme of their lyves, amounting by yere to £27 16s. 8d., whereof certificat is made in an other boke by the particuler serveyour. Also £4 13s. 4d. was distributed yerely to the pore, but not by any ordinaunce of the first foundacion.

10. The parishe of Kyngeley.

The chauntery or preistes seruyce.

Hugh Adderley, clerk, did enfeff Thomas Houncesley and other in Fee of certeyne londs and tenementes, to the entent that the issues and proffettes therof should be holly employed for perpetuall fyndyng of a priest dayly to celebrate at the Alter of Jesu for all Cristen sowles. And to kepe scole, and to teche pore mens children of the seid parishe grammer, and to rede and sing.

The yerely value, £7 13s. 8d.

Reprises, 32s. 8d.

Remayneth, £6 0s. 12d.

15. The parishe of Kynvare.

The preistes seruyce or stipendary there.

John Perot, in the sixt of May, in the 6th yere of the reign of Kyng Henry the 8th [1515], did enfeff Edward Gray, Knyght, and other of certeyn londs and tenementes in fee, to the entent that the proffettes therof for 90 yeres from thensforth shold be employed for fyndyng of a prist to syng devyne seruyce in the churche of Kynvare, and to syng Masse at the Alter in the Chappell of our Lady there. And after the seid yeres ended, that the seid feffees and their heires shold dispose the proffettes therof about devyne seruyce in the seid chappell, and other workes of charite for euer, as to them shold seme convenyent. And sithens that tyme dyuers other persones haue gyven diuers other londs for mayntenaunce of the same seruyce for euer, All whiche were employed vpon one preist, who hath kept the same seruyce, and also kept a free scole for children of the seid parishe.

The hole yerely value, £6 7s. 4d.

Reprises, 2s. 3d.

Remayneth, £6 5s. 1d.

Memorandum : there be of the seid possessyons copyhold londs and rentes out of copy hold londs holden of the manere of Kynvare, by yere, 57s., wherout goth the aforeseid yerely reprise of 2s. 3d. But the seid Manere is Auncient Demeane, and (as it is sayd) the copyholders do not hold at the will of the Lord, but to them and their heires, according to the Auncient custome of the Manere there.

16. THE PARISHE OF SHENSTON.

The chauntery or preistes seruyce there.

Henry Hunt, executour of the testament of James Keyley, buylded a chapell adioynyng to Shenston churche, And by dede according to the last will of the seid James, did ordeyn that Antony Fitzherbert, Knyght, and other, being the feffees of certeyn Londs and tenementes of the seid James, shold employ the issues and proffettes therof to the perpetuall mayntenaunce of one preist perpetually to celebrate Dayly Masse at the Alter of Thomas Beckett within the seid chappell for all Cristen sowles, And ordeyned that the seid priest shold distribute vpon one holy day in euery yere for euer, 13s. 4d. in bread, drink, and chese to the persones present, And also shold teche yong children of the seid parishe grammer, or otherwise, accordyng to his knowlege.

The yerely value, £8 10s. 3½d.

Reprises, 29s. 11d.

Remayneth, £7 0s. 4½d.

19. THE PARISHE OF ECCLESHALL.

The Guylds there.

The enhabitauntes of Eccleshall did among themselfes, without incorporacion, erect two Guylds, one of our lady, an other of Seynt Kateryn, and did purchase and opteyn of diuers persones londs and tenementes towards the mayntenaunce of their seruyce priestes there for euer, whiche were in nomber somtyme two, and one at the least, who were found partly of the hole revenues of the same londs, and partly of the gatheringes among themselfes. And one of the same priestes haue alwais kept a scole, and taught pore mens children of the same parishe freely.

The yerely value, £4 0s. 10d.

Reprises, 18s. 8d.

Remayneth, 62s. 2d.

21. The parishe of Cannok.

The priestes seruyce, comonly called our Ladys seruyce, there.

Londs and tenementes gyven by seuerall persones for perpetuall mayntenaunce of one priest to syng dayly masse at the Alter of our lady, in the churche of Cannok, euery mornyng for ever, Whiche priest was called our ladyes priest. And the same priest thise 30 yeres past hath kept a grammer scole in the same parishe, and taught children of the seid parishe for the most parte freely.

The yerely value, 119s. 5d.

Reprises, 24s. 11½d.

Remayneth, £4 14s. 5½d.

Plate, White, 4½ ounces.

Ornamentes, 5s. 2d.

Gyven also by dyuers persones for the perpetuall maynteuaunce of the same priest.

Ten kyen, price, £6.

Redy mony, 26s. 8d.

Memorandum : londes and tenementes belonging to the seid seruyce, by yere, 107s. 11d. ben copyhold ; Reprises out of the same, 24s. 8½d ; Remayneth therof, £4 3s. 2½d. ; The residue, 11s. 6d. by yere ben free londe ; Reprises out of the same, 3d. ; Remaneth, 11s. 3d.

22. The parishe of Pagettes Bromley.

The priestes seruyce or stipendary there.

Londes and tenementes gyven and appoynted of long tyme past, by whom it is not knowen, to the fyndyng of a priest to celebrate in the parishe churche there for euer ; whiche priest hath alwais kept a scole, but not freely.

The yerely value, 30s. 8d.

Reprises, 5s. 2d.

Remayneth, 25s. 6d.

Staffordshire. Certificate 43.

(Edward VI.)

Edwarde the Sixt, by the grace of God, Kyng off Englande, Fraunce, and Irelande, defendour of the Feithe and of the churche of Englande and also of Irelande in erthe the supreme Hedd. To our trusty and Welbelouid Sir George Blounte, knyght; Edwarde Leveson and William Vnedale, esquiers; and to Richard Forsett, Robert Harecourte, and Hugh Lee, Gentlemen, greatyng. Where diuerse Colledges, Chauntries, Frechappelles, Fraternyties, brotherheddes, guyldes, manours, landes, tenementes, and hereditamentes and other thinges gyven to vs by an acte of Parliament, made in the Firste yere of our reigne, towchyng the dissolucion of Colledges, Chauntryes, Frechappelles, guyldes, and Fraternyties, Were concelid, omytted, and lefte vnpresentid to our late Commyssionors appoynted for the Survey of the same in our Countie of Stafford to our detrement, losse, and disheryson. We, trustyng in your fidelities, Wysdomes, and discre[cre]cions, haue appoynted, ordeyned, and made you our Commyssioners, and by theise presentes do gyve vnto you fyve, Foure, thre, and two of yow full power and aucthoritie to enquyre and examyn as well by the othes of suche persons as ye shall thyncke convenient as other wise by your Wysdomes and discrecyons what Colledges, Chauntries, Frechappelles, brotherheddes, guyldes, manours, landes, tenementes, goodes, catalles, or other thynges whiche ought to come to vs by reason of the seid acte, were and are omytted and concelid from vs as is aforeseid, and also of the Foundacions, vses, qualities, contynuaunces, values, condicions, and state in euery degre of the same and of euery of them and to survey the same and of your doynges and procedynges therin. We will and comaunde you fyve, Foure, three, or two of you to certifie vs vnto our Courte of The augmentacions and revenues of our Crowne at Westminster in the Quindene of the Holy Trynytie, next comyng in Wrytyng in parchement vnder your seales or vnder the seales of fyve, Foure, thre, or two of yow together with this Comyssion and we will and

comaunde all Mayers, Shryves, Baylyffes, Constables, and all
other our officers, mynysters, and subiectes that they and euery
of them shalbe obedyent, aydyng, favouryng, and assistyng
to you and euery of you from tyme to tyme in all thinges
touchyng or in any wise concernyng the execucion of this our
Comyssyon as the case shall requyre, and as they shall be on
our behalf by you commaunded uppon the perell therof to fall.
In Wytnes wherof we haue caused theise our lettres of Commyssyon to be made patentes.   Wytnes, Sir Richard Sakevile,
knyght, at Westminster, the 15th day of Marche, in the thirdde
yere of oure reigne [154$\frac{8}{9}$].

(Duke.)

The Certificat of Edward Leveson, Esquyer, Richard Forssett
and Hughe Lee, gentillmen, made in the quindesin of the Holy
Trynyte in the third yere of the reigne of our souereigne lorde,
Edward the sixt [1549], by the grace of God, kyng of Englond,
Fraunce, and Irelond, Defendour of the feith and of the churche
of Englond and also of Irelond, in erthe the supreme hed.
And certyfyed vnder our seales the same day and yere into the
Court of our seyd souereigne lord of the Agmentacions and
revenues of his grace, his Crowne by vertu of a Commyssyon
out of the seyd Court to vs and other directed concernyng
the enquery, Survey and Certyfycat of Certeyne Colleges,
Chaunteryes, Freechappelles, and other thynges recyted in a
Commyssyon herunto annexed, And into the same Court by vs
to be Certyfyed as by the same Commyssyon to vs was comaunded.

2. THE TOWNE AND BURGH OF STAFFORD.

The morowe masse preist and scole maister there.

One Croft in Ricarscote gyven, tyme out of mynde, by whom
it is vnknowen, employed to the use of the seyd scole priest in
Stafford, and so entended to contynue for euer.

The yerely value, 2s.

9. The paryshe of Bradeley.

Our Ladys seruyce there.

Fower Mesuages and certen londes in Bradeley in the seuerall tenures of George Cokkes, Richard Parker, Elen Horton, and Agnes Oley, gyven tyme out of mynde by whom it is vnknowen; butt they haue bene always in the order and disposicion of the paryshoners there, and the churchwardens there alwais receyued the proffettes of the same, And employed and for euer entended to employe the same vpon one preist whiche was called our ladys preist to celebrate dayly masse and other devyne seruyce in the seyd churche there. And the seyd mesuage and londes were called our ladys londes And one Sir John Austen, Clerk, was the last incombent of the seyd seruyce, who also did teache children of the seyd paryshe frely, And so did dyuers other incombentes of the same seruyce before hym. And the same sir John Austen did depart from the seid seruyce about thre yeres past. Sithens which tyme there was no priest found there.

The yerely value, 31s.

18. The paryshe of Kynvare.

The Chauntery there.

Dyuers parcelles of lond and rent belongyng to the Chauntery there, whiche before were presented to be copyhold be frehold; that is to say, one rent of 2s. out of the londes of William Moseley in Kynfare, one pece of medowe by Gospell Ashe in the tenure of Richard Shaxton, one howse and a Croft in the tenure of John Smyth, And one medowe, called Clambroke medowe, in Kynvare aforeseid.

The yerely value with the rentes aforeseyde, 6s. 8d.

Staffordshire. Certificate 44.

28. The Chauntery of Shenston

a Schole.

The clere yerely value aboue all reprises, £7 0s. 4½d.

Rauff Parker, clerk, incombent, whose clere porcion is 118s. 0½d.

Distributed in brede, drynk, and chese among the persones present on an haliday, 13s. 4d.

The incombent is bound by the foundacion to teche yong children of the said paryshe grammar, or otherwyse, accordyng to his knowelege.

This Schole is thought meet to be removed to Walsall, a greate towne about 3 myles thence.

36. THE CHAUNTERY OF KYNGELEY
a Schole.

The clere yerely value aboue all reprises, £6 6s. 2d.

John Berdmore, clerk, incombent, whose clere porcion is 79s. 11¾d.

Pencion, 79s. 11d.

The incombent is bound by the foundacion to teche frely children of the said parishe, whereupon he hath yerely gyven to the fyndyng of a scolemaster there, 31s. 8d.

Memorandum: aftre the death of the incumbent of Kingley the whole 111s. 7d. to remayne to the Schole.

45. THE CHAUNTERY AND SCOLE OF TAMWORTH.

The clere yerely value aboue all perpetuall reprises, £11 3s. 0¼d.

Richard Broke, clerk, incombent, whose clere porcion is £10 13s. 2¼d.

The incombent bound by the foundacion aswell to teche a fre scole as to sing morowe masse dayly in Seynt Georges Chappell there.

49. THE CHAUNTERY OR SCOLE IN STAFFORD.

The clere yerely value without perpetuall reprises, £4 13s. 4d.

Humfrey Peckeman, priest, incombent, whose clere porcion is £4 5s. 0¼d.

The incombent hath hitherto kept a free scole for certeyn yeres past.

Continuatur Schola quousque.

It is certified in the certyficat of tenthes by the name of the

Chauntery of Thomas Beckett, then called Seynt Thomas the Martir ; but whether the foundacion were to kepe a scole or not, I knowe not.

50. THE CHAUNTERIES IN WALSALL CALLED ASTONS CHAUNTERIES.

The clere yerely value of the one aboue all perpetuall reprises, £8 6s. 2d.

The clere yerely value of the other aboue all perpetuall reprises, £8 16s. 10½d.

William Ridware, Clerk, incombent, whose clere porcion is £7 19s. 6½d.

Pencion, £6.

Sampson Bourne, Clerk, incombent, whose clere porcion is £8 9s. 5d.

Pencion, £6.

Skoles, Preachers, Poor, Nothing.

51. THE CHAUNTERIES IN WALSALL CALLED HILLARIES CHAUNTERIES.

The clere yerely value of the one aboue all perpetuall reprises, £6 14s. 9d.

The clere yerely value of the other aboue all perpetuall reprises, £6 5s. 5d.

Richard Bradeley, Clerk, incombent, whose clere porcion is £6 6s. 1d.

Pencion, 100s.

Robert Parker, Clerk, incombent, whose clere porcion is 117s. 1d.

Pencion, 100s.

Skoles [&c.], Nothing.

52. MOLSELEYS CHAUNTERY IN WALSALL.

The clere yerely value aboue all perpetuall reprises, £6 17s. 4d.

Thomas Bourne, Clerk, incombent, whose clere porcion is £6 3s. 4d.

Pencion, 100s.

Skoles [&c.], Nothing.

53. FLAXALLES CHAUNTERY IN WALSALL.

The clere yerely value aboue all perpetuall reprises, £8 13s.
Edward Hill, Clerk, incombent, whose clere porcion is £8 3s.
Pencion, £6, able to kepe a Cure.
Skoles [&c.], Nothing.

54. VERNON AND BEMONDES CHAUNTERY IN WALSALL.

The clere yerely value aboue all perpetuall reprises,
£10 11s. 0½d.
Thomas Dobson, Clerk, incombent, whose clere porcion is
£8 14s. 8½d.
Pencion, £6.
Skoles [&c.], Nothing.

~~Thomas Dobson, appointed to be Assistaunt to the Cure, and to haue £3 yerly quousque~~ (sic).

Memorandum : in the seid parisshe of Walsall be at the least one thousand howselynge people. By reason wherof it is nedefull to haue a preist there to be assistent to the vicar there and to preache.

Per me Ricardum Forssett, superuisorem.

Forasmoche as the chauntrie priestes in Walsall be all vttrelie vnable to Ministre or assist Ministracion, it is therfore ordred at speciall request of my lord of Warrwik, that allowance be made to the inhabitauntes there of tenne poundes yerlie for the lyving of oone able man to be the assistaunt to the said cure, And the same allowaunce to contynew quousque, &c.

55. SPERNOURS CHAUNTERY IN WALSALL.

The clere yerely value aboue all perpetuall reprises, £9 17s. 2d.
William Staresmore, Clerk, incombent, whose clere porcion is
£9 3s. 10d.
Pencion, £6, able to kepe a Cure.
Skoles [&c.], Nothing.

56. The Chauntery in Walsall, founded by the Mayre and Burgeses of Walsall.

The clere yerely value aboue all perpetuall reprises, £6 14s. 11d.

Thomas Smyth, Clerk, incombent, whose clere porcion is £6 7s. 9¼d.

Pencion, 100s.

Skoles [&c.], Nothing.

57. The Guyld of Walsall.

The clere yerely value aboue all perpetuall reprises, 34s. 3d.

No priest found therwith.

Scoles [&c.], Nothing.

58. The Guyldes in Eccleshall,
wherin be 800 howselyng people.

Founded by lycens of King Henry the eighth.

The clere yerely value aboue all perpetuall reprises, 62s. 2d.

Geffrey Geslyng, priest, appoynted for the seid Guyld to celebrate dayly, and also to teche children. Howbeit the same priest hath ben removeable at will and plesure of the Masters of the guyldes.

Able to serve a Cure.

Continuatur Schola quousque.

59. Our ladyes seruyce in Cannock.

The clere yerely value aboue all perpetuall reprises, £4 14s. 5½d.

Laurens Peryn, Clerk, synging for the said seruyce, removeable at plesure of the wardens of the seid seruyce, who hath yerely had for parte of his salary the seid £4 14s. 5½d.

He hath kept a scole freely there, but not bound so to do by any foundacion.

Continuatur Schola quousque.

Memorandum : londes, parcell of the seid seruyce clere by yere, £4 2s. 11½d., ben copyhold londes, holden partly of the Manere of Cannok, and partly of the Manere of grete wirley.

z

65. THE SERUYCE OF A PRIEST IN PAGETTES BROMLEY.

The clere yerely value of the londes gyven to the seid seruyce, 25s. 6d.

John Stephanson, Clerk, hath serued in the seid seruice, who hath had clere by yere, 13s. 6d.

Pencion, 13s. 6d.

He hath kept a scole there, but not frely.

Memorandum : No mencion is made in this Certificat of any Colledge, Chauntery, or other thynges beforeseid beynge within the Duchy of Lancaster.

Townes in the seid Countie wherin it is most nede to haue free scoles : Stafford, Woluerhampton, Tamworth, Walsall, Burton upon Trent, Leeke.

Where most nede is to haue hospitalles for relief of the pore ; Stafford, Walsall, Tamworth, Burton upon Trent.

The tenthes are deducted out of this bok.

Examinatur per me Ricardum Forsett superuisorem, &c.

Sum to the pore, £12 18s. 2d.

Sum to the scholes, £32 12s. 10½d.

Reparacion of bridges, 20d.

Staffordshire. Schools Continuance Warrant, 24.

Forasmoche as it apperith [&c.] that there hath been a preacher of godes woorde mayneteyned in Lichefelde [&c.], with the reuenues of the late Chauntrie called Yattons Chauntrie, in Lychefelde aforesaid ; And that he hath had yerelie [&c.] £11 0s. 17d.

And that there hath been a Grammer Scole contynually kept in Shenston [&c.], with the reuenues of the late Chauntery there ; And that the Scolemaister there hath had [&c.] £5 18s. 0½d. [&c.].

And that there hath been a grammer Scole contynuallie kepte in Kyngeley [&c.] with the reuenues of the late Chauntrie there ; and that the Scolemaster there hath had [&c.] £3 19s. 11¾d. [&c.].

And that a grammer Scole hath been contynuallie kept in Stafforde [&c.] with the reuenues of the late Chauntrye there; and that the scolemaister there hath had [&c.] £4 5s. 0¾d. [&c.].
And that there hath been a grammer Scole contynuallie kepte in Walsall [&c.]; And that the Scolemaister there hath had [&c.] 62s. 2d.

And that a grammer Scole hath been contynuallie kepte in Cannocke with the reuenues of our lady service there; And that the Scolemaister there hath had [&c.] £4 14s. 5½d. [&c.].
Wee therefore [&c.] haue assigned [&c.] That the said preacher of goddes worde in Lychefelde aforesaid shall contynue, and that Henry Sydall, Bacheler of Dyvynytie, shall contynue [&c.] preacher of goddes worde there, and shall haue [&c.] £11 0s. 17d. [&c.];

& that the said grammer Schole in [Shenston] [&c.] shall contynue, And that Rauff Purke, Scolemaister there, shall haue [&c.] £5 18s. 0½d. [&c.];

And that the said grammer Scole in Kyngeley aforesaid shall contynue, and that John Bondmore, Scolemaister there, shall haue [&c.] [79s. 11¾d.];

And that the said grammer Scole in Stafford aforesaid shall contynue, And that Humfry Pockeman shall contynue Scholemaister there, and shall haue [&c.] [£4.5s. 0¾d.] [&c.];

And that the said grammer Scole in Walsall aforesaid shall contynue, And that Geffrey Gestlyng, scolemaster there [&c.], shall haue [&c.] 62s. 2d.;

And that the said grammer Scole in Cannocke aforesaid shall contynue, and that Laurence Peryn, Scolemaister there [&c.], shall haue [&c.] £4 14s. 5½d.

Comitatus Staffordie. Particulars for Schools. Roll 9.

(Edward VI.)

STAFFORD GRAMMAR SCHOOL.

Parcelle possessionum   [*faded*]   Marston, in ecclesia Collegiata Staffordie, in Comitatu predicto, nuper fundata existencium; valent in Firma   [*torn*]

Libera Capella siue hospitale sancti Johannis Baptiste, prope Staffordiam, in Comitatu predicto; valet in

[Firmis]   [torn]   Reprise. Redditus resolutus [torn]   Summa totalis clare   [torn]   6s. 6d.

Memorandum : the seyd Chappell, comonly called Saynt Johns chappell, above excepted, is mete to [the] placyng of the Kynges evydences of the seyd Countye, for his maiestye hath none other convenyent   [faded]   County beyng within the Survey of thaugmentacion Courte, so mete for the same purpose.

Possessiones   [faded]   Capelle Sancti Leonardi, prope Staffordiam, in Comitatu predicto; valent in Firma [faded] li.

Obitus perpetuus   [torn]   e Robyns, in ecclesia de Staffordia, in Comitatu predicto; valet in Redditu, 2s.

Obitus perpetuus Willelmi Dentyth, Clerici, in predicta ecclesia de Staffordia ; valet in Redditu   [torn]

Obitus perpetuus Roberti Welles, in predicta ecclesia de Staffordia ; valet in Redditu   [torn]

Obitus perpetuus Johannis Myllys, in predicta ecclesia de Staffordia ; valet in Redditu   [torn].

Summa totalis, £20.

18 die Novembris, Anno Regni Regis Edward vj., quarto [1550].

Make a Graunte of the premisses to the Burgeses of [the town of] Stafford, and to their successours for ever, to thentent a free scole within [the said town], to be erected and founded, may be with thissues and proffettes therof   [torn] mayntened and vpholden, all which premisses amount to the [yearly sum] of £20 ; one chappell within the towne of Stafford. [torn].

To haue thissues from Michelmas laste past.

(Signed) Ry. Sakevyle.

The Countie of Suffolk. Certificate 45.

(Edward VI.)

Sir Roger Townesende, Knight, John Gosnolde and Nicholas Bacon, Esquiers, Ambrose Gilberte and Christopher Peyton, gentilmen, commissioners.

5. LONDES AND TENEMENTES LYING IN EYE.

Put In Feoffamente by John Fluke and others for the fyndyng of a Scoole Maister In Eye aforeseid for ever, whiche sometyme was a Layeman and sometyme a prieste, And the seyde scoole hath contynued tyll Michaelmas, Anno Primo Domini Regis nunc Edwardi 6ti, saving that the same Scoole was voide of a scoole Maister sumtyme, by the space of halfe a yere, Bicause they coulde nott be provided of oone In that tyme, And for the same cause yt is nowe Voyde.

The yerely valewe therof Amountyth to the some of £7 6s. 8d. Wherof

In Rentes Resolutes to dyvers Lordes, 34s. 7d.

And so Remaynyth Clere to the use of the seide scoole Maister, Whiche the Inhabitantes of the same Towne of Eye doo take to their owne vse, 112s. 1d.

7. LAVENHAM.

Londes and Tenementes in Thorpe Morieuxe and Reston in the Countie of Suffolke.

Put In Feoffamente by Lawrence Cooke, of Alpheton, alias Lawrence Parker, to the entente the Aldermenne of seynte peters guilde shoulde take the profittes of theyme yerely And to finde oone Pryeste to singe for ever In the parrishe Churche of Lavenham.

And Sir Alleyn Chynnereye, Clerke, is nowe the stipendarie prieste thear, of the age of 56 yeres, having none other

Lyvinge, And teacheth Childerne In the seide Towne of
Lavenham; who is Secundarye to the Curate of the seide
parisshe, who wythowte helpe of a nother prieste is not able to
serve the Cuer thear, The same Towne of Lavenham being a
populus Towne, having in yt by estimacion 2,000 people.

The yerly valewe therof, wyth 6s. 8d. of the fearme of 20
Acres, parcell of the seid londes holden by copie of courte Roll
of the erle of Oxforde, Amountyth to the some of £7 6s. 11d.
Wherof

In the yerely tenthes, 10s. 8d.

In Rentes Resolutes for the Freeholde, 21s. 5d.

And In Rente for the Coppieholde, 6s. 8d.   38s. 9d.

And so Remayneth Clere to the use of the seide Incumbente,
108s. 2d.

22. LONG MELFORDE.

The mannour of Bower Hall wyth other londes and Tenementes thear vnto belonging, lyeng in Pentlowe, in the Countie
of Essex.

Put in feoffamente by John Hill, of Mellforde, deceassed, to
contynnew for 99 yeres, And further, so long as the Lawes of
the Realme wyll suffer, to the use to haue oone stipendarie
pryeste to singe in the parryshe Churche of Mellforde for the
Sowle of the seid John Hyll and other, And to haue for his
salarye the profittes of the seid Mannour, excepte the quyet
Rentes and the woode belonging to the same Mannour, as by
the Laste will of the seid John yt appearythe Which quyet
Rentes and the profittes of the woodes he willed to be dysposed
yerly to dyscharge the taxe, or to be dystributed in dedes of
Charytie emong the porest of the seid Towne, And oone Sir
Edwarde Tyrrell, clerke, of the age of 50 yeres, having no other
Lyving, is the encumbente thear, and is ayding to the Curat of
the seid parryshe, who wythowte helpe wer not able to dyscharge
the seid Cuer, the Towne being very populus; he doth also
teache A grammer scole thear.

The yerly value of the seid Mannour amountyth to the some
of £11 3s. 4d.   Wherof

In yerly tenthes, 14s. 6d.

In Rentes Resolutes, 18s. 2d.

In the fee of the Baylye, according to the wyll, 6s. 8d.

To be dystributed emong the poore people yerly the quyet Rentes, amountyng to 58s. 1d.   £4 17s. 5d.

And so Remayneth Clere to the use of the encumbent, £6 5s. 11d.

The value of the plate, Jewelles, and ornamentes as appearyth by an Inventory Remaynyng, videlicet :

One challis, gilte, poyessaunte 17 ounces.

One Vestemente, wyth all that belongyth therto, 40s.

24. CLARE (CHILTON).

One free chapell theyr founded.

By whome, or to what vse, Intente or purpose, wee knowe nott, but In the 24th yere of Kynge Henry the 6ᵗᵉ [1445–6], Rycharde, then Duke of Yorke, Lorde of the honour of Clare, by his deade dyd gyve the seide free Chapell, wyth all londes and tenementes to the same belonginge, to the Masters or wardeyns of the gylde and brotherhoode of seynte John baptiste, in Chylton, hamlette of Clare, vppon condycion that the same Masters or wardeyns with the same, And the profittes yerely commynge of the seid Guylde, shoulde fynde for ever oone prieste to saye Masse oone Daye In the weke in the seide Chapple, to praye for the sowles of the same Duke and other.

And oone Sir Roberte wyncome, Clerke, of the age of 30 yeres, havinge no other lyvinge, well learnid, doth nowe aswell the seid devyne service, as also the Reste of the weake he singeth in the Churche of Clare, whiche is a greate and populus Towne, and helpyth the curatte to dyscharge his cure. And also he teacheth oone grammer scole to the goode and vertuous Instruccion And educacyon of the yowthe theyre.

The same is no parrishe Churche, but standythe in the hamlett of Chylltone, And dystaunte frome the parrishe churche of Clare oone quarter of a myle.

The yerelye valewe therof amountythe to 26s. 4d. Whereof
In Rentes Resolutes by yere, 20d.

And so Remaynethe clere towardes the mayntenance of the
seide priestes servyce, 24s. 8d.

33. ORFFORDE.

The Chauntrey of our ladye.

Founded by John Pishale and Roberte Grigge, Clerkes, to
endeavour for ever to fynde oone prieste to synge In the Churche
of Orforde at an Alter thear, called our ladies Alter, to praye for
the soules of the seid Founders and others.

And oone John Grenewoode, Clerk, of the age of 38 yeres,
well learnid, and teachith children, having no other Lyvinge,
is nowe Incumbente therof.

The yerly valew therof amountyth to £7 15s. 7d. Wherof
In the yerly tenthes, 25s. 5½d.

In Rentes Resolutes to dyvers Lordes, 20s. 3¾d. . 45s. 9¼d.

And so Remaynyth Clere to the use of The encumbente,
109s. 9¾d.

46. BURYE SEYNTE EDMUND.

Memorandum : yt is to be concyderid that the seid Townne
of Burye is a greate And a populus Townne, Havinge In yt
twoo parrysshe Churches, And In the same parrisshes above
the nombre of 3,000 Howselinge people, And a greate nombre
of yowth, And the Kinges Maiestie hathe all the tythes, both
predyall and personall, And all other profightes yerely commynge
or growinge wythin the same parrisshes, fyndinge twoo parrishe
priestes theare, whiche seide twoo parrysshe priestes bene nott
able to serve and discharge the seide cures wyth owte ayde and
helpe of other priestes.

And Further theare is no scoole nor other Lyke Divise
founded wythin the seide Townne, or wythin 20 myles of ytt,
for the vertuous educacyon and bringing vpp of yowth, nor
eny hospytall or other Lyke foundacion for the cumforte or
Relieffe of the pover, of whiche theare is excedinge greate

nombre wythin the seide Townne, other then arre afor mencyoned, of whiche the seide Incumbentes doo nowe take the hoole
yerely Revenues and profittes, And distribute no parte therof to
the ayde, comforte, or Relieffe of the seide pover people.

In consideracyon wherof yt maye please the Kinges seide moste
excellente Maiestie, of his moste charytable benygnitie, moved
wyth pyttie In that behalfe, to converte the Revenues and
profyttes of the sume of the seide promocions In to sume godly
foundacyon, whearby the seide pover Inhabitantes, dayly theare
moultiplyeng, maye be releved, And the yowght instructed and
browghte vpp vertuously, or otherwyse accordinge to his moste
godly and discrete Wisedome ; And the seide Inhabitantes shall
dayly praye to god for the prosperous preservacyon of his moste
excellente Maiestie longe to endewer.

47. The Colledge of Seynte John baptiste, in Stoke
next Clare, in the seid Countie of Suffolk.

Founded by Edmunde the Erle of the Marches and Vlton, lorde
of vigmore and of Clare, the 19th Daye of Maye, In the 7th yere
of Henry the fyfte [1419], As appearyth by the Foundacion of
the same Edmond being shewid, bearing Date aforeseid, by the
lycence of the seid King firste hadde, bearing date the 16th of
Octobre, In the seconde yere of his Reigne [1414], And after-
warde In the exchequer the terme of seynte Michaell, the 9th
yere of the seid Kinge Henry the fyfte Reigne enrolled [1421].

To the entente to Fynde oone Deane, 6 Canons, 8 vicars, 2
Cheffe Clerkes, 2 Meaner Clerkes, oone Verger, oone Porter,
and five Choristres, And syns the firste Foundacion dyvers
other benefactors hath both encreased the nombre and Lyving
As 2 pryestes, The oone constituted by Mr. William Pykenham,
sometyme Dean thear, to be vicare to the Deane of the same
Colledge and his successors, And the other constytuted by
William Lovell, sometyme verger thear, to be Deacon of the
same Colledge, As more pleynly by the proporcion in the Rentall
sett forth at large Doth appeare.

The yerly valew therof Amountyth to the some of £383 2s. 6½d.

The Baylies Fee, wyth the Stewardes, by yere, £8.

The Tenthes peide to the Kinges Maiestie, £32 8s. 5d.

Rentes Resolutes to dyvers lordes, 43s. 7½d.

Pencions, porcions, Sennage, proxes, procuracions, And vysitacions, by yere, £23 3s. 10d.

Decayes of Rentes, 3s. 8d.

Reparacions of the Chauncell of the Churche in Buers, wythe mayntenance of a bridge ther, yerly, 20s.

To the Poore, 28s. 4d.   £62 7s. 10½d.

And so Remaynyth Clere to the use of the seid Deane, Canons, Vycars, And is employed to dyvers vses, As by a Declaracion therof at large appearyth, £314 14s. 8d.

Goodes, Cattalles, plate, Jewelles, Ornamentes, and household Stuffe, as appearyth by twoo Inventories Remayninge, videlicet :

Plate Gilte, 148 ounces ; Parcell gilte, 136½ ounces ; White, 207 ounces.   [491½ ounces.]

Ornamentes and Howshold Stuffe, praysed together at £69 0s. 8d.

Leade Remayning apon Dyvers places thear, as by a particuler Survey therof at Large appearyth, 62 Foodders.

Belles there Remayning, weying, by estymacion, 8,220 łi. weyght.

Arrerages of Rentes, £105 9s. 2¼d.

Mathewe Parker, Deane, Doctor of Dyvinitie, of the age of 44 yeres, having dyvers promoysions Amounting to the some of £30.   £67 0s. 2d.

Thomas Whitehead, clerke, oone of the prebendaries or Canons, of the age of 75 yeres, well learnid, having dyvers promoycions Amounting to the some of £60.   £16 15s. 1d.

Richerd Baldwyn, Clerke, another of the prebendaries, of the age of 54 yeres, well learnid, having dyvers promoycions Amounting to the some of £30.   £17 15s. 4d.

George Lilbourne, Clerke, of the age of 50 yeres, well learnid, having dyvers promoycions the valewe wherof wee can nott Learne.   £8 9s. 4d.

Thomas Bacon, A nother of the prebendaries, of the age of

52 yeres, well learned, having dyvers promoycions the valew wherof wee can nott Learne.   £16 17s. 4d.

Reynold Baynbridge, a nother of the prebendaries thear, well learnid, of the age of 63 yeres, Having dyvers promoycions Amounting to the some of £30.   £16 15s. 5d.

William Harper, Clerke, oone of the prebendaries, of the age of 40 yeres, well learned, having dyvers promoycions the valew wherof wee can not Learne.   36s.

William Dikons, Clerke, oone of the vicars, of the age of 62 yeres, well learnid, being Master of a free Chapell in Norffolk of the clere yerely valewe of 46s. 8d.   £8 8s. 8d.

Thomas Aldred, Clerke, Another of the vicars, of the age of 63 yeres, well learnid, having a pencion of £7 owte of the late Monasterie of Crowlande.   £8 8s. 8d.

Thomas Augar, Clerke, another of the Vicars thear, of the age of 56 yeres, well learnid, having a pencyon of 100s. owte of the late Abbey of seynt Johns in Colchestre.   £8 8s. 8d.

William Mynting, of the age of 40 yeres.   £8 8s. 8d.
John Bradforde, of the age of 48 yeres.   £8 8s. 8d.
Marmaduke Lystre, of the age of 55 yeres.   £8 8s. 8d.
And John Sampson, of the age of 60 yeres.   £8 8s. 8d.
Clerkes and Vicars, having no other Lyvinges.

Hughe Turnour, of the age of 60 yeres.   £6.
Nicholas Gladwyn, of the age of 54 yeres.   £8.
Thomas Poley, of the age of 38 yeres.   100s.
And Fraunces Cony, of the age of 30 yeres.   £4 15s. 4d.
Laye menne And Clerkes wythin the seid Colledge.

Thomas Parker, of the age of 66 yeres, verger.   £7 18s. 8d.

Michaell Knott.   66s. 8d.
Jaymes Harpour.   66s. 8d.
William Poorie.   66s. 8d.
And John Chapman.   66s. 8d.
Choristres, of the age of 15 yeres, having no other Lyvinges.

Radolf Ratclyffe, gentilman, porter.   66s. 8d.

William Sydey, gentilman, Audytor And Steward of the seid
Colledge.   56s. 8d.
William Cracherood, gentilman, baylyff to the Deane.   £6.
William Noote and Jaymes Inkingson, baylies to the vicars.
                                                  40s.
Thomas wilson, Clerke, Scole Master in the Colledge.   40s.
John Crosier, Clerke, Scoole Master of the Free Scoole.   £10.

And John smyth, of the age of 50 yeres, Cooke in the seid
Colledge ;

Every oone of theym having for their Stipend and Salary
of the Revenewes of the seid Colledge as is paramounted
apon their heades, And the Residewe of the seid Colledge was
employed in and apon the Reparacions of the seid Colledge, and
other Incydent charges.

Item : the vicorage of the Towne of Stoke is apropried vnto
the seid Colledge, And the Deane hadde alweyes the proffyttes
of the same, who dide dyscharge the Cure.

Comitatus Suffolcie. Particulars for Schools.

Edward VI. Roll 11.

BURY SAINT EDMUND'S GRAMMAR SCHOOL.

Parcelle Terrarum et possessionum modo ad manus Regis
proveniencium virtute nuper Actus parliamenti.

Cantaria in [Kir]keton, alias [Shot]ley, in Comitatu Suffolcie ;
valet in

[Firmis], 100s. Inde

. Reprise, videlicet in Quadam Elimozina annuatim distributa
pauperibus ville de Kyrketon predicta, per annum, 11s.

The Kynges magesty to dyscharge thys.

Et valet Clare, per Annum, 100s.

Thaforeseyd Londes and Tenementes, with thappurtenaunces,
was putt in feoffament by Rycharde Straught, sometyme vicare
of Doncourte, and diuerse other, for the finding of one Stipendarye preste to sing in the parisshe Churche of Shotley, and to
doo certayne other deades of Charitie during the terme of 99
yeres ; And after thende of the seyd terme the londes to be

solde, and the moneye Therof Commyng, to be employed apon the seyd preste service, soo long as any parte therof remaynith, as by a deade of feoffament therof apperith ; And ther was a former particuler hereof made to Edwarde Grimston, Esquier, by your worshippes warraunte.

[Can]taria vocat   [torn]   [M]elford in [Comitatu [Su]ff[olcie] [Firmis], £6 9s. 8d. Inde

Reprise videlicet In Quadam Eleptosina annuatim distributa pauperibus ville de Melford predicta, per annum, 6s. 8d.

The Kynges majesty to discharge.

Et valet Clare, per Annum, £6 9s. 8d.

Thaforeseyd londes and Tenementes, with thappurtenaunces, was put in feoffamente by Sir William Clopton, knight, to thentente to have one obite kepte yerly, and to dispose yerly 6s. 8d. amonge the poore people in Melford, And to have one preste to sing in the Churche of Melford, and to be called his preste, to praye for the sowles of the seyd Sir William and others during the Tearme of 99 yeres, and after so long as the lawes of the realme will suffer.

[torn]   um de   ingham, in Comitatu
    nuper Cantari   [voca]t Freye Chauntry
in parochia Sancte   a in Ciuitate
    [cu]m omnibus terris   eidem
    spectantibus   pertinentibus ; valet in
Firma Manerii de Calinghamhall, £8.

Thaforeseyd Mannor, with thappurtenaunces, was putt in feoffamente by Sir John Freye, Knight, deceased, for the maynteynaunce of a preste to sing in the parisshe Churche of Littell Seyntt Bartilmewes, in London, for euer ; And to praye for the soules of the seyd John and others, As by the will of the seyd John itt apperith.

Redditus in Kirketon, alias Shotley, in Comitatu Suffolcie valent in Firma, 46s. 8d. Inde

Reprise, videlicet in [Redditibus resolutis] [8s. 8d.].

Quadam Elimosina annuatim distributa pauperibus, per Annum, 10s.

Reparacionibus ecclesie de Shottley predicta, per Annum 6s. 8d.

The Kynges majesty to dyscharge.

8s. 4d.

Et valet Clare, per Annum, 38s. 4d.

Thaforeseyd londes and Tenementes, with thappurtinaunces, was put in feoffament by Nicholas Fikkett, deceased, for euer, to thentent the proffittes therof shulde be yerely bestowed according to his laste will and Testament; viz., 3s. 4d. to the maynteynaunce of the sepulcre light in the parisshe Churche of Chelmeton, 3s. 4d. to be delt euery good Fridaye to tenne poore menne of the same parisshe, 6s. 8d. to the Reparacions of the parisshe Churche of Shotley, 6s. 8d. to the maynteynaunce of the sepulcre light in the seyd Churche of Shotley, 6s. 8d. to twentye poore menne of the same Towne, And the resideue of the proffittes of the same londes to the maynteynaunce of An obite in the parisshe Churche of Shottley aforeseyd, as by the will of the same Nicholas itt apperith.

Totalis clare, £21 8s.

Examinatur per me, Christoferum Peyton, Supervisorem.

28 Julii, Anno Edwardi vj^u., 5 [1552].

Make a graunte of the premysses vnto William May, Doctour of dyuynitie, and deane of Paules; Nicholas Bakon, John Eyer, and Christofer Peyton, Esquyers; William Tassell, Stephen Hayward, gentlemen; Roger Barbour, John Buttry, William Baker, Thomas Coxsage, Robert Sharpe, William Cheston, Thomas Horsman, Thomas Stacye, and Thomas Andrewes, of Bury seynt Edmonde, yomen; and to ther heires and Assignes, to the use of a Scole ther to be founded by the Kinges Maiestie, in like maner and forme as the scole of Sherborne is graunted, Reservyng vnto the kinges maiestie, his heires and Successors, in the name of an yerely rente, 28s.

The said graunties to haue the proffittes from the feaste of the annuncyacyon of our lady last past [155½].

(*Signed*) Ry. Sakevyle.

The Countie of Sussex. Certificate 50.

(Edward VI.)

A Briefe declaracion.

No. 2. THE CYTIE AND SUBURBS OF CHECHESTRE.

The gramer scole in Chichestre.

Anthony Clarke, Scholemaister, prebendarie in the said Churche of the prebend called Vyley [Highleigh], Impropried for a gramer Schole for ever.

Wherof

The said prebendary of his benevolens alloweth towardes the Fyndyng of an vssher yerly, £4.

£4 ; not thought within the compace of The acte.

Also the deane and Chapiter Haue graunted and paid syns Michaelmas, Anno primo regni Regis Edwardi sexti, to the Finding of the said vssher, 52s. 4d., and Have graunted to continewe the same accordinglie out of the lyvinges of the said Deane and Chapiter for ever.

8. HORSHAM.

Memorandum : there is a grammer scole of the foundacion of one Collier, of London, deceased, who by his last will and testament did endowe the Mercers of London with certein possessions for the fynding of a Scholemaister and vsher at Horsham, vpon divers condicions mencioned in the same Will remaining with the wardeins of the said Mercers, which they denie to shewe vnto me, and therfor I cannot make certificat of the said Intentes as aperteyneth.

Fiat processus versus merceres Londonienses ad ostendendum Testimonium, &c.

14. SULLINGTON.

The Chauntrey of Sullyngton.

Thomas Sakevyle, Incumbent, being student at a grammer scole, of the age of 13 yeres, and hath the premisses towardes his exhibicion, £3 17s.

Pencio, 77s.

20. BYGNOR.

The Chauntrey or Free Chappell of Bygnor.

George Vaughan, Incumbent, beyng a servyng man and no priest, 35s. 3d.

Respiciatur pencio.

33. LEWES.

The grammer Scole in Southouer nexte Lewes, of the Foundacion of Agnes Morly.

There is a grammer schole Founded there to have a prieste Scholemaister to teache children and to say Masse for the Founder, and to have for his labour and for an vsher, £5, and the rest for reparacions yelie, and for other charges to be kepte in a chest in which there is nowe £72 or there aboutes remaynneng for the receptes, Wherof it were convenient to have your letter, lest they do bestowe yt otherwayes, which is lyke they will doo, Which Scholemaster and vsher shulde alwaies be named by the prior of Lewes and his successors.

There is nowe no scholemaster there, but only an vsher, and for that it is a populous towne and moche youth, The inhabitauntes do require to haue some lerned man to be admitted to the same, bicause nowe the Kyng, in the right of the late monastery of lewes, Intitled to be Founder; and the proffittes of the said londes, besides the Scholehous, is clere towardes the reparacions and charges aforesaied, £19 6s. 8d.

There is one Otley, parson of Rype, which is very well lerned, mete to be scolemaster there, if he will take it vppon hym.

Continuatur schola quousque.

35. COUKEFEILDE.

The grammer Scole in Cuckefeilde.

Robart Hedon, preiste, of the age of 32 yeres, is Scholemaister there, to teache the children, and to pray, and to say Masse for the founders, and so is appointed by the Foundacion; there is Landes, tenementes, and hereditamentes appoynted therfor of the clere yerelie value of £11 8s., wherof to the Scholemaister, £10 ;

vsher, 20*s.*, and the rest for reparacions and other charges, and is infeoffed to certein persounes named in the said Foundacion, the Founders names Edmund Flower and William Spyser, £11 8*s.*

Continuatur Schola quousque.
Examinatur per me Anthonium Stryngar.

Warrwicus (et Leicestria). Certificate 31.
(Henry VIII.).

John, Bysshop of Lincoln, Rycharde, Bysshopp of Couentre, and Lycheffylde, Sir Rychard Manners, Knyght, Sir Rycharde Cattisbye, Knyght, William Lee, esquyre, John Beamounte, esquyre, Wylliam Rygges and Clement Throkmerton, gentelmen, Commyssyoners.

1. CIUITAS COVENTRIE.

Gilda Sancte Trinitatis in Bablake, in ciuitate predicta. Videlicet in

Gofforde Strete	£13 19*s.* 4*d.*
Micheparke Strete	£6 12*s.*
Dede lane	75*s.* 4*d.*
Lytleparke Strete	£10 13*s.* 8*d.*
Barterames lane	17*s.* 4*d.*
Frerelane	£4 14*s.*
Brodeyate	13*s.* 4*d.*
Smythefforde Strete	33*s.* 4*d.*
Essex lane	33*s.*
Fletstrete	£7 7*s.* 4*d.*
Spone strete	£15 18*s.* 8*d.*
Spone ende	15*s.* 8*d.*
Wellstrete	£4 5*s.* 8*d.*
Cookestrete	12*s.*
Palmerlane	24*s.*
Crosethepyng	£7 8*s.* 8*d.*
Le Draperye	£9 0*s.* 16*d.*

A A

Redditibus diuersarum Clausurarum et pasturarum iacentium infra precinctum Comitatus Ciuitatis predicte, £18 10s. 4d.

Redditibus assise Ciuitatis predicte, 38s. 8d.   £112 3s. 8d.

Reprise, vt In Redditibus resolutis .   .   . £13 15s. 7d.

Decimis   .   .   .   . £4 10s. 8d.

Stipendio cuiusdam Capellani, vocati le Warden Capelle de Babelake, in Ciuitate predicta, per annum, £6 13s. 4d.

Stipendijs octo Capellanorum diuina seruicia, infra eandem Capellam Annuatim celebrancium, cuiuslibet eorum ad [blank] per annum, in toto, £37 6s. 8d.

Stipendio [blank] Ludimagistri cuiusdam Scole vocate a grammer scoole ibidem, ad £6 13s. 4d. per annum.

Stipendijs duorum Clericorum Cantancium ibidem, cuiuslibet ad £4 per annum, in toto, £8.

Stipendijs duorum puerorum similiter ibidem Annuatim Cantancium, cuiuslibet eorum ad 20s. per annum, in toto, per annum, 40s.

Regardis datis diuersis personis quondam fratribus gilde predicte, modo pauperibus, Annuatim in pecunijs numeratis, et ex Antiqua consuetudine sic vsitata, per annum, £10.

Feodo Thome Gregory, Clerici, Contrarotulatoris eiusdem gilde, sibi concesso per litteras patentes, per Annum, £6.

Feodo Martini Bydell, Collectoris omnium Reddituum eiusdem Gilde, sibi similiter concesso per litteras patentes, per Annum, £6.

Feodis Thome Brewer et Thome Eaton, supervisorum Reparacionum omnium Tenementorum et Cotagiorum predictorum, sic eis pro termino vite concessis per litteras patentes, per Annum, 66s. 8d.

Feodis Senescalli et diuersorum aliorum officiariorum ibidem, per Annum, £6.   £110 6s. 3d.

Et Remanet clare, per Annum, 27s. 5d.

The seyde Gylde was Founded by Kyng Edwarde the seconde, Kyng E. the thirde, quene Isabell, hys mother, and Prynce E., there sonne, to Mayntayne and Fynde 9 prestes in a Chapell in the seyde Cytye of Couentre Caulyd Babelake, there to praye For euer For the soules of the seyde Founders.

·The romes of the ·seyd prestes be all Full and none voyde. And do celebrate and sey devyne seruyce by note daly in the Forseyde Chapell of Babelake, and euery of them Hathe a seuerall chamber within the precyncte of the same Babelake, worthe to be lett euery chamber by yere, 4*s.*, and not ·aboue Charged, Also the Reuennewe of the same Yelde ys ymployde as in ·the reprises before ·mensyoned playnly Dothe Appere.

2. Terre et tenementa Appunctuata predicte Gilde sancte Trinitatis in Bablake, per vltimam voluntatem cuiusdam Johannis Bonde, iam defuncti . . . . £49 11*s.* 7*d.*

Reprise . . . . £43 8*s.* 11½*d.*

· Et·Remanet clare, per annum, £6 2*s.* 7½*d.*

The seyd londes and Tenementes was geuen to the Forseyd Yelde ·of the Holy Trynyte by one John Bonde, of Coventre, Draper, as by the laste Wyll and Testament of the same John beryng Date the 18th daye of·Marche, Anno Domini Millessimo quingentesimo sexto, playnely dothe Appere, And to the entente to bylde and establysshe within the precyncte of the seyde Babelake a substancyall Almonshouse with a Chapell in the same·House, where in there sholde be kepte, mayntayned, and Founde For euer ten pore men and one Woman to Dresse there meate and Drynke, And also one preste, beyng a Doctour of Dyvynytie, or elles a Master of Arte, and libertye to saye Masse within the seyd Chapell, And that he sholde be bounde yerely to preche 40 sermons within the same Cytye, or ten myles compasse of the same, And He to haue for hys stypende one Chamber within the seyd Almons House, one gowne Clothe with a Hode, And 20 markes in Redy money, as in·the same Wyll more ·at large yt dothe appere.

25. Cantaria de Derettende in parochia de Aston ac infra Dominium de Byrmyngham, in Comitatu predicto.

Valet in

Redditibus et Firmis omnium Terrarum et tenementorum dicte cantarie pertinencium soluendis ad Festa Annunciacionis beate Marie Virginis et sancti Michaelis Archangeli, equaliter,

prout per Rentale inde Factum et renouatum particulariter
Apparet, per annum, £13 19*d*. Inde

Reprise, videlicet in

Redditibus Resolutis diuersis personis sequentibus, Videlicet :
Domino Lyle, ad Manerium suum de Byrmyngham, 4*s*. 1*d*. ;
exeuntes de certis terris ibidem Magistro selyngham, ad Manerium suum de Hundsworthe, 7*s*. 2*d*. ; eidem Magistro Selyngham,
16*s*. 2*d*. ; exeuntes de certis terris et tenementis in Bordysley
eidem Magistro Selyngham, 32*s*. 4*d*. Thome Ardern armigero,
20*d*. exeuntes de certis terris in saltele ; Thome Holt armigero,
2*s*. exeuntes de certis terris in Dudston ; Domino Ferres, 4*d*.
exeuntes de certis terris in Bordesley ; et Johanni Shilton, 17*d*.
exeuntes de vno tenemento in Byrmyngham : in toto per Annum
65*s*. 2*d*.

Stipendiis duorum Capellanorum diuina seruicia infra Ecclesiam 'parochialem de Aston celebrancium, cuiuslibet eorum ad
100*s*. per annum, in toto per annum, £10.   £13 5*s*. 2*d*.

Et sic in Superplusagio, 3*s*. 7*d*.

There ys no Foundacyon of any suche Chauntry, but a
certayne composicyon, or ordynaunce, made Betwene the prior
and Munkes of the late Monasterye of Tykfforde, Whiche Ware
parsons of Aston and' Deretende, on that one partye, and Sir
John Byrmyngham, Knyght, and the inhabitans of the same
hamlet cauled Deretende, on that other partye, by the assent
and consent of one Robert, Bysshop of Coventrye and Lycheffeld.
That the seyd inhabitans of Deretende myght haue one chap-
leyne to celebrate dyvyne seruyce within a chapell there of saynt
John, newlye erected and mayde ; And also to Mynyster vnto
them all sacramentes and sacramentalles, Beryinges except, by
cause thay be 2 myles dystaunt From there parisshe churche, so
that in Wynter season the seyde parisshyoners coulde not go to
there parisshe churche without greate daunger of perysshyng ;
and there be Aboue 200 houselyng peaple Wythe in the seyde
2 hamlettes,

And at thys present tyme there be 2 prestes, Where of the
one seruyng the Cure, and the other teachyng a grammer
schole.

There, Hathe bene no other landes belonging to the same chapell syns the tyme before lymyted more then ys before expressed, And the Inventory there of hereafter dothe Appere.

28. GILDA SANCTE CRUCIS DE BIRMYNGHAM, IN COMITATU PREDICTO.

Valet in

Redditibus assise ibidem, prout particulariter per Rentale inde Factum et renouatum Apparet, per Annum, 23s.

Firma diuersorum Tenementorum ibidem prout per Rentale predictum inde Factum et renouatum particulariter Apparet, £22 14s. 10d.

Firma diuersarum terrarum et pasturarum infra Dominium et Forrensicum, prout per Rentale predictum inde renouatum Apparet, £6 4s.

Firma certarum aliarum terrarum et pasturarum in Egebaston, prout per Rentale predictum inde renouatum Apparet, per Annum, 21s. . £31 2s. 10d.

Inde Reprise, videlicet in

Redditibus Resolutis diuersis personis sequentibus, videlicet : Domino Lyle, 11s. 8½d. ; pro diuersis redditibus Heredibus pepwall, 9s. 3d. ; Roberto Myldmore Armigero, 21d. ; pro certis terris in Egebaston, cantariste ibidem, 17½d. ; Roberto Myldmore, 2s. ; pro terris predictis predicto Domino Lyle, 32s. 6½d. ; pro diuersis aliis redditibus cantariste ibidem, 17½d. ; Heredibus pepwall, 9s. 3d. ; Roberto Myldemore Armigero, 2s. 9½d. ; Rectori ecclesie beate marie, 6d. ; prefato Domino Lyle, 4s. 2d. ; et Johanni sporier, 6d. ; in toto per annum, 77s. 4½d.

Stipendiis trium capellanorum diuina seruicia infra ecclesiam parochialem de Byrmyngham Annuatim celebrancium, cuiuslibet eorum ad. 106s. 8d. per Annum, sic eis concessis per litteras patentes pro termino vite eorum; in toto, per Annum, £16.

Feodo Willielmi Bothe, pulsatoris organorum infra Ecclesiam predictam, cum 10s. pro redditu siue Firma vnius tenementi iuxta Ecclesiam ibidem sibi concessi, ut parcella eiusdem Feodi, per litteras patentes, pro termino vite sue, per Annum, 73s. 4d.

Feodo [blank] clerici gilde predicte, sibi concesso pro termino vite sue, per Annum, 6s. 8d.

Feodo Thome Groves, Custodis Domorum et gardinorum gilde predicte, sibi concesso pro termino vite sue, per Annum, 13s. 4d.

Feodo gardiani gilde predicte, per Annum, 6s. 8d.

Diuersis obbitibus ibidem, per Annum, 20s.

Denariis Annuatim solutis pro vino, cera, olio, et aliis necessariis infra Ecclesiam ibidem expendendis, per Annum, 20s.

Allocacione Reddituum diuersorum Tenementorum et cotagiorum superius oneratorum inter se ad 44s. 4d per Annum Eo quod dimittuntur diuersis pauperibus, quondam Fratribus et sororibus eiusdem gilde, pro termino vite eorum, absque aliquo inde Reddendo, prout sequitur, videlicet: Christophero Bagley et Agneti eius vxori, 5s.; Isabelle Waldern, vidue, 3s. 4d.; [blank] et eius vxori, pro tenemento apud Deretende, 4s.; [blank] vocate the commen Midwyffe, 4s.; Jacobo Johnson et Agneti Walton, 5s. 4d.; Thome grovys, 3s.; Elene Smythe, vidue, 4s.; Radulpho Grete, 5s.; Agnete Bydle, 4s.; [blank] vocato le belman, 6s. 8d.; in toto per Annum, 44s. 4d.   £29 20½d.

Et Remanet clare, per Annum, 41s. 1½d.

The sayd Gylde Was Founded by Thomas Sheldon and other in the 16th yere of Kyng Edwarde the seconde [1322–3], to Fynd certayne prestes to syng dyvyne seruyce in the parisshe Churche Aforseyde for euer, And to praye For the soules of the same Founders; And in the same towne of Byrmyngham there be 2,000 houselyng peaple, And at Ester tyme all the prestes of the same Gilde, With dyuers other, be not sufficient to Mynyster the sacramentes and sacramentalles vnto the seyde peaple. Also there be dyuers pore peaple Founde Ayded and suckered of the seyde Gylde, as in mony, Breade, Drynke, Coles; and When any of them Dye, thay be buryed very honestlye at the costes and charges of the same Gilde, With Dyrge and Messe accordyng to the constytucyons of the same Gilde.

85. GILDA SANCTE TRINITATIS ET SANCTI GEORGIJ IN VILLA
WARWICI.
Valet in
Redditibus, £32 10s. 5d.
Reprise, videlicet in
Redditibus Resolutis, 68s. 1½d.

Stipendijs quatuor capellanorum diuina seruicia infra Ecclesiam de Warrwico Annuatim celebrancium, cuiuslibet eorum ad 106s. 8d. per Annum; in toto per Annum soluendis ad quatuor Anni terminos equaliter, £21 6s. 8d.

Feodo Ricardi Hawes, generosi, Auditoris gilde predicte, sibi per litteras patentes pro termino vite sue concesso, per Annum, 13s. 4d.

Feodo Ricardi Warde, Clerici, Collectoris Reddituum ibidem, sibi similiter per litteras patentes pro termino vite sue concesso, per Annum, 40s.

Denarijs solutis 8ᵗᵒ pauperibus Gilde predicte, in qualibet septimana, 8d. ex antiqua consuetudine sic vsitata; in toto, per Annum, 34s. 8d.

Feodo Johannis Weryng Cantatoris, pro bono et laudabili seruicio suo ac diuina celebrantis in choro Ecclesie parochialis beate marie Warwici, sibi concesso per litteras patentes pro termino vite sue, per Annum, 20s.

Feodo Philippi Sheldon, vnius Cantatorum in Ecclesia ex consideracione predicta, sibi concesso per litteras patentes pro termino vite sue, per Annum, 26s. 8d.   31 9s. 5½d.

Et Remanet clare, per Annum, 20s. 11½d.

The seyd Gylde Was Founded, in the name of a Master and Bretherne of the same yelde, to Fynde 4 prestes to celebrate dyvyne seruyce For euer, and to praye For the Founders soules; that ys to seye, 2 of the same prestes to syng within the parisshe churche of Warwick, and the other 2 to syng within 2 Chapelles Bylded over 2 seuerall Gates of the seyd Towne, and the remaynder of the Revenewe Aboue Mensyoned ys ymployed toward the repayryng of A greate Bridge contaynyng 13 Arches. Bylded ower the Water vpon Aven and dyuers Hyghe Wayes For the Better resorte and accesse of the markett Folke com-

myng to the same towne, Withowt Whiche yt Wolde be a
greate Decaye to the Hole Towne.

Also the seyd Master and Bretherne Hathe solde certayne
parcelles of lande to the yerely value of 39s. 8d., ouer and
besydes the rent before rehersed, syns the Feaste of the annuncyacyon of our lady, in the 36 yere of the reigne of our souereigne lorde the Kynges maiestye that nowe ys, and receyvyd
therefore £39 13s. 4d., Whyche Was expended and bestowed
For the optaynyng and establysshement of the Kynges
maiestyes Foundacyon of the parisshe churche of Warrwick
and the Kynges newe scole within the same Towne.

And the Inventory of the same Gylde here after Dothe Apere.

42. COLLEGIUM DE STRATFFORD SUPER AVEN IN COMITATU
WARRWICI PREDICTI.

Valet In [Firmis], £127 18s. 9d. Inde
Reprise, videlicet in
Redditibus Resolutis .   .   .   . 27s.
Stipendio, Antonij Barker, Gardiani Collegij predicti, per
Annum, £68 5s. 1d.

*Where of ys payd to Doctour Bell, late Bysshoppe of
Worcester, for a Pencion yerely, £22.*

Stipendio subgardiani ibidem, per Annum, sibi concesso per
litteras patentes pro termino vite sue, £6 13s. 4d.

Stipendio cantariste ibidem, per Annum, £6 13s. 4d.

Stipendio curatoris ibidem, per Annum, £6 13s. 4d.

Stipendio Ricardi Burowes, capellani ibidem, sibi per litteras
patentes pro termino vite sue concesso, per Annum, £6.

Stipendio Thome Clarke, capellani ibidem, per Annum, £6.

Stipendio curatoris de Lodyngton, per Annum, 106s. 8d.

Stipendio Ricardi Sharpe, Ludi Magistri, ac pulsatoris organorum ibidem, sibi per litteras patentes pro termino vite sue
concesso, per Annum, £6.

Stipendio Ricardi Bedell, vnius cantatorum infra Ecclesiam
Collegij predicti, sibi per litteras patentes pro termino vite sue
concesso, per Annum, 106s. 8d.

Stipendio vnias alij Clerici cantantis infra Ecclesiam predictam, per Annum, £4 13s. 4d.

Feodis [blank] senescálli, Receptoris, et superuisoris omnium
terrarum et possessionùm dicto nuper collegio pertinencium,
sibi per litteras patentes pro termino vite sue concessis, per
Annum, 100s.   £127 18s. 9d.

Et remanet clare per Annum, nullum, quia summa deduccionum
predictarum coequalis est summe Totalis oneris superuisoris.

The seyd College Was Founded by one John Stratfforde,
sometyme Archebysshoppe of Canterburye, For one Warden,
Fyve prestes and 4 querysters, to Mayntayne Dyvyne seruyce
Within the parisshe churche of Stratfforde, Whyche be there
nowe Resydent, And the seyde Warden ys parson of the same
churche as in the ryght of the seyd college, and the same
parisshe ys 10 myles compasse, And he hathe the cure of 1,500
Houselyng people Within the same parisshe, so that Withowte
the helpe of the seyd prestes he ys not able to serue the seyd
Cure.

Also there ys belongyng to the same Collegiate Churche
2 chapelles, the one caulyd Bysshopston, and the other Luddyngton, beyng members of the seyd parisshe, And eche of them
Dystaunt From the seyd churche 2 myles, And the preste of
the same chapell of Bysshopston hathe the mynute tythes of
the village of Bysshopston for seruyng the cure there, Whiche
ys not comprised aboue in the Reuennewe of the seyd college,
nor yet within the Déduccions of the same; And the other
Curate, of Luddyngton, ys payde by the Warden, as apperythe
aboue in the Deduccions of the same college.

43. Gilda de Stratfforde, in comitatu predicto.

Valet in
[Firmis], £50 23½d. Inde
Reprise, videlicet in
Redditibus Resolutis, 20s. 10d.

Annuitate [blank] Dalam, preceptoris Scole gramatice ibidem,
per litteras patentes pro termino vite sue concessa, per Annum,
£10.

Annuitatibus quatuor Capellanorum gilde predicte, cuiuslibet eorum ad 106s. per Annum ; in toto, per Annum, £21 6s. 1d.

Feodo Johannis Combes, Senescalli omnium terrarum et possessionum dicte Gilde pertinencium, sibi per litteras patentes pro termino vite sue concesso, per Annum, 20s.

Feodo vnius Coci seruientis predictorum quatuor capellanorum gilde predicte, per annum, 10s.

Feodo, vnius Clerici seruientis infra Capellam eiusdem Gilde, per Annum, 4s.

Feodo Oliueri Baker, custodis 1 horalogij infra predictam capellam, per Annum, 13s. 4d.

Feodo Balliui siue collectoris Reddituum ibidem, per Annum, 26s. 8d.

Expensis Magistri et sociorum suorum ac diuersorum tenencium et Fratrum eiusdem gilde, pro vno prandio ibidem Facto die Finiente compoti sui Annuatim, ex Antiqua consuetudine sic vsitata, per Annum, 53s. 4d.

Denarijs Annuatim solutis pro vino et cera infra predictam capellam expendis, per Annum, 40s.

Decasu siue Vacacione diuersorum tenementorum ibidem, per Annum, 30s.

Reparacionibus super diuersis tenementis, communibus Annis, ibidem Factis, per Annum, 100s.

Denarijs Annuatim solutis predictis quatuor capellanis pro diuersis lez Dirges, per Annum, 6s. 8d.

Oblacionibus Annuatim solutis Gardiano collegij ibidem ad Festum Michaelis tantum, 4s.

Denarijs solutis quatuor pauperibus gilde predicte, videlicet : in pecunijs numeratis, 53s. 4d.; et pro 30 quarterijs carbonum, 10s.; in toto, per Annum, 63s. 4d.

Decimis Domino Regi Annuatim solutis, per Annum, 20s. 10¾d.   £51 19s. 8¾d.

Et sic videtur in superplusagio, 37s. 9¼d.

The same yelde Was Founded by Kyng Henry the 4th, by the name of a Master, 2 proctors, an Alderman, and to erect as many prestes as the reuennewes of the same Wyll extend vnto, and there be at thys present tyme 5 prestes, Where of one A

Scolemaster of Gramer, and celebratyng Dyvyne seuryce Within
a chapell stondyng in the Myddes of the same For the greate
quyetnesse and comffort of all the parissyoners there, For that
the parisshe churche stondyth owte of the same towne Dystaunt
From the moste parte of the seyd parisshe Halffe a myle and
more, and in tyme of syknes, as the plage and suche lyke dys-
seses, dothe chaunce Within the seyde Towne, than all suche
infectyue persons, With many other ympotent and pore peaple,
dothe to the seyd Chapell resort For there Dyuyne seruyce ; and
in the same Towne there ys a markett Wekely kepte, and
Havyng in yt abowt 1,500 houselyng peaple, to gether with
7 lyttle hamlottes therto belonging, Whiche hathe no other
resort but only to the same chapell and parisshe churche.

47. GILDA DE BRAYLES IN COMITATU PREDICTO.

Valet in

Redditibus suie Firmis omnium terrarum et tenementorum
predicte Gilde pertinencium, soluendis ad quatuor anni terminos
ibidem vsuales, prout per Rentale inde Factum et renouatum
particulariter Apparet, per Annum, £18 13s. 2½d. Inde

Reprise, Videlicet in Redditibus Resolutis, 59s. 6½d.

Stipendio Johannis Pyttes, clerici, vnius capellanorum gilde
predicte, sibi per litteras patentes pro termino vite sue concesso,
per Annum, £8 20d.

Stipendio Willielmi Broadway, clerici, etatis 73 Annorum,
per Annum, 108s. 4d.

Diuersis obbitibus ac elimozinis datis diuersis pauperibus
ibidem, per Annum, 11s. 8d.

Decimis Domino Regi Annuatim inde solutis, per Annum,
26s. 8d.   £18 7s. 10½d.

Et Remanet clere, per Annum, 5s. 4d.

Founded by Rycharde, Erle of Warrwick and Sarum, by the
name of A Warden, Bretherne and Systerne, For Fyndyng of
2 prestes For euer to celebrate Dyvyne seruyce Within the
paroche churche there, and to pray For the soules of the
Founders of the same.

And there be within the seyd parisshe 4 hamlettes, And in

euery Hamlet A Chapell, and euery of them beyng a myle at
the leste Dystaunte From the same parisshe churche, And be
members of the same parisshe, and haue Messe seyde there
Dyuers tymes in the yere; Also the same parisshe ys a greate
compasse, And Hathe almoste 2,000 houselyng peaple, so that
in tyme of plage or suche lyke syknesse the parson of the same,
With owt other Helpe, ys not able to serue the Cure there.·

Further, the same yelde do Fynde at there proper costes A
Fre Scole of Gramer For the Erudycyon and bryng vpp of
dyuers and many pore scolers.

The Citie off Coventre and the Countie off Warrick.
Certificate 53.

(Edward VI.)

Sir Fulke Gryuell, knighte; Clement Throkmorton, John
Hales and William Rynnocke, esquiers; and Thomas Fisher,
gentillman, Commissioners.

1 COVENTRE.

The trinite Guylde, which was

Founded by king Edward the seconde, and by hym Incorporate by the name of Master and bretherne of the Guilde of
the Holye trinite, our ladye, saint Marye, Saint John Baptist,
and saint Katheryne the Virgin, which Corporacion was after
Confirmed by King Edward the thridd and prince Edward his
sonne; To the which guilde Quene Izabell, somme tyme quene
of England, by lycence of king Edward the thridd afforesaid,
gave a platt of grounde whereon is nowe builte a Chappell called
Bablacke, where was songe daylye Divine service;

Vnto whiche guilde belonge landes and possessions to the
yerelye value of £178 13s. 6d. Whereof

In diuers Reprises going owte of the premisses, videlicit,
In chiefe Rentes to diuers persons, £15 17s. 11d.

In the Kynges majesties yerelye tenth, £4 19½d.

In the Fee Ferme of the Citye off Coventre, paid with parte
of the revenues of the same guilde, £10. In Fees and Annuytes

to diuers persons, £45 3s. 4d. In stipendes of diuers other ministers of the Churche, £17 6s. 8d.

In the stipend of a Schoole master teaching in a Free Schoole theare, £6 13s. 4d.

In allowaunce gyven For certein tenementes letten to diuers poore people, bretherne and sisters of the same guilde, Rent Free, £10 7s. 8d. In expences at 4 seuerall obittes kept by the Mayster and Bretherne (with 14s. thereof to poore people), 111s. And in Expences at a generall meting For the elleccion of a Newe Master of the same guilde, 20s.

Amounting in the hole to £116 18½d.

And then Remaineth, £62 11s. 11½d.

Memorandum :

Plate and Jewelles Belonging to the same guilde, videlicet, 2 Chalices of Sylver, waying 41 ounces.

Goodes and Ornamentes, as by an Inuentorie Indentyd thereof Apperyth, are praysed at £17 4s. 4d.

Leade theare, being abowte and appon the Chappell of Bablacke, by Estimacion, 16 fowder.

Bell Mettall theare, waying by Estimacion 20 cwt. 13℔.

These things were all bye the kings majeste goven to the Citye of Coventre bye his lettres patentes.

A Free Schoole theare

Mainteyned with the possessions of the same guilde, wheareof Sir Robert Coventre ys Schoole Master, who hathe yerelye For his stipend £6 13s. 4d., allowed amongest the Repryses of the same guilde.

4. THE TOWNE OF BRAILES.

The Guilde of brailes was

Founded by one Richarde, late Earle of Warrick and Sarum, and Incorporate by the name of Warden, bretherne, and Systers For the Fynding and mayntenaunce of two Priestes to celebrate Dyvine seruice in the Paroche Churche of Brayles, and to praye For the Solles of the Foundours,

And haue Londes and possessions to the yerelye value of £18 13s. 10¼d. Whereof

In Rentes Resolute to Diuers persons going owte of the premisses, 56s. 10½d.

In the Kinges Majesties yerelye 10th, 26s. 8d.

In the yerelye Annuyte of Sir John Pyttes, Schole Master, £8 20d.;

And in the stipend of Thomas Okeley by lettres patent, 40s.; in all, £14 5s. 2½d.

And then Remaineth £4 8s 8d.

Memorandum :

Plate and Jewells belonging to the same guylde, none.

For yt was sollde beffore the same guilde came to the Kinges majesties handes.

Goodes and Ornaments thereunto belonging are praysed at 23s. 9d.

A schoole Mayster theare

Mainteined with parte of the possessions of the same guilde, and one Sir John Pyttes, Clerke, a man of honest conuersacion and well learned, teaching in the same schoole, hathe For his Stipende yerelye, by letters patent, £8 20d., going owte of the same premisses, and thereffore deducted amongest the Reprises thereof.

20. THE TOWNE OF STRETFORDE.

The College of Strettforde was

Founded By one John Stretforde, some tyme Arche byshopp of Cantorburye, For one Wardein, Fyve priestes, and Foure Choristares, to mainteign dyvine seruice in the paroche Churche of Strettforde, For the mayntenaunce of whiche Choristers one Rauffe Collingwood, sometyme Warden theare, gave all his landes in strettfford, Drayton, and bynton, by hym purchased to the same intent and Charged amongest the Revenues of the said College, whiche Revenues amounte to the yerelye Reate of £127 18s. 9d. Thereof

In Rents Resolute, 20s. 3d.; In Annuites and Fees, £13; In stipendes to diuers ministers, videlicet, the Wardein For his stipende yerelye, £68 5s. 1d.; And to the other ministers For theyr stipendes and diett, £64 18s. 8d.

£147 4s.

And then Remaineth nil; Quia in surplusagio, £19 5s. 3d.

Memorandum :

Plate and Jewells belonging to the same Colledge amounte in weight to 249 ounces.

Goodes and Ornamentes thereunto belonging, as by Inventorye Indented thereof apperyth, are praysed at £6 10s. 8d.

The guilde of strettforde was

Founded by king Henrye the Fourthe, and incorporate by the name of A maister, two proctours, and one Alderman, to main-teign as many priestes as the Revenue thereof will extende vnto to minister and syng Divine seruice in a Chappell therefore erected, stonding in the middest and face of the same towne, called the guilde Chappell, whereunto belonge lands and pos-sessions to the yerelye value of £49 18s. 8½d. Whereof

In the kinges majesties yerelye 10th, 62s. 8d.; In Rentes Resolute going owte of the premisses, 20s. 10d.; In Fees and Annuytes, 46s. 8d.; In diuers stipendes of the ministers of the Churche, £31 6s. 8d.; and in Almes to 12 poore men and theyr wyves, £4 10s.; in all £42 6s. 10d.

And then remaineth £7 10s. 11½d.

Memorandum :

Plate and Jewells belonging to the same guilde, videlicet, twoo Chalices, parcell guilte, waying 47 ounces.

Remayninge in the handes of the maysters of the guild.

Goodes, Ornamentes, and Howshollde stuffe thereunto Be-longing are praysed at 33s. 4d.

Theare ys maynteygned with parte of the Revenues of the same guilde a greate stone bridge Leading over the Ryver of Avon, conteigning in Lengthe 400 yerdes, stonding appon 18 Arches, and ys the chiefe Commodyte of the same towne and of all the Contreye thereaboute; wherefore yt is verey nedeful that yt be allwayes Repayred, or ells yt wilbe the onelye decaye and Empoueryshment of the same towne.

Theare are allso Relieved with parte of the Same possessions 24 poore people, videlicet, 12 poore men and theyr wyves, euerye couple having a house and a garden Rent-free of the same possessions, and yett not above charged, and have yerelye amongest them going oute of the same landes £4 10s. allowed amongest the reprises of the same ; over and besydes, theye haue £4 more of the discrete provision of the mayster of the same guilde.

A free Schoole theare

Mainteigned with parte of the Revenues of the same guilde. And one Sir William Dalam, priest, aboute the age of 60 yeres, ys schole mayster theare, having For his stipend yerelye £10, going owte of the same possessions by letters patent and allowed amongest the stipendes of the ministers of the Churche theare.

Memorandum :

Allso Theare Be twoo Chappells at ease (members of the said paroche churche) callid Byshopton and Loddington, eche of them being twoo myles distaunt From the said Towne of Strett-forde, having (euerye of the said Chappells) one priest to minister in them, the priest of Byshopton being one of the nomber of the guilde of Strettforde, and hathe for his salarye and Lyving all the mynute tythes of the towne of Byshopton not charged emongest the Revenues of the same guilde. And the priest ministring at Loddington afforesaid, being one of the nomber of the Colleage of Strettforde, hathe onelye a pencion going owte of the possessions of the same Colleage and allowed emongest the Repryses of the same.

Anthonye Barker, Clerke, of the age of Fyftye yeres, Bacheler of Diuinte, Warden of the said Colleage of Strettforde, is par-sone theare, and hathe the same in the Right of the said War-deinship, which parsonage ys yerelye worthe of yt sellffe in tythes £75 2s. 8d., charged in the hole value of the said College.

Hoseling People in the same paroche, 1,500.

Yt is allso a thinge vereye mete and Necessarye that the guilde Chappell of stretford stand vndefaced, for that it was allwayes a chapell of ease, for the Separacion of the Sicke persons from the hole in tyme of Plague, and standith in the face of the towne.

55. The Guilde of brimincham

Was Founded by one Thomas Sheldon and other in the 16th yere of kyng Henrye [*sic*] the Seconde, and incorporate by the name of Master and Brethern of the guilde of the Holye Crosse in brymyncham For the maintenaunce of certein priestes, Where-unto belonge Landes and possessions to the yerelye value of £32 12s. 5d. *prima facie*, Which are nowe and have bene of longe tyme conuerted as well to dedes of charyte and to the Commen-welth there, as hereafter shall appere, £32 12s. 5d. ; whereof

In Rentes Resolute, as well to the erle of Warrick as to diuers other, going owte of the premisses, 55s. 10½d. ; In stipendes of priestes and other ministers of the churche, £20 6s. 8d. ; In Fees and annuytes, 60s. ; For bread and Wyne For the Churche, 20s. ; For keping the Clocke and the Chyme, 13s. 4d. ; And in Allowance For Reparacions of the same possessions, consisting moste parte in tenementes, Communibus Annis, £4 ; in all, £31 15s. 10½d.

So remaineth 16s. 4¼d.

Memorandum :

Plate and Jewells to the same guilde belonging, videlicet, three Chalices of Silver, waying 24 ounces, and a nutte with a cover waying 4 ounces ; in all, 28 ounces.

Whereof 2 chalices, waying 16 ounces, are left For a diuine seruice.

Goodes, Ornamentes, and Howshold stuffe are praysed at 41s. 8d.

Theare be Relieved and mainteigned appon the same posses-sions of the same guilde, and the good provision of the master and bretherne thereof, 12 poor persons, who have their howses Rent-free, and all other kinde of Sustenaunce, as well Foode and apparell, as all other necessaryes.

Allso Theare be mainteigned, with parte of the premisses and kept in good Reparacions, two greate stone bridges, and Diuers Foule and Daungerous high wayes, the charge whereof the towne of hit Selfe ys not hable to mainteign ; so that the Lacke thereof will be a greate noysaunce to the Kinges majes-

B B

ties Subiectes passing to and From the marches of Wales, and an utter Ruyne to the same towne, being one of the fayrest and moste proffittuble townes to the Kinges Hignese in all the Shyre.

The said Towne of Brymyncham ys a verey mete place, and yt is verey mete and necessarye that theare be a Free Schoole erect theare to bring uppe the youthe, being boathe in the same towne and nigh thereaboute.

Howselinge People in the same Paroche of Brimyncham, 1,800.

The Certificate For the assignement off all the pencions as well within The Citie off Coventry as the Countye off Warrwick. Certificate 57.

(Edward VI.)

CIUITAS COVENTRIE.

1. Guilda Sancte Trinitatis in bablack, in parochia Sancti Michaelis, in Ciuitate predicta.

Terre et tenementa dicte guilde, cum terris eidem appunctuatis per thomam bonde, valent clare per annum, £201 3s. 0½d.

Willielmus Madder, Capellanus, ætatis 40 annorum; Willielmus Wright, Capellanus, etatis 50 annorum ; et Johannes Symondes, etatis 58 Annorum, alias non habentes promociones, habent pro Salarijs suis quilibet eorum, 106s. 8d.; in toto, per Annum, £16.

3 *penciones eorum cuiuslibet,* 100s. £4 [*sic*].

Rowland Gosnell, etatis 36 Annorum, minister ibidem, et Rogerus stoneley, etatis 30 Annorum, minister ibidem, quilibet eorum, 53s. 4d. ; in toto, per Annum, 106s. 8d.

2 *penciones eorum vtriusque,* 53s. 4d.

Respectuatur.

Margareta Lane, vidua, habet per Annum, 20s.; Et duo pueri, vocati queristours, habent pro salarijs suis quilibet eorum, 20s. ; in toto, per Annum, 60s.

Pencio Margarete Lane, 20s.

Respectuatur.

Memorandum : the Warden And diuers other Ministers there have Fees and Annuites by patent going owte of the premisses, Wherefore I have here omitted there Names and Fees.

2. The poore.

Allso with the proffittes of the premisses are kept ten poore men and one poore woman.   Everye man having wekelye 7½d., and the woman 5d., amounting yerelye to £17 6s. 8d.   Besydes eche of them 3½ yerdes of clothe For theyr gownes, and the woman 3 yerdes at 2s. the yerde, which amounteth to 76s. And, besydes, 23s. 4d. in money to by theyre fewell yerely, Amounting in the hole to £22 6s.

3. The poore.

Allso James Gilbert, Thomas Spencer, and Margarete Cooke, Who, being Fallen in decay and being of the same brotherhed, have Eche of them 20s. yerelye, with diuers suche other that have theyr howses Rent free, 60s.

4. Scholemaster.

Theare ys allso appon the premisses one fre schoole, and one Robert Coventre of the age of 40 yeres, is schoole master there, and hath For his stipend £6 13s. 4d.

Continuatur Schola quousque.

5. Preachour.

Theare ys allso one Sir baldewyne Norton, of the age of 40 yeres, A precher, who hathe For his stipend £13 6s. 8d., And 20s. For his gowne ; in the hole, £14 6s. 8d.

24. GUILDA DE STRATFORDE SUPER AVON, IN COMITATU PREDICTO.

Terre et possessiones dicte guilde pertinentes ; valent clare per annum, £43 11s. 10½d. ; vnde

Quatuor Capellani ibidem habent per litteras patentes quilibet eorum, 106s. 8d., alias non habentes promociones, In toto, per Annum, £21 6s. 8d.

Item clericus ibidem habet per Annum, 4s.   Et Oliuerus baker, custos horalogij ibidem, habet per Annum, 13s. 4d. ; in toto, per Annum, 17s. 4d.

Scolemaster.

Memorandum : Appon the premisses ys one Free Schoole, and one William Dalam, Scholemaster theare, hathe yerelye for teaching theare, *by patente*, £10.

Continuatur Schola quousque.

Poore.

There is Allso gyven yerelye to 24 poore men, bretherne of the said guilde, 63*s.* 4*d.*, videlicet ; 10*s.* to be bestowed in Coles, and the Rest gyven In Readye money, besydes one Howse theare called the Almes Howse, and besydes 5 or £6 yeven them of the good provision of the master of the same guilde, and the same 53*s.* 4*d.* to be payed them euerye quarter, 13*s.* 4*d.*

63*s.* 4*d.*

27. GUILDA DE BRAYLES, IN COMITATU PREDICTO.

Terre et possessiones dicte guilde pertinentes, per annum, £14 10*s.* 8*d.* ; vnde

Thomas Okeley, Custos Organorum, etatis 40 annorum, nullam aliam habens promocionem, habet pro salario suo per litteras patentes, 40*s.*

Allocatur charta.

Scoole master.

Memorandum : Appon the premisses ys one Free Schole, And one John Pyttes, being Schoole master theare, hathe For his stipend, £8 20*d.*

Continuatur Schola quousque.

52. NONNETON.

Memorandum : one John Leke gave by his laste will certein landes in the paroche of Nonneton, to the value of 4 markes, to the Mayntenaunce of a priest to pray For his parentes ; the which hathe allwayes bene accomplyshed accordinglye, vntill nowe, abowte syxe yeres paste, yt was concluded amongest the parochians theare by the consent of the Heyres of the same Leke, that the Revenues thereof, with more gyven of theyr Devocion, shollde be convertyd to the mayntenaunce of A Scoole Master theare, the which For that yt hathe not bene conuertyd to the use of A Chauntrye within these syxe yeres I take it to be owte of the compas of the statute, and therefore I have omitted the certificat thereof.

Examinetur in Curia Augmentacionum.

Examinatur per me Clementem Throkmorton, superuisorem.

Examinatur per Johannem Dodington.

Coventry and Warwickshire. Schools Continuance Warrant, 6.

Forasmoche as it apperith [&c.] that a Grammer Scole hath been contynually kept in the said citie [*of Coventry*] with the revenues of the said late Guylde [*of the Holy Trinity in Babelacke*], And that the Scolemaster there hath had [&c.] £6 13s. 4d. [&c.],

And that a Grammer Scole hath been contynuallie kept in Stretforde vpon Avon [&c.], with the revenues of the late Guylde in Stratford vpon Avon aforesaid, And that the Scolemaster there hath had [&c.] £10 [&c.],

And that a Grammer Scole hath been contynuallie kept in Brayles in the said Countie with the revenues of the late Guylde in Brailes aforesaid, And that the Scolemaster there hath had [&c.] £8 20d. [&c.].

Wee therefore [&c.] haue assigned [&c.], that the said Scole in the Citie of Coventrie aforesaid shall contynue, And that Robert Coventrye, Scolemaster there, shall haue [&c.] £6 13s. 4d. [&c.] ;

And that the said grammer [*scole in Stratforde vpon Avon*] aforesaid shall contynue, And that William Dalam, Scolemaster there, shall haue [&c.], £10 ;

And that [*the said grammer*] scole in Brailes aforesaid shall contynue, And that John Pyttes, Scolemaster there, shall haue [&c.] £8 [20d.].

**Comitatus Warrwick. Particulars for Schools.
Edward VI. (Roll 5.)**

BIRMINGHAM GRAMMAR SCHOOL.

Parcelle possessionum nuper guilde Sancte Crucis, in villa de Brymincham, in Comitatu predicto.

Diuersa terre, tenementa et possessiones, tam infra burgum quam Forrenseca de brymincham, dicte guilde pertinencia; valent in

Dalende, videlicet in
Redditu horrei in Dalende, in tenura Henrici Russell, per Indenturam, per Annum, 20*d*.
Redditu vnius tenementi, ibidem in tenura Johannis Eliate [*d*°.], 3*s*. 8*d*.
Redditu vnius tenementi, ibidem vocati Edale Halle, in tenura eiusdem Johannis [*d*°.], 7*s*.
Redditu vnius tenementi, ibidem in tenura Johannis shilton [*d*°.], 5*s*.
Redditu vnius tenementi, ibidem in tenura Willielmi Collmore [*d*°.], 14*d*.   18*s*. 6*d*.

Chapell strete, videlicet in
Redditu vnius tenementi in chapell strete, in tenura Johannis veysye, per annum, 4*s*. 6*d*.
Redditu diuersarum parcellarum terre vocatarum the Folldes, in tenura eiusdem Johannis [*d*°.], 3*s*. 4*d*.
Redditu vnius alius Fold ibidem, in tenura eiusdem Johannis [*d*°.], 3*s*. 4*d*.
Redditu vnius tenementi ibidem, in tenura Johannis Eliot, per Indenturam [*d*°.], 10*s*.
Redditu vnius tenementi ibidem, in tenura Johannis Massye [*d*°.], 16*d*.   22*s*. 6*d*.

Englishe markett, videlicet in
Redditu vnius tenementi in the englishe markett, in tenura Ricardi smalbroke, per Indenturam, per annum, 6*s*. 8*d*.

Redditu vnius tenementi ibidem, in tenura Ricardi Alatt [*d°.*], 9*s.*

Redditu vnius tenementi ibidem, in tenura Thome Sompnour [*d°.*], 9*s.*

Redditu vnius tenementi ibidem, cum vno crofto iuxta Redhill, in tenura Johannis Veyseye [*d°.*], 8*s.* 6*d.*

Redditu vnius tenementi ibidem, et vnius crofti apud Molle strete ende, in tenura Roberti preston [*d°.*], 6*s.*

Redditu vnius tenementi ibidem, in tenura Roberti Collins, [*d°.*], 6*s.* 8*d.*

Redditu vnius tenementi ibidem, in tenura Johannis Eliat ad voluntatem, [*d°.*], 8*s.*   53*s.* 10*d.*

Newe strete, videlicet in

Redditu vnius tenementi in newe strete, in tenura Willielmi Elson, per Indenturam, per annum, 2*s.* 8*d.*

Redditu vnius crofti ibidem, in tenura eiusdem ¦Willielmi [*d°.*] 10*s.*

Redditu vnius horrei cum gardino ibidem, in tenura Johannis Shilton [*d°.*], 3*s.*

Redditu vnius Crofti ibidem, iuxta Feckelane, in tenura Willielmi Sheldon ad voluntatem, 18*d.*

Redditu vnius Domus siue Aule, vocate the towne halle, alias the guilde hall, cum gardino ibidem, per annum, 5*s.*   22*s.* 2*d.*

Highe strete, videlicet in

Redditu vnius shope in the Highe strete, in tenura Thome yemont alias Perynn, per annum, 14*d.*

Redditu vnius shope in the shambles, in tenura Johannis Shilton, per Indenturam, [*d°.*], 4*s.*

Redditu vnius shope, ibidem in tenura Thome baker, [*d°.*] 3*s.* 4*d.*

Redditu duarum shoparum, ibidem in tenura Willielmi Peynton ad voluntatem, per annum, 6*s.* 8*d.*   15*s.* 2*d.*

Molle strete, videlicet in

Redditu vnius tenementi in Molle strete, in tenura Willielmi peinton, per Indentarum, per annum, 8*s.*

Redditu vnius tenementi ibidem, in tenura dicti Willielmi
[d°.], 3s. 4d.

Redditu vnius tenementi ibidem, in tenura Johannis Veysye
[d°.], 5s.

Redditu vnius tenementi ibidem, in tenura Thome Marshall
[d°.], 3s.

Redditu vnius crofti ibidem, iuxta the [tenement] crofte, in
tenura Johannis Shilton [d°.], 7s.

Redditu vnius tenementi, ibidem in tenura Johannis Smythe
ad voluntatem, per annum, 10s.

Redditu vnius crofti, ibidem in tenura Marie Vernon [d°.], 4s.

40s. 4d.

Egebaston strete, videlicet in

Redditu vnius horrei in Egebaston strete, in tenura Willielmi
bodgye, per Indenturam, per annum, 3s. 4d.

Redditu duorum Cottagiorum ibidem, in tenura eiusdem
Willielmi, per annum, 4s.

Redditu vnius tenementi ibidem, in tenura Rogeri Davyes, per
annum, 3s.

Redditu duorum tenementorum ibidem, in tenura Thome Mak-
worthe, per Indenturam, per annum, 16s.

Redditu vnius tenementi ibidem, in tenura Willielmi Corpson
[d°.], 10s.

Redditu vnius tenementi ibidem, in tenura Henrici Burcotte
ad voluntatem, per annum, 5s.

Redditu vnius gardini, ibidem in tenura Johannis Shilton [d°.],
12d.   45s. 3d.

Mercers strete, videlicet in

Redditu siue Firma vnius tenementi in Mercers strete, in
tenura Thome preston, per Indenturam, per annum, 8s.

Bulringe, videlicet in

Redditu duorum tenementorum apud the bulringe, in tenura
Johannis Shilton, per Indenturam, per annum, 24s.

Redditu vnius tenementi ibidem, et vnius crofti apud the
pynnefolde, in tenura Roberti Rastell [d°.], 6s. 8d.

Redditu vnius tenementi ibidem, in tenura Willielmi Michell, per Indenturam [d°.], 6s.

Redditu vnius tenementi ibidem, in tenura Thome Marshall [d°.], 10s.

Redditu vnius tenementi ibidem, in tenura Johannis Shilton [d.°], 4s. 6d.

Redditu vnius tenementi ibidem, in tenura Willielmi peinton [d°.], 5s.   56s. 2d.

Well strete, videlicet in
Redditu duorum tenementorum in Well strete, in tenura Thome pest [d°.], 3s. 4d.

Redditu vnius tenementi, ibidem in tenura Henrici Foxhall [d°.], 28s.

Redditu vnius tenementi, ibidem in tenura Willielmi Willington [d°.], 3s. 6d.   34s. 10d.

Parke strete, videlicet in
Redditu vnius horrei et gardini in parkestrete, in tenura Roberti Rastell [d°.], 2s.

Redditu vnius horrei et gardini iuxta godes earte lane, in tenura Willielmi peinton [d°.], 12d.   3s.

Forennseca, videlicet in
Redditu vnius crofti iuxta Lake Medowe, vocati Longe Crofte, in tenura Johannis Shilton [d°.], 9s.

Redditu vnius tenementi, cum certis terris vocati bynges, in tenura Johannis Shilton [d°.], 30s.

Redditu vnius pasture vocate Rottonffield, in tenura eiusdem Johannis [d°.], 13s. 4d.

Redditu vnius crofti iuxta Heybarne yate, in tenura Johannis Veysye [d°.], 8s.

Redditu vnius crofti apud Philipps poole, in tenura Ricardi Smalbrooke [d°.], 6s. 8d.

Redditu vnius Crofti ibidem, iuxta Dodwalles, in tenura Henrici Biddle [d°.], 16s.

Redditu vnius pasture vocate Wallmores, in tenura Henrici Foxhall [d°.], 36s. 8d.

Redditu vnius crofti, iuxta [tentor] buttes, in tenura Ricardi Walker [d°.], 8s.

Redditu vnius Crofti apud Honde Crosse, iuxta Colborne Fieldes, in tenura Johannis [blank] [d°.], 3s.

Redditu vnius parcelle pasture et prati apud bynges, vocate saint Marye wood, in tenura Henrici geste, per annum, 8s.

Redditu duorum Croftorum apud Wynesdon grene, in tenura Johannis Osborne, per annum, 2s. 6d. £7 [1s. 2d.] [£23 1s. 0d.]

Reprise, videlicet in

Redditu Domino Johanni, Comiti Warwick, exeunte de terris et tenementis infra burgum de brymincham, per annum, 15s. 4¼d.

Redditu Resoluto eidem, exeunte de terris et possessionibus existentibus in Forennseco, ibidem, per annum, 25s. 7¾d. [41s.]

Et Remanet clare, £21.

Per me clementem Throkmorton, superuisorem.

Mr. Duke, I pray you drawe a boke vnto certen persons to be [namyd] to you b . . .

Annuales redditus reseruandi domino Regi, 20s.

Et sic remanet clare [blank].

Primo die Aprilis, Anno regni Regis Edwardi sexti, quinto [1552].

The Kinges maiesties pleasure is that a Free Scol . . . Brymyncham, in the Countie of Warrwick, with landes to the y[erely valewe] of . . . by his Highnes to the mayntenaunce thereof, And that the . . . Inhabytauntes of the Towne, Parishe and Lordship of Brymyncham . . . perpetuall succession as Gouernours of the possessions, reuenues, and goodes, . . . haue powre to receyve the landes to be appoynted for the said Scole . . . gouernaunce thereof, wherfore there must be a bill thereof devised according . . . made of the landes aboue rehersed, with the Issues and proffites therof from . . . Michaell the archangell last past to the Gouernours of the possessions . . . Scole, and to their Successors, with suche other necessary and reasonable . . . the late boke made for the Ereccion of the Scole of Shirborne.

Ryc. Sakevyle.

Westmorelande. Certificate 11.

(Edward VI.)

For Commissioners see under Cumberland, p. 44.

17. THE TOWNE AND PARYSHE OF KIRKEBY KENDALL,
where are 6,000 houselinge people.

The stipend or Fre grammer schole there.

Off the Foundacion of Adam Pennyngton, by his laste will
and testament, for 98 yeres to kepe a fre grammer schole in
Kendall, And to celebrate and praye for the soulle of the founder,
and further willed by the same will that the same shulde
contynue for ever if the lawe wolde permytte, Which scole is
kept and observed accordinglie.

Adam Sheperde, Bacheler in dyvynite, a preacher and Schole
Master there, hath the clere yerely revenue of the same for his
salarie, £10.

The landes and tenementes belonginge to the same be of the
yerely value of £15; whereof

In Reprises, £5.

And so remayneth clere by yere, £10.

20. APPULBYE.

A stipendarie in the parishe Churche there.

Vsed to celebrate Masse and other devyne service in the
parishe Churche there, And to kepe a fre grammer schole.

Edwarde Gibson, Incumbent and Schole Master there, hath
the clere yerely revenue of the same for his Salarie, 119s. 10d.

The landes and tenementes belonginge to the same be of the
yerely value of £6 0s. 10d. ; wherof

In Reprises, 12d.

And so remayneth clere by yere, 119s. 10d.

The goodes and Ornamentes belonginge to the same be valued
at 41s. 8d.

21. BURGH VNDER STAYNSMORE.

The fregrammer Schole and Stipendarye in the parishe
there.

Of the foundacion of John Brounscalles, to kepe a Free grammer schole and to saye devyne Service there, And also to teache scholers to wryte, which is observed accordinglie.

John Beckes, Schole Maister there, apte and mete for the same, hathe the clere yerely revenue of the same for his salarie, £7 11s. 4d.

The landes and tenementes belongynge to the saide Schole be of the yerely value of £7 11s. 4d.; whereof

In Reprises, nil.

The Countie of Westmerlonde.
(Edward VI.)

Q.R. Anc. Misc. Aug. $\frac{76}{5}$, Rental and Surveys Roll, 846.

BORGH UNDER STAINMORE.

m. 4. Seruice of A Scole master teching gramer within the towne of Burgh vnder stanesmore, as appereth by A compocicion. Sur John Bek, nowe master ther.

Furst one Mansion with a garthe in the towne of Burghe vnder Stanesmore, in tenour of Sur John Bek, by yere, 4s.

[*Together with divers other rents*], £7 11s. 4d.

Memorandum : ther is A chapell in Burghe, with a littell garthe, called Gypgarthe, whiche chapell is covered with lede, contening by estimacion [*blank*] foders of lede : And the said chapell and garthe is worthe to be letten 3s. 4d. by yere.

Jowels, plate, ornamentes, gooddes, and cattalles pertening to the said fre scole of Burgh:

Furste, one Chales, parcell-gylte, weying 6 ovunces, at 3s. 8d. le ovunce, 22s.; Two vestementes, 4s.; two corporax with cases, 8d.; 4 alter clothes, 20d.; 2 candelstikes of Bras, 12d.; one pax and 2 crewettes of Tyn, 3d.; the messe bookes, 20d.; 6 bookes of the byble, called glosa ordinaria, 13s. 4d.; The hole byble in latten, 20d.; 9 other bookes, as ortus vocabulorum et catholicon, 20d.; one chiste, 12d.; one chare, 6d.; one mete table, 4d.; one bynche, A Fyrme, and 2 tristes, 6d.; A Rakand, 4d.; and 2 bedstokes, 6d.   51s. 1d.

APPLEBY.

Londes and Tenementes pertening to Fynding of A Scoldémaster keping a Fre gramer scole on the Towne of Appylbie.

Sur Leonard Langhorne, master of the same Scole.

Furst, one burgage in Appylbie, in tenour of Swithin Milner, set betwexte A burgage of Alexander Appilbie, of the northe, and one burgage of the gramer scole, of the southe, paing therfor yerlie, at Martynmes and Whitsondaie, 5s.

[*Divers other rents.*]

Item a gres close in tenour of Sur Leonard Langhorn, vicare, lying of baksyde o' the Scolehouse, and payeth by yere, 6s. 8d.

Item one burgage, called the Scole, paing yerlie, 6d.

[*In all*] £6 10d. ; wherof

Reprises

Paid to the heyres of Thomas Ros for on burgage in scolehouse-cloce, 12d.; for the subcedie to the Kinges maiestie, 12s. 6d.; for perpetuall tenementes, 9s. 2d.   22s. 8d.

And so Remaynethe, £4 18s. 2d.

Plate, ornementtes, Gooddes, and cattalles, pertening to the said Scole in Appylbye.

Furste, one challes dubled gylte, weyng 7 ovunces, at 3s. 4d. the ounce, 23s. 4d.; but it is doubtefull whether it is syluer or not; one broken chales, weing 4 ovunces, at 3s. the ounce, 12s.; thre vestementes, 15s.; 7 alterclothes, 4s.; one Messebooke, 16d.; and 3 corporax, 2s.; 57s. 8d.

Comitatus Westmorlandie.   Certificate 103.

(Edward VI.)

7.   KYRKEBYKENDAL.

A grammer schole.

The stipendary prest or scholemaster of the Free grammer schole there.

Adam Shepperde, Incumbent there, £10.

The clere yerely value of the landes, £10.

Continuatur schola quousque.

Comitatus Wilteš cum ciuitate nove Sarum.
Certificate 59.
(Henry VIII.)

Johanni, Sarum Episcopo, Thomæ Seymour, militi, Roberto Chydley, armigero, Thomæ Leygh, et Willelmo Grene, generosis, commissioners.

1. Cantaria fundata per Andream Holse, in Ecclesia cathedrali Sarum.

Valet, videlicet in

Quodam stipendio siue Salario septem librarum sex solidorum et octo denariorum pro Sustentacione cuiusdam Capellani ad celebrandam missam in capella beate Marie Magdalene, in Ecclesia cathedrali Sarum, per Magistrum, Socios, et Scholares Collegij beate Marie de Wynchester, prope ciuitatem Wyntonie, annuatim soluto secundum ordinacionem fundatoris eiusdem.

Qua quidem cantaria sic per Andream Holse fundata, certas terras et Tenementa in Feoffamento posuit ad vsum dicti Magistri, sociorum, et scolarium clari annui valoris quadraginta marcarum, per qua causa dicti Magistri, Socij, Scolares, et Successores sui, per quoddam Scriptum concedunt inter alia bene et fideliter tenere, perimplere, et solvere dictam Summam ad duos Anni terminos, videlicet, ad festa pasche et sancti michaelis Archangeli, equis porcionibus, prefato capellano et Successoribus suis pro tempore existentibus in dicta Ecclesia Sarum, vel infra vnum Mensem post quemlibet terminorum predictorum, £9 6s. 8d.

Cum 40s. pro quodam annuo obitu.

3. Collegium Sancti Edmundi Sarum.

Valet videlicet in

[*Redditibus et Firmis*], £93 16s. 4d.

Reprise, videlicet in

Feodo Edwardi Crescet, generosi, Senescalli omnium Maneriorum et aliorum Tenementorum domus siue Collegij sancti Edmundi, nove Sarum, cui prepositi et Socij eiusdem domus per quoddam Scriptum suum dederunt et concesserunt officium predictum, prefato Edwardo, pro termino vite sue, Habendum pro Exercitione officij predicti quandam Annuitatem siue Annualem redditum quadraginta Solidorum per Annum exeuntem de possessionibus Collegij predicti, prout per idem Scriptum concessionis predicte plenius Apparet, 40s.

Feodo Nicholai Sulden, Collectoris Redditus omnium Tenementorum infra Ciuitatem nove Sarum predictam, per Annum, 20s.

Redditu Resoluto exeunte de terris predictis Reuerendo in Christo patri Johanni, Sarum Episcopo, annuatim soluto, 41s. 10d.

101s. 10d.

Et Remanet clare, Reprisis deductis, £88 14s. 6d.

Comitatus Wiltes. Certificate 56.

(Henry VIII.)

Johannes, Sarum Episcopus, Thomas Seymor, Miles, Robertus Chydley, Armiger, Thomas Leigh, et Willielmus Grene, generosi, commissionarij.

1. ECCLESIA CATHEDRALIS BEATE MARIE INFRA CIUITATEM NOVE SARUM.

Cantaria ex fundacione Egidij, quondam sarum Episcopi, qui constituit Vnum capellanum perpetuum ibidem et proficua eiusdem cantarie consistunt in quadam annuali pencione, 66s. 8d., exeunte de possessionibus nuper collegij, vocati scholars devawse, quam quidem Pencionem dictus capellanus recipit nomine salarij siue stipendij sui per Annum.

Eadem cantaria fundatur in ecclesia cathedrali predicte.

[*Annuus valor terrarum, &c.*], 66s. 8d.

Abusus aliquis non apparet [*eo quod Reuenciones et proficua eiusdem cantarie vtuntur et consumuntur secundum primam fundacionem eiusdem*].

[*Valor ornamentorum, &c.*], 69s.

3. Collegium sancti Edmundi, in ciuitate nove Sarum.

Vnde quis sit fundator non constat, sed benefactores multi, in quo collegio ad hoc presens Remanent Vnus Magister siue prepositus et quatuor capellani, quorum vnusquisque recipit pro salario siue stipendie suo annuatim, £6 13s. 4d.; necnon vnus Barbitonsor et vna lautrix, quorum vterque recipit pro salario, siue stipendio suo, per Annum, 10s. 8d., et residuum proficuorum terrarum et possessionum, tam spiritualium quam Temporalium, eiusdem collegij annuatim proueniunt ad manus Willielmi Seyntbarbe, Armigeri, Magistri, siue prepositi collegij predicti.

Idem collegium est parochialis Ecclesia in se.

Idem collegium [valet per annum], £93 16s. 4d. Inde in

Feodis, 60s.

Redditibus resolutis, 41s. 10d.

Et Remanet, £88 14s. 6d.

Abusus aliquis non apparet, eo quod nulla Fundacio dicti collegij remanet recitans intencionem eiusdem, sed Reuenciones suspradicti collegij, ultra £26 13s. 4d., pro stipendiis dictorum quatuor capellanorum, annuatim proueniunt ad manus predicti Willielmi Seyntbarbe, Armigeri.

8. Hospitale sancti Johannis in Hatysbury.

Ex fundacione Domine Margarete Hungerford, in quo adhuc Remanent Duodecim Homines pauperes et vna Mulier, pro quorum Manutencione dicta Margareta Hungerford dedit et concessit certas Terras et tenementa, Quarum terrarum Reuenciones et proficua, preter et vltra sustentacionem dictorum pauperum, annuatim proueniunt ad manus Johannis Benet, seruientis cuiusdam Willielmi Sherington, Armigeri.

Idem Hospitale fundatur prope ecclesiam parochialem de Hatysbury.

Idem Hospitale [valet per annum], £43 3s. 7½d. Inde in

Feodis, 13s. 4d.

Et Remanet, £42 10s. 3½d.

Abusus apparet, quia per primam fundacionem fundata fuit

quedam Schola gramatica, ultra sustentacionem predictorum
duodecim pauperum, cuius Schole gubernator annuatim reciperet
pro salario suo, £10, et nunc ibi remanent neque schole Magister
neque scolares in eadem.

"[*Valor ornamentorum*, &c.], 67s. 4d.

Comitatus Wiltes. Certificate 58.

(Edward VI.)

The booke of Survey of the Colleges and chaunteries, et
cetera, there, Datum Anno regni regis Edwardi VI[u]., secundo
[1548].

The countye of Wilteshire and cyttye off Newe Sarum.

Here Followyth the Reporte off the Surveye off all colleges, chauntrees, Free chappelles, Fraternytees, Brother-
heddis, Stypendaryees, Obbittes, lyghtes, lampes, and Anniuer-
saryes, Hauynge beynge within 5 yeres nexte before the 4th
daye of November laste paste, with all Mannours, landis, possessions, Hereditamentes, Stockes of money, Stockes of Cattal,
Goodis, Jewelles, Plate, and Ornamentes, to them or any of
them belonginge within the sayd countye and cytye, taken by
John Thynne and William Wroughton, Knyghts, Charles
Bulkeley, John Barwycke, and Thomas Chafynne, Esquires,
Wylliam Thornhyll and Laurence Hyde, gentylmen, By vertue
of the Kingis maiestie, his letters of commyssyon to them in
that behalf directed, beyrynge date the 14th daye of Februarye,
in the seconde yere of the reigne of oure moste dradde souereigne
lorde, Edwarde the syxte, by the grace of god, of Englande,
Fraunce, and Irelande Kinge, Defender of the Fayth, and in
Earth of the Churche of Englande, and also of Irelande, the
supreme Hedd, as hereafter is declared.

26. Westeleys Chauntre at Endforde.

Rychard morres, of the age of 56 yeres, incumbent, videlicet :

John Westley, decessyd, gave one thousand shepe to fynde a
preeste to synge at Endforde for euer, of whiche thousand shepe

dyed 692, wherevpon one parson Burde gave 578 shepe toward
the increase of the sayd stocke, whiche be nowe 886, praysed at
16*d*. the pese, and so letten to diuerse men for the yerely rent of
£7 14*s*. 6*d*.

The plate belongynge vnto the sayd chauntre, 30 ounces 1
quarter.

The goodis and Ornamentis belongynge vnto the sayd
chauntre, prised at 22*d*.

Memorandum : the sayd Incumbent is a verey honeste poore
man, and hathe none other lyvinge, but only this chauntre, And
a man ryght Able to serue a cure, and hathe alwayes occupyed
hym selfe in teachinge of children there.

30. The priorye or freechappell of saint John in Calne.

Robert Blake, of the age of 26 yeres, incumbent, videlicet :
The Rentis, &c. [*in Calne and Ufcote*], £4 8*s*. 4*d*. Whereof
Reprised for An yerely rente, &c., 3*s*. 5*d*.

And so Remaynyth clere, £4 4*s*. 11*d*.

Memorandum : the sayd Incumbent is no prieeste, but hadde
the sayd priorye or Freechappell gyven vnto hym for his Exibytyon to Fynde hym to scole.

33. A Chauntre in North Wroxall.

William Spenser, of the age of 20 yeres, incumbent, videlicet :
[*Lands in Northwroxall*], 44*s*. 8*d*.

Memorandum : the sayd Incumbent is a student in Oxforde,
but no prieeste ; and, ferthermore, a verey poore man, hauynge
no parentis, or any other lyvinge to kepe hym to scole.

36. Landis gyven for the mayntenaunce of a prieste within the parisshe of Westporte, in Malmesbery.

John Wimbolle, of the age of 54 yeres, stipendarye, videlicet :
[*Lands in Westport, &c.*], £6 9*s*. 3*d*. ; wherof
Reprised for [*Rents*], 14*s*. 6*d*.

And so Remaynyth clere, 114*s*. 9*d*.

The goodis apperteynynge vnto the said seruice, prised at 60*s*.

Memorandum : the sayd Incumbente is a verey honeste man, well learned, and ryght able to serue a Cure, albeit a poore man, and hath none other lyvinge, savinge one yerely pentyon of £6 owte of the late Monastery of Malmesbery. Also he dothe occupie hym self in bryngynge vppe yonge children in learnynge.

Also, the said towne of Malmesbery is a great towne, and but 2 parisshe churches, wherin be 860 people, wich Receyve the blessed communyon, and no prieeste to helpe the vicars in admynystracion of the sacramentis savinge the said stypendary preestis. Wherfore the inhabitauntis there desyre the Kingis moste Honorable Councell to consider them accordinglye.

42. CRYOURS CHAUNTRE.

Founded within the parisshe churche of FISSHERTON ANGER.

John Powell, of the age of 36 yeres, incumbent, videlicet :
[*Lands in Fisherton and Bemerton*], 119s. 8d. ; Wherof
Reprised for [*rents*], 17½d.
And so Remaynyth clere, 118s. 2½d.

Memorandum : the said Incumbent is a verey honeste man, and hadd the sayd Chauntre gyve vnto hym for and to his exibytyon to scole, Albeit he is no prieeste.

43. HORTONS CHAUNTRE.

Founded within the parisshe of BRADFORD.

William Furbner, of the age off 56 yeres, incumbent, videlicet :
[*Lands in divers placcs*], £11 18s. 3d. ; Wherof
Reprised for An yerelye rente, 12s. 4d.
And so Remaynyth clere, £11 5s. 11d.

The plate belongynge vnto the sayd chauntre, 17 ounces.

The goodis and Ornamentis belongynge vnto the said chauntre prised at 23s. 4d.

Memorandum : the sayd Incumbent is a verey honeste man, well learned, and ryght able to serue a cure, Albeit a verey poore man, and hathe none other lyvynge but the sayd chauntre; and, Ferthermore, he is bounde by the fundatyon to kepe a Free scole at Bradforde, and to gyve to the clerke ther yerely 20s. to teache children to synge, for the mayntenaunce of devine seruice, and also to distribute to the poore yerely 13s. 4d.; all which things he hathe done accordinglye.

Also, the sayd parisshe of Bradforde is a greate parisshe, within wiche be the number of 576 people, wiche receyve the blessed Communion, and no preeste to helpe the vicar there in administracion of the sacramentis savinge the said chauntre prieeste. Wherfore the parissheuers desire the Kingis mooste honourable councell to consider them accordinglye.

45. TERUMBERES CHAUNTRE.

Founded within the parisshe churche of TROWBRIDGE.

Robert Wheatacre, of the age of 42 yeres, incumbent, vide-licet:

[*Lands in divers places*], £23 3s. 10d.; Wherof

Reprised for yerely rentis, £7 14s. 9d.

And so Remaynyth clere, £15 9s. 1d.

The goodis and Ornamentes belongynge vnto the sayd chauntre, prised at 4s. 3d.

Memorandum : the sayd Incumbent is a verey honeste man, Well learned, and ryght able to serve a cure, Albeit a verey poore man, and hathe none other lyvinge but the sayd chauntre. And, Ferthermore, he hathe occupyed hym self in teachynge a scole there euer sith he came fyrste theder.

Also, the said parisshe of Trowbridge is a great parisshe, wherin be the number of 500 people, whiche receyve the blessed Communion, and no prieeste besidis the vicar to helpe in administracion savinge the sayd chauntre prieeste. Wherfore the Inhabytauntes there desyre the Kingis moste Honourable Councell to consyder them accordinglye.

54. A CHAUNTRE WITHIN THE PARISSHE CHURCHE OF SAYNT MARYE, IN MARLEBOROWE,

of the Fundatyon of Foster and Pengryve.

William Liwys, of the age of 60 yeres, Incumbente.

The towne of marleborowe is a great towne, wherin be 3 parisshe churches, and in the same 1,056 people, whiche receyve the blessed Communion, in euery of wiche parisshe churches there is a vicar indowed; Albeyt their lyvingis be so small and their cures so great that withoute helpe of some ministers they be not able to serue the sayd cures, and in consideratyon therof all the landis before mentyoned were gyven to haue contynuance, as before is declared. Wherfore the Mayre and Commons of the same towne desyre the Kingis mooste honourable councell to consyder them accordinglye.

Also, there is an Hospitall within marleborowe (Wherof the incumbente is ded) of the clere yerely valewe of £7 16s. 11¾d., wiche the sayd mayre and commons humbly desyre the Kingis Highnes and his mooste Honourable councell to converte into a Free scole for the inducement of youth within the same towne, and in the countrey nere thereaboute.

75. The Free chappell of Asserton,

in the parisshe of BARWICKE SAYNT JAMES.

Gyles Chestellthwayte, of the age of 26 yeres, Incumbente.

William Hulet holdith at will the Freechappell, with a cotage and a close of pasture adioininge, containing by estimation 1 rods [sic], togeyther with all maner of tythes, cummynge and rysynge in and vpon the Ferme of Asserton, and of 14 of acres the tennaundryes lande, and payith at the festis of the annunciacion of our lady and saint michel, 106s. 8d.

There is a bell in the sayd Chappell wayinge, by estimation [blank] lib, valewed at 20s.

Memorandum: the said Incumbent is a lay man, and hadd the sayd Freechappell gyven hym for his exibytyon at scole, whoe hadd in the said chappell a chalesse of siluer, with a payre of vestementis, wiche said Chalesse and vestementes he solde before the Feste of saynt mychaell, in the 38th yere of the reigne of King Henry the 8th.

80. THE FREECHAPPELL OF BACKEHAMPTON,
in the parisshe of AVEBERY.

John Warner, of the age of 40 yeres, Incumbente, videlicet :
[*Lands in Backchampton*], £4 8s.

Memorandum: the said Incumbente is Warden of Allsowles
College in Oxforde.

88. HEYTYSBERY.

Also there is one Hospitall in Heytysbery, called saynt
Johns hospitall, wiche was founded by one Margaret lady
Hungerforde for the sustentacion of a Scolemaster, 12 poore
men and one woman for euer.   The revenues wherof (ouer and
besydis 13s. 4d. goynge oute of the same) do amounte to the
clere yerelye valewe of £42 10s. 3½d., Albeyt there hathe bene
no scolemaster by the space of these 5 or 6 yeres, but the pore
persons only ; and, ferthermore, Sir William Sheryngton perceyvith the issues of the same, but by what Auctoryte we know
not ; the perfecte Survey of the premissis we haue not taken for
the cause afore declared.

ASSHETON KEYNES.

Adam de Purton, Knyght, gave by his dede, made before the
conqueste, all his landis and hereditamentes lyinge in Crudwell,
in the countie of Wilteshire, to the vicar of Assheton Keynes,
and to his successors vicars there for euer, to the Intente the
sayd vicar for the tyme beynge shuld fynd a prieeste to synge
for the soule of the sayd Adam, Cycelye and Sare his wives,
within the sayd churche for euer, wiche landis Amounte to the
yerelye valewe of 35s., Albeit Rychard porte, nowe vicar of
Assheton Keynes, sayth vpon his othe that there was no
prieeste founde or mayntened by the same within the remembraunce of man ; and, ferther, sayth that he is charged with
the sayd somme in the Courte of tenthes as parcell of his said
vicarege.

The Countie of Wilteshire and cytye of Newe Sarum.
Certificate 105.
(Edward VI.)

PARISHE OF SAYNT THOMAS IN SARUM. p. 4.

*   *   *   *   *

Also there be within the sayd parisshe of saynt Thomas the number of 1,652 people wiche receyve the blessyd Communion [*&c.*].

And furthermore the Cytye of Newe Sarum is a goodly Cytye and well peopled, as it is well knowen, full of youth, in consyderatyon wherof if hit myght please the Kingis Highnes and his moste honorable counsell to appoynt a Scole mayster there for the Inducement of youth, hit wold not only serue the sayd Cytye, but also the countrey nyghe adioyning.

This is to be considered for a Schole.

CRYOWRS CHAUNTRE, FYSSHERTON ANGER. p. 9.

Founded within the parisshe Churche of Fyssherton Anger.
John powell, of the age of 36 yeres, incumbente.

The clere yerely yalewe of the said chauntre ouer and besydis 10s. 11½d. deducted for the tenthes, 107s. 3d.

Pencion, 100s.

Memorandum : the sayd Incumbent is no prieeste, but a laye man, and hadd this Chauntre gyven hym for and to his exhibytyon to the Schole.

HORTONS CHAUNTRE, BRADFORD.

Founded within the parisshe of Bradforde. William Furbner, of the age of 56 yeres, Incumbente.

The Clere yerely valew of the sayd Chauntre ouer and besidis 13s. 4d. deducted for the tenthes, £10 12s. 7d.

Memorandum : the sayd Incumbent is a verey honest poore man, well lerned, and well able to serue a Cure.

Also this Chauntre was founded purposely for the mayntenaunce of a Fre scole, and for none other Intente, Wiche the sayd Incumbent hath kepte accordinglye euer sith the foundatyon.

Also he is bounde by the Foundatyon to Distribute to the poore yerely 13s. 4d., and to the clerke there 20s. to teache children to synge, all wiche he hath done accordinglye.

Also the sayd parisshe of Bradford is a great parisshe, Wherin be the number of 576 people, wiche receyve the blessed communion, and no prieeste to helpe the vicar there in administration of the sacramentis savinge the sayd chauntre prieeste. Wherfore the parissheners desire the Kingis moste honourable councell to consyder them accordinglye.

Continuatur the Schole with the accustumed wages.

TERUMBERES CHAUNTRE.

Founded within the parisshe churche of TROWBRUDGE.   p. 10.

Robart Wheteacre, of the age of 42 yeres, Incumbent.

Nota a Schole.

The clere yerely valewe of the sayd Chauntre neuer heretofore contributory to the tenthes, £15 9s. 1d.

Memorandum: the sayd Incumbent is a verey honeste poore man, well lerned and well able to serue a Cure, Whoe hathe alwayes kept a Freescole in Trowbrydge, and yet dothe, for the Inducemente of Children.

Also the sayd parisshe of Trowbridge is a great parisshe, where be the number of 500 people wiche receyve the blessed Communion, and no priest besydis [*illegible*] vycar to helpe in administracion savinge the sayd Chauntre prieeste. Wherfore the inhabitauntis there desire the Kingis mooste honorable councell to consider them accordinglye.

Appointed the schole to continue quousque with the accustumed wages.

THE PRYORYE OR FREECHAPPELL OF SAYNT JOHNS IN CALNE.   p. 13.

Robert blake, of the age of 26 yeres, Incumbente.

The clere yerely valewe of the same ouer and besidis 4s. 3¼d. deducted for the tenthes, £4 0s. 7¾d.

Pencion, £4 0s. 7d.

Memorandum: the said Incumbent is no prieeste, but hadd

the said priorye or Freechappell gyven vnto hym for his Exibityon to fynde hym to the scole.

HEYTISBURY HOSPITAL.

p. 16. Also there is one hospitall in Heytisbery called saynt Johns Hospitall, wiche was Founded by Margaret Lady Hungarforde for the sustentacyon of a scole master, 12 poore men, and one woman for euer, the Scole master to haue yerely £10, the revenues Wherof (ouer and besidis 13s. 4d. goynge owte of the same) do amounte to the clere yerely valew of £42 10s. 3½d. Albeit there hathe bene no scole master by the space of 5 or 6 yeres but the poore persons only; and Ferthermore Sir William Sheryngton perceyvith the Issues of the same, but by what Auctorite we knowe not; the perfyte Survey of the premissis We have not take [sic], for the cause above declared.

Decima inde, 76s.

Remanet, £38 14s. 3½d.

This to continue.

WARMESTER. p. 17.

*   *   *   *   *

Also the said towne is well peopled [*number of people*, 400], and specyally with youth, a place vercy mete to haue a Freescole in, if it myght so stand with the Kingis pleasure and his moste honorable councell; toward the Erectyon wherof, if it myght please the Kingis Highnes to gyve the said landis, the inhabitauntes there wold bye so moche more as shuld make hit vppe £10, wich, if hit maye take effecte, will do moche good in all that countrey.

Nota, a mete place for a Schole.

Examinatur per L. Hyde, Deputatum.

Johannis Thynne, Militis, superuisorem.

Wilts. Schools Continuation Warrant, 1.

Forasmoche as it apperith [&c.] that a grammer Scole hath been contynnuallye kepte in Bradforde, in the said Countie, with the reuenues of the late Chaunterie called Hirtone chauntrie, in

Bradforde aforesaid, And that the Scolemaster there haith had for his Stipende and wages yerelie, £11 5s. 11d. [&c.].

And that a grammer Scole hath been kepte contynuallie in Trowbrigge in the said Countie, with the reuenues of the late Chauntrie called Terumberes chaunterie, in Trowbrigge aforesaid, And that the Scolemaster there hath had yerelie for his stipende and wages, £15 9s. 1d. [&c.].

We therefore [&c.] have assigned and appoynted that [&c.] the said Scole in Bradforde aforesaid shall contynue, And that William Furbner, Scolemaster there, shall contynue in the same Rome of Scolemaster, and shall haue for his stipende and wages yerely, £11 5s. 11d. [&c.],

And that the said grammer Scole in Trowbrigge aforesaid shall contynue, and Robert Whiteacre, Scole master there, shall haue and enjoye the rome of Scolemaster there, And shall haue for his wages yerelie, £15 9s. 1d.

Countie of Worcester. Certificate 25.

(Henry VIII.)

Commission addressed to John, Bishop of Hereford, Nicholas, Bishop of Worcester, Sir Robert Acton, Knt., John Pakyngton, Esq., Thomas Burgoyn, Esq., George Gifforde, Esq., & Richard Cowper, gent. (*Certificate made by the four last-named.*)

THE DEANRIE OF BURFORD.
12. ROCK.

The Chauntrye of owre blessed lady and saint George, Wythein the parishe Churche of Rokke, otherwise called Raka.

The said chaunterye was Founded by Humffrey Connysbie, Knyght, in the fryste yere of the Regne of owre Souereigne Lorde Kynge Henrie the eight, by his graces lycence vnder the Greate Seale of Englonde, For one preste to saye masse and other dywyne seruice Within the saied Church for his grace is prosperitie, and Alsoe to Fynde and mayntayn A Free Scole, For the continuance Wherof the said Humffrey gaue certen landes and Tenementes to the saied Chauntery, As by the said license shewed vnto the said Commissioners may Apere.

The yerely valew Accordynge to the boke of 10ths, £6 10s.

The yerely valew Accordynge to thys surveye, £7 14s. 8d. Wherof In

Tenthes yerely payable vnto the Kynges magestie, 13s.

Rentes Resolutes, likewise yerely payable vnto His grace, 12s.

For the sustentacion of An obite, 15s. 8d.; in the whole, 40s. 8d.

The clere yerely valew, 114s., Wiche is Imployed to the sustentacion And mayntenaunce of A preste And Reparacion of the houses.

The valew of the ornamentes Accordynge to An Inuentorie, 7s. 2d.

The Countie of Worcettour. Certificate 60.

(Edward VI.)

5. THE PARYSHE OF SEYNT NICHOLAS,

within the Citie of worcettor, wherin be of houselyng people the nomber of six hunderth.

The Guylde or fraternytie of the Trynytie, in the paryshe of saynt Nicholas aforesaid.

John Olyuer, bacheler of arte, Incumbent there, of the age of thyrtie yeres, well learnyd, and of honeste conuersacion.

The yerely valewe of all the landes and tenementes belongyng to the said guylde as apperythe by the particuler of the same, £13 17s. 7d. ; wherof

In repryses yerely owt of the same, 26s. 6d.

And so remains clere, £12 11s. 1d.

Plate, 18 ounces.

Goodes, presid at £11.

Prechers, None.

A Scoole, as in the Memorandum vnder wrytten apperyth.

To the poore owt of the clere yerely valewe, 107s. 4d.

Memorandum : hit was presented by John Callowe, Maister of the said Guylde; Thomas wylde, and Richarde Dedycote, baylyfes of the said Citie ; Robert yowll, aldermann, of the

same Citie; Thomas Parton, Citizen; Thomas Johnson and
Richard hasyllocke, Stewardes or wardens of the said Guylde,
that there hath byn tyme owt of mynde a Free scole kept within
the said Citie in a grete hall belongyng to the said Guylde called
the Trynitie hall, the scole master wherof for the tyme beyng
hath hade yerely for his stypend ten poundes, wherof was paid
owt of the reueneus of the said landes by the Master and
stewardes of the said Guylde for the tyme beyng, £6 13s. 4d.,
And the resydewe of the said stypend was collected and gathered
of the deuocion and benyuolence of the brothers and systers of
the said Guylde; And, further, hit was presentid that by the
space of foure or fyve yeres or more last past or there aboutes
the walls of the said Citie, and one great stone brydge with
ten Arches within the same Citie, called Syuerne brigge, and
the said tenementes, howsis, and cotages belongyng to the said
Guylde, were ruynous and in greate decaye, By reason wherof
they lefte the kepyng of the said Scolemaster by the said space
of foure or fyve yeres or more, and Imployed and bestowed the
said money that dyd vse to fynde the saide Scolemaster, to the
necessary reparacions of the said walles, brigges, howses, tenementes, and cotages, and the same being repayred, they, before
the Feaste of seynt michaell the archaungell last past, prouyded
and haue founde an honest lernyd Scolemaster within the said
hall in lyke maner as they before tyme dyd; that is to say, one
John Olyuer, bachelor of Arte, who hathe there at this present
tyme aboue the number off a hundred Scolers.

10. The paryshe of Kyngsnorton,

within the said Countie of Worcettor, wherein be of houselyng
people the nomber of nyne hundreth.

There be three stipendaryes or seruices within the said parishe,
wherof one hath allweys tought a fre Gramer scole, the parishe
havyng nede there vnto, as in the remembraunce vnder wrytten
doth more appere.

Herry Saunders, Master of Arte, of the age of fortie yeres, one
of the said stypendaries and scolemaster there, of honest conuersacion, and well learnyd; laurence Blackewey, one other of the

said stypendaryes, of the age of thirtie and syx yeres, learnyd, and of honeste conuersacion; John peart, being no priste, but vssher of the said scole, well learnyd, and of honest conuersacion.

The yerely valewe of all the landes and tenementes Imployed to the vse of the said stypendaries or seruyces, £25 10s. 3½d.; whereof

In repryses yerely owt of the same, 46s. 1d.

And so remains clere, £23 4s. 2½d.

Prechers, None.

Scoole, as in the remembraunce vnderwrytten dothe appere.

To the poore out of the clere yerely valewe, 13s. 4d.

Memorandum : that the said paryshe is 7 myles brode euery waye, and fortie myles compas, and that many of the same parishe do dwell foure myles frome the parishe churche, and, therfore there is one Chappell buylde by the parysshoners there at a village called Moseley, where that Sir laurence Blackewey dothe mynyster the sacramentes and other necessarie vsagis in the said churche to dyuers the Inhabitantes of the said parishe dwellyng nere to the said chappell, which is twoo myles dystante frome the said paryshe churche ; And, furder, that the hole landes belongyng to the said parysshoners, as apperyth by a rentall, dothe amounte to the clere yerely valewe of twentie foure poundes ten shillynges ten pence halfpenny, of whiche landes dyuers of the said parysshe be enfeoffed by sundry dedes declaryng no vse, Neuerthelesse they have vsed to bestowe parte of the rentes therof some tyme to the fyndyng of one pryste, some tymes to the fyndyng of two prystes, some tyme three prystes, of whiche prystes one dyd alwayes kepe a free Scoole, And when they hade but one or twoo prystes they then bestowed the reste of the Issues and proffytes of the said landes in mendyng and repayryng of decayed brydges and highe wayes, releuyng of the poore people, and other cherytable almes and good dedes, And for thes twoo yeres paste withe the same they have founde an vssher as aforesaid to ayde the same Scolemaster, now beyng charged with the teachyng and Instructyng of an hundreth and twentie scollers, And a pryste to serue in the said chappell of Moseley.

11. THE PARYSHE OF BROMSGROVE,
wherin be of houselyng people the number a thousande.

Landes and tenementes employed to the mayntenaunce of a Stypendary pryste within the said parishe churche.

Wyllyam Foyns, Incumbent, of the age of thyrtie yeres, learnyd, and of honeste conuersacion.

The yerely valewe of all the landes and tenementes employed to the vse aforesaid, as apperyth in the particuler of the same, £11 11s. 8d.; wherof

In repryses owte yerely of the same, 2s. 10d.

And so remains clere, £11 8s. 10d.

Prechers, None.

Schoole, as in the memorandum vnder wrytten apperpth.

To the poore yerely out of the same, 14s. 6d.

Memorandum: that seven pounde parcell of the foreseid some of £11 8s. 10d. hath byn allwayes employed towardes the fyndyng of a scole master, being a pryste, who was not only bounde to kepe a scole there, but also to ayde and assiste the ·Curate there, consyderyng the said paryshe is very large, and some vilagis within the same being foure myles dystante frome the parishe churche; And the ouerplus of the said some of eleven pounde eight shillynges and ten pence hathe byn bestowed yerely vpon the reparacions of the said churche, setting ·of Sodyers forewarde to the warres, repayryng hygh wayes and bridges, and suche like cherytable dedes within the said paryshe.

20. THE PARYSHE OF OLDE SWYNEFORD, [STOURBRIDGE]
wherin be of houselyng people the nomber of 700.

Landes and tenementes Imployed to the vse of one stypendary pryste within the chapell of Sturbrydge within the said paryshe.

Nycholas Rock, Incumbent, of the Age of fyftie and foure yeres, lernde, and of honest conuersacion, but for certen Impedymentes not able to kepe a Cure.

The yerely valewe of the said landes and tenementes, as in the particulers therof playnly apperyth, £6 6s. 7d.; wherof

In Repryses owt of the same, 6s. 6d.

And so remains clere, £6 0s. 1d.

Prechers, None.

A Scoole, as in the memorandum vnder wytten apperyth.

To the poore out of the same yerely valewe, 20d.

Memorandum : that the said stypendary pryste hath all wayes vsed, and yett dothe vse, to kepe a Scoole in a markett Towne called Sterbrydge, beyng within the said paryshe, and a myle dystante frome the paryshe churche, whiche Stypendary pryste stode charged to teache the pore mens chyldren of the same paryshe Frely ; In whiche Markett Towne the said stypendary pryste dyd alwayes vse to saye masse in a chapell there, and hathe also vsed in tymes of necessytie to ayde and assyste tha curate there, the parishe beyng very large and brode.

21. THE PARYSHE OF CHADDESLEY CORBETT,

wherin be of houselyng people the nomber of fyve hundreth.

Landes and tenementes Imployed to the vse of a Stypendary or scolemaster within the said paryshe.

The yerely valewe of all the landes and tenementes, as in the particuler of the same playnly apperyth, 103s. 8d. ; wherof

In repryses yerely out of the same, 5s. 4d.

And so remains clere, £4 18s. 4d.

Prechers, None.

A Scoole, as in the memorandum vnder wrytten apperyth.

Memorandum : that the said some of foure poundes, eightene shillynges, and foure pence was alwayes employed to the vse of a pryste that did vse to teache the chyldren of the paryshe, but yet they did not shewe forthe no foundacion therof.

24. THE PARYSHE OF ROCKE,

otherwise called Raka, wherin be of hoselyng people the nomber of two hundreth and three score.

The Chaunterye of our Lady within the parishe churche

yarde of Rocke aforesaid, founded by Syr humfrey Conyngby, knyght, to continewe for euer.

John Ree, Incumbent, of the age of three score and tenne yeres, learnyd, and of honeste conversacion.

The yerely valewe of all the landes and tenementes belongyng to the said Chaunterye, as in the particuler therof playnly apperyth, £6 8s. 4d.; wherof

In repryses owt of the same yerely, 12s.

And so remains clere, 116s. 4d.

Prechers, None.

A Scoole, as in the memorandum vnderwrytten apperyth.

To the poore yerely owt of the same, 3s. 4d.

Memorandum: that the Incumbentes of the said Chaunterye have allwayes sethens the firste foundacion therof tawght a gramer scole, takyng nothyng therfore of the pore men, accordyng to the foundacion of the same chaunterye.

35. EVESHAM. THE PARYSHE OF SEYNT LAURENCE,

within the said Towne of Evesham, wherin be of houselyng people the nomber of fyve hundreth.

Landes and tenementes there Imployed to the vse and fynding of thre stypendary prystes within the said parishe churche.

John Wylmotes, of the age of three score yeres; Richard Swaton, of the age of fyftye two yeres; and Wyllyam lane, of the age of fyftie yeres, Incumbentes of honest conuersacion, and competently learnyd.

The yerely valewe of all the said landes and tenementes, as apperythe in the particulers therof, £13 17s. 2d.; wherof

In repryses yerely out of the same, 25s. 7d.

And so remains clere, £12 11s. 7d.

Prechers, None.

A Scoole, as in the memorandum vnder wrytten apperyth.

Memorandum: hit was presented that sethens the reign of the noble prynce of famowse memory, kyng Edward the thirde, there hath byn payd by the Abbottes of the late Monastery of Evesham for the tyme beyng yerely the some of ten poundes, with meate and drynke, frely, withe in the said late Monasterye, to one scolemaster for the kepyng of a free Gramer scole in the said Towne of Evesham, vntyll the surrender of the said late Monasterye ; Sethens which tyme the kynges Maiesties Receavor of his highnes Revenues there, for the tyme beyng, hath lykewyse payed yerely too the said Scolemaster ten poundes for his teaching of the said Free scoole vntyll the feaste of the Annunciacion of our lady last paste ; And the said towne of Evesham is a greate Markett towne, and a greate thorowghfare frome the Marches of Walys to london ; And that there is noo scole within twelve Myles of the said towne of Evesham.

Summa of the hole yerely valewe videlicet of
The Chaunteryes Gyldes, fraternyties [&c.], £349 5s. 9d.
Repryses yerely, £24 15s. 6d.
The yerely paymentes to the poore £12 18s. 1d.
Summa of plate, goodes, ornamentes, and stockes of Cattell, £24 3s. 8d. ; and of plate, 66½ ounces.

The County of Worcester. Certificate 61.

(Edward VI.)

THE CYTIE OF WORCESTER.

PARISHE OF SAYNT NICHOLAS.

6. The Guyld of the holy Trynyte, within the said paryshe and Cytie.

Memorandum : there is a house called the Trynitie Hall, with certen landes and tenementes belongyng to the said Guylde to the clere yerely value of £13 17s. 10d., whych hath byn always employed as hit was presented before the Kynges Maiestyes Commyssioners there, to the mayntennaunce of one scolemaster ther to teche Freely Gramer, £6 13s. 4d. ; And to diuers pore people Inhabyting in 24 Cotages or Almshouses adioynyng to the Trynite Hall there, 107s. 4d. As aforesaid. And so remayneth of the said some but 37s. 2d., which some the

presenters did afferme to be not sufficient for the yerely repayryng of the said Hall, cotages, and Almeshouses.

Memorandum : that John Olyver, Clerke, is now scolemaster
there, and hath yerely tenn merkes For his wagis.

*Continuatur quousque the pore; for the Schole may cease,
for ther is one other in the towne of the Kinges fundacion;
and this is no Schole of any purpos, as it is credebly said.*

THE DEANRIE OF WYCHE.

9. THE PARISHE OF KYNGSNORTON,
wherein be of houselyng people the nomber of 900.

There be three Stipendaries within the said parishe.   The
Incumbentes wherof :

Henry Saunders hathe for his stipend, being a Scolemaster,
£10.

Contynewe the Schole quousque.

Laurence Blackeway hathe for his stipend, seruing at the
chapell of Moseley, yerely, £4 13s. 4d.

Continuatur quousque the chapell of Ease.

John Peart, being no prist, but vssher of the Freescole ther by
the space of these 2 yeres last past, hath for his pencion 100s.

Continuatur the vssher of the Schole quousque.

Precher, none.

Scolemaster, the said Henry Saunders.

To the poore, 13s. 4d.

Vssher of the said scole, John Peart.

Memoranda : hit was presented before the kynges Maiesties
Comyssioners there that the said parishe is 7 myles brode euery
way and 40 myles compas, and that many of the same parishe
do dwell 4 myles from the parishe churche, and therfore there
is one chapell buylded by the parishioners there at a village
called Moseley, where the sir laurence Blackway doth mynyster
the sacramentes and other necessarie vsages in the churche to
dyuers the Inhabytantes of the said parishe dwellyng nere to
the said chappell, which is 2 myles distant from the said parishe
churche.

And hyt was furtder presented that the hole landes belonging
to the said parishioners, as apperith by a rentall therof, dothe
amounte to the clere yerely value of £24 10*s.* 10½*d.*, of which
landes dyuers of the said parishe be enfeoffed by sundry dedes
declaryng no vse; neuerthelesse they have vsed to bestowe
parte of the rentes therof sometyme to the fyndyng of one prist,
sometymes 2 pristes, some tymes 3 pristes, of which pristes one
did alwayes kepe a Free scole; And when they hade but one or
2 pristes, then they bestewed the reste of the issues and
proffites of the said landes in mendyng and repeyryng of
decayed brydges and high wayes, releuyng of the pore people,
and other cheritable and godlye dedes, And for theis 2 yeres
paste with the same they have founde an vssher, as aforesaid, to
ayde the same Scole master, now being charged with the teaching and instructing of an hundred and 20 scollers, And a pryst
to serue in the said chapell of Moseley.

10. The parishe of Bromsgroue,
wherein be a houselyng people the number of 1,000.

There is one Chauntrye, called Staffordes chauntery, within
the said parish, And one scolemaster being prist within the
same parishe, the Incumbentes wherof:

Thomas Jamys, chauntery prist there, hath yerely paid out
of the Maner of Sorford, in the Countie of Northampton, in the
nature of a rent charge, £6 13*s.* 4*d.*; vnde pro decimis domino
Regi, 13*s.* 4*d.*   £6.

Pencion, 100*s.*

William Foonys, now Scolemaster there, hath yerely for his
wages out of certen landes and tenementes to the yerely value
of aleven pounde fortene pence, wherof dyuers of the parishoners
bee enfeffede, declaryng no vse therin, £7.

Continuatur the Schole quousque etcetera.

Prechers, none.

Scolemaster there, the said William Foonys.

To the pore people, 14*d.*

Memorandum: hit was presented before the Kinges Maiesties

Commissioners that the said landes of £11 14d. being in feofment to dyuers of the parishioners there, no vse declared therin ; Neuerthelesse, £7 parcell of the said £11 14d. hath byn employed towardes the fyndyng of a Scolemaster, being a prist and assisting the curate there, consideryng the paryshe is very large, And the nomber of the houselyng people as afore-said, some dwelling 4 Miles from the church and more, And the ouerplus of the said £11 14d. hath byn bestowed yerely vpon the reparacions of the church there and settyng forth of Soldyars to the kynges warrs, repeyryng of highweys and bridges, and suchlyke charitable dedes within the said parishe.

The Deanry of Kethermyster.

16. The parishe of Olde Swynford [Stourbridge],
wherin bee of houselyng people the nomber of 700.

There is one stipende prist within the said parishe, the incombent wherof :

Nycholas Rocke, stypend prist there, hathe yerely for his stipend and salarye £6 4d.

Prechers, none.

Scolemaster, the said [blank].

Continuatur Schole quousque, etcetera.

Memorandum : hit was presented before the kinges Maiesties Commyssioners that the said stipendary prist hathe alwayes vsed, and yet doth, to kepe a scole in a Market towne called Sturbrydge, being within the same parishe, And a mile distante frome the parishe churche, And stode charged to teache the poore children of the same parishe Freely, In whiche market towne the said stipende prist dyd vse to saye masse within a chapell there, And hath also vsed in tymes of necessitie to aide and assist the curate ther, the paryshe being very large and brode.

17. The parishe of Chadsley Corbett,
wherin be of houselyng people the number of 500.

There is one Stipende prist in the said parishe, the in-

cumbent wherof hathe yerely for his stipende and salary
103s. 2d.

Prechers, none.

Scolemaster, none namyd as yet.

Memorandum : the parishoners there did present that they
hade vsed to give the said some of 103s. 2d. to a priste that did
vse to teache children, but they namyd no prist nor they did
shew no foundacion.

Respectuatur.

THE DEANRY OF BURFORDE.

20. THE PARISHE OF ROCK,

wherin be of houselyng people the nomber of 260.

There is one chauntery within the said parishe, the Incumbent wherof. John Ree, Chauntery prist there, hath yerely,
the 10th deducted, 114s.

Prechers, none.

The chauntery prist was bound by the foundacion to tech
there all pore mens children Free.

To the poore, 3s. 4d.

Continuatur the Schole quousque.

Memorandum : the Incumbentes of the said chauntery have
alwayes, Sethens the first foundacion of the said chauntery
taught a Gramer scole, taking nothing therfore, of poore mens
children, accordyng to the foundacion of the same Chauntery.

THE DEANRY OF POYKE.

28. THE PARISHE OF LYGHE,

wherin be of houselyng people the nomber of 340.

There is one stipendarye prist within the said parishe. The
Incumbent, John Kaysse, hath yerely for his salary and stipend
in rentes 42s. 8d.

Pencion, 40s.

Prechers, none.

The said prist hath vsed to teache a free scole.

Respectuatur.

The Deanry of Evesham.

31. The parishe of seynt lawrence, in Evesham,
wherin be of hoselyng people the nomber of 600.

There is within the said parishe one chauntery and 3 perpetuities, or Stypendary pristes, the Incumbentes wherof ar:

Thomas Saunders hathe yerely for his stipende, 106s. 8d. *Apoyneted to assist the Cure with his accustomed wages.*

John Wylmottes hathe yerely for his stipende and salary, 106s. 8d.

Pencion, 100s.

William Swaton hathe yerely for his stipend clere, 106s. 8d.

Pencion, 100s.

William Lane hathe yerely for his stipende with [*blank*] markes goyng out of certen Mills, called harvington Mills, £4.

Pencion, £4.

Prechers, none.

There hath byn alweys and yet is a free Grammer scole, and the scolemaster there hath hade £10 by yere as more at large hereafter apperithe.

Memoranda: hit was presented before the Kinges Maiesties Comissioners that sithens the Reign of the noble prince of famose memorie, Kyng Edward the therde, there hath byn paid by the Abbottes of the late Monasterie of Evesham for the tyme being, yerely, the some of £10, And borde and tabelyng frely in the late Monasterie, to one scolemaster for the keping of a free Scole in the said Towne of Evesham vntyll the surrender of the said late Monastery, Sethens whiche tyme the Kinges Maiesties Receuer of his hignes reuenewis there for the tyme beyng hath lykewise paid yerely to the said Scolemaster £10 for teaching of the said free Scole, vntyll the feast of the annunciacion of our lady last past, And the same Towne of Evesham is a Greate Market towne and muche resorted.

In consideracion wherof, And forasmoche as Sir John Robyns, now vicar of the said parishe of seint lawrence, within the said Towne, being an honest man and well lernyd, his benefice being valued in the booke of tenth at £9 by yere, by reason that as well all the Gentelmen, being seruauntes within the said late Monasterye, as the yomen and other seruantes there to the nomber of some score housleyng people and more, dide vse to paye there prive tythes and offeringes to the vicare there for the tyme being, which wase worthe £4 and aboue yerely more then it is at this daye, Soo that his hole lyving is not 100s. by yere for keping of that Geate Cure; Hit myght therefore please your Good Mastershipps to appoynt the said sir John Robyns to kepe the foresaid free Scole, now being voyde, or els by your dyscrecions to appoynte to hym some lyving, If it maye soo stande with the Kynges Maiesties pleasure.

Examinatur per Willelmum Grene, Superuisorem ibidem.

Forasmuche as by letters from Sir philyp hoby, knight, I ame Credible aduertised that one sir humfry Attewood, alius taylor, preist, was incumbent and master of the said Schole vntyll white sonday last past, at wiche tyme he Departed for lake of wages, and that he is a man of veary good learninge and honestye, And that the said vicare is, nayther for Learninge nor honestie, nothinge so mete nor sufficient for that Rome as he, Therfore Apoynte the said Atwood to this office of Scole Master with the accustomed wages of £10, notwithstandinge any other comaundement hertofore gyven, wherin suffer him to Remayne vntill further order shall be therin taken.

Worcester. Schools Continuance Warrant, 11.

Forasmoche as it appereth [&c.] that a Scole and dyuerse poore people inhabytinge in 24 Cotages or Almeshowses in Worcettour haue been yerely kepte and susteynid with the revenues of the Guylde of the Holy Trynyte within the parishe of saynt Nicholas, in the Citie of Worcettour.

And that a grammer Schole hath been contynuallye kepte in Kyngesnorton [&c.].

And that a grammer Schole hathe been contynuallie kepte in Bromsgrove [&c.].

And that a grammer Schole hathe been contynuallie kepte

in Rocke [&c.], and that the Scholemaster there hathe had [&c.] 114s. [&c.].

And also that a grammer Schole hathe been contynuallie kepte in Evesham [&c.], And that the Scolemaster there hathe had [&c.] £10 [&c.].

Wee therefore [&c.] haue assigned [&c.] that the saide schole in the parishe of Saynte Nicholas, in Worcetour aforesaide shall continue, and that the Scholemaster there shall haue [&c.] £6 18s. 4d. [&c.].

And that the said Schole in Kyngesnorton aforesaide shall contynue, and that Henry Saunders, Scholemaster there, shall haue [&c.] £10 [&c.].

And that John Porte, Vssher of the Schole in Kinges Norton [&c.], shall haue [&c.] 100s.

And that the saide Schole in Bromsgrove shall contynue, and that William Fones, Scholemaster there, shall haue [&c.] £7.

And that the saide Schole in Rocke shall contynue, and that John Ree, Scholemaster there, shall haue [&c.] 114s. [&c.].

And that the saide Schole in Evesham shall contynue, and that John Robyns shall haue [&c.] £10.

Comitatus Wigornie. Particulars for Schools. Roll 12.

STOURBRIDGE GRAMMAR SCHOOL.

Parcelle possessionum nuper Collegii de Fodringhaye, in Comitatu Northamptonie, in manu Regis per Actum parliamenti inter alia existencium.

Markeley et Suckeley, in Comitatu Wigornie; valent in

Pencionibus et porcionibus, videlicet, in Markeley 40s., et Suckeley, £4, parcellis dicte nuper Collegii de Fodringhaye, per annum, £6.

Parcelle nuper. Canterie, siue servicii sancte Trinitatis, beate Marie et Sancti Clementis, in parochia Sancti Laurencii, in villa de Evesham, in Comitatu Wigornie.

Parcelle terrarum et tenementorum, in villa de Evesham, in
Comitatu predicto, dicte nuper Cantarie pertinencium; valent
In [Redditibus], 118s. 4d. Inde
Reprise videlicet in Redditu Resoluto, 20s. 2d.
Et valent clare, per annum, £4 18s. 2d.

Parcelle nuper servicie, siue Canterie beate Marie et Sancti
Georgii in parochia Omnium Sanctorum, in villa de Evesham, in
Comitatu predicto.

Parcelle terrarum et tenementorum in Eveshame predicta,
dicte nuper Servicie pertinencium; valent in [Redditibus], 23s.

Parcelle nuper Canterie, siue servicie beate Marie et Sancte
Katerine, in parochia Sancte Elene, in Ciuitate Wigornie, nuper
fundate.

Parcelle terrarum et tenementorum in Ciuitate Wigornie,
eidem nuper Canterie pertinencium; valent in [Redditibus], 33s.

Parcelle possessionum nuper Guilde Sancte Trinitatis, in
Ciuitate Wigornie predicta fundate.

Parcelle terrarum et tenementorum in Ciuitate Wigornie
predicta, dicte nuper guilde pertinencium; valent in [Reddi-
tibus], £4 5s. 10d. Inde Reprise videlicet in Redditu Resoluto,
9s. 4d.

Et valent clare, 76s. 6d.

Memorandum : the Chapell of Sturbrige, with the parcell of
grounde wherin the same ys scytuat, containing per estimacion one Rod, the valowe wherof appointed to be certyfied in the
warraunte directed from the Right wurshipfull Sir Richarde
Sackvyle, knight, Chauncellour of the Counte of Augmentacions, etc., ys not mencyoned in valowe in the Surveye of
Chauntryes and [faded] certyfied by the Surveyour vnto thau-
ditour. Neuertheless, the landes and tenementes ar[e] [faded]
and belongninge to the Service foundid within the said Chapell
of the yerely v[alew of] £6 6s. 7d., byn all sold amongest others
to William Wynlow and Richard [faded] and their heyres,

by the kinges maiestis lettres patentes in that behaulf showid
unto . . .

Examinatur per me Johannem Hanbie, Auditorem.

Primo Junii, Anno Regni Regis Edwardi vjth., quinto [1551].
The premisses to be graunted to certen persons, and to there
heires to have continuance [*faded*] For the free teaching of
Children within the towne of Stourbridge, within [the county]
of Worcester. And the sayd persons to be called gouernors of
the sayd [*faded*] King Edward the vjths foundacion, To hold
the premisses in Socage, And [*faded*] thissues from the annuncyacion of our lady last past, with a clause to be contayned
in the sayd patent that the kinges maiestie may cause visitacions to be made of the said Scole when his highnes shall
think convenyent.

Totalis clare, £17 10s. 8d.

(*Signed*), Ry. Sa   [*faded*]

The Counties of York, the Cytye of York, and Kyngeston upon Hulle. Certificate 66.

(Henry VIII.)

THE DEANERYE OF THE CRISTIANYTIS OF YORK.

Robert, archbishopp of Yorke, Syr Mychaell Stannop, knight,
Syr Leonard Bekwith, knight, Wyllyam Babthorp, Robert
Chaloner, Robert Hennage, Richard Whalley, esquyers, Thomas
Gargrave, Richard Norton, Humfrey Bowland, gentlemen, Com-
missioners.

23. The Chauntery of Oure Ladye withyn the sayd Churche
[of Yorke, *i.e.* the Cathedral Church].

Crystofer Bentley, incumbent. The same is made by th'
archebysshope, deane and chapyter of Yorke dayly to syng
masse wyth note by one chapleyn, the chorysters and theire
master, except princypall feestes ; and so, because the saide

chapleyn is so sore charged with day[ly] singing the saide masse, and but small stipend, the deane and chapter did graunte to the said chapleyn, for tyme beyng, the chaunteries of Seynt Andrewe for the space of 30 yeres, now expyred.

The same chaunterie is withyn the said churche. The necessitie thereof is for the mayntenaunce of Goddes servyce; the same is observyd and kept accordyngly.

[Rent in all], £8 19s.

Whereof Paiable yerely to the Kinges Majestie for the tenth, 7s.

To the master of the chorysters for singing and playing, £4.

To the deacons for mynystryng, 8s.; and to the chorysters, 12d. In all, £4 16s.

And so remayneth £4 3s.

91. Thospitall of the Name of Jhesus and Our Blessed Ladye juxta Fossegate, in the Parisshe of the Holy Crosse in Yorke.

Thomas Pykeryng, incumbent ther. Of the fundacion of John Rowclyff, beynge first founder therof, as apperyth by the Kynges letters patentes, berying date xij^{mo}. die Februarii, anno regni regis Edwardi tercii, xlv°. [137?], by which lettres pattentes the said Kyng licencyd the said Roclyff to purchase landes and tenementes to the value of tenne poundes, and to gyve the same to a pryste, which shuld be keper of the said hospytall, and to the brethern and sistern of the same hospitall, to th' entent that the said pryst shuld have th' order of the same, and to praye for the said Kyng and his heires, Kinges of England, the founder, and all Cristen soules, and that the said master shuld paye wekely to 13 poore folkes and to 2 poore scolers, every of theym, 4d.

And for that the said founder, in his lyff, purchasyd but one house and 26s. rent, which was not suffycyent for to bere the said charges, nor none other person sithens that tyme hath purchased any more landes, as the Kynges commyssioners can perceyve; therfore the governour and kepers of the mysterye of merchauntes of the cytie of Yorke, incorporated the 12th

day of Julye, in the 8th yere of the reigne of Kyng Henry the
vjth, and auctorysed and licencyd by the same corporacion to
purchase landes and tenementes to the yerely value of £10, and
to fynde a pryste of the prouffytes of the same, did entre in
to the said landes gyven to thospitall aforesaid, and of that
proffyites and other landes do gyve yerely to a pryste to syng
contynually in the said hospitall, over and besides all charges,
£6 13s. 4d.; whereof

Paiable yerely to the Kynges Majestie for the tenthes,
13s. 4d.

And so remaneth, £6.

Goodes valued at 26s. 1d.   Plate, £6 10s. 2½d.

The Deanery of Bulmer.

106. Our Lady Service or Guylde in the said parysshe
of Toplyff.

John Bell, incumbent. The same guylde is without foundacion. There is dyvers landes and tenementes purchasyd, gyven,
and put in feoffement towardes the fyndyng of the said pryste,
and is bounde to say masse and to pray for the prosperytie of
the parochienns lyvyng, and for the soules of them departed ;
and, further, to kepe the queyer with 6 chyldren all haly and
festyvall days, which 6 chyldren the same incumbent is
bounde to teche to syng, and to fynde proper song bokes for the
servyce ther.

The same guilde is within the sayd parysshe church of
Toplyff. The necessitie therof is in singynge masse and other
divyne service, and bryngyng up childer aforesayd. Ther is no
landes solde ne alienatyd sythe the 4th day of February, anno
regni regis Henry VIIIth, 27th [153⅗]. The same guylde is
nether charged to the fyrst frutes nor tenthes.

Goods, &c., nil.

[Rents in all], £4 17s. 7d.   Wherof

[Outgoings], 5s. 7d.

And so remayneth, £4 12s.

111. The Chaunterye or service at the Alter of Our Lady is
wythin the sayd churche of THRESK.

Thomas Raper, pryste, incumbent of the said chauntrye, of
the nominacion of John Norton and Roger Lasselles, and other
feoffees, of diveres landes and tenementes in Thresk aforseyd
and Esteharlesey, in the countye of Yorke. Whiche landes
were gyven by dyvers weldysposed persons, to th' entent that
the profyttes therof shuld be gyven to a pryste, whyche shulde
helpe to do devyne service in the sayd churche, and to teche a
gramer scole within the sayd towne.

The same chaunterye or service is within the sayd parysshe,
and the foundacion is used accordingly. The necessytie therof
is in singynge masse and other devyne service, in bryngynge
up and techyng of chyldryn aforseyd. Ther is no landes [&c.]
sold [&c.] sithe the 4th day of February, anno regni regis
Henrici VIII^ti., 27th [153½].

Goodes, 6s. 8d.; Plate, £1 12s.

[Rents in all], £5 18s. 4d.

[Outgoings], 8s. 10d. 1 lb. peppor.

And so remaneth, £5 9s. 6d.

THE DEANERYE OF RICHMONDE.

158. Th' Hospitall of Seynt Nicholas, wythyn the PARYSSHE
OF RYCHMONDE.

Memorandum.—There is a chappell wythyn the sayd towne
of Richmond, called the Trynytie chappell, covered with lead,
and distaunte from the churche 1,000 fete. The necessite is
that in tyme of the plage the inhabitantes without infeccion
to resorte to the same for savegarde of there bodyez, fyndyng
in the same the prystes of theyre owne charges yarely to put
in and out at the pleasure of the inhabitants of the same towne,
with such wages as they do agre unto. Havyying no lands nor
tenementes to the sustentacion of the same.

Item, thare be in the parysshe churche 2 other prystes re-
sevyng in like manner there wages of the inhabitants, whereof
the scole master is one.

Yorkshire, North Riding.   Certificate 63.
(Edward VI.)

THE WAPENTAKE OF LANGBARGHE.

63.   Landes gyven for the fynding of a Grammar Schole in NORTHALLERTON aforeseyd.

Memorandum: That there is within the sayde parishe of Northallerton one grammar scole, having certen landes and tenementes gyven by certen well-disposed persones, to the yerely value of £8 8s., to the intent and for the better bringing up of the children of the towne and others of th' inhabitantes of the countrey, the which is used accordingly.   £8 8s.

THE WAPENTACKE OF GYLLYNGWEST.

83.   A Grammer Scole.   RUMBOLDE.

Memorandum: That there is in the sayde paryshe [Rumbolde] one gramer scole for the better brynging up and instructyng of the inhabatauntes children there dwellyng.

The master of the sayde scole is Michell Horner, having yerely for his stipend or wages, £3 6s. 8d., paid out of a stocke which remayneth in the handes of the paryshoners of the same parishe.   £3 6s. 8d.

THE WAPENTACKE OF HANGAEST.

89.   A Stipendare or Service.   BEDALL.

Memorandum: That there is in the sayd paryshe [Bedall] one stipendarye preste, called John Grege, doing dyvine service in the sayde churche, and teching a grammar scole in the sayde towne, for the which there was certen landes and tenementes geven to the yerely value of £7 11s. 4d.

92.   A Grammer Scole.   WELL.

Memorandum: That there is also in the same paryshe [Well] one Sir Robert Redshawe, bacheler of divinitie, a preacher of Godes Worde, and scole master of a free grammer scole for the better bringing up and instructyng of children, founded by the ryght honorable John Latimor, and receyvet yerely for his salary or wages the some of £6 13s. 4d., of the master of the hospitall of Well, and the vicare of the same. £6 13s. 4d.

THE WAPENTACKE OF RYDALL.

137. The Paryshe of MALTON aforeseyd.

Memorandum : That there is within the said towne of Malton one gramer scole, of the foundacion of the right reverend father in God, Robert, lord archbisshop of Yorke, for the better instructing and bringing up of youth. And there is landes and tenementes belonging to the same, of the gifte of the said lorde archebisshop, of the yerely value of £20, and that one Thomas Norman, prest, is now master of the said scole. £20.

THE TOWNE OF RYCHEMONDE, AND THE LIBERTIES OF THE SAME.

148. A Gramer Scole.

Memorandum : That there is one gramer scole kept within the said towne of Richemonde, and that one John More, prest, is nowe master of the said scole, and haithe for his stipend yerely during his life £6 13s. 4d., graunted to him by the burgesses and bayliffes of the said towne, as apperithe by his pattent. £6 13s. 4d.

North Ridding, in Comitatu Eboracensi.
Certificate 108.

NORTHALLERTON. m. 4 (b).

A Gramer Schole within the said parishe of Northallerton, of the landes of the Guylde there, John Foster, clerke, Scholemaster there, having a salarie or stipende to the clere yerlie value of £5 1s. 4d. paide oute of certayne landes there gyven for the mayntenaunce of the said Schole. £5 1s. 4d.

Continuatur the Schole quousque.

ROMBALDE. *m.* 4 (*b*).

A Grammer Schole within the said parishe of Rombalde.

Michaell Homer, Scholemaster there, having wagis or stipende to the yerelie value of 56*s*. 8*d*., paide out of a certeyn stooke of moneye remayning in thandes of the parisheners there. £2 16*s*. 8*d*.

Respectuatur quousque the King's title do better appare.

BEDALE. *m.* 5.

A Stipendarie preeste, which of late hathe been uside to teache a Grammer Schole within the said parishe of Bedale. John Gregge, Incumbent or Schole maister there, having in recompence of his sallarie certen landes of the clere yerelie value of £7 11*s*. 4*d*.

Continuatur the Schole quousque.

WELL. *m.* 5.

A Grammer Schole within the said parishe of Well.

Robert Redshawe, Bachellare of Dininitie, Scholemaster there, having a clere yerelie stipende or sallarie of £6 13*s*. 4*d*. paide by the saide master of Well [Hospital] appoynted by the saide Lorde John Latymer to have contynuaunce for ever. £6 13*s*. 4*d*.

Respectuatur quousque titulus Regis examinetur.

MALTON. *m.* 6.

A Grammer Schole in the parishe of Malton aforesaide, founded by the Archebisshop of Yorke that nowe is.

Thomas Norman, clerke, Scholemaster there, having for his stipende or salarie certayne landes and tenements to the yerelie value of £20.

~~Not within the Acte~~ [*sic.*]

RICHEMOND. *m.* 6.

The Grammer Schole within the Towne of Richemond, the Scholemaster there, John More, havynge a yerly stipend payd by the baliffs and burgeses of the said towne. £6 13*s*. 4*d*.

Not within the Acte : tamen quaere.

Yorkshire, North Riding. Schools Continuance Warrant, 22.

Forasmuche as it aperith [&c.] that a grammer Schole hath been contynually kepte in Northallerton [&c.], with the reuenues of the late Guylde there, And that the scholemaster there hath had [&c.] 101s. 4d. [&c.].

And that a grammer Scole hath ben contynually kepte in Bedale [&c.], And that the Scholemaster hath had [&c.] £7 11s. 4d. [&c.].

We therefore [&c.] haue assigned [&c.] that the said Scole in Northallerton aforesaide shall contynue, And that John Foster, Scholemaster there, shall haue [&c.] 101s. 4d.

And that the said Scole in Bedale aforesaid shall contynue, And that John Gregge, Scolemaster there, shall haue [&c.] £7 11s. 4d.

Yorkshire, East Riding. Certificate 73.

BEVERLEY.

[Petetion to the King to the effect that the Collegiate Church of St. John of Beverley, with an income of £1,000 a year, including the fabric lands, amounting to upwards of £60 a year, was in the hands of the Crown.] Furthermore, pleaseth it your grace to understande, that the said towne of Beverley is a market towne, and the greatest within all Estryding of your Majesties countie of York, having a grete nombre of youuthe within the same, and fyve thowsaund persons and above, whereof some of them be apte and mete to be brought up in learning which are not, for so muche as there is neither gramer schole or any other schole as yet founded, wherewith they might be brought up in any vertuous studdie. For present remedy wherof, it may pleas your grace, of your moost noble, habundante clemency and goodnes, not only to graunte unto your said humble and faithfull subjectes the said £60 and above, which was and is assured to them by graunte and gifte, as aforementioned, but allso that there may be erected within the said

EE

towne of your moost princely fundacion one fre gramer schole, to the further encrease of such youthe as there remayneth at this present daye and in tyme to come, so shall the same youth be educated and taught of all thinges to serve God, to lyve in due obedyence and feare of your heighnes [and your petitioners will ever pray].

Endorsed : Th' inhabitantes and burgesses of the towne of Beverley.

Yorkshire, East Riding. Copy Certificate Hull Corporation Records.

(Henry VIII.)

KINGSTON UPON HULL.

The Chauntrie of Bisshoppe Alcocke, in the parisshe Churche of the Trynities, in Hulle.

John Amer, incumbent. The same is founded at th' aulter of Our Ladie and St. John the Evaungelist, in the churche of the Trynities, in Hull, by John Alcocke, sometyme bisshope of Worcestor, to pray for the soules of Kinge Edward the 4th, the founder, and all Cristien sowles.

And the saide incumbente is bound to kepe a free scole of grammer within the saide towne of Hull, and teche all scolers thither resorting, without takinge any stipend or wages for the same, and shulde have, for his owne stipende, £10, and shulde paie yerelie to the clerke to teche childern to sing, 40s., and to 10 of the best scolers in the scole, every of them, 6s. 8d., by yere, £3 6s. 8d., so longe as the possessions of the saide chauntrey shulde be able to bere the same, or els the same to be defaulked by the maire and vycare of Hull, as appereth by foundacion dated the yere of our Lord God, 1499.

The same chauntrey is within the said churche of the Trynities in Hull. The necessete therof is for keping of the fre scole in Hull, which is continued at this daye, accordinge to the said foundacion, the payment of 40s. to the clerke and £3 6s. 8d. to the scolers, only except, by cause the revenues of the possessions will not extend to the same.

Ther is no landes ne tenementes solde, alyened ne entryed unto syns the 4th day of February, anno regni regis Henrici VIII., 27th.

Goodes, £1.   Plate, £2 6s. 8d.

[Rents] in all, £14 6s. 4d ; Whereof

Paied in all, £2 11s. 3¼d.

And so remayneth, £12 0s. 0¾d.

HULL AND HULL SHYER.

(Edward VI.)

The Paryshe of the Trenytie, in the Town of Kyngeston upon Hull.

The Chauntrye of Byshope Acoke, in the same parishe churche.

John Olyver, bachelar of arte, incumbente of the saide chauntrye, beinge of th'aidge of 46 yeres, of honeste conversacyon and lyvinge, and well lerned, who kepethe a free gramer scole, and hathe no other promocyons, but onlye the revenuys of the said cauntrye.   And ther is within the same parishe the nombre of 1,500 howseling people.

The yerely value of the landes belongynge to the same chauntrye as apperethe by the particuler rentall thereof, £15 14s.

In reprises goinge out of the same, £2 11s. 9¼d.

And so remayns, £13 2s. 2¼d.

Plate, 11 unces.

Gramerscole.

Memorandum : That th' above named John Olyver his bounden by his fundacyon therof, showed unto us, to kepe a free gramer scole, and too teache and instructe all suche yowthe as resortethe thydder, takinge for his payns in teachinge, and for his salarye, as in the fundacion more plainlye apperethe ; and so dothe according at this presente.

Yorkshire, West Riding.   Certificate 67.
(Henry VIII.)

DEANERY OF DONCASTRE.

62. The Chauntery of Seynt Nicholas within the
parysshe churche of RUSSHETON.

Richard Thornton, incumbent. Founded by Robert Drax,
late prior of Monk Burton, by reason of a wrytyng mayd penul-
timo Julii, anno Domina 1503, and sealed with there convent
seal, whereby it apperyth that the prior and convent gave certain landes and tenementes to Thomas Worteley and other, to
th' use and intente that they shuld grant a rent of 7 markes by
yere, furthe of the landes aforesayd, for a pryste to sing masse
in the sayd chappell, and to helpe dyvyne servyce in the quere,
and to teche 13 pore chyldren frely, and to make an obyte.

The same is wythyn the sayd parysshe churche. The necessitie is as a fore is mensioned. There is no landes, tenementes solde ne alyenatyd sins the statute.

Goodes, 10s. 2d. Plate, none. Landes, &c. In all, £5 18s.
And so remaneth £5 4s. 4½d.

67. THE COLLEGE OF JESUS OF ROTHERHAM,
wythin the towne of Rotherham.

Robert, Busshoppe of Hull, incumbent. The same was
founded by Thomas Rotheram, sumtyme archebysshop of York,
of tenne persons ;
That is to say,
One proveuste, havynge for hys stypend yerely £13 6s. 8d.,
and 18s. for a gowne, £14 4s. 8d. ;
One scole master of grammar, havyng yerely for hys stypend
£10, for his gowne 16s., and for hys fewell 3s. 4d., £10 19s. 4d. ;
1 scole master for songe, havyng yerely for hys stypende
£6 13s. 4d., for hys gowne 16s., fewell 3s. 4d., £7 12s. 8d. ;
1 scole master for wrytyng, havyng yerely for hys stypende
£5 6s. 8d., his gowne 16s., and fewell 3s. 4d., £6 6s ;
And 6 pore chyldren, chorysters, to be chosen in to the sayd

College by the sayd provoste, of the pore sorte, which be apte to lernyng, wythyn the sayd parysshe of Rotherham and Eglesfelde. The same chyldren to be brought up in knowledge of grammer, song, and wrytynge, untyll the age of 18 yeres, duryng which tyme the sayd chyldren to have theyre fyndynge in mete, drynk, and clothe, of the possessions of the sayd college, amontynge yerely to the charge, by estimacion, £21 9s. 2d.

And the same scolemasters be bound to contynuall residence in the sayd college, and to teache all chyldren, frely, resortyng to the sayd college; and further in the sayd college have all the chaunterye prystes, in the parysshe churche there, all theyre chambers and loging, to th' intente they shulde here and se lernying in the sayd college, and not to be vagrant abrode in the sayd towne.

And the provoste of the sayd college is bounde to preache the Worde of God in the parish churche of Rotherham, and in all other places therunto adjoyning, and to kepe a yerely obyte for the founder, and at the same to gyve to 13 poore people theyre dyners, and every of them 1d. in money, amountyng to the yerely charges of 3s. 4d., in all amountynge to the some of £60 15s. 1d., as apperyth by foundacion, dated 22nd die Julii, anno Domini 1484.

And further, by reason of a second dotacion, the sayd college is charged to pay yerely to a chaunterye pryste in the church of Rotherham, of the foundacion of Henry Carnebull, £6 13s. 4d.

The same College is wythyn the towne of Rotherham, and dystaunt from the parysshe churche 160 fote. The necessitie thereof is preachyng the Woord of God, the instruction of chyldren in the knowledges of grammer, song, and wrytynge, in the sayd countrey, beyng very barayn of knowledge, and also the contynuall brynging upp of 6 poore chyldren, and the maynten-aunce of Godes service in the parysshe church of Rotherham, wyth the kepynge together all the prystes in the sayd churche of Rotherham.

And the same is observed accordyngly, and no landes solde nor put awey sithens the statute, savynge onely that one Hugh

Wirhall, of Doncastre, about the 14th of December, in the 36th yere of the Kynges Majestiez reigne, entrid into certen landes and tenementes in the towne and feldes of Greysbroke, of the yerely value of 23s. 4d., and the same hathe convertyd to hys owne use, wherof, before that tyme, the sayd college was in possession by the space of thirtye yeres.

Goods [&c.], £54 7s. 8d.; Plate, £267 0s. 4d.

Some of the sayd College, £127 7s. 7d. q.

Paiable in all, £20 2s. 1d. q.

And so remaneth £107 5s. 10d.

[Lands, &c.] First, the mansion house of the said college, wyth a garden and orchard wythyn the clausture of the same, inserounde with a brick walle, conteyning by estimacion 2 acres;

And one house nere unto the seyd college, wherein the free scoles be kept and taught, 56s. 8d.

DEANERY OF REPON.   Certificate 68.

1. THE CATHEDRALL MOTHER COLLEGIATE AND PAROCHE CHURCHE OF REPON.

Marmaduke Bradley, clerke, prebendarye of the prebend of Thorpe, and residentiarie ther.

The same is a paroche church, havynge an incorporacion therin of 7 prebendaries, which have for ther levynges the tythez, offrynges, and other profectes pertenyng to 7 curez; 6 of the same prebendaries have 6 vicars inducted under them in the said church, called vicars choralles, which 6 vicars are bound to discharge the said prebendaryes of all ther cures and service in the said church, every of the saide vicars havynge yerlie of the said prebendariez for ther stipendez, £6. The 7th prebendarye is made of the parsonage of Stanwich, and is called the chantor of the said church, who haith a vicare indowyd underneth hym at Stanwych, to discharge hym of all cure and service in the said churche. The necessitie is to maynteyne Goddes service in the saide churche, the kepynge of hospitalitie of 6 prebenderies for the releif of poore

people, wherof two prebendaries be contynually resident and
the other 5 absent.

*   *   *   *   *

Memorandum : ` . . . Item, ther is 9 chauntries founded
in the said churchez by diverse persons as herafter by ther
particuler foundacions may appere, the incumbents whereof
be bounde to be present in the quer of the said church at
all the service done in the same, and to helpe the saide vicars
to mynystre sacrementes in tyme of necessitie, and be named
petichanons.

13. THE THRE DEACONS, 3 SUB-DEACONS, 6 CHORESTARIEZ, 6
  TRIBLERS, 1 ORGANE PLAYER, AND ONE SCOLEMASTER OF
  GRAMER.

In the same church be 3 deacons, 3 sub-deacons, 6 chorestariez, 6 tribblers, 1 orgayne player, and one scolemaster of
gramer ; that is to say,

The 3 deacons for ther yerlie stipende, £5 0s. 10d.

The thre subdeacons for ther yerlie stipende, £4 0s. 10d.

The 6 chorestaries for ther yerlie stipende, £3 0s. 8d.

The 6 triblers for ther yerlie stipend, £2 12s. 6d.

To the said 6 chorestariez for ther lyvereys, £1 4s.

To the organe player, 13s. 4d.

And to the scolemaster, £2.

All which be payde yerlie furth of the common of the sayde
church.

Sum of the rental, £18 12s. 2d. qui remanent.

DEANERY OF CRAVEN, YORKSHIRE. **Certificate 70.**

4. The Chaunterie of Saynt Nicholas in the said
   churche [SKIPTON IN CRAVEN].

Stephen Elys, incumbent. Havyng no foundacion, as he
allegyth, but by reporte one Peter Toller, clerke, founded the
same. To th' entent to pray for hys sowle and all Cristen
sowlez, and to helpe to do and manteyn dyvyne service in the
said quere, and also to keep a grammer skole to the children of
the same towne.

The same is in the said churche, beinge used according to the
foundacion. Ther is no landes aliened sithens the statute.

Goods, *nil.* ; Plate, *nil.*

[Rents in all], £4 13*s.*

Whereof paiable in all, 10*s.* 7*d.*

And so remanyth £4 2*s.* 5*d.*

11.   The Chaunterie of Our Lady and Saynt Anne
in the Paroch church of LONGE PRESTON.

John Fernesyde, incumbent.   Of the foundacion of Richard
Hamerton, knight.   To th' entent to pray for the sowle of the
founder and all Cristen sowles, and to helpe to do dyvyne service in the quere ther, and to ayde the vicare in tyme of
necessitie in mynystracion of the sacrementes, and to teache
one grammer scole and also a songe scole to the children of the
said paroch, and also to make one especiall obyte yerlie for the
sowle of the founder, and to distribute at the same in breade
emongest poore people, 6*s.*, and to make a sermon hymself, or
els by his deputie, ons in the yere, as apperyth by a composicion
dated 14th die Maii, anno regni regis Edwardi IV., 8th [1468].

The same is in the saide paroch church and used accordinglie.
Ther is no landes alienate sithens the statute.   The necessite ys
as beforesayd.

Goodes, &c., 18*s.* 3*d.* ; Plate, *nil.*

[Rentes in all], £5 11*s.* 8*d.* ; Whereof

Paiable yerelie to the Kinges Majestie for the tenth, 8*s.* 9*d.*

And so remanyth £5 2*s.* 11*d.*

17.   The Chaunterie of the Roode in the same
paroch churche of GYGLESWYKE.

Thomas Husteler, incumbent.   Of the foundacion of James
Skarr', prist.   To th' intent to pray for the sowle of the founder
and all Cristen Sowles, and to synge masse, every Friday, of
the Name of Jhesu, and, of the Saterday, of Our Lady.   And
further, that the said incumbent shulde be sufficientlie sene in
playnsonge and gramer, and to helpe dyvyne service in the same
churche.

The same is in the saide church and used accordinge to the foundacion. Ther is no landes aliened sithens the statute.

Goodes, &c., 19s. 2d.; Plate, £2 2s.

[Rents in all], £6 1s. 0d.

Wherof paiable [in all], 14s. 8d.

And so remanyth £5 6s. 4d.

DEANERY OF BARROBRIGGE, YORKSHIRE. **Certificate 71.**

1. The Chaunterie of Our Ladye withyn the said
parish churche [ALDEBROUGH].

Christopher Spence, incumbent. Havyng no foundacion, but presented by certen feoffees of severall landes gyven by syndry persons of the said paroch for fyndyng of a preyste ther, to pray for his benefactors and all Cristen sowles, and to helpe to do dyvyne service in the sayde churche, and the seid incumbent doth teache a gramer scole to the children of the sayde paroche.

The same is withyn the sayde churche and used accordinglye. Ther is no land alienated or sold sithens the 4th day of February, anno regni regis Henrici VIII., 27th.

Goodes, 12s. 6d.; Plate, nil.

[Rents in all], £6 10s. 9¼d.; Wherof

Paiable [in all], £1 16s. 10¼d.

And so remanyth £4 13s. 11d.

DEANERY OF POUNTFRETT, YORKSHIRE. **Certificate 65.**

46. The Chauntrie or Service of Our Lady in
the saide Church of WRAGBYE.

Thomas Gylle, incumbent. Ther is no foundacion of the same, but certen landes and tenementes purchased by the parocheners ther, to th' entent to fynde a preyst to pray for the sowles of the founders and the parochians departede, and to teache children in the said paroche.

And of the profectes of the said landes the saide parochians doth pay yerlie to the said preiste, towardes his levinge, £5, and the residewe they bestowe of the necessities of the said paroche, as it is alleged, albeit the hole rentall is charged in this certificate, as herafter may appere.

And there hathe bene thre incumbentes of the same successivelie, and not charged to the pamente of the tenth.

Sum of the rentall, £6 15s. 2d.

Westrydyng of the Countye of Yorke. Certificate 64.

(Edward VI.)

Robert, Archbyshop of Yorke, Robert Chaloner, Thomas Gargrave, and Henrye Savyll, Commissioners.

7. STYLLINGFLETE PARISH.

The Colleage of Saynt Andrew, in Nether Acaster, within the sayd parishe of Styllingflete.

There ys a provost and three fellowes, being all preistes, wherof one doth kepe a free schole of grammer, according to the foundacion, and the sayd colledge ys distaunt from the parishe churche one myle.

The necessitie thereof ys for the inhabitaunts of Acaster aforesayd, being in nomber 200, the ryver of Owse, which is a great streame, runnyng betwixte the said colledge and the parishe churche, and in that place without a bridge.

Goods, 17s. 4d. ; Plate, six ounces, parcell gylte.

The yerely value of the freehold landes and tenementes, belonging to the sayd colledge, £37 15s. 0½d.

Wherof Resolutes and deductions, £2 10s. 8d.

And so remayneth clere to the Kinges Majestie by yere, £35 4s. 4½d.

Wherof The Provostes stypend of the sayd Colledge, William Alcocke, provost of the sayd colledge, of th' age of 67 yeres, indifferently learned, hath and receyved yerely for his stypend, £10, and hath none other lyvyng.

The stypend of 2 fellowes of the sayd colledge :

William Barton, of th' age of 63 yeres, and John Rawdon, of th' age of 49 yeres, 2 of the fellowes of the sayd colledge, have and receyve yerely for theyre stypendes, every of theyse, after the rate of £6 by yere, and have none other lyvings.

The scholemasters stypend of the sayd colledge :

William Gegoltson, schole master, of the sayd colledge, indifferently learned in grammer, of th' age of 38 yeres, hath and receyveth yerely for his stypend out of the revenue of the sayd colledge, £5, and hath none other lyving.

8 & 9. ROTHERHAM PARISH.

The Colledge of Jesu in Rotherham aforesaid.

In the sayd towne and paryshe of Rotherham, being great and wide, there ys no preist found to serve the cure besydes the vicar and paryshe preist, which hertofore have ben accustomed to have helpe of the chauntrie preists aforeseyd, as nede hath requyred. The number of houslyng people ys 2,000.

The sayd colledge was founded for a preacher to preach 12 sermons every yere, three scholemasters of free scholes, viz. : grammer, song, and wyrtyng ; 6 pore children, a butler, and a coke.

Goods, £32 10s. Plate, gylte, 517½ ounces ; parcell gylte, 520½ ounces. Plate, white, 24¼ ounces.

The yerely value of the freehold land belonging to the seyd colledge, £130 16s. 1¼d.

Wherof Resolutes and deductions by yere, £7 19s. 7¾d.

And so remayneth clere to the Kinges Majestie yerely, £122 16s. 5½d.

The stipend of the preacher in the seyd colledge :

Robert, Bushop of Hull, provost of the sayd colledge, and founded for a preacher, as ys aforesaid, of th' age of 44 yeres, hath yerely for his salarie or stypende out of the revenue of the sayd colledge, £13 6s. 8d. ; with a gowne clothe, price 18s. ; wood and coles sufficient for his chamber ; and the yerely allowance for the fynding of 3 horses. Also he hath in other promocions and lynings, viz. : of the Kinges Majestie one yerely pencion of 250 markes, and a prebend in the churche of Yorke of £58 by yere.

The grammer scole in the seid colledge :

Thomas Snell, scholemaster there, 36 yeres of age, bacheler of arte, of honest conversacion, qualities, and learnyng, hath and

receyveth yerely for his stipend, £10; for his gowne clothe
12s.; for fyre to his chamber, 3s. 4d.; his barber and launder
free; which amounteth yerely to £10 15s. 4d.; and hath none
other lyving.

The songe scole in the seyd colledge:

Robert Cade, scholemaster there, 38 yeres of age, hath and
receyveth yerely out of the revenue of the sayd colledge,
£6 3s. 4d. for his salarie; 12s. for his gowne clothe; 3s. 4d. for
fyre to his chamber; his barber and launder free. In all,
£7 8s. 8d.; and hath none other lyving.

The wryting scole in the seid college:

John Addy, scholemaster there, 61 yeres of age, hath and
receyveth yerely out of the sayd revenue, viz.: for his salarie,
£5 6s. 8d.; for a gowne clothe, 16s.; for fyre to his chamber,
3s. 4d.; his barber and launder free. In all, £6 6s.; and hath
none other lyving.

The 6 choristers, or pore children, in the seyd colledge:

The sayd children have yerely meat, drinck, and clothe, out
of the revenue of the seyd colledge, which is worth to every of
theym after the rate of £3 6s. 8d. by yere; And hath none
other lyving.

The butlers and the cokes stipends there:

John Pakyn, butler, of th' age of 40 yeres, and Robert
Parkyn, coke, 45 yeres of age, hath every of theym yerely for
his wages, £1 6s. 8d., with meate, drincke, and lyvery.

Pore people:

There hath ben yerely distributed in almes to pore people, 6s.,
according to the ordinaunce and will of the founder.

36. BRAYTON PARRISHE (GATEFORD).

The Chauntry in the Chappell of Gateford, within the seyd
paryshe of Brayton.

Robert Broke, incombent, 47 yeres of age, apte to teach a
gramar schole, hath none other lyving then the proffitts of the
chauntrie. The chappell is distant from the parishe churche of
Braynton aforesaid, twoo myles and di; And the contree is
fowle in wynter.

Goods, 6s. 4d.   Plate, 8 ounces, parcell gylte.

The yerely value of the freehold lande, £4 19s. 8d. ; Wherof Resolutes and deductions, by yere, 2s. 8d.

And so remayneth clere to the Kinges Majestie, by yere, £4 17s. 5d.

41 & 42. SKIPTON IN CRAVEN.

The Chauntry of Saynt Nicholas, used as a Free Grammer Schole, in the Paryshe Churche there.

The sayd parryshe of Skipton is great and wyde, wherein there is a vicar and a parysh preist only to serve the cure. The nomber of housling people is 1,300.

Stephane Ellis, incombent and scholemaster, 42 yeres of age, a good grammaryan (having scollers to the nomber of 120, and hath kept scole there theis fyve yeres past), hath, over and besydes the proffits of this chauntry, one other chauntrie in Kyldwike, to the value of £4 by yere, for the better maynteynance of his lyving, unto hym gyven by the right honorable Henry, now the' erle of Cumberland, to th' entent to kepe a schole as is aforesaid, as by his deade apperith, dated the 35th yere of the late King of famous memorye, Henry th' eight.

The yerely value of the freehold land, £4 16s. 4d.

Wherof Resolutes and deductions, by yere, 3s. 4d.

And so remaneth clere over and above the deductions, £4 13s.

46. KYLDEWIKE IN CRAVEN.

The Chauntry or service of Our Lady in the parysh Church there.

In the seyd paryshe of Kyldwike is a vicar that serveth the cure himself, and hath none assistance, the nomber of houslyng people is 1,290, and the parysh is 8 myles in circuite or therabouts.

Stephane Ellys, scholemaster of the freescole in Skipton aforseyd, hath the issues and proffitts of the seyd chauntrie for the better mayntenance of his lyving, as is aforeseyd.

The yerely value of the freehold land, £3 13s. 4d.

Coppiehold, £1 3s. 4d.   [In all], £4 16s. 8d.   Wherof
Resolutes and deductions by yere, 9s. 4d.
Resolutes of the coppiehold, by yere, 8d.
So remayneth clere of coppiehold yerely, £1 2s. 8d.
And so remayneth clere to the Kinges Majestie yerely,
£3 4s.

47. GARGRAVE IN CRAVEN.

The Chauntry of Our Lady in the Parysh Churche there.

In the seyd paryshe of Gargrave is one preist, founde by the
parochiners there, as well to teache theyre children as to assist
the vicar in serving the cure, the nomber of houslyng people is
900.

Nycholas Cleveland, incombent, indifferently learned, 55 yeres
of age, hath none other lyving then the proffitts of the seyd
chauntrie.

Goods, 3s. 2d.   Plate, 9 ounces, parcell gylte.

The yerely value of the freehold land, £1 15s.

Coppiehold, £4 4s.   [In all], £5 19s. ;   Wherof
Resolutes and deductions of the freehold, by yere, 4d.
Resolutes of the coppiehold by yere, £1 2s.
So remayneth clere of coppiehold yerely, £3 2s.
And to the Kinges Majestie of freehold, yerely, £1 13s. 8d.

50. GYGGLESWIKE PARRYSHE.

The Chauntry of the Rode in the seyd Paryshe Churche.

Rychard Carr, incombent, 32 yeres of age, well learned, and
teacheth a grammer schole there, lycensed to preach, hath none
other lyving then the proffitts of the seyd chauntrie.

Goods, 6s. 8d.

The yerely value of the freehold land, £6 1s. ;   Wherof
Resolutes and deductions, by yere, 6s.
And so remayneth clere to the Kinges Majestie, £5 15s.

A some of money geven for the meyntenane of scholemaster
there.

The seyd John Malhome, and one Thomas Austeler, disseased,

dyd gyve and bequeth by theyre last will and testament, as apperith by the seyd certificat, the some of £24 13s. 4d. towards the meyntenance of a scholemaster there for certen yeres, wherupon one Thomas Iveson, preist, was procured to be scholemaster, which hath kept a schole theis three yeres last past, and hath receyved every yere for his stypend after the rate of £4, which is in the holle, £12.

And so remayneth, £12 13s. 4d.

56. KIGHLEY PARISH.

The Chauntry or service in the Paryshe Church there.

In the seyd paryshe of Kighley is one preyst, found by the parson there to serve the cure, the parson hym self not resydent. The nomber of houslyng people is 700, and the paryshe wyde.

William Hillingworth, incombent, 56 yeres of age, hath his lyving of certen lands in feoffement to certen persons of the seyd paryshe, to th' use of fynding of a preist to say masse and teache children.

The yerely value of the freehold land, £3 5s. 5d.

Resolutes and deduction, by yere, 3s. 11d.

And so remayneth clere to the Kinges Majestie, £3 1s. 6d.

59. SEDBURGH PARRYSHE.

A Chauntry there called Lupton Chauntry, founded for a schole and so contynued.

In the seyd paryshe of Sedbargh is one preist founde, besyde the vicar, to serve the cure there, the nomber of housling people, 1,100, and is a wyde paryshe.

Robert Hebblethwayte, scholemaster there. The same was founded by Doctor Lupton to pray for his sowle and to kepe a free schole, as apperyth by foundacion, dated the 9th day of Marche, anno regni regis Henrici VIII^ti., 19th [152⅚], and hath ben so used hetherto, and is verie necessarie for the bringing up of youth in that wyld contree.

The yerely value of the freehold land, £11 0s. 11d.; Whereof

Resolutes and deductions, by yere, 3s. 11d.

And so remayneth clere besyde the deductions, £10 17s.

61. WAKEFIELD PARRYSH.

The Chauntry, called Thurstone Chauntry, in the seid Parysh Churche.

Edward Wood, incombent, 52 yeres of age, well learned, and teacheth youth there, hath none other lyving then the proffittes of the said chauntrie.

Goodes, 12s. 6d.   Plate, 11¾ ounces, parcell gylte.

The yerely value payd in annuall rent, £4 13s. 4d.

Resolutes and deductions by yere, *nil.*

And so remayneth clere to the Kinges Majestie, £4 13s. 4d.

Westriddinge of the Countye of Yorke.   Certificate 109.

9. THE COLLEGE OF AKASTER, in the parishe of Stillingflete.

The Provouste stipend there:

William Alcocke, Provouste there, Freholde, £10.   Copihold, *nil.*

Pensio, £6 13s. 4d.

The stipend of two fellowes there :

William Barton and John Rawdon; the clere yerely value of their porcions in freholde, viz.: William Barton, £6; John Rawdon, £6.

Pencio utriusque, £5.

The Stipend of the Scolemaster there ;

William Segollson, Scholemaster there.   Freholde, £5.

Appoynted to remayne as Scolemaster and also to serve the cure their quousque, And, because he must do both, allowe hym £8.

Scoole.   Memorandum : that the seid Scole was founded for a free Grammer Scole as apperith by the certificat, and so hathe ben contynued ever syns the foundacion accordinglie.

Case of the People.

Item, whereas the said College hathe been usid as a parishe

churche, mynystringe sacraments and sacramentalls to 200 howseling people, and the seide hamlet of Akaster is within the parishe of Stillingflete, the River of Owse runnyng betwixt without bridge or boote there, it is necessarie a stipendarie preste or mynyster in perpetuite to serve the seide cure.

14. THE COLLEGE OF ROTHERAM THERE.

Clare Domino Regi, £116 19s. 10½d.

Grammer Scole.

The stipend of the Grammer Scole there.

Thomas Snelle, Scolemaster there. The clere yerelie value of his stipende there with other allowances, £10 15s. 4d.

Continuatur quousque.

The stipende of the Songe Scoole there.

Roberte Cade, Scolemaster there. The clere yerelie value of his stipende with other allowances, £7 8s. 8d.

Pencio, £6.

Writyng Scoole.

The stipend of the Writing Scoole, John Addie, Scolemaster there. The cleare yerely value of his stipend, with other allowances, £6 6s.

Pencio, £5.

The stipende of sixe choristers there.

The saide childerne have yerely meate, drinke, and cloth out of the Revenue of the saide College, whiche is worth to every of them after the rate of 56s. 8d. ; by the yere, £20.

Respectuatur pencio.

The stipende of the Butler and Cooke there :

John Pakyn, Butler, and Robert Parkyn, Cooke, hath every of them for his wages yerelye, 26s. 8d., with meate, drinke, and lyverie, £2 13s. 4d.

Forasmuch as they hadd no perpetuytie but servaunts re-movable at the wyll of the Master, therforc they have no pencions.

F F

59. SKIPTON.

The Chaunterie of St. Nicholas there, used as a Fre scole.
Steven Elles, Incumbent there.
Freehold, £4 4s. 10d.   Copihold, *nil.*

Memorandum : that the seide Chaunterie was founded for a free gramer scole for the good educacion of youth, and hathe been contynued accordinglye eversyns the foundacion.

Necessarie with the seide Revenue to be contynued, or some like stipende therto appoynted.

72. KIRKEBY MALHOMDALE.

The Chaunterie of the roode there.
Richard Cane, Incumbent there.
Freholde, £5 6s. 8d.

Memorandum : that thincumbent of the seide Roode Chaunterie being well lerned and licensed to preache, kepith a Grammer Scole there, which is necessarie to contynue with the seide Revenue or other stipend for the good educacion of the abboundaunt yought in those rewde parties.

Continuatur quousque scoole.

74. GIGGLESWIKE.

Scoole maynteyned with a somme of money.

Memorandum : that in the seide parishe one John Malhome, prest, and Thomas Husteler, diseased, did give and bequethe by their last will and testament, as apperith by the certificat of Giggleswike, the some of £24 13s. 4d. towardes the maytenaunce of a Scoole master there for certyn yeres, whereupon one Thomas Iveson, priest, was procurid to be Scolemaster, which hathe kept a Scole there these three yeres paste, and hathe receyved every yere for his stipende after the rate of £4 the yere, the hole £12, and so remayneth £12 13s. 4d.

Continuatur Scole per quantitatem pecuniæ.
Examinatur per Henricum Savill, Supervisorem.

81. SEDBERGHE.

The Chaunterye there, called Lupton Chaunterye.
Robert Hablethwaite, Incumbent there. Freholde, £10 17s.
Scoole.

Memorandum: that the seide Chaunterie was foundid for a free Scoole for the good educacion of yougthe, and hathe byn usid and contynued accordinglie ever syns the seide foundacion as apperith by the certificat.

Necessarie, with the seide Revenue, to be contynued, or some other stipende therto be appoynted.

Continuatur quousque.

94. NORMANTON.

The Chauntery of Our Lady there, usid as a Free Scoole.
Richard Johnson, Incumbent there.
Freeholde, £3 4s. 7½d. Copiholde, 12s. 10d.

Memorandum: that the seid Chaunterie was founded for a Free Scole for the good educacion of yougthe, as well in grammer as wrytinge, and hathe been contynued and used accordinglye.

Yorkshire. Schools Continuance Warrant. Duchy of Lancaster. Div. XXV., Q. No. 8.

Wee [etc.]. Forasmuch as it apppeareth [&c.].

And that a grammer scole hath beene heretofore continually kept in the chapel of Burrowbridge, in the parish of Aldeburgh, in the county of Yorke, with the revenues of the chauntry of our Lady founded there, And that the Scolemaster there had for his wages yearly £5 3s. 10d., which scole is very necessary to continue.

And that a grammer scole [&c.], parishe of Pickaringe, in the said countye of Yorke, with the revenues of a gilde called the Lady Gilde, founded in the church there, And that the Scolemaster [&c.] £1 1s. 1d., which scole [&c.]

And that a Grammer Scole [&c.], Midleton, in the said countie [&c.], with the revenues of the gilde of Our Lady, founded in the parish church there, And that the Scolemaster [&c.] 18s. 4¾d., which scole is very meet and necessary to continue.

And that a Grammer Scole [&c.], Tikkehill [&c.], with the revenues of chauntry of S. Elyn, founded within the Church there, And that the Scolemaster [&c.] £4 18s. 11¾d., which scole [&c.].

And that a Grammer Scole [&c.], Bolton upon Derne [&c.], with the revenues of a chauntrey founded in the church there, And that the Scolemaster [&c.], £4 13s. 4d., which scole [&c.].

And that a Grammer Scole [&c.], Pountefrett [&c.], with the reuenues of the service of Corpus Christi founded in the parish church there, And that the Scolemaster [&c.], 59s. 2d., which scole [&c.].

And that a Gramer Scole [&c.], Rooston [&c.], Chauntry, founded in the parish there, And that the Scolemaster [&c.] £4 6s. 11d., which scole [&c.].

And that a Grammer Scole [&c.], Wragbye [&c.], And that the scolemaster [&c.] £6 16s. 4d., which scole [&c.].

And that a Grammer Scole [&c.], Owston [&c.], Chauntry of Our Lady founded in the parish church there, And that the scolemaster [&c.], £4 3s. 11¼d., which scole [&c.].

And that a Grammer Scole [&c.], Calthorne [&c.], with the revenues of Boswell Chauntry founded for the Parish there, And that the Schoolmaster [&c.] £5 4s., which scole [&c.].

And that a Grammer Scole [&c.], Normanton [&c.], with the revenues of the lands given to the maintenance of Our Lady's service, founded in the parish church there, And that the Schoolmaster [&c.] 59s. 2d., which scole [&c.].

Wee therefore [&c.] have appointed [&c.], And that the said Grammer Schole in Alborough aforesaid shall continue, And that Christopher Spence, scolemaster there, shall continue and bee in the same rowme, and shall have for his yerely wages £5 0s. 10d.

And that the said Grammer Scole in Pickering aforesaid [&c.], and that Richard Judson, Scolemaster there, shall bee and remayne in the same rowme, And have [&c.] 35s.

And that the Grammer Scole in Middleton [&c.], and Thomas Monketon, Scolemaster there, shall bee and continue in the same rowme, and shall have towards his liveing 18s. 4¼d. yerely.

And that the said Grammer Scole in Tykehill [&c.], and John Hardwicke, Scolemaster there, to bee and remayne in the same rowme, And to have for his wage yerely £4 13s. 4d.

And that the said Grammer Scole in Pountfret [&c.], And that the Scolemaster there to have for his wages yerely towards his liveing, 59s. 2d.

And that Grammer Scole in Rooston [&c.], And that Richard Thorneton, scolemaster there, shall have the same rowme, And to have for his wages yerely £4 0s. 11d.

And that the said Grammer Scole in Wragbye [&c.], and Thomas Gill, scolemaster there, to bee and continue in the same rowme, and to have [&c.] £6 16s. 4d.

And that the said Grammer Scole in Owston [&c.], And John Rayner, Scolemaster there, to enjoy the same, and to have [&c.] £4 3s. 11d.

And that the said Grammer Scole in Calthorne [&c.], And that Richard Wygfall, Scolemaster there, to enjoy the same rowme, and to have [&c.] £5 4s.

And that the said Grammer Scole in Normanton [&c.], And Richard Johnson, Scolemaster there [&c.], 59s. 2d.

Comitatus Eboraci. Particulars for Schools.
Edward VI. Roll 6.

SEDBERGH GRAMMÁR SCHOOL.

Omnes Possessiones nuper Cantarie fundate in Ecclesia Omnium Sanctorum, Eboraci ; valent in [Firma], £6 8s. 4d.

Omnes Possessiones nuper Capelle de Coleye, infra parochiam de Hallifax pertinentes ; valent in [Firma], 33s. 8d.
Inde Reprise ut in [Redditu . . . resoluto], [4d.].
Et remanent clare per Annum, 33s. 4d.

Omnes Possessiones nuper cuiusdam guilde in Sedborgh, vocate the Roode guilde ; valent in [Firma], 26s. 8d.

Parcelle possessionum nuper Cantarie vocate Hunters Chauntrie, in Ecclesia parochialia de Hallifax; valent in [Firma
. . .], 20s.
Inde Reprise ut in [Redditu . . . resoluto . . .], 2½d.
Et remanent clare per annum, 19s. 9½d.

Omnes Possessiones nuper ad supportacionem vnius lampadis
in Fishlaik pertinentes; valent in Firma . . 4s.
Inde Reprise ut in Redditu . . resoluto . . , 1½d.
Et Remanent, clare, per annum, 3s. 10½d.

Parcelle possessionum nuper Cantarie beate Marie in Ecclesia
parochialis de Thurne pertinencium; valent in Firma . . , 8s.

Parcelle possessionum nuper Cantarie beate Marie in Barne-
bye super Dvnne pertinencium; valent in [Firmis], 74s. 7½d.
Inde Reprise ut in [Redditibus resolutis], 15s. 9½d.
Et Remanent clare, per annum, 58s. 10d.

Parcelle possessionum nuper Collegii Jhesus in Rotheram;
valent in [Firmis], 47s. 4d.
Inde Reprise ut in [Redditu resoluto], 4s. 4d.
Et remanent, clare per Annum, 43s.

Omnia terre, tenementa et possessiones nuper Cantarie Sancti
Nicholai in Ilkeley pertinencia; valent in [Firmis], £4 7s.
Reprise, nulle.
Summa Totalis clari annui valoris omnium et singulorum
premissorum, £20 13s. 10d.
Examinatur per Henricum Savill, Supervisorem ibidem.

20 die Februarii, Anno 5 Regni Regis Edward vi^{th} [155⁹].
Make a graunte of the premysses for a free grammer Scole to
be erected in Scordborgh [sic], in consideracion of a Scole there
before, the landes whereof are solde by the kinges maiestie and
to make a Corporacion of 12 persons of the Towne and parishe
of Sedberg to be governours of the possessions, reuenues, and
goodes of the said Scole, to whome the premysses shalbe assured,

and to their successours, and that Robert Hebilthwayte, late Scolemaster of Sedborgh aforesaid, to be named Scolemaster there, and to haue the yssues and proffittes of the premysses during his lief in consideracion that he was Scolemaster there before.

And that after his deceasse the master and Fellowes and Scolars of Saint John's Colledge in Cambridge to haue the nominacion of the Scolemaster in consideracion of twoo Fellow-shipps and 8 Scolerships establisshed in the same Colledge for Scollers of Sedbergh aforesaid, according to an ordynance thereof made there at the charge of Doctor Lupton, deceassed, which founded the late Scole of Sedbergh. And if the said Master and Fellowes and Scollers of Saynt John's Colledge do not elect the Scolemaster within one moneth after notyce geuen to them of the death of the Scolemaster, that then the Gouernours to elect hym with thassent of the Bisshop of the dyocesse, and the Scolemaster to haue the nominacion of the Ussher.

With a Lycense also that the said Gouernours may receyve by way of gifte or purchas other landes and heredytamentes hereafter to the value of 20 ᴸⁱ, with suche other convenyent clauses to be conteyned in the said graunte, as in other like Free Scoles erected by the Kinges Maiestie.

(Signed) Ry. Sakevyle.

North Wales. Certificate, 110.

(Edward VI.)

13. MONTGOMERY.

The Fraternyte or late Service of our lady in the said Towne.

Rentes of landes and Tenementes, 26s. 9d.

And vpon the increase and yerelye profyttes of a Stock of Cattell preysed to be solde at £330 15s. 4d., £40.   £41 6s. 2d.

Entre this in the warrant of contynewance.

Mathew David, Clerc, verie aged and impotent, Stypendary prest by the brotherheade seale, £8.

Alloce hym the yerelie Somme of £6.

William Ilkes, Clerc, Stipendary prest, £8.

Pencion, £4.

Sir hugh woodes, another stipendarye, 106*s*. 8*d*.

Pencion, £4.

Rychard Smythe, Orgaynplayer, 100*s*.

Pencion, 66*s*. 8*d*.

John Elkes, keper of the Quyre, being a poor man, £4 0*s*. 8*d*.

Allowe hym 40*s*. *yerelie.*

John Bocher and Mathew ap Richard, Querysters, eyther of them, 13*s*. 4*d*.   26*s*. 8*d*.

William ap John, holywater bearer, 6*s*.

It appearyth by the depositions of the Proctors, wardens and presenters ther, that those same dyd fynde and hiere one prest or lerned man continually, by the space of 30 yeres by past, to keape a Free Schole in the said Towne, Albeit that Sir William Ilkes, above named, beyng cheyfelye hyred for that purpose, taught but yonge begynners onelye to write and syng, and to reade soo farre as the accidens Rules, and noo grammer, sytheus the feast of Sainte Michell the archangell last past.

Memorandum : that albeyt by the good husbandry, Industry, and ouersight of the late Incumbentes, and of the Wardens and kepers of the said flocke and Cattell, ther accryeved commonly of those same, being kept onely vpon the Commons, wastes, and Montaines without any charge for ther pasture, suche yerely profittes and encrease by the space of certeyne yeres expyred as above, yet the same gayne and profittes (many wayes oncertayne hertofore) cannot for many consyderacions so continue nowe a certeyne yerely Revenue vnto the King[es] Maiestie, whiche is to be consydered in the assignement of recompences vnto the above named Incumbentes, etcetera.   Forasmoche as by the said vncertentie the clere revenue and yerelie gaine of the said Cattell is not like to contynue above the Somme of £16 10*s*., which is the even rate of oon yere's value redu[ced] vpon the proporcion of the price of these same as ab[ove].

North Wales. Schools Continuance Warrant, 17.

Forasmoche as it appearith [&c.] that John Elkes, keper of the Quyre in the Churche of Mongomery [&c.], beyng a very poore man, had yerelie for his lyvyng out of the Revenues of the saide late Fraternytie of our lady in Mongomery £4 8d. We therfore [&c.] have assigned [&c.] that the said John Elkes shall haue yerelie 40s. in recompence of the said £4 8d. which he had yerelie out of the same late Fraternitie.

Sowth Walles, including Monmouthshire. Certificate 74.

Sir Thomas Johns, knyght, Dauid Broke, Sargyant at Law, John Bassett, John Rascall, and John Phillip Morgan, gentilmen, Commissioners.

THE COUNTIE OF GLAMORGAN.

9. THE PARISH OF LANDAF.

There is within the same parishe one service callid David Mathewes service, wherevnto belongith certeyne lands and Tenementes gyven to the intent to haue a prest to celebrat masse in the Churche there for ever, and he to teache Twentie Children, and to be removable at the will and pleasure of the heyres of the said David Mathewe. The valew whereof as particularly it may appere by a Rentall delyverid into the Court of The augmentation, amountithe to the yerely somme of 115s. 10d., whereof

Renttes Resolute, to Dyverse persons, as it apperith by the said Rentall, by yere, 12d.

Stipendes or Wagis :

In the stipend or wagis of John Syngar, stipendarie prest there, of the age of 43 yeres, having none other spirituall promocyon, by yere, 114s. 10d.

There is within the same parishe one Colledge callid our
Lady Colledge, founded by one Adam hutton and one John,
Duke of Lancaster, and Dame Blaunche, his wif, for a master, 7
Fellowes, and 2 Queristers, and about 60 yeres past, the same
as is reported, was vnyted to the Cathedrall Churche of saynt
Davis, to the intent to haue a master of the same Colledge
founde, and 27 vicars Corall, 8 Queristers, and other servantes.
And the same is scituat on the northe syde of the Cathedrall
Churche there, being covered with leade. That is to say, the
Churche conteyning in Leingh 24 yardes, and in bredeth 9
yardes; the vestre in Leyngh 7 yardes, and in bredeth 5 yardes,
one steyre coverid with leydd, conteyning in Leyngh 6½ yardes,
and in bredeth 3½ yardes. To the which Colledge ther apper-
teynyth in parsonages, having vicars Indowed to the yerely
valew of £89 6s. 8d., and in Landes and Tenementes to the
yerely valew of £6 10s. 4d., all whiche amountith, as it may
particulerly appere by a Rentall exhibitid into the Court of the
Augmentacion, to the yerly valew of £95 17s.; whereof

Stipendes or Wages of the Master and Vycars there, with
others;

In the stipend or wagis of Stephen Grene, Master there,
being of the age of 38 yeres, having other promocions to the
somme of £42 by yere, £20.

And in the stipendes or wagis of Dyvers and soundry vicars
Corall, by yere, videlicet:

In the stipend or wages of William Castell, on of the vicars
Corall, of the age of 60 yeres, having none other promocion,
£4;

Peter Fenne, one other of the same vicars, of the age of 50
yeres, having yerely of other promocions foure poundes, 40s.;

John Batho, one of the same vicars, of the age of 36 yeres,
having yerely of other promocions Thyrtie poundes, 40s.;

John Williams, one other vicar, of the age of 44 yeres, having
none other promocion, 40s.;

Roger Phillip, Sexten there, of the age of 51 yeres, having none other promocion, 40s. ;

The same Roger, vicar Corall, 40s. ;

William hire, of the age of 58 yeres, for his pencion out of the said Colledge, £6 13s. 4d. ;

The same William, vicar Corall there, for his wages, 40s.;

Phillip Perie, vicar there, of the age of 34 yeres, having none other promocions, 40s. ;

William Thomas, vicar there, of the age of 54 yeres, having none other promocion, 40s. ;

Lewes Morris, master of the Children, of the age of 34 yeres, having none other promocion, £10.

Morres Blackney, vicar there, of the age of 35 yeres, having none other promocion, 26s. 8d. ;

John Lea, vicar there, of the age of 80 yeres, having none other promocion, 26s. 8d. ;

Hugh Jackson, vycar there, of the age of 38 yeres, 26s. 8d. ;

Juan lloyd, vicar there, of the age of 72 yeres, 26s. 8d. ;

William Walter, vicar there, of the age of 26 yeres, 26s. 8d.;

William pillip, vicar there, of the age of 38 yeres, 26s. 8d. ;

David lloyd, vicar there, of the age of 34 yeres, 20s. ;

Griffith Jones, vicar there, of the age of 36 yeres, 26s. 8d. ;

David ap hoell, vicar there, of the age of 38 yeres, 20s. ;

John hoell, vicar there, of the age of 58 yeres, having in other promocions fyftie thre shillinges foure pence, 20s. ;

James Jones, vicar there, of the age of 48 yeres, having in other promocions fyve poundes, 20s. ;

And frauncis Robert, vicar there, of the age of 24 yeres, having none other promocion, 20s. ;

In all, £51   £71.

Plate and Ornamenthes remayning :

There is within the said parishe and Colledge certeyne plate and other ornamentes, which hereafter particulerly may appere. That is to say, one Challes, with a patent of Silver, weyng 11 ounces, valewed at 42s. 2d.; one other Challes, with a patent of Silver, weying 11 ounces, valewed at 41s. 3d. ; 4 frontes for an Alter, valewed at 4s. ; 4 Coopes, valewed at 5s. ; 4 other Copes,

10s.; 2 other Copes, 8s.; 3 vestmentes, with Albes, 20s.; 3 mase Bookes, 4s.; and a pax of Sylver enamelyd parcell gilt, weying 17 ounces, 56s. 8d.; in all, as it may appere by an Inventorie, £9 11s. 1d.

Plate Gooddes and Jewelles solde of late:

The master of the said Colledge hath of late solde certeyne plate. That is to say, one Challes, with a patent gilt, weying 37 ounces, valewed at 115s. 8d.; one other Challes, with a patent gilt, weing 26 ounces, valewed at £4 17s. 2d.; one other challes, with a patent gilt, weying 17½ ounces, valewed at 64s. 2d.; 2 Crewettes, parcell gilt, weying 6 ounces, valewed at 24s. 9d.; A Cencer of sylver parcell gilt, 35 ounces, valewed at £6 10s. 2d.; and a Bell, weying 3 hundred weight and more, or there aboutes, valewed at 60s.; in all, £24 11s. 11d.

THE COUNTIE OF BRECKNOCK.

47. THE PARISHE OF BRECKNOCK.

There ys within the said parishe one Colledge callid Crist Colledge, Founded by our laite souereigne lord, of most famus memorie, Henry the eight, late king of England, in the 32nd yere of his graces reigne, to Fynd one Reidder of Holy scripture, one Gramer master, one hussher, 20 scollers, and one stipendarie prest, They having thos stipendes hereafter men-cyonyd. Wheronto there dothe aperteyne and belong Landes and tenementes, spirituall promocyons, and pencyons, as more planely it maye appere in the Rentall thereof, the whiche amowntithe to the some of £72 16s. 8d. The rewle wherof, grauntyd by the said laite king his letters patentes, to William, laite bysshopp of Saynt Davyd, and to his Successors, £72 16s. 8d., whereof

The Stipendes and wages :—

In the stipend of James Faber, Gramer Maister there, £13 6s. 8d.;

To the same James, for reding of Devine lector there, £6 13s. 4d.;

To Richard Watkyns, Vssher of the scoule there, £6 13s. 4d.

To D[avi]d Edwardes, Chapeleyn, to singe masse Daly there, and to teache the yonge Children resorting to the said scoule there a. b. c., £6 13s. 4d. ;

To 20 poore Scollers, after the rate of 24s. by yere the peice, £24 ;

And to Griffyth Mathew, Clerke, steward of the said howse, and overseer of the Reparacions there, 66s. 8d. ;

In all, £60 13s. 4d.

Et Valet Vltra, clare, £12 3s. 4d.

South Wales. Certificate 75.

(Edward VI.)

The Certificate to the Right Worshipfull Sir Walter Myldemay, knight, and Robert Keylwey, Esquyer, Commyssioners to the Kinges maiestie for the Sale of all Colleges, hospitalles, and Chauntryes, etcetera, by the Surveyour of Suthwales.

COMITATUS BREKNOCK.

The College of Breknock, otherwise called Christes College, in Breknock.

There doth apperteigne and belong to the said College landes and tenementes, tithes and pencions of the clere yerely value of three score twelve poundes sixtene shillings and eight pence, the same College beyng founded by our late Soueraigne lord, of most famous memory, kyng henry the eight, in the 32nd yere of his reigne [1540–1], to finde a Reader of holie Scripture, one grammar master, one vssher, Twenty Scolers, and one Stipendary preste, £72 16s. 8d. Wherof

In the Stypend of James Faber, Grammer master there, £13 6s. 8d.

Item in the Stypende of the same James for redyng of the Divinitie lecture there, £6 13s. 4d.

Continuatur quousque.

In the Stipende of Richard Watkyns, vssher of the Scole there, £6 13s. 4d.

Item in the Stipende of David Edwardes, stipendary preste there, £6 13s. 4d.

Pencion, £6.

In the Stipende of twenty pore Scolers, after the Rate of 20s. a pece, that is to say, William Jenkyn, Rice ph[illip]e Thomas Barlow, William Thomas, Thomas Williams, David ap Jeuan, William Jones, Walter ap Rice, Howell ap Watkyn, Hopkyn Awbrey, John ap Jeuan ap John, John Williams, Meyson ap David, John Jevans, David Thomas, William John Walter, Thomas Walter, Jankyn ap Hugh, llūs Williams, Morgan Mathewe, £20.

Continuatur quousque.

In the Stipende of Gruffith lloyd, Clerke, stewarde and Receyvour there, £3 6s. 8d.   £56 13s. 4d.

South Wales. Schools Continuance Warrant, 19.

Forasmoche as it apperith [&c.] That a grammer scole hath bene contynually kepte in Breknok [&c.] with the reuenues of the late colledge there, called the colledge of Breknok, otherwise called Christes Colledge, in Breknok, And that the scolemaster there hath had [&c.] £13 6s. 8d., And that the vssher of the same schole hath hadd [&c.] £6 13s. 4d., And that twenty pore scholers of the seide Schole haue hadde towardes theyr exhibicion £20 yerely emongst them, that is to sey, euery of them, 20s. [&c.].

We therefore [&c] haue assigned [&c.] that the seid gramer schole in Breknok aforesaid shall contynue, And that James Faber, scholemaster there, shall haue [&c.] £13 6s. 8d., And that Richard Watkyns, vssher of the same Schole, shall haue [&c.] £6 13s. 4d. [&c.], And that the payment of £20 yerely toward the fyndying of 20 poore scholers [&c.] shall be contynued.

Bedford. Certificate 1.

THE CHAUNTRY OF CORPUS CHRISTI IN THE PARISHE
CHURCHE OF S. PAULE, BEDFORD.

The ferme of 3 cotages in Schole lane in the tenure of 2
poore folkes [&c.], 12s.

Total, £10 15s. 4d.

[Founded by licence of 4 July 20, Henry VII.].

Devon. Certificate 15

56. BARNESTABLE.

The nomber of the houseling peple, 2,000.

The Chauntrye called Saynt Nicholas, his chauntrye.

Founded by diuerse persons, who gave certayne landes to the
sayd chauntrye or guylde, to the entent that a pryste shulde
be founde, contynuallye to praye for them in the paroche
churche of Barnestable aforesayde, And he to have the profytt
of the same landes gyven to that entent and purpose.

The yerelye value of all the landes and possessyons belonging
or appertayning to the sayd Chauntrye, £7 11s. 8d., whereof

Defalked For rente resolute yerelye going owt of the sayd
landes, 2s.

And so Remayn clere to the vse of [blank] now Incumbent
there, the 10th in this value not reprysed, £7 9s. 8d.

There is no ornamentes, Jewelles, plate, goodes or catalles belonging to the sayd Chauntrye; but the Incumbent celebratythe
with those ornamentes, which arr valued before, in our ladyes
stipendarye.

Memorandum, that one of the sayd prystes dothe teache scole
within the sayd towne of Barnestable, which is a great haven
towne, and charged with the reparacions of a great bridge.

The Busshopprycke off Duresme. Certificate 17.
(Edward VI.)

Sir Thomas Hilton, Nicholas Strelley, Roberte Brundlynge,
Knyghtes; Robert Meynell, John Tempest, Henry Whitreson,

Esquyers; Thomas gower and Raufe Rokesbye, gentlemen. Commissioners.

Certificate signed by Hilton, Brundlynge, Mennell and Whitreson only.

19. THE PARISHE CHURCH OF NORTON,
havinge of howselinge people, 700.

The porcion of Tythe within the seyd parishe of Norton.

Incumbentes, havinge the seyd tythes porcioned emonge them, to studye at the vniuersite: Jerom Bernerde, John Tonstall, Nycholas Thornell, Nycholas Lentall, [*blank*] Phillipe, Rowland Swyneborn, Anthony salven, and Lancellotte Thwayte.

The yerly valewe, £48.

22. THE PARYSHE OF DERLINGTON,
Havinge of Howselinge people abowte [*blank*].

The Chuntery of all seynts, or the Free scole in the parishe churche of Derlington.

Thomas Rycherdson, of the age of 30 yeres, Incumbent.

The yerely valewe, £4 19s.

The Repryses, 6s. 8d.

The Remaine, £4 12s. 4d.

The Deanrye and prebendes of Derlington, in the parishe churche afforesayd.

The Incumbentes ther, Cuthbert Marshall, Dean and Vicar, beinge a prebendary; Robert Bushall, prebendary; John Hewes, prebendary; William Carter, prebendary; Symond Bynkes, prebendary.

The yerely valew, £53 6s. 8d.

Repryses, that is to wytt, in wages of 4 Curates found by the Deane, £15 5s.

The Remaine, £38 20d.

Rente bequethed to the afforseyd Gramer Skole:
The yerely Valew, 3s.

CHRONOLOGICAL LIST OF SCHOOLS.

This List is intended to be confined to Schools mentioned in the Chantry Certificates and Continuance or Re-foundation Warrants above printed.

The first column gives the date of foundation or first known mention of School. The second column, headed S.I.R., contains the date given in the Report of the Schools Inquiry Commission, 1867, mostly taken from the earlier reports of the Commissioners for Inquiry concerning Charities 1818 to 1837. The third column gives the name of the place where the School is, or was. When this is printed in italics, the School has ceased to exist, and the endowment is lost, or misappropriated. "El." added means that the School has been degraded to an Elementary School; "Ex." that it has been converted into an Exhibition Fund.

It is rather surprising to find that of the 204 schools in the list, 132 still exist, though 19 of them have been degraded to Elementary education, and 4 are only Exhibition Funds.

It must not be assumed that the date given in column two in all cases refers to the same foundation as that of which the date is given in column one. In some cases the two dates clearly refer to two different foundations, e.g. Trowbridge. In others the identity, legal or historical, may be a matter of opinion. When Archdeacon Magnus gave the existing endowments of the Grammar School at Newark in 1532, was the School the same School as that which had been going on for hundreds of years before, and the jurisdiction over which was the subject of legal dispute and solemn settlement in 1238? When Dame Agnes Mellers endowed the Grammar School at Nottingham in 1512, which appears apparently unendowed from 1382 downwards, was this the same School? When Sir W. Laxton got a grant of Oundle School endowment, together with the Almshouse connected with it, and vested them in the Grocers' Company in trust, the question may be easier historically, but not perhaps legally.

It must not be understood that in any case legal identity is asserted.

Date.	Date in S.I.R.	Place.	Date given is that of
1066 (bef.)	1566	Bedford	Foundation of Collegiate Church.
,,	1652	Beverley	,, ,, ,, ,,
,,	1547	Crediton	,, ,, ,, ,,
,,	1555	Ripon	,, ,, ,, ,,
,,	1868	St. David's . . .	,, ,, Cathedral ,,
,,	Hen. VIII	Southwell . . .	,, ,, Collegiate ,,
,,	1550	Stafford	,, ,, ,, ,,
,,	1548	Tamworth . . .	,, . ,, ,, ,,
,,	1545	Warwick	,, ,, ,, ,,
,,	—	Wells	,, ,, Cathedral ,,
1075"	1509	Wimborne . . .	,, ,, Collegiate ,,
1091	1497	Chichester . . .	,, ,, Cathedral ,,
1091	1583	Lincoln	,, ,, ,, ,,
1108 (bef.)	1548	Pontefract	Grant of School to College of S. Clement in Castle.
1198 (bef.)	1550	Bury St.Edmund's	House bought and given rent free for School-house by Abbot Sampson.
1288 (bef.)	1582	Newark . . . , :	Assertion of jurisdiction by Chancellor of Southwell Minster against S. Katharine's Priory, Lincoln.
1244 (bef.)	Hen. VIII	Basingstoke. . .	Mention of brotherhood of Holy Ghost.
1274	Elizabeth	Penryn	Foundation, or re-foundation, of Glasney College.
1291 (bef.)	1568	Darlington . . .	Mention of Collegiate Church in Pope Nicholas' Taxation.
1809–10	1499	Crewkerne . . .	Licence for Chantry.
1814	1598	Ashburton . . .	Deed as to endowment of Chantry in Chapel of S. Lawrence.
1821 (bef.)	Unknown	Northallerton . .	Appointment of Master by Prior of Durham as Ordinary.
1824	—	Harlow	Foundation of Chantry by John Staunton, rector.
1829 (bef.)	1555	Boston	Master appointed by Lincoln Chapter during vacancy of chancellorship.
,,	1528	Grantham . . .	Master appointed by Lincoln Chapter during vacancy of chancellorship.
	1547	Grimsby	Master appointed by Lincoln Chapter during vacancy of chancellorship.
,,	1552	Ludlow	Patent confirming Guild of Palmers of St. Mary.
1831	1668	Witney	Licence for Chantry of J. de Stanlake.
1832	—	Gateford	Licence for Chantry.
1834	1545	Ottery S. Mary .	Licence for College to Bishop Grandisson of Exeter.
1845	—	Whitwell	Licence for Chantry to R. Wightwell, Canon of Lincoln.
1849' (bef.)	1551	Louth	Foundation of Trinity Chantry, annexed 1877 to Trinity Guild.

Date.	Date in S.I.R.	Place.	Date given is that of
1363	1585	Evesham	Foundation of Chantry in Charnel.
1364	1702	*Braintree*	Collation by Bishop of London to S. John's Chantry.
„	1578	Coventry (Bablake)	Licence to found Trinity Guild with two chaplains.
1369	—	*Rayleigh*	Foundation of Trinity Guild.
1375		Chelmsford . . .	Foundation of Chantry by Sir J. Mowntney, Kt.
1379	1549	Wisbech	Incorporation of Guild (1464, schoolmaster mentioned).
1380	Hen. VII	Launceston (Ex.) .	Licence for Chapel of S. Mary Magdalen to Mayor and Burgesses.
1381	—	*Hereford (S. Owen's)*	Licence for grant to Chantry.
1382 (bef.)	1512	Nottingham . .	Master mentioned in Town Records.
1382	1884	Winchester . . .	Licence for College to William of Wykeham.
1384	„	Wootton-under-Edge	Foundation of School by Katherine Vele, late Lady Berkeley.
„	—	*Henley*	Licence for S. Katharine's Chantry.
1387 (bef.)	Unknown	Ledbury (El.) . .	„ „ „ „
1392	—	Great Badow . .	Licence for Coggeshall Chantry.
„	—	*Bocking*	„ „ Doreward's Chantry.
„	1658	Coggeshall . . .	Licence for Chantry.
„	—	Dilwyn	„ „ „ to Roger Berde and others.
„	1596	Wellingborough .	Licence for Guild.
„	—	*Writtle*	Licence for Chantry to Sewall Bromfield and others.
1394	1676	*Cockermouth* . . .	Foundation of Chantry by H. Percy, Earl of Northumberland.
„ 1396	1566	Bromyard . . .	Licence for Chantry of B. V. M.
	—	*Boroughbridge* . .	„ „ „ „ „
1399	1612	Preston (Lancs.) .	Admission of Master by Archdeacon of Richmond.
1400	—	*Bolton-upon-Derne*	Licence for Chantry.
1402 (bef.)	1558	Stratford-on-Avon	Mention of Master in Guild Records.
1406 (?)	Hen. IV.	Oswestry	Foundation of School as stated in School book.
1412	1585	*Middleton (Lancs.)*	Foundation of Chantry by T. Langley, Bishop of Durham.
1414	1541	Durham	Foundation of Chantry by T. Langley, Bishop of Durham.
1419	—	*Stoke-by-Clare* . .	Conversion of Monastery into College.
1440	1442	Eton	Letters Patent of Henry VI. founding College.
1440 (bef.)	—	*Gosfield (Essex)*. .	Death of founder, T. Rolff.
1441	—	*S. Anthony's, London*	Appropriation of S. Benet Fink's Church for School.

Date.	Date in S.I.R.	Place.	Date given is that of
1442	—	Newport (Salop) .	Licence for foundation of College to Thomas Draper.
1445–6	—	Deddington . . .	Licence for Guild.
1445	—	Wokingham (Okyngham) . . .	Death of founder, Mullen, Dean of Salisbury.
1446	1627	Newland (Gloucs.)	Licence for Chantry to R. Gryndour.
1446	1548	Tamworth . . .	Licence for Chantries.
"	—	Chilton-by-Clare .	Grant of Chapel of John Baptist to Guild by Duke of York.
1447	1447	Wye	Foundation of College by Archbishop Kemp.
1448	1649	Alnwick	Licence for Chantry to Earl of Northumberland and Alnwick, Bishop of Lincoln.
"	—	Deritend (Aston) .	Foundation of Guild by Earl of Warwick and Salisbury.
1449	1552	Towcester . . .	Foundation of College by Archdeacon Sponne.
1451	1547	Chipping Norton (El.)	Licence for Trinity Guild.
1453	1548	Appleby	Deed mentioning School-house.
1455	1639	Cawthorne (El.) .	Licence for Boswell's Chantry to Langton, Kt.
1462 (bef.)	Unknown	S. Michael-upon-Wyre (El.)	Death of founder, John Butler.
1464	1556	Oundle.	Licence to Joan Wyat.
1466	1677	Newbury	Foundation of Stipendiary Priest by Henry Wormestall.
1468	—	Long Preston . .	Foundation of Chantry by Sir Richard Hamerton, Kt.
1472	—	Heytesbury . . .	Foundation deed of School and Hospital by Lady Hungerford.
"	1495	Lancaster . . .	Will of John Gardiner endowing School.
1474	Elizabeth	Bodmin	Licence for S. John Baptist's or Nayler's Chantry.
1477	—	Ashwell	Licence for Guild.
"	—	Prittlewell . . .	Licence for Guild of Name of Jesus.
1478	1592	Wakefield . . .	Licence for Roger Nowell's Chantry to Thurston Banaster.
1480 (c)	—	Acaster.	Foundation of College by Stillington, Bishop of Bath and Wells.
1480	—	Thaxted	
1482	1486	Hull	Licence for Chantry to J. Alcock, Bishop of Worcester.
1483	Ed. IV.	Rotherham . . .	Licence for College to T. Rotherham, Archbishop of York.
1484	—	Long Melford . .	Will of John Hill.
1487	1487	Stockport. . . .	Will of Sir Edmund Shaa, late Lord Mayor.
"	—	Chipping Campden	Deed of John Ferby and wife.

Date.	Date in S.I.R.	Place.	Date given is that of
1489	—	*Aldwinckle* . . .	Foundation of School for 6 children.
1492 (bef.)	1548	Skipton in Craven	Death of founder, Peter Toller, Rector of Linton.
1495	Ed. VI.	Lichfield	New Statutes for S. John Baptist's Hospital.
1501 (bef.)	—	*Banbury*	Conversion of S. John Baptist's Hospital to School.
1501	—	*Lambourne* . . .	Licence for School and Almshouse to John Eastbury.
1502	1502	Macclesfield. . .	Will of Sir John Percival, late Lord Mayor.
1503	Ed. VI.	*Blisworth*	Death of founder, Roger Wake.
″	1548	Bridgenorth . .	Entry in Town Records.
″	Ed. VI.	Royston (El.) . .	Deed of foundation.
1505	1505	Cromer (El.). . .	Will of Sir Bart. Read, late Lord Mayor.
1506	—	*Manchester* . . .	Deed of Richard Beswike.
″	1506	Brough (El.). . .	Deed of John Brownscale.
1507 (bef.)	1571	Burford	Conveyance to new Trustees for Guild Priests.
1507	Hen. VIII.	Cirencester . . .	Grant for School by Ruthall, Bp. of Durham, and others.
″	1558	Giggleswick. . .	Lease by Prior of Durham to J. Carr, close of land for School.
1508	—	*Week S. Mary* . .	Licence for Chantry to Dame Thomasine Percival.
1509	Ed. VI.	Rock (El.) . . .	Foundation of Chantry by Sir H. Connysbie, Kt.
1512	1512	Lewes (Ex.) . . .	Foundation by Agnes Morley.
1514	1509	Blackburn . . .	Foundation by 2nd Earl of Derby and parishioners.
″	—	*Chesterford* . . .	Licence for Chantry to William Holden.
″	—	*Owston*	Foundation of Our Lady's Chantry by Rt. Henryson.
″	1525	Saffron Walden .	Licence for Chantry to John Leche, Vicar.
1515	—	Houghton, King's (El.)	Deed of William Dyve, Mercer, of London.
″	—	*Liverpool*	Will of John Crosse.
″	1525	Manchester . . .	Deed of Oldham, Bishop of Exeter.
″	1571	Kinver	Deed of John Perot to Sir E. Gray and others.
1518 (c)	1727	*Cannock*	80 years before Chantry Certificate.
1519	1519	Bruton.	Foundation by Fitzjames, Bishop of London.
1520	1526	Warrington. . .	Will of Sir T. Butler, Kt.
1521	1521	Middleton Tregonnell, Milton Abbas	Conveyance for endowment of School.
1521	1521	Cuckfield	Will of Edmund Flower.
″	″	Tenterden . . .	Grant for School by Wm. Marshall.
1522	1558	Taunton	Building of Schoolhouse by Rd. Fox, Bishop of Winchester.

Date.	Date in S.I.R.	Place.	Date given is that of
1523	—	*Hornby.*	Will of Lord Monteagle for School and Hospital.
1524	Elizabeth	*Leyland*	Deed of Sir Hy. Farington, Kt.
1526	1526	Childrey (El.) . .	Will for School and Almshouse, by W. Fettipace.
1527	1690	Malpas (El.). . .	
1528 (bef.)	1532	Horsham	Deed of W. Spicer, Rector of Balcomb.
1528	1551	Sedbergh . . .	Foundation deed of Dr. Lupton.
1530	1745	*Kirkoswald* . . .	Foundation of College by Lord Dacre.
1532	1530	Stamford	Will of E. Ratclif.
1535 (bef.)	Ed. VI.	Bromsgrove . . .	Mentioned in Valor Ecclesiasticus.
„	—	*Higham*	„ „ „ „
„	—	Kingsley (El.) . .	„ „ „ „
„	—	*Orford*	„ „ „ „
„	—	*Shenston*	„ „ „ „
„	—	*Thirsk*	„ „ „ „
„	—	*Weobley*	„ „ „ „
1541	1542	Brecon	Foundation of Collegiate Church by Henry VIII.
„	1541	Walthamstow . .	Foundation of School by Sir George Monox, Alderman.
1542	—	*Well*	Will of John, Lord Latimer.
„	—	Thornton (Lincs.)	Foundation of Collegiate Church by Henry VIII.
1545	Hen. VIII.	Cirencester . . .	Conversion of Chantry to School,
„	1545	Berkhampstead .	Foundation of School by Dr. Incent.
1546	1546	Malton	Licence for School to Archbishop Holgate.
1548	1547	Brackley	Conversion of Chantry to School by Magdalen College, Oxford.
1548 (bef.)	1640	Alton	School mentioned in Chantry Certificate.
„	—	Barnard Castle. .	„ „ „ „
„	Elizabeth	Bedale	„ „ „ „
„	—	*Blandford* . . .	„ „ „ „
„	—	*Boroughbridge* . .	„ „ „ „
„	—	Bradford, Wilts (El.)	„ „ „ „
„	—	*Bucknill*	„ „ „ „
„	—	*Chaddesley Corbett*	„ „ „ „
„	1586	Cheltenham. . .	„ „ „ „
„	—	*Cowarn.*	„ „ „ „
„	—	*Eardisley*	„ „ „ „
„	1551	East Retford . .	„ „ „ „
„	—	*Eccleshall*	„ „ „ „
„	1566	Eye	„ „ „ „
„	—	*Finchingfield.* . .	„ „ „ „
„	1686	Gargrave in Craven (El.)	„ „ „ „
„	1604	Godshill (El.) . .	„ „ „ „
„	—	*Hornchurch* . . .	„ „ „ „
„	1713	Keighley	„ „ „ „

Date.	Date in S.I.R.	Place.	Date given is that of			
1548 (bef.)	1525	Kendal	School mentioned in Chantry Certificate.			
"	—	Kingsland . . .	"	"	"	"
"	1629	Kington	"	"	"	"
"	—	Kingsley	"	"	"	"
"	—	Kinnersley . . .	"	"	"	"
"	Ed. VI.	King's Norton (El., Ex.)	"	"	"	"
"	1606	Kirkby Malham-dale (El.)	"	"	"	"
"	1647	Lavenham (Ex.) .	"	"	"	"
"	—	*Leigh*	"	"	"	"
"	1554	Leominster (El.) .	"	"	"	"
"	Ed. VI.	*Liskeard*	"	"	"	"
"	—	*Lyme Regis* . . .	"	"	"	"
"	? 1645	Madeley	"	"	"	"
"	—	*Marledon*	"	"	"	"
"	—	*Mattersey*	"	"	"	"
"	—	*Middleton* (Yorks)	"	"	"	"
"	—	*Montgomery* . . .	"	"	"	"
"	1552	Morpeth	"	"	"	"
"	Elizabeth	Nantwich. . . .	"	"	"	"
"	1565	Netherbury . . .	"	"	"	"
"	1592	Normanton(Yorks)	"	"	"	"
"	—	*Odiham*	"	"	"	"
"	—	*Ospringe*	"	"	"	"
"	—	*Pagett's Bromley* .	"	"	"	"
"	—	*Pembridge* . . .	"	"	"	"
"	—	Pickering	"	"	"	"
"	—	*Richard's Castle* .	"	"	"	"
"	—	*Romaldkirk* . . .	"	"	"	"
"	—	*Rothwell*	"	"	"	"
"	Unknown	Saltash (El.). . .	"	"	"	"
"	—	*Staunton on Wye* .	"	"	"	"
"	1552	Stourbridge . . .	"	"	"	"
"	—	Tickhill	"	"	"	"
"	1861	Trowbridge . . .	"	"	"	"
"	1549	Truro	"	"	"	"
"	Unknown	Wragby (El.) . .	"	"	"	"

INDEX

₊ The numbers refer to the pages. Where no part is mentioned, the reference is to Part II.

Butler & Tanner, The Selwood Printing Works, Frome, and London.